The Dream Divided

Nancy Niblack Baxter

The Heartland Chronicles, Book III

The jacket of this book,
a depiction of the Battle
of Perryville, was designed
by artist Richard Day.

Guild Press of Indiana
6000 Sunset Lane
Indianapolis, IN 46208

Also by Nancy Baxter

Gallant Fourteenth: The Story of an Indiana Civil War Regiment 1980

The Heartland Chronicles
Book I   The Movers   1987
Book II   Lords of the Rivers   1988
The Miamis   1988

Acknowledgments

Colonels John Coons and Lige Cavins and Generals Nathan Kimball and William Harrow, Gus Van Dyke, Will Landon and Tommy Brooks and his brother Lewis all existed, and their own written records form the basis of the narrative of this book. Jess Harrold, John McClure, his cousin Henderson Simpson, Tommy Thompson, Joe Roseman, Isaac Crim and most of the other enlisted men in the Fourteenth also lived the lives ascribed to them in the Civil War. Other men I have depicted are composite pictures of types of soldiers in the conflict.

The account of the Fourteenth Indiana and the Eightieth Indiana Regiments in this book are derived from their own records, found in the archives of the State of Indiana and historical libraries in which regimental letters, journals and accounts have been preserved and my own collection.

The homefront picture is reconstructed from historical record. Most of the events occurred, including Morgan's Raid, the Battle of Corydon, the proliferation of the Knights of the Golden Circle and the Sons of Liberty and Oliver P. Morton's controversial struggle to suppress political dissent which both he and Lincoln considered treasonous. The Northwest Conspiracy in the desperate last years of the war was viewed as an authentic threat by many Northern officials and was planned in the way I depict. The letters of Thomas Jefferson Brooks and Lewis Brooks from the Perryville campaign are original and held in my family collection. Mary Jane, Annie, Bob and John McClure really existed and their story is similar to the one depicted in the book. I have tried to reconstruct the history of these families and the state in as historically accurate a form as I could and to keep the settings as authentic as is possible. Some characters, of course, have been invented, and it is well to remember that this is fiction.

I wish to thank my manuscript editor, Susan Snelling of Austin, Texas and my historical editor Tom Shaw of Ft. Snelling, St. Paul, Minnesota. I also appreciated the help of the late Art Funk of Corydon for taking me over the roads that Morgan the Raider followed in his raid into Indiana; the Indiana Historical Society Library for the original documents and letters of the Fourteenth Indiana Regiment; and my husband for his encouragement and practical help in this book. I am indebted to Dr. John Beale for use of the Tilghman Vistal letters, some of which are reproduced in the book.

Family Trees of the McClure, Poore and Brooks Families

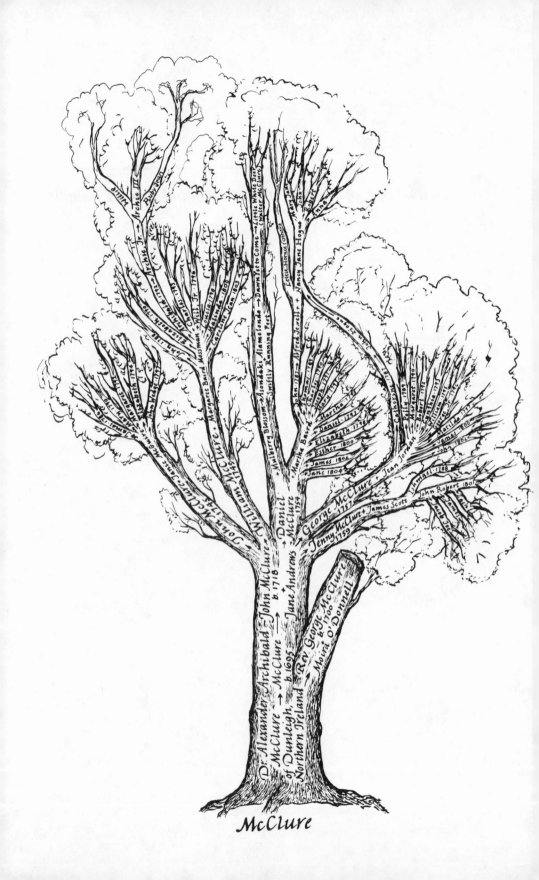

McClure

Betsey Chute
Hannah
Harriet 1815
John 1818
Amelia P. 1819

Mehitable T.
Alvan

Susan + Thomas J. Brook
Amanda
Wendell

Amanda 1798 - 1799
John Poore 1775 - 1818
+
Hannah Chute 1780 - 1872

Poores

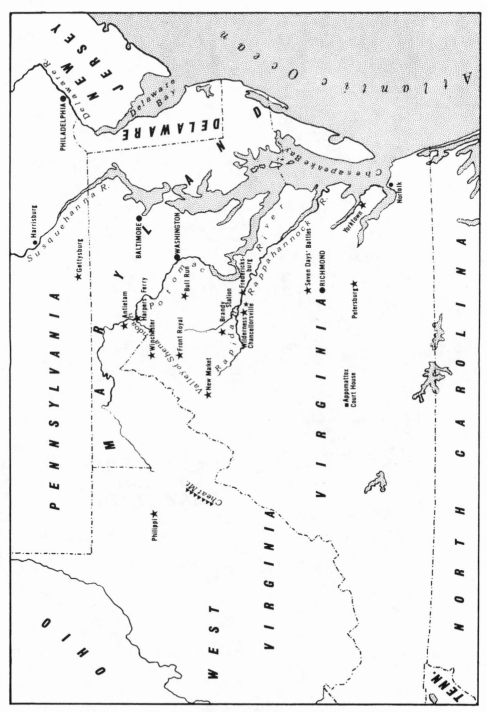

Map of the Fourteenth Indiana's Theatre of War

From *The Morgan Raid in Indiana and Ohio* by Arville Funk

This book is dedicated to the Senior History classes at the Daycroft School, Greenwich, Connecticut, 1982-1986, who loved to hear the old stories come to life. Debbie, Rahna, Robin, Dan and all the rest—you made me want to tell the tales for everybody.

And to my ten dear grandchildren. You I hope will love to read these stories in the future.

October, 1861

Chapter One

Shards of shrapnel-like freezing rain pelted the mountains of western Virginia, turning the branches of trees into frozen cascades, icing the canvas tents until they collapsed on the sleepers within. To the east, glimmers of light pierced the darkness. Dawn, October 4, 1861, was coming with grim inevitability to General Reynolds' Corps of the Union army.

Only thirteen miles away, the army of Robert E. Lee lay spread out over the hills, ready to meet whatever this day brought. Its commander was determined to secure western Virginia and present it to the year-old Confederacy which so desperately wished to control the mountain passes, roads and railroads which led to Richmond and Washington City.

A dark-complexioned, spry man with lieutenant's bars on his shoulders leaned against a tree whose branches hung almost to the ground with the weight of the ice. The collar of his overcoat was hoisted up around his ears, his slouch hat pulled low to deflect the rain.

"Eleven horses froze last night," David Beem said laconically to the young lieutenant from another company who stood near him.

"Eleven? Seems like a lot, even for this damned icebox of a climate. Beem, it's a wonder we didn't have at least eleven men freeze, too, sleeping three men in a tent. Their feet stick out, poor devils." This second man— Will Houghton was his name—rubbed his hands together against the cold. They were slight, nervous hands that might have belonged to an artist or pianist.

David Beem was silent for a moment, scanning the dotting of tents belonging to the six hundred men of the Fourteenth Indiana Regiment that had been hastily set up the night before in the wind and rain. The camp was altogether too random for his liking, with poor ditching. Rivulets of water coursed off the higher slopes and ran through the pup tents where men huddled feet to head, breathing each others' foul air, trying to keep each other warm. Well, it couldn't be helped. They had been moved to a front position, where they must wait until the dawn came, perhaps longer. So the orders read.

The freezing rain stopped suddenly, as if someone had shut it off at a spigot in the skies. The camp was silent except for the clitter-clatter of gibbering tree branches. Finally, a few desultory snowflakes began to descend in spirals.

"At least the overcoats came in," Houghton said, spitting phlegm on the ice. A persistent cough had been bothering him. Houghton was the lieutenant of Company C, Martin County Indiana, and the mountain weather was as foreign to him as everything else out here in the high hills of western Virginia. "It would have been a hell of a disgrace to meet Lee bare-assed the way we've been for two months," he said finally.

After he spoke, Houghton ran the tip of his tongue tormentingly over his chapped lips. He pondered what he had just said. The thought crossed his mind that his mother would consider his language very coarse indeed. He cleared his throat sternly to banish the idea. His mother was a long way off. She was asleep between clean, soft sheets in Loogootee, Indiana. The tall clock was probably chiming five o'clock; soon his father and his sisters and brothers would be gathering in the warm kitchen for ham and eggs and hot bread with butter.

"Oh, we got the overcoats all right," David Beem commented, his voice edged with bitterness. "But not before Governor Morton himself went to Old Abe in Washington about it and told the old man that the credibility of the whole war was at stake when the Federal government allowed its best men to freeze and die of exposure on Cheat Mountain."

"The bravest and the best," Will Houghton said, taking a cup out of his haversack. "Beem, that's what that fat woman said last April at the train station when we marched off to win glory in three short months. I wish she could see this." He laughed, a good, deep laugh, with more sadness than amusement in it. Three months had extended to four, and they had not even seen a battle before the United States Congress extended their tour to "three years or the duration." There had been terrible arguments about it, out here at the outpost on Cheat Mountain, but the Fourteenth had stayed.

Securing western Virginia was a hideous assignment. Boredom, cold and illness had leached everything from Will Houghton except the desire to live—and to fight. The two officers stood silently, watching the morning routine begin in the frozen camp. The orderly sergeants of each of their companies had already supervised reveille. Now the men were turning out of the tents, tousling their hair, sneezing like horses into the cold air, urinating in the woods or right in the path.

Houghton and Beem watched the first sergeants bring the men to attention, listened as rough voices called out, "Hyar,"—the brief morning roll call of a day of battle. The two lieutenants walked out from beneath the tree;

they would soon need to supervise the endless routine of duties their captains had ordered to get the regiment ready to move to the front lines.

"Shall we test this morning's mud from the coffeepot?" Beem asked. "It ought to keep us alive till we move out at—what's the latest news?—midnight, I think. It's changed three times." The two men separated, moving into the circles which marked each company's quarters. Here grizzled men huddled around campfires, slapping fat side meat into frying pans, where it sputtered and sizzled.

"Whooee, damn!" said one huge young giant of a soldier trying to pull a skillet of corn pone from the coals as Houghton approached Company C's camp. "Last of that good corn meal they brought in last week, lieutenant," the tall soldier said. "And that damn travelin' salesman of a sutler won't be 'round today. He got drowned crossing the stream, did you hear?"

"I heard, Crim," Houghton said. "Wish I didn't think it served him right, charging a dollar a chicken. The pone smells like Indianney, though. Hard crackers and salt pork don't suit as well as the good hot bread you had back in that cabin in Hindostan Falls when you were a young'un, do they?"

Houghton smiled at the young man as if he were his grandson, although Isaac Crim, at eighteen, was only three years younger than Houghton himself. An officer had to maintain distance, he told himself, dignity, even with peers. That was what they taught Houghton anyway, at the officering classes in the evenings on Cheat Mountain. An entire volunteer army with no military experience was going to school here in the first days of the conflict between the states, October, 1861. They hoped to learn some basic lessons before the mortal tests they would soon have to face began. Houghton sponged it up, every drop of it, what they taught in the tactics lessons. Glory School, some called it. Well, if that's what it was, he wanted to be the most apt pupil. Might as well have something to keep him going through this war. The elusive search for glory would do.

"I sort of admired the sutler," young Crim was continuing. "He knew how to pull in almost every penny in Company C. Like he had a magnet in his pocket. Whisky under the straw of his wagon, and when the colonel caught him at it, brought it in anyways in the hoops of his woman's skirt. I'd like to make a third of the money he did."

Houghton nodded congenially. One of the things they were teaching him, and that he already knew by personal inclination, was that you were a combination mother confessor and older brother to these men so far from home.

Crim went on complaining. There were a certain number of gripes per day that had to be gotten out, Houghton noticed. It was almost like trips to the sinks or privy woods, an elimination of poison. So he let them talk. "Thirteen dollars a month ain't nothin', and they never pay us nohow." Houghton looked at Crim inquiringly. "Been tryin' to think up a scheme to get some coin in m' pocket. Thought I might sell newspapers, if I could get 'em. Boys're gettin' tired of the *Cincinnati Enquirer* all the time."

"There'll be time for that. Now, use your energy for the secessionists. We're finally going to find out what a southern gentleman's profile is like in person."

Houghton scanned the skies. Day had flickered into existence behind gray-black clouds. Smoke from the cooking fires ascended towards skies which could hold still more snow. Just so there was no more sleet, Houghton thought. Sleet slashed through the shoddy, makeshift uniforms the men wore while they waited for the Union supply system to lumber into existence and send them Yankee blue. Sleet got the guns wet, those old muskets rounded up hurriedly at the first call in April, the new English Enfields the sharpshooters used to pick off the enemy effectively. Sleet chilled marching men to the bone, causing the croup and chest fever. Over three hundred men had to remain behind today on sick call, up in camp on the summit of Cheat Mountain, and he had been tempted himself. They could spare no more troops. "God, please no sleet," Houghton thought. Meeting the rabidly determined troops of this West Point general, Robert E. Lee, would be bad enough without the shaking chills too.

He hitched his pants over thin hips, coughed till the muscles of his gut tightened in pain, and spat yellow mucus again, this time on dried weeds by the side of the road. "Mustn't give in to it, not now," he told himself, returning to pour coffee from the pot over the campfire grill and sit down Indian style by the sputtering brush fire.

Crim cut up the cornbread and handed Houghton a piece. "I'll jest take a bit the pone to some of the Hindostan Horrors," he said, referring to his messmates. Houghton sat, grimly contemplating the sky on which so much depended for this coming day's battle. Then he looked at the smoky fire. "Not a proper cooking fire," he noted. All his life he'd managed the family woodlot, and he guessed he knew how wood should be cut and used. Well, the boys went for everything that called itself a tree. It still surprised him how fast an army could reduce a respectable forest to desolation.

After a while Crim returned and eyed Houghton. "Lieutenant, I gave Bo Reilly some of the pone, and he couldn't keep it down. He's a throwin' up all over the ground. Spilt all the rest o' the pan, too, as he jumped up to puke. Says it ain't because he's scared that the battle's comin', though."

An older man with a sparse, salt-and-pepper beard and piercing eyes came up behind them, cup in hand. "Tell Reilly not to waste good pone. When it hits the sacred soil of Virginia, it turns to shit," he said. The men guffawed.

Houghton stood up to give his place to Ham Mitchell, the oldest and one of the best-liked men in the company. He had fought in the Mexican War and returned to raise a family of six teenaged boys. He would not allow any of them to leave his hillside farm when the glory regiments pulled away after Ft. Sumter—he knew that war really meant sickness, a dreary life outdoors and interminable discomfort, if not pain and death. So he came instead. Ham had adopted Bo Reilly, possibly as a surrogate for the boys back home he missed. He had seen Bo, and lots of others like him, through the misery of these months on outpost duty.

"I'll go talk to Bo. Maybe tell him about the charge on Monterrey in Mexico, 'bout how we saw it through."

"Not about when the Indiana regiments ran away though. Keep clear of that," Houghton advised.

"I will, for sartain," Mitchell agreed, heading down the lane. Houghton watched him go, sensed his determination to help his "new son" face the trial of manhood war would force him to experience in a few hours. Word had just come that they would not move forward until evening—possibly even midnight.

"Well," Houghton told himself, "it will come when it will come." Hamlet's words suddenly echoed in his mind. He was a student of Shakespeare in the schoolhouse in Mt. Pleasant and had read *Hamlet* three times. Truly, he thought, there was plenty for the morose Dane to comment on out here in western Virginia.

The cheerful, half nervous sounds of men preparing for their first battle filled the camp as the afternoon wore on, the jingling of iron ramrods, the hallooing across the clearing, the snapping of percussion caps used to fire the guns, the spit-in-the-face-of-destiny songs men sing around campfires soon kicked into extinction. Houghton was part of the group of officers circulating about; he stood, watching the tents being struck, and heard the singing. Raw, sexual energy, often part of the kindling wood of bravery in battle, burst forth:

Sally was a farmer's girl
Some said she was a slut
But every time I saw her
I admired her pretty—

Butter from the butter churn
She turned till it had fits
But when she leaned above me
How I longed to kiss her—

Hands which milked the cows so neat—

He smiled, ruefully refusing to even consider what his mother would think of that. Scrambling down the muddy incline, he went to instruct C

Company's captain to check on a musket that wasn't working. Time was passing; they still had to stow the tents, cook rations and eat supper.

Ten o'clock tattoo, taps at ten fifteen, then two hours of fitful, troubled sleep for all of them disturbed by the sounds of ice finally melting off the trees and falling with eerie, echoing clatter through the woods.

Houghton raised his head from his blanket after midnight to look into the serious face of his neatly accoutered cousin, Lewis Brooks, captain of their own Company C, Martin County. "Lieutenant, rouse the boys. Colonel Kimball will be by to give us some final words in a few minutes."

Lewis always spoke to him formally, as "Lieutenant." It was his way. As if they had not grown up together in Mt. Pleasant, sat at the same desk listening to their aunt teach from the McGuffey *Sixth Reader*, hadn't sampled hard cider in the attic of the Houghton barn, hadn't stolen watermelons and taken them to the back of the churchyard at Hindostan Falls. For a moment he stared into the darkness, savoring the memory of their splitting watermelons on tombstones. Those dank, yellow stones had fallen and shattered before they were born, after the terrible cold sickness had wiped out the first town, the giant river boom town their fathers had built, but they had laughed and spit seeds at them anyway. No, Lewis could be formal if he wished for the sake of military protocol, but they had shared too much not to be knit like brothers.

But then, that was true for most of C Company—they were like brothers. Houghton thought about it often. They were childhood friends who had played at soldiers together with stubby wooden swords and toy muskets and somehow grew up and found that now their game of soldiering was real. Together, in times of careless laughter, they had climbed the maple-clad hills, roved through cornfields, and swam the cascading streams of Martin county; together they were now, in danger and trial, boys grown suddenly old in a few short weeks.

The officers roused the troops as the hour for the advance finally neared. Time began to pick up pace for Houghton, as if someone had sprung the spring in the big clock in the sky. Images tumbled one over another. Colonel Kimball riding up to say, "Remember you are from Indiana. Follow me and do as I do. If I run, you run. If I go forward and fight bravely, you do so"— then, "Right face! Forward march!" Over muddy ground, still rank with pools of urine, through the smell of green wood smoke, past a heap of baggage discarded as being useless and heavy for the already overburdened packs—home-knit underwear, cans of blackberries, leather bound Bibles—

The Fourteenth marched briskly eastward, down the mountain. Bo Reilly, who had vomited most of the day in spite of the ministrations of his older friend, nodded at Houghton as the lieutenant fell into step beside the column. Bo's face was grave and grimly set, and if he felt fear, he hid it. He was the son of Will Houghton's best friend back home, and he was fifteen.

As the men filed down off the mountain, they came to the narrow Cheat River Bridge. They could see, but not hear, the river roiling with the recent downpours, rushing over the boulders in its path. Pray God the bridge held while six hundred men passed over it, Houghton told himself as he stepped out of line. He had been instructed to observe the crossing and let the colonel know when it was completed. And so he watched the regiment pass, with its anxious but determined faces from ten counties in southern Indiana, the cream of the pioneer stock. The farmers of hilly central Indiana, Company H, with David Beem among their officers, showing no sign of acknowledgment as he passed because duty forbade it; the sturdy wild woodsmen of Parke, Greene and Vermillion Counties, looking cocky and casual, the toughly resilient Germans from Evansville and the city gentlemen from Terre Haute with calm, inscrutable faces.

And, marching by with G Company of Vincennes, was his friend Sergeant Augustus Van Dyke, who tossed him a mocking smile and a lift of the eyebrows as he passed, as if to say, "And so, we are finally in battle. It will be as pointless as the endless outpost duty we've had for three months." Sooner than Houghton had expected, the six hundred men were over the bridge.

Houghton advanced on the double quick to report the completion of the crossing and then rejoined his company. They passed the artillery being hauled on wagons through the mud by sweating teamsters. Then on, on, through eight miles of dark and silent night, till the first streaks of dawn came. The regiment halted, loaded its muskets and rifles, then hurried on. They stumbled on roots and rocks and the backs of each other's shoes, and though they did not speak they made altogether too much racket.

They caught up to the ambulances, the Ninth Indiana's and their own. Some of those "bravest and best" who marched here would be in those wagons, groaning and lurching, within hours, Houghton thought and found himself looking at Bo Reilly. Bo's head, also, was turned toward the jolting covered wagons, whose interiors revealed bare boards on which folded blankets lay. "Not a comfortable way to retreat from this battle. A feller oughter avoid that fate," Houghton heard Ham Mitchell say with a chuckle to Bo Reilly.

Down, down the steep, treacherous mountain road. Some men slipped and slid almost a hundred feet, while one or two, taking the path at the side, rolled head over heels. There, finally, was the Greenbrier Bridge, strategic entryway that Lee was trying to hold. It was here that the show of force would be made; the Confederate pickets must be threatened, the power of the Northern army shown. Lee must see he was facing a behemoth of strength even here in this remote place; he must retreat; take his army where it was really needed; and let western Virginia become a Northern state. And all of this upheaval was to be accomplished by the boy's gang of Martin County and the other counties like it from Indiana and Ohio, who, hearts thudding a violent tattoo, nausea rising in their throats, sweating and shaking from fear and excitement, were pounding down into the valley and towards the bridge to destiny.

And there was gunfire, crisp and incongruously cheerful in the dawn light. Pop! Pop! Like firecrackers, firecrackers back home at Christmas. There was a moment of silence and then the "Hoosier whoop" as the men rushed towards the bridge on the double. Over the bridge Houghton saw the Ninth Indiana regiment which had preceded them spread across a meadow in line of battle; orders from the front of the column filtered back, "Form behind them."

Other units came up behind them—the Seventh and Seventeenth Indianas. Ohio regiments were here too—it was, as Kimball had told them, most of General Reynolds' corps. At last they would fight. Men had died at Bull Run, while Houghton and the others were foraging to locate secessionist cows and pigs! This would be different, the blessing of the cause with the sacrament of blood. Baptism of blood: you heard the phrase often around camp; except for a few isolated encounters, they had not really spilt their blood to save the Union. Odd, Will Houghton thought, he had not until this moment considered that the spilt blood might be his own.

Images, oozing and then congealing, hot and fast, like bullet lead in a pan. Enemy tents visible, with the strange insight coming to him that these foul traitors hung their washing on the bushes, too, and had smoky campfires. Van Dyke, his sergeant friend, helping to lead Company G to drive out the Rebels from the woods at the left with yells exactly like the Indian scalp yell—"Aw-weee ohhhh."

Companies C and H, Beem's, climbing through tanglewood and clumps of bushy, leafy laurel, brambles ripping at the shoddy uniforms of the boys, a shell, the first they had experienced, tearing over their heads and exploding in the enemy ranks, horses' limbs flying in the air.

Answer from the enemy artillery, loud, ear-splitting booms as shells exploded fifty feet over the heads of C Company. The boys, cheering, louder than ever, to drown out noise and panic, as they advanced through smoke. Musketry beginning, loud and startling, as the Rebel skirmishers, rousted out, retreated, shells bursting all around. One soldier kneeling to tie his shoe. A shell falling a few feet from him, making a small crater, and its impact sending him tumbling head over heels into other men. Gravel in the men's eyes, dirt in their mouths, sulphur on their tongues. And blood, the sacramental blood, spilled next to Houghton and Bo Reilly, horribly, as Ham Mitchell's thigh was shattered by a shell and he crumpled in the road, dying. The view of Ham's home on the Mt. Pleasant Road as Houghton had last seen it, with children's wagons on the path and the cornfields beyond, flashed into Houghton's mind as he helped Bo Reilly cradle the dying man's head. There were tears streaming down the fifteen-year-old's blackened face, and ever after it became the face of all the war to Houghton.

The show of force was over; Lee was, presumably, suitably impressed and withdrew his men to a rear position. As Houghton formed C Company in line for the return to camp, an artilleryman staggered into the clearing. He was hit in the arm, just below the shoulder; blood poured from the wound, and his forearm and hand twisted and turned strangely from the sliver of coat sleeve which held it to the stump. All the company watched as the artilleryman took out his pocket knife, cut off his coat sleeve and the piece of flesh by which his arm still hung and let it fall to the ground. Then he picked up his severed arm and staggered off to the rear.

On the steep hills above, Houghton could see tall pines, majestic with the recent snowfall, intermingling their deep green and white colors with the yellow and crimson of maple and mountain ashes in a flagrant display of beauty, as if nothing at all had happened beneath their boughs.

The Fourteenth Indiana regiment settled into its new camp in the valley of Huttonville beneath the mountains a few days later. They were infinitely relieved to be out of the cold rains and fog of the western Virginia mountains. Let someone else forge a new state for General Rosecrans and the Union; let the Twenty Fourth Indiana take its turn at picket duty for a while, fighting the sniping Rebel backwoodsmen on the top of a mountain peak with summer clothes on.

"Old Lee's retreating anyways, tail between his legs. Secesh can't hold up to the straight firin', teeth clenchin' Yankees of the Fourteenth," so said Henderson Simpson of the Tiger Tail Mess of Company G, as he and his messmates sat around a sputtering fire in front of their new cone-shaped tent.

"These tents are no damn good for November. Have to make our own squirrel nests," his cousin John McClure said, turning an apple on a stick over the fire. He hitched his pants up. His uniform did not fit particularly well; he was almost as slight as a girl and the size "small" was not really small enough around the waist.

"Regular log cabins for the winter, that's what we need," McClure went on. "Some of the boys are from the backwoods and m' own grandpa taught me how to make a log cabin. John Hogue was his name—captured by the Indians."

"The officers are in private houses in the town up the road there, moppin'up roast pork gravy these Virginia women are paid to cook 'em," Henderson Simpson said a little sourly.

"We have to fend for ourselves," McClure said, looking into the eyes of the six other men who were cooking over the fire. "Forage. But today Sergeant Van Dyke got permission for us to make our own winter quarters."

"How are we going' to do that without woodsmen's tools?" Isaac Crim wanted to know. He had a "visitor's pass" that let him dine away from C Company, with the Tigertail Mess. Crim knew little about building cabins. He had been born in the woods near the old fallen ruins of Hindostan Falls, but bred in the city in Illinois. He had been visiting his grandfather when the war came, and signed up and marched away from Martin County, Indiana.

"We got axes," McClure told him. "Hew us down logs, eight foot lengths. Notch 'em out, clap 'em on four foundation logs. If we all work together, we can build a cat and clay chimbley, too, from the sticks I see about in the edge of that woods over a piece." He pointed and Crim and the others in the mess looked past a few rude houses to the beechwoods beyond.

"Chimbley shouldn't smoke," McClure went on, his dark eyes astute. "We don't want to cough. Take the time to vent it right so it don't smoke. Even make us a puncheon floor. Hew the logs in half."

"Sounds like a gob lot o' work," sighed Tommy Thompson. He was one of the "Young Americans" marching militia group, like McClure and Simpson. He had joined with the rest of the men from the neighborhood outside Vincennes.

"Better'n freezin' our asses," McClure went on, poking at the fire. "The better the shelter, the more comfort and health you can claim in this man's war." John McClure seemed quite definite about it, and so Thompson nodded. He was nineteen like McClure and Simpson, but looked at least two years younger than his two friends. There was an innocent vacuity, a lack of abstract thought in his manner. At some level he was aware of it himself; it often caused him to frown in perplexity and stamp his palm with his fist, searching for a word that eluded him.

"You tell me what the purpose of our existence here is," McClure demanded of the group of ruddy faces around the fire.

Simpson answered, "Guard the Staunton Road. Keep the Rebels from uniting their western and eastern armies while McClellan decides how he wants to go to Richmond."

"By air balloon, tunnel under the earth through hell, or steamboat from

San Francisco by way of the tip of South America,'' someone else added. The men laughed. General George McClellan was presently reorganizing the Union's eastern army around Washington after the disaster at Bull Run. In July at that small creek, not too far from the capitol itself, green fighting men from both sides had blundered, faltered and retreated upon themselves into a debacle that proved nothing but that many lives could be lost in a few hours. Most folks thought McClellan was taking a great deal of time to whip the troops into shape when he ought to have been proceeding to the Rebel capital.

"No, tell me what our purpose as soldiers o' the Union army is," McClure insisted. Then men shrugged, waiting for his answer.

"I say it is to insure our own comfort," he said firmly. "To live, breathe and exist to find comfort. Efn we can do that in the middle of all this bad food, the wormy crackers, the rotten, crawling salt pork, the cold, and the bad leadership, then I say we help Lincoln. We will be fit and ready to fight for him."

Crim shook his head in disbelief. Build a cabin? He felt lethargic, almost immobilized, now that they were off the mountain. All he wanted to do was lie about and eat the apples and chestnuts they found in abundance in this village. As for winter, well, they could cobble something up in the way of shelter after Christmas when it grew really cold.

"Too many men in this man's army are lazy. Lie about playin' aces on jacks and talkin' about women's ankles and bosoms when they should be fixin' their socks," McClure went on. "Runnin' whoopeein' after the battle's over when they could be lookin' over the other side's fallen men to see what they could use. Captain Beem's men took three prisoners at Greenbrier, but they also commandeered three good rifles and ten pairs o' leather shoes from corpses. We didn't do that. Lazy as hell, I tell you, and I don't mean lazy about goin' on duty, bein' first in a charge in the ranks. No need to be a fool about that to do your duty. I'm as careful about myself there as any other, I say. What I'm talkin' bout is bein' a wise look-out, for yourself in camp and on the march. Before this winter's over, you're goin' to remember what I said. . .''

Augustus Van Dyke took the cigar from between his teeth and walked away from the conversation he had been listening to as he cleaned his gun. He was tired of it, and there was nothing to be learned. It did pay him, as a non-commissioned officer, to listen to enlisted men, especially when they did not know he was about. They knew which way the wind blew. When a sort of mutiny occurred on top of Cheat Mountain about the forced ''three year or duration'' service the Congress imposed, Van Dyke had listened to the men's murmured conversations. Although many of the officers resigned, although some men declared the regiment disbanded and left, the men said they knew they must eventually submit and stay.

So Van Dyke had decided to stay and look for advancement with the regiment, come what may. It would not have done for it to be nosed about in Vincennes that one of the leading lawyers in town left when others stayed.

He threw the cigar into the laurel bushes and stood watching it a minute, then decided to go over and grind it out with his heel. One had to be wary and watch friends as well as the enemy, if one could ever get to them. Every non-com here wanted to be an officer, to replace the mealy-mouthed political friends of the governor of the state that had been appointed and elected.

Every officer wanted up the ladder of command and was willing to campaign, deceive and bribe in subtle ways, and write to Washington weekly to get there. That idiot Coons, who had just been made captain of Van Dyke's own company, had done that when he wrote to Governor Morton that the Fourteenth needed overcoats. That was what Van Dyke was trying to get his friend Will Houghton to understand, how to guard your flank as you charge forward toward being a captain, or even a colonel. Coons had been a lieutenant when he wrote the letter; now, he was a captain.

Will would not believe him. Well, Will was too pure for his own good. He thought this war was about the Union. Restoring the nation the patriots had fought to win and doing it with honor. No, it was about advancement. That was the meaning of the game. To gain ease and power and political favor, when and if this thing was ever over and won by the United States' troops.

Will did not understand that. He was still playing the glory game. But then Will had not been brought up by a failure of a father who whipped him black and blue, or a distant, drinking mother, as he, Van Dyke had. Time and the Rebels would teach Will a thing or two.

Van Dyke looked down the road into town, which was unusually empty. He reached inside his coat pocket, felt the pistol he kept ready and waiting. General Reynolds was a fool for forbidding the officers to keep personal pistols, he thought. Afraid we would violate the "laws of war," or hurt "innocent non-combatants." Everywhere in this Rebel state were Southern sympathizers. They shot from ambush, they picked off Union men on the roads, pretending to be army sharpshooters. No bushwhacker would leave him without the chance to fire his own shot. You had to have a hundred eyes in this war, and all of them open, if you were going to survive.

Eternal vigilance, that was the only way. Well, he had already seen about getting a contraband negro to do the cooking. A man had wandered into camp, and he, Van Dyke, had picked him up first off, before someone else preempted him. Certainly wasn't going to cook and clean for himself while there were former slaves about, wanting protection. And he had preempted shelter for the winter, too, though it certainly wasn't Queen Victoria's palace. Now, he had better figure out a way to become a second lieutenant; life would be pretty grim this winter unless he did. He had a plan.

Slowly Van Dyke walked towards the village about a half mile up the road, to see if the mail brought any of the list of amenities he had requested from home. He had ordered dried cherries and raisins, tinned cookies, a knitted scarf, and some fine coffee and oolong tea. It would not be easy for his mother to find these things, and it might mean the family would have to go without them. But he would have his contraband servant offer freshly ground Columbian blend and oolong with the tinned shortbread to the colonel, Colonel Kimball. Van Dyke had already asked him to stop by to drink tea, in honor of his mother's birthday. Not that Van Dyke ever celebrated the occasion before. There had always been too little money and too much work on their scrabbly spread to light birthday candles, even if his mother could have afforded the sugar and vanilla beans to concoct a cake.

But Colonel Kimball was his mother's second cousin, and they had played as children together in Ohio, before Van Dyke's mother married the turnip farmer who was his father and wore out her life with childbearing and chapped hands and other families' washing.

Kimball did not know about the worst days; he only knew Van Dyke was the son of his old golden-haired cousin. He had seemed pleased to be invited to tea. There would be another officer's place coming up in G Company soon; Lieutenant Denny was drinking himself into a court martial, no question about it.

Van Dyke's thoughts were interrupted by a group of raucous, swearing Southerners on the road; most cast passing, scornful glances at him. "These mountaineers look like chickens," he thought scornfully. One maiden riding in a buckboard smiled at him and touched her curls. He had never had trouble in that direction, that was for certain. Most people considered him extremely handsome; indeed, he considered himself so. But handsome did not spell advancement.

He continued on his way, his thoughts rambling about moodily. Denny would saturate himself once too often and at an inappropriate time; he would pull a knife on the wrong person, and it would happen soon. Van Dyke had known it from the moment he saw his law partner's son sign the rolls into Company G, there in the heady days after Sumter. Denny would drink himself into shame in the army as he had drunk himself into shame in Vincennes. Van Dyke would be right there, and Kimball would know him, could appoint him, even if the men voted for someone else. Even if Coons, the Captain of Company G, pulled the rug out. He and the men might just do that, they might make that mistake. A lot of the men were taken by, were supporting, his fellow sergeant Will Landon, a cocksure wise cracker who had about as much officering ability as a parrot with a sore leg.

These days Kimball was appointing lots of his own officers; he was suspicious of the democratic powers they had all used in the recruiting days. In that heady time they had elected leaders as if they were voting for Queen of the May. Too many popular, sawdust-brained rag dolls had been elected to command. Kimball knew this, and he was regulating democracy whenever he saw fit.

A few spots of rain fell and then lay like ink splotches on the fine dust of the road. Van Dyke picked up his pace, hoping a general rain would not develop; he did not have his raincoat. His thoughts drifted back to the advancement quandary.

Getting known and noticed, that was it, especially if you were a poor boy who had risen to the law by dint of your own hard work. And by the light of oil lamps at midnight in the dusty law offices of Denny and Sharp in Vincennes, and by your own carefully cultivated charm. He would be noticed, and appointed, and now might be the time, with Denny's character flaws bounding to the surface faster than driftwood on the Wabash after spring rains.

The tea party had to be just right. It had to show Sergeant Van Dyke as a gentleman, demonstrate his élan, in case anyone knew his scrabble-farmer background. The officers corps smacked of Napoleonic esprit de corps, of gallantry, and nobility of soul. So Houghton was always telling him. Will Houghton read books about Napoleon. That was what Kimball liked, anyway. Dratted old sheep. The colonel wore white gloves and liked to think he was one of the men. Last week the men in Company G had all swooned when, as they sang "Maggie, Coming Home" in the tent, a baritone voice joined them, and turning around, they saw it was the colonel.

Van Dyke looked about him at the trees by the side of the road. Pines, too many pines for his liking. And those stupid little bushes, laurel they called them, in the underbrush, giving a sameness to every acre. It was a lean country, sallow, with thin soil. Even the hogs couldn't find enough to eat out in the brush here.

He walked on, visualizing the tea party. The food had to be fresh and plentiful. Food was an obsession out here. Deprived of decent cooking and sometimes even basic sustenance, men turned into food lechers who slavered for a taste of something really savory. Colonels were no different under their plumed hats and sashes. Van Dyke had bribed the so-called chaplain, old Brother Welsh, to let him take mail duty for a week to be certain he got his things as soon as they came in.

Freshly ground coffee was a thing not heard of in camp; most of the men used grounds at least four times, even carried them about in little bags to suck on while they marched. Supposed to give you nutrition and provide moisture to your body, but the stale grounds were awful. He would offer Kimball freshly ground brew. He already had a small grinder, in top-drawer shape. Had "appropriated it for military service" up on Cheat Mountain, when they were scouting and had come upon a mountain family, Johnnies of course, just ready to eat a Sunday dinner. Roast veal, new potatoes, apple pie and coffee, and he snatched the grinder, too. Well, the damn locals deserved it, cohabiting with the Rebels.

Would Kimball be impressed? Or would he realize the tea was not just a gentlemanly tribute to one of his mother's favorite relatives? Mustn't seem as though he were crap-nosing it. No, the mother thing would take care of his excuse in that direction.

He reached the brigade's mail office, a small one-story frame house that had belonged to the schoolteacher in the village of Huttonville and was confiscated by the Northern Army. He entered, spoke to the mail officer, took up the Fourteenth's mail and was pleased to see his own packages were in. Yes, there was the tin of cookies. Well packed—they had not crumbled in the mail. Thank God! He checked the other items; found the coffee had not been included. Drat the old woman. Why hadn't she followed his instructions exactly! Just like her. Well, Kimball would like the tea. Van Dyke could smell its freshness all the way through the package.

He walked back along the road through the village, past a train of drovers herding beeves to the town. Good food was beginning to come in, but there were precious few luxuries. He had even spent fifty cents on a lemon for the tea. Raisins—he heard the colonel loved them. Then too, there would be the band. He had slipped a dollar to George Washington Lambert, the regimental band leader. They were to stop by and serenade the colonel, as if by chance.

Yes, it would be a good birthday for his dear old mother. He would see to that. He would invite Will Houghton and perhaps even Will's friend Beem, even though Beem was a prig. Have two officers to his party, in honor of his mother, of course. They'd write her a letter; all would sign it, that was the ticket. Will Houghton always made a good showing, and Kimball liked him best of all the officers in the Fourteenth. So the rumor went.

That was only one of the reasons Van Dyke liked to be with Will Houghton, he realized. There were other reasons: Will did uplift his own shoddy materialism with all his high-flown idealism. Van Dyke could use that; he knew it if he admitted the truth. Then too, Will was fascinated with battlefield tactics, and the subject really bored Van Dyke. He could learn a lot from hearing Will talk of feigned retreats, entrenchments, all the rot he was learning in his Glory School. It was Van Dyke who had coined the phrase, after all, laughing as Houghton told him of studying to be an officer in Lincoln's Army. If, and when, action ever should come, Will would be ready and Van Dyke would have sponged up a good deal of strategy like a sop of bread in beef gravy, just being near his friend.

As Van Dyke neared the oyster seller's cabin he had commandeered for his own digs, he paused a moment. It suddenly occurred to him to wonder why Will Houghton, one of the most respected men in the regiment, liked him. Well, probably there was a lot more good in him than he realized. Yes, that was undoubtedly it, and Colonel Kimball would realize it too and appoint him to take that drunkard Denny's place. The door of Van Dyke's cabin was wide open; he could see into it as he approached. Good, his contraband Clem was cooking, there at the fireplace. The colored man's name was Clemson Smith, and he was round, shaped like a bowling pin more than anything else, with a fringe of gray hair on a shiny brown pate.

Several coloreds had wandered into camp the other day, having liberated themselves into the hands of the United States Army, and Van Dyke and a few other officers had been quick to be their new U.S. Army "massas." "Hey there boy, Clem, here are the supplies for the tea I told you about. See you hop to it. Get that table inside clean. The place still stinks of seafood," he called out.

Kimball would like it that he had a colored servant, even though he knew that it could not be a permanent arrangement. Kimball was a Democrat; he didn't support freeing the slaves. Only the most radical Republicans favored that. The status of contrabands was not at all clear, and as soon as the spring campaign began, Clem would have to go. The slave was, after all, someone's property, even if that someone was a Rebel. Van Dyke thought he'd have to tell Kimball that Clem was a freeman, following him by contract. Yes, that was it. He raised the oolong tea to his nose to take one more long, reassuring sniff, and entered his house. He would set to and get the cleaning underway. Time enough to get the mail to the boys when that was done.

Van Dyke looked at his black servant. He was sprinkling flour into a turkey stew which hung over the fireplace and puttering over a tin stove, from which an incomparable, cinnamon odor was issuing.

"Why does it make me uncomfortable to look at this nigger?" Van Dyke wondered. It wasn't the rotund body, the shiny black shoes and checkered vest which made him look so different from the few other Negroes in the camp. No, not his dress. Possibly it was the spectacles and the cool, intelligent eyes in back of them. Clem did not resemble the Negroes Van Dyke had seen in Cincinnati, listlessly moving down the broad sidewalks without a gleam of interest in their eyes. They wouldn't jump even if the river rose over their feet.

"You been here a week, boy, and you've cooked excellent food. You can take a hunk of meat and a few turnips and an onion you dig yourself and turn out a fricassee worthy of the Old Yellow Tavern in Vincennes."

"Yes, suh." Clem was adding water from a canteen, carefully lifting the turkey meat and vegetables to keep them from burning. "Stews de easiest thing t' fix on the road where you don't got good stoves."

"I don't know a thing about you."

"No, suh." The contraband was silent, then, realizing he was expected to give information, began cautiously, "Ah'm from Virginny. And ah'm a free man. I look at it dat way. Massa Lincoln will make us free soon and I am jest anticipatin' my liberation. Took m' walking papers and went a little early."

Anticipatin'. This nigger used unnecessarily big words. Uppity. But he could cook. Clem was opening the door of a little tin oven which sat on the coals and Van Dyke could see a pan of apple dumplings inside. Apple dumplings! Perhaps there would be some left for tomorrow's tea.

"You said when you came into camp that you were from a plantation in King's and Queen's County."

"Yes, suh. I had been with one massa for twenty years, den I was sold at auction when my massa went bankrupt. I had been at de farm in King's and Queen's county eight years. Married me a house servant and den I got to assistin' in de master's kitchen with her and learnt to make good pastries, tortes. Dey had parties ever' fall and spring."

"Go on," Van Dyke commanded, sorting the mail. He would deliver it before taps.

"The war come and all de Southern regiments were a-comin' into our area to sign up. 'Fore we knowed it, my massa and his sons had formed a regiment and went to the wars. "

"What was their unit?" Van Dyke wondered if it was one they had met on the mountain.

" 'Crampton's Chevaliers' dey called derselves."

Van Dyke thought that was just like the Rebs. Always cloaking their treachery and trouble in fancy French names and gray satin.

"Us niggers was on our own for some weeks. Et up everything in de larder, but we took care o' de mistress and de girls best we could."

The Negro man opened the tin oven door to stir some sugar syrup he had poured over the dumplings.

"Where'd you get that tin oven?" Van Dyke wondered.

"I had lots o' things with me when I come in with my mule. Didn't you see de saddle packs? Wasn't goin' to take m' walkin' papers without de means to make m' living. If we're goin' to be free as de white man, we are goin' to have to work like de white man."

"If that day ever comes. Which I doubt," Van Dyke said. Such talk aggravated him mightily. He couldn't even conceive of niggers walking free on the streets of every town in America, applying for jobs, saying "How do, Gus," to him in front of the soda parlor in Vincennes. This damned descendent of an ape—still, Van Dyke's curiosity drove him on.

"You left the plantation," he said, contemplatively.

"Farm, suh. We calls 'em farms in our part o' Virginny. Well, dey called us up to Bull Run. Said all de negras in de county was to dig trenches and help at de battle. All of us went."

"Bull Run," Van Dyke mused, looking up from the mail. How he and the other men in the Fourteenth had wished they could be there last July when they heard a giant battle was to be fought outside Washington. When the extent of the debacle was known, they had not been so sure.

"My job was to run charges to de cannoneers and to swab cannons. Was terrible work. I was frightened out of m' wits. Wisht, all of us wisht, we could jest run on over to de Yankees. But we would 'a been shot. Finally a piece next to us exploded, woundin' some of de Secesh men I worked for. I took to m' heels and went back for a while to de farm. Wanted to be with m' family, wife and two boys. Finally, though, decided to leave and join de war."

"You can't fight. No black men can, or ever will."

Clem Smith looked up, his eyes calm but sure. "We will fight, jest as we will be free. Massa Lincoln will see to dat."

"What makes you think he is going to do that, boy? Not a man in the regiment would like that. The old railsplitter'd be rubbing our noses in crap, boy, if he did that."

"Crap or not, it's a-goin' to come. You better start to get your nose ready, now, massa, for a bad stink.

"You are the sauciest nigger I ever did see." Van Dyke's face was growing red.

"Why dat make you mad, massa? I jest tell truth. We are de webbing, so to speak, of de Rebel army, and the Yankees cain't afford to let us stay de way we are."

"Webbing? Speak English."

"Look at a piece o' weaving, massa. Specially tow work. You can see de webbing and de filler. The troops are de filler of de Rebel army. But back o' them is de webbing." He held up his hand and Van Dyke stared at the palm, dusty gray black, and broad as a wooden roof shingle. "What keeps it all together, criss-crossed everwhere? We are de webbing, de slaves back home. Planting de corn de soldiers eat, raising der stock, taking care of de women and children dey left behind. Free de slaves, take out dis webbing, and you take de heart of de army."

He picked up an old piece of hemp bagging he used to cover his hand when he opened the oven door. "See dis, massa?" He showed it to Van Dyke.

"Pull out de webbing, thus." He pulled two threads, then three more through the piece and dropped them on the dirt. Then he handed Van Dyke the few straggly threads left.

"Ruint your garment," the colored man said and turned again to his stove. "No, massa, you are wrong about bein' freed, and you are wrong about de fightin'." Clem Smith, squatting on the uneven puncheons before his tin oven, looked calmly up at Van Dyke. "We will fight for de Union sometime soon, and when we do, we'll be jest as good soldiers as de white folks." His eyes were firm, without a trace of mockery, and yet something in them enraged Van Dyke. What was it? Self confidence. The one thing that made Negroes bearable was that they kept their eyes down, looked like beaten hound dogs. Everybody said so. It was their nature. And yet this one—it was all he could do to keep from whacking this nigger across the face. And yet what was it Smith said about the Rebel army? Could it be true? Some men in the regiment talked of the slave backup system for the Rebel army, but he had never paid attention to them. Could it be true that having the slaves freed could help end the war?

He changed the subject. "Clem, I'm having a little soiree tomorrow afternoon, a tea. For the colonel."

"Oh?" The colored man had another piece of bagging on his hand and was taking out the apple dumplings.

"I—I want everything to go just right. I had some sweet biscuits shipped in, and I want you to make tea. Maybe some other things, if we could find them. It's important to me—to have it right, the colonel there and everything, you know."

"I understand, massa," Clem said without looking up. "Leave it to me."

"I should take the mail to the men," Van Dyke thought. His head suddenly began to hurt. Tomorrow morning would surely do for the letters. He wanted to be in fine fettle for his party tomorrow. This was not a duty day. He would send Clem up the road with his invitations to Beem and Houghton, then be up early tomorrow to perfect his plans.

The brigade band played almost on tune next day at its special appearance outside the oyster seller's shack. The tinny notes floated through the window, which was opened because of the mildness of the day. "Schubert's Serenade," Van Dyke said with a tilt of his head that said that was nothing, he knew all of Schubert's music.

"I'm sorry your company officers, Lieutenant Denny and Captain Coons, couldn't be with us. You say you invited them?" Colonel Kimball asked.

He was seated on an oyster box with a pillow case over it. The room smelled relatively good. Van Dyke had put pine boughs about.

"Well, I thought of it." As if he would ask that son-of-a-bitch hypocrite Coons or a drunkard to his tea. "Actually, Captain Denny is often—indisposed—these days." He looked across the box at Houghton and Beem. He had to be careful. He did not want anyone, not even his friends, to know how actively he was scheming for Denny's position. But Denny had already headed into the tents today with his bottle; that was only the simple truth.

"Is this real cream, Sergeant Van Dyke?" Nathan Kimball peered into a tin cup.

"Well, yes sir. My freedman, here, Clem, managed to get it." Houghton was stirring the tea in his cup, Beem enjoying the biscuits one after another. But it was the apple dumplings which were the tour de force of the party. Kimball had put a finger into the cream cup and was licking cream, savoring the rare treat before he poured it onto the dumpling.

"Boy, how did you get this cream?" the colonel said, stroking his beard and turning to look at the contraband.

"We boys in Virginny have got good at beg an' borry," the colored man said. He was passing round a plate of cracked walnuts. "Lots of dese folks have stashes o' things in der root cellars. Dey keeps cows in de woodsheds dat nobody knows 'bout. I have some small things I brought from the farm, scarce as hen's teeth, needles and pins, buttons to trade."

"Bright boy, this," Colonel Kimball said, looking pleased. He had gold teeth and they glittered when he smiled. "How'd he get to be a freedman?"

"Well," Van Dyke began, uneasily. He didn't want this nigger's status to come up. "Somewhere in the early part of the war, when his master went off to the army, he was freed. I guess it was part of an obligation."

"Yes, suh," Clem said, playing along because it suited his claim of freedom. "Now I have to get m' wife freed too. And m' boys. T'aint no good to have de rooster out o' the barnyard if de hen and chicks are still pent up. I'm goin' back and take care of de rest of m' flock."

"Free Negroes, all over," Kimball mused, squeezing a piece of lemon into his tea. "Who would have thought it?"

"We're all going to have to get used to it," Beem said. "It is simple justice." Kimball did not look up at his H Company lieutenant. Everyone knew Beem was an abolitionist.

"They say President Lincoln is going to declare free all the slaves of Rebel traitors whose property we confiscate," Houghton said. He had read it in the New York papers.

"It will go further than that," Van Dyke said.

"I hope not," Kimball said. "It would make our job harder. The men are opposed to fighting to free the slaves."

Van Dyke looked at the older man and decided to take a daring plunge.
"It may make our job easier sir." Kimball, a little surprised, turned to
look at Van Dyke inquiringly. "Well, ultimately—"

Van Dyke stuck a spoon into his apple dumpling and licked his lips. "Sir,
the Negroes are standing in the wings of the whole Rebel operation. They
are the whole labor force. To free them would hurt the war effort terribly."

Kimball peered at this sergeant, whom he had hardly noticed before this
week.

"Well," Van Dyke went on, "think of them as the webbing in a piece of
fabric. To withdraw it would—" he was conscious of Clem Smith's presence, quiet and unassuming, behind them at the washtub in the corner, "hurt
the Rebel effort and possibly allow us to win. It would be a small price to
have freed slaves about, with all their problems, if we saved the Union."

"Hmm. Never thought about it that way, sergeant. Please pass the walnuts. Free the niggers, beat the Rebs. Maybe has some sense to it. Have to
think about that for a while."

Later that afternoon Van Dyke finally brought the mail to Company G. He
had his contraband with him. He liked to parade him around a little, give a
certain status to his position. They finished passing out the envelopes and
small packages to the men and left the group of tents, walking briskly. Van
Dyke handed Clem the pouch of letters he had just collected from the men
and the one written at the tea party to his mother. She would certainly be
surprised to have such a fine letter from Van Dyke; he had written her only a
couple of times since he joined the service. He sent Clem down the road to
the mail station.

He needed to straighten out tonight's duties before taps. No need to check
with Denny; he would be three sheets to the wind by now. And Landon
would be impossible to find, writing his "dispatches" to the paper or short-
sheeting some fellow officer's cot. Better find Coons. Actually, it wouldn't
hurt to cultivate Captain Coons a little, even if he was a first-class horse's
hind end. Van Dyke wanted to be sure to do all things right if attention was
going to be cast on him, if he was to be considered for lieutenant.

"Look at that! There's a nigger walking down the road, Henderson,"
John McClure yelled at his cousin. "Brass Ass Van Dyke has freed a slave,
it do appear, and has taken him under his PROtection.

"So I see. Brass Ass emancipation. Best not get downwind of the black
ape, cousin. Ain't good for your health." Henderson Simpson walked to the

pot Isaac Crim was stirring. Simpson's round, ruddy face glowed with the heat of the unexpectedly warm day. "How doth the stew, my friend?"

"As good as a rubberized rooster and wormy flour can make it," Crim said. "I'm jest so pleased to be asked to dinner. Didn't I hear that some Christian soul around here has two bottles of brandy to share with his campmates?"

"All too true. If the provost ain't about, call that campmate out and we'll dine a mite. Dilute our troubles in dissolvin' spirits." They did, and awkward, gangly Bushby Quillen came and sat before the fire, opening his stash of forbidden liquors.

"Got 'em from Lieutenant Denny. He bought 'em. Is back there drinkin' himself into forget-it-all land," Quillen said.

"He'll be in trouble if they find out he's bought for enlisted men. He ain't supposed to do that," McClure said. Still, he held up his cup for some of the brandy. There was a silence around the campfire. Everything had happened so fast in the last week and a half, since the Battle of Greenbrier. It was as if they were finally in the war they had waited so long to join, and it made their thoughts serious, almost sad. The brandy did not help.

"Ah, if only the home folks could see us now. They'd pine and droop to know our sacrifices, don'tcha know," the sentimental Tommy Thompson said.

"You speak true. Many a sad fair one, I s'pect, is dropping tears right now as she reads the account of our sufferin's at the Battle of Greenbrier," Simpson added. "Landon sharpened his quill and dipped it in ink for several pages to the *Vincennes Western Sun*," he grunted. " 'Bout us in the battle."

The mushy chicken and onions were dished onto slabs of hardtack crackers; more cheap brandy was poured into tin cups.

"Here's to the weeping fair ones." Cups were raised and touched.

"Here's to all the folks back home. May the comfort of our recent glory in battle console 'em for the loss of sons, fathers, brothers far from the joys of home." Henderson stood, making the toast.

"Hyar, hyar." Cups touched, with the clink of tin.

"Is that nigger gone? Keep him away from me. Ugh. Might get bugs," Quillen opined, then mumbled into his cup. "Hate 'em wors'n Indians."

Several cups later, as the embers faded, untended, around the campfire in G Company mess, someone offered the fifty-first toast.

"Hyar's to our officers, bold and noble. Putting the glory of the regiment before personal gain. We can give them all our trust."

"Hyar's to Sergeant Van Dyke and his nigger. May we not see too much o' the latter."

("Hyar, hyar.")

"Here's to Denny for supplyin' the liquor. May he get tubs more of it where this come from."

("He will, he will.")

"Hyar's to Ham Mitchell of Company C—and the others no longer with us. May the folks of our dear state, our loved ones, not repine nor worry that we may be next. May the blighted firesides, the grievin' villages find comfort for our loss to the wars."

"Yes, here's to the folks back home. The reason for fightin' this yere war."

(Drunkenly and a little sadly, "Hyar, hyar.")

Slowly the campfires died, the lights went out on the encampment of the Fourteenth Indiana regiment, on a mild October night in the first year of the Civil War at Huttonville, Virginia, far from the state of Indiana.

October, 1861

Chapter Two

Catherine McClure Hogue strode along the wooden sidewalks of Main Street in Vincennes, Indiana. Rain had sluiced down the last three days, causing rivulets of sand to course over the pine boards, burying them in some cases. Catherine held up the flounces of a skirt that concealed a still slim figure.

"Fine state of affairs," she told herself, "that a seventy-four-year-old woman has to serve the needs of fashion by wearing barrel hoops and fripperies that tumble down like a waterfall." She passed Ephriam Baird's store and paused to look in the new plate glass window. "How do they do that?" she wondered, looking at the slick glass, only bubbled in a few spots. "Pa thought leaded glass panes were marvelous and said Grandpa McClure almost killed himself in the wilderness of Pennsylvania gettin' hold of bottle glass to put in one window hole of the log cabin. But a whole pane? 'Tis a genie's miracle, rubbed from a magic lamp."

A sign painted right on the glass said, "Ice cream saloon. Five fine creams to suit your taste."

Then, on she went past Fire Station Number One, Thomas Riley Fancy Goods, and James Davidson, Boots, which were all little, two-story clap-board buildings, and around the corner to the livery stable on Third street.

"Mornin' Mrs. Hogue. Will you be rentin' a rig?" the proprietor asked.

"I'm proposin' to get a horse and calash, Willis. Goin' to the Orphans' Benefit," she said, looking the man over with a sharp eye. His name was Willis Mawkins; he had just bought the place. He wore a watch chain and sported an almost oily mustache. His grandfather had been a hired hand at her father's farm, and his father had helped her late husband, John Hogue, with haying. Thirty, forty years ago, was that? The years, like the little children that used to tumble about their home, had trooped over the hills and out of sight and she had not even known they were gone, either children or years. When she turned about, all was changed.

"Won't Miss Lettie be goin'?" Mawkins asked her, taking a cigar out of his pocket.

THE DREAM DIVIDED • 27

"She isn't goin' out much these days. Doesn't cotton to folk, I don't know why."

This was both true and untrue. Her daughter Letitia, with whom she lived here in Vincennes, was home behind drawn curtains, being "sickly," toying with tonic bottles and Barbhof's female elixir. And with the sleeping drops.

"I'll take the gentle one, the mare you set me up with last time," Catherine told Mawkins, pulling greenbacks from her purse. The man pocketed the money and went to harness the calash, wiping his face with a large linen square monogramed on the corner.

The nine o'clock sun was hot in a cobalt blue sky following the rains. Southern Indiana in the fall was like that, like Caintuck, or Tennessee or Texas, even, Catherine thought. Winter never really lit till January 15, and then it quickly flitted away, like an eighteen-year-old girl cousin come to visit. Just as well; the orphans' benefit would be out in the yard of the old McClure homestead on the road east. The first part of it, that is. The ball would be at Duggerville, on the Wabash. It was a real she-bang, three counties involved.

The weather made Catherine think about her grandson John. The telegraph had said that the boys on Cheat Mountain were in a violent, freezing rainstorm when they prepared for battle at Greenbrier Bridge. She knew her grandson John was safe; the casualties had been telegraphed, but the details of the battle were not yet in the *Western Sun*. A few folk had asked about him, but most everybody was too busy with the orphanage play parties to fret much about the far-away boys. They were reasonably safe and having a fine time, folks said, cavorting around on the mountain tops, camping out like Indians, cooking good things over open fires. Soon 'twould all be over, anyways. So the reasoning went.

"I'll bring the rig back tomorrow, Willis," Catherine said, letting him help her onto the board and taking the reins.

"Aren't you going to the ball out on the river at Duggerville tomorrow night?" the man wondered.

"Invited, but declined. The picnic at the old home place will be more'n enough for me. These bones are too old for 'the gallop' or 'polka trot.' 'Tis for the young belles. My young cousin Jacob Joe Scott is going, and his brother Zach, so their father tells me. Besides, the Duggers are Democrats." She smiled enigmatically.

She might have said Copperheads, but she restrained herself, not knowing Willis's politics. Turn over a rock in southern Indiana these days, and you turned over a Southern sympathizer, hissing like a poison viper. And she had better things to do than take tea with the folk who gave aid and comfort to the Confederacy, the very Rebels who wanted to blow her grandson John off the face of the earth.

She clucked to the horses and headed out of the road north at a brisk pace. The play party picnic was to start at eleven-thirty o'clock. Half of three counties would be there, so the *Western Sun* had said. Musicale group from Bruceville to play flutes and piccolos, Women's Shakespeare Club to do a recitation from *The Merchant of Venice*, and even the Evansville Crescent City Fireman's Band would play.

After twenty minutes or so she turned onto the old Washington road. It used to be called the Buffalo Trace and it ran east, from Vincennes to Washington to Mt. Pleasant and the ruins of Hindostan and east to Louisville. 'Twas on this oldest road in the state that all of the McClure homesteads lay. History seemed to hang from the branches of the old oaks and beeches which had been left in front of these homesteads, virgin timber from a time when forest and Indian dominated the land.

Her father George McClure had been one of five McClure children to come to Indiana from Kentucky with their eighty-year-old, widowed mother. Four middle-aged sons they were, veterans of the Revolutionary War, and their families, along with one daughter Jenny Scott, who was the mother of her dear cousin John Robert.

Catherine and John Robert were among the last of a generation, many having already trooped over the hill, and she and John Robert spent much time together, for the sake of the old times. Not that they lived in the past. No, John Robert was active in his Quaker affairs, she with the Upper Indiana Church and the—Abolitionist movement. Best say it out loud in your mind, even though if it were said aloud it could cause a clap of thunder from the skies in southern Indiana.

She trotted the horse a while; then the mare whinnied and seemed to want to slow down; Catherine never knew quite what to do when a horse did that. She snapped the reins; the mare continued to loll along. She gingerly applied the pretty women's horsewhip Willis Mawkins had given her, and the mare condescended to stretch its legs a mite.

Catherine was an indifferent horsewoman and she knew it; always had been since the days when she was allowed to curry the beautiful English stallions and geldings in her Uncle John's stable in Caintuck, in the days before the family came to Indiana. A dozen beautiful, blooded quarter horses had been delivered to Bardstown by her Aunt Janie McClintock McClure. Now dead these thirty years, disgraced in Tennessee after living with a strange old herb healer she'd taken up with after Uncle John died. Gone, trooped over the hill, out of sight.

Uncle John and Jane's horses had seemed like huge, giant horses from dragon tales when the McClure cousins were small. They had foreign names, Belle Ame and Fincastle's Dream. They stomped and snorted when you didn't expect them to. At least she had always finished the currying job without running out of the barn the way her cousin Jack did. Aunt Martha and Uncle Dan'l had made him come back in and finish the currying, said he'd grow up to be namby-pamby if he didn't "steel himself to duty," even when he was afraid.

Poor Jack. Good Jack. He had died at Hindostan Falls, in the great Cold Sickness, doctoring the sick, including her own father, who had died anyway, like all the rest in that terrible Hindostan epidemic. Jack had learned to steel himself to duty, certainly Hindostan had proven that. But he had never learned to like horses.

Thinking of Jack made her think of his grandson, John R. McClure, and it still seemed odd to think that John was the grandson of both she and her cousin Jack at the same time. 'Twasn't incest when two second cousins married as her Nancy Jane and his Alfred McClure had, but it was a powerful lot of wild McClure for one bloodstream to absorb. Contrariness, pugnacity and odd, elfin winsomeness—there must be enough of all those McClure traits flying around John McClure out there in western Virginia to keep the whole regiment supplied. Well supplied, too. She chuckled to herself, remembering how her ancestors had crossed from Northern Ireland in a hurricane, fought Shawnee and Munsee Indians, and finally became the talk of Knox County by getting drunk and slugging it out at the crossroads, taking all comers just for the sake of a Scotch-Irish fight.

She was coming now to the first of the McClure farms, the beautiful rolling fields of her long-dead uncle, William McClure, who had earned them by captaining a company for George Rogers Clark in the Revolution. The fields were now farmed by his daughter's descendants. To the north of the road, her uncle John McClure's stand lay, shrunken to a third of its original size by Aunt Janie's indifference and bad management, part of it now the Emisons' farm. And, to the right and down the road was Uncle Dan'l's acres—over a thousand of them, green with a beard of winter wheat, a tidy part of them now owned by her young grandson John R. McClure, though he had never yet lived on them.

John ought to make a good soldier. Any McClure should—they had fought for Washington, Clark, Harrison—no draft dodgers they. There were other McClures in this Civil war: her uncle Will's great-grandson, Archie McClure III was one of about a hundred who had gone. Well, but then Archie was in a Mississippi regiment. He, whose great-grandfather had fought to establish the nation, was now fighting to tear it apart. Not odd, really, when you stopped to think that most of Will's kin had lived over there at Duggerville for a couple of generations now. Near the house with the big southern pillars, where the Duggers had kept "bond slaves" for thirty years after Indiana became a free state. Where slave-trading had gone on in secret ways. Where slimy-skinned Copperheads lived now, pretending to be patriotic Americans.

Would the next battle see her beloved grandson John wounded or dead? While these Southern-sympathizing people stayed alive and well all around her, railing away against winning the war? It made her angry when she thought about it, and her heart jumped in an alarming way. Best not think of it.

There was so much evil these days. It was getting so she didn't want to think about it, as if her brain would burst if she did. She applied one of the new theories she had read about recently in a book: cerebral calisthenics. Control your own thinking with vigor, do exercises of good thinking! Nip bad thoughts before they become blue moods! Just force them out of your mind and replace them with good thoughts. One, two, one, two, bad thinking all go shoo! That was it.

It was a theory originated by a Dr. Evan Parsticle and his wife Clothilde. Some of it was pure rubbish—Mrs. Parsticle advocated "marital restraint," boasting that she and her husband had not completed the marital act for twenty years now. They allowed all the "bodily energies" to peak at a moment before the marital climax, then pulled back from each other without completing the act. "Thus energies are reabsorbed into the psyche, generating new and noble deeds for the future." So Mrs. Parsticle said.

Piggy bath. Pure hog wash. Catherine guessed she should know what the release of "marital energy" was like, living with a tall, blonde Scandinavian giant of a husband for almost forty years. Well, the Parsticles' ideas about cerebral calisthenics were better; they were helping her face her grandson's fighting in the war. Her mind kept slipping to what a battle would be like, cannons booming and shrapnel flying. She heard recently of one poor county boy who was decapitated at Rich Mountain. Head blown off and lying by the trunk—just discipline yourself, Catherine. No thoughts of John lying under a tree, head blown half off, John drowning in a torrent fording a stream, John captured and taken to a dreadful Rebel prison—one, two, bad thoughts shoo!

Now the sun was high in the sky, and the air was growing warmer by the minute. She came to the old home place, where her father George McClure had built his homestead in 1803, when she was a fair young girl. Her heart leapt, in spite of her firm resolve, thinking of the world in those days when they lived lives out of storybooks. John Hogue had been captured by Miamis and had killed more than one bear, a real hero of the woods, while she was feisty and defied her family, running off to join the Shakers. He had won her, carrying her away from the Shakers on a thundering horse. Over the hill, to the north, was the place where John Hogue built the stockade to keep out the Indians in the troubles of 1812, where he brought her as a bride, where their children were born. Over the hill, far away, in another time. Must live today. She scorned old people who tottered around whining about the past.

Look, beyond the home place was the Mifflin mansion, deserted these six years but now being refurbished and turned into the Protestant orphans' asylum. It stood on land her brother Billy, who owned the family homestead and had bought the old Mifflin place too, had donated. This was what all the fuss was about. There were many orphans from the changing economic times and cholera, and they couldn't all go to the Catholic orphanage south of town. There would be many more left parentless from this war.

These counties needed a home-like place to bring the orphan children up. Her own grandchildren, including John, had been orphaned after all, hadn't they? And the court gave them to their other grandmother, a bitter old woman, and after her death to her prune-faced daughter while she, Catherine, was not allowed to see them until just last year. (Cerebral calisthenics, one, two, one, two.) And, then, just as she was reunited with her grandson John McClure, he went off to war, almost the very month. (Bad thoughts go shoo.) And here she was, seventy-four, a widow, most of her children moved away or dead, the only daughter she had with her suffering from hysteria, the only son left in these parts unmarried and morose and—(one, two.) Taking her handkerchief out, Catherine Hogue wiped away the tears which coursed down her dusty cheeks and drove onto the homestead of her youth. Mental calisthenics be damned. She'd cry a tear or two if she wanted to before she got to this party. Wasn't the past worthy of it?

Friendly hands reached out to help her down, care for the rig and horse. "Cat—you're here, late as always," her youngest brother Billy said, with a ringing laugh. There it was, the long, angular face so like her own father's. And here was her son, Horace, who lived with his uncle out here and served as a hand on the old place.

"Hello, m' dear," Catherine said, kissing her son. Every time she saw him, which wasn't often enough, he was grayer. Thirty-six he was and fervidly for the Union. He carried newspapers about with him, discussing every battle, and he had tried to join the Fourteenth Indiana, but they had turned him down. A game leg from a hunting accident years ago, caused him to limp, bodily and mentally, she told herself with a pang.

Her spirits lifted as she saw the band assembleing on the platform her brother and son had erected for the festivities. Men were in their Sunday best, and this only Thursday. She passed through the crowd, catching shreds of conversation.

"Russia has recognized the Union. The Czar sent his messenger."

"Best corn crop we ever had around here. Cribs full to bursting."

"Big cities these days all are like Sodom and Gomorrah. I read it in the paper. Rats in the soldiers' hospital in New York City. Run right over the patients' faces at night. What next?"

"That's them Easterners for you."

Black frock coats and trousers, fancy silk vests and silk hats, layered hoop skirts, parasols, bonnets with birds leaning and pecking towards her—she made her way through them all. Well, it was her cousin John Robert Scott who was stepping onto the stand. Of course, it would be John Robert, who was first when the church doors opened, first to dig in his pocket when the Benevolent Society came around for the poor relief. But not first to pay for uniforms for a company of the war regiments. Ah, no. He was a Quaker.

"My friends and relatives," he smiled right at Catherine. Bless his heart. "You have come from all these parts hereabouts to support a very worthy cause—the new area Orphans' Home. After we've had our program and bid on the dinners, there will be a tour of the facilities down the road there. We'll chase the ghosts away and see the new wing that's being built on the old house for these children. The straw hats you see turned upside down on the table are for your donations. Remember, you do not have to pay in full today, just tell us what you want to subscribe.

"Friends, it's at times like this that southern Indiana shows the substance it's made of. We put aside sectarian concerns—why, you Methodists and Disciples are standing right next to Presbyterians and Roman Catholics here today, and when you come up to put your donation in the straw hats, it doesn't matter if you're a Democrat, a Know-Nothing, or a Republican." (Cheers when each group was mentioned.) "Put all parties aside, just for today. We all stand together for our homeless children. We have a program and then dinner, and I think you can still be home by dark. If you've come too far, as you've probably read in the paper already, the farmers up and down the road have generously opened their homes. To start us off—" He introduced the Crescent City Firemen's Band and they oompahed out in bright red uniforms, sat in chairs, and played several concert selections, heavy on tuba, light on piccolo.

The Bruceville Musicale performed next, heavy on piccolo, light on tunefulness. For their third number Mrs. Almeady Beckwith announced she would be singing to the flute accompaniment. "I'll be performin' for you a little 'riginal composition of m' own, 'Weeping willow, shed your tears.' " Heads nodded in approval, hands clapped a little.

Simpering out at the audience, she awaited the fluttery introductory passages in a sort of heavenly euphoria. Her face reminded Catherine of the glowing countenances of angels on a children's Christmas book she had bought for her granddaughter, Annie. Except that the angels were young cherubim and Almeady Beckwith weighed almost three hundred pounds.

> *"Weeping willow, shed your tears*
> *Droplets in the vale*
> *My love lieth in the ground*
> *Face so cold and pale."*

Too much vibrato had always made Catherine want to laugh. "Oh, God," she prayed, "do not let me giggle at all that vocal tremolo and wiggling."

> *"Raven, take your ebony wing*
> *Cover up your beak*
> *Fly now to his resting place*
> *Hill so bare and bleak—"*

"Piffle," thought Catherine. "These silly songs. How can a raven fly if its wing is covering its—*beak* was it. I don't know which is worse, Almeady's vibrato or those tootling flutes."

Just then there was a genteel commotion towards the rear. Catherine turned to see two beautifully clad women, accompanied by two young men, disembark from a handsome carriage driven by a black man. Bright, polished cotton dresses swished the grass as they came to the side of the group, near the platform. The men with them set up tiny, elegant upholstered camp stools and the women sat, oh so carefully, putting up parasols to keep the sun off their complexions.

"The Duggers. Leave it to them to enter like Queen Victoria and her court," Catherine thought. A murmur, composed in exact portions of disdain and envy, rippled through the standing crowd.

The Bruceville Musicale finished, curtsied, and retired. John Robert Scott came again to the platform. "Ladies and gentleman, I'd like to introduce Mr. Greene, the editor of the *Vincennes Western Sun*. He's just received a message that will be of interest to you."

A florid man with long, wavy red hair leapt onto the platform. He displayed a piece of paper. "A messenger has just brought the report of Sergeant Landon, our battlefield correspondent in the Fourteenth Indiana Regiment. I thought I might anticipate the story in tomorrow's paper by sharing this with you." He put on spectacles and cleared his throat.

" 'On Cheat Mountain October 6, 1861. Friend Greene: I promised you details of the "bully fight" the Glorious Fourteenth was engaged in at the Greenbrier Bridge. We were ordered by General Reynolds to show a 'reconnaissance in force,' which we did do, galloping over the bridge, forming in line of battle behind the Ninth Indiana and driving back the skirmishers they sent against us until we were called to retire. Our noble Colonel Kimball wished to pursue but—' "

The crowd, which had turned on its heels to chit-chat when the last entertainment ceased, was just beginning to attend to what was being said. Someone was shushing them; clapping his hands for order. It was Catherine's son, Horace. If there was something to be said about the Union, he wanted it to be heard.

Editor Greene went on, a little louder, and the crowd began to listen more intensely. " 'Eleven killed and fifteen wounded. Three of the killed and four of the wounded belonged to the Fourteenth, none from Vincennes. We took thirteen prisoners. Bully for—' "

To the side, the Dugger group had stood up. The men lit cigars and turned away from Editor Greene's reading. The women brushed away crumbs from their skirts, although the younger woman, tall and slim, with cascades of dark hair tied back in a yellow ribbon, seemed to try to maintain courtesy, twisting her head towards the speaker. The subdued laughter of the woman who was obviously her mother, however, rang across the crowd. Heads turned towards the group.

"Althea Dugger should have better manners than that," Catherine said to herself. "Brought up in Tennessee in a mansion, sent to Ladies' School. She should be bright as a copper candlestick about manners. Maybe the years of living with Lucius Dugger corroded her," Catherine thought. "Handsome daughter, though, very." The swaggering, cigar-smoking young pups she recognized as Calhoun Dugger and Willie McClure, brother of Archie III and her own cousin. It was Willie's brother that was fighting for the Confederacy. Her son Horace had turned, fixing his stare on them.

Editor Greene cleared his throat and continued reading: " 'During the engagement, unfortunately, the Ninth Indiana shot and wounded one of their own comrades. Such accidents occur frequently out here, because—' "

Calhoun Dugger and Willie McClure turned their backs squarely on the speaker. They blew thick smoke rings shaped like donuts, which floated towards the speaker's platform, dissipating in snake-shaped wisps around his head. They were obviously not interested in hearing of the gallant doings of the Fourteenth Indiana Regiment. A woman's words, spoken slightly louder, began to float out of the conversation. "Do tell, Calhoun. That is, indeed, humorous." Althea Dugger's laugh grew more strident.

But harsh words rose out of the crowd, also. "Quiet, over there. Shame!"

"Son Horace, again," Catherine noted, an edge of apprehension beginning to niggle at her consciousness. "We're supposed to be forgetting politics for the orphans' asylum."

Editor Greene paused, looked towards the group on the embroidered chairs, and went on reading. " 'The Thirty Second Ohio held 3,000 Rebels in check who were attempting to attack us from the rear and cut off our retreat—' "

"Ha, ha, ha. Tell that story again, sir. Funniest thing I ever heard tell." Calhoun Dugger's voice was really very loud now. Suddenly, someone jumped from the crowd, like a jack-in-the-box on a spring, making fists and punching. "You goddamned Copperhead. Why don't you pay attention when he's reading about the men who're dyin' for us out there?" It was Horace.

And the fight was on.

Other men from the crowd rushed to the fray, some trying to pull back Horace, some pulling back the ladies, others trying to pummel Calhoun and Willie, who already had bloody mouths and were shouting invective, which other Southern sympathizers joined—

"Bloody Abolitionists! Freedom haters! Nigger kissers!"

"Copperheads! Damn your Democratic, stinking hides—" Catherine and the other ladies gathered their flounces and fled. Still, finally, there was no real reason to fight on a beautiful October afternoon; the spirit of the event seemed to affect the fighters, and the melee fell apart almost as quickly as it had begun, dissipating the way fights do from the outside in. Men drifted away, sweating and mumbling, while the Duggers dabbed at their wounds with dainty handkerchiefs and took out glass jars of mint liquor to calm their nerves.

She saw her cousin approaching the platform again and decided to speak to him. "John Robert," she called out, "everyone in the country seems to be fighting, even the folk in our county."

"Yes, cousin, I can never understand any of it. Peaceful persuasion, that's it. Thank God my boys are not in the war." He had twins; one was an objector of conscience, the other a Southern sympathizer. Neither one of them might ever fight in this all-volunteer war.

"Speaking of fighting," John Robert Scott asked, deferring his trip to the platform to approach her, "How are your grandchildren? I was glad to hear Editor Greene speak of the Fourteenth Indiana and see that your grandson John McClure was unscratched in the recent conflict." His voice was lowered as he spoke of personal matters, between the two of them. "And Bob and Annie and Mary Jane—living there with their aunt Jewell. Have you been able to see them? The court order should still be in force."

"Yes, I see them but not enough. Mary Jane is twenty-two and sweet. Bob is sixteen and works on the farm. Annie, well, Annie is unusual. She is just ten."

"Ten? I thought she was older. You know I have never seen her, but from a letter you sent me I had gathered she was older."

"Was I that careless with my pen? Well, sometimes I think she is going on sixty-five. Curly-headed little hoyden. She has lived through a lot."

"We are ready to finish the program, Catherine," John Robert said, taking her hand in his. She kissed his cheek and let him go.

The sun went under the one, fat white cloud that was in the sky. Everyone drifted back towards the platform, dropping pledges in the straw hats. The Wheatland Women's Shakespeare group appeared and gave shaky interpretations of three key scenes from the bard, including Hamlet's mad scene with Ophelia. "They're leaving out the bawdy references to bedplay," Catherine told herself. "Nobody seems to notice." If it wasn't in the 1850 *McGuffey's Reader*, they hadn't read it.

"I knew there was talk about bedplay. Used to page through my mother's copy of Shakespeare to find it. What an educated woman she was. Well, these folk around here have minds as small as armadillos' and shells twice as tough. Tomorrow night they'll be handing round their dance cards and sipping sherry with the Dugger family as if nothing ever happened. And maybe it didn't. Ideas around here are so confused these days I don't even know myself."

She went to find her son to see if his wounds, earned on the field of honor, needed dressing.

"Tell me, Mother, again, why it is we have to endure such insults," Delia Dugger said ruefully to her mother as they drove rapidly back through the slanting sunlight of late afternoon along the road into Vincennes. "I can't understand why we had to stay and eat fried chicken and talk to everybody as if there hadn't even been a nasty, senseless brawl."

The girl sat up rigidly straight, her slim hands on her knees, a shawl pulled tight about her shoulders against the coming chill as the sun sank, brazen orange beyond the horizon. Her brother and his friend Willie McClure sat opposite her and her mother, slumped in the corners of the carriage, asleep. Rumpled clothing and cuts on their lips and cheeks attested to the recent fight.

"We have our views, with which others may differ," Althea Dugger said. "I cannot tolerate listening to Yankee battle rites described, their escutcheons shined, at the very moment Southern boys are fighting to preserve freedom."

"Calhoun and Willie brought everything on themselves. You are supposed to have taught us courtesy, and I do not see how provoking those people at that picnic was courteous her daughter said shortly."

Her mother sighed and dabbed at the corner of her rather prim mouth with a fine cambric handkerchief. "Above courtesy, my dear child, is honor."

"And Mother, a ball—a fancy dress ball, now when Archie is fighting in Tennessee and all these Lincolnites are revelling over the loss of western Virginia—" Archie McClure had been her ideal when she was a child. She used to play down on the levee with the "common" McClures—Archie III, Willie, and their small sister, Ruby Jean.

Althea Dugger leaned over to her daughter and put her hand on Delia's wrist. "Listen to me, Delia. We are one of a handful of families in this neighborhood, in this part of the North, who really understand the cause this war is about. Oh, there are plenty of Southern sympathizers here, people who wish the war all the ill they can conceive of. But they are pocketbook Rebels. Their garners are full of corn, and they can't ship it south to New Orleans any more. So they want the war to stop so they can continue getting rich. I'm not talking about them."

Her daughter looked searchingly at her mother. She knew Althea Dugger was as steely and strong as the strings on the piano in the ballroom at their plantation, Rivertides, but at this moment her voice had an edge to it that was unusually brittle. Perhaps the scuffle at the picnic had unnerved her more than she allowed.

Althea Dugger went on, "Then there are the Democrats who hate the governor and want to see the Republicans frizzle in hell, fried with their own greenbacks. They purr like tomcats about the need to 'negotiate peace,' to 'stop this senseless war with our own national brothers in the South,' but their claws are pulled. They don't know what all of this killing is about."

"And what is that, Mother?" the young woman said, lifting her chin slightly. She felt she and her family were paying a heavy price for something she did not understand, some musty ideal that had to do with a South she knew only in her mother's stories. Mystical old houses in western Tennessee surrounded by tobacco and cotton fields, dusky colored folk bringing trays of candied fruits throughout long evenings made fragrant with the perfume of flowers, duels fought because of honor trampled on and horses hoofs, ringing down roads to right wrongs.

"This war is about a way of life, and the freedom to live it. Nothing more, nothing less." Althea Dugger's syllables, still softly edged by the drawl of the South, clipped across the heavy air of the carriage like scissors. Delia's brother was beginning to snore gently. Willie McClure roused himself and began to fish in his waistcoat pocket for a match and cigar. He smoked and they rode without talking for many long moments. Twilight faded into stolid gray as they came into Vincennes.

When Althea spoke again, it was almost to herself. She did not look at either Delia or Willie. "My great-grandfather fought in North Carolina in the Revolutionary War.'' Rev-o-lu-shnary, she said, savoring the word as if it were a forkful of ragout. No doubt about it, Delia thought, her mother's accent was different even from the soft syllables of southern Indiana folk. ''He sided against his own kin to fight the Britisher Tarleton and secretly join the Colonist general, Nathanael Greene. The Rebel group met in barns in the night, they rode in ambush. He risked his life for the independence of America.''

Calhoun Dugger had finally stirred and awakened, but he was not listening to his mother; he raised the curtain and looked out at the lights of Vincennes. He told himself that it would have been better to have stayed somewhere along the road, but they needed to return to get the elaborate plans perfected for this ball his mother had her heart set on, to set the darkies straight about the fripperies and foolishments that had to be done, be sure the nigger men had gotten all of the ice from the icehouse, every last bit of it for the frozen delicacies. Or at least his mother would, and Delia. She was the smart one, anyway.

''The moon's risin' '' he said to his mother and sister. He pointed at it with an unlit cigar, as it stood, huge and perfectly symmetrical over a field of pumpkins out the other window of the carriage.

''Nothing was said about slavery in the Declaration of Independence,'' his mother was saying. ''My great-grandfather's dearest friends signed the Declaration, and they wouldn't have done that if slavery was forbidden. No, we spent all those lives and fortunes so each state, each section, could make their livings as they saw fit, as the needs of their lands dictated. My Daddy came to the Tennessee frontier when Indians were there and made it bloom and blossom. He made his fortune his own way, with slaves. And the South is still going to do that. Each man has a right to his own property, and men banding together can decide to have their own country, if they don't like what others are pushing on them. That's what my ancestors died for before, and that's what the South is dying for now.''

In the charged atmosphere of the afternoon and this ride under an October moon through an eerie, still countryside, it occurred to Delia Dugger to ask her mother a question she had never asked before. ''And why, Mother, if you love the South so much did you leave it? Why not go back there now, when everything you care about is shattering?'' Cigar smoke hung in the air; it made her voice come forth harsh, a little carping. She didn't want it to sound that way, because she did care about her mother very much.

Fully a moment passed before her mother answered, and when she did Althea Dugger did not look her daughter in the face. ''I loved Tennessee more than anything in this world when I was a young woman. I still do. It was a world where we created gentility and duty and civilization out of nothing. Those things, really, were everything.

"I was a very young girl when your father came down the river, doing business returning fugitive slaves. He came to bring back one of our field darkies, and he stayed for a week. He was not of my class, of course, you could tell that by the way he dressed and sat a horse, but he captured my interest, later my heart, by the way he came across the fields one day in April. He scorned the road; instead he flew across the fences and the stream and came red-faced and laughing to the very porch where I sat with my sister, taking the cool breezes." Althea Dugger smiled a sad smile and seemed lost in the past.

"I was only eighteen, but Papa was afraid nobody would ask for me. He told me I was too hard of face and will. 'Be gentler, Althea,' Papa always said. 'A soft and gentle voice is a very excellent thing in women.' Anyway, Lucius Dugger was as handsome as a man had any right to be. His forwardness with horses I mistook for boldness of character."

Delia opened the side windows to let the cigar smoke out. She did not wish to look at her mother. Her father had been gone only two years, and she believed she did not want to hear anything to his detriment.

"I was wrong. He was bold only with horses. In all else he was a mild, hesitant man. Good but timid. We married, he brought me north, away from my sister and the fields of Tennessee. When I came I found a squalid camp on the river, with dregs from all the riverboats playing banjos and drinking whisky night after night, as the big, wide, White River emptied itself into the Wabash. Up the hill they took me to meet an old widow lady of the hardshell Baptist persuasion holding forth as if she was the Queen of Sheba. That was your great-grandmother, Delva Dugger.

"She was tyrannizing her son, himself an old buzzard of a man, your grandpa, James Byrd Dugger. Named after the Byrds of Virginia—they were distant cousins of Grandma Delva's. The Duggers always did put on airs. They put pillars on their house, even though it had derelicts sitting with their feet up, in the parlor, eating chicken and greens. They pretended they were bluebloods, when their folks had been Scotch-Irish claim buyers and slave-traders. Still, there was a heap of money there when I came, and I decided to put it to good use."

"Mother—do you really want to tell me all this?" Delia asked, slightly bewildered. She had never really heard the story this way. The fracas they had endured during the afternoon seemed to have set her mother's nerves on edge; when she was irritated she spoke with clipped tones and frankness. Now she was chuckling, ruefully.

"I got your father to use the money to build his own life, on a higher hill, above the old place, away from his grandmother and parents. An architect from Louisville designed three full floors, including a ballroom, Grecian pillars. We put everything we had into it. Your father recouped a good deal through buying and selling for the New Orleans market.''

"And now the war has dried up the river trade," Delia murmured.

"We are still people of means. Your father had a decent head for investment. Better than he did for farming. He was about as good a manager as a field mouse was. Charming with the grain brokers and farmers, but—" She shrugged her shoulders. " 'Twas the horse racing. I managed the hands myself. He went to Louisville. The races at Louisville and Nashville took his energies. You know that, though.''

Calhoun had sunk again into the corner of the carriage. Delia wondered how her brother could sleep through this. What Willie McClure thought, she had no idea. Well, his own ancestors, Captain Will and his son Archie McClure, were notorious through three counties for their hell-raising. So perhaps none of this was new. Still, it upset Delia. It was Mother herself who had taught her that ladies did not show the dirty undersides of their petticoats. "What an odd mood you're in, Mother," Delia said.

"You asked me," Althea Dugger said a little shortly. "It's a good time to talk about it, because tomorrow night you will be hostess to people who do not understand us or believe as we do, and unless you understand what is at the heart of the Cause, you cannot stand and smile the way we must.''

"Why must we smile? Why must we have a ball right now? When Cincinnati stands in danger of attack, it seems odd to spread a fine table, have servants serve wines, hire an orchestra to play Chopin's waltzes.''

For the first time her brother roused himself enough to speak. "I jest hope I can keep my hands off my horsewhip for these god-damned Lincolnites who caused all this trouble when they didn't need to.''

"Of course you will keep your hands off your horsewhip, and you will hold your tongue too," his mother said, in the style of one who was used to thinking for her son. "I think we should all regret what happened at the picnic today. These are our neighbors. This is our home. I am not a Tennessean any more, I am from southern Indiana.'' The clipped tones took on a rather tired edge. Delia watched her mother's profile, chin lifted, defiant mouth slightly open, silhouetted in the gathering darkness. She was, unquestionably, a beautiful woman, and Delia could understand how her quiet father had been captivated.

"I love Rivertides," her mother went on. "My children were born in those rooms, my husband died and was laid out in the parlor there. I can never leave it. But our hearts are with the Cause, the freedom of the South. The Confederacy must be allowed to go its own way freely, without the tyranny and oppression and murder this war is bringing about. And as long as we live here, we are the South, for these friends and neighbors. We must hold our heads up and be the gentlepeople we are.''

"They will eat crow when Lee wins. I hope he shows them all no mercy," Calhoun growled.

"When the South wins, as it must, then we will find it in our hearts to be merciful. And we will be vindicated. In the meantime—"

Althea's vigor seemed to have waned. She took out a box of bonbons and her long, slender fingers selected a cream fondant.

"In the meantime we dance, we eat, we smile," Delia said, casting her glance into the clumps of dark trees which clad the hills by the Wabash River, at the edge of the horizon.

Gaslight, and the glow of hundreds of old-fashioned candles, lit the windows of Rivertides Farm as guests approached its circular drive. The sounds of Stephen Foster's, "Ring, Ring the Banjo" drifted out of the double doors, which were opened by a colored man in livery to admit smartly dressed men and women. Stable hands took care of buggies and rigs.

Two men appeared from a clump of trees where they had tethered their mounts. One hesitated, walking almost purposely a few steps behind the other, as if to deliberately distance himself from the obvious fact that they were brothers. Actually they were twins, although that fact was not immediately obvious, for the brother striding confidently towards the steps was three inches taller, and his blonde, handsome face sloped down to a strong, half-cynical smile, while brother who followed behind, though just as strong and blondely handsome, had a look of innocent anticipation. It was as if he were expecting something good to happen behind every door, even this new, aristocratic one, guarded by a silver-haired colored man that looked for all the world like a slave in this free state. Still, the two young men were fraternal twins, born ten minutes apart twenty-three years ago, in 1838, to Mahalia and John Robert Scott. They had lived their childhood across from the ruins of old Fort Knox, where William Henry Harrison had gathered his troops to fight the Battle of Tippecanoe.

Jacob Joe Scott spoke in a low voice to his brother. "I guess I'm glad we came, even though I didn't want to when thee suggested it, Brother. I thought we should represent Father—"

"Remember, Brother, none of your thees and thous. You're breaking yourself."

"Not that I want to, but regular speech does fit society better than Quaker. Anyway, I can switch back when I am with my friends."

"I don't know why the Duggers invited Father. It's hard to imagine John Robert Scott in these surroundings." The taller brother laughed and bounded forward, causing his brother to shake his head. There was more than a slight edge of bitterness and cynicism in the laughter that floated down the shadowy lane.

They mounted the steps, and the door opened. The colored man's white teeth flashed at them out of his shining black face. He showed them to the staircase, and they climbed eventually to the third floor, where another colored servant took their card and announced to the assembly, "Mr. Zachary Scott. Mr. Jacob Joe Scott."

"The floor is covered with sand in the shape of stars," Jacob Joe breathed in admiration, admiring the blue-and-red spangled ballroom floor as they stepped into the assembly of people.

"Stars and stripes, or stars and bars?" Zach asked with amusement.

"Doesn't matter. As soon as the 'gallops' and mazurkas start, we will all trample the designs like the sands of time under our flying feet."

"Tell me, Zach, who all these people are. You know more of 'em than I do."

"I have gotten about in society, for better or worse, Brother, that I do concede," Zach Scott said. Jacob Joe turned to look at his brother for a moment. Zachary Scott had been expelled from Earlham College for helping organize a drunken party, had been involved with ladies with some tinge of shame more than once, had read a little law in Vincennes and had used it to help set up questionable groups to support the Southern cause—let it pass. Jacob Joe had recently decided that "live and let live" politically in these troubled times was the only practical attitude. Especially in families.

Zach pointed with a white gloved finger. "There's Editor Greene, from the Vincennes newspaper. A Democrat loyal to the Union. At least for now. And George Badollet. One of the young Vincennes beaux. Do you know him?" His brother shook his head. "Well, he gets around in my circles. His great-grandfather was a friend of Thomas Jefferson."

"Badollet is a Democrat?"

"Of course," Zach answered, flashing his brother a dazzling smile. "Am I close to anyone else but Democrats?"

"No, for better or worse," his brother replied. "Who is the gentleman, there with the lady in white satin, the man with the portly stomach and long, beaming face."

"Ah, that's a big catch for the Duggers. Congressman Clement Vallandigham from Ohio. He's come over to stay a week, I hear."

"The Copperhead leader," Jacob Joe said with scorn.

"The defender of States Rights in our beloved country, you mean, brother," Zachary said with a very small, enigmatic grin.

"All I know is he is opposes the policies of the government towards the war every step of the way. But wait, I see someone I do know. 'Tis Thomas Jefferson Brooks. And his wife—"

"Who is your old friend, Mrs. Poore's daughter. I remember now. Well, take me over and introduce me."

They shouldered their way around the edge of the beautifully lighted ballroom. Suspended chandeliers caught the gleam of jewels on a hundred ring fingers and necklaced bosoms. Jacob Joe and Zach murmured their excuses when they brushed satin gowns, bumped trousered legs. The gentry of southern Indiana swept about making conversation before the ball music began.

Thomas Jefferson Brooks stood in a modest, black frock coat with a plain black silk vest, looking more ready for business in a counting house than dancing at a ball. Jacob Joe doubted the Brookses danced; they, at least Mrs. Brooks, was a devout Methodist. She recognized the young man as soon as he approached.

"Why, it's Jacob Joe Scott. Whatever has brought you to this shining parade of fashion?" she said. Her husband smiled and took out a cigar, but said nothing.

"Mr. and Mrs. Brooks, this is my brother, Zach. I believe you have not met." Susan Brooks nodded with a little tilt of the head and a touch of a quizzical smile, that said she had heard of Jacob Joe's twin, and that what she had heard wasn't all fine. He nodded to her diffidently.

"I should ask why you are here, Mrs. Brooks," Jacob Joe said buoyantly. "Martin County is quite a drive."

"We are staying up the road at my brother, John Poore's. Did you know he had moved here? And as for why we have come to join the fashionable herd, it was because we were asked. Thomas's business acquaintances, the Duggers—"

"Disreputable rivals, you mean," said the man in the black coat, tamping his cigar into a champagne glass that he had emptied after being served by a colored servant. "The Duggers have fought me for forty years in this neck of the woods."

"I did not know you had rivals, sir, in the trade," Jacob Joe said.

"Not rivals, exactly," Thomas Jefferson Brooks answered. "More irritants. Somewhere between chilblains and poison ivy. No sooner had we built the inn and mill at Hindostan Falls than they appeared on the scene, trying to steal the trade. Lucius Dugger's grandfather tried to undercut me in the flatboat trade that was building Hindostan Falls into one of the biggest towns in the Midwest."

Zach allowed his eyes to stray about to the tables loaded with flowers from the glass hothouse upstairs and the gleaming silver candelabra.

"I heard something of how you came to Indiana, crossing the Ohio on foot when you were only eighteen," Jacob Joe said.

"Those were the days when if a man had the will and a few hundred dollars to stock a store, he could make a modest fortune in a year and a half. Hindostan. The town sprang up overnight like an ant village, people poured in—''

"I taught school," Susan Brooks said, her eyes sparkling. "Almost every week there would be a new pupil, sometimes two or three or more, month after month." Jacob Joe nodded his head, trying to listen, but he could not help watching his brother, who was not paying a bit of attention to the conversation. Zach's eyes had stopped and were fixed on the receiving line.

Thomas Jefferson Brooks went on, his voice low. "Then, when Hindostan had its—terrible days, the days of the Cold Sickness—Lucius Dugger's father Jay Byrd attacked the boats coming to get food supplies for us from Duggerville. Stove them in so they wouldn't contaminate his town, he said."

"I did not know that, sir," Jacob Joe said. From the corner of his eyes he, too, scanned the receiving line standing by that gorgeous, loaded buffet table. He would needs go through it soon. The only one of the Dugger family he had met was Calhoun Dugger, who was standing several yards away, alone, looking at the women. He was a friend of Zach's and had been at the Scott house. A shadow crossed his mind. Before—Calhoun and Zach rode off into the night to do shadowy damage to the Union cause.

"My mother would not receive the Duggers, I know," Susan Brooks said. "If they should ever call on us at Loogootee."

"The likelihood of which is nil," her husband said, with a chuckle.

"Well, Mother crossed swords with Luke Dugger, the grandfather, in a court case involving the freeing of some of his indentured servants."

Zach finally came back to the conversation. "Indentured servants. That was what people in our state called slaves," Zach said, looking into her eyes, "Long after Indiana was admitted to the Union as a free state."

"Yes, I suppose you could call holding human beings in illegal bondage that. Mother won her case."

"And the enmity of the Duggers, I assume." Zach said, taking a glass of champagne from a passing servant.

"I have tried to convince her that the new generation is trying to put on a more respectable face, that we as Christians must not hold the misdeeds of the past against the Duggers—''

Thomas Jefferson Brooks patted his wife's gloved hand. "Yes, yes my dear. And even if they are still a bunch of Rebel-loving *snobs*"—he raised his voice purposely on the word—his wife took her small hand and put it over his mouth.

"They are our hosts," Susan Brooks said, smiling sweetly and cocking her head on the side. What simple charm she had, Jacob Joe thought. Her husband was one of the richest men in Indiana, a man they called the

"Yankee trader" because he and his brothers, before they built their trading empire along the Buffalo Trace, had originally been from Massachusetts.

Susan Brooks, who now put her arm through her husband's with obvious adoration, was the mainstay daughter of a pioneering family who had fought the wilderness to survive and won largely because of her serene strength. She was every inch a natural lady, courteous and naturally poised. Dressed simply in a deep wine-colored silk in the old style, without hoops, with a lace shawl her mother had made over her slim shoulders. She was a true aristocrat, Jacob Joe thought.

Suddenly he realized he had not asked about the soldiers in the Brooks family. The beauty of the ball had turned his head, and truly, it was difficult to remember that even in the midst of plenty and gorgeousness in this autumn of 1861 here in the Northwest, men were fighting and dying only a few hundred miles away.

"I read in the paper that your son fought bravely at the Battle of Greenbrier," Jacob Joe said.

"Yes," Susan Brooks said. "Lewis was commended by General Reynolds for his leadership of Company C in the Battle of Greenbrier."

"You have one son in the service."

"And another one who wants to go," Thomas Jefferson Brooks volunteered. "Tommy, Lewis's younger brother, is chomping at his bit to be with the others."

"I know how he feels—sometimes. But I am a Quaker." Jacob Joe said it in a low voice. He would not have ventured to tell his full heart to just anyone, but the Brookses would understand.

"The war brings many strange quandaries on us," Susan Brooks told him comfortingly. "My sister's boy, Will Houghton, is a lieutenant in the Fourteenth Indiana Regiment, and she is always beside herself with worry."

They went on to discuss other things, and finally Jacob Joe made his polite farewells to the Brookses; Zach nodded and took his brother's elbow to move him towards the banquet table and the Dugger family.

"Who have you been staring at?" Jacob Joe demanded. "I thought you knew all those people."

"The girl. I have been with Calhoun much, know the mother and knew the father, too, but the girl they have kept cloistered. I had no idea—"

"No idea she was so beautiful. Father mentioned it to me. He saw her at the picnic."

"Ravishing. I have never seen anything like her." Jacob Joe sent a quick look at his brother. There was a sincerity, a twinge of emotion in Zach's voice that Jacob Joe was not used to. Then, however, his voice took on its usual razor edge. "They have kept her from me. Thought I would carry her off, ravish her in the woods. Possibly even told her the diabolical stories about me.''

"Diabolical? Isn't that too strong a word?''

"You never know, brother, perhaps it is, perhaps not. But here we are.''

They turned to the receiving line, which gleamed like the fashion plates from the latest pages from *Godey's Ladies Book*, with tiers of silk fuchsia and ivory silk, loops of pearls and ear bobs and dainty, soft bleached leather slippers. A widowed aunt from Louisville, the "greeter," gushed over them and brought them to the host and hostess.

Zach introduced his brother to Calhoun Dugger, who in turn introduced Jacob Joe to his mother Althea, shiningly resplendent in gold satin with a pearl bodice, and assorted cousins who had come from around Louisville and Memphis for the event.

Jacob Joe exchanged a few remarks with the girl he had seen from across the room, one of the Louisville cousins, a young girl with braids tied with looping bows. She was a round, vivacious girl named Sophie Lavenham, daughter of the widowed aunt Addie who was the greeter, and she wore hibiscus blossoms from the flower house that faced the river, off the second floor conservatory of this fine mansion.

"Sir, do I hear that you are a Quaker?" she asked, her eyes dancing.

"Can that information have come to your ears, Miss Lavenham?"

"My aunt Althea has told me of your many missions of mercy in the county, and that your father, I believe, was responsible for the plans for this orphanage we are all goin' to subscribe such spectacular sums to tonight.''

Jacob Joe felt caught up in the splendid exhilaration of the moment. The notes of a clarinet tootled across the room as the orchestra tuned up; he smelled the dark chocolate of the mountains of bonbons on the tables, the salty richness of toasted pecans. The girl's jasmine scent reached up and surrounded him.

Quaker women weren't the only ones in the world, Jacob Joe thought. He could converse just as easily as his brother did with these elegant women. Especially now that he had forsworn "thees" and "thous."

"Well, it is certainly true that my father has long been involved in charitable causes," he said joyfully. "Why, he was part of the underground railroad twenty years ago, although he no longer—"

The young woman's eyebrows arched and her mouth opened in alarm. He had said the wrong thing to this Southern woman. Drat it. Politics again. Keeping them straight in southern Indiana was like trying to recite the Latin declensions. You never could remember what was what and you blurted out the wrong thing before you knew it. But then she was smiling again.

"Are you as free and bold in your dancing as you are in your conversation, Mr. Scott? Have you learned the newest dances? Do you dance the schottish?''

"Perhaps you will teach me, Miss Lavenham. May I invite you to test the floor?'' Jacob Joe bowed a little in invitation. Neither of them had come escorted, so they could dance the first dance together. "Shall we scatter the sand stars around a bit?'' Jacob Joe smiled. His boyishness and eager sincerity always charmed women, although he never had time to look for a special love. He was too busy teaching school in eastern Indiana, and more recently in setting his father's farm in order.

Miss Lavenham took out her dance card, and Jacob Joe signed his name with the pencil that was attached to it with a yellow ribbon. Then, he took her arm and they strolled from the receiving line to the dance floor. The orchestra leader took out music and handed it to the orchestra. Jacob Joe looked around the room for Zach. While he had been speaking to Miss Lavenham, he saw, his brother had disappeared.

"I look forward to some substantive discussions with you, Mrs. Dugger,'' Clement Vallandigham said as he beamed on his hostess at the beginning of the receiving line. He bent to kiss her hand.

"I regret I was unable to personally help you settle in upstairs. I hope the accommodations are to your liking, sir,'' Althea Dugger said, touching the white rose which bloomed on her bosom.

"Above my fondest wishes. I only regret my dear wife could not have been here to see the rose-fern wallpaper and that delicate Chippendale desk by the fireplace.''

"It came from North Carolina, sir. From the fine house of my grandfather in the Piedmont country. One of a few magnificent relics saved. My grandfather gave his health and fortune to the struggle for independence. But he lived long enough to see his country win the victory for the cause he fought for.''

"Let us hope, madame, that history will repeat itself,'' he said in a lowered voice.

Althea Dugger gave him a long look, then smiled briskly. "Sir, as honored guest, will you join me in leading the grand march to begin the ball?'' Her guest smiled and took her arm. Calhoun Dugger stood next to the raised platform where two clarinet players, two fiddlers and a guitarist, all in black frock coats and shiny trousers were raising instruments, poised to play.

Noticing his mother and Clement Vallandigham come to the center of the room, Calhoun clapped his hands smartly. "Gentlemen, please bring the lady for whom you serve as escort to the center of the room. Form in order for the Grand March.''

Jacob Joe listened as the exalted strains of "Hail, Columbia" floated over the crowd.

> Hail, Columbia
> Happy land
> Hail ye heroes
> Heaven-born band

Mr. Vallandigham and Althea Dugger, smiling and radiant, stood just beneath the orchestra's platform. The honored guest from Ohio raised his arms and the dancing partners glided sedately forward in a row, from the back of the room. As they approached him, he divided them into two parts, couples moving to right and left, alternately. As they came about for a second pass, Vallandigham and Mrs. Dugger raised their arms in a London Bridge and the couples ducked smilingly under. Then Vallandigham and Mrs. Dugger led them round and round the room until, with one triumphant set of chords, the clarinetist-leader brought the patriotic piece to an end.

The band swung into a splendid Chopin waltz; Jacob Joe bowed to Miss Lavenham and swung her onto the floor; other men and their partners dipped and glided about, the sand crunching genteelly under the slippers of the women, the short, fashionable bootees of the men.

Althea Dugger looked at the whirling couples with satisfaction, then gazed up at her guest. "Sir, we have much to talk about. May I suggest a walk about the house? We have almost an hour till supper time. It is stuffy in here, is it not?"

"Of course, madame," Vallandigham said, taking her arm.

Down a flight of stairs in the hothouse conservatory, the moon cast fantastic shadows through the pots of plants on the stone floor. Beyond the tiers of leaded windows was the river, aglow with the moon's light.

"The Wabash is rippled with the wind tonight," Zach Scott said to the girl by his side. "They say the ghosts of Kickapoo war parties ride the waters on nights like this. So my grandfather, James Scott, used to say. He should have known; he killed Indians every place he could, in Pennsylvania, Kentucky, Ohio."

Delia stood taut by one of the plant pots. "Sir, I think we must return. The grand march is over. I do not know why I let you convince me to take the air just as it was beginning."

" 'Twas as stuffy in there as a Chicago boxing ring." Zach reached out to touch the leaves of the plant, fine lacy leaves, which slipped through his fingers. "Golden raintree, did you say, Miss Dugger?"

"Golden chain. A member of the locust plant. Related to the coffee plant. Mr. Scott, I think we must—"

He turned his face to her suddenly, "Do you have sensitive plants in the greenhouse?"

"No. I have heard of them—little plants with drooping leaves?"

"They look as these golden chain leaves do. When you touch them, as I just have, they pull back, close up. They feel too much."

"How odd." Delia Dugger looked up at him. The smell of gardenias hung heavy, sweet in the air.

"Like my brother. Like Jacob Joe." Zach smiled, offhandedly, and the girl tried to read his expression.

"I do not think I understand, Mr. Scott," she said.

"He feels too much. Life touches him, wounds him, he withdraws. He went to college, let out his leaves a bit, though he didn't want to go. Now he has returned. In his heart he wants to go to the war, but he cannot. He feels the pain of"—here he laughed—"all those being killed, the lands over which they tromp, the orphaned children. Feels it like a real pain, sometimes in the pit of his stomach."

Delia's eyes were large in the darkness. "That is odd and sad."

"He says he feels it rising, like a mist over the river to cover him—the pain of the war, I mean."

"I have heard of women who were sensitives, in the South."

Zach laughed again, a short bitter, laugh. "My grandmother was one of them—a sensitive. Jenny McClure Scott. Fat lot of good it did her. She ended up insane. Sat in our home like a boulder for thirty years."

The girl reached out and took his arm. "I am sorry, Mr. Scott."

"Don't be. Folk should not go about with their leaves out, ready to shrink at a moment's touch. I do not believe in feeling. It is dangerous."

"Surely not—" the young girl by his side whispered. He turned, took the hand that lay on his arm.

His eyes flashed. "But having you near me like this, I can for once—"

She withdrew her hand and pulled back from him. "Sir, we must go back to the ballroom—" and at that moment footsteps clattered on the cobblestones at the entrance to the hothouse; the young couple turned in confusion towards them.

There was a moment of silence, finally broken by Althea Dugger's humorless laugh. "I see you are admiring our botanical specimens, Mr. Scott. Many of them I brought up with me from Tennessee and others have come from New Harmony. They are rare in this part of the country. Mr. Vallandigham, I believe you know Zachary Scott."

Zach bowed low. "We have met—at other times."

"Perhaps, sir," said Althea, turning her head towards Clement Vallandigham, "you would escort Delia back to the ballroom. I do not believe her dance card is complete, and I know she would be honored to have you sign it yourself."

Vallandigham, smiling, offered his arm to the girl. "We will follow along soon," Althea Dugger called out after them.

Palmetto trees in pots shot long, spear-like shadows in the silent conservatory. Althea Dugger glided towards a camellia bush. She took a spindly shoot in her hands and pinched it between thumb and forefinger, then dropped the broken twig into the dirt at the bottom of the pot.

"Mr. Scott, you have been at Rivertides before, and you have not met my daughter."

"No, not till tonight. Why is that, madame?"

Althea Dugger did not answer for a long moment. She took the gardenia from her bosom, looked at the fringe of brown on its petals and stooped to pick another from among richly glossy leaves by the window. "You are not received, sir, among families I know."

"Society is blind to merit in our time, don't you think? Shallow as a coffee saucer," Zach said, looking unperturbed through the darkness at her.

"There was the matter of the French girl in Vincennes. And after that the lawyer's daughter—"

"Surely you do not credit trifling gossip, madame. Besides, that has not stopped you from welcoming me before."

Althea's voice was strained, harsh. "We need each other. I do my part in the daytime in the halls of political counsel. You—you and Calhoun do your parts in the nighttimes. We are all walking the same dangerous road. There will be much more trouble before this is over. We need to know, and cherish, our allies. Have you talked to Vallandigham?"

"I have. I met him this morning, at the tavern in Vincennes," Zach told her.

"He believes sentiment in Ohio is building. That Kentucky may soon fall to the South, and when it does, thousands will come to our ranks, throw off the yoke of the Yankee ape, Lincoln."

"Vallandigham is often a fool. Prestige he has, and a sharp orator's tongue, which got him elected him to Congress from Ohio. But he thinks Southern sympathizers are behind every lilac bush in the old Northwest."

"And they aren't?"

"Not yet. Time must pass. There is work to be done, miles to be ridden, in Illinois, Indiana, Ohio. What we have done in organizing in the last year is as nothing compared to what will come soon, as the Yankees lose battles and the people sicken of the war. But many months will have to pass before we can even guarantee the southern part of the state. Calhoun and I leave in the morning again. There is a new castle of the Knights' organization being raised in Orange County, near Paoli, and we must be there.''

"Be careful. Sentiment is as strong as mother-of-vinegar here 'bouts. The war is working in our favor. The Yankees are doing poorly. One Southerner is worth five of them, cowards that they are! But if there is a Northern victory, hatred will fly back against us. I was at a picnic yesterday where there was a fight—''

"I heard. My father was there. Well, there are fights everywhere. The papers are all vitriol on both sides. Hatred and malice ride about like the horsemen of the apocalypse.''

There was a thumping sound on the dance floor above them; the dancers must be doing a polka. "We must return. Our presence will be missed, and there are many true-blue Yankees here tonight,'' Althea said. She turned to face Zach Scott squarely. "Delia is gently brought up. I do not wish you to see her again, speak to her in the familiar way I saw in here—''

"And if I am quite good enough to be the confidant of your political bosom, may I not be good enough to know your daughter socially?''

"Socially? I am not sure you are a gentleman, Mr. Scott.''

Zach's mouth was a cynical line, his voice full of restrained anger. "A gentleman? Beauregard and McDowell both were gentlemen at Bull Run and they gave orders bordering on stupidity. Several of the regiments who turned tail and ran in confusion were aristocrats of your gentile South as well as the North. Let the 'gentlemen' bungle away the military effort. It will take more than honor to make the Northwestern states drop this war and make peace immediately. Is that not what we want?''

Althea looked a little reproachful. "Your voice, sir, is loud, but your point is well taken. I know Mr. Vallandigham regards you as one of the bulwarks of this momentous effort—''

"And you? I do not intend to be your errand boy, kept at a distance. My ancestors earned their way in the Revolutionary War as well as yours, for that matter. And they certainly have earned their place here in Indiana. As for my personal habits—they are my own business. I am discreet.''

"Your speech is too smart for my liking. Still—if all you intend towards Delia is social interchange—''

Zach smiled mysteriously. "You have my word of honor.'' Somehow, she did not catch the irony.

Althea took his arm and sighed. "Shall we go on up to the ballroom?''

Two hours later, carriages rattled off down the driveway, horses hoofs fading into the moonlit night. Tired houseguests yawned their way up the huge staircase to find fires burning and satin coverlets turned back in their small visitor bedrooms.

Delia, Calhoun and Althea Dugger stood watching servants carry out the remains of the midnight plate supper. Chicken salad with raisins and nuts, ham jambalaya in its chafing dish, mounded jellies and coconut cakes— ruins of their former splendors, they were carted off for the servants in the kitchen.

Calhoun started ripping at the studs in his collar. "Damned good bash. Raised over $8,000 for the orphanage."

"Mr. Thomas Jefferson Brooks' gift was the most impressive," Delia said. "To get up, take out a $1,000 bill from his pocket, plunk it into the bag, as if it were nothing. Yet he did not seem boastful when he did it."

"I thought that might happen when I asked Mrs. Brooks to be chairman of financial gifts," Althea affirmed.

"Why, Mama, that sounds self-serving," Delia said, looking at the other woman archly.

"One must know who one's allies in a cause are and keep them happy," Althea said, without looking at her daughter. Calhoun was striding from the room, frock coat under his arm, unbuttoning his embroidered vest as he went.

Her mother turned to look at Delia with cool eyes. "By the way, be very sparing of your presence to Mr. Zachary Scott. He is danger itself," she said.

"Do not be so dramatic, Mama. I am almost twenty and shall make my own acquaintances from now on. At any rate, I might like a little danger in my life. It would be better than these infernal gardenias and ribbons and dance cards." And with that she, too strode from the room in a very unladylike way, bumping a tray of departing fruitcake and julep cups as she went.

January, February, March, April, 1862

Chapter Three

On a particular day in January, 1862, snow hung like a soggy blanket over western Virginia. The only signs of warmth in the frost-bound world were wispy threads of smoke floating out of the chimneys of "log tents," and up pine-clad hills surrounding the encampment of the Fourteenth Indiana regiment in winter quarters.

Inside one well chinked and roomy cabin, at a rude table, sat the regiment's assistant surgeon and one of his company medical orderlies. Before them was a bowl of soapsuds into which they were dipping lancets, blood cups, and small saws.

"I don't know why I wash these instruments," the surgeon, who spoke with a strong German accent said. "Nobody else does. Still, you tell me that this is how your mother does her surgery and infection never sets in—oddly, it does seem to work. So I do it."

The young man before him nodded, smiling, and continued to dip the scalpels and suture needles. "My mother says it is important to heal cleanly. I have seen the other surgeons sponging pus from wounds and then using the same sponges to sop up blood in a fresh wound."

"You have been very useful to me, Walter," said Assistant Surgeon Joseph Burkhart to the young man across the table from him. "I do not know how I could have stood this life without you. You are like mine own boy—"

The assistant surgeon was a thick sausage of a man. His strongly guttural tones bore the marks of the province of Baden.

"Thank you, sir," his young assistant acknowledged the compliment. "Perhaps common interests and trials have bound us together." The young man was speaking obliquely of the fact that his older friend was one of the "Deutschies," the Germans from Evansville whom the other men of the regiment singled out for jokes and slurs. He betrayed his own origin—and therefore his rejection—just as markedly in his own face, which was straight and narrow with high cheekbones and dark skin. Walter McClure was a

Potawatomi-Miami Indian. Only his soft, brown hair proclaimed that his native heritage was attenuated with white blood.

The older man chuckled. "Fortune was with me that day Herr Broadbent told me to reorganize the medical practices in the regiment. To appoint company assistants to see to the, how do you say it, the hygiene of the men—."

"With all respect, he said it, sir, so that you could use your own ideas to make order out of the chaos he had caused."

The older man poured the suds over a bone saw he held in a metal bowl and carefully scrubbed its teeth. "My boy, you know I cannot hear you say such things."

"Then I will say them to myself. You do not have to hear a word, sir. But you are the capable one, and Dr. Broadbent—if we should give him that term at all—"

"Herr Broadbent is appointed by the governor of the State of Indiana."

"Whose cousin-in-law he is. With only a year as an assistant and after reading some medical books—'tis disgraceful. Why our horse doctor in Peru has had more experience than this 'head surgeon.' "

"Well, he has learned to cut off a leg well enough, I think," the older man said. He took out a meerschaum pipe and filled it from a small pouch. "Only an ounce or two of tobacco left," he mused.

"Whereas you—"

"I am only a village doctor. Trained as an apprentice in the old country, with simple practices. Put men in light quarters, away from the sinks and disease of the sick others, give them broth and bread."

"What you have done for Lieutenant Houghton's lung fever is remarkable. I thought he was done for, sir—"

"A good, warm fire, a kindly woman we could pay to give him good food and hot tea. Clean blankets."

"Ah, those are my mother's healing prescriptions, too."

The doctor dried the saw with a piece of newspaper. "You have told me but little about her, my young friend," he said. "I would like to hear more."

"Dawn Yet To Come of the Potawatomi," Walter said, looking out at the frosty landscape. "*Manitto Wabo*, special healer, she is called by those in the Miami tribe—the ones left, that is."

Walter McClure was silent, thinking of his home in Peru, Indiana, where the scattered remnants of the once powerful Miami Indian nation and a few survivors of the Potawatomi, like his mother and himself, lived among whites who were indifferent to them. The rest of the tribes, like all the rest of the Indians in the Northwest, had gone to Kansas and Oklahoma, forced from their homelands by the land greed of the whites and by changing times.

"Mother was one of the first healers to try sunlight and herbs and cleanliness for best healing," Walter said. "She was, is still, known among all the Potawatomi. Her uncle was a shaman, a medicine man, and he had the gift, but he misused it to frighten people and make them give him gifts and trade goods. Mother believed love was the best potion. She gave it as a gift, and got it too, from those she healed."

"You have the gift of healing, too."

"Perhaps, in a different way. I have been to school, and someday I wish to teach my own people. But I do what I can here."

"You do much for C Company, Houghton's and Brooks's company, and the other McClure—John R. takes care of G. He is also a good sanitary helper." Something occurred to the surgeon. "You have the same name. Are you somehow—"

" 'Tis a common name in Indiana. There are scores of us in the southern Indiana regiments. The McClure name causes trouble for me just now. John R. McClure hates me because I have it, and because I am a 'redskin.' The men in the regiment call me 'Redskin' McClure, and call him 'Whiteskin'."

"But you have not answered my question."

"My name was, uhh, given me by the courts." It was not a lie. The courts of Miami county had awarded him the name officially, but he was entitled to it, also. Still, no one in the regiment knew why.

There was a silence. Thinking of his mother, Dawn, made Walter think of her herbal teas. He stood, moved to the small fireplace and put a teapot from the sutler on the hook over the fire.

"What is it now, my boy? Indian brew, I suppose?" the older man asked indulgently, putting away lances and scalpels in the leather case he had brought from Evansville.

"Elderberry tea, from desiccated fruits my mother sent me. I will give you some. It is good for the bowels."

"Well, it will surely be better than what we try now. Only ten men in the regiment have not seen me about the bowels going too much."

"It is the awful beans, mildewed and cooked in rancid side meat. Every time we have beans we have quickstep."

"Walter, you have more knowledge than the surgeon general himself about potions for the body."

"And the heart and mind, too, sir. Indian medicine changes the thought within a man, tells him to be strong, in harmony with the Great Spirit. With God, I say, since I am a Christian."

The surgeon looked at his young friend, puttering about the fireplace, and felt the sense of shared friendship which bound them together, a friendship built on faith. It was hard for the two of them as the only two Catholics among the small town, revive-us-again Protestants in the regiment.

"When I was growing up in Baden—" Burkhart began, contemplatively.

"Yes, sir?"

"Well, times were different, then. Reverence was a word we all knew. 'As God wills it,' was what my dear mother always said, about everything. She said it the day my sister was saved from the river, the day my father decided to come to America so we young sons could avoid having to fight in the army—as God wills it."

"My mother is the same way. 'Each has a path to the stars,' she says. 'The Great Spirit guides that path; man must not interfere.' "

"And she is right." The surgeon was silent, puffing at his pipe, his mind rambling to that large farmhouse in Germany, where fields sloped down to the river Necker, at a tumbling lot of starchly-clad children, the barking dogs, the huge tables set under trees and laden with crusty rye bread and meat soup. He thought of the church in the nearby village, where he had been baptized, and where every Sunday, well-scrubbed with hair combed, the family made their procession to Mass.

And to the young woman with the beautifully coiled braids and embroidered bodice. He had wanted her to join him in the new land, to take up the cap of marriage and announce the banns before they left. After all, her parents were gone; she was free to choose. It was not to be. Her eyes clouded in fear at the idea of America. To leave her god-parents and her sisters and the old churchyard where the sacred dead lay? She could not do it, she had told him, tears dropping into her lap. And he went alone to pray before the Virgin at church, that somehow his heart might heal in the new land, and that the training he had as a surgeon's apprentice might solace him and help someone, even though he could not help himself. And the Virgin had answered him, because he had found a new life in the heart of the new land, in Evansville, where he was physician to the large, newly-arrived German immigrant population. Thanks be to God!

Burkhart took a handkerchief and wiped road dust off the leather instrument case. "The men are disgraceful about their religion lately. They do shame, I say," he said finally.

"They do not go at all to the services. I do not think they like standing about in the rain hearing the chaplain on a barrel spout off about the *Book of Revelation*."

"Well, so they say. Brother Webb has much interest in the book of Prophecy. The Horseman of the Apocalypse are always galloping through his sermons," answered the older man. He looked with interest at the elderberry tea his young friend was pouring into a tin cup for him.

"Did you hear about Landon's mock sermon the other day?"

"No, I did not. You mean Landon who writes to the Vincennes paper about the regiment?"

"The same. He is a skeptic about religion, even a non-believer. He and a friend mounted a barrel out in a grove in the woods and told G Company they would preach on the Book of Revelation. I went out to hear. Landon beat his breast and spoke on 'The Whangdoodle mourneth for its firstborn and fleeth to Mount Humbug.' Everything was mock-serious. Some of the men laughed. I did a bit, I admit. Lieutenant Van Dyke was there, and he laughed a good deal. I believe he could have delivered a similar sermon, but he would be afraid it would hurt his 'advancement.' Captain Beem of H was outraged and said he'd better never hear more of it."

"Ah yes, Captain Beem."

"A fine soldier, sir. I can say for your ears only that I was glad when H's captain resigned and Lieutenant Beem was advanced."

"Yes." Surgeon Burkhart dropped his tone, confidingly. "These resignations are for the best, my boy. The laws of chemistry are in operation and the unfit are precipitating out." He smiled a broad, toothy smile, showing teeth stained brown from the meerschaum. Walter returned the surgeon's smile, with a warming in his heart. It was wonderful to have a friend to whom he could speak his mind. The surgeon was the first man in the regiment to really talk to him, to look past the term "Indian" the others saw plastered on his forehead like a bandage.

Talking to Burkhart as they prepared for morning sick call, helping him with his instruments and medicines in the chilly evening hours, Walter had developed confidence in this strange new world he had chosen to join. Recently he determined not to let the men's shallow attitude keep him from knowing people. Just today he'd resolved to overcome the men's prejudices through his own courtesy. He found a little book not too long ago called *The Courteous Gentleman: Succeeding in Society*, in a store in town. Well, he was determined to try that. It was all based on expressing an interest in other people, and he thought he could do that.

The surgeon was still thinking about David Beem. "He has been in often to see to the quartering of the sick in H Company. He cares for them."

"It is odd there are so many ill. Here we are in winter quarters and they are fairly decent, at the foot of the mountains of western Virginia, not up on the top of them any more, and the enemy's far away," Walter answered.

"That very thing has made them sick," the German stated, drinking off his elderberry tea. Walter McClure raised his eyebrows questioningly. "Yes, it is the morale. It is winter; we do not fight the war. We had the one battle, at Greenbrier, now we rest; the Rebels rest. Our regiment is no longer a military unit, just a bunch of lonely men, out in the lonely hills, far from family. They are ill cared for and iller fed, waiting to be summoned to a war which has just now got started. Men do not take care of themselves in such circumstances. We do not even maintain military schedule: drill and dress parade are too hard with the men scattered about and the weather freezing. The men's spirits sink, they let go.'' Both men were silent, listening to the winter wind rise outside the cabin, whirling snowflakes about.

"You must go to see Captain Beem tomorrow,'' Burkhart said. "Tell him about the new camp regulations. See if he will agree to them. He outranks me, I do not know—''

"You have finished the sanitary regulations, then, sir?''

"Yes I have. Broadbent gave me, what do you say, jurisdiction in the matter. So he can be free to practice surgery if it is needed. He wishes to make a reputation so he can go into practice in the city after the war.''

Walter scanned the list. "The men may not like these rules.''

"They will save their lives. There was awful camp fever on Cheat Mountain. Swelling of the limbs, extreme pain, high fever, delirium, well, you saw it, I do not need to tell you.'' His finger was tapping determinedly on the table. "It was caused by the overexposure and filthy streets and tents the officers allowed the men to live in. There is still too much typhoid and pneumonia here, and it is caused by low spirits and unspeakable conditions in this camp. Captain Beem is a leader.''

His voice was insistent. Useless death angered him. "If Captain Beem and Captain Brooks of your own Company C agree to post and use the regulations in their companies, the rest will follow. They are the two moral leaders. More men are dying in this war from fevers than in our battles. We bury some each week here in winter camp. It will be useless to win the battle for freedom if we lose the battle with the typhoid.''

"I will start with Beem tomorrow,'' Walter McClure sighed. He thought of going among the men of H Company, of the partly good-natured taunts about his dark skin, of the comments made under the breath when they thought he was out of earshot.

Slowly he put away the packet of herbs, smelling their pungent sweetness. For a moment he stood again where elderberry vines, purple and green, bent low in clumps near a cemetery at home. It was the Godfroy Cemetery, where Miami chieftains, his relatives, slept near that most beautiful of rivers, Mississinewa.

Their battle with an intolerant people was over; his was just begun.

" 'Sanitary Regulations, Fourteenth Indiana Regiment,' '' David Beem read from the piece of paper Walter McClure handed him in his captain's quarters after guard mounting and drill the next morning.

" 'One. New blankets are being issued. Burn ragged old shoddy ones from former camps and boil and hang out new blankets every two weeks.' ''

He nodded agreement. Sitting on his own cot, he motioned Walter to sit on the dirt near him.

" 'Two. During cold weather, air tents daily. Do not sleep without ventilation, no matter how cold the night.

" 'Three. There will be no urinating in the streets at night. Urine is running down the hills, contaminating our stream. Use the latrines. Latrines will be re-dug regularly.' " Walter shifted his legs to get comfortable.

" 'Four. Meat should be broiled instead of fried. Heavy fried foods weaken digestion, making the system vulnerable to disease. A new fund has been set up to purchase dried fruits and vegetables.

" 'Five. The military regulations in force about excessive liquor drinking are reinforced by the surgeon. Intoxication is damaging to internal organs and affects performance of duty. Do not drink.' " Beem turned away and said in a low voice, "That is, of course aimed at our unfortunate Lieutenant Denny and the others of his ilk." He looked out the door of his captain's hut at the winter landscape. "How they marred Christmas for all of us," he said bitterly.

From his position on the cot he turned to face Walter squarely. "These seem excellent to me, McClure. Tell the assistant surgeon I will implement them. You go show them to Captain Brooks of C Company, and I will talk to the rest of the captains about them. The present policy calls for company-wide adoption of sanitary regulations. These will do, certainly!"

"Thank you, sir."

Walter McClure scrambled up from his position on the ground. His face was beaming, and Beem realized that the surgeon's assistant did not often receive praise. Beem watched him sympathetically. Anyone the least bit different took it on the chin in the unit, of course. Beem knew what that was, too. He read his Bible and poetry magazine only here, behind the closed door in the officer's hut he shared with Lieutenant Porter Lundy, so the men would not taunt him behind his back as "Polly Priss."

"Will you have a cup of coffee, McClure?" Beem asked the young man. The tripod was over the makeshift fireplace at the end of the rude hut. He and Lundy cooked for themselves. Van Dyke and the rest of the non-coms and officers might have their own contraband servants; Beem wasn't going to have "house hands" work for him.

"Yes, sir," Walter answered. Still standing deferentially, he took the tin cup proffered by Beem and dropped a white square in it from a blue envelope in Beem's other hand. "You have sugar, sir, I see." (If invited to tea, take note of the small amenities provided by your host, the *Courteous Gentleman* advised.)

"Well, yes." Beem smiled just a little. "My fiancée sent it."

"Sir, you're—are you engaged to someone from Owen County?"

"Indeed I am, McClure," Beem sat down again with his own cup. He leaned back and stretched out his legs, lightly positioning his black brogans on the dirt of the hut floor so as not to disturb the shine. "Should have been married by now, if it hadn't been for this slight argument we had with our Southern brothers."

"You were the first man from Indiana to join, so they say."

"I do not know that for sure. But when the news came, I did pick up my rifle and went to find my old friend, Jesse Harrold of this company—have you gotten to know him?"

"Sergeant Harrold, sir? I do have that pleasure, sir." (Show interest, but be sure to maintain formal, courteous language. Over-familiarity is the bane of an ever-coarsening world, said the *Courteous Gentleman*.) "He has been teaching blacksmithing to the cavalry some, has he not?"

"Yes, Jess was a blacksmith before the war. When I walked into his shop, he put down his tongs and took up his own gun from the corner of the shop. Well, he and I and Lunday and the rest met on Main Street in Spencer, and got up a company. And here we are." He looked pensively at his tin cup. "Beans, bravado and boredom, while Buell fights to hold Kentucky, and McClellan drills troops around Washington to go take Richmond. All far from us. So my dear Mahala wraps sugar in a little envelope and mails it to Virginia, to sweeten my life."

Walter McClure stirred a scant spoonful of the sugar into the coffee. (If offered food or drink, take only small portions. One does not wish to appear hoggish.) "How does—how does she feel about that, sir?" His face burned; he did not know if he had transgressed the laws of social intercourse by asking such a personal questions of an officer. He wanted to know more about this good man he felt mutual interests with. Was it all right? The *Courteous Gentleman* did not cover military situations.

But Beem seemed tolerant, even expansive. He changed positions, stretching his short legs towards the fire and taking a long drink of coffee.

"She hates it. Says she is embarrassed in Spencer because I did not marry her before I left. Feels deserted and lonely. She wants me to quit the service."

"Quit the Fourteenth, sir?" Walter McClure was surprised. Officers did resign commissions, but for a lonely woman?

"There are Copperheads in Owen County, like every other section of Indianney. They say the war is useless, the Rebels destined to win, the price much too high for the middle states to pay. High prices, widowed wives, orphaned children—and try as they will not to hear it, our folks back home listen."

"Some out here say that, too, sir. Some in the regiment itself." Walter McClure's voice was low.

"I know, McClure. And you know who they are as well as I do. Southern sympathy was the reason some of the officers have resigned their commissions and gone home already. That is how I have my place, because a weak sister wanted to go home. But how many enlisted men have deserted or been discharged through influence? Three hundred men. One third of us, McClure. They came as volunteers and now that it seems as if it may be a long, sad war, they want to go home. Just at the time we will be called into real action."

"Real action?"

"That's what I said."

Walter put his cup on the trunk and sat ramrod stiff. "Sir, have you heard something?"

"Only the rumors. Colonel Kimball has been to Washington to see if he can get us a fighting assignment. He believes it may come through soon. As soon as the roads clear up, we will join the army in the Shenandoah Valley, then possibly go to meet McClellan's army."

"They may go by sea to Richmond, some say."

"Ah, the city of Jefferson Davis. Nobody's gotten there yet." Beem smiled and allowed himself a little wool gathering. "I hear Jeff Davis has a regular royal court there. Dances every night, full dress balls, with pressed chicken and tea cakes made from spices brought through the blockade. Perhaps we can sample one or two eventually." He winked and nodded.

"Sounds like some of the events the rich Copperheads are having back home, sir, from what I hear. The men say there was a big ball south of Vincennes. Big Southern supporters were there, mixing with our own folk."

Beem snorted, then was silent. "There is a castle of Copperheads in my own hometown. Their lodge. Knights of the Golden Circle. These things are spreading all over, like a rotten disease."

"Fire in the rear, back home. That's what it is." Walter was silent a moment, then said more hopefully, "But now we are to have fire, real fire, at the front."

"I hope so, McClure. We don't need the Copperheads to finish off the Northern cause with their scheming back home. We're doing it ourselves. The Northern Army is going to die of boredom and defeatism if this war goes on much longer like this."

"Thanks for the coffee, sir," Walter McClure said, rising and brushing sticks from his trousers. "I wish you well in your—wooing." He smiled, more confidently this time. Did he really need a book to tell him how to care about other people?

Beem stood up too. With an open, confiding look on his face that seemed to ignore the fact that he was an officer talking to an enlisted man, he said,

"I may be a bridegroom soon. I've been promised a long weekend leave, and I may just go and marry the girl."

Walter was grateful to be included in the confidence, and he was also impressed. Not many passes were given out here—Beem must have found favor with Kimball and the higher powers. Well he should have! When combat came, he himself would wish to serve under David Beem. Still, his own Captain Brooks and Lieutenant Houghton were also honorable soldiers.

"Congratulations on the coming event, sir," he said, offering his hand. "When the Miami and Potawatomi marry, they go to the lodge of the loved one and bring gifts. Then they promise to stay together, always in love. That is all there is."

"Wish it were that simple. We'll have oceans of lemonade, stacks of cake. Doting maiden aunts giving us teaspoons and uncles giving us bad advice."

"I hope the advice is not to"—he was being very bold indeed—"not to resign your commission and go home."

"That advice I should not take," Beem said seriously. "I am in for three years, or the duration. Whatever that may be."

"Whatever that may be," Walter Mcclure thought as he returned to give his report of success to the assistant surgeon. With McClellan in the doldrums, Buell in the mud and the Fourteenth Indiana in limbo, the duration could be a very long time indeed.

After the "Roast Beef" call for dinner, Walter McClure walked down the lane to find the encampment of his own C Company. Captain Lewis Brooks was coming out of an officer's tent. He was having to do double duty since his cousin Lieutenant Houghton was still in the "sick house."

Walter handed the list of regulations to the small, dapper man whose uniform was so immaculately brushed.

"Yes, yes, seems appropriate to me," said Brooks. "Certainly has validity. Anything to reinforce the discipline. Good work, McClure. We shall see them effected on the morrow! Except for the drinking one. Can't seem to do much about that one, no matter how hard we try, eh? Still, good work!" He clapped Walter McClure on the back.

Turning, the young man returned to the surgeon's tent with the news that the regulations seemed to have been well received. A group of men were standing by the burnt-out dinner fire, preparing to assemble for afternoon drill.

"Hey Redskin, got any bear grease for my hair? It couldn't stink any more than it does now," someone shouted down the road.

"Redskin, any letters from your sister, the squaw?" The speaker was

Isaac Crim, a tall young man of his own age and also from C Company. He was not a bad sort. Like the rest of them, he wore horse blinders when it came to folk not of his own kind.

The men began sending other taunts towards Walter McClure; from somewhere, comfortingly, he heard one voice raised in his defense.

"Leave off the target practice, men." It was Bo Reilly, the youngest man in the regiment. But he was out-shouted.

"Speaking of target practice, you're not shootin' with us anymore, are you, Redskin," Bushby Quillen shouted. A wiry man with a short beard, he was the cruelest of all. He yapped insultingly all the time, like a feisty terrier. Still, Walter had to consider what Quillen had just said. It is true that after the Battle of Greenbrier, Colonel Kimball and Captain Brooks asked that he detach from C Company to become orderly to Surgeon Burkhart. He had made nothing of it except that he was needed. Did it have anything to do with the fact that he was an Indian? Could the men believe he brought "bad luck" or some such thing?

Walter sent a noncommittal wave to Crim and the rest and walked on down the lane. "Your sister, the squaw." They did not know him, he thought, or they would know he did not have a sister. His father had died when Walter was only a baby; his mother had no other children. Not that any of that mattered to most of the men in the regiment. He was a caricature, a cartoon from an illustrated magazine, with a balloon above his head saying "Me want wampum," just as the E Company Germans in the regiment were fat, harsh, lager-drinking "krauts." If he told them that he had a wart on his chest, a mother he loved, who taught school in Peru, Indiana, and plans for a future life as a schoolmaster himself, they would not know what that meant. It was nothing new. He had been called names in Peru, Indiana, too, only there it was "Tecumseh" instead of "Redskin." He knew it would be this way, and he had come anyway. He felt outraged that men would sunder a nation rather than give up slavery. He had to do something, even if that meant getting his pride stepped on and his heart wrung by small-town bigots.

He approached the row of stockaded tents that was Company C's domain. A skinny dog trotted out of the woods towards his tent. It was the ugliest dog Walter McClure had ever seen, with ribs sticking out and a damaged eye leaking rheum down the side of its muzzle. Unaccountably, the dog turned and wagged its tail. Walter McClure picked up a flat stone to toss at it, then, standing still in the street a moment, changed his mind. He whistled to the dog and called it over. "Come here," he called, and, when the dog came over, Walter knelt to pat its scruffy fur. Then he began to laugh, with secret, mischievous satisfaction. "Whiteskin," he said emphatically, telling the dog its new name.

When he finally entered his tent, he picked up the small green book he had been studying to learn the skills of courtesy. He fingered the raised filigree design on its cover and then he walked back to the now-deserted campfire of Company C. He laid the book on a cracker box in plain sight.

With the dog at his heels he bounded back to the tents. "They need it more than I do, Whiteskin," he shouted laughingly at the dog.

*　　*　　*　　*

A month later, as the first snowfall of the winter fell on Martin County, Thomas Jefferson Brooks sat in the parlor of his Loogootee, Indiana home. A plate had just been put before him by the hired girl, food fixed lovingly by his wife Susan: on it were sausages, eggs, fried mush and syrup and stewed apples with cinnamon. Savoring the food like a man who had known hunger in his time, he tested each item on the plate once, grunted his satisfaction, then ate everything quickly.

"Thersa, come get this," he called and pushed it aside before she arrived, so he could continue the letter he was writing. An oil spot from the sausage fat on his hand appeared on the paper; he dabbed at it with blotting paper and put his pen into the inkwell before him. He read what he had written.

To: Captain Lewis Brooks
Fourteenth Indiana Regiment
Phillipi, Virginia

February 10, 1862

My Dear son Lewis:

Your missive of January 20 from the Fourteenth Indiana Regiment has reached us and as always your mother and I and your brothers and sisters heave a sigh of relief that you are alive and well.

And that your cousin Will is better now from the swelling of the lymph glands and lung fever. Your Aunt Harriet Houghton has been wild with worry, as you can imagine. You know she is as nervous as a cat on a griddle in her normal mood; now that her baby is at the wars, she dances on the edge of hysteria about half the time. I am glad your assistant surgeon Burkhart found him a good home and a foster mother to plump his pillows and bring him potato soup as he sits before a bright fire.

We rejoice about the news, which you out there must have heard by now, from Ft. Donelson in Tennessee. This unknown general Ulysses Grant has won us two victories. He has sailed right past these strategic forts on the Tennessee River and made them his own, with fine strategy, really and little loss of life. How we have needed a victory to prop up this sagging war. May it be the first of many.

Lewis, you say you do not like the court martials you must act on. Yes, the insubordination and drunkenness you describe are shocking. I suppose Colonel Kimball's punishments, making the sots parade about in barrels to the Rogue's March, is a just one. But to think that Clay Welch, the son of a friend of ours from Loogootee Methodist Church, would be one of those wearing a barrel for drunkenness—it is discouraging. Still, you must help him. You say he feels as if his reputation is damaged and that of Company I also—tell him reputations are of more worth than the present greenbacks— there is always a chance to redeem a reputation.

But—what you tell me of Christmas there in Virginia in winter quarters shocks and saddens me. Of course, there would be little cheer for you, but for so many men to have had a drunken brawl on Christmas day, to have one die, stabbed in the lungs and another drown in the freezing river with a bottle in his hand. Shame on our southern Indiana boys. I will honor your request not to "show" your letter around. I do not agree, though, that we must preserve the "honor of the Fourteenth" at all costs. That, you all will have to earn. So far the glory you have earned could be kept in a house-wife's thimble. I think the core of the apple is sound, but it is rotting, unused in the barrel.

You say the lieutenant of G Company, Mr. Denny, has finally been arrest-ed for drunkenness and will be forced to resign. I had already heard, son, for all Vincennes is agog with it. Lieutenant Denny was a drunkard before he joined the service and only got his commission because his father was a Republican friend of the governor's. I should know; his father is my lawyer, and I have met Governor Morton in that very office. Never has a war been so politically controlled. Men may plan strategies and fight battles, but it is the fat pols at home who will win or lose the war as they plot to stay in power.

At least the change means Sergeant Van Dyke, who you say is a compe-tent officer, will be made Second Lieutenant. I am interested in the comment that you do not trust him very much. I did meet him in the law office, too, but did not know him well enough to form an opinion.

"How is it in Martin County, now?" you ask.

Well, not very good, I answer. The Butternut Southern sympathizers behind every spirea bush are busy denouncing every minute: they rail against the Republicans, Lincoln. What they denounce most loudly is the Massachusetts industrialists who are making money selling shoes and coats to the government. What the folks around here are really saying is that the price of corn is 20 cents a bushel and there are no longer any markets in the South to buy it. The war is making the average man poor.

Our neighbor, Thornton Slicer from down there by the mill at Hindostan, has already distinguished himself by trying to run a load of bacon past the army at Cairo, Illinois. His boat was confiscated, but not before he fired a few shots as they came out in boats from shore. He is a fool as well as a Copperhead; you know that.

All along the Ohio River business houses that sell to New Orleans or Memphis have closed down because there is no trade; my own hog and corn trade is slower than it has ever been. I do not blame the farmers around here for hating the Easterners—those Eastern railroad bosses are charging almost a dollar a bushel to get grain to New York City where it can be sold for less than the shipping costs.

Because of this war there is abject proverty in Louisville, Cincinnati, Evansville. I have seen it myself just lately.

The papers are as full of raging sentiments as a barnyard is of hog ordure—"The blood and murder party, with its railsplitter President, has killed the goose that lay the golden egg." "Lincoln is under the foot of the Eastern war manufacturers. The war policies make us in the Northwest servants and slaves." "We do not share sentiments with the Easterners. Rather, we hate them and their special interests. Most are rank abolitionists who would free all the slaves and send them up north to take all our jobs. Let us make peace and invite the South back into the Union, at their own price."

So say the Democrat papers. Still, they will not make us join the South or some other treasonous action, I think, as the Copperheads wish. Mr. Clement Vallandigham keeps talking and writing in Ohio, but the rest of us are not listening very much.

Enough of these political froufrous and trumpetings. You know my opinion of politics and letter writers. Let us talk of home. Your sister, Susie, is a happy married woman, but I fear that your brother-in-law Sandford Niblack will never realize a cent in the mercantile business. Still, I have just set him up with a store in Wheatland. We must take care of our own.

Your brother, Tommy, mopes about at Brooks store. I thought giving him full management of it would assuage his desire to go to "see the Elephant," but it has not. Not everyone must go to the war, I tell him. Certainly, with Lib's delicate health and that of Baby Lewie and the responsibilities of the family, no one would dare call him a dodger. He feels left out, useless as a fifth wheel on a wagon.

I tell him I need him at the store and put all the screws to him that I can. It is hard enough having you, Lewis, out in the field, exposed daily to the attack of a bullet or the typhoid fever. I do not think even Lincoln himself asks that I send all my sons to the war.

Your older sister Emily is busily chasing the small ones while that dear husband of hers, Doctor Campbell drives about trying to get serum to vaccinate for the smallpox, which has hit near the Orange County Line. Grandmother Poore is staying with them to help with the children while Emily picks lint and wraps bandages at the church most days for the Ladies' War Aid Society. She talks some of being a nurse, if there were somebody to nurse nearby.

You say something about trying to get a higher commission if a new regiment is formed in Martin County. I believe you could go for colonel, son, and my new political connections with the governor might forward that effort.

Your mother told me to write that "your younger brothers Eustace and Seymour are in health. Pray they stay so, with the smallpox so near. Every day is a trial and proof of God's grace." So says your mother.

And I say keep your gun polished and repaired and tell all the Martin County boys to stay away from bad women around the camps. We hear they are there, though you would not tell your father so. I heard tell one surgeon general has banned 'em from around his camp near the city. Getting the clap is no fun. So they say, I could not prove it. I say this not for you, but for the men in your company. Do not show this letter, as you always say to me.

Next week I go to Indianapolis to see Governor Morton. If I cannot sell hogs in New Orleans, I shall try to sell them and broker other goods for the war effort. I shall become a military purveyor, member of one of the shoddiest of fraternities in this war. Ah well, perhaps I shall uplift it. We shall see.

Either that or bad company there in the state capital will be my downfall. Come to think of it, I may take Tommy. Perhaps that will make him feel as if he's swimming in the mainstream a little bit more than he does now in Loogootee.

Your loving father,
Thomas Jefferson Brooks

Slowly he put the letter in an envelope with a soldier in its upper left hand corner and the words "Blessed Union, survive!" printed beside the cap. Then he returned to attacking his eggs and mush.

A month later, his mother-in-law opened a letter in the same kitchen. She smiled as she recognized the handwriting of a young friend.

To: Mrs. Hannah Chute Poore
From: Her Old Friend John R. McClure, Camp at Phillippi,
Virginia

March 3, 1862

Dear Miz Poore:

I thot I would while away the hours here at Camp Bordom riting to you and tell you how life is here in this man's army. Please excuse the hand. I never was much of a riter.

I no you have heerd from your grandsons Captain Lewis Brooks and Lieut. William Houghton. But I thot you might wish a word from that boy that you have sent cookies and nit sox to, that orfaned child you opened your heart to after the death of his parents on the Ohio River, as you no so well, so long ago now.

I guess you know both armies are in winter quarters here in western virrgina. After the Bull Run flop twas too mudy to march either "on to Richmond" or "on to Washington" so mostly we sit here and wait to get out onto the roads in spring.

Our Northern boys have been more active lately. We marched towards Winchester and back for a skirmish with the enemy, and earlier we got on the cars and rode through freezing whether to a town where we got off, made fires to thaw our feet, stayed the night and found the rebbels had gone already.

Tiger Tail Mess has sibbley tents, I am the mayor so they say of G company. Ever day I patrol to be sure wood is cut for the fires in the cookstoves in the middle of the tents and the streets is clean and limed down. Issac Crim (he says his Pa knew you at Hindostan) has a laundry and for 5 cents a shirt does our wash. To my way healthy men are those who stay clean. They will be whinners and live to the end of the war.

My tittle is "Company Sanitation Oficer." The ass. surgon give me it. Also there is another McClure who is C company's oficer, a Indian. How he got the name I do not no but he stole it sure nuf. Probly to mock me. He also had a dog that he called Whiteskin secret-like to mock me too because that is my nickname sometimes. But it got killed misteriosly.

I talk to him as litle as posible, after all the trouble our fambly had with redskins I don't want to sit and chitty chat with 'em. He can read, to boot. Sits there and puts his nose in The Pit and the Pendumlum to make the rest of us look bad. Fries my eyes to think how uppity everbody is gettin in America.

The oficers still have contrabands to cook and clean. Sergeant Van Dyke's, though, up and left him one night. Said he had to go get his wife free. Can't imagine what a niger's marriage would be like, but maybe they love their wifes too like regular people. I wish you was here to give me one of your good sermons on the brotherhood of man. I am mad haf the time at the nigers in camp who roll their big eyes and talk of "Massa Lincoln and how he is gwine to free usnes." Best he never does it. Sorry Miz Poore I no how you feel but you have to no how I feel too, you always tole me to. Hard nuf out here without we have to git an equality going and when we git back all the nigers come to Wheatland Indiana and take the work up so we can't get any jobs.

The men in the Fourteenth are mostly fine fellows and I love 'em all like brothers, Miz Poore. We are still all of one mind as we were in Vincennes at the train station. It suprises me after all the troubles we ben through and not much fightin yet, but tis true. It jest does me good to think that we are all together to put the Union back after our ancestors fought so hard to start it in the first place. So Grandma Catherine tells me, Some of Our grandpas had fought Tecumsey at Tippecanoe. Tommy Thompson's great grandpa Sam'l came acrost the Buffalo Trace in 1803 with my great grandparents. She said his great grandma was a Baird as mine was. Thompsons and McClures fought with Clark. Ralph Emison come out with us but he had to go back because he got tiephoid and it weakened him. But there are lots of us are relatives from a way back.

How time does circle around, don't it?

Here we all are together on mouldy blankets in the same darn Tiger Tail Mess.

I better tell you about the big shebang when General Lander died. He was general of our division here and he was the cusingest, tiradingest, raw, horse-whip spur of the moment man I ever did see, and the fever got his body as the devil stood in line for his soul.

For his funneral we was got in line at 11:30 in the morning and stood there till our hands froze off. The flags was at half mast and draped in black. Finally they marched us to the depott, where we stood till our feet froze off. Then there was booms and we knew canons were being shot off at general headquarders. Thousands a men, the whole division was there, a sea of blue. Bands played the death march. Guns kept a firin and the casket approached. The parade was chaplins, then officers and then the corpse borne on the shoulders of his staff, who might have been the only ones to a loved him. Especially since we all had stood about in the below zero weather to see his remains. Anyways, we saluted the old man with "pressent arms." After the corpse was put on the cars, the bands played "the girl I left behind me," and we high-tailed it in ranks back to our camps.

Well, for fun we done these things in the last two weeks: went to church down the road a piece and when we got there found out some rough characters had took over the church and were playing cards in the pews while their fidlers played tunes at the altar. In the middle of it all, the preacher come over to the church for Sunday services but left, sad at such goins on.

(2) Had a big country breakdown with square dances and country reels, but no gals.

(3) Had a big snowball battle of the whole brigade with tactics like flanking and fayned retreat.

(4) Requisishuned the toughest hog in five counties, a regular old Noah, from a Rebel farmyard nearby, which I have to cook now for supper

(5) Drilled, drilled and drilled some more.

Later. Looks like it may pay off, Miz Poore. Guess my ole hog will have to wait. Lieutenant jest come to tell us to cook rations to get onto the road. Some Secesch named Stonewall Jackson is in the Shenandoey Valley nearby, and our job is to see he don't cause any trouble as the Young Napoleon's push to Richmond gets underway.

I would preciate any mail. Show my Grandma Catherine this letter if you see her and tell her to tell Aunt Jewell—oh well, nevermind. They ain't speaking now, anyways.

> Your dear friend
> John R. McClure

And that same John McClure himself opened a letter four weeks later in camp:

From: Catherine McClure Hogue
To: Private John R. McClure
Fourteenth Indiana Regiment

> April 15, 1862

Dear Grandson:

Mrs. Poore showed me your letter when she was in town visiting. She is now in Cincinnati with her daughter. She says to tell you everyone is fine in her family and she now has fifty-eight grandchildren and fifty-nine great-grandchildren.

I am glad you are staying firm in trying circumstances. Boredom is a great enemy to good behavior. Your cousin, Jacob Joe Scott, often seems bored to me these days, ill at ease. He runs the farm for Cousin John Robert. They have bought a McCormick reaper and they are going to loan it around for harvest teams this summer. Still, he does not seem to have much heart for it. I'm afraid the promise he made to his ma so long ago, as she died, that he would stand a Quaker and not go to war is eating at him.

Particularly because Zach, his brother, is up to no good, agitating for the South. I see the letters Zach writes in the Vincennes Western Sun under the name of The New Boston Tea Committee. Says the North tyrannizes. Pother such stuff. As if Abraham Lincoln were some sort of tyrant because he has to arrest people and consider a draft for this war. And these slimy slave holders think they are George Washington and Sam Adams. Pother I say. And to boot I think Zach is breaking his father's heart causing such agitation and supporting the slave system. John Robert had a spell a while back and lay in bed for over a week, and I know he is partly pining about that boy.

John, I hope you do get to church. Things sound at sixes and sevens in that camp and our family has always been a church-going one.

You say there is an Indian name of McClure. That's odd. Pa in his old age used to chuckle that there was an Indian named McClure he knew about, but I think he said twas in Ohio. He was vague about it, I recall.

News from here. I am planning to meet your sister, Mary Jane, in town at the soda bar for a fizz drink this next week. It is the only way I get to see her, because your Aunt Jewell is ornerier than ever about us McClures. She tit-tattles every time she can on us—I know you can't do anything about all this, and I guess I shouldn't put you in the middle of the mess.

Lately she's been gossiping to all the folk in her neighborhood about your Aunt Lettie. Aunt Lettie has finally got a beau, well I admit he's not much and the prospects raise my hackles a bit. She is seeing Willis Mawkins, the livery man. You may remember his pa used to work for your Grandpa John Hogue.

My, I do still miss that good husband of mine! Especially when five o'clock comes. He always used to come in off the fields, no matter what he was doing at five, and when the clock chimes I look up, even though it has been so long. Fixing supper and winding up the day will never have much meaning for me, I think, any more.

I hope your Aunt Lettie finds some happiness. If she were to marry that slick little man I think I could stand it if she had some meaning to her life.

You are part of the meaning of mine, John dear. We know you are on the roads of Virginia, hard to reach, and I am apprehensive and reading the Ninety-first Psalm. My mother used to turn to that. "He that dwelleth in the secret place of the most High shall abide under the shadow of the Almighty." I know that is really where you are, in the shade of the Almighty's power, although it seems it's Stonewall Jackson's shadow that is pursuing you and the regiment.

Love always,
Your Grandmother Catherine

A week later, Thomas Jefferson Brooks and his twenty-four-year-old son Tommy sat on cracked leather sofas in the waiting room of the governor's office. Indiana's State House was run down, a middle-aged lady down at the heels. Through the transom they could hear water dripping somewhere down the hall, and a mouse had scurried along in front of them as they came for this appointment with Governor Oliver P. Morton.

Thomas Jefferson Brooks was aware of the respectability of this venerable state house. It was obvious in the frescoes of justice and mercy which adorned the inordinately high ceiling in this anteroom, tribute to the early founding days of the Republic in which it was built. Still, the bright spittoon which sat by the settee and the telegraph office next door spoke of its modern connections.

"They ought to tear this old relic down," Thomas Jefferson Brooks told his son. "It arrived in Indiana about the same time I did."

"Pa, you came in 1818. Indianapolis wasn't even here," young Tom said absently. "The statehouse isn't that old—it just hasn't been kept up well." Tommy acted as if he were used to his father's slight exaggerations, and as they walked down the hall towards the governor's office, the senior Brooks thought of this. Well, maybe he was exaggerating a bit more these days; the family was "funning" him about it. Susan Brooks had a retort to the children who mocked. Anyone who had become a frontier millionaire in Indiana honestly could afford to exaggerate a little, she said.

"I'm glad you have that opinion now, Susan," Thomas Jefferson Brooks had said once recently, curling up his mouth in a smile when she said this. "There was a time in Hindostan when you thought I was Chicanery Charlie. I'm glad you concede I made my fortune honestly."

Susan had just paused and put on her "parlor of the Methodist Church" look. "Well, almost all honestly," she said primly.

A secretary to the governor sat at a huge desk outside the door to the inner office. "Governor Morton will see you now," he said.

Tom was instantly off the settee; it took his father a few grunts and slides across the deep seat to accomplish the task.

"Sit down, sir," the governor said gravely. "I do recall our meeting in lawyer Denny's office in Vincennes."

"Unfortunate scandal about his son."

"Scandal, sir?"

"Well, my son wrote of the—indiscretions and dissipating that beset poor younger Denny."

Morton looked at the two sternly. "Many of those, I am afraid, may have been trumped up charges, thrown at Captain Denny by jealous rivals for his post."

"Oh?" was all Thomas Jefferson Brooks could think of to say.

"Yes. I have seen to it that he is reassigned in another regiment, just now forming."

Younger and older Brookses said nothing, but smiled and nodded weakly. "Consarn," thought the elder Brooks. "Why I have to plunge right into the pork barrel?" Patronage by the governor was a sore point all over the state.

"Governor, you were kind to see us. First of all, you are aware I have applied for a commissarying license," the father said.

"I do think my new commissary head has called that to my attention."

"There are so many applying, and as I have been unpolitical—"

"Your party?" Morton had a small, neat beard; it seemed to wag with the question.

"I voted for your ticket and Abraham Lincoln. Before that I was a Democrat."

"And so was I."

"You were, sir?" Tommy burst in with surprise and a little laughter.

"You didn't know that?" Morton's face grew rosy, and he smiled. "You are young. Believe me, my older constituents in the state never let me forget the fact. I was a Jacksonian Democrat until I stomped out of a meeting one night."

"What over, if I may ask?" Tommy seemed fascinated by this man with the strong, confident look and equally confident voice.

"They were discussing the Kansas-Nebraska Act and I felt I could not support it. Let the states choose—why, if every territory and state were to decide these issues, soon Massachusetts might decide it wanted slavery and would vote to change its constitution and include slavery. Beginning of the end. I saw it from the start."

"Yes, sir," the elder Brooks said, watching the governor make and unmake fists. "No one could fault the speed with which you called for troops and funded them through the legislature."

"I was glad to support my President." He eyed Brooks curiously. "What was it you wanted to say about your license application?"

"You have had some trouble with your other suppliers. There are still complaints about the hams being too salty, the coffee watered down."

"Yes." He smiled a little, which seemed to encourage Tommy to his usual exuberant brashness.

"There was a story in the Fourteenth Regiment, sir," Tommy said, "that the coffee at camp in Indiana was so weak that a soldier could carry a bean dragged through the whole length of the Mississippi, bring it out at the Delta and the drink would be stronger than what they were supplied with."

The elder Brooks coughed, but Morton whooped and said, "I have heard that. We did find that parched beans were supplied to the soldiers in large numbers, along with the good ones. And the beef was slimy and spoiled. I must admit I was a little new at getting a war organized. I put in friends and enemies alike to be fair, and I didn't always get competent people in the rush. We replaced the original commissary superintendent on my staff. I think my new man is doing a better job.''

"Only partly,'' the elder Brooks commented. "There are still complaints almost every week in the papers.''

"The *Indiana Sentinel*, broadsheet of the treacherous Democracy—''

"Not only Democrat rags. Let me tell you my plan.''

Morton nodded. Tommy popped his knuckles, excited about sitting in the halls with The Great.

"You are using Indianapolis people,'' Thomas Jefferson Brooks began, "who are factoring with second and third parties who then contract with farmers. Nobody knows when some skinflint puts in last year's hams, wormy wheat. These people sit behind these big desks''—he instantly wished he had chosen another allusion—"and never get out to the country.''

Behind his big desk Morton appeared unmoved, looking at him expectantly; and now Tommy's face was also turned, wondering what his father would say.

"I know everybody in five counties in southern Indiana. Between my family and my wife's—well, we've been around a while. Half of 'em have owed me debts and are beholden to me anyway. Let me deal directly with the farmers, be your jobber for all the rich farmland down there, and we can supply you faster and more reputably. Our hams'll never turn green.''

Morton stroked his beard. He picked up a pitcher of water and poured himself a drink, slowly. "And so you wish to be a direct broker, without middlemen.''

"Reporting to you.''

"Well, of course, I have a commissary chairman. I couldn't go behind his back. Besides I don't have enough hours in the day—''

"You went to President Lincoln yourself when the boys on Cheat Mountain didn't have overcoats. You made a trip on the train and went right into his parlor, where his wife and children were sitting.''

"So I did. A captain from G Company had written me. Coons, by name. I saw Lincoln. And the overcoats came up next week.''

"High time, according to my son. But they know about that out there in the camps. They know you care for the boys. I must admit to you that I do too. I don't want to think of them marching and fighting and eating rot.''

"No.'' Morton was thoughtful. "Perhaps it would be worth a try. Have you report to me at least for a while. Good for the public to know, too.'' He turned his chair and looked out the window. Apple trees were coming into bloom. The air entering the window was fragrant with their sweetness. "Just a year," he said. "A year ago this week. What will another year bring? We need more men, better ordnance, modern guns. It will take years to win."

"Years, sir?" Tommy seemed surprised.

"Yes, years. I knew they were all fools who said we would take Richmond in three months with 70,000 men."

Thomas Jefferson Brooks hitched his chair forward a little. "That brings me to my second question. My son, Lewis Brooks—"

"Ah, yes. I have heard of him. Recommended for promotion."

The elder Brooks breathed a sigh of relief. "I had hoped so. He has had an honorable record."

"So Colonel Kimball tells me." Then after a pause, "Kimball is a Democrat."

"So are many fine officers you appointed. My son Lewis is a staunch Republican. A speaker for the old values, supporter of the Union."

"We can use those."

An apple petal came in from the window and lodged on Thomas Jefferson Brooks's sleeve. He did not brush it off. "I believe you are thinking of forming another regiment from Martin County," he said.

"Yes. I am told there are still men who will come to the colors."

"I sir, I wish to," Tommy stood and said in a bright, eager voice. "But both my wife and son are ill. And with Lewis gone I sustain my father."

Morton looked archly at the pair. "Indeed? He seems to be sustaining himself very well, from what I can see."

Brooks, senior's, face flushed. The governor had hit a sore spot. His son flashed a triumphant look at him.

"I cannot make your son Lewis a colonel," Morton went on. "That spot is spoken for already. But he can raise the regiment himself and be second in command. Your son is as good as a lieutenant colonel already. We will issue the call in mid-summer. But as for this other boy of yours, here—"

A bee entered and was buzzing about, and Tom leaned away from it. "I am a loyal Unionist. Even an Abolitionist," he said.

Morton looked surprised. "Even so? We haven't abolished slavery yet officially. It may come to that, eventually."

Tom picked up a copy of the *Indiana Sentinel* and was using it to usher the bee towards the open window. "Yes, sir. I took a trip to New Orleans and what I saw there turned my mind against the South and its hated institutions. Why, I saw a slave whipped on the streets. And there were rich women there who kept slaves for—" He caught his father's warning eye. No need to go too far. The bee refused to go to the window; it flew towards Morton. Resolutely the governor took the copy of the *Sentinel* and whacked the bee squarely against his desk. It lay there, dead, and Tommy stared at it for a moment.

"Loyal are you, very loyal? Well. . . " Morton seemed to be considering something. He brushed the bee onto the floor and lowered his voice. "I may have something for you. Something that could serve our cause. Would you be interested in some. . . investigative work?"

Tommy nodded eagerly.

"You say you run your father's store?"

"Yes. Largest general store in the state, even now, when Indianapolis stores are so large."

"Many people come in?"

" 'Tis one of the centers of life in our part of the state."

"Ahh. Well, you know, not everyone in Martin County is as loyal as you are."

"Sir," Tommy said confidingly, " 'tis a hotbed of Southern intrigue. The Knights of the Golden Circle—"

"I'm aware of that—lodge. And it is about them that I have grave concern. We are at a crucial point in the war. We have not won battles, morale is low now, prices are falling, times are hard. Mr. Clement Vallandigham keeps writing letters to all the newspapers in the Northwest, implying that the war is wrong. We must not allow a sub-rosa group of fanatics to steal our state."

"Steal it, sir?"

"I use the word correctly. May I be frank? I take very seriously the movement to stop the war effort. It is strong in Indiana, and if these people get into the ascendancy, they could hurt the Northern effort immensely. Lincoln depends on Indiana; he has told me he regards it as the keystone state in the war effort. The Knights of the Golden Circle can control the next election here in the state. They demand peace immediately, and they are even considering an armed uprising to get Indiana to join the Confederacy and stop the war. Should the Rebels penetrate into Indiana as they well may soon, and should there be an uprising—"

Both Brookses were silent. They had heard rumors, of course, but to hear the governor of the state speak so chilled them.

He went on. "Martin County, though it is by no means the only center of activities, is one of the areas in which this sentiment is spreading like wildfire. I need to get information from within the county."

Tommy nodded eagerly. "What sort of information?"

"New lodges starting—they call them castles. Numbers joining. Plans, even. Would you hear of such things in your store?"

"I have kept my politics very quiet," Tommy said seriously. "It does not do to carry campaign cards with men you sell whisky and shoes to. They believe me a Unionist, I suppose, but it would be easy enough to let them believe I was angry at the course of the war—"

"Do so, then, Tom Jefferson Brooks, Junior. You are my spy to the Knights of the Golden Circle. Sniff them out, sir, and you will be rewarded with the thanks of your country!''

Tommy Brooks nodded eagerly. The governor stood and shook hands again across the desk ending the interview.

The two Brookses left the office returning to the depot. They took the train back to southern Indiana, God's Country—now the center of enthusiasm in Indiana for the infamous Knights of the Golden Circle, or the Devil, as some described them.

Mary Jane McClure sat on a horsehair chair in the parlor of the farmhouse where she lived with her aunt Jewell, uncle Archie, her sister Annie and her brother Bob. A likeness of her younger brother, John R. McClure, in his soldier suit in the Fourteenth Indiana Regiment, sat on a little table with a marble top. Mary Jane was working a piece of cross-stitch of a cat tipping over a pitcher of water on top of a table.

"Mary Jane?" A strong voice floated down from upstairs.

Mary Jane did not look up. "Yes, Aunt Jewell?"

"Did you fetch the last of the apples and set them to soak for the pie?"

"Yes, Aunt. Oww!" Mary Jane popped her finger into her mouth. She had pricked her finger. Embroidery needles were sharp. Maybe it was because you didn't use them as much as darning needles. She sucked the drop of blood on the tip of her finger away.

"And did you set the dough?"

"Yes. To make eight loaves, I think you said."

The clock ticked.

Her uncle Archie was sitting by the window, using the light of the setting sun to read the *Vincennes Western Sun*. "Barnum's fixin' to marry off Tom Thumb," he commented. "Goin' to have a reg'lar church affair." Uncle Archie was really talking to himself, thought Mary Jane. He had forgotten Mary Jane was in the room. He often blocked things out in his life, especially the enormous presence of his wife, a presence which otherwise would have blotted everything else out, like a spy balloon in front of the sun.

"Tom Thumb and his bride are both the same size. Wonder how they— well, I guess it's all in proportion, anyways."

Young Annie McClure had come into the room. "Hello, Annie," Mary Jane said. The girl did not answer but settled herself on the piano bench. She hardly ever carried on a conversation which went beyond asking for things for herself. Mary Jane was not sure if Annie knew other people really claimed existence in the world.

Aunt Jewell came down the stairs and stood like a dark cloud in the door of the parlor.

"Did I hear you say something to Bob about a letter from John in Virginny?"

"Well, yes, Aunt Jewell," Mary Jane answered. "Grandma Catherine read me John's latest letter when I—well, when I saw her. I had ice cream with her at the confectionary shop."

"I reckon you did," her aunt said in tones as frigid as an ice house. "Did she mention how her own daughter is hangin' round the livery shop spending time talkin to that trashy hired man, Willis Mawkins? The whole town is talkin'. Ain't no way for a respectable old maid to act. Don't know why you have to see that woman anyways."

"Now Aunt, you know I do see Grandma now and then. After all I am a grown woman and my own parents are dead." Down and up went the needle, a little nervously, making x's. Then up with the needle, twist thread three times for French knot. Bam. Into the cat's eyeball.

"So you do say," her aunt said. "Don't twiddle around, Mary Jane. Tell me about the letter." Her husband, sensing a change in the weather that boded storms, picked up the *Western Sun* and made for the kitchen.

"I wonder if Bob has cleaned that chicken pen like I tole him to," he said. "He always tries to git out of it."

"He don't like the smell of the chicken shit," Annie said without looking at her uncle.

"Shet your mouth or I'll whop you, young woman," her aunt said, sensibilities outraged. "Why, sech talk. Wherever do you get off cursing like that."

"John said stuff like that all the time. You jest didn't hear him," Annie said. The odd thing, Mary Jane told herself, was that Aunt Jewell never did whop Annie. Jewell Simpson seemed to be a little afraid of the girl.

Annie, for her part, began thumbing through the pile of ballads, looking at the pictures on the front, of girls with golden ringlets clasping their hands in delight or despair, while big dogs looked encouragingly up at them, of families sitting looking at soldier boy pictures, of idyllic, tinkling brooks. Then she began playing, "Somewhere My Love Lies Dreaming," with one finger.

"Well, Aunt," Mary Jane went on, "John had sent a letter to Grandma Catherine. Said he was going to write you next week."

"Did he now?" Jewell seemed a little mollified. "I have to depend on John to tell me what Henderson's a-doin'. He sure don't write to his ma. Well, what did your brother say?"

"Let's see. He got the pitcher I sent him. They had a big fight out there. Fought Stonewall Jackson's troops at Winchester."

"Stonewall Jackson. I hear he's a Christian. Thanks God after ever' battle."

"He thanks God for helping him kill people," Annie said from the piano bench.

"Clamp up, I tole you, girl," Aunt Jewell said, frowning so heavily her eyes disappeared into the folds of flesh in her face.

"*Anyways*," Mary Jane went on. "Called it the Battle of Winchester Heights, Kernstown, John said, and 'twas the biggest battle they was in yet, and they won. Fought in the open, ran acrost a field and wiped out the Rebs. Henderson got grazed with a bullet, but it didn't even break the skin."

"Oh, no. I wish that chile would write me. How 'bout John?"

"He waren't hit."

"Waal," Jewell said with a sigh. "I hope they ain't—gettin' in no trouble. Card playin' and all that. Did John say anything 'bout Henderson playin' cards?"

"No, aunt. But I think we can be pretty sure Henderson ain't goin' to take no chances with anything like that." Not unless he thought he could win, that is. Mary Jane knew her cousin well.

"Is John readin' his Bible and prayin'?" Aunt Jewell knew better than to ask if Henderson were doing Bible reading. His Bible was in the attic under a layer of dust an inch thick.

"No, but John is readin' the *Pilgrim's Progress*—" she stopped, realizing she had blurted her way into something uncomfortable.

"*Pilgrim's Progress*? Where'd he get that?" her aunt demanded.

Mary Jane was silent.

"I said where in tarnation did he get that ole book? We ain't got it around here."

Or any other book for that matter, Mary Jane observed to herself.

"I think—I b'lieve Grandma Catherine gave it to him when he went off to the wars," she said as casually as she could. "At the train station."

"Ohh, I knowed it," Jewell said, putting her hand to her head as if in pain. " 'Tis that old volume of my pa's, Jack McClure's. Old Grandpa Dan'l McClure give it to him, was from some old preacher crost the sea in Ireland they was related to. All full of claptrap bout some men wanderin' around in swamps and deserts. Men kept in cages, giants blabbin' around. Not a bit o sense in it." Annie was playing louder than ever, emphasizing some notes:

Somewhere my love lies DREAMING
DREAMING the happy hours away.

"Wall, John seems to like *Pilgrim's Progress*," said Mary Jane. "Says it comforts him."

"Leave it to the McClures to give him a worthless book like that. Your grandfather, my pa, Jack, had about as much sense as a soft-boiled egg. Runnin' off and doctorin' and gettin himself killed at Hindostan Falls whilst my poor, dear mother pined away—And your own pa, my brother Alfred. Crazy as a loon, runnin' off to join the Quakers and underground railroad. I always hate to curse my own kith and kin but they never was a more story-tellin', taffy-brained, liquor-guzzlin', fist-fightin' bunch of Scotch-Irish wastrels than—"

Interrupted, she looked up in amazement. Annie had set her mouth and was pounding with her fists on the piano, in five sharps and six flats. *BAM, BAMITY, BAM.* "Waal, I never," Aunt Jewell said, more mildly than Mary Jane would have expected. She was silent a long moment and Annie looked up defiantly.

"I do suppose we are goin' to have to get you some pianny lessons so you don't bang so," Aunt Jewell said and departed haughtily to the kitchen to check the bread.

A few minutes later Archie Simpson returned and sat in a rocking chair to watch the sun go down. All was silent in the room. "Sure would like to see Tom Thumb and his new bride," he said. "Sure as hell would like to do that."

Late May, June, 1862

Chapter Four

Hindostan Falls, 1862, almost forty years after the epidemic which had overnight destroyed it as a town, leaving its cabins to molder into the swampland of Martin County, was an eerie testament to the frailty of human endeavor.

On a sultry night at the very end of May, while the men of the Fourteenth Indiana regiment were campaigning in the Shenandoah Valley, heat lightning flickered over the ruins of the town, illuminating its earth-covered foundations and the streets grown high with Jimson and burdock.

Three figures wearing low-brimmed hats and oiled coats rode up a lane towards the town and dismounted near the northern edge of the overgrown cemetery. They led their horses towards a large barn on a lonely farm which now abutted the old town property.

The tallest of the trio spoke in a low tone to the others, "Meeting is at nine; we're a half hour late. If the road hadn't been so damned awful out of town—"

"They don't keep the son-of-a-bitch up," his short, stumpy companion answered. "Nobody comes out here no more, 'cept to go to the old mill there. Perfect spot though, for a gatherin' of witches on Allhallows Eve." He began to laugh, loudly.

"Shut up, you fool. We're running enough risk," the other man retorted. "You don't know who's about. You had no business asking so many questions in that store in Loogootee. I thought the man—Brooks was it?—was curious about us."

The tall man turned to the third person in the party, a slim figure who shadowed him a few paces behind. "And as for this escapade of *yours*—I don't know why I ever allowed myself to be talked into letting you come with us."

"Because I would not stay behind, and I would not let Calhoun come without me." One of the weak, far-off flashes illuminated the face of Delia Dugger, her hair pinned severely up and under the hat, her rounded body hidden beneath wide brimmed trousers and a covering mackintosh.

Holding their coats down against the wind, the trio reached the barn. Calhoun Dugger growled at his sister. "When Ma comes back from Louisville, if she finds this out—"

"I'll tell her myself," his sister said impatiently. "I want to live life a little, and I have been pining to know what you and Zach were doing with your castles and initiations."

"Well, we are here, and I don't think we were followed from town," Zach said, as they picked their way around the fragments of several Conestoga wheels and rusting iron tools. "Cal, light the lantern." The other man lit a sulphur match, sheltering it carefully with his hand. He touched it to a wick in the lantern and shut the glass down. Once, twice, he swung it past the darkened shutter that was the barn's window. Then he extinguished it quickly. "Now knock once, then twice, quickly," Zach commanded.

"Why so much folderol?" Delia's voice was irritated.

"Do as I say. The governor's men are all over the state, trying to nose us out. At first this Martin County group were meeting in a cave up the river, but we have switched to the barn here. Throw 'em off the track."

Calhoun knocked in the required way; slowly the huge door creaked open a crack. The three filed in, into the smell of straw, manure and candle wax from a few flickering candles held by shadow-figures in the corner of the barn. A ring of dark shapes loomed at them through the darkness, shimmered into focus, and became a circle of men wearing black robes. The wind moaned and thrashed, sending branches thumping onto the roof of the barn. The storm which had been threatening all evening was building.

A man wearing odd shin plates of steel and what looked like a home-made hauberk approached and held up a candle. He seemed to recognize Zach. With his hand, he motioned them to stand before him. Then the following conversation, in hushed, ceremonial tones, ensued.

"Who cometh?" said the man.

"A worthy fellow of the Knights of the Golden Circle who desireth initiation," answered Zach.

"It is well. He shall be examined to confirm if his devotion to God and country match his daring."

"I can attest to his loyalty on the blood of my patriot ancestors." Here Zach took out a small sharp penknife and slashed a tiny cut in his arm. He dipped the knife in blood and made a cross on the forehead of Calhoun. The low rumble of thunder echoed outside.

The man with the candle looked piercingly at Calhoun. His voice resonated through the gloom. "The keeper of the seals shall instruct you in the lore of our secret order."

From out of the darkness a very heavyset man lumbered forward, carrying a book. He opened its pages and read: "This order of brothers is yet young.

Its principles, though, are as old as the nation itself. It was founded on the sacrifice of blood which was shed for freedom. When we were young as a nation, our compact with each other was based on the fact that each unit of the new nation had its own freedom. The founding fathers believed the government could not compel obedience from individual states. They were free to hold their own views and have their own economic institutions. Today the will of the government is being forced on us all. Men are no longer free to hold their own property in the way they deem best. A bitter war against nature itself is being waged unfairly, against our sacred Constitutional privileges. Initiate, do you understand this?"

Calhoun nodded.

"Do you who would be our brother recognize the Constitution of the United States as your highest authority? Will you defend it against tyranny wherever it appears, even from the highest portals in the land?"

"I will." A crash of thunder split a tree which must have been only a few yards from the barn.

"Will you defend the freedom of a man to hold whatever property he wishes—defend it with your strength and your spirit?"

"I will."

"Will you fight against this unjust war which tramples on freedom? Even with your life if necessary?"

Calhoun hesitated, then whispered his affirmation, as rain began to pelt like pebbles onto the shakes of the roof.

Two men suddenly clasped Calhoun's arms firmly and held his face almost into the candle. "Repeat after me," the leader said, raising his voice, "I do solemnly promise I will never reveal or make known anything about the Knights of the Golden Circle except to a brother." His voice rasped above the rat-a-tat on the roof.

Calhoun repeated the oath, accompanied by the thunder claps of the heat storm.

"And that I shall yield obedience without hesitation to every order given me." Again, Calhoun gave his assent.

"And further, I will never take up arms under the flag of the discredited government or serve in its army. I will never serve as a despised mercenary to this hated government. This I do solemnly promise, so help me God."

Stumbling a bit, unnerved by the thunderclaps and noise on the roof, Calhoun completed his oath. A man stepped forward to show him a secret handclasp, grasp the wrist, put finger to the pulse of the other person. The leader, seemingly noticing Delia for the first time, said, "Who is this that has come with you?"

Someone rudely shoved a lantern in Delia's face. As she flinched, Zach put an arm about her casually to steady her.

"A sympathizer to our cause," he told them calmly.

Grumbling came from the circle and the heavyset keeper of the seals who served as leader said, "You know we are wary of outsiders unless they join our brotherhood. Who can tell men's loyalties these days?" His voice was edged with steel; tenseness stood as a tangible presence in the room.

Zach's voice was calm and sure. "I personally vouch for our new friend. He will become an initiate, brothers, when he has learned our ways. Is that not enough?"

The leader seemed mollified. "If you say so, brother. Now, new initiate, to your knees!" He motioned Calhoun to the barn's floor. The first fury of the storm seemed to have spent itself, and the pelting downpour eased into a steady rain, the thunder grumbling away over White River and to the east.

"I dub thee Knight of the Golden Circle. Rise to become a brother. You join an army 10,000 strong, an army which may soon rise and send its battle cry across the whole Northwest."

Candles came out from robes and the leader lit his and passed the light about the circle. The group closed with a repeated oath of loyalty.

"To that day! Day of freedom in the Old Northwest without the tyrant ruling! Loyalty! Uprising! Southern Confederacy!" Their voices, strident and strong, boomed over the noise of the storm. Then the circle broke to welcome the new initiate. Men sat on the floor of the barn discussing strategies for disrupting the Union war effort in the counties of southern Indiana. Delia stood a little aside, letting voices drift at her through the darkness. "New castles like this forming every day." "Ten thousand men in Indianney alone, did you say?" "Illinois better yet . . . Vallandigham speaking in Ohio . . . Crowds carry him on their shoulders." She shook her head, reached her hand back to be sure no wisps had escaped from the confining cap, then smiled a small, mysterious smile.

An hour later the rain had not stopped. "Drat, the road will be a quagmire. We will have to stay in the barn tonight," Calhoun muttered as the black-robed men left the building, pulling up their oiled coats about their ears. "The rest are all from up the road—we can't get back to the hotel at Loogootee tonight."

"Go get the horses, Calhoun," Zach ordered.

"To that cemetery, in this storm?"

"We'll bring them in here. Slicer—"

"He was the huge man who initiated me?" Cal wanted to know.

"Yes. He owns the barn, the land around here. He says we can stay the night if we keep the horses out of sight. Go now." The door opened and closed with a wet gust.

Everyone was gone. Delia walked to the far corner of the barn, took off her mackintosh, and spread it diffidently on the straw.

She rose and turned to Zach. "Why do you speak to Cal as if he were a mule?" she demanded.

"Because he is a mule. A good-natured, decent one that I happen to like. Besides, you treat him the same way." Zach had come close to her; she was aware, as she was lately when he had been at the house, of how tall he was. She was not a short woman, yet he loomed four inches taller than she. The candle he carried flickered on the thin, cynical line of his mouth, the light-yellow, tight curls which framed his face. She could smell his breath, the sweet, spicy odor of cloves. She knew he chewed them, probably to cover the odor of the spirits he often drank. He was close to her, very close. She did not step back. Something about him, a strange, exotic attractiveness enveloped her. She fought the magnetic pull of that mocking smile and wished for Calhoun to return.

"I think I should excuse myself. I need to go—" She could not finish the delicate reference. The oddness of the moment struck her suddenly. A gently-bred woman, here in a barn, spending the night in the presence of a strange man.

He laughed, not harshly. "To the woods?" He bowed low. "I regret I cannot provide a comfort station. Now that you are a gentleman, you must do as the rest of us do and take your own leak among the dripping trees."

Anger lit her eyes. "How dare you speak so?" She brushed past him, and as she did so, he put his hand on her arm for just an instant, through the light shirt she had worn. The touch of his hand was unexpectedly hot in the moist coolness of the barn; it scorched her like a burning brand.

His voice followed her across the room. "I have not asked how you like being a Copperhead. A Knight of the Golden Circle."

"I am not one. That I save for you," she flung at him defiantly. "I do not know how I feel about it. Midnight oaths, uprisings, promises made in blood—it is like a bunch of pirate games. I fear all this army of 10,000, if that be what it is, is nothing but a bunch of wild boys."

Or are they? she asked herself. As she pulled at the door of the barn and felt the wind and rain rush at her, she was more disturbed than she would admit.

*   *   *   *

A thin line of men crawled its way through the blue-green valleys of the Shenandoah the next morning, June 1, 1862.

The Fourteenth Indiana was chasing the elusive Stonewall Jackson. The Southern hero of Bull Run was trying to block the movement of the Northern army in the valley, to keep it from joining and reinforcing McClellan as he prepared to advance on Richmond, the Southern capital.

Actually, there were two major Northern armies in the Shenandoah, and

Jackson was just completing an ingenious strategy to divide and conquer them. That strategy, worthy of the brilliant, innovative general, was, however, probably lost on the bone-tired, dogged men slogging through the mud towards Luray, Virginia.

"Why'd you say again you come to see the elephant anyways, Bo?" a voice drifting out of the ranks of C Company demanded. It was Will Landon of G, now a lieutenant along with Van Dyke. Not one but two lieutenants had to be replaced, and there had been a double promotion. He and the rest of the men were playing one of the many verbal games which helped make the dreary marches more bearable. This one had originated when they first came to Virginia, before Rich Mountain.

"Well, now lessee," Bo Reilly yelled back towards Landon. " 'Twas that the ice cream at the strawberry socials at the church was not quite up t' par, and I thought I could get better eatables at the Abraham Lincoln res— too—raunt."

"The menu shore is good, ain't it? Fat back consumay, hard tack soo-flay and puree o' rotten potato," Landon shouted. The men chuckled and shifted their shoulders to ease the pain of overloaded backpacks.

Bo patted his rib cage and smiled. They had had nothing but basic tack and pork for about four weeks, and they had marched over three hundred miles. The worst part was that Chief of the Army General McDowell, had forbidden foraging. "To protect the honor of the army in a land which has had much deprivation," he stated.

"Shit, they don't know what deprivation is," Bo Reilly said out loud, as he thought of it.

The rules of "See the Elephant" varied with the circumstances. When they were in the frigid railroad cars in February, dashing after Secesh who escaped through the cold winter night before they got there, it was "I never got to see the country none, and I wanted to get away from the oppressive heat of the Wabash valley."

But whatever the circumstances it was always correct to answer, "Because I wanted a good purge." No one was ever free from "the trots."

"Why'd you come, Captain Houghton?" said Isaac Crim, placing slight emphasis on the word "captain," to recognize the new rank of the officer walking beside him. Houghton himself had been promoted just this week. His cousin, Lewis Brooks, had officially resigned because he had been named Lieutenant Colonel of a new regiment forming at home.

Will Houghton paused just an instant to pull his gum rubber blanket around his shoulders and head. Drizzling rain was beginning to fall again. He smiled trying to think of an answer for the elephant question. Flippancies did not come very easily to him.

"Hey, sir, it was because the girls ran you out of town," Bo Reilly said laughingly. "There were too many broken hearts in the neighborhood."

Houghton smiled weakly and waved Reilly off. There was an element of real truth in what Bo had just said. There had been Bo's own sister, Belle, and Peachy Ellison. Did he really break their hearts? He courted them quietly enough, or was it that they courted him? Whatever it was, he was successful enough in keeping it from his mother, who would have gone to bed with a headache if she knew he had even given a dandelion to a girl, let alone sat with one at the spelling bee or played kissing games at parties.

Peachy had been particularly hard. She flirted outrageously, dawdling to walk with him after church, having her mother invite him to dinner. His mother thought it was because Will was being rewarded for mowing the churchyard lawn. Peachy had walked with him in the garden. She seemed to want him to take her hand and she put her arm about his neck and kissed him hard, there under the elder trees. Three times. The smell of marigolds was always connected with those kisses in his mind, and the memory was not particularly pleasant, he did not know why. And when Belle Reilly ran her fingers lightly over his arm he had felt—nothing. Why? Sometimes it bothered him.

"Pick it up. We're supposed to be saving Fremont's skin, and if we don't get there, Jackson will have flayed the old man alive," he shouted in a more surly voice than was usual for him. Then he felt a little guilty at his petulance. "Their feet hurt," he told himself. Well they should. Many had no shoes and were actually walking slowly by the side of the road barefoot, scores of them. The war was marking its passage with the bleeding feet of its soldiers, at least in this theatre. Most had no gum blankets to ward off the worst of this infernal, never-ending rain, which was now pouring down. Houghton tried to ward it off; it was trickling off his hat into his face, coming off the road and soaking the bottoms of his trousers.

He leaned for just a moment on an ivy patch on the hill beside him to pour water out of his boots. Resuming, he thought, "How many miles more?" What was a mile? An arbitrary measurement, from Roman times. A certain number of feet. His mind flew back to the Mt. Pleasant schoolhouse; pictures formed of Bo's brother, George Reilly, Lewis Brooks, and half of the rest of the company sitting on the benches, with the smell of just-cut hay drifting in the windows—drilling on the numbers in a mile—5,280 ft. Well, but it was not that he was thinking of. How many steps in the line of march. That was what counted. Someone in Beem's company had counted them. One thousand, eight hundred paces. (Where was Beem. Why hadn't he come back from his weekend wedding? He hadn't had to march any of these miles.) Depending on whether it was military strides or double time. One thousand, eight hundred painful, dreadful steps along this rocky, mountain valley road.

And the bitter thing was that they had marched all this way at the command of chess players in Washington. The more Houghton thought about it, the angrier he grew. His thighs were chafing; he had some sort of rash, and it hurt to march.

Flatulent, comfortable men sitting before fires, drinking chocolate, eating little biscuits stamped with flowers. Houghton pictured their military planning session. "Now let's see," Houghton pictured the scene (their voices just slightly nervous because they were moving men to the edge of death and back) "I see possible danger here if Jackson moves too quickly and Washington is unprotected. He might come down on the double quick" (and get us and our tea cakes).

"Best take Shields' Division from the Valley and move it over, uhh, *here*" (pointing at map) "to Fredericksburg to protect the capital" (with all its velvet settees, fans and white gloves and the Willard Hotel). Chess, that's what it was. Rook forward to white knight.

"Let's see, they should be able to get there if they try in six days. Only 130 miles. Well, a few mountains, that's true."

Damn their fat rear ends. As soon as we got there, the chess game began again.

"Humph. We seem to have sent too many men to Fredericksburg and the Shenandoah Valley is unprotected now." (Reading telegraph dispatches, being careful not to get crumbs on them.) "Jackson seems to be taking full possession of it. Let's move Shields' Division back again. Immediately. Can't spare time for rest. Too bad. Well, let them wait until tomorrow, anyway." Castle back to white bishop.

Two-hundred-sixty miles, finished a few days ago, to arrive back at Front Royal, fight a brisk, decisive battle, win and head out in hot pursuit of the elusive Jackson, to Luray, where they hoped they would stop and defeat him and maybe—checkmate.

Well, they would be there soon.

The Fourteenth continued its march down the pike and as Houghton had predicted, through the gradually diminishing rain, a town loomed. Luray. Over the rise appeared the shapes of comfortable houses, churches, a three-story office block. People were frying potatoes there, probably getting married and having babies, just as if the Fourteenth Indiana Regiment were not marching halfway to hell.

Getting married—Beem was a married man himself. He was supposed to have returned two days ago. Not that he could have found them in all this mud and mess. But they needed him. When he came, Beem could decide what to do with Horde from his own H Company.

"Poor Horde," Houghton thought disconsolately. Horde's stomach had been his downfall. McDowell and Shields were right when they said "no foraging; it causes difficulties." The men drifted into all of the Seven Deadly Sins when they went off to "requisition" pigs and potatoes. After they had their hands on a few things forced from the cellars of reluctant Rebels, they went into minor frenzies, foraging for whisky, clothing, horses, contraband servants, and maidens willing to give them candy or even their virtue. Yes, a bit of that occurred when foraging parties went around. Behind fences, in the tall grass and up in the lofts of barns.

Horde had been eating a tray of pears with a farm girl, sitting on a fence near a stile, when a rabid dog ran into the farmyard. The girl hopped off and ran away, but as Horde jumped down he tripped over the foot of the stile, and the dog bit him.

Now he frothed at the mouth and was carried in a cage with the few sick men and the tents at the end of the tiny baggage train that was traveling with the regiment. He had screamed, out of his head in pain and anguish for two days now, and there was no field hospital to put him in. He couldn't be left to be nursed along the road; no farmer would board someone with hydrophobia.

There were so many times when Houghton felt as if he were in a bad dream with lurid, distorted happenings rattling around on the inside of his heated brain, claiming to be real life. Here was an army marching with a man chained inside a cage, sanitary assistant Walter McClure going about telling everyone who handled him to wash their hands and pumicing their hands with an odd stone he carried about. And news filtering through the ranks that Jackson had eluded the net in spite of all the marching and fighting and was securing the bridge to make good his escape.

They marched through this blessed town of Luray to the campgrounds on the far side. A few wisps of smoke still rose from the campfires the Rebels had abandoned only half a day earlier. The group filtered across the field by companies to wait for the tents to come up so they could pitch them.

John McClure and Henderson Simpson lay on their backs flat on the ground. They gazed for several moments at the shapes of the Blue Ridge high above them. The mountains loomed heavy and misty through the sunset, with wreaths of smoke hovering about their summits. The sun was setting behind one of them, sending orange-red streaks out into blue-black clouds.

"One range on the east, 'nother'n on the west," McClure said.

"Massenhutten, they call them on the west," Simpson said. It was indescribably comfortable to be lying on the ground instead of walking. Behind

McClure and Simpson, the others in the Tiger Tail mess pounded stakes into the ground, putting up the Sibleys.

Silence again, which Simpson finally broke. "You chomping grass?" he asked his cousin.

"Not grass. Timothy weed," John McClure answered.

"Grass will make you bilious."

"Timothy don't. Sweet as rock candy. You and I used to chomp a lot of it back home."

"That's true, cousin."

"Ma wrote to say Floss Barger asked about me," Simpson said with a satisfied smile.

"I 'spect she did, Henderson. You and Floss Barger got about a bit, if you were to speak the truth of the matter."

Finally, after a pause, Simpson blurted out, "I wisht I had a cake of soap. I like to wash myself now and then. Them damned Eastern regiments in Fredericksburg made fun of us, said we smelled like ammonia. We can fight rings around a Maine regiment, smell or not. But I sure wisht I had a cake of castile."

John McClure did not answer the petulant comment. His round-faced, boyish-looking cousin was as erratic and impulsive as a four-year-old in a cakeshop. He ought to know that better than anyone. John McClure had grown up in the same house, had been raised by his aunt and uncle, after his parents had drowned in the river and he and his brother and sisters were made orphans. He had learned to accept that Henderson had all kinds of wants and needs, not the least of which, so he constantly said was—

"I'm afeerd I'm goin' to get the crabs," his cousin said.

"Well, there are a-plenty of 'em and all kinds of varmints about. You can use green soap if you do."

"I want to be clean and neat when I get the chance to—you know."

Henderson had been waiting for "you know" for quite a while. Other units, stationed close to towns spoke in reverent terms about the blisses of "you know," available easily all around the towns by gift or purchase. Henderson thought of little else, voicing his opinion that life was not intrinsically fair. 'Twasn't right that a nineteen-year-old American boy who yearned so much for something should be deprived of it in the flower of his youth, first by living in a place where girls were kept on leashes like Pomeranians, and then, by lack of opportunity in the boondocks of western Virginia.

He lowered his voice as he and his cousin John began speculating about the thing most yearned for. Van Dyke, standing smoking and leaning against a tree, caught snatches of the conversation. "Shaped like two little lips, jest waiting to be kissed.'' "A whole variety of tits. You can see them through their blouses. Some like muskmelons, some—''

Van Dyke yawned and walked away from the conversation. Farm boys, waiting to be laid. They'd get their share in due time. He'd been like that when he was nineteen, before he'd had his share. Women seemed to gravitate to him. He had just broken an engagement and was writing to a girl of good family in Cincinnati. He would keep himself clean in this war. It was that sort of thing that could ruin the march to advancement. He had already been made lieutenant. He would confine himself to friendship with men like Houghton who were going to get ahead and, if he felt anything else, plunge himself in an icy mountain stream for a while, if he had the chance.

Van Dyke stubbed out the cigar he had just bought for fifteen cents from one of the local peddlers who had flown into camp, shirttails flying, when the troops were spotted on the road. Must have their wives baking cheap cakes for days. The grays march in, bring out the coconut and 'lasses puddin'. They go down the road and the boys in blue come in, get out the devil's food. This neck of the woods had already changed hands five times in the course of the war.

He walked to Houghton's tent. Inside, Will sat talking to David Beem, now also a captain and just returned from leave. For an instant, Van Dyke hesitated. Beem was Houghton's friend, and he, Van Dyke, was Houghton's friend too, but he and Beem were not friends with each other. Still, it would be interesting to find out what had happened back in Dumbville, Indiana. Where was it? Spencer. Might pass a half hour or two—

He went forward and offered his hand. "Welcome back, captain. Shall I offer my felicitations?'

"Lieutenant Van Dyke, I am a married man." The smile on Beem's face was as wide as a trencher.

Houghton looked up from cleaning his boots. "David was telling me about the Copperheads back home—''

"Just before I got back the Knights of the Golden Circle had come into a Union loyalty meeting. They had guns. A veteran of the Twentieth Indiana was there and shot one of them. Good thing I wasn't there.''

"Did anyone die?''

"No, but the loyal farmers are going around armed. That should keep the snakes in their holes for a while.''

"How—how did it seem to be home,'' Houghton asked, his eyes wistful.

"For me, not as I expected. I had dreamed of it, yearned for it for so long. And I admit a lot of it was beyond the dreams. The food. They had angel food cake with canned peaches and whipped cream. And a wedding cake as big as a table. All of Owen county was at the wedding, and there were salted nuts and fondant and creamed chicken and ham with currant sauce.''

The three men had a moment of almost reverent silence, tribute to the foods of southern Indiana.

Beem finally went on. "But all the festivities seemed petty. And tiring. I felt like a maiden aunt at a Sunday School cradle roll picnic, I guess. My father was afraid I was gambling my wages away, and my cousins gossiped about the intrigues in those small towns as if they were at the Russian Court."

"I remember," Van Dyke said. "Mrs. Cronin left her estate to her brother in Kansas instead of her mean children. Betty has 'got in trouble.' That sort of thing."

"Arguments over land being sold, and the preacher. Especially the preacher."

Van Dyke and Houghton nodded. They remembered those arguments, once a blue moon ago, far away.

"The preacher's wife turned into a witch, before her monthly time, so rumor went, and the Ladies' Aid Society has to come and get her children to keep 'em. I got so I wanted to cover my ears. I knew what the boys were marching through back here in Virginia. All I wanted to do was to be here with them."

"And the reputation of the regiment?'

"It is strong. They asked me at every turn about our fight with Stonewall two months ago at Winchester Heights, Kernstown."

"Did they? What did they say?" Both Van Dyke and Houghton seized on the subject like a dog on a meaty bone.

"That we fought well. They knew the details from the papers—knew Shields was wounded and Kimball took command. They knew we fought the Stone Wall right in the open fields, with closed ranks of Rebels. They had heard of how Colonel Murray, of the Pennsylvania regiment that we relieved, was carried through our ranks with his brains dropping out."

"And did they know we stood? That we won our glory with the wounded and the dead? That no one ran, even the new recruits?" asked Van Dyke.

"They did. But one thing." His angular face was hesitant, solemn. "Some say Stonewall was fighting with less than 5,000 men. The Richmond papers have just come out and said so."

Houghton was astonished. "Impossible. We had almost twice that many." They sat for a moment, silent, and then Houghton murmured. "So the victory wasn't really won but taken."

"And we have to wait to buy our glory a little longer," Beem said.

"Ahh," said Houghton with disappointment. The folks back home had known it before they had. It never occurred to any of them that the number of men Jackson had was so small. The slyness of the man! He had fooled an entire army. This general would have to be watched.

They heard glad halloos outside. "The quartermaster. I hear there are turnips and stew beef." Houghton rose and sought the stew pan.

"What about Horde?" Houghton asked Beem as he passed. "You've heard he's completely mad?"

"Yes. My lieutenant, Lunday, is guarding him. But it is an awful quandary." Houghton stopped to listen to him.

"No one will get near enough to clear the poor devil's pants or sponge off his brow," Beem said.

"Colonel Kimball has been having me watch him. But he has no orders about what is to be done. We may move at any time. We've been flitting around like a flea on a hot griddle for the past month, and we can start jumping again any time. I think Colonel Kimball is hoping that poor Horde will die."

"What does the chief surgeon say?" Houghton wanted to know.

"Call him in here," Beem suggested.

"No, don't ask him. Ask the assistant, Burkhart. He's the only one that knows an ass from an ankle," Van Dyke said. He fished in his pocket for another cigar.

"Take supper with me tonight," Houghton suggested to his two fellow officers. "We'll talk about Horde. I feel as responsible as you do. The poor fellow."

"Feel more worried about the regiment," Beem told him. "If he gets loose, or someone gets breathed on taking care of him, we'll all be targets of madness. The atoms of miasma travel through the air or by touching wounds, so the doctors now say."

As Houghton went to get the food for his meal, Beem went to look for Surgeon Burkhart. Soon he and the orderly Redskin McClure were poking their heads in the tent flap. Houghton had just returned; Beem slipped in through the door to join him.

"You want to know of Horde's prognosis, sirs?" Surgeon Burkhart said, looking earnestly in at them.

"Yes. Can he be moved? What are the stages of this thing. Is he—is there any hope of recovery?" Houghton wanted to know.

"I saw him this afternoon. He is completely mad, of course and in awful pain. He cannot drink water, of course; it sends him into—what you say— fits. So he is drying up. The end is sure, but it may not come for a week or ten days. My assistant McClure here, has seen these cases before."

"It is one of the worst diseases for suffering. One can only pray for the end," Walter said sadly.

"A week—that long. Are you sure that it is—inevitable?" Beem asked.

"Of course. There is never remission in these cases. We must guard against his biting, scratching someone. Somehow that transmits the disease.''

There was a sad silence in the tent. To think of dying in such a miserable way, wallowing in your own filth, shunned. It was nothing like the shining sacrifice they had all envisioned when they followed the bands into the recruiting places.

The surgeon finally spoke. ''We must take leave of you. We are going to get ourselves a few onions and whatever fruits there are for the scurvy cases.''

''Thank you, Doctor,'' Beem said.

After supper Beem, Houghton and Van Dyke visited Horde in his cage. He howled at them like a wild animal. His eyes were red and odd, his hair matted with pieces of cornbread and excrement.

''Did you grow up with him, Beem?'' Houghton asked, turning his face away for a moment.

''No, he was from the hill country east of us. He couldn't read a word. Still lived in a log cabin.''

Houghton nodded, wordlessly.

''I wrote to his mother. Told her there was little hope,'' Beem said. At the word ''mother,'' the madman began to jiggle the bars of the cage violently. Was there a spark of humanity in there? The men looked in alarm at the lock on the cage's door.

''What if he should escape?'' Van Dyke wondered anxiously. ''Run through the camp and attack the men? What would we do?'' No one dared answer the question.

''If he were a dog or horse we would go get a gun and—'' Beem did not finish the statement. Such a thing was too awful to contemplate.

''Everything is upside down here,'' Beem went on. ''We kill people all the time when we are supposed to be Christians and not kill. Our beards grow and our bodies stink, so we are more like wolves than men. The enlisted men curse and swill, the commissary officers steal us blind and—''

''And?'' Houghton demanded.

''And someway,'' Beem said ruefully, ''I lost track of right and wrong somewhere as we came down off Cheat Mountain. Right seems wrong and wrong is right out here. I must admit I have no idea what to do.''

Both of the other men looked long and hard at the captain of C Company, awed by the responsibility he now bore.

''Terrible quandary,'' Van Dyke said again, blowing smoke rings in the dark of his officer's tent after supper. Beem had gone to see to his company; Houghton had stopped by Van Dyke's tent.

"What in the world can we do?" Houghton wondered, watching the smoke rings dissipate over the head of Van Dyke's tent-mate, the captain of Company G, William Harrow. Coons, as a result of his overcoat letter, had been promoted to major, and Harrow had the company captain's job.

Harrow sat at a portable desk, poring over the quartermaster's report. There were serious charges of graft floating about, and he aimed to prove food was being filched and sold. He seemed oblivious to both the choking cigar smoke and the conversation.

"A veritable moral dilemma," Van Dyke went on. "Socratic, really. What is the value of a human life?"

"Not much, out here." Houghton answered. The light of the oil lamp pulsated. In this faint, warm glow the world seemed oddly benign. Van Dyke stubbed out one cigar, fished in his pocket for another.

"Only one left," he mused. "Well, I'm out of money, too."

"If they don't come down here soon with our pay, these men are going to mutiny," Houghton said. Harrow coughed from his corner. The smoke was finally getting to him.

The smell of sulphur added its bitter pungency to the air as Van Dyke scratched a match on the sole of his boot, then, unaccountably blew it out, throwing the match onto the muddy floor. "Think I'll save that last cigar for tomorrow. Greet the morning with a smoke. In honor of a day—or two—of leisure, we hope, at Luray, Virginia."

Houghton smiled at his friend. Van Dyke's face was so strong, so serene in the lamplight. Van Dyke picked up his Enfield rifle, flicked a few pieces of dust from its barrel, put it down again carefully, by his bedroll. Van Dyke had one of the best souvenir rifles in the regiment, one of the new ones. He had captured it at Kernstown from one of Jackson's dead Rebels, and he was keeping it surreptitiously in case, he said, one of the men needed it. He had not got rid of his pistol, either. No one knew he had it. It was strapped inside his coat.

A shadow crossed the tent door. "Come in, Redskin," Van Dyke said. Walter McClure was mopping his face with a towel. "Hot, isn't it, Captain?" he said, smiling deferentially. Van Dyke nodded.

"Horde is worse," Walter announced. "He is panting on the ground, eating mud. There's nothing more we can do but wait," he said. Van Dyke thanked and dismissed him.

"Decent man for an Indian," he said. "Always knows his place. I don't quite understand him. He doesn't smell any worse than the rest of us."

"Better than some," Houghton conceded.

"I keep trying to decide what I think," Van Dyke said, lying back on his cot, his cool eyes staring at the canvas top. "That contraband I had. Smith. He left before we went to fight at Kernstown."

"Yes?"

"He talked to me a lot. Used a lot of 'massas' and so forth, but what he said was full of sense."

"I suppose some nigras are smart," Houghton mused. "My grandmother Poore always said so. My trouble is I never got to know any colored people in Martin County. There just weren't any around."

"That's because our state passed a law barring free Negroes from Indiana," Van Dyke said. "They are the inferior race," he continued, sitting up. "I've read lots of articles in magazines about it. When evolution was starting with the apes and all, it got to the Negroes and stopped for a while. Then another branch developed further into the white race."

"So they are lower down the chain from us."

"That's what it said. So it made me mad when Clem Smith knew so much. He was making me nervous. I don't want my views overturned by niggers—or Indians."

They were both silent. In the corner, Harrow's folding chair creaked as he shifted his weight. Van Dyke looked over at him, hunched over the report he was writing. Van Dyke still didn't understand this new captain fully, though he had spent a good deal of time analyzing the man since Coons had been elevated and replaced by this Evansville lawyer.

Harrow spent all of his time, literally all of it, on company affairs. He was a hard-ass, brittle-voiced captain's captain who liked to be saluted just right, and he would have spent fifteen minutes polishing the brass bugles on his captain's hat if there had been any polish. Harrow never frittered away time gassing with other officers. Military regulations were his Bible. He was a rebuke to everybody else just by being who he was, and he could be ruthless, stern as a Transylvanian dungeon keeper if he felt like it.

"You know, Houghton," Van Dyke said, eagerly, glad to change the subject, "this thing with Horde reminds me of a case we had in the law office a year before the war. Woman by the name of Galt had a cancer in her breast the size of an orange. Suppurating all the time. The treatment was to put salts of iodine on it and she screamed, cried, whimpered like a baby all the time from the pain. They gave her morphine, but it didn't but take the edge off the pain."

Houghton winced; even Harrow turned from his work and gazed curiously over at them.

"Finally her husband couldn't stand it any longer. He upped the dose of morphine that the doctor left. Trouble was her son, his stepson, was in the house and saw it happen. Accused him of murder."

"And what happened?" Houghton asked.

"I thought you would have known. It was in all the papers. Well, maybe you didn't read it. Jury found him not guilty."

"Who's to say?" Houghton wondered, shaking his head.

Harrow had bent over his figures again.

"Like Horde. Socratic problem," Van Dyke mused, staring into the gloom.

"Beem could never do that," Van Dyke said.

"What Mr. Galt did?"

"No?"

"No. Even if it were right."

"Beem's too god-damned moral." There was a sneer in Van Dyke's voice. Houghton looked up sharply.

"Beem is a Christian gentleman," he said.

"Christian gentlemen aren't good at hard choices."

Harrow suddenly shouted out from his table. "That son of a bitch!"

"Who, Beem?" Van Dyke asked, non-plussed.

"No, Wood! He has been stockpiling and selling to the sutlers secretly over the last two months. While we starved!"

"So what are you going to do?"

"Tell Kimball."

"You know Wood is his protégé," Van Dyke protested. "From the home county. Besides, Kimball doesn't listen to these things well. Says it upsets the apple cart, gives the regiment a bad name. And he may think you're sharpening your hatchet on Wood."

"I don't give a damn."

Van Dyke shook his head. "You are in line for promotion. major, maybe even lieutenant colonel. You could jeopardize your chances. Why—"

Harrow stood and folded up the camp stool. He came over to leer at them malignly. His balding head gleamed in the lamplight. "Why? Well, maybe I've been waiting to get that horse's rear end Wood for quite a while. Maybe I'm hungry myself and hate him for stealing our cheese and raisins. Maybe my guts are just looking for a good wrenching. I don't think I'll have a bit of trouble sticking a knife up his ass. Anyway, you said it all."

"What did I say?" Van Dyke demanded. The idea of someone's consciously risking his chances of promotion was beyond his comprehension.

"You said Christian gentlemen aren't good at hard choices," said Harrow in a matter-of-fact voice. He took the lamp in his hand and headed for the tent flap. "No one ever accused me of that crime."

"Of being a Christian gentleman?" Van Dyke wanted to know.

"You have it," Harrow said and headed out the flap with his papers.

Van Dyke and Houghton walked through the camp for a final evening check with the sergeants of their companies. Someone was coming towards them, his face shielded by his elbow. He was combing his mustache.

"Landon," Van Dyke said sourly, as he recognized his bumptious fellow second lieutenant.

The muscular correspondent to the Vincennes paper came closer. "Hail, fellow fighters for the Union," he said in his rather drawling voice. "Are we still hoarding Horde behind the fence? I think we may have the wrong person. Harrow's cloistered right now with the top brass, ranting and raving and foaming at the mouth himself about our quartermaster." He laughed, a sort of braying chuckle which made his head bob back and forth.

"It isn't funny, Landon," Houghton said sharply. "And see that you don't write to the Vincennes paper about all of this."

"It was just a jest," the lieutenant said, slightly offended by Houghton's tone.

"He rubs me the wrong way," Houghton said, when Landon was out of range.

"You can see what I live with, Will," Van Dyke said. "My immediate superior is a huge mouth and my fellow lieutenant is a huge buttocks. There's truth to what Beem says about craziness out here."

Ruefully Houghton nodded as the drum beat taps.

Stonewall Jackson slipped the noose the Yanks had prepared. He secured the bridge at Port Republic as he intended and the Fourteenth was called out of camp at Luray to reinforce troops attempting to stop him in one last, desperate stand. Arriving too late, units of the Fourteenth could only watch the grim retreat of other Northern units and then return for a few much-needed days of rest at the camp in Luray.

Thick clouds of dawn mist rolled down off the mountains as the bugle sounded reveille.

"Get them out of there fast," Houghton shouted to his lieutenants, gesturing toward the Sibleys where C Company slept, arranged like spokes out from the wheel of a wagon. "Colonel Kimball says we must be ready to march in an hour. We have a new assignment."

Beem was nearby. "How is Horde?" Houghton asked him.

"Point of death, but not dead yet. The orderly—McClure—still doesn't know how long it will be." Houghton groaned and looked up to see Van Dyke, who had come up panting, on the run. He too asked about Horde; Beem answered briefly and departed.

"Will, have you heard that Harrow has been commissioned to major?" Van Dyke asked, wiping sweat from off his upper lip. The heat was oppressive, as it had been all month. If it wasn't pouring rain, it was frying ants on the baked dirt of the roads.

Houghton looked at him with his mouth open. They began to hurriedly walk towards G Company's tents.

"His report has been 'noticed'," Van Dyke said, his tone somewhere between admiring and envious.

"Well, he held the discipline as well as any of us in this hellish valley campaign. And Wood does deserve to be nailed. But so fast—" Just the suggestion of a smile crossed Houghton's face. Landon appeared and listened on the edge of the conversation, as was his habit.

"So the stealing of the sidemeat and the stewstuff has been stopped," he said whistling through his teeth with each "s." "Well, some other fool will come forward and start filching forthwith."

Houghton nodded grimly. It was hard to keep up with the command changes in Lincoln's army these days. Generals, field officers, non-coms— all were shifting about as fast as the armies were. Add the personnel changes due to all the desertions, exhausted ranks and frustrated resignations, and it was obvious that the Northern army was trying to define itself.

"Harrow hath gone above," Landon said with exaggerated seriousness, pointing like a finger on a tombstone. With a wave of the hand Houghton said goodbye and turned back to C's tents; Van Dyke headed on to the G encampment. "Room above for more in that upper room," Landon shouted at him. "Maybe room for me!"

Watching Landon whistle off down the lane towards the latrine, Van Dyke looked at him with narrowed eyes. "Never," he reassured himself. "The top brass may flirt with clowns, but they don't promote 'em." He hastened on to put Company G in motion, to be noticed being efficient. His eyes narrowed into impassivity, as he thought of another little duty he had to perform.

"John, Lieutenant Van Dyke is out there. He is saying we are movin' out today," Henderson Simpson said, pulling on his blue trousers.

"Whaa?" said his cousin, John McClure, sleepily.

"Harrow says Jackson just whopped Fremont at Cross Keys. He's out of the valley and we have orders to go back over the mountains."

"Shiiit!" John McClure rolled over on his blanket and pounded the ground.

"Wait a minute, not on shanks' mare. On the cars!"

"The cars?" His cousin seemed dazed.

"We're goin' out of the Shenandoah Valley. Well, we do have to march to the cars and it's a jaunt. But then we ride. Goin' to join the army.''

"I joined in Vincennes already, seems to me. Corner of Fourth and Main. Worst damned day of m' life—''

"No, privy-head. Shields' Division is goin' to join McClellan's army headin' to Richmond.''

"On to Richmond?''

"On and off to Richmond, more like it. Still, we're goin'.''

"This means war.''

"This means food. Whisky. And—'' He snickered and put his hands together forming a triangle.

"'You know?' '' McClure asked.

"Yaa. Whooppeeooo.''

Captain David Beem went to the campstool by his bedroll. Breakfast and sick call were over; he would have to hurry if he was going to have his men ready to march to the cars. He picked up a picture and looked at it. Then he lay down the picture and picked up a drying rose which lay beside it.

"A rose from the wedding?'' his tentmate, Porter Lunday, asked. He had not mentioned it before, leaving Beem the privacy of his bridegroom's memories. Lunday was a stoop-shouldered, hulking man with a high forehead and gentle, sensitive eyes. He was quietly intelligent, with an immense capacity for kindness, and he remembered everyone in H Company's birthday with a list he kept in a box.

"From Hala's bouquet,'' Beem said shyly.

"It's been ten years since I smelled wedding roses,'' Lunday said. He had started up a mercantile in Spencer and borrowed from the bank to stock the promising store. His wife was trying to run it while he was gone. The picture by his bunk showed a woman with a halo of soft blonde hair and a tentative, lop-sided smile, and two little boys.

Both men scooped up their meager possessions and began to arrange their baggage.

"Have you seen this?'' Beem asked Lunday. "It was on the floor of Horde's cage. It must have fallen out of his pocket.'' Another picture, this one an old daguerreotype, of a woman in a beribboned dotted Swiss gown of the early fifties.

"His mother,'' Lunday said, looking sadly at the picture. "She lived in a log cabin. Probably spent half the egg money on this likeness. I'm glad she can't see him now. I hope she never knows.''

"Leave it to me. When it finally happens, we'll say he died peacefully in the service of his country.''

"The death letters must be the hardest," Lunday said, handing the picture back to Beem. "Almost makes me not want to be a captain. I could do all the rest of it—stowing the Sibleys in the wagons, being sure they follow us to where we have to camp, yelling at the commissary for food, listening to mama's boys who weep for home—" Lunday's eyes were anxious. He had brought his little brother into his own home and was raising him, and he was not sure he was doing a very good job of it. He was afraid the boy might be coming out here as a recruit.

"And you will do captain's duties like a veteran, Porter," Beem said encouragingly. "They say an opening's coming in A Company soon, and I will recommend you."

Lunday was still thinking about writing the death letters. "I've asked myself if I could really lead a company," he said. "To have to write a letter to someone who loved, deeply depended on one of my men and tell that loved one that never, never again—" Lunday shrugged, unable to articulate his pain. Beem nodded, understanding. He had watched Lunday carry spiders outside the tent rather than step on them.

"Well, the death letters are not as bad as the court martials, but they're bad enough. I never tell the last details."

"Yes. It'll be best for her to remember him as he was. A man."

Beem looked at Lunday searchingly. "Was Horde ever like that? I have trouble remembering when I bring him food. Was he ever a man? Maybe if I look at this picture, tell myself he had a mother—"

"Why didn't he die?" Lunday said with emotion. "Just expire, breathe his last. He's lasted all these days, almost dead, when the surgeons thought he was on his last legs." Then, quickly he added, "I'm sorry I said that."

"We've got to get this tent to the baggage men," Beem sighed finally. "But before we do—would you help me put Horde's cage in the wagon? I can't conceive how we are going to finally put it on the train. And when we get to Alexandria—I don't think the hospital will accept a hydrophobia case."

"They'll have to."

"It may take several of us to organize this. When I checked him this morning, he was growling on the ground."

Rapidly the men made their way down the company street to a grove of trees where the man was kept. An overwhelming smell accosted them as they neared the cage.

"The saddest thing of all is how much he's become like the dog who bit him," Lunday said as they approached the cage.

There was a moment of silence as they drew near. Beem stared into the cage. "Not any more," he said, shortly. "He's a man again, at last." There, lying on his stomach, not moving, was Horde.

"There's a bullet hole in his back," Beem said. They stepped closer. His hands were clawing the ground, but his face, turned toward them, looked peaceful through its grime.

"Who—" Lunday looked wonderingly at his tent-mate. "Powder burns. Shot with a pistol—who has one of those?"

Beem did not answer him. He did not know. "Organize a burial detail for him. Two men who can keep their mouths shut. I'll tell the colonel he's gone to his rest. Nothing more."

Lunday turned and trotted back to the camp.

Beem bent down to look under the cage. He picked something up from beneath one of its wheels.

"What's wrong is right, what's right is wrong in this war," Beem thought. Slowly he walked down the path. As he went, he carried what he had picked up from under the wheel of Horde's cage. It was stub of a Havana cigar. He turned it over a couple of times with his fingers, feeling the smoothness of the tamped tobacco. Then he tossed the cigar far into the woods, where it landed on some laurel bushes. He took out the picture of Horde's mother, with the ribbons flowing around her waist, and looked at it as he walked hurriedly back to camp.

When he reached it, Houghton gave him the news. The new captain who was to replace Harrow would be named within the week.

"Van Dyke, you think?" Beem wanted to know.

Houghton shrugged. "Gus is strong," he said.

"I know you admire him. But he has the ethics of a coyote."

"Strong enough to take out a pistol and put an animal out of its misery when none of the rest of us could. I was the only one who saw him go, I think."

Beem nodded, resigned. Well, it would make sense in a war where mad men frothed on the ground because they would not die and other men threw themselves into battle willingly a few miles away. And it was Van Dyke who had the gumption to end the quandary, after all. Coyote ethics sometimes blundered into a certain truth—the truth of necessity. Maybe the war could use Van Dyke after all.

Two days later the men of the Fourteenth Indiana Regiment descended on the wharfs at Alexandria, Virginia with a roar, the Hoosier yell. "Ahweeoooh," they shouted, pummeling each other as their officers tried to get them to stack arms in an orderly way.

"Remember, you have a six P.M. departure," the new Major Harrow yelled at G Company, pointing to the steamship which floated at the end of a wide, rickety pier. "Remain right here and under no circumstances go beyond the bounds of this wharf."

No sooner had he turned his back than over half of the men in his company sprinted up the hill. Men from other companies joined them and the hill was alive with dirty men heading away—up the hill to wash themselves at the pump, and then into the shops to buy pork pies and tarts, and beyond that into the shadowy depths of the narrow streets of the city. Beem, Lunday, Houghton, Harrow, Van Dyke—all ran after them, ordering, pleading, to no avail. The Fourteenth Indiana veterans were making a statement about the extent of what volunteers could be asked to do. The paymaster had come while they were on the cars. It was time for recreation and refreshment and they were going to take it, come what might.

A bell tinkled as Bo Reilly and Isaac Crim entered a bookstore on Hill Street. "Can I help you soldiers?" a man wearing an old-fashioned starched collar asked. He had crippled, arthritic hands and his eyes were chilly, dull.

Crim's and Reilly's eyes met. Probably a Rebel. "We want to browse among your volumes," Crim said to him.

"Do what strikes your fancy," the old man said. "I got all kinds o' books here. For every taste." The two men went to the shelves and tables.

"Now, we'll buy two bags and each take as many as we can carry," Crim said. "I have what I made on the shirt-washing and with half your pay, we should have plenty. You pick out religious books and I'll get the novels."

"Crim, let me pick the novels. You know I ain't very religious," Bo protested.

"Do what I say. If I'm goin' to take such a pup as you for a partner in my business, you have to be subordinate to m' wishes."

"What's subordinate mean?" Bo demanded.

"The opposite of insubordinate," Crim retorted. "You know what that means. Anyways, get started selectin'."

Reilly went to the table marked "Spiritual Consciousness" and began picking up volumes, some inlaid with pictures of Jesus, some embossed with roses and crosses. He began talking to himself. "Waal, here's *Practical Lectures on the Decalogue*, 200 pages. Too high-churchy even for the chaplain. Especially, I should say for Chaplain Webb. No wonder he's a-going home. Nobody in their right mind who preached purity could take this regiment. And here's *The Golden Land: Visions of what Heaven is Like*. That's more like it. And *Wedge of Gold: A Book of Presbyterian Sermons*. Might float; we got plenty of fallen-away Presbyterians, and their consciences'll hurt 'em enough to buy that."

Crim had picked up a novel and was turning it over, muttering, "*Patsy*

Willis: The Story of a Poor Orphan's Pilgrimage. That sounds soulful enough. I'll get five o' that one." He began to stack books on the side of the table. *Wuthering Heights*. "Sad enough to make even Landon weep." *The House of Seven Gables*, "That's a scary one," and *Moby Dick*, "Consarn long and costs fifteen cents, but maybe one of the intellectuals'll read it."

"What we really want is more of these modern novels," he commented to himself. He added *The Slave's Dilemma, Lost in The Wilds of Africa* and *Alas, Victoria: A Maiden's Virtue Defended*. Then he put in a couple of copies of *Uncle Tom's Cabin*. Lately the men had been asking for it.

Bo Reilly called to him in a loud whisper. "Crim, come look at this."

He had found a morocco book beneath the "Adventure Stories" table and was reading from it with wide eyes. "It's called *The Bird of Paradise and Other Exotic Flowers in the Garden of Love*. It's from England. Listen to this: 'As the older people entertained themselves into the wee small hours of the morning, Young Lord Winston, his brother, Launcelot and the two young cousins they had met only this morning slipped out the door of Coventry Hall. They had pledged that they would initiate the eager young girls into the pleasures of the large gazebo at the far end of the garden.' "

"There's more, Crim," Reilly said, his eyes wide. "Let's go back behind that stack. That way that Old Grandad can't hear us."

They stepped further back into the empty store and stood behind a bookcase. Crim looked over Bo's shoulder and read:

The girls stepped out of gowns, chemises and stockings and presented their shining young bodies triumphantly before the ravenous young men. Moonlight shone bright above them all. The young men exchanged deep-drinking kisses with the girls. Quickly Lord Winston picked up young Lady Lucretia and laid her on the divan. His hands sought her roundly bulbous boobies. Then, as she moaned passionately in her gentle, feminine voice, Lord Winston's hand went lower and touched the mound of Venus—

Bo Reilly looked up in reverent awe. "Mound o' Venus. I never read anything like that in a book before."

Crim looked suspiciously at the front desk of the shop, where the old man sat complacently reading the *Baltimore Sun*. "He must know this book is back here," he said. "Old lecher." Bo took the book and read more.

She arched her hips to meet his ardent advances. Meanwhile, on the other side of the gazebo—

Crim pursed his lips thoughtfully. "This book could have some value in our bookstore. We could consider it a lease. Read it for ten cents—"

"That's high," Bo said, raising his eyes from the book. "Still, it is the most gol-durned, ding-blasted interestin' stuff I ever did see. Wish there were pitchers."

"Should be a hot item. We'll start with you, Reilly. That'll be ten cents if you want to finish it." He gathered up *Patsy Willis, Sermons from the Decalogue* and *The Bird of Paradise* and all the rest of his traveling library and went to pay for them.

"That old crotchet had an evil gleam in his eye, seems t' me," Bo Reilly said as they left the store.

"Dirty old Rebel. Guess they figure if they can't beat us on the battlefield they can corrupt our morals with dirty books," Crim answered.

"Well, and we bought it," Reilly said, becoming a little dismayed at himself.

"So we did," Crim said, and began to whistle down Hill Street to buy himself a pastry.

John McClure and Henderson Simpson strolled down a narrow lane near the wharf. They went into stands where toys were sold, played with a set of metal horses leading a circus wagon. Then they stopped and bought a copy of *Frank Leslie's Illustrated Magazine* and thumbed through its pages as they walked down the street.

"Am I clean enough?" Simpson asked his cousin.

"How in the hell am I s'posed to know. Can't you think of anything else? Let's enjoy the town."

Simpson enunciated each word carefully. "We have got until six o'clock tonight. I am not leaving until I do it. Hey ho, there's Lambert." He had spied George Washington Lambert, a corporal in the Terre Haute company. He was one of the rotating regimental directors of the brigade band, and he had a reputation for getting around with ladies. Now he was gazing into a millinery window opposite them.

"Wait here," Simpson told his cousin. Then he sidled across the street and exchanged a few words in a nonchalant manner with Lambert.

"So?" McClure said, half-exasperated.

"Says he's been told there's action at the Golden Corset."

"Sounds like there would be," McClure mused. "Lead on, oh fool eternal."

They passed a candy shop and met Tommy Thompson, who was coming out with bags of fondants and hard candies. He was alone and bored, and somehow he agreed to accompany them, although hesitantly. He was betrothed back home to Lina Everett.

Following Lambert's second-hand directions, they wound their way through four or five streets and finally came to a dilapidated two-story, Federal-style building. A pot of wilting geraniums sat sadly by its door.

"Big knocker, what?" Simpson said, snickering at the ring on the huge door. Just then it opened and a man came through, looking both ways as he emerged. He gave the soldiers a haughty look, twisted the end of his handlebar mustache and departed down the street.

"I don't wike the—wooks—of this," Thompson said. He had cinnamon balls in both of his cheeks and it distorted his speech. Red candy juice was dripping down the edge of his mouth. "It would be better if we could find a good game of fah-woh. Make a few dollars, spoo-urge on food. Ain't gonna have time to spend it soon."

They climbed creaky stairs and knocked at the door at the head, to be admitted by a woman with stiff, blonde ringlets. The smell of cooking sauerkraut floated out from somewhere in back.

"You boys come to see us?" the woman asked with a bored smile. As their eyes became accustomed to the dusky interior, McClure saw the pocks, really sores, on her arms.

"No'm. We must be in the wrong place. Beg your pardon."

He dragged Simpson down the stairs; Thompson followed.

"What'd you do that, for John R.?" the dismayed Simpson demanded.

"Damn it, Henderson, don't you remember that lecture the surgeon give us? Sores are one of the marks of syphilis. I don't want you to get the clap."

"You a—wong for the wide, too McClure? Glad we're here to take care of this poor young man—huh?" Thompson dug in his sack for another candy.

"Well, I don't want to get the clap, neither," said Simpson, beginning to grow more agitated. "But how can we tell?"

"I don't know. We'd best just—" Suddenly someone stepped from the shadows and put a gentle hand on McClure's arm.

"Hello, Yank."

He turned and looked down into the face of a young girl. "Why, hello, miss," he murmured. She was as slim as a young apple tree and her voice was as sweet as a child's. She had red ringlets and a pretty face sprinkled with freckles. How old could she be? Fourteen? Fifteen? Her bosom, swelling beneath a simple morning dress, her rounded hips, proclaimed she was one of the most beautifully mature women he had ever seen. "Do I know you?" John asked irrelevantly.

"Not yet. But ah hope you may, sir." She smiled up at him. Henderson was alarmed. This was not the way it was supposed to go. He was supposed to be the one—

"My lodgin's are only a block down this way. You and your friends are welcome to come take tea with me and m' sister."

He yearned towards her melting tenderness in a way he had never experienced before in his life, and a wave of desire rushed over him. Still—"I don't know, Miss—" Why was it at crucial moments in his life, when he was about to "fall from grace" in some way, the picture of his father, drowning amidst the ice floes as he tried to bring fugitive slaves across the river to freedom, jumped in jarring fashion into his mind? It was no time to think of that. She had some kind of cheap scent on, orange blossoms, wasn't it? Her skin beneath the freckles was as pink as a baby's.

They entered through a small, well-kept garden into a tiny dollhouse of a flat.

"We live here by ourselves."

"Where are you from?" Simpson wondered.

"Georgia. Our pa went to the wars. Ma is sick. We send money home the best we can." Her eyes looked far away as she paused a moment on the doorstep. "No one knows us here."

"I'll stay outdoors here, boys, on the stoop, don'tcha know," Thompson said. "Wait for ye and look at Lina's pitcher and enjoy the breeze. Take y' time."

Henderson, John and the girl went inside, into a shabby but clean flat. There was just the parlor, with a small stove and two small bedrooms. The sister was a year or so older, taller, with a plain, cynical face. She began to prepare tea on the stove.

The next hour passed as a dream for John McClure. As if he were sitting above on the mantel of the tiny fireplace, he saw himself stirring tea, pouring in sugar, eating little sugar cakes and nodding his head. When he looked up, Henderson and the sister had gone into one of the bedrooms.

Smiling into his face, the girl took him by the hand.

"I don't know what to do," he whispered as they sat on the edge of the bed. "I've never—"

"It's all right. I had to learn, too. It's nice. I'll show you."

Later he remembered her voice, with its Southern drawl giving him instructions in an almost singsong way, freckles as numerous as stars all over her breasts, the bumpy feel of her light brown nipples as she took his hand and let him explore. The smell of orange blossoms on her wrists. Then, sweet, melting pleasure, like warm featherbeds and the feel of silky cat fur and lying in the middle of a bed of lily of the valley in spring all put together—the consciousness of overpowering urgency and the wish to be less urgent, and, oddly, at the end, meeting the eyes of Jesus, standing at the door of the heart in a picture on the wall behind the bed, just above his eyes. And peace, as he had never known it.

Then there was raucous banging at the door.

"Simpson, McClure, I know you're in there." It was the voice of Lieutenant Van Dyke. "Major Harrow is madder'n hell at everybody. You have to come now or else."

McClure reached for his trousers as the girl fled behind a screen.

"We're coming." Quickly he dressed. He took a dollar out of his pants and carefully laid it under the pillow.

"Goodbye and thank you, Miss—" his voice ended in a question. She emerged, dressed in her chemise.

"Eva," she said. She took his hand and kissed it, smiling into his eyes. "You're a nice young man," she said.

"Maybe you can go back to Georgia soon."

"It may be. I hope to."

"What unit is—is your pa in?"

"Stonewall Jackson's Division. Ashby's Brigade. Don't know if he's all right. Ma ain't heard in three months."

God! Ashby's Brigade had been at Kernstown. He had probably fought against her father, maybe even—what kind of a goddamned war was this when you could kill a man one month and screw his daughter the next? And never even know either of them.

Van Dyke was in the parlor. Lieutenant Houghton was with him. Thompson was standing behind them, agitated at having betrayed his friends. Henderson Simpson emerged from the other bedroom, tucking in his shirt, and gave Thompson a scathing look.

"I'm sorry, men. They found me outside on the stoop, don'tcha know. What could I say?"

"It's all right." McClure fiddled with the brass buttons on his army blouse. He was embarrassed before Houghton and Van Dyke; he did not like having them see him this way.

As they marched down the street, the officers behind them, McClure felt giddy. His eyes did not seem to focus, or was it that he was allowing them to glaze. Some sort of odd mood had descended on him.

"I couldn't do a thing," his cousin whispered in his ear. "Nothing would happen. At the big moment, I kept thinkin' of the spring house at home for some damn reason. Ma separatin' cream." Henderson said. "Damn it all anyways. Didn't mean a thing. How 'bout you?"

"No, me neither," he lied. "Van Dyke and Houghton come in at the wrong moment. You're right. Didn't mean a thing."

He put his hand to his nose, sniffing the sweet smell of orange blossoms.

By six o'clock the officers had rounded up the regiment for departure on he steamboat for the James River and renewed warfare. Several were stowed below, dead drunk. Isaac Crim and Bo Reilly were among the last to be located; Houghton had found them in a tavern, drinking ale. At least Reilly was.

Beem stepped up to the gangplank and said to Houghton. "McClellan has lost the first battles at Richmond. General Lee has turned the army's flank around the Chickahominy River."

"Are they retreating?"

"Hard to tell from the dispatches. They may have just fallen back to strike again. We are to reinforce. We go to Fortress Monroe on the James River and from there inland towards Richmond, as we are needed."

"Almost everyone is on board," Houghton mused, looking about.

Lieutenant Will Landon was brushing his coat. He had been oddly unavailable, taking a nap while the others scouted the troops out of the taverns and cookshops of the town.

"You haven't heard the rest of the news," Beem went on. "Harrow has just been promoted to colonel.

"Colonel! Jumped from major in this amount of time!" Houghton said, wonderingly.

"Well," Landon said, his mouth twitching merrily beneath his small, neat mustache. He had been vocal in his dislike of Harrow, called him "the madman." "How the fox does run ahead of the pack." He spat. "Cold blooded heartlessness doth win the day." Still, his eyes were calculating. They still had not announced who would replace Harrow as captain of G Company. Was he still in the running? There was another captaincy in A Company, and Harrow would now have the word on it.

"For unusual service to the Federal government," Beem went on. "Kimball has passed Harrow's recommendation on to Washington and the top brass is court-martialling Woods for graft in the commissary. The old man says he must have honesty in the regiment, even if it involves his friends."

"Anything else?"

"Kimball himself has just been made a brigadier general for winning that battle at Kernstown. Coons is now lieutenant colonel. Van Dyke becomes captain of G."

Landon, unabashed at the news that his rival had succeeded, strode up the gangplank, stroking his mustache in a calculating manner.

"Woods gone, Harrow advanced. So right prevails after all. What do you think about this Harrow thing, Will?" Beem wanted to know.

Houghton thought a moment, watching the stevedores preparing to cast off the huge lines.

"I think the Fourteenth will be heading into the crucial campaign of the war, outside the gates of the Confederate capital, led by the most foul-mouthed, steel-hearted man in all the army,'' he said.

"Well, maybe that's not all bad—"

"Here come the last of my men," Houghton cried.

Bo Reilly, still carrying his bag of books, clung to the ropes on the edge of the gangplank; Crim tried to pull him forward as the new Colonel Harrow, came up from the rear.

"Not—goin'. Jest goin' to stay right here and sleep in that nice little park—" Bo said.

Harrow looked coldly on as Houghton rushed over to aid the men up the gangplank. Van Dyke appeared from the hold and watched Landon move smugly to the colonel's side. Landon had changed his color, like a chameleon and was standing, court jester-like, near Harrow, the "mad man's" side. Landon was pointing, identifying the delinquents, leaning and murmuring in his superior's ears. For all the good it did him. He, Van Dyke had just caught the fish of the moment, after all, hadn't he? It would be sweet shit to have Landon address him as "Captain Van Dyke."

"Reilly, you say? Get him aboard," Harrow barked. "I don't know why you officers allowed this disgrace this afternoon. I blame you. I ought to prefer charges against some of you."

Houghton looked up without surprise. Harrow evidently believed that conceding one iota of discipline in the Fourteenth Indiana Regiment would result in the immediate loss of the entire Northern army.

Bo Reilly shouted drunkenly back at Harrow, "On to Richmond. On to glory."

"On to that goddamned, fucking steamboat or I'll blow your balls off, soldier," Harrow roared, grabbing an Enfield and pointing it at the gangplank. With noticeable tact Landon retired. In a hurry Houghton and Beem and Van Dyke carried the collapsing young man up into the hold, where the rest of the drunks had been deposited.

The boat steamed down the Potomac. The river was a band of gold in the sunset, and behind it was the skyline of the nation's capitol, with its truncated, incomplete capitol building. Soon Houghton saw on the shores the stately outline of Mt. Vernon. He, Beem and Lunday stood, waving their hats at it, as the wind blew their hair.

"George Washington," Lunday said, pointing and smiling, the wind blowing the hairs about his premature bald spot high into the air. "Do you suppose he knows about all of this, about us?"

The other two men nodded, thrilled with the emotion of the moment.

Below were almost a third of the Fourteenth Indiana. Landon was checking them. Most were asleep in the cocoon of alcoholic slumbers, preparing themselves to burst forth in their imagined glory at the siege of Richmond by almost the entire army of the United States of America. Some sang raucous songs, punctuated by the drunken curses of the rest.

I had a pig, my pig pleased me.
I fed my pig under yonder treeeee—

Harrow walked haughtily by, going to his stateroom. Landon had come out on deck again. He pointed after the new colonel. "He has truly ascended, now, and sitteth on the right hand of Father Abraham," he said in a stage whisper.

My pig said fiddle-eyeeee feeee

sang the drunken voices.

"On to Richmond, on to glory," Van Dyke said mockingly. The rest looked at him, shrugging, as the sun finally dipped behind the horizon in a blaze of orange light, illuminating the classic lines of Mount Vernon, home of the Father of Our Country.

August, 1862

Chapter Five

Lettie Hogue stood before the long mirror in the hall of the house she and her mother shared on Busseron Street. Because she was tall, she had to lean down to accomplish pinning a hat with three bouncing birds on it to the bun on the top of her head. "You are determined to go?" Catherine Hogue said, standing behind Lettie with her hands on her hips.

"Of course, Ma. I told you I start work today at two. It's now one o'clock. That gives me an hour to finish my primping and walk down the street three blocks."

She turned and smiled with dazzling irony. "That should be enough time to make me beautiful, don't you think, Ma?" she said. Catherine Hogue melted. She came up and put her arms around her daughter.

"You're already beautiful enough right now. Lettie, you know I love you. 'Tis just that this working business. It makes you seem like a coal miner or a drummer who sells hosiery."

"Some women are working today, Ma. A few. Well, you yourself taught school until you met Pa. You were always trying to be your own woman."

"I know. But in an office—"

"And there are nurses now, all over the place, because of the war. They are paid. And so, if I do the ledgers for Mr. Mawkins, just as a man would, I should be paid."

"By Mr. Willis Mawkins. You have been keeping company with him. There will be talk."

"There is always talk in Vincennes, Ma. You know that. It never bothered you when folk talked of you."

"That's me. I mean you. The last of my children."

Lettie stepped back from her mother and held her at arm's length. "Ma," she said determinedly, pursing her lips. "I am thirty-four years old. I am so tall and gangly that no man ever asked for me."

Her mother interrupted. "Letitia, you are willowy. I was always tall."

"Yes, and you married Pa, who was six feet, four inches tall. You possess a gargantua for a daughter, someone who towered above everybody in the academy class and at church, too.''

"Speaking of church, Reverend Paden was asking after you."

"Tell him I send my regards. That I have been poorly some Sundays lately.''

"I told him. He says your Sunday school class was the best in the church.''

Lettie picked up her pocketbook from the table. "That was before we moved into town. It takes an hour to go out to Upper Indiana Church, and I like walking to the church at the end of the block. When I go. I'm having a fallow period now. On second thought, don't tell him that. I doubt that Reverend Paden would understand fallow periods in a Christian's life. He's so perfect himself, he has never been fallow.'' She put her hand on the edge of the door.

"I have been, though," her mother answered. "Your pa was too. Once he had to explain to Upper Indiana Church why he tormented an Indian woman as a witch, and she killed herself for grief.''

Lettie turned to her mother with wide eyes. She had never heard that story about the man she idolized. "Well, it's hard for me to believe Pa could ever torment anybody. Maybe it was because—did you say the woman was an Indian? He had been stolen by the Indians, and I remember him talking about being a captive." She did not meet her mother's eyes, looking instead through the open door. Her voice was dreamy. "My memories of Pa always have sort of a rosy glow. I came so late to you both. Nancy Jane was already sixteen when I was born, the others—well, I forget what they were but only a little younger. There was Horace, but he always walked down his own lane. Pa seemed like a giant from a fairy tale. Not that he ever noticed me much. I wish I could have found someone like him. Never mind. If I have not been happy, I am now. I have a beau—''

Catherine walked to the door, leaned against it, reaching up to cover her daughter's hand with her own as if to prevent her leaving. "A divorced beau—''

"Of a mature mind. Handsome, and with a good business. And he wishes me to do his ledgers on a regular basis. I am very good with figures. I was always first in arithmetic in my class, don't you recall?'' Brightly she unclasped her mother's fingers from her own and tweaked her cheek. "Besides, he will pay me three dollars a week.''

"And what else must you do besides total figures and keep balance sheets?''

Lettie's face reddened. "How can you think me base, Ma? He is my employer. That is what this is all about. And what I think of him is my own affair. You have always taught me to make up my own mind about life. So why are you—''

Catherine nodded. "Lettie, you were last and a special dispensation. I thought the change of life had come to me and 'twas you instead. Nancy Jane is gone now these twenty some years, your brothers high-tailed it to Texas and Iowa and—well, Horace is Horace and not really much good to me. So of course I fuss about you like an old hen."

She kissed her daughter and saw her through the door. Watching her walk down the wooden sidewalk she thought, darkly, "And Willis Mawkins is probably better than Barbhof's female elixir all day long in a darkened room."

Lettie walked briskly along Busseron to Fourth and turned at the corner at Fourth and Main to head towards the livery stable near the river. The birds bounced about briskly on the hat, giving her a feeling of buoyancy and enthusiasm. It was a beautiful day. Yesterday a late August heat wave had given way to showers, and the air above the Wabash was washed clean, sparkling above the river. It was unseasonably cool, perfect weather, really, she thought.

She entered the office of the livery. "Good afternoon, Mr. Mawkins," she said, taking the pins out of her hat and then setting it on a cabinet by the wall. "I am ready to begin closing the books for July."

"Very well, Lettie." He came nearer to her. She smelled a trace of the lather of his shaving soap. Or was it mustache wax? "I hope you do not mind the familiarity. All of us here use first names."

"No. But I shall call you Mr. Mawkins, even though at other times I may use a more familiar term."

"I understand." He squeezed her hand, released it and moved away.

"I do not know why that made me feel nervous," she said to herself. "He was being sincerely welcoming. Nothing more. Just as I told mother." She patted her hair to see if all the hair was still captured by the bun, licked her lips and reached for the ledger and pencil that were on the desk.

Services were over at Upper Indiana Church the next Sunday. There had been rain during the services, darkening the skies, and then it had stopped as suddenly as it started. The last of the worshippers drifted away under clearing skies, climbing into surreys and rigs and carriages, clucking at horses. Only one man remained and he stood alone by the edge of the church yard as the minister, Reverend David Paden, came out and locked the door.

"Ah, Mr. Scott, I see you are staying to visit your ancestors," he said.

John Robert Scott looked up and nodded at the tall, lean man with eyeglasses and a shock of coal black hair.

"It's one of the reasons I have been coming to the church lately."

"I wondered about that."

"The other, larger reason is that my own Quaker congregation is half a county away. I'm too old and my legs are too swollen to ride that far of a Sunday morning."

"I'm sorry and not sorry about that," the minister said, smiling. "There are so many churches about these days that this old church needs parishioners. You are very welcome here. How will you get home?"

"My sons are coming for me after a while. I told them to give me a few minutes on my own. Jacob Joe, you know, lives with me and runs the farm. Zachary—well, he drops in from time to time. He travels a good deal." He hesitated, wondering if the minister had heard that his son was a Southern sympathizer. "Anyway, he is coming for dinner today with us. The hired gal is fixing fried chicken."

"No better dish for a family on Sunday."

"And cherry pie. I picked the cherries and she canned them so we could have a cherry pie when Zach came. It's his favorite. 'Twill be like old times to have them there together."

"Good day to you, then, and may you have a happy family gathering," the minister nodded. He tipped his hat and sauntered to his horse. Clattering along the yet-damp roads, he rode north towards Bruceville, where he lived with his wife and seven children in an old house on the main street. "Abraham Lincoln spoke to the Whigs in the late 40's in the house next door to that one," John Robert Scott said out loud to himself. It was odd, but true, that lately he had been carrying on conversations with himself, as if he had to try to make sense of a frighteningly changing world, and that the only way he could do that was to converse with one of the few people he hoped was really rational. It was, then, a very specific and pointed kind of reverie he engaged in as he walked slowly towards the far north corner of the churchyard, where the Revolutionary War veterans and families were laid to rest.

The heavy, bent grasses were wet and shining with globular drops which caught the sun. "Lincoln's family lived near ours in Kentucky," he said to himself. "I wish I had been born to know those days. Everyone was so full of boundlessness—they could have jumped in the sky if there were a way to get up there. Lincoln's family moved into southern Indiana just after ours came across the Buffalo Trace. Fought their way through three miles of wilderness with an axe before they got to the homesite. They were Movers too—and moved on into Illinois. But the McClures stayed. Stayed, and were buried here." He had reached the McClure plot. Trees had grown to the very edge of the plot, a second growth woods which had not been here when he was a boy. Uncle Dan'l's property, this was, and he had given it for this first Protestant church in Indiana.

John Robert Scott walked through the tall, bent-over grasses of late August, and saw the stone of Dan'l McClure. "Dan'l," he said the word over in his mind. "That was what most folk called him, and that was what he wanted on his stone. One of the best men I ever knew—1754 and 1838, it says. The cholera took him, or he'd be here yet, exhorting us to good works, shaking his head, chuckling at the children. Next to it, Martha Baird McClure. Of Bardstown—Bardstown all Catholic now. No Bards. So many tombstones here, children and children's children, clustering about Uncle Dan'ls grave, as they clustered about him in life." He bent to pull ivy and Virginia creeper from the round, brown tombstones. "William McClure," he said softly, again aloud. "Uncle Will. Captain of troops for George Rogers Clark. What is it about standing in a cemetery that makes us want to address the folk beneath the ground? Uncle Will, you led the Pennsylvania Caintuckians against the Shawnee at Piqua in Ohio. What do you think about this war?" He chuckled a little at himself for his foolishness of speaking to the long-dead.

"And there—Margaret McClure and assorted of Uncle Will's family, victims of cholera, typhus or just worn out bodies—all buried next to him. Aunt Meg, a soft, warm, laughing woman. Twenty years younger than he.

"Uncle George's and Uncle John's graves—'Veterans of the War of Independence.' As is Pa." He walked to the graves at the end of the yard, perpendicular to the rest, with roots of the overhanging ash and elm threatening to do them danger.

" 'James Scott. Jenny Scott, his beloved consort. Asleep in Jesus.' " His thoughts moved inward. "Why is it I always think of the human bodies beneath the ground? Pshaw. Should be thinking of the spirits in heavenly places. But can't help it—in twenty, thirty years, what happens to a human body in a fragile casket. Is there anything left? A heap of bones? The same ones that were the bodies that had spawned and borne me? Moles, maybe? At my ma and pa? Ugh. When the French dug Napoleon up after thirty years, his features were in perfect shape; he looked young and handsome, a miracle they said, testimony to the power of the French Revolution (or the crazy man who took it over. Glad for my education). Thank heavens Mahalia June is buried at Mariah Creek Baptist Church; don't need to think of her in terms of bones and dust."

He gave a panoramic glance around the cemetery. "Look at all these stones," he thought. "What's on them, the men's that is, except for an occasional Bible quotation, is war service. The battles they fought. The causes they shot cannons and guns for at other humans. Dr. John McClure, Sergeant Parke Dragoons, Battle of Tippecanoe. Bones moved here from

Hindostan Falls. (Glad I didn't have to move them.) Gave his life caring for the sick in the terrible epidemic there, but all that's remembered of him was the Battle of Tippecanoe. His horse had run away from him, Cousin Catherine always said, and he led a final assault against the Indians against his will. A fluke, and this tombstone says he is a hero.''

He moved among the stones, speaking again softly to himself. ''Not all of these stones have battles on them, but they might as well. George McClure, 'With George Washington at the Battle of Princeton'; John McClure, 'Battle of the Brandywine'; Archie McClure, 'Battle of Tippecanoe'; Robert McClure, 'War of 1812, Battle of the Thames.' He bent, picking up a piece of stone that had chipped off, and putting it back on the stone of the original Jane McClure, who had come from Ireland. Her own husband's grandfather, so they said, had fought in the Battle of the Boyne over there.

He walked over to one of the larger tombstones, an Emison one, and sat down. He mopped his brow with a handkerchief. It was getting towards noon. Hot. The boys were late.

His own Friends church was right. All the fighting these tombstones represented was so futile. Or was it? Somehow he could hear his father's voice. ''The land y' stand on today is in the United States and not a part of Canada or England because these men came acrost Illi-noys with Clark and took the fort from the British. Is that worth anything to you?''

Of course it was. It had to be, and really, he did not know anymore. He really did not know. All his life he had thought that war was completely wrong, killing a man a sin, outright, no matter how it was done. He had stood adamantly with his sons for no war service. But now Abraham Lincoln was beginning to issue proclamations freeing the slaves in some cases. Soon there might be an official, complete emancipation. Releasing an entire population from hideous, unbearable bondage. And men would have to die or kill others to make it stick. They had not started that way, but that was what would happen. So was that right in the eyes of God or not? He did not know; he simply did not know. The Bible had answers for almost everything, but when it came to shades of right, it was not specific. You had to decide, and those decisions, which had elements as delicate and finely wrought as a spectrum seen through glass, were what Christianity was about.

Did God have a long-term plan? His mother had thought so. Jenny thought that if there was war, it didn't matter. The real plan was Love. There might be wars and rumors of wars, but God was Love, and that was stronger than any power on earth. Poor Jenny McClure Scott had lived in the shadows of insanity for thirty years, speaking not a word. He was only a stripling when she had left off being herself. But before that—he had adored her. She was sprightly and imaginative and warm, and she looked into the heart of living and saw things nobody else saw.

One night, when he was about nine, and she was putting him to bed, he began to cry and fret about Tecumseh. The Indian leader had been riding about, threatening war and he, little John Robert was afraid. "Don't be scared, John Robert," his mother Jenny had said. "You are safe here with us. And safe in my love. Why, didn't I love you enough to bear you when I was almost past child-bearing age, loved you enough after I had given up—" Her eyes had gone out the window, to the light of the sunset over the Wabash.

He knew what she meant. His older brother Ish, the only other child Jenny had borne, had by that time turned completely bad. But his mother never stopped loving Ish, no, when he went to join Aaron Burr, and even later, when he killed a man in Vincennes. Her love was as strong as piano wire, as strong as granite, though finally, in an uneven contest, it had snapped and her mind had broken.

"You were a child of promise," she said. She told him how the doctors said she had almost died when she bore Ish and how she should not conceive again, of how they felt she could not carry a child to term, especially beyond forty.

And of the vision she had had in this worrisome time, of sitting on a hill above a creek in Kentucky. While others were tending to a relative who had just died, she wearily rested from the trials of the hot day. Mopping her brow, leaning against a tree, she had seen a sort of mist come down and she seemed to pass into another time. She spoke of seeing troops dressed in odd uniforms come down to drink water in a very dry time, and begin to skirmish over the water rights. A general battle had begun, and when she saw one young man in her vision, she felt such overpowering love that she felt she could reach out and touch him, warn him of snipers in the trees. She had raised a hand and spoke the warming, but the scene disappeared before she knew whether he had heard her.

With tears coming to her eyes, she spoke of the love she had felt at that moment, overwhelming, reaching out beyond the pale of war. "Love is stronger than war and fear and death," she had told him, putting her head beside his on the pillow.

"My love for you, before I even saw you, carried you happily and healthily through all the months of danger. You were born to console and support your parents late in their lives. Love goes beyond time and even beyond death."

And her own love had done that. He felt it with him now, thought in some irrational way as she had said, it would support his own should they ever need it, beyond the years.

John Robert Scott stood up slowly. He felt wrung out, exhausted. " 'James Scott. Fought with the Pennsylvania Militia and with George Rogers Clark'," his father's stone said. Then a radical thought, which had been forming for weeks but just now found articulation, hit him. John Robert thought it might be all right to support this war, it just might. That wouldn't mean personally fighting, he guessed. Just support. He must tell Jacob Joe, because they had so often hotly debated it. The sound of a rig coming up the road made him turn about suddenly.

His sons rode into the church road, tied up the rig and strode across the churchyard to him. He turned eagerly toward them; he was glad they had come. They were so seldom together these days, it would be a happy family afternoon, with the fried chicken and laughing—but no. As they neared he could see their faces were red and angry. They had been arguing.

Jacob Joe was breathing heavily as he came to his father. He refused to look at his brother Zach, who stopped behind him, nonchalantly, with his hands in his pockets.

"Father, do you know what this son of yours has done?" Jacob Joe demanded.

"No, but—"

"He has been put on Governor Morton's proscribed list. The list of dangerous Copperheads. He disturbed a Union meeting in Brown County last month, and now Morton is circulating his name on a list."

John Robert Scott reached towards his son's arm. "Zach—" he said, with anguish.

Zach brushed the touch off, haughtily.

"It shouldn't be a surprise to you, Father, that I'm not a Union man."

"But to have your name put on a list with traitors—" His father's mouth hung open.

In the strained silence, Jacob Joe Scott's voice finally rang out again. "Daniel Voorhees of Indianapolis, Jesse Bright of Salem, and Zachary Scott of Knox County. The only one they don't know is the Northern Mask. He stays secret, but our family has no secrets any more. We know our traitor."

"Who is to say who the traitors to our country are, brother?" Zach articulated between closed teeth. "I do this because I believe in it."

"So now you are the fine hero believing in something, Zach," his brother confronted him with a raised fist. "Or is it that you're just playing the role of the Evil One, like when we were boys and you tied two dogs' tails together to see them yip and scream?"

"Boys—" John Robert tried to put hands on his two sons shoulders. "Don't do this—especially here. This is sacred soil."

"Tell him your part, then, my angel brother," Zach sneered.

Jacob Joe turned white. "You wouldn't—"

"Your son is joining the Union Army. This good Quaker is going to get a musket and shoot people's guts out. You brought him up well according to your tenets, father.''

"What?'' John Robert asked, shocked. "Why did I not know this?'' His Quaker son going to kill. Still, as he had just been thinking that the war was a worthwhile one. Perhaps Jacob Joe did have to make up his own mind and would be serving the cause of God better this way. It was all so confusing, and he was so tired—he started to speak his mind, but Jacob Joe interrupted him.

"Father, I was going to tell you my own way. Lewis Brooks is raising a new regiment in Martin and now Knox County, and I have signed on. I know I promised Ma on her deathbed that I wouldn't go to war, but I have told you if Lincoln freed the slaves, I would think again.''

"Son—'' John Robert started to say, "I—''

Jacob Joe was not listening. He turned in a frenzy on his brother. "Son-of-a-bitch, why did you tell father this?'' he cried, and grabbed the lapels of his taller brother. "I could kill you!''

"I pray you, don't—'' His father attempted to separate them, anguish written on his face. Suddenly he turned away, unable to speak. A stabbing pain gripped his heart. He clutched at it. His sons did not see him; they were struggling over the tombstones. Zach was swinging his fists, Jacob Joe closing to pummel his brother's chest.

Their wrathful voices rang out over the quiet churchyard.

"Always were—such a mad dog. Frightening—even Grandmother Jenny, letting Mother die without you there—''

"I'll plaster your stupid, Quaker mouth shut—''

"Must tell Jacob Joe my mind on the war—'' John Robert struggled to speak through unbelievable spasms of pain. He sank to the ground and finally one of his sons saw him.

"Father—'' Jacob Joe said, turning, choking back his rage. They rushed to him. "Whatever is the matter?''

"I—ah, ah—'' was all he could say and then his eyes clouded over.

"His heart—has pained him lately. He is dying,'' Jacob Joe cried.

Zach knelt beside the old man. He said nothing but his eyes were surprised, stricken.

Jacob Joe's voice was frigid with fright and anger. "I shall go ride for the doctor. Stay with him—if you think you can spare the time.''

Leaping over tombstones, he ran towards the horses.

His brother put his ear to their father's chest. He could not hear a heartbeat. Still, the old man was trying to speak. A faint whisper. Zach bent low. "Tell—Jake—the war—it's all right. 'Tis a just cause. I don't mind. Tell him.'' And then a bubble formed on his lips and he was still.

"It's too late, I think he's gone—'' Zach called after Jacob Joe. There was no pulse, no heartbeat. The sound of his own voice echoed in his mind, strained, high. "Jake—" But his brother was already untying the mare. He could not hear him. He spat on the ground so Zach could see it.

Zach was left alone, the sound of hoofs thundering down the road rattling emptily in his mind. So, Jacob Joe would blame him for this. Let him. Jake had always hated him anyway. Let him rot in his ignorance of what their father really felt.

He stood up, watching the wind drift a few oak leaves down over the tombstones. Then he turned his back. The face of the man on the ground was blue, and he could not bear to look at it.

And at home Ella, the hired girl, took fried chicken from a pan and, humming a happy tune, set it on the table. Then she waited all afternoon, worrying and wondering why nobody ever came to the party.

They laid John Robert Scott to rest the next Sunday. Half the county stayed for the funeral after church. The choir sang, "Lead kindly light, amidst the encircling gloom."

"John Robert Scott was a son of America and the gospel," Reverend Paden said. "He gave himself to the service of his community and to Christ and thought both were inseparable. Early on he was part of the underground railroad, going to the South to free kidnapped slaves. He headed our orphanage drive—his works were as the stars. He lived the Lord's saying, 'As you do it unto them, you do it unto Me.' "

Catherine Hogue represented the family on the front bench. Zach and Jacob Joe sat stony-faced, one on each side of her. They had only agreed to come on the condition she would divide them on the bench.

Afterwards, Catherine cornered them together. At her pleading, they reconciled enough to stand side by side at the burial and then agreed to greet mourners together.

Catherine took her place in the hushed silence before the long, open grave site. "Ashes to ashes, dust to dust. In the promise of the Resurrection," Reverend Paden was saying in a soft voice. A whippoorwill sang, oddly during the daylight hours, his sad song in the trees; the smell of trampled grass rose from the ground. Catherine's eye rested on clumps of goldenrod poking up next to many of the old McClure tombstones.

Lettie stood at her side and Catherine whispered in her daughter's ear, "My favorite cousin laid to rest. We crossed the trace together, watched the troops go to Tippecanoe, brought the children here ourselves to look and know the past. Now he, too." The simple wooden casket was lowered by pallbearers into the ground near where his mother and father slept. Catherine wept. "So few, so few of us here and so many there," she said, leaning on Lettie.

"Mother, you always tell me not to be sentimental," Lettie said softly.

"Of course, of course. It's a McClure trait and I must fight it. Pa grew so 'menti-sental' in his last years." She smiled as they walked from the grave, then frowned.

Looking up, Catherine saw her granddaughter Mary Jane and Mary Jane's aunt and guardian, Jewell McClure Simpson, coming towards them. The three of them had kept their distance in the church and at the graveside; now they could not be avoided.

"I know what you are thinking, Mother," Lettie said sharply, "but this is a funeral of someone you love. You are going to go right up to them. See, Mary Jane is pushing Cousin Jewell towards us." A middle aged woman with tiny, yellow-white sausage curls, wearing pearls that dangled over an enormous bust, approached, being steered by her niece, like a freight boat being eased from the rear into dockage. Young Annie followed indifferently in their wake.

"I don't know," Catherine whispered as they came on. "Jewell is always so hateful. Just like her mother. Five minutes with her makes my stomach hurt."

"Well, if you two ladies don't speak," Lettie continued in a low voice, "you are not going to keep me from talking to my nieces, the daughters of my dear sister, Nancy Jane. Now here they are."

"Law, it's Aunt Lettie and Grandma Catherine," Mary Jane said in a loud voice. She came up and pecked Catherine on the cheek. "However are you folks on this occasion? Sad, ain't it?" Mary Jane McClure had a wide, bucktoothed smile and miles of chestnut-colored hair piled high on her head. She was as solid as a young pony.

"We're as fine as could be expected, Mary Jane," Lettie said, firmly. "Losing cousin John Robert is a blow, isn't it, Ma?"

"To be sure," Catherine said, "I'm as numb as a turnip. It isn't easy to bury the last of your youth."

"Too bad the twins' older brother, Cousin James, couldn't be here," Lettie said.

"Yes. The custom is the oldest son's s'posed to bury," Mary Jane said. "I hear tell he's been so busy makin' money as a lawyer in Kansas he don't have time for fambly any more. The estate's passin' in equal parts to him and the twins, but Zach is executor."

"Well, and my own last two sisters aren't here at the funeral either. It hasn't been much fun returning to the bickering that Jacob Joe and Zach have done lately—" Catherine put in. She was speaking to her granddaughter, not to Jewell Simpson; the riveting gaze she fixed on the girl reinforced that.

"No, these here spats 'mong relatives poison the air," Mary Jane said.

Finally Annie roused herself. "I'm hot, Aunt Jewell. Can we go get some of that there lemonade the Ladies' Aid is serving under the elm tree?" Her aunt shook her head "no," and did not move; Jewel Simpson was continuing to distance herself from the conversation.

"Mary Jane, what do you hear from your brother John at the wars?" Lettie asked.

"Still down by Richmond, the Fourteenth is," the young woman answered. "Have you all heard from him?" This question was directed at her grandmother.

"Not for a month," Catherine Hogue said. "But you must have."

"Have a letter here. Thought I might see you here and you'd be interested, grandmother." All this while Jewell Simpson pointedly avoided looking at Catherine Hogue, casting her eyes instead on the line of mourners beginning to greet Zach and Jacob Joe on a rise near the church.

Mary Jane took the letter out of her dress pocket and smoothing it on her knee, read it out, while Lettie looked over her shoulder.

July 13, 1862.

Dear Sister,

Well, we are here. All quiet on the James. 'Twasn't quiet when we come here. We steemed up just as seven bad days of fighting were over to take Richmond. As you know by reading of the papers, we didn't take it. And it seemed to me that the whole Army of the Potomac was standin around slappin mosquitoes and pickin mud off their uniforms. The wounded was crowdin about waitin to get into the field hospitals. This army of the Potomac was the dirtyest bunch of reperbates I ever seen, worse than the Brant brothers when they hanged 'em for killing that old lady out by Bicknell. Remember that? Anyways, we were fresh troops so we was called out to cover a retreat back to this infurnal river. Fourteenth got shot up in that retreat, called it the Battle of Haxols. I called it, for G company anyways, sit for three days in the trenches and swat at mosquitoos and rain pours down, while the canons fire over you. The old Fourteenth did itself proud, though, and was comended for bravery in part of the action. Then we all, all McClellan's army of the Potomac, snuck back like cornered cats to this river, which is about as nice as the dismal swamps around Shakertown.

Lee is on the other side, close enough we can call over to his rebbels. Sometimes some cross over and trade coffee grounds for good Virginny tobaccy. Not me. I don't hunt posums one day and go play kissin games with em the next.

McClellan says he don't have enough men. We hear he asked Lincoln to send down 50,000 more. That's all we need. Fifty thousand more soldiers to tromp around and trip on the grapevines in the Chickeyhominey swamp, to pitch their tents on the sand of this riverbank and get sick. And throw their garbage around to draw flies. I never nowed so many flies existed. I am writtin this letter under a blanket.

Still, the Sanitary Comission has been bringing things in. They bring us lemonade by the galon to keep the scurvy away. Also, there are lots o wounded. And they bring 'em ice water. They sprinkle kemical powder about and it takes away the e-floovia that comes out of the privy holes that are everwhere to make us sick.

We are idle a lot now. Some play harmonicas, some read books. A corporal in C company, Crim by name has a bookstall bussines. Takes dime novels along everwhere and sells em. Henderson loves em, partickerly one. Lots of men play cards—By the way sister, the way you write it seems you don't put much confidenc in me, you are afeerd I will go to gambling. I thought you nowed I had more sense than to go gamble my money away. Now I'm not but so if I did, what? You don't have a kernal of understaning about what livin is like out here. You must reckon that you folks are seein good times to what us fellows do out here.

Love, Your Brother John

Mary Jane stumbled several times over the wording while she read the letter, but her Grandmother Catherine pretended not to notice.

"He seems well, thank God," was all Catherine said.

"Waal, that was a month ago," Mary Jane observed.

Jewell Simpson finally spoke. "Yes, we can all be glad." She looked at Lettie. "Do I hear, Cousin, that you are keepin' company?"

"Well, yes, Cousin Jewell. How did you—"

"And with the livery man there in Vincennes."

"Yes, Mr. Willis Mawkins has visited a few times at our home."

"I do seem to recollect he was your pa's hired hand—a grass widower divorced from one of the Chenoweth girls?" Jewell smirked, and Lettie cast a sidelong glance at her mother.

"Your recollector seems to be servin' you satisfactorily, Jewell," Catherine said. "Better'n your fat-grinder. Seems to me you've picked up plumpness recently."

Jewell sniffed; Catherine smiled and, taking Lettie's arm, headed for the rise under the elm tree where Jacob Joe and Zach Scott were receiving condolences.

"Boys, we take leave of you," she said, kissing each of them on the cheek. "Zachary, we know we will see you round and about these parts." Zach nodded courteously and turned to speak to a woman in a fuchsia silk dress who was putting a gloved hand on his sleeve.

"Jacob Joe," Catherine said, leaning towards him, "in all the confusion of the funeral I haven't spoken of your going off to war. You leave—when is it?"

"Within the month. I must finish up a few things before leaving the estate in the hands of—my brother. Still, I do not intend to stay in the house with him. I will pack and stay in Vincennes."

"Where will you go?"

"I am joining the regiment at Louisville."

"The Fourteenth isn't at Louisville."

"Cousin Catherine, there are other regiments," said Jacob Joe, smiling. "Even other regiments in Vincennes."

"Not for me."

"That's what every grandma in town says. There's only one true bearer of the colors, only one group goin' to glory. I'm joining the Eightieth Indiana, the regiment Lewis Brooks is raising. We are sure to be assigned to Kentucky."

"I wish you well. Our folks came from Caintuck; I hope you find all you wish there."

*   *   *   *

At almost the same time in that awful mid-August heat, the Fourteenth Indiana regiment, sweat-drenched, begrimed and emaciated from camp sickness, wearily watched the troops of the Army of the Potomac go on the road. Dust clogged their hair, their eyes, and even their toenails inside the government-issue brogans.

"Any word when the water issue will be better?" Will Houghton asked David Beem.

"None. But I am almost prepared to drink the water in the James again I am so thirsty."

"You know what the sanitary commission says about that."

"I know. Pure mud and effluvia. But I—all the boys—are desperate."

"We should go on the road soon, and there will be streams all along the way."

"Sunk to trickles by the heat." They were silent a minute, watching mule carts, ambulances, supply wagons jolt along onto the road north.

"How many more hours before this army is finished going on the road and we can follow them?" Beem asked.

"Maybe three more."

"It's been sixty-one."

"Hours? You've counted?"

"Lunday did. Day and night they have gone, never a letup. McClellan and the whole Union army giving up the ghost. What if Lee attacks us on this retreat?"

"He won't."

Beem had a list before him. He was filling out the new sort of captain's report the brass was demanding, being certain each accoutrement was complete. He did not want to account for sixteen dollars' worth of U.S. Government issue himself. "What do you think of morale?" Houghton asked his fellow officer.

"The spirit of the Fourteenth has never been better," Beem said.

"I concur," Houghton said, "and I ask myself why. The most awful defeat the Northern Army has ever suffered, seven wretched days of defeat before Richmond, men dying of dysentery in the wasting heat in this swamp, gangrene poisoning wounds, and still the men laugh and curse and press on. What's driving their will?"

"Hatred," Beem laughed tiredly.

"I know," Houghton replied. "I've learned how to hate, myself. I was always taught all men were brothers, but seeing the jagged wounds in the hospitals, the piles of dead we buried here—"

"Or didn't bury," Beem countered. "A man came in from Hooker's division—did you see him? Brought a message to Colonel Harrow. He said the stench is so awful down there they can hardly bear it. The Rebels felled trees over the hundreds of dead at Malvern hill and just left 'em."

"No, but I saw those pools back in the swamp when we were on picket. Those poor devils, from both sides, who crawled there wounded and died, trying to get to the water. No one attended them."

"Van Dyke's company found ten or twelve Yankees—from Pennsylvania I think it was—mired in quicksand up to their armpits, shot by the Rebels while they couldn't move," Beem was cleaning his face with his own sweat.

"I think I would kill any Rebel I saw on sight with my bare hands," Houghton said. "There isn't enough blood in all the South to atone for what these traitors have taken us all into. I want to make the South a wasteland. Burn every home. Destroy every field. Sew the fields with salt as the Romans did the Carthaginians."

Beem looked at Houghton. Being uninterested in history, he knew very little about the Romans and Carthaginians, but he got the point. Somehow he had never allowed himself to think of the end of the war and what it would mean. He knew he struggled against hatred in himself. "I don't feel personal hatred towards individuals. Being a Christian should keep us from personal hatred." It was getting harder all the time to feel this way, but it was important to him.

"Wipe out Charleston and Atlanta," Houghton insisted. "To say nothing of the traitors back home."

"It is difficult not to despise them," Beem conceded.

"Father wrote to say the Copperheads keep meeting," Houghton went on. "Now they're making plans to resist the draft, should Lincoln set it up. They openly parade, calling down scorn on the Stars and Stripes. What I can't understand is we have men back home who have been out here. My cousin Lewis—Captain Brooks is there. What's he doing?"

"Chasing glory, like a falling star," Beem told him, wryly. "Perhaps I'm just feeling dismal today. I should be more fair. Truly, he's an honorable officer and the new regiment, where he'll be lieutenant colonel, will win glory."

They looked over towards the enlisted men, as they lounged playing cards on turned-over cracker boxes, drinking from canteens, and wiping their mouths on their shirt sleeves. Waiting. Beyond them, on a sort of pulpit made out of log stumps stood on end, so they would not be seen sitting down on the job, officers and non-coms played cards. Landon was snickering and slapping jacks and aces about with Sergeant Jess Harrold of Beem's company.

"I wonder that I feel so fit myself," Beem finally said. "Over a third of the regiment has gone now. Dead, sent home to recover from wounds, drifted into the woods and away from us. But those of us that are left are brittle. I feel—well I feel like petrified rock."

Houghton looked at him. "You talking about those trees that turn to stone out on the desert?"

"Well, they don't really turn to rock." Beem's special interest was geology. He read about it in *Harper's Magazine* and every book he could find. "Volcanos erupted in California or wherever they are, and covered the huge trees with ashes. Big spruces, I guess they are. And the trees rot out under the ash, leaving holes. Little by little dissolved rock comes into the hole and forms a rock tree. I'm a rock tree now."

"A chunk of granite for the Union?" Houghton asked with a small smile.

"As much as I ever was the day I formed H Company. This war is right."

Houghton nodded. Beem coughed and spat dust. "In the midst of all this I have a letter from Mahala."

"Oh? But then you get a letter from her every day." Houghton smiled, looking affectionately at his friend.

"She wants me to resign my commission. Again."

"What is it?" Houghton looked suddenly alarmed.

"Nothing. She just doesn't understand. Usually I screw up my patience and write her loving, consoling letters, but today I had enough. Maybe it's the dust and heat. Want to read it?"

"Well, it's yours—private, isn't it?"

"No," Beem said, picking up a letter from the camp stool and putting it in his friend's hands. Houghton read it; Beem seemed to expect him to.

It is not my intention to write you a lecture this beautiful morning, my dear wife, but I do intend to write you something about your way of thinking concerning certain things of which you speak in nearly ever letter I get from you. I think I haven't got a letter from you without your saying in it that you couldn't stand it to be separarated from me so long, that it is hard for women to be separated from their husbands and so forth. Well, of course it is or ought to be, and I am glad you say you will stand it the best you can, but you must remember that this world makes us experience a great many things disagreeable to us and that the more cheerfully we endure hardships and disappointments, the better it is for us. Besides, your situation is favorable compared to that of many other women, and if you think that your case is hard, many others have reason to despair.

Laughter erupted around Landon and Harrold's gambling stump. The men were whooping at some comment the newspaper correspondent had made. How did a man get to be so witty, anyway, Houghton wondered, with grudging admiration. The few times he tried to tell a joke the men looked mystified. He always forgot something important or mis-told the final line. Well, it didn't matter. He went on reading.

How is it with at least a hundred other men in Owen County, who have large families to take care of? If their wives can stand it, as they must, you can do the same. Were I a woman, I should be ashamed of a husband who would not fight for his country. A good government is the best thing on earth. Property is nothing without it, because it is not protected, a family is nothing without it because they cannot be educated. Hence, every man ought to defend it and a man who refused to do so when he can is no man at all.

Now my dear wife, you may think that this is plain talk, but I say just what I mean, and I think you will say it is right. This war has a great many hard features about it. Friends have to be separated for a time at least, perhaps forever, a great many die of disease, thousands fall on the field of battle and a great many sweet little wives like yourself have to be left at home. All I can ask of you is that you be cheerful like a good Christian ought. For my part, I have no doubt I am a good deal happier than I would be at home, and I lie down at night with a lighter mind and a more grateful heart than many a big, lazy pup at home who is too cowardly to come out and defend the old flag of Freedom.

Houghton, moved in spite of himself, returned the letter to his friend. "If that doesn't do it, nothing will. Sometimes I think not a one of them back home understands any of this."

Beem nodded. "Still, I wish I had just one of those lazy pups here today as this army goes onto the road. I'd make him lap up dust." They turned and surveyed the long line of march for a time.

Van Dyke appeared. His face was like a dark cloud.

"What's the matter?" Houghton wanted to know.

"Shit, we're one musket short in G." He glanced at Beem. "I see you've been at the accounts, too."

"Everything's here in H—"

"Not in G. Fairbairn says his gun is gone. Doesn't know where. I don't see how he could possibly lose it here in camp. They have no business making us personally responsible."

"Colonel—*General* Kimball now, says it was the only way," Beem told him, indifferently.

"Still I hate it. Makes me wish I was a lieutenant again."

Both men turned to look at him with surprise.

He looked towards the gambling lieutenants and non-coms. "Landon has some part in this. I know he does."

Houghton smiled a little, grimly. "The matter of the gun? Gus, you're obsessed with Landon. He's an opportunist, it's true, but to make away with Fairbairn's gun. Why would he want to do that?"

"To get my job. He wants captain as bad as I did. He'd just as soon see me shoved aside. Little things count, and he doesn't mind making me look bad."

"Ridiculous," Beem said. Still, he looked over at the tall stump card-playing table. It was easy to get irritated at lieutenants, particularly. Lunday, of course, was different, he was a fine officer, but the rest in this regiment— they were ill fitted for officering in this amateur army, They postured about and shirked whenever they could, especially when there was a strong captain. Even Jess, his friend, who was a sergeant, sometimes shirked. He had to look him up for duty, and he slept too often under oak trees. It had become a bone of contention between them. Beem sighed. It was hard to sustain the friendship of Spencer, Indiana, in the middle of the Seven Days' battlefields. It was hard, very hard, to maintain Christian optimism in a civil war.

The men in G company were eating a cold meal. "No fires to cook. Hell, I don't see what the harm would be," Tommy Thompson said.

"They thought we'd be on the road by this time." John McClure was forking through a sort of cold stew. "This is the last of the potatoes. And onions, too," he said.

"What the hell is that you got, Simpson?" Thompson asked his friend.

"Apple pie," Simpson smiled up. "Waal, I took the dried apples Sanitary Commission brought down and mixed em up with honey I carried all the way from Alexandria. Put 'em in the middle of a flapjack and fried it."

"Not bad?"

"Cold as a provost's heart. But edible."

"The surgeons are mad at the Sanitary Commission, don'tcha know," Thompson said.

"Surgeon Burkhart isn't," McClure said, looking up from his meal.

"No, not him. He's different anyways. But the rest of the corps, so they say. Don't want a bunch of civilians, specially women, butting into their affairs. Bunch of volunteer gasbags, they call 'em."

McClure rose angrily from his haunches. "Hell, if the surgeons get their way, we won't see apples and onion any more. 'Twas too good to be true, I knowed it when I saw the Sanitary Commission coming with them burlap sacks full of good stuff."

"Just about the time something starts to work, some politician or military brass comes in and tinkers with it," McClure said. "The Sanitary Commission comes in, brings ice to the wounded, gives us lemonade and apples. That's good, so they want to get rid of it."

"Hell," Simpson said, "the army's just one big backwards party."

"What d'ye mean?" asked Thompson. Somehow he always felt a little dull in the presence of the other men. Maybe it was because he never learned to read very well. The schoolmarms had always kept him after three o'clock, but nothing ever seemed to work. He could puzzle it out, but it was uphill all the way.

"You remember," McClure told him. "In Knox County the gals are always looking for new kinds of play parties, and they hit on the idee of backwards parties. Were all the rage the year we left—" a shadow crossed his face.

McClure continued the explanation. "One of 'em invites the other ones over for a sleepin' party. Everone has to come backwards—all the clothin' is backwards, the chairs are put at the table backwards, they have to reach backwards to eat—"

"Whatever makes sense in the real world is crazy in the army. And what makes sense to the gas balloons in Washington or headquarters is really crazy. Backwards party," Simpson added.

"It all fits," agreed Bushby Quillen. "McClellan comes up the peninsula with 100,000 strong and says he doesn't have enough men. Fights till he gets to the doors of Richmond and says he can't go on."

McClure waxed enthusiastic. "And the President says, 'General McClellan, you're doing a perfectly horrible job and I'm going to keep you on at the head of the army.' "

"Ahh," said Thompson, wondering at the wisdom of his friends, who seemed to know as much as even the politicians in Washington.

"Now, if you want me to I'll go on with the story," said Crim to the C Company group sauntering about on the dusty ground, waiting to go on the road. He looked up from the book he held in his hand, facing a group which included Bo Reilly, Redskin McClure, and several others, mostly from the old Mt. Pleasant neighborhood.

" 'Tis a powerful good novel, Crim," Bo Reilly said. Their bookstall business had boomed, so well, indeed, that they were almost out of stock. Crim smiled, nodded his head enthusiastically and read:

Little Patsy trudged along the weary road to Albany, the worn tintype held fast in her pudgy hand. Her poor little feet, in their thin slippers, were blistering from the stones on the rough road. "Ah, if I can just catch a glimpse of him, hold his shaggy head to my chest," the little girl breathed. Soon the gates of the prison loomed heavy before her, their cruel gates forbidding entrance.

"She's walkin' all the way to see her pa? He's in prison?" Bo Reilly demanded incredulously. "I seem to remember that Albany, New York is awful far from—"

"Shut your mouth and let Crim go on. It passes the time," a chorus of voices shouted.

Crim read:

Little Patsy tried to decide how one should get a prison gate to open. It certainly wouldn't respond to 'Open Sesame' in the book she had seen years ago in school.

"She's ten. How come she ain't in school any more? Wanderin' all about the roads, alone, at her age—" Bo demanded.

"Shut up, I said. Reminds me o' my little gal, brave and bold," Bushby Quillen commented. He was listening enrapt, stroking his white-streaked beard. "Mebbe 'twas summertime."

"Mebbe she was too poor," Joe Sholts opined. He was a jaunty, down-to-earth man, one of the few clean-shaven men in the regiment, who wore his cap at an angle when he could. He was able to juggle four apples at a time to entertain the men and could whistle exactly like a bird, but he did not ever offer philosophical comments.

"What do you mean, too poor? School's free now," Reilly maintained.

Walter McClure decided to venture something in the conversation. "Well, perhaps New York doesn't have common schools. Ours are just ten years old." He dare not say more. Every time he shown brighter in intelligence than the "boys," they cut him as a "show-off Injeean."

After a contemplative look, though, the group nodded acquiescence to the theory.

"Can I go on?" Crim demanded a little haughtily. His straw-colored hair was almost black with dust and perspiration and huge sweat circles stained his blouse, but his expression could not have said "wounded dignity" better if he had been General McClellan himself. He put his knee up on a box and rested the book on it.

A man appeared, dressed in a guard's uniform. "Little miss, you surprise me, so far out in the country in this dark place. What can have brought you to the state prison?" Little Patsy did not flinch. Her bravery and courage had carried her far; she would not allow any vicissitude to stop her quest. "Sir, I have come to see my dear father. He languishes behind these stern walls. I hope you too are a father to dear little ones—"Touched, the guard opened the gate, then bent down to touch her golden curls. "Who can resist such heavenly innocence?" he smiled. "Tell me your father's name, little angel."

Captain Van Dyke appeared. "Two more units to go," he said. "We are definitely the last. They are leaving one cavalry unit to watch the Rebels, but we should be on the road to cover this movement within the hour."

Nobody paid any attention to him. He went on to the next group.

Crim continued.

Little Patsy was led through a giant doorway of a rock ribbed building. Cold, musty smells assailed her delicate nose. She raised a hand to her face as if to defend herself from the sad terrors of the place.

"Poor, poor Patsy," Bo Reilly said sadly.

On, through blocks of cells, where shadowy forms lurked in the corners, sighing, partaking of their meager, inedible food.

"Sounds like us," Sholts said.

Finally they stood at a cell more remote from the rest, where spiders spun their filmy webs, where water dripped its everlasting cadence onto the moldy floor.

"Gol-ding, they got 'im in the dungeon," Quillen said, stamping his hand with his fist. "What'd he do?"

"Mebbe embuzzled something or exhorted money," Bo said.

Crim began to glare at the group and continued the narrative:

"Father, my dear father, come to the bars," the child pleaded. Her tears fell on the cold stones. "I have something to show you." She looked at the dim photographic likeness she held in her hand. On the far side of the cell, a man bending over a chair, hopeless and despondent, brightened as if a shaft of heavenly light had fallen on him. "Is that the voice of the past? 'Tis like the voice I heard when I bent on my knees to beg of beauty the sacrifice of marriage. The voice that crooned over a cradle long ago—who—"

Crim stopped. He closed the book emphatically and put it in his pack.

"What happened?" "Who was the pitcher of?" "Where's the child's ma?" voices demanded.

"That's all for now. You'll have to patronize my bookstall to find out what happened to Little Patsy."

"Crim, you bastard—tell us what happened. What'd the father do?—"

"I have three of these fine novels left. Twenty-five cents each."

"Twenty-five! Last week they was ten cents."

"I kept 'em till last. Now I want to liquidate so's I can have something to spend back in civilization, when and if we get there. I had to pay men to help me carry 'em all the way from Alexandria and to keep my stock clean in— bad circumstances. You already beat t' pieces my lease book, *The Bird of Paradise.* The market demands—"

He was mobbed by comrades both protesting his tactics and desiring his wares. By the time Houghton began to put them all on the road, he had sold not only all the Little Patsy books but the last of his religious tracts as well.

Will Landon and Jess Harrold kicked the stumps of their makeshift card-playing table into the trampled brushland they were about to depart. The eagle eyes of their captains were upon them, honing in like lighthouse beams. Landon sauntered nonchalantly to near where Van Dyke stood, but he did not speak to his captain. Drops of sweat stood on his forehead, beaded around the mustache. He did not know where his sergeant was, probably off in the woods on an emergency trip. He had better do the job himself, post haste.

"All right you government order flea palaces, you lumps of blue that smell like mutts and have bumble bees in your brains," Landon yelled with tardy officiousness, "let's get your underpaid, underfed bodies on the road to perdition."

Harrold scuttled over with Lieutenant Lunday to straighten the ranks of H Company, under Beem's critical eyes. When Harrold was satisfied and the ranks finally began to move, he slung his rifle over his shoulder and strode past Beem.

"What's that gun?" Beem yelled at Harrold. "It's an English rifle, top class."

"Waal, some of us got 'em off the battlefield there near Haxols. You know that, Davey."

"Some of us—you didn't, sergeant. Don't call me Davey." Beem was grimly silent for a moment. "Wait a minute, Fairbairn in G had one of those." He placed himself under the nose of his boyhood friend, who had the build of a short stevedore. "Sergeant, I want to know where you got that rifle."

"Waal, Davey, well Captain Beem, I won it, don't you know—" His eyes were evasive, uncomfortable. "From Lieutenant Landon, said he found it lyin' about."

"I knew it. Van Dyke was right, after all. Landon got hold of that English rifle and set him up for trouble. Son of a gun." He gestured for Harrold to swing the rifle off his shoulder and turned towards the ranks of G Company. The government would have to do without six dollars of missing accoutrement fine, Van Dyke would get his money back in his pocket and Landon's prating, cocksure smile would be wiped off his face with a stern reprimand, at least for a while.

Beem matched his stride to Lunday's. "I hope to God we have something better to think about than all this petty bickering when we get back towards Washington," be said to his lieutenant.

Lunday did not answer. He took a finger and ran it across teeth black with dust, nodded, spat and began the march to the boat that would take them away from Richmond and failure.

*   *   *   *

"Memphis is occupied by Northern troops, Calhoun," Althea Dugger announced as she read the newspaper at the breakfast table at Rivertides.

"I know, Mama," her son said in the almost apologetic tone he often used with her. "Seems hard to think we lost Memphis. The Mississippi ports are gettin' swallowed up. New Orleans was the worst loss. They say that General Ben Butler is running that old city like—"

"Never mind Beast Butler. This is an opportunity for us."

"Pardon, Mama?"

"We have smokehouses full of bacon, sacks of cornmeal and even salt, don't we?"

"Yes. But I don't see—"

"You never do see, son. The South is starving. That's what every report we hear says."

"I suppose they are."

"We have bacon and meal and flour, they have—well, they will find means to buy our stocks in Memphis."

"How?" Calhoun demanded, wearily. He helped himself to marmalade and toast from the toast holder. "How will we get down South to sell the stuff?"

Delia came down the stairs into the sunny dining room and slid into her chair. Listlessly she watched the shrunken stream of the river go by. "Lower yet today," she said to herself. "What a grim, warped summer it is," she murmured. "The river so low you can walk across it in places. Half the nation in battle, the other half in distress. Almost like some troll had enchanted us all and placed a cursed spell on the land."

"Delia, you are eating like a bird," her mother said, looking at the girl's thin wrist. "I've been meaning to talk to you about this. I've just asked for the accounts of the plantation, and I'm goin' to replace Shriver as manager. There's nobody to hire to replace him. Men all gone to the war—things are not going well."

"What's that have to do with my eating?" Delia wondered, fiddling with a silver butter knife in front of her.

"We cannot afford the luxury around here of being Southern women, who starve and preen themselves, so they will look like willow wands. Each of us here, without the men about"—quickly she glanced at Calhoun—"except for your brother," she amended, "are goin' to have to go out on the plantation. I don't like it but—supervise the work of the harvest. You ride as well as your father did, sit a horse superbly, and I need you to take over some of the work. If I can plan and supervise the work on these acres, you will have to help with the work. To do that you must eat. Have some ham. We have corn puddin'—"

Delia looked distastefully at the loaded table, at the hot popovers the servant, Zenobia, was setting in front of her mother. "Mama, I am not hungry. And I'm not interested in riding any more. Or in anything else."

"You were interested enough in riding halfway across the state." Delia looked up and met her mother's eyes. There it was again. A reprimand for the escapade to Martin County, the night spent under a strange roof with a man not her own relative, the return, dishevelled and damp, to the whispers of the servants. Her mother did not often mention it, but when she did, she cut as fine and as neatly as a scalpel.

"Life isn't interesting to me," Delia said. "I have nothing to do, and riding around following your orders on the plantation isn't going to change that. Working in the fields for a month or two would be a novelty, but I'd know all the time I would be returning to what I've always been—an ornament. I can't help thinking that I'm like Aunt Addie and my cousins in Louisville. Living there at the hotel. Born and bred to be ladies. I hate that."

Althea nodded and smiled, her eyes proud. "My mother raised Adahlia and me, both of us, to be ladies. To follow proper rules. Keep our skin pale as snow, sit with ankles crossed, never admit rudeness to our thought or homes. And certainly, never to do men's work, as I—and you—are going to have to do."

"Well, my cousins are perfect ladies, then. They get up in the morning, put on morning dress, sit on the porch until dinner. Then dine, sit in the parlor until supper. Then—"

"Never mind, my dear. Anyway, your cousins do a lot more work these days than you imagine, now that your uncle is gone and they must run the hotel. They pretend to be idle, but since times are hard, they are doing servants' work, too. It is not what we were raised to, but even here training tells. A true lady can rise to any occasion, meet any challenge with dignity—if the cause is right. Keeping on with head held high—that is what life is all about." Althea Dugger turned her head away from her daughter, but her lips were pursed, her eyes veiled.

She took the paper and pointed at the front page. "Calhoun, it says here that traders can receive licenses to sell their goods in Memphis. I want you to go there, to my home state, and take boatloads of things from Rivertides. Prices are down here, and we need gold, you know that."

"We don't have enough stuff for more than one boatload, Mama," Calhoun answered indolently. "And to make any profit, we'd have to stock five or six."

"Well, then, let's canvass all our neighbors. We'll set Willie and all the rest of the McClures down at the landing to riding about, contracting on credit for all the hams and salt and meal and flour they can find."

Delia had picked up the paper from the table and was scanning the article on Memphis markets opening to traders. "Mama," she said, "what makes you think sympathizers like us will be given traders' licenses?"

"Hunger and need are willing to accept calling cards from very unsuitable friends," her mother said emphatically. "Those Yankees running the city will be eager for our produce. The people under their care are malnourished. Our hams and maple sugar are the best in the Northwest.''

Delia could not argue with that.

''I may go on the trip with Calhoun,'' Althea said, with sudden inspiration. ''I am dreadfully worried about my parents' plantation, our old home Fairchance, now that they have fled to Mississippi. If I could find a way to go to see it, find someone to get us a pass. I know! Aunt Adahlia and your cousins in Louisville have been cooperating with the Northern government, enjoying Yankee money in their hotel.''

''Hunger and need are willing to accept even Yankee calling cards,'' Calhoun said wryly.

''Yankees do not have calling cards, at least the ones around here don't,'' Althea went on, coolly. ''I have considered Addie and her children turncoats until this hour. Now I see their value. Calhoun, call Trotter. He is to ride to mail a letter that cannot go by telegraph to my sister in Louisville. She can arrange our safe passage down the river—say it is for trade purposes.''

''But what will I do if you make this long trip to Memphis?'' Delia wailed. ''How long do you plan to be gone?''

''After the produce is gathered, two months, maybe three, will see our schemes through to fruition.''

''And I, back here?''

Althea looked at her daughter as if noticing her for the first time that morning. ''You my dear,'' her mother said, with a bright, sudden smile of inspiration, ''will run the plantation. Carry on all the duties and obligations as I do. You will be mistress of Rivertides. After all, you have to learn to carry on with your head held high as much as I do!''

Delia's face brightened.

''Oh, yes, young miss. You have been crying for me to give you your own head in the horse race. Perhaps you need to run something real and gain some sense, so that you will not run off in odd directions—'' Delia raised her eyes to try to catch the meaning of the gleam in her mother's eyes.

''Now I give you your way. I will be busy managing this new commercial venture in Memphis. You are mistress of family affairs and may run them in the way that suits you, only as long as necessary, of course. How does that strike you?''

''Perfectly, Mother,'' Delia smiled, pleased at herself and the turn of events. Had her mother really decided to trust her with something important or was it just expedient to have her run the plantation? It did not really matter; she would be on her own. Suddenly Delia was hungry. She turned to her brother, whose cheeks were as full as a chipmunk's. ''Calhoun, will you pass the ham?''

Her mother smiled at her daughter and patted her hand.

As the colored woman passed her hominy and eggs, Delia suddenly looked up. "Morgan—Morgan the Southern cavalry raider—he is riding about Kentucky and Tennessee," she said to her mother. "Many say that he could head for Ohio, or more likely, Indiana."

"Well?" her mother asked.

"What shall I do? They say he is brutal, destructive."

"Ask for his calling card and do not admit him if he is not a gentleman," said Althea with a mocking smile. "That is the advice my mother always gave me, which she said covered all the events in a lady's life. Otherwise, sort it out for yourself." Her mother rose from the table, leaving her children to finish by themselves.

Hannah Chute Poore bent over the dry, cracking earth in the garden she maintained in the back of the house that belonged to her daughter and son-in-law, Susan and Thomas Jefferson Brooks.

"Hottest, driest summer since—was it 1838?" she thought as she tied up tomato plants to neat stakes. "That was the summer I stayed with little Emily and Lewis while Thomas and Susan went to Massachusetts. So hot the canal boats grounded in the middle of the Wabash and Erie canal. Then came drenching rains, and, as Thomas told it, cut new channels for the canal right before his eyes, as he stood watching from a packet boat."

She snipped off suckers. "Here, Eustace, Seymour," she called to her teenaged grandchildren, who were pushing each other wildly in a huge rope swing under a large tulip tree at the back of the yard. "You are supposed to be helping me irrigate."

She wiped her dusty hands on her apron. "Good children, but a little soft," she told herself. "The last ones in a large family are often soft, like river clay, as if the marl has run. Everybody's tired and doesn't want to give them the fine, strong molding they need." At least that's the way it was here, with their mother busy in the Methodist church and Father Thomas Jefferson in Indianapolis with Governor Morton seeing to supplying the food the state was still sending to the army, even though the Federal government was beginning to supply the troops itself.

"Gramma, you want us?" Eustace was a sallow-looking boy of about seventeen with a firm, determined mouth and odd, out-of-control hair.

Hannah clapped her hands. "Spink-spank. Take those hoes, you too, Seymour, (here speaking to an owlish lad of sixteen who had an implacable look on his face), "and dig out little channels. Start them back there, at the edge of the garden. We'll carry buckets of water and pour them in, then let it run, so" (here she outlined with her finger the path the water would take). "These tomatoes are going to quit bearing if they don't get water."

Reluctantly the two boys picked up hoes and began to channel out trenches for the irrigation water.

"Now I'm going to go in with this basket of tomatoes and do the rest of my canning."

Slowly she straightened up. Her back had been bothering her these days. Well, it was an eighty-two year old back—it had a right to complain. Had come all the way from Massachusetts in 1818, riding over bumpy Conestoga roads through Pennsylvania to Pittsburgh.

Had borne (joyfully) the burden of a loving husband and ten children— she set down her basket at the edge of the garden and stooped to crop the foliage of the grape hyacinths, now a sallow, summer yellow. She had brought the ancestors of these bulbs from Massachusetts, had carried them over all that long road to a new life. And set them in the log cabin home her husband built for her in Orange County, west of here, where she had raised the younger children. "Old bulbs you are," she said as she snipped the thin, yellow leaves, "but still producing. There's life in you yet."

"Let them settle in for fall," she thought. "The bulbs have fed themselves and now they will lie dormant. If a grain of wheat will grow it must lie in the ground." She had read that very verse in the Bible today at morning prayers, and she could not get it out of her mind. Why was she thinking of it today? Because her back hurt a bit? She might, probably should have several more years before she lay down to rise up again as new grain. Or was it because she was worried about her grandson, Lewis Brooks, off to form a new regiment in dangerous Kentucky? Well, it was a good verse from Scripture and there must be some reason for it standing out for her that way. That was what she usually found, when she read a verse in the morning, there would be a call for it to sustain her or hers during the day.

She looked beyond the house, to the street in Loogootee, where her other grandson Tommy Brooks was coming through the picket fence, brushing the heads of the tall dahlias that lined the path as he strode past them.

"Tommy, I'm going in the house," Hannah called. He was coming to help her can, bless his soul. Had taken the afternoon off at the store and would lift the washtub, fill it with buckets of water, make the fire, all those things it was no longer easy for her to do. That was the way Tommy was, a ray of pure joy. No one in the family could explain him. They just basked in his unselfishness, his impulsive joy.

She went in through the back door and met her grandson in the back kitchen.

"Hello, Gramma. Are there hermits in the jar?" He reached into the cookie crock and took out three fresh cinnamon cookies Hannah had made the night before.

"The fire's going in the stove, Tommy, just stoke it up and feed it and put the washtub full of water on it so it boils,'' she said. It hadn't been difficult for her to learn to can when her daughter Susan brought home the glass jars four years ago. It was a miracle, fresh peaches floating in sugar syrup, green peas in January, cherries for pie anytime. "I want to say something to your parents,'' she told Tommy.

"They're in the parlor,'' he said.

Hannah walked slowly into the parlor where Thomas Jefferson Brooks sat on the horsehair settee. He had just come in from the train and was telling his wife the details of a trip south for Governor Morton.

"—got to New Madrid in Missouri and checked directly with the regiments. They received the uniforms the governor sent them.'' He rose to take off his coat and carefully fold it, laying it on top of the piano.

"What was New Madrid like?'' Susan Brooks asked, hungry for details of foreign soil.

"Well—just a bunch of falling-down shacks on the river bed. The earthquake, they had in '11, y' know, wiped out the town and swallowed up the shoreline. But it's booming up on the hill with all the troops about. That's the jumping-off place for us to take Vicksburg. Someday they'll do it.''

"What?'' Susan Brooks wondered.

"Why, cut off that Mississippi artery and strangle the South. At any rate, as I was saying, finally the uniforms arrived. I had sent them at the governor's orders for the commissary in *March* and it took all this time—''

"Well, I don't understand why they wouldn't let the boys have the new uniforms.''

"Politics. General Halleck didn't like Morton intruding in his stomping ground. Kept writing to tell Morton there were plenty of uniforms in his command, he would see that they were taken care of, all the while the men were walking around with ragged shirts and bags on their feet, coatless in the rain, unprotected from the mosquitoes in the bogs.''

"And General Halleck never sent the U.S. government uniforms.''

"Never. Finally we sent our own uniforms on, and I checked to be sure the coats, trousers, hats, shoes had arrived. But it was distressing to see our Hoosier boys, I tell you, Susan.'' He could not seem to sit still, bounding around like a rabbit. He finally noticed his mother-in-law at the door and escorted her to a chair.

"I was saying, Mother Poore, that I saw our regiments from Indiana digging rifle pits, dragging siege guns through the mud, doing the work of mules.''

"There are difficulties in taking the Mississippi river towns,'' his wife said.

"Yes. Anyone who is there is in a furnace of heat and filthy mud.''

"Anyone—'' Susan Brooks said, with a pang. It was possible that

Lewis's Eightieth Indiana regiment might be sent there eventually. They were at Cincinnati now, just organizing. The fighting in Kentucky and Tennessee was particularly bitter. Twenty-three thousand men had fallen at Shiloh earlier in the spring. The Rebels were going for the jugular vein in a Northern command that was riddled with dissention and poor generaling. It was not a good theatre to be entering.

"Well, Lewis is an experienced soldier," his father said.

"A noble one, who will put himself in the forefront of the troops," his mother affirmed, leaning her head on her hand on the table and turning her face from them.

There was a long silence. "If only he could have been satisfied with the glory he earned in the Fourteenth," Thomas Jefferson Brooks said in a measured way. "They always let him deploy his company first. He hasn't even had a furlough—"

"Lewis told me, 'Duty has no furlough,' " his mother said softly.

"He would say that," Brooks said with grudging pride. "And now son-in-law Campbell is going to the Eightieth. Emily is left with those little children."

"Son-in-law is an expert. The army in Kentucky does need good surgeons," Susan said.

"More than my daughter needs a husband, I guess," Brooks said glumly, then added, "Family's coming to pieces at the seams. Susie will have her husband, at least. You can bet Sandford Niblack won't go. Niblacks never expose themselves to danger if they can help it. And we can be sure of Tommy. His work as a spy for Governor Morton should keep him satisfied." Her husband stomped about a little impatiently. He pulled off his tie and undid his collar.

"Heat's awful. Almost as bad as it was at New Madrid," he said. His wife looked at him in surprise. He prided himself on his dapper neatness, even at home. But now he tossed the tie across the piano and headed, somewhat tiredly, up the steps to pour water from the pitcher into the wash bowl and clean himself up from the trip.

"Gramma, water's boiling," Tommy called out from the kitchen. In the parlor Hannah Poore stood and smoothed her dress.

Susan turned from the table. "Mother, I'm afraid we've been ignoring you," she said, touching the older woman's shoulder affectionately.

"I'm fine. Have to dip the tomatoes now, take off the skins."

She filled a colander with red tomatoes and dipped it into the boiling water she would soon use to can. "Time one minute, Tommy," she instructed her grandson. Soon the skins began to pop and split back, revealing the rosy pulp beneath.

"Now we'll core and stuff them into the cans." She handed her grandson a paring knife. "When we're done you can have a piece of that blueberry pie in the pie chest," she said, pointing to the oak cabinet in the corner of the kitchen.

The kitchen was comfortably silent for a while. Finally Tommy spoke. "Gramma, did your parents ever hold you down?"

Hannah listened to the ticking of the clock outside in the hall. She could smell the cinnamon from the hermits, a pleasant, reassuring smell in a kitchen. "Hold me down?"

"Well, you were a girl—woman, maybe it's different. Put you under their thumb, refuse to let you live."

His eyes looked perplexed, almost angry, and so his grandmother answered carefully. "Well, my father died early. My mother was—a Puritan woman. I loved her dearly, but she lived by laws. She expected us to, also." Hannah's mind drifted away for a moment, to the seacoast towns near Boston, to Newbury, where she had grown up.

"The Chutes were always determined people," she went on. "I guess they kept their children under their thumbs. But when I wanted to marry at eighteen, they did not stop me." She smiled, and the image of twenty-three year old John Poore entered her mind, earnest, ardent, yet timid as a deer. She had him such a short time in such a long life.

Hannah's thoughts returned to fix abruptly on her grandson. She was not really listening to what he was saying. There was trouble here. She sorted it out for a moment and then said, "You want to go to war."

Tommy nodded, wordlessly. His paring knife poked viciously at the center of a tomato.

"Dry, aren't they? Should be much juicier. What a hot August it's been—I thought you were serving Governor Morton."

"Oh, I have been," Tommy said stridently. "Standing behind the counter of the Brooks Store, measuring out lengths of ribbon and digging out pickles from the barrels. Listening for traitors."

"You found one."

"I suppose so. When the group from Knox County came in, I kept my ears open and was able to pass on information about the Knights of the Golden Circle."

"And Morton put one of them on the proscribed list."

Tommy breathed and watched his grandmother nervously. "The son of your old friend from the underground railroad—Zach Scott."

"Well, he should be put on the list, I guess, if he's running about talking traitor talk. They aren't arresting anybody for that yet, thank heavens. But it bears watching."

They were stuffing tomatoes into the thick, yellow glass jars. Juice was oozing down their hands.

"How many should I put in, Gramma?"

"Shove them down, Tommy. The jar needs to be packed tight. They make their own juice. We just add a little salt and snap the lid tight over them."

There was a moment of silence, then he looked up. "Gramma, I am going with Lewis. I have to."

"Yes. I thought you would."

"It will break Pa's heart."

"His heart will mend. Your conscience will not."

"Why, why does he feel this way about me? Fuss and fret over me as if I were a ten-year-old. I'm a married man," Tommy asked desperately, not looking at his grandmother.

Hannah grew thoughtful and finally answered. "You were born after he got good at fathering and really enjoyed it. You came after a hard delivery and he helped you into the world. He breathed into you the breath of life, and if it hadn't been for him, you would not be living. You are a special son, as Adam was to God when he breathed into him and he became a living soul. Besides, he does not have faith to fall back on."

"Pa? He goes to church sometimes."

"Yes. But he is not a believer. Faith helps us let our children go. Faith in them, faith in our upbringing of them, best of all faith in the God that loves them more than we do."

"I need to know that myself, with little Lewie."

"Yes, the weak ones that depend on us are even harder to let go. My father was an invalid, depending in his last days on Mother for all his needs. And the night he died, she came downstairs, oh so slowly, with her face stiff and white as a starched shirt. Then she broke down. She said it was twice as difficult to lose him because he had depended on her, like a child."

"I'm not dependent on Father."

"Yes, but he doesn't know that. He thinks he is still breathing life-giving air for you. He still has the umbilical cord tied to you, and he does not have the knife of faith to cut it."

"How can I help him?"

"It will be hard. He is afraid—that the war is shattering everything he has worked for, that his life is slipping through his fingers and is in the hands of a bunch of soldiers and politicians who will bungle everything. Afraid most of all of death."

"Mine?"

"Of course. And through the risk of death to you, his own. Your father has always fought a battle with death. He used to make pilgrimages to cemeteries, peering around tombs, looking for—who knows what?"

"Is that so odd? Most of us are afraid to die." The jars were loaded and ready to put in their wire rack beneath the bubbling water. Tommy looked into his grandmother's eyes. "Gramma, I'm not afraid to die. I'm afraid to die never having lived."

"I know, Tommy. Tell your father that. He'll understand. He'll have to. Tell him the truth."

He picked up the basket. The yellow jars jiggled against each other. He plunged them deep into the water, then dipped his hands in the sink to clean them.

Then he walked to the kitchen door, through the dining room and into the parlor. "Pa. I'm glad you're back downstairs. I want to tell you something."

Hannah went to the door and softly closed it. Outside she could hear the young people's voices. They were sloshing water from the buckets into the irrigation troughs. Suddenly her back hurt. She put down the tea towel she had been holding and took off her apron. Then she sank into a chair and slowly closed her eyes.

"If a grain will live it must lie in the ground." That again. Well, the day was almost over, and there was no use for it. Well, another day, perhaps. The Bible verse was just waiting, ripening for future use. In the ground— well, she could wait for that one to mature, come to think of it.

August, September, 1862

Chapter Six

The Fourteenth Indiana and the rest of the regiments of the Army of the Potomac retreated slowly from Richmond the end of that summer of 1862. Disaster struck, however, before that retreat could be completed.

In a masterly plan, Lee began moving at the very end of August into the heart of the North. He saw that the forces of McClellan, which were retreating from the James River, would soon join the army of John Pope not far from Washington. Lee decided to move rapidly, cut off, and whip incompetent John Pope, whom he had long scorned, and then head for the rich farmland of Maryland and Pennsylvania. Encountering Pope at Bull Run, Lee beat and humiliated both general and men in two days of cleverly-conceived, searing fighting.

The Fourteenth Indiana, fresh off the steamboat from the James River country, marched all one afternoon and all night to help Pope, to aid in preventing the defeat. It arrived late on the scene, after Pope had suffered 15,000 casualties and his men were rushing back to the fortifications around the capital in a dismaying rout. Men who had run by the hundreds into the woods were filtering into camp as the Fourteenth pitched tents at the rear of Pope's troops.

"We will be needed," Dr. Burkhart told Walter McClure in the middle of all the confusion. He and his assistant headed towards the field hospital and ambulance area.

They found the Division surgeon under a tree, operating by lamplight. Burkhart volunteered his help. The surgeon listened but did not look up. "Amputations," he said, gesturing with his head towards a table fifty yards away.

Some men had been waiting hopefully about the operating station for almost twenty-four hours for their chance to escape death from infected wounds by the only means they knew of—amputation. They immediately turned to follow the new doctor to his station.

Walter McClure opened the instrument case and went to get chloroform and towels. As he returned with the bottle in his hand a young man whose arm was hanging limp and helpless stopped him. "Please, sir, I know you help the surgeon. I beg you take me first."

Walter turned and looked at the young soldier. Although his features were marked with pain, he had managed to scrape the mud from his uniform with his good arm, and he, or someone had somehow combed his hair and washed his face.

"What part of the battle were you shot in?" Walter asked.

"I wasn't shot; I was hit with canister. My clothing was so fouled and I am so covered with dirt, I fear the wound is goin' to fester. Take my arm off, I beg you, or I'll die."

Walter put his hand on the soldier's shoulder and directed him to the table. He whispered a few words to Dr. Burkhart, who was examining the men and placing them in a line according to the priority of their wounds.

"Ah, they are all in danger of blood poisoning with the filth the Rebels shot out of the cannons," the surgeon sighed. He helped the young man up, then to relax him while Walter prepared the chloroform, asked, "And where are you hailing from, soldier?"

"New York—I'm in the Seventh New York Zouaves. We lost 125 men." His voice was low, with an edge of control that sounded as if it were being won at a great price.

"Ah. And where was that fighting?"

"Whilst we were waiting for reinforcements, our unit and some western Virginia regiments were holding the line for General Pope—what's that towel?" The voice was edged with fear.

"Relax, my boy. 'Tis the chloroform. Private McClure is pouring it out, getting ready to drip it for you—"

"I've heard it can kill—"

"I can tell you true, son, that I have never seen a chloroform death. If we did not have it, you might die of shock. Now just breathe the smell, it is a little strong, no? Like over-ripe flowers? Tell me about the Zouaves."

The surgeon's methods were having their effect; the boy relaxed and grew almost conversational. "We were firing shrapnel at point blank range, they were firing. There was a terrible struggle around the guns, men beating each other over the heads with rifle butts, cursing and then . . ."

He was asleep. "Hand me the scalpel, Private McClure," the surgeon said. The lantern flickered on the tree, and behind them late cicadas, buzzing in the briars and underbrush, blended their sounds with the groans of the wounded.

John McClure couldn't sleep, lying in the tent, enervated after the walk along hard roads in the dark. G Company had made camp amidst thistles and brambles and his hands were cut pulling up blackberry bushes.

"You asleep, Henderson?" he asked,

"I'm a-tryin'. M' nerves are on edge."

"Me, too. Wasn't only the walk. 'Twas that stupid fight on the road."

"I don't know how stupid 'twas. Them damn sutlers had it coming. Cakes high as the sky and us so hungry for somethin' else but crackers and coffee."

"Well, I guess it was all right to tip the cart over."

"Sure. That old, fat fart had it comin'. He had dog meat in them pork pies."

McClure did not look up. "If that's so, howcome you all et 'em so fast?" he asked his cousin. "Picked 'em right up off the ground after you turned over his cart and 'et em dirt and all."

"Dog meat's better'n what we been eatin'." Simpson rolled over to McClure's bedroll to make his point. "Anyways, who are you to act as judge? You wolfed down some of the cake I brought you."

"Waal, I was as hungry as the next man. It's jest that I didn't like seein' our men fightin' each other over pies."

Simpson returned to his side of the tent and began pawing through his knapsack again. "Onct you get riled up to fight, it don't take much to press the rile button."

" 'Spose so." McClure lay down and pulled a blanket around his head. It was warm, but the gnats were a bother, particularly bad in this section of the woods where the men were camped.

"Anyways," Simpson went on, "I got me two real apple pies in this here sack and I intend to eat 'em both tomorrow, come what may. And that ain't all."

"What do you mean?" his cousin murmured. His voice was growing sleepy.

"As soon as everything is quiet I'm goin' to take a little trip to the back of the camp. When we come in I saw somethin'. Over where Pope's men are. I seen me some pretty nice little tents put up there in the woods. Had fancy underwears dryin' on them."

"You mean—"

"There's ladies in them woods. For sale." He chortled to himself and held up a cake of soap. "I carried this all the way from the James. Got it in a swap with a Johnnie Reb. I'm a-goin' to clean me up fine and walk down the lane. Finally I'm—"

Van Dyke rattled the tent. "Out, men," he said.

"Whaa? We're jest gettin' to sleep," McClure's voice floated out at the officer.

"All of you. I've been looking for the sergeant—can't find him—to tell you to go out on picket duty immediately. Lieutenant Colonel Coons says General Kimball has had word Lee may continue this advance. He may push towards Washington; the army can't let him move further."

Amidst curses and grunts, the men of the Fourteenth rolled themselves out of their bedrolls. Simpson squatted on the muddy ground on his haunches. Disconsolately he packed his gear. At the last, on top of his dirty stockings, he laid the sack with two small apple pies with the crusts caved in. On top of that he put the cake of soap. Then he closed the pack.

About noon of the next day, General Nathan Kimball sat pulling at his whiskers and drinking coffee in his officer's tent. On a small travelling desk lay a half-finished letter home, its neat, round handwriting testifying to the orderliness of the writer.

Lieutenant Colonel John Coons, second in command of the regiment under Harrow, rode up.

"Sir, Colonel Harrow and the Fourteenth are continuing to man the pickets," he said.

Kimball gestured him out of the saddle. "The Fourteenth," he said to himself. "My thoroughbred regiment. And they use them as workhorses. The high command sends them into tight spots because it knows they will not run. Which is more than we can say for Pope's army."

The young officer dismounted and tied his horse to a stump. "There is considerable shelling and rear-guard action out where the pickets are," Coons said, his manner as smooth and affected as a French officer's.

"I don't see how you got through," Kimball said in his even voice. "The road is a seething mass of confusion."

"We picked our way around the wagons," Coons told him, seating himself diffidently on a log that stood by the flap of the tent. "Will Pope's men will ever get all of these units back to the Potomac?"

Kimball nodded gravely. "We can hope and pray," he said, and then moved with dignity to the coffee pot and poured the lieutenant colonel a cup of coffee, wiping the pouring spout with a piece of paper to stop drips. He had a reputation in the regiment of having habits as quiet and methodical as a church clerk's. For that, he was Coons' ideal. "The sages in Washington are packing the government to go to New York," Kimball went on. "A special train is awaiting Lincoln, to take him north. They are in a panic," he added, handing the coffee to his subordinate.

"Expecting—what?"

"Expecting General Lee on the doorstep of the capitol building momentarily."

"Where is McClellan? Is he in command?" McClellan was a particular favorite of Coons, because he represented the West Point element in the army. West Point, the home of the gray line, parade-ground, fresh-brushed discipline. At "the Point" they wore shined shoes and tall, spiffy hats.

"No one knows," Kimball told him. "General Halleck still seems to be commanding general. He is signing orders—"

"Do we have good intelligence on Lee's movements?"

"No," Kimball said. His eyes were hollow, lined with black. There had not been much sleep for any of them, officers or men, in the last week. "But I do not think he will go to Washington. The retreat is beginning to be secure here, and that will block an attack on the capitol."

"Thank God for that," Coons said. "The men are angry. You know how they talk."

"I do," Kimball nodded.

"They say Pope has the head of a mule and the tail of a yellow-bellied polecat. That Jackson began to annihilate him before Pope even knew Stonewall was on the field."

"Hoosiers through and through," Kimball smiled slowly and glanced at his unfinished letter. There were so many things to take care of here, and his wife was fluster-pated about handling things at home. She wrote about piano lessons, pigs to be sold, that sort of thing, and he had to write to her while the Rebels might be marching on Washington.

Coons went on. "Pope's own men are in mutiny. They are calling for "Little Mac" McClellan to take over again."

"Well, maybe he will be given command. In the meantime we will be securing the retreat."

A rider came up from the direction of the rear lines, a lieutenant from another regiment. "Sir, I have a message for you from headquarters." He handed it to Kimball, who quickly read its contents.

The lieutenant went on. "Also, sir, I just heard a rumor that may be of interest to you. One of our officers returning from the shelling area near the old Bull Run battlefield says the Fourteenth Indiana has just been captured and is being taken behind enemy lines."

"My God," Kimball said, his deep voice unexpectedly loud.

Coons took the officer aside and began earnestly questioning him. But Kimball buttoned his coat and went for his hat.

"Lieutenant Colonel Coons, I trust your horse is relatively unjaded. Please have my adjutant get mine. We are going to find the Fourteenth."

It began to rain tentatively, then in earnest, turning the clogged roads into mud wallows. The horses made their way to the rear amidst the whine of shells. Eventually Kimball and Coons saw the trenches near Manassas, which marked the outermost line of the Northern army—ugly scars on the shell-pocked countryside, protected with felled trees.

"Sir, there they are—the rumor was wrong."

"Yes. So I see."

Captain William Houghton came out of the trenches, along with Colonel Harrow.

"So, men, I see the Rebels have not taken you to Castle Lightning yet," Kimball boomed heartily.

"Castle Lightning, sir?" Houghton wondered.

"The Rebel prison in Richmond. Word had it you were there."

"I could almost wish we were under some roof, sir," Harrow snarled. "It's been raining on us in this exposed position now for over an hour, and we're exhausted and drenched."

"Withdraw your men, colonel. Our orders have come. I had intended to send my adjutant to tell you that, but decided to say it myself."

"Sir, I believe you were concerned about us," Houghton said seriously.

"Well—the boys from the old neighborhood, you know. Can't have the Rebels marching them about as prisoners. Just wanted to see," Kimball said a little gruffly, and turned his horse about.

"Son-of-a-bitch and I'll be damned. The old man cares about us enough to ride through the rain to the front," Harrow said, watching him go.

"Sir, I think you might have known that," Houghton said coolly. "That brotherliness is one of the things that makes us the unit we are."

"Indolent, lecherous, mad for liquor—" Harrow countered stridently.

"Courageous, bold and hard as iron," Houghton replied.

"Ignorant Hoosiers from the woods—"

"The woods breeds men."

"Insubordinate, scornful of military discipline." Colonel Harrow was chewing on a plug of tobacco he kept in his cheek and spat against an oak tree stump after he said this. Brown juice ran down the gnarled bark. "Why, if we were put into a real clutch," he went on, "with regular army people on the other side, we would be shamed. I've watched these men whine and snivel at Cheat Mountain and Alexandria. These are the men who push over sutlers' carts and take the bacon they want. Volunteers." His voice was sneering. Houghton looked steadily at him. Well, the colonel's father had been a career officer in the Fourth U.S. Infanty, and Harrow always wanted to join the "regulars."

Still, Houghton couldn't let him slander the veterans of Greenbrier, Kernstown, the retreat from the Seven Days' Battles. "Volunteers," answered Houghton. "Here because, in the long run, we want to be. And Westerners, which is the best of all things to be. You've seen the Eastern regiments!

"This brigade, with the Fourteenth and the Ohio and western Viriginia regiments, is one of the finest units in Lincoln's army. Headquarters knows it and sends us in when it needs unfaltering strength. When we are really tested, we will show our preeminence. We will earn glory.''

Harrow stared at the earnest young man. "Oh, yes, I remember. Houghton—the boy with the highest marks in glory school. An unconquerable idealist. Well, we will test your theory about the Fourteenth's mettle.''

"So it seems.''

"Lee has the deck of cards and is holding all the aces. He is going to go on the march with his huge army.''

"Where do you think he will go?'' Houghton asked, watching his canny superior.

"Where would you go? There is no food in Virginia and no pasturage for horses. North, to the green fields and the plenty of Maryland. Past that into Pennsylvania. He will go to carry the war into the very homelands of the North.'' Harrow looked away, towards the northwest, where mountains pushed at the sky.

"And we cannot let that happen.''

"No. This army will finally have to fight to win. McClellan is in the process of joining us; we will have enough men, finally. All depends on this battle. Lee cannot be allowed to go north. It would finish us. The Copperheads back home are just waiting to find an excuse to force the end of the war. No, we will meet Lee and when we do, the battle will shake the earth!''

"The Fourteenth will not be found wanting,'' Houghton said proudly. "Westerners can never stand to be second best.''

"I hope you and your shiny ideals will be as bright when this is over as they are now.''

"So do I. I shall go relieve the picket, sir.'' Houghton turned and walked towards the trenches. Harrow watched him go, shaking his head.

*   *   *   *

Delia Dugger went to her wardrobe press and opened the doors. Reaching among the taffetas, lawns, and cotton dresses, she pulled out a brown polished cotton. That should do, without hoops. She held it up to herself, stood on a chair and faced the full-length glass in the corner of her room. No, it would not do. The frills would drag the dirt, the skirt restrict her movement.

What was she going to wear? She had promised Willie McClure's eleven-year-old sister, Ruby, that she would direct their combined farmhands in the apple picking, and she had to meet her in the Dugger orchards in a few moments. A woman and a child running the farms at Duggerville! What strategies the war forced upon them.

Her eye lit on the steamer trunk in the lying-in chamber beside her bedchamber. Yes, that was it. She went and lifted the heavy lid, then pulled out the man's clothing she had worn on the ride to Martin County. Quickly she slipped out of her shift and into the trousers and shirt. She pinned her hair up under a felt slouch hat and surveyed herself in the mirror.

God in heaven! She looked like one of the colored field hands, and like a man to boot. She went into Calhoun's room and found a long leather jacket he wore for hunting and put that over the top of the outfit. The insects were awful today; the jacket would keep them from her arms. Returning to the glass she took one last, long look at herself and bent over with laughter. Pray God she did not meet anyone she knew socially. She had known Ruby Jean, of course, since the girl was a baby. Ruby Jean knew Delia was high spirited and did as she liked and would not be surprised to see her in man's clothing. But anyone else—well, the clothes were comfortable. She had been surprised last time at the freedom of movement the trousers and the shirt gave her, the casual way the cotton clung to her limbs, warm and free.

She bounded down the stairway. Trotter had saddled her mare and stood with it outside the open door. Brisk it is, she thought, for the first of September. Clear, fine weather, with no hint of rain. Good for harvesting— what was it she had promised Thomas Jefferson Brooks?—five hundred bushels of apples.

Swinging into the saddle, she headed down the north lane to the orchards. There, waiting for her, were the colored and white hands—those that hadn't gone off to war or weren't working in the cities—of both the Duggers and McClures. There was Ruby. Ruby Jean and Delia would be the overseers and split the receipts; the money from the sale of the fruit would be welcome in these hard times.

"Delia, is that you?" said Ruby Jean. "Not ridin' side-saddle and with that hat on—for a minute I thought 'twas Calhoun only young and thin." The child looked seriously at her, her green eyes peering out of a round, sallow face. She seemed as humorless and uninteresting as a possum; still, she was a stolid, hard worker and could pick these apples all day.

Delia looked at the crew. She had even called the cooks and housemaids out. Thomas Jefferson Brooks had agreed to buy the apples on the condition that they would be delivered to Indianapolis by the cars, slightly unripe, firm and unbruised, by September 5. He was contracting for thousands of bushels of Indiana apples for the spring market. It was a new idea, he explained to Delia when he wrote to her with the contract.

"I've purchased an ice house in Indianapolis," he wrote. "We will store the apples for the government at a uniform temperature during the fall, using ice. Then during the winter we will protect them from freezing. They will be available to the soldiers in late winter and early spring at the very time other fresh fruits are missing. For this I will be able to pay you a slight premium.

The governor has found ways to bypass the uncooperative Democratic legislature and is funding purchases for the soldiers in his own way.''

Delia did not care about the politics of it all. She simply knew she had hands to pay, and the money would take them into the winter.

"I want you all to pick carefully. Do not shake the trees,'' she commanded. "Bring me that ladder, Ruby Jean.'' The girl pushed it over and Delia mounted the ladder easily. "I know you househands haven't done this. Watch me. Pull the branch over to you, keep the apple sack on a high rung of the ladder and pull apples carefully from the branches to place in the sack. Then pass down the sack to the hands on the ground. Do not pour the apples and do not allow them to drop. They must be unbruised. I'll help, too, and so will Ruby Jean.''

The young girl looked at Delia adoringly when Delia handed her the picking sack, and Delia smiled sweetly. Then, up into the tree she went again.

"What do you hear from Willie?'' she called down to Ruby Jean. Delia had received a letter a week ago from her mother; her aunt had pulled the proper strings in Louisville to get a pass for Althea, Calhoun and Willie to go down the river to Memphis with the supplies they'd already collected to sell. But that had been seven days ago.

"Step-ma heard yesterday,'' Ruby Jean called out. "They were preparin' to leave. Willie and Calhoun took the freight boats with the hands; your ma is takin' the steamboat. They have reservations at the Gayoso Hotel in Memphis. It's all takin' longer'n they reckoned.''

Delia nodded and then devoted herself to gently placing apples in the sacks. By eleven o'clock the sun was high and the day warmer than she had expected. She doffed her jacket and pitched it onto the ground. The tree she had started on was almost finished; there were only a few apples she could not reach, but they were some of the largest, best ones. She stood precariously on the top of the ladder, putting her head into the branches.

Then she heard a young man's voice below. "You there, young man, pardon me. I am looking for Miss Dugger. I have been up to the house and no one was there. Do you know where the mistress is?'' As he spoke, Delia descended until finally she stood face to face with Jacob Joe Scott. She took off her hat and let her hair go free, laughing gaily.

His mouth flew open. "Miss Dugger!'' he said in astonishment. "I took you for one of the colored men.''

"It is I, Mr. Scott. I am boss of this plantation now, and I am dressing the part. Believe me, you wouldn't wish to pick apples in a dress either.''

"No, no, I suppose not.'' Slowly, Jacob Joe began to smile. Delia looked at him and thought of his brother. Zach had smiled once or twice like that, when he thought no one was looking. It was a smile she loved, not his usual cynical, uncaring smirk.

She chided herself. She had not seen Zach for over a month, not since her mother and Calhoun had left to take the produce load south. Why should it cause her a pang and an unsettled feeling when she saw this young man smile in a way so like his brother's? She did not care a fig for Zach Scott, with his insolent ways.

"Come, let's walk back to the house," she told Jacob Joe. "The hands can carry on without me now. They are going to pick all this orchard today and when they are finished move on to the McClure's stand down the hill. We are furnishing the Indiana commissary supplies for the troops. Ruby Jean, have one of the hands ride my mare back." The girl nodded.

Bottle flies buzzed about their heads and they swatted as they walked the lane, through trees laden with fruit. "The flies are attracted to the last of the peaches," Delia said. "The big reds. Here let me pick one for you."

She leaned over into the peach trees they were passing and plucked a large, luscious, gold-red peach.

"I won't be seeing the likes of this for a long while," Jacob Joe mused, rubbing the fuzz off on his trousers. "I am on my way to the wars, Miss Dugger. I thought I would stop and pay you my respects."

Delia was only a little surprised. "Thank you, Mr. Scott. I appreciate your kindness," she said. They reached the house and sat down in the large rockers on the porch, overlooking the Wabash.

"I want to offer condolences," Delia said. "My mother wrote to your brother on the death of your father, I think."

"Did she? I did not see the letter, but then Zach and I are not on good terms now. Yes, I cannot get used to Father's death. It was so sudden, and I feel as if we did not get to make a good parting. He did not approve of my going to the war."

"How—how did it happen?"

"His heart failed him as Zach and I were arguing." Jacob Joe's eyes reflected the torment the memory aroused. "My father never spoke a word after that. I had no time to part with him—nothing. I leave with his disapproval. It afflicts me greatly."

Delia did not know what to answer, so she remained silent.

Jacob Joe reached over to swat a fly on the porch rail. "I am going because I must," he said.

"Will you be in Kentucky?"

"Yes. The Rebel, General Bragg, is trying to wrench Kentucky away from the Union. The Rebels are beginning an invasion, and the Eightieth Indiana has been ordered to the area around Louisville. I will join them this next week. I thought perhaps I might entreat you to tell me"—here he looked uncomfortable—"the address of your cousin."

"My cousin? Which one?" Delia smiled brightly.

"Well, was the charming young lady I met at the ball last year not your cousin, Sophie Lavenham? We danced twice and spoke during the evening several times, and since I will be going through Louisville, I thought I might pay her family my respects."

"Ahh," Delia breathed. "The ball. I remember all that—the orchestra playing, the beautiful food. It seems so long ago. Somewhere else. It's as if I see us dancing there, in a dream, in another time."

"Yes. I do believe it was another time," Jacob Joe said, sadly.

"Still, I can tell you how to reach my cousin's house—hotel, that is. Her family runs the Lavenham House in Louisville. Yankees stay in it, now." She went in for a pencil and tablet of paper. "I can tell you how to find your way to Sophie's family."

She drew a chart of Louisville.

"Can I not persuade you to stay for dinner?" Delia asked.

"No, I must be off. I am boarding a steamboat down at the landing. But if you had a cool drink—" He lifted his eyebrows and smiled, a disarming, sweet smile that charmed her and that she hoped her cousin would appreciate.

She brought him lemonade with ice, in a silver cup. "Odd," she said. "I gave this same cup yesterday to another member of your new regiment."

Jacob Joe raised his eyebrows in inquiry.

"Tommy Brooks. He was seeking his uncle John Poore's house up the road here, to say goodbye."

"Well, I know him and will be glad to have a fellow raw recruit to learn the ropes of soldiering with. Goodbye, Miss Dugger."

As she took his hand in parting, he seemed to hesitate a moment. "I went home to the farm for only a couple of days, and I left suddenly. If you see my brother, tell him—"

"Yes?"

"I may never see him again, and we did not part as Christians should. Tell him—" Then his features seemed to freeze. "No, never mind. I cannot feign a forgiveness I do not feel. Tell him nothing for me."

Delia Dugger nodded. Jacob Joe Scott walked briskly down the lane and disappeared around the bend, heading for the steamboat dock. She watched him go, then pinned up her hair again to return to the orchard.

Louisville, the military launching point for the battle to hold Kentucky, was a confusion of activity when Jacob Joe Scott disembarked the steamboat at the end of the day. Stevedores were loading bales of cotton destined for Indiana, being shipped by merchants frightened at the rumors that the Rebel Kirby Smith might be heading towards them. Newly arrived blue-clad soldiers were looking, as Jacob Joe was, for the location of their regiments stationed around the city. Officers with muster rolls were checking recruits in, summoning wagons to carry gear, checking food stocks coming off boats.

Regiments were being assembled and rushed to reinforce the Northern forces holding the state. Jacob Joe bought a newspaper from a boy; its stories of Morgan the Raider and his strike-and-run victories over the Yankees, and rumors of Confederate reinforcements pouring over the Tennessee border to begin the invasion gripped his interest. He walked off the levy, chewing on taffy he had purchased at a stand. Some sort of decisive action was imminent, that was for certain, Jacob Joe told himself. He was eager to find his unit, but for only a few hours he wished to please himself in a life in which his choices, if not his very existence, would soon be in jeopardy.

He took out the map Delia Dugger had given him, looked up a the street sign and headed away from the river.

Federal blue was everywhere on the narrow streets; brass buttons, officers strutting about trying to prove they were "persons of importance." The Lavenham House stood up a quiet side street of Louisville, where purple wisteria vines drooped low over the porches.

Jacob Joe turned a bell ringer switch. Rinng—then a pause—rinng. Jacob Joe could imagine little hammers pounding on the bell inside.

The door opened. A slight young woman with her hair pinned back in a bun, from which it was escaping everywhere, answered the door.

"Sir? Do you wish accommodations?" she asked, in a clear, musical voice.

"For the night, I think. I am really seeking the Lavenham family to pay my respects. I met them in Indiana at a party last year."

"Ahh," said the girl, brushing her cheek with her hand. Jacob Joe noticed it was one of the most beautiful hands he had ever seen, perfectly white with rounded, oval nails which had almost no cuticle. She opened the door and he came in, turning to face her inside the hall of the stately house which served as a hotel.

"I am Jacob Joe Scott of Knox County," he said, bowing a little.

"Sir, I am pleased to make your acquaintance. Dora Lavenham is my name. I recall my sister spoke of you—"

"Your sister?"

"Sophie was at the ball. I could not be there, as someone had to stay to maintain the house. We have been busy.'' Dora walked down the hall, indicating Jacob Joe should follow her.

"At the time of the ball,'' he said, speaking as he walked, "I did not realize your family operated a hotel.''

"No,'' she laughed. "We pretend it is only a temporary expedient, that soon we will return to being waited on instead of waiting on folk. But it is an honorable operation, and we make a living at it, particularly since so many Yankees like the cleanness of our rooms and the table we set.''

They reached the door of the music room. Jacob Joe looked inside this comfortable, cozy retreat. Roses twined on the wallpaper; in the corner stood a huge walnut piano with a Yankee captain standing beside it. He was looking down adoringly at the young woman who was running her hands over the ivory keys. "Oh, oh, oh, oh—I dream of Jeannie with the light brown hair,'' she sang in a rather forced soprano.

Dora walked to the piano, smiled and tilted her head towards Jacob Joe, who stood framed in the doorway.

The beautiful sister looked up and raised just the tip of a finger in a gesture of charming recognition. Well, almost. "Ah, it's—'' Sophie could not bring up the name.

"Jacob Joe Scott, Miss Lavenham. I could not expect you to recall so brief a meeting,'' he said, smiling broadly. The Yankee captain looked mildly irritated and flecked at a piece of lint on his blue coat.

Sophie Lavenham rose and gave Jacob Joe her hand. Her chestnut curls, held back by a yellow velvet ribbon, danced about her bright, piquant face. "Why, sir, we are ever so glad to see you. What brings you to our— house?''

Jacob Joe bent to kiss her hand in the old way. "I wanted to call to see you before I went to the wars.''

"You are going—'' her eyes, which had bubbled like hot springs a moment before, cooled suddenly. "What unit will you be joining, sir?'' she asked.

He understood. In this border state which had as many different loyalties as a sassafras tree has odd-shaped leaves, Sophie's sympathies were with the Confederacy. He should have assumed it; after all, the Duggers were her relatives.

"The Eightieth Indiana Volunteers,'' he said. The Yankee officer came over, saying, "Sir, I offer you my hand.'' He introduced himself and his unit, one of the ones which would soon be going down the river to help capture Vicksburg.

With a wave of her hand Sophie directed them all to sit on the parlor chairs which clustered about a diminutive fireplace. A light blue china vase on a polished Chinese table held dahlias, and Jacob Joe looked at them fondly, remembering his mother's garden.

"I notice your admiration of our vase, sir," Sophie said. " 'Tis Wedge-wood, brought all the way from North Carolina by my grandfather, Frank Fryerson, when he came to Memphis. He had a fine genteel home, sirs."

She proceeded to tell of the North Carolina house of her grandfather as she had been told of it, of its porches opened to get the breezes, its fine lawns, of orangeries and pigeon houses and other wonderful things. "His brother and he moved within a few years of each other to the East, Grandfather to take up residence in the wildwoods of Tennessee, his brother to go to Mississippi. Uncle Bartie is a well known planter in Mississippi. He had a hundred slaves. I have been to see the place. 'Tis there I think my grandmother and grandfather have fled now that the—" her smile froze and she closed her eyes for only a moment—"now that the Memphis area is occupied."

The Yankee captain, sitting on the settee, had stretched his long legs out. He was eating candied pecans from a pewter dish on the table. He did not know he had been insulted by the tone of the girl's voice.

"Now gentleman, I must confer with my mama about our supper tonight," Sophie said. "We want to make you as comfortable as we can. Consider this your home. We will be havin' some mint julep for you on the veranda at six."

Jacob Joe watched her leave and suddenly was smitten with a pang of guilt. All this time he had been listening to the charming prattle of Miss Sophie, he had not thought once to wonder where Miss Dora, the other sister was.

As if in answer to his unspoken thought, she came into the music room from the kitchen. She was wearing an apron. "I have been doing the silver all day. Ugh, what a job! But then one must keep up appearances. We are expected to be Old South and Old South means huge amounts of silver." She smiled and tugged back one of the loose strands of her hair with that elegant hand.

"Miss Dora, do you have a moment or two to show me your garden?" Jacob Joe asked.

The girl flushed, pleased. "Why, of course. Just let me get out of this apron, Mr. Scott. I have had Joball take up your carpet bag to the Lobelia Room. All our rooms are named after flowers. I hope it will suit—"

"I'm sure it will, Miss Lavenham," Jacob Joe said, smiling. She bustled out into the hall and from there into some back room to leave her apron.

Soon they were strolling in a rather overgrown late-summer garden.

"I love to keep the herbs—salify, basil, sage—and if I had the time, I would grow all the fancy flowers. Irish bells, delphinium, tea roses. Love of gardens runs in our family, as Sophie said.''

"I see why your Aunt Althea has such a conservatory!''

"Yes. And my mother would have one, too, if we still had our plantation.'' She bent to pick off a blown rose. The golden stamens dusted her hands.

"Did you—where was your plantation?''

"South of Bardstown. It was beautiful. Truthfully, though, I like it better here.''

"Do you?''

"Yes. My father was a failure on the plantation. We tried everything. Hemp, cotton, tobacco. He could do nothing and—well, the sheriff wasn't coming, but that is only because he was a friend.'' Jacob Joe looked at her wonderingly. She wore her heart out on her bonnet, for all to inspect. And a good heart it was, so it appeared.

"We sold the plantation and came to Louisville. We bought this old house and now all is going swimmingly.''

"Your father is a success?''

"Was. He passed on last year of the fever.'' Her eyes were sad. "No, he was not a success, but we ran it for him and told him he was. Thus all faces were saved.''

They strolled to where a tottering gazebo crowned a slight rise at the back of the yard. Some thick, gnarly grape vines were set into a small arbor; this still propped up the old circular building.

"This is lovely, so picturesque,'' Jacob Joe said. "My mother would have loved it, I think.''

"Would have? Is she gone?'' The path ended; they turned about and started to walk towards the house.

"She had a wasting disease,'' Jacob Joe said. "It robbed her of the use of her muscles, slowly, a year at a time, like a robber filching things from a house a little at a time, until there was nothing left she could use. I became the cook around the house, learned to fix almost anything. But I also used to carry her into the garden where she sat in her chair. Her hands itched to dig among the dahlias, but she could not work her will on them. They would not obey and pick up the trowel. I became her hands and learned to dig, delve, make the furrows for the seeds, take the board and tamp them down. I think I inherited my love of the land from her.''

"You, too?'' Dora Lavenham looked searchingly at him. They had reached the door to the house.

"Miss Lavenham, I am so glad you showed me the garden,'' Jacob Joe said.

"Are you, Mr. Scott?'' Again, that flush that spread across her pale face.

"Yes. Now I can take the breezes tonight, my last night of freedom with—" He broke off the sentence. His eyes were eager, looking at the house. Sophie's voice floated out, still dreaming of Jeannie with the light brown hair. He stood, transfixed a moment.

When Jacob Joe turned around to usher Miss Dora in, he found her gone.

During dinner, at a table crowded with officers ready to report to Buell's army, the talk was of the invasion of Kentucky.

"Ma'am, I note you are not taking the steps others in Louisville are taking to flee to Indiana," the intense young officers asked of the house's proprietress, Adahlia Lavenham. "Are you not afraid that Louisville will be occupied by General Bragg's army? He is trying to take the state for the Confederacy."

"No," the older woman answered calmly. Jacob Joe looked at her, trying to decide how much she favored her sister, Althea Dugger. Same bright, curious eyes, same rich, dramatic voice. She seemed to be a plumper, sharper-edged version of Althea. There was something veiled about her, however; she made you pause at the edge of knowing her, did not invite closer scrutiny.

"I am not afraid," she said. "They have been stopped at the very gates of Cincinnati. Besides, I have not supported either side. My views adapt themselves to those of my guests."

"And so, ma'am," the red-bearded Yankee said, "you will take the blue tablecloth off this table and put on the gray one if the Rebels take the city?"

"I think I shall put the lime-green one on the table, captain, to avoid all political imputations," Addie Lavenham said with a tight little smile. "No, we at the hotel are in business, sir. We serve fine wines and foods, not political causes."

"May you be able to do so, madame, for years to come," the captain said, raising a small glass of apricot cordial. Then he excused himself. He needed to pack the papers he had brought with him, he explained, and arrange to ride at dawn towards the Cumberland River, where the Northern army was advancing.

"Where is Colonel Morgan, sir?" Mrs. Lavenham asked as he placed his chair under the table. John Hunt Morgan was the toast of Kentucky; defiantly he aided Bragg's advance by conducting raids on the pursuing Yankees.

"Rumors are that he is stocking up supplies near Lexington to ride hard and fast against the Yankees," the captain answered. Everyone followed him into the hall. "He is a cocksure raider, that is for sure. But we do not fear him. Small fry. Bragg is our big fish. We will move all these troops out of Louisville soon and get him." His voice echoed up the stairs, where he was bounding to collect his gear. Jacob Joe excused himself from the company and sat in the music room until Sophie Lavenham appeared to show him her collection of doll tea sets and sing him a few songs until it was time to retire.

*   *   *   *

In the East, the Fourteenth Indiana was marching to stop Lee. They were part of the relentless army, a juggernaut which rolled after the commanding general as he made moonlight passage into the Northern farmlands.

Lee had split his army in four, then five parts to try to accomplish as many goals as possible on his campaign into the heartland of Maryland and Pennsylvania. Several of his generals clustered in the mountain passes around Harper's Ferry and prepared to seize the Federal arsenal and supply depot there.

Then, in an odd chance of war, a Northern soldier found Lee's secret orders and took them to McClellan, now in command of the army again, and with that new knowledge "Little Mac" moved to force Lee's army out of the passes where they lurked. The armies met in battle at South Mountain on September 14, 1862.

The Fourteenth stood in a reserve position in the Battle of South Mountain, then camped on its summit the evening after the awful battle.

The night was brisk that evening after the battle; campfires illuminated the dirty, bearded faces of men who had bivouacked in a different place every night for over a week, with no knapsacks and only cold rations.

"How many of the Rebels are down there in that town way beneath us, sir?" Isaac Crim asked Captain Houghton.

"At Sharpsburg? Some say 120,000 men."

"God. That many?"

"Well, that's what headquarters believes. General Kimball thinks it's far less."

Houghton was eating a piece of honeycomb he had found on the trek up South Mountain. He looked up to see David Beem approach, his step buoyant. Houghton smiled, broke off a piece of it and handed it to his friend.

Beem sat down, cross-legged, and Houghton watched him survey the faces around the campfire. What was Beem thinking? Was he as nervous as Houghton himself about the coming battle up here? Men from all companies were mixed around this campfire; with so many ill or gone, there were only three good full companies left, and they had become close comrades. There was Sergeant Jess Harrold, Beem's boyhood friend, the blacksmith who dropped his hammer and took up a rifle the day they received the news from Sumter. And there, next to Harrold of H, was Bo Reilly of Houghton's company. His face was in the shadows as he slowly eating corn meal mush from a tin; in between bites his jaw hung slack with nervousness.

Beem slapped the young man on the back. "Can this be Reilly? The regimental clown? Quiet as a man at the ladies' quilting circle meeting?"

Reilly turned his face until the shadows caught it. Tiny freckles spread beneath his eyes and across his nose. "Did you see the Confederates beneath us, Captain Beem? On the side of this mountain? I walked down a piece."

Beem soberly nodded. "I did, too. Hundreds, fallen on top of each other—trying to hold us back while Lee's men retreated off this mountain."

Bo Reilly stared into the fire. "I can't get 'em out of my mind. I've seen lots of corpses in this war, but these were the worst. Pinched, thin faces, like they was starvin'.

"Mebbe they were," Crim put in quietly from the shadows of the flickering fire.

"I stooped to look at their rations," Bo said. "Captain Beem, there were only little balls of corn meal, fried up like bullets. That's all they had."

"Yet they fought like tigers," Captain Houghton put in.

"Almost won, mebbe they will yet." Bo Reilly said, then was silent.

"They had all different uniforms," Crim put in. "Some dark brown, some light as dust."

"The Southern regiments are outfitted by their states," Houghton told him. "There's a lot of variation."

"Some of 'em looked like they just had on farmers' shirts," Bo said.

Houghton watched the boy pull a blanket up around his shoulders. The wind was coming up, bringing the scent of rain.

"You take that from a dead man, Bo?" Houghton asked, pointing to the blanket.

"Well, that Rebel can't use it now. 'Tisn't his war any more. They're all unburied out there, Captain."

"I know," Houghton said, softly. "The Secesh had to leave them to go off the mountain and regroup to meet us. We haven't buried our dead yet either."

"Both sides, walkin' over the bodies of their dead to get into camps to rest so's they can kill some more. Fought yesterday, fought today, fight tomorrow. Wonder if it'll ever stop," Bo said, in a strained voice.

"Sometime." Houghton's eyes grew canny. He wanted to change the subject of what would happen tomorrow. Or would it be the next day—whenever it was, the thought of these two armies clashing in their totality was so horrible it was beyond speculation.

Beem changed the subject for him. "Bo, I don't think I ever asked what made you come to the wars when you should still be sitting in school in Martin County?"

"Hell, Captain Beem, I don't know. Wisht I was there, in school, at this very moment. Remember the school, Captain Houghton?" He looked up with eager eyes at the man he admired. "You and my brother were the big boys there in Mt. Pleasant. You could say the Presidents in order and all the rivers on the earth. I 'member listenin' to you while I sat with the little tykes. I had first and second grade there, sweet as honey and nice as pie."

Houghton smiled and nodded at this good young man, his friend's little brother, whom he had known since Bo could barely crawl. "I remember, Bo, how you used to carry in kindling for the stove. Nobody ever asked you to. And the day we locked the teacher out because he didn't bring us a Christmas treat, you crawled through the window and let him in. You were teacher's pet."

"Aww, Captain. I jest felt sorry for the feller. He couldn't afford to treat us, not on what they paid him."

There was a round of chuckles and the men poked the fire.

Bo went on. "Well, I can tell you how I come to join the Fourteenth, Captain Beem. Captain Houghton knows it; he's known us since before I was born. M' brother George was behind my coming, in a ways. Not that he could help it. George had been sickly all winter. He was coughin' a lot and Ma and Pa were worried out o' their heads it was consumption." Bo's eyes constricted; his gaze was far away.

"Then come the firin' on Fort Sumter," Bo went on. "George got it into his head he was goin' to join the regiment Colonel Kimball and Captain Brooks was a-raisin'. Said he didn't care if he was sick, he weren't goin' to be the shirker. Every family was sending the first son. But he started coughin' and took to his bed, and said he'd get up soon and go. Ma started cryin' and Pa shook his head, and I went down to the middle of town and signed the roll." Bo smiled a little, showing a broken-off upper tooth. "Captain Brooks knowed I was underaged but I told him I was goin' in George's place and he let me pass. Nobody else questioned it cause I was tall enough to be eighteen, I 'spect."

Someone started to sing over to the west. It had to be the only other campfire the regiment built—for G Company. The sounds drifted through the crisp, chilly air.

Dearest love do you remember, when we last did meet
How you told me that you loved me, kneeling at my feet.
Oh, how proud you stood before me, in your suit of blue
When you vowed to me and country, ever to be true.

Van Dyke appeared. "G Company is singing those sentimental songs. I can't stand it." The voices sang on:

Weeping sad and lonely, hopes and fears how vain
When this cruel war is over, praying that we meet again.

"You don't like the singing because it makes you sad?" Houghton asked, looking up at his friend with a smile. He knew the answer was "no."

"Because it's maudlin. They torture themselves until they weep thinking about the hearthsides and sisters and mothers. Sweet torture."

"Well, it relieves the tension," Beem said, not looking at Van Dyke.

"I suppose so."

"Captain Houghton, come with me to the singing. I'd like to join in," Bo said. Houghton nodded and he and Beem followed Bo Reilly to Company G's campfire.

"I hope they sing 'Somebody's Darling,' " Bo said as they approached the circle of bright, lean faces.

"I hope they don't," Van Dyke said. He had decided to follow his fellow officers, in spite of his disgust at the emotional singing. "McClure always asks for that one, and we left him at Rockville."

They had arrived at G's campsite, and the men looked up at them. "You talkin' bout John McClure, Captain?" Tommy Thompson had overheard the last of the conversation. "When will he be back?"

"The doctor didn't know," Van Dyke answered. "Lieutenant Landon stayed down with them, over thirty of them. McClure seemed to catch his death of lung fever out there on picket duty for Pope's army. He and Simpson—Simpson was out all night and when he came in he was sicker than a dog. The colonel sent him home, finally. Good thing. This way he's avoiding disciplining for going down among the tents of the camp followers."

Thompson looked up at the faces of the officers. He was glad they had come. Here, as they sang, he could hold his own. His strong baritone was the best in G Company, and G was the best singing group in the regiment.

"Sit down," he said cordially. "Reilly—you too, Captain Beem, Captain Houghton. We were just getting ready to sing—" here he smiled mischievously at Van Dyke. The men tuned up a little and then broke forth, in three parts.

Somebody's darling, so young and so brave
Wearing still on his sweet, yet pale face
Soon to be hid in the dust of the grave,
The lingering light of his boyhood's grace.

Van Dyke and Houghton had not seated themselves with the rest, but stood in the grove of oak trees, talking softly.

"How many can you field when we fight, Will?" Van Dyke wanted to know.

"Thirty-nine. Just thirty-nine," Houghton admitted. "The rest don't have shoes, and their feet are bound with rags. Or we left them at Rockville in the hospital." The notes, sung in close harmony, blended sadly:

> *Somebody's darling, somebody's pride*
> *Who'll tell his mother*
> *Where her boy died?*

Van Dyke looked out over the mountain valley, over gaping holes where shells had exploded, at disfigured uprooted trees and at a lone man, covering the bodies of the dead with blankets. "Or we left them at Greenbrier, or Kernstown or under the mud in the swamps of the Chicahominey," he said.

"There, too," Houghton agreed ruefully. "Thirty-nine of the hundred bright boys of Martin County are all I have left."

> *Who'll tell his mother*
> *Where her boy died?*

The notes died away. There was silence. Then Tommy Thompson spoke up, softly, pointing towards the mountains. "The Rebs have gone into the passes of that next range. Where will we fight them?"

"There's a large valley area near Sharspburg," Van Dyke answered. "Colonel Harrow and I rode out to it on reconnaissance a while ago." His voice boomed out of the shadows, as if it issued from a disembodied specter. "They seem to have settled in there."

"What's the area like?" Thompson wanted to know.

"It's an area of Dunkards—religious people like the Amish. Good farms, strong farmhouses, open fields and fences."

" 'Twill be a battle of the ranks," Bo Reilly said, almost in a whisper. "Mostly before, we have fought the pickets—or in trenches lately, as they sniped or fired shot at us. When we fight them now, they will march across the field, bands playing, colors flying, jest like Napoleon."

"And so will we, 80,000 of our men, 100,000 of theirs," Thompson said. He was looking at a picture of his sweetheart, Lina.

"One line will follow the other," Van Dyke said from his dark shadowed spot amidst the trees. "When one line is gone, another will arise. Then another."

"To be mowed down like a scythe cuttin' wheat," Bo murmured, his young voice awed, near to trembling.

They sat for a long while silently, and then someone rose and put a few more logs on the fire.

"Can we sing a hymn, boys?" Bo finally asked.

They turned and nodded. Tommy Thompson smiled a little sadly at him.

"What would you like, Bo?" Houghton asked. As the youngest man in the regiment and the pet of all, he had the right of choice.

" 'Eventide.' I think it might help me."

Tommy Thompson set the note; the others began. The fire flickered brightly; the voices resonating through the clearing were strong, full of courage, and even faith, interpreting the hymn's stately harmonies.

> *Abide with me, 'tis eventide,*
> *The day is passed and gone.*
> *The shadows of the evening come,*
> *The night is coming on.*
> *Within my home a welcome guest,*
> *Within my heart abide,*
> *Oh, Savior, stay this night with me,*
> *Behold, 'tis eventide.*
>
> *Oh, Savior, stay this night with me,*
> *Behold, 'tis eventide.*

The slow, solemn harmonies of the beautiful hymn echoed over the mountain top.

Thompson put the picture of his sweetheart away in his pocket, stood up and brushed off his pants. The smell of rain was in the mountain air, perhaps even the smell of autumn, with its crushed leaves and pungent campfires.

Beem and Houghton walked through the encampment. As they reached C's campsite, Walter McClure approached Houghton. "Please, captain," he said.

"Yes, McClure?"

"I—I want to shoulder my rifle and fight at Sharpsburg when the battle comes."

"How do you know Lee will not slip away, as he has done before?"

"We are covering his only road of retreat. He is backed up to the Potomac."

"That is true. But I think we will need you with the surgeons, McClure. To carry out the wounded—"

"Let their comrades do that this time. I have spoken to Surgeon Burkhart, and he can get along. I came to fight and I wish to stand with the others."

Houghton looked at him searchingly. Certainly he did need Walter

McClure, any man he could get. But Walter had not fought since western Virginia.

Walter persisted, "I'll certainly be as good as the raw recruits we took on back in Washington City."

Houghton had to concede that was true. He was having to teach these men to hold and shoot a gun. What good would they be against the Fifth and Twelfth Alabamas, who fought like wart hogs and shot like Comanches, and all those famous Virginia brigades they kept hearing about?

Houghton drew in his breath and made a decision. "All right, Redskin. It's your war now, too. Clean your gun and get ready to fight."

The fighting did not immediately commence, and the Fourteenth and much of the rest of the army marched down the mountain to Sharpsburg. On the evening of September 16, they camped by a creek and ate a cold supper.

"Houghton," Van Dyke said, as they watched the men clean their rifles and check ammunition, "why did Little Mac wait so long to call us down to fight Lee? Every hour he waited was one more hour for more Rebels to prepare for the battle."

"Lieutenant Colonel Coons says it's because he wanted to perfect his plans."

"Finicky son-of-a-bitch," Van Dyke retorted. "Maybe too finicky."

"You can't tell the Fourteenth that. Or any other soldier in this army."

"You're right. Did you see the way they welcomed McClellan outside Frederick? He rode by and thousands of hats went into the air. The shout started at one end of a line of ten thousand soldiers and went all along it."

"Mac loved it. The soldier's idol. But now he must prove that faith. Tomorrow, here on this very ground."

The wind rustled the dry poplar leaves in back of them. It was starting to drizzle. Some men were already stretching out, open-eyed and apprehensive, staring through oak openings towards Antietam Creek.

"The Colonel has orders for silence tonight for the enlisted men. No talking," Van Dyke said almost bitterly.

"Yes. I'm not quite sure why. Lee knows where we are."

"Stupid order. I hope we're better commanded than we have been."

"General French will command our corps well. He is a good officer. Round as a tub of lard but no coward."

"Hooker is going in first. Harrow and Coons are polishing their swords. They are ready to take us in right now. Kimball will stay in the rear."

Light rain filtered on the rubber blankets the men used to cover themselves. Houghton noticed Bo Reilly reach up and pull the blanket over his head, then curse as his feet stuck out in the rain. Houghton looked down; water ran in rivulets off his own boots.

"The officers and men both will have their chances," Houghton said. "Harrow can judge if we Western volunteers stand cowards or heroes. We will see if I am right and we cover ourselves with glory."

"Or blood."

"Both. They seem to go together," Houghton said, putting away his haversack.

Beem checked the men of H Company. Jess Harrold was sleeping without a blanket.

"Sergeant, do you need covering up?" Beem asked his old friend.

"Lost my blanket, Captain. But I'll borry me up another one from a Reb tomorrow."

"Sleep well, Sergeant," Beem said, reaching down to clasp his friend by the hand, to tousle his shaggy head. "Most of the men are tossing and turning like dervishes."

"I'm too ornery and evil to lie awake," Harrold said. " You know that well as anyone. I could sleep through hell."

As Van Dyke walked about checking the men of G Company, Bushby Quillen called him aside.

"Captain—did I hear tell that Redskin McClure was goin' to be in the line tomorry?"

"He asked Captain Houghton's permission to fight with us instead of standing ambulance duty."

"Captain, I don't want no goddamned savage fighting beside me. Keep him away from me." Quillen's voice was edged with hatred. Joe Sholts, beside him, mumbled assent.

"Why not?" Van Dyke asked coldly.

"Cain't trust 'em. Sneaky. Everbody knows they fight from trees and won't come out like men. I'm a-gonna be nervous enough tomorrow without havin' a ugly Shawnee beside me."

"He isn't a Shawnee. He's a Potawatomi. Part Miami, too."

"All the same. All like niggers. Besides, he knows how I feel about him. Some of the rest of the men, too. Prob'ly jest lookin' for an opportunity to knife any of us in the kidneys. If I have to depend on him to help me over a fence or cover me in a retreat—waal, I don't want to be within a country mile o' that Injeean. Besides, he's bad luck."

"We all will be within a country mile of each other tomorrow and I think you may be glad to have any man by your side. I will be. Now be quiet. It's a no-talk night."

Houghton did a last check of the men under the soggy blankets.

A quiet, nervous hum issued from one of the lumps. It was Bo Reilly, singing himself to sleep. Houghton sat down against a tree. The stately words of the hymn reverberated in his mind as Bo hummed them.

Oh, Savior, stay this night with me
Behold, 'tis eventide."

A sad, portentous silence settled over the encampment.

"Fog. Rolling up from the creek and river beds. It has such a soft, harmless look about it," Houghton thought the next morning as he drank coffee made from the water of Antietam creek. "Napoleon's men saw the rain the night before Austerlitz, and they thought it a good omen. Our men fear it." The guns had begun, stridently and to the right as the camp prepared to advance on this ironically beautiful fall day in Maryland.

The men had roused themselves and were ready, their eyes almost eager. Soon they would be going soon across someone's farm, where other soldiers were already fighting. There were cornfields and a church over there, beyond the creek and pleasant homes, so folks said. Homes that looked like some in Loogootee and Mt. Pleasant. The people had fled into the village nearby.

The companies of the Fourteenth had formed in line, along with the Seventh West Virginia, the Eighth Ohio, and a new recruit regiment from Pennsylvania. A few paces away Houghton noticed Van Dyke arguing with Bushby Quillen; Quillen was pointing at Redskin McClure. The discussion became heated, the words "damned Shawnee" could be heard. Bushby Quillen was waving his arms. Finally Van Dyke pushed the soldier into line. Walter McClure looked up inquiringly at Houghton.

"Never mind, Redskin," Bo Reilly, who was standing next to the Indian, said. Then Walter McClure's lips began moving.

"What're you doin', Redskin?" Bo wanted to know.

"I'm saying a prayer."

"Hail Mary?" Bo knew Walter McClure was a Catholic.

"No. A Potawatomi prayer." Houghton heard the band striking up at the regiment's rear. George Washington Lambert was directing "The Yellow Rose of Texas." Why had he selected that idiotic Rebel song?

"Let me tell you my prayer," Walter McClure said softly as the commanders, Lieutenant Colonel Coons and Colonel Harrow, swords raised, rode past to ford the stream.

Reilly nodded, licking his lips, as the line moved forward through dry leaves and trodden grass towards the knee-deep water.

"Great Spirit," Walter McClure's young voice resounded, "Give me the manhood to right this wrong. Make my limbs strong as those of the bear's, my courage as great as the wind's, my heart courageous as the Eagle's. Let me live and die for my tribe. May no one take my spirit, but if it is my time, let me give it to God freely."

The sounds of cannonade and musketry made it difficult to hear, but Houghton could catch the words amidst the clink-clank of the canteens. The men were straightening accoutrements, raising their guns to cross the creek.

"A good prayer, McClure," Houghton shouted. He wanted to reassure Bo as much as anything else. He felt a special responsibility for him, indeed, somehow Bo represented the whole point of officering to Houghton. Bo, from his home grounds, his best friend's little brother, now under his command, dependent.

Looking at Bo, but shouting at all his men, he called out, "Men, we're told ours is a mop-up action for the corps which has gone earlier, but we do not know what we will encounter. May we find glory for our regiment and nation. It appears the brigade is almost ready. In just a moment Lieutenant Colonel Coons will give the order to wade the creek." Houghton turned for a moment's reflection. The band was playing a new march he did not know, and that unsettled him, vaguely.

The order came. The regiment's colors fluttered in the September breeze. Two circles of stars with one star in the center, stained with powder, frayed from Greenbrier, Kernstown, Seven Days, and all the rest. Glory, he heard the word all around him. It seemed to float in the very fog, now being pierced with shafts of morning sun. What was glory? Was it in this flag? In this line so bravely spread out across this autumnal field? In the hearts of Bo or Isaac Crim? Was that glory?

He did not know. The water came up about his boots. He almost lost his balance and rocked an instant in the stream, flowing rather swiftly from the recent rains, then he pressed on, up the muddy bank.

The Fourteenth stacked knapsacks on the other side of Antietam Creek, then reformed in almost perfect order. Houghton looked briefly down the line at his little company, thirty-nine men, and past them to the officers he knew and valued, all with their own shrunken companies. There was Beem, beside him Porter Lunday, with his heart as big as all of Maryland. Was the picture of Lunday's wife in his pocket? There was Van Dyke, grim and leather-faced and irascible. Coons and Harrow were ahead on horses, personally leading. Kimball, monitoring the brigade's movements, would be in the rear.

French's Division of Sumner's Corps—that was who they were. Sumner had already sent word back that Hooker's troops, who had gone in earlier, were supposed to be having an easy time of it ahead of them. His communications with headquarters, though, had been vague. French's Division were to simply finish off what Hooker had started an hour or so ago. On, on across the fields. Houghton's heart thrilled with the splendor, the bands playing, the bayonets gleaming silver in the sunlight, the flags fluttering, the pure, unadulterated beauty of combat. Then they came to the cornfields where the battle was in progress.

"What's this?" Houghton thought, his mind abruptly shifting as reality replaced illusion, and the real scene jumped into view. His heart leapt into his throat. "This is not a mop-up action. These men are closely engaged—in a slaughter." Sights and sounds came at him. Cornstalks cut off, there to the left, his feet cold and wet. He barked an order. "Halt a moment; they seem to be deciding where to put us in this melee—"

Screeching noises, a shell a minute, "Advance! Corn sheared flat, as if with a scythe. Everything gold and green. Fog lifting. Sheen of bayonets almost blinding for a brief moment. Front of our line, up there, is going to 'Fix Bayonets, shoulder guns'—but—order coming—'right shoulder shift.' What is going on?"

The gray smoke cleared for a moment; he could see the cornfield and farmhouse before him, and his mind spun as if it were a kaleidoscope. "God, the corpses. Hooker's—or is it Sedgwick's—men have been in a maelstrom for these two hours. Corpses on top of each other. Here it comes! Duck—ah, there are two men in F down. Bits of bodies, rifles, fence posts flying all over in the air. More musketry, cannon shot. On, on. We do not falter, we march! Better than on drill. Brave Fourteenth. What is that silence from the Confederates? Four lines of them coming at us and they do not shoot—maybe just a single line there, hold their fire until close enough— there it is. Oh God. The Northern line goes down like bowling pins."

The lines in front broke and ran.

Van Dyke's hoarse voice sounded through the scream of the shells, "The Northern Sixth Maryland's turning tail."

The word spread quickly and soon the men of the fleeing regiment were among them; young, fresh faces with only a stubble of beard, eyes an agony of terror. These were raw recruits and this awful battle their first. Their bright, untrampled colors were being carried off with hoopla by the Rebels.

"Yellow asses, go back," Crim shouted, others took up the cry. A few shamefacedly returned, but most scampered for the woods.

Suddenly Harrow shouted a command from Kimball's courier: occupy a small rise south beyond the farmhouse. Near it was a sunken road; the Rebels were forming there, on the bodies of the dead from the early morning's engagement. The battle was clearly centering its whirlwind vortex on this spot. It was a desperate moment. Walking through heaps of the dead and scores of wounded, Houghton and the other officers placed their troops facing the Rebels.

"Ammunition," Houghton thought. "We have ten rounds per man. Not enough today. And there are guns—they have started above us, big ones. Lee has brought in reinforcing artillery from elsewhere on the field. Aiming all at us."

He looked up and as the dark smoke cleared, he could see the enemy positioning themselves in full force was only sixty-five feet away in the sunken road.

"I have become an automaton," Houghton thought numbly later. For two hours they had stayed here at the road. The Confederates reinforced their lines, came in with flags flying, they shot at them, the lines shattered and collapsed and individual soldiers dropped down to defend their ditch. None had come across it.

"This must be hell and I have died and am being punished by seeing everyone I care about in this regiment wounded or dying," Houghton thought through the numbing shock that possessed him. He could see Beem through the black smoke, numbly glaring through the smoke at the Confederates. Lunday lay, face up, by Beem's side, his eyes staring in death. Ten yards behind Houghton, with his brains spilling out, was Bryant, who was the preacher's son from Mt. Pleasant.

McCord, a distant cousin of Bo Reilly's from the Bedford Road, had died in Bo Reilly's arms and Reilly had cried like a baby as the dying man said, "Farewell, Reilly, farewell, captain. Go and avenge my death on the traitorous bastards—"

Crim was grumbling to himself; Houghton looked at him through the smoke.

"Can't hardly stand the air," Crim said loudly. It was unbearably oppressive here at this sunken road. The moisture in the air and the temperature which was near eighty lay about the men like a smoldering coverlet.

Houghton had almost forgotten he was an officer. Now he lay on his stomach shooting with the few men who were left. He re-loaded the rifle he had picked up from a dead man, using the last round of his ammunition. It was difficult to load; bullets had to be jammed into guns fouled by too much shooting.

He looked into Crim's face, sooty, mixed with sweat. An apparition from hell; they all were. Stuck here for eternity. Heaven was Martin County ten billion years away, and they would never see it again.

Bo Reilly was on his mind; he had just sent him as one of the two men who bore Lieutenant Colonel Coons blood streaming from a wound, to the rear. Walter McClure had volunteered to help; Bo had picked up the other end of the stretcher and started before Houghton could stop him.

" 'Twill be dangerous, Bo, to go through the lines that way. Let someone else—"

"I'm ready, captain. I want to earn my glory, too." He nodded to Walter, and they were off, trotting for the rear.

His glory. Where in the hell was it anyway, today, here? Even the band members had made their way to the front and were entrenched with the rest of them, getting wounded and dying, too. Blood, moaning, death and maiming that never stopped. Piles of bodies with legs and arms sticking out like children's toy dolls in a heap. Glory School hadn't covered what was happening on Antietam Creek.

Major Lige Cavins of D Company had assumed command for the wounded Lieutenant Colonel Coons. There was hardly an officer still unwounded. Five lieutenants had been killed. A sergeant was commanding A; no one seemed to be commanding companies B and I, and their fragments had assembled around Houghton.

"Those bastards are putting up white flags," Thompson shouted from his spot near a bullet-riddled tree.

"Mebbe they're surrendering," Bushby Quillen opined. The men stopped loading their rifles and waited in eerie silence. Sharp musket fire rat-tat-tatted across the ditch again.

"Some sort of trick," Harrow shouted out. "Watch for an advance; they seem to be changing fronts."

"Colonel, we're out of ammunition," Houghton shouted. "Major Cavins has gone to the rear to try to locate more—"

Harrow was not listening. A courier had made his way to him.

"Fourteenth, attention. We are commanded to retire."

An outburst of outrage rocked the line. "Shit, do you think we're goin' to go after we've held this line three hours and lost half the regiment doin' it?"

"Shove the order up your gun barrel."

"My cousin got his arm shot off and just bled to death holding this craphole. His dying words were 'Stay on and fight.' Do you think I'm leaving after that?"

"Colonel, I'm afraid my legs won't take me away." Houghton recognized Harrold's voice. There was a raucous bravado in his tone: "I've been wounded four times and they don't function very well."

Harrow sprang into his saddle and raised his sword sternly. "Attention, Fourteenth, I say, I have—"

Little by little the Fourteenth rose like ghouls in the acrid, heavy air, but not to follow Harrow into retreating.

"What the hell are they doing?" he demanded of Houghton, who no longer ducked to avoid the whistling bullets.

"They refuse to act the part of beaten dogs and sneak away from glory," Houghton shouted. Harrow's lip curled in disbelief. The men of the Fourteenth Indiana were not listening to their own colonel, but instead were wandering about, bending low over the bodies of their fallen comrades, getting ammunition.

Harrow spurred his horse. "Shoot, you goddamned volunteers, then," he shouted back at the men. Still, Houghton thought he detected something like admiration in his tone.

Cavins returned. He passed among the skeleton staff of officers; soon Beem, Van Dyke, Houghton and a couple of the Ohioans put their hats on their swords and led a charge against the Rebels.

"Off this hill at last," Beem shouted passing over the bodies of the fallen Rebels. "They are running like coons from the hounds," he shouted at Houghton, joyfully and then turned to see the shock in his friend's face.

"Will, you're wounded."

"Nothing. Just a ball in the shoulder. Let's drive them on."

Giving the Hoosier yell, the tattered remnants of the Fourteenth and the rest of Kimball's brigade drove the Southerners out of the bloody lane they had held all morning. "Bring the colors forward!" Cavins shouted as Beem and Houghton urged the men on. D.C. Hill's division was finally melting before the sustained onslaught that had cost this part of Lincoln's army so much.

Houghton, holding his painful shoulder, turned around and looked behind him. Where was the rest of the Northern army? Certainly not here. Only the dead, the dying, the deep smoke and somewhere off to the side some tom fool Eastern regiment parading around in the wrong place with a green flag. What hole had McClellan's army fallen into? Any fool would have had reinforcements ready to push the Rebels back and take the field. For the first time in the day he cursed with all the energy he had. The pain of poor leadership was worse to bear than the pain of a Minie ball buried deep in his shoulder.

As the afternoon faded into early evening, the fiery struggle between the two giant armies fizzled and then flickered out with the dying of the light. It was as if the spent forces sank onto the battlefield with a giant collective sigh, exhausted from the cataclysmic effort that had wrung all vital energy from them without giving either side victory. The Fourteenth Indiana Regiment and the rest of the Northern army settled into dismal bivouac on the bloody battlefield. A chill wind began to blow and the men, unprotected in the evening air, listened to the eerie and disturbing moans of the wounded all around them.

Beem brought Surgeon Burkhart to Houghton; the surgeon probed the wound and found that the ball had passed almost through him. He poked out the ball, bound up the shoulder and Houghton stood, staring into the distance.

"Are all the men accounted for?" he asked.

"No. Several missing. Jess Harrold can't be found."

"But he was wounded four times."

"I know. But during the last charge he somehow made his way to his feet and onto the field—" Houghton shook his head in amazed silence.

"Mooother—" An agonized voice cried out nearby. "Tell them we never gave an inch, Mother." Houghton looked towards it briefly, then went on.

"McClellan has sent his commendations to the regiment," Beem said.

"Commendations," Houghton said bitterly. "What we needed him to send was a full reinforcement, instead of the damned Irish Brigade marching around with all their satin sashes. Their colonel was so drunk he fell off his horse. Worse than nothing. We could have won—"

"French has sent a praising dispatch to Kimball. He is calling us the Gibraltar brigade. Says we have covered ourselves in glory."

"Gibraltar. A rock surrounded by the blood of the bravest and the best." Tears came to Houghton's eyes and he turned from Beem. The faces of McCord and Bryant and the other fifteen men wounded in his company flashed before his eyes. "Where's Bo Reilly?" he suddenly demanded.

Beem shook his head sadly. "Nobody seems to know."

"We're going to look for him—and for Harrold," Houghton said, wincing in pain as he rose.

They wandered among the fallen and imploring victims of the battle, tormented because they could not stop to attend them. Harrold was not to be found; he was located the next morning by the burial detail out on their grisly work by the Rebel line. His head streaming blood, delirious, Harrold had wandered in and out of the Rebel pickets to finally collapse by a tree.

About midnight Beem and Houghton wandered into one of the outlying field hospitals. There they found the stretcher of Colonel Coons. His wound had been stitched up and he lay, unconscious, between life and death. Beside him, unattended because he was dead, lay young Bo Reilly. A Rebel bullet caught him as he had almost reached safety. Walter McClure was by his side; he had refused to leave until someone came to take Bo away, and he was tending Colonel Coons. They arranged for Bo's burial.

"We could walk over the entire length of that wretched lane on Rebel corpses," Beem said as they returned to the bivouac area. "I can't stop hearing the din. I don't think it will ever leave me, as long as I live." He put his hands over his head as if to drive out the sounds of the battle that still raged within his skull, tormenting his thought.

But all Houghton could think of was Bo Reilly. There, lying on his back, Bo's face had a quizzical look on it. The freckles stood out on the bridge of his nose, and Houghton remembered him standing sturdily beside the teacher in the Mt. Pleasant schoolhouse, defending the poor old man from tormenters. A good, purely good young—boy. There were so many like him on this execrable field, whose lives had been springs of decency and promise, dried up in a moment's time. The future was robbed of them, the nation would be poorer.

"Surgeon! Captain! Stretcher bearer"

"Mother—"

"God, somebody kill me, please I beg you."

Glory. They had achieved it; he understood now. It meant honor and sacrifice and endurance beyond all hope. But it also meant stark horror and pain, and men begging like babies for somebody to shoot them on a darkened, chill field. And Bo, never going home to walk the fields by the schoolhouse at Mt. Pleasant, Indiana again.

Houghton's brain was spinning, tortured with the noise of artillery, constant musketry, the cries of the wounded, his own exhaustion. "Oh, Savior, stay this night with me." Hands reached up to Beem and Houghton. They bent to give drinks from their canteens, filled with the bloody water of Antietam Creek, as best they could.

Houghton's shoulder began to throb. He felt weak and dizzy. Beem, alarmed, made him sit down by a tree. The world began to spin, and instead of the imploring voices of the moaning wounded, he heard the chorus of strong young men around a campfire. Four part harmony, slightly off key, expanded to fill his mind, larger than the pain.

> *Oh, Savior, stay this night with me,*
> *Behold, 'tis eventide.*

"With Bo and with them all, oh God," he prayed. And then he slipped into unconsciousness.

Late September, October, 1862

Chapter Seven

Horace Hogue opened the drawer of the cabinet in his tiny kitchen on the old George McClure farm. He took out three sets of worn silver knives, forks and spoons. For a moment he stood running his gnarled finger over the twining roses in the pattern, then marched to the table and carefully set three places for supper.

Brushing away a few toast crumbs, he set linen napkins beside the forks. He stared at them as they lay on the table. Wrinkles. He had borrowed his sister-in-law's flatiron and tried to iron them nicely after he washed them in his small tub, but all he had done was scorch the linen.

He went to the cupboard. Opening the door he carefully took out three plates, white china with tiny green and pink tea roses around the edges, and cups and saucers of the old-fashioned sort, with no handles on the cups. He held them up to be sure they weren't dusty, then carried them one set at a time to the table.

Each one at the right of the knife, wasn't that it? The voice of his mother interrupted his concentrated musings. "Well, Horace dear, those are the very cups your father and I went to housekeeping with."

Catherine Hogue was there to have supper with him. "We were given twelve by Uncle Dan'l and Aunt Martha. Glad you are using the set I gave you. Lettie, of course, isn't using hers." She did not intend the comment as a slur at her unmarried daughter, who had followed her into the room, nor did Lettie interpret her mother's words in this way.

"Well, I have small use for china cups of my own at home, Mama," Lettie said. "You know that. But still I am glad to have them. They're the most delicate things I own. Odd they have no handles, though," Lettie said.

"Well, in our day things weren't so dainty. Men took their coffee and poured it into the saucer and blew on it to cool it."

"Yes, well." Lettie pulled off her gloves and put them on a small chiffonnier by the doorway.

"But then none of you young folk want to hear about the bears and

Indians and ugly things your grandfather George and his father endured in Pennsylvania and Kentucky, do you?'' Catherine said.

"Here, Ma, sit down," Horace said. "I fried a nice slice of ham and cooked some potatoes."

Catherine looked proudly up at him as he seated her and Lettie at his small table. Really, Horace was a good man. It wasn't his fault that he married so young and poor little Grace had died bearing that tiny, dead child. After that, he never wanted to look at another woman, had withered on the vine and sunk inward, like a frosted pumpkin. But he loved his mother and sister and his nation, too, with a fierce, defending love.

The three family members cut their ham and covered the brown fried potatoes with pepper and salt. They passed around cinnamon apples, corn relish, and hot biscuits, chatting about this and that in soft voices as the shadows deepened. Horace rose and lit the oil lamps.

There was a pause in the conversation. Then, as if he had waited as long as he possibly could, and now could restrain himself no longer, Horace blurted out, "Ma, Uncle Billy is selling the farm."

Catherine Hogue's mouth flew open. She put her fork down by her plate and looked her son directly in the eyes. "What do you mean, selling the farm?"

Horace tried to evade the piercing glance. "Says he cain't save it. The bills aren't paid, and corn and wheat so low you cain't give 'em away because of the war. Says he got into real trouble buyin' the property next door, too—the orphant home property. He has to do something, so he's offerin' this farm for sale."

Catherine Hogue said nothing. She looked off through the darkened window, towards the hill in the back of the property. Finally, she cleared her throat a little and said, " 'Twas there, on that hill, we first viewed the land. Came in among the girdled trees before Tecumseh even thought to threaten half the state. Raw and rough 'twas, with slashes, as if the land were hurt. Grandma Jane brought flowers with her and birds flew over our heads. Pa reared the house, there, up there on the hill, and we moved it on rollers later, towards the road."

"Still," Horace persisted, "Billy says he is a-goin' to sell it and move into town."

"Well, he is goin' to have to think again," Catherine stoutly affirmed. "He is not the only one in this family, even though he did inherit the acres. No, I have a stake in this land. My heart is tied to it, and it aches to think it might pass out of the family." She rose from the table and picked up a lamp. In spite of her children's protest, she went out the door into the blustery autumn night and headed towards the big house. Lettie and Horace followed behind her.

"Why'd you have to say anything?" Lettie demanded of her brother.

"Jest a-suppose I was to let her hear after the fact?" Horace answered, his face contorted with anxiety.

Billy McClure was smoking a pipe by the old fireplace in the downstairs room. His wife, Esther, was combing the long hair of their youngest child, a beautiful girl of eleven who squirmed with impatience and pain in the hands of her mother.

"Billy," Catherine demanded at once, "what's this I hear about selling off?"

"Now, Cat," her brother said soothingly, getting up.

"How he looks like Pa," Catherine thought to herself. "That blush that illumines the freckles all the way to his red hair line. Pa, Pa, I miss you still. How you would fret to hear the acres are in danger."

"Cat—this damned war," Billy offered, spreading his hands apologetically. "All the profiteers in the East are in cahoots with old Lincoln and they're driving me to the poorhouse. I can't sell a bushel of corn at a profit."

"Still, we can't be selling Pa's farm. It was a grant from George Washington for fightin' with George Rogers Clark in the Revolution."

Billy hit the palm of one hand with his fist. "George Rogers Clark—all this family ever talks about is some dusty old history. I don't care a damn for the family tree, just as I don't care a damn about whether the North wins. We ought to settle it up, amongst us all—" His wife nodded firmly. This second wife of his, Esther, married after Billy's other children were gone, was from Kentucky, from around Danville, and her folks had owned slaves.

"Just a minute, Billy," Horace said. He had come up behind his mother and had quietly put a hand on her shoulder. "You are talkin' out of turn. You ain't goin' to tell us to settle the war after Shiloh and Antietam. Our boys' blood is not goin' to be spilt for nothin'."

Billy McClure gave his nephew a sideways glance. "We ain't talkin' about spilt blood, Horace. After all, I guess I'm enough of a patriot. I marched off to the Battle of Tippecanoe when I wasn't hardly sixteen. We're talking about wheat and harness and accounts at the store. Horace, you don't know what it is to run a farm."

"We have to do what we have to do, Cat. This world ain't heaven, you know," Esther said. "My old home had soldiers marching through it this very month," she added. She took the brush and pulled back hard on Effie's hair, regathering it decisively into her hand to braid it.

"I know what Billy said about the North ain't right. And what you're doin' about the farm, ain't right neither—" Horace said.

Young Effie let out a squawk. "Ma, you're pullin' too hard, I told you."

Catherine had been pondering. "Billy, in a way this is my farm, too. You know that. Polly and the rest of 'em don't care any, old and infirm as they are. But I can't let it go out of the family. Pa's memory would be disgraced to have that happen. They came so far, lived through so much, to claim these acres. This land has seen so much. John and I were married in this very room. Nancy Jane and Jack's Alfred used to climb onto mother's lap when you yourself were only half grown here.''

"I know, Cat. But what can I do?'' Billy set his pipe down on the table and looked searchingly into his sister's face.

The old grandfather clock chimed in the corner. Esther had settled down and was calmly braiding Effie's hair; still, tension hung among them all, and they did not speak for a long moment.

"I'll tell you what, Billy,'' Catherine said with inspiration. "I could sell my house and let you take out a loan from me. With the sale of the house, and with what I have in the bank, I'd have enough for you. Only until times get better, as they will.''

Her brother looked at her. He said nothing for a long moment, then, "I don't know. It's all you have. Anyways, seems like a man ought to be able to take care of his own.''

"We all have to be able to help in these bad times, brother,'' Catherine said. "Perhaps I can move in with Horace.''

"Yes, there's room, Ma,'' Horace said. "It might solve the problem. Then, when Uncle Billy could pay off the loan, you could get something else in Vincennes.''

"God knows I don't want to lose the farm,'' Billy said, ruefully. "I'd do almost anything to keep it from happenin'.''

All this while Lettie had been silent, watching the scene from the doorway, as a spectator might observe a play. She spoke at last. "I don't intend to come out here to this lonely farm. I'll take lodgings in the town.''

There was a silence, while this knowledge sank in. "And how will you live, Niece?'' Esther McClure finally wanted to know. She tied bows on the braids she had made, and Effie hopped away from her mother's chair.

"I have my—salary,'' Lettie said, smiling proudly. Catherine looked towards her with eyes that revealed complicated emotions—pride that Lettie was really on her own, helplessness that she would not be providing a home and—fear for the daughter who depended on tonic far too often to ease her pain.

As they walked down the lane to Horace's small hired man's cottage, Catherine said, "I think we'll all be comfy. The other house in town wasn't right for us. 'Tis only for a few months, a year at most.''

Horace dropped into step beside his sister. "A lot can happen in a year,'' he said to Lettie. "See that you watch yourself. Women, even modern ones, don't belong alone in lodgings,'' he said.

Lettie lifted her head. "Not your concern, anyway,'' she said haughtily.

Then she stepped rapidly ahead to hold the door open for their mother, who turned to look at both of her children with tired eyes.

A handsome carriage pulled up in front of the Thomas Jefferson Brooks house in Loogootee, and a driver opened the door. A slight woman poked her head out, looked nervously up and down the street, then alighted hesitantly.

A voice called out from the screen door of the house, "Harriet, come on in, for heaven's sake. You haven't been over here in such a spell you seem like a foreigner." It was Harriet Houghton's sister, Susan.

The screen door opened and Harriet crept in. "You know how I feel when I go out. 'Tis a miracle I do go out after so many years of bein' afraid of a cat's shadow. But I mustered my courage."

"Well, that says a lot for your finding religion," Susan Brooks said. "Mother has just made sugar cakes. Let's set and have some tea." She led her sister into the parlor. Harriet went to the piano and picked up the picture of her son Will in his Army of the Potomac suit. She sighed. Hannah Poore came in with a tray of tea cakes, watching to be sure they didn't slide off onto the floor and crossed to get a peck on the cheek from her daughter.

"Mama, I have a letter from Will," Harriet said, fishing in her pocketbook. "It's from the battlefield there at Sharpsburg, and I wanted you to hear it. It's—awful."

"He is all right," Hannah Poore said with apprehension. "The paper said he was wounded."

"Yes, in the shoulder. He'll recover," Harriet said. She took out eyeglasses, put them on her nose, and began to read the letter. " 'September 19, 1862. Dear Mother: I could a tale unfold. 'Twas an awful fight, Mother! I'm wounded—don't start, it's only a scratch, merely a Minie ball struck my left arm. No bones broken, wounded but doing nicely and my spirits are excellent. But the boys, Mother, are nearly all wounded or dead who were with me.' "

Harriet went on reading the letter, of the days before Antietam, of the wounding of so many of C Company at the awful, bloody, sunken road. Will Houghton's grandmother, Hannah Poore, sat stone still, listening anxiously to the details of proud, fierce fighting and death.

"Listen to this," Harriet Houghton said, pointing her finger at a line of the letter as she read, " 'The bullet went into my arm and rested against the bone. The surgeon, Dr. Burkhart, squeezed it out the hole it went through, and it is healing now. It was as nothing compared to the other wounded. The surgeons were covered with blood from head to toe from amputating, and I felt guilty asking Dr. Burkhart to come for my small wound. Still, it might have poisoned.' ''

"Ahh," said Susan Brooks, white-faced. She sat down, and her mother looked at her, surprised.

"Susan, you have always been so strong. Here, drink some of this tea and eat a sugar cake to give you strength." Hannah Poore put the plate under her daughter's face, but Susan waved it away.

"I helped bury Pa there in the wilderness," she said, "and Thomas and I took care of so many sick and dying at Hindostan Falls. But the thought of all those young men, their fine strong limbs gone in one bloody day. I read they have piles of arms and legs. And I keep thinking of Lewis and now Tommy off in Kentucky." She flopped her head down to keep from fainting, finally felt the blood returning to her face and sat up.

"Harriet," she said, thinking suddenly of her sister. "It's you who usually do this sort of thing. Yet there you are, unmoved."

Harriet Houghton was walking about with the picture of her son in her hand. "Just before the battle at Antietam Creek," she said, "as reports came in of Lee's progress and the army's pursuit, I did not think I could have any more fear and still live. I was livid with fright for Will. Somehow it seems different now. Knowing he has gotten through it calms me." She looked up at her brother-in-law, who had come into the room. Thomas Jefferson Brooks had his account books from the mill under his arm, but seeing his wife weak and white in a chair, he dropped them on a table and went to her with concern in his eyes. Harriet Houghton folded the letter into her purse and crossed the room to the couple.

"Susan, Thomas—I know you are out of your wits about Lewis and Tommy. What have you heard?"

"Nothing," Thomas said a little sadly. "Except that he had arrived at Louisville and was waiting with another recruit, Jacob Joe Scott, for Lewis and the regiment to arrive from Covington. They are probably there by now, and are supposed to be taking off in pursuit of that Rebel general Braxton Bragg."

"The papers say Bragg missed his chance," Harriet said. "That he remained too long without attacking the Northern army and now cannot hope to fight and win. Still, he's drifting around Kentucky. The Northern troops can't let him stay there."

"So the papers say," Thomas Jefferson Brooks said dryly. "But I am learning never to trust them. They say whatever they think will look good in forty-eight point type on a given day, and they never get close to a battlefield."

"Let us pray they are right and the Confederates are leaving Kentucky," Susan Brooks said. "The Rebels are realizing the North is close to closing off the Mississippi River. A fight there in Kentucky would be awful."

"And if fortune should favor the South there," her husband said, "our Indiana Copperheads could do real damage to the Union cause here in Indiana, where folks are so tired of the war and out of money. The political opposition they raise can damage Governor Morton's—and the President's—strength in running the war."

"Doesn't anyone want a tea cookie?" Hannah Poore was asking.

"Ah, Mother," Harriet said, glancing fondly at the older woman. "Living so long in the woods, where we never saw any sugar but a maple block, has made you love treats."

"Well, there's nothing like a sugar cake to ease a troubled heart. If the trouble isn't too bad, that is," Hannah said. Harriet walked to the table, picked up a cookie and then set it down.

The door burst open and the teenaged Brooks boys, Eustace and Seymour, dashed in. "Ma," said Eustace exuberantly, "we've been to the music store and bought that ballad everyone has been singing. "It's called the 'Vacant Chair.' "

He put the new sheet of music on the piano. "Aunt Harriet, play it," he said, starting to turn the first page, which showed a family dining room with a big table and chairs around it. On the table was a soldier's picture, much like that of Will Houghton or Tommy Brooks.

Harriet Houghton sat down and played a little of the sad verse, then, on the refrain, said, "Eustace, you sing it for us."

The young man cleared his throat. Grandmother Poore, Susan, Thomas and his younger brother Seymour all gathered behind him.

We shall meet, but we will miss him,
There will be one vacant chair
We will labor to caress him
When we breathe our evening prayer.

Seymour joined in, his young voice strong and full of feeling. The notes of the piano, which needed tuning, sounded harsh and tinny.

At our fireside, sad and lonely
Often will the bosom swell
At remembrance of the story
How our noble soldier fell.

Harriet Houghton stopped playing and limbered up her fingers a moment or two. "I suppose," said Eustace, "it is the same for the Southern families as it is for us."

"Maybe it is," his mother Susan said. "I never think about them."

"I do," Eustace said with an odd sound to his voice.

They sang the chorus, and Harriet began the next verse.

> *How he strove to bear the banner*
> *Through the thickest of the fight*
> *And uphold our country's honor*
> *In the strength of manhood's might.*

"I think about it," Eustace said, with strength in his voice. "And it seems so wrong to me that the country goes on killing, maybe even my brothers. Southern families have sons too, and they could be crying at this very moment. We should end it all."

The adults were strangely silent. Thomas and Susan Brooks turned away, finally, and went to the window, looking out onto the street of Loogootee.

Grandmother Poore walked to the table where the sugar cakes lay, untouched. She picked them up and carried them to the kitchen as the plaintive music continued to float out behind her.

Slicer's barn above Hindostan Falls was lit again by murky candlelight. On this cool autumn night, the Knights of the Golden Circle were seated on stools after their rites and ceremonies.

The huge rock of a man who was their leader spoke. "Brothers, our cause has seen some triumphant moments this fall. Governor Morton's tyranny is bein' opposed by new peace Democrats elected by the people. They are sick of the war."

There was an affirmative rumble of the black-hooded men around the circle.

"Now the real matters the war is about are comin' to light," Thornton Slicer (for that was who it was) continued. "The President has issued an infamous paper making the niggers equal to white men."

The small man dressed in knight's chain mail who served as Marshall of the Ceremonies spoke: "He ain't goin' to take it back, neither. Waited till the battle there in Maryland was over and spit it out. Mebbe the sojers will rebel and jest leave the army."

"They ain't yet," another voice said.

"Some o' the officers are resignin'? I heerd tell that a couple from the Fourteenth are thinkin' of it."

"Nobody important. No, I don't think it's a-gonna happen thataway,"

Slicer went on. "Politics and secret freedom societies like ours'll end this war without destroyin' the Southern cause. Vallandigham is at work for us in Congress."

"The governor is out to get all of us who oppose him. He put those spies on us," said a very young voice across the room from Slicer.

"Some say 'twas Tommy Brooks," Thornton Slicer answered. His voice was evasive; he owed a lot of debts to the Brookses and did not wish to involve them in what he was doing. Besides, one of their own—"I don't know. I know they never really know when or where we meet and it's goin' to continue that way. We'll be rotatin' our meeting times and places. Down in the cave sometimes, too. Keep 'em on their toes. They don't dare do nuthin' anyways. We're within our rights o' free assembly."

"For now, brothers," the little man said.

"I don't know what more we can do right now," Slicer said. Then he looked into the shadows, to a spot out of the circle where a tall man stood, watching but not participating in, the proceedings.

"Council Member S., can you tell us if we have any more orders from the Northern Mask?"

Zach Scott answered in his low, even voice. "No. We are all watching the political scene. Democrats are going to be elected in every office in Indiana, except perhaps the governor's office. And our leaders are waiting to see what course the military action takes. The Northern Mask is, of course, in touch with John Morgan."

"Is Colonel Morgan comin' with his cavalry to take Indianney?" an older man wanted to know from across the room.

"Not at present," Zach answered. "But his raids are effective in Kentucky and when the opportune moment arrives—"

"I can't wait," the very young, eager voice said. The hood slipped back and by the light of the candles Zach recognized the young man. It was Eustace Brooks, who had just recently joined the Hindostan castle of the Knights of the Golden Circle.

"Well, we will all have to wait," Zach said sardonically. "So the Northern Mask says, and he calls the shots. He is the one who is the link between the political part of what is happening and what we in the secret societies do. He even comes and goes in Virginia, in Richmond."

There were nods of respectful surprise, and Zach felt he had gone a bit too far in revealing the inner workings of the group. These people in the castles of the Knights did not need to know everything; even he did not know how the intrigues in the peace movement operated. Utmost secrecy in the inner circles which connected with the Confederacy was necessary.

"We must wait for Northern losses, for more distress, discouragement. When we have seen ten thousand more die in this senseless butchery, then the people may rise and support us. Then we can act. If the news for Lincoln's army is bad, it is good—for the peace that will grant the South independence or let it come back to the Union with slaves. Or, if they won't agree to peace, to raise the Northwest to join the South!''

There was another affirmative rumble through the circle, and the men rose from the benches. Zach joined them. They assembled and crossed hands to give the closing ceremony.

Together they chanted, "We do promise to fight for freedom and state independence and to defy tyranny, even if it means with our arms and lives. Down with Lincoln, and the Constitution forever. Hurrah!'' They gave the secret handshake, clasping each other by the wrists, and filtered towards the door and out into a night whose only light came from far-away stars.

*   *   *   *

David Beem sat in his tent near the battlefield. He was writing to the wife of Porter Lunday. He dipped his pen in his inkwell:

I now have to perform the most painful duty of my life, and one which fills me with grief and sadness. Tell his children that their father died a glorious death. When they arrive at maturer years, they will know they lost an affectionate parent in the great struggle for a priceless government. I am filled with regret at our inability to send his corpse to you at present. The great number killed at Antietam Creek and the want of facilities for embalming have rendered it absolutely impossible. Myself, Colonel Harrow and General Kimball did all we could to have it done. It may be a satisfaction to you, however, to know we buried him decently in a country cemetery under a beautiful tree.

Blotting the letter, he folded it and put it in an envelope. Then he took the picture of the lovely woman and two fair-haired children looking like angels and tied them carefully into a neat parcel, along with the letter and the Bible Lunday had always carried. He stared at the still-open parcel, reconsidered, then took out the photograph and put it in his own Bible.

Houghton came in, and Beem rose to greet him. He told him that he was keeping the photograph. "I want to remember what he lived and died for," he said, not meeting his friend's eyes. "And—they probably have a copy at home.''

"I imagine so,'' Houghton said, sensing the anguish behind the words. Beem handed him the letter he had written, and Houghton read it with a sigh. "Yes,'' he said, "it seems to mean so much to them to be able to have the body buried back home. But it is almost impossible after this battle.''

"So many burying details, so many unidentified graves.''

"George Reilly, Bo's brother, has died back home," Houghton told him. "Mr. Reilly is bereft of his only two sons in one week. He is leaving Loogootee this morning to come here to get Bo's body to bury next to George's."

Beem was dismayed. "No, he can't do that! Bo's body will have been buried over two weeks by the time he gets here."

"I know—I told him by telegram not to do it, but he insists."

"How will you—"

"Dig it up. Find the spot the burial detail thinks it is, unearth the boxes and look inside."

"My God, Will."

Houghton rubbed his hands together briskly in the chill of the late September day, felt just as sharply inside the tent as out. "It was hard enough to bury Bo; now it will be ten times harder to disinter him. They can't even let the poor boy rest in peace."

Beem looked at him earnestly. "Who will you get to help?"

"I've asked Walter McClure."

"A good choice. Do you want me to go?"

"No. You had enough of this grisly work with Lunday and the rest of your company. Two of us will be more than enough for this job."

Will Houghton and Walter McClure leaned against their shovels by the long mound where the Union dead of Antietam were laid to rest. They had long, binding bandages over their noses and breathed only through their mouths to avoid sickening at the overwhelming stench of death.

"Luckily Lambert remembered where they put him," Walter McClure said.

"I wouldn't want his job. It seems nice to be in the band, staying out of range of the shelling, generally, having young ladies clap their hands as you march through the towns. But then they always seem to draw burial duty as compensation—"

"Which one of these—" Walter gestured towards three plain pine boxes which lay side by side in the pit they had unearthed.

"There are no names." His voice was oddly muffled through the bandage; still, it was clear enough to understand.

"We'll have to jump down and raise the lids," Walter said.

"Wait, let's not do it quite yet. Let's just rest a moment more." Will Houghton could not quite bring himself to do it yet, to disinter from a foul grave the fair-haired child of his youth. He gazed towards the hills in speculative thought.

"When we fought at Antietam Creek," he said, "and even now, as our generals try to decide what to do here in the East, it seems as if we are the only fighting force in the world.''

"Yes," Walter agreed. " 'Tis hard to think there're other groups of us who have to go through this sort of thing, several armies really, fighting this war. Everything really isn't happening just here." His voice came in little pants, as he inhaled through his mouth.

"Today," Will Houghton said, "they are marching in Kentucky. Following Bragg, trying to push him out and secure the waterways there. Captain—that is, Colonel Lewis Brooks will be leading his Eightieth Indiana Regiment. The colonel of the Eightieth resigned and my cousin has been given his position as colonel."

"Yes. We miss him here."

"He was destined for greater glory. Or death—here, had he stayed." His arm described a large arc, the awful, hideous ugliness of the field after the battle.

There was a silence. The scars of destruction were everywhere on the edge of this gouged-out, blackened cornfield. Unexploded shells, broken cart wheels, mixed with scattered playing cards, canteens, even ragged coats. And to the side lay a pile of mangled horses, partially covered with brush and burned.

Finally Walter McClure spoke again. "In the time of my father, when the Potawatomi buried, everyone who had known the warrior walked in single file without speaking a word. They threw gifts into the grave and sang and blessed the Great Spirit for having sent their friend to be with them for the time he was alive. They asked Him to receive their friend and welcome him with joy and love. Then they covered the grave lightly, wishing the body to go back to the elements from which it came."

"A good custom. We had no time for any memorials to these thousands—" Will Houghton's voice broke. Over four thousand men had died on the fields around Antietam Creek.

"Just as well. The way white men usually bury it seems as though they want to make the body immortal. Expensive morticians who embalm. And for the rich, burial vaults, steel caskets—"

"Not for these," Houghton sighed.

"No, not for these." Walter folded his hands and tilted his head towards the heavens. "Since no one said a prayer, I will say the Potawatomi prayer for the moving of the bones."

He indicated with his hand that Houghton should bow his head. "Great Spirit, our Father who art in Heaven, bless these men and forgive us for disturbing their resting place and these, the bones of our friend. Grant our hearts rest and take the plague of this battle from our minds. May the spirit of our friend know we come in peace. May he not send bears to turn and chase us in the hunt, nor ride the winds on his pony, we pray, in search of us on stormy nights. In the name of the Father—'' He concluded the prayer and crossed himself. Houghton looked up to see Walter McClure jump down into the common grave near the battlefield of Antietam. Then, the young captain smiled a small smile as he thought of Bo sending bears against his old friends. No, he wouldn't do that. Bo was too afraid of bears himself. Houghton's smile grew wider. The Potawatomi prayer was a good one. Bo would understand; he'd have to. Suddenly, he felt more at peace than he had for many a day.

*   *   *   *

That same week, in late September in Tennessee, Althea Dugger went into the headquarters of William Tecumseh Sherman for the second time in one day. She sat quietly in a straight-backed chair, smoothing her skirt, waiting for the general to see her, as he had not been able to do all week. Finally he came out, looking haggard and worn. ''Mrs. Dugger, I will see you now,'' he said, ushering her into a small office out of which he ran the Northern-held territory along the Mississippi around Memphis.

''Sir, I hope my son Calhoun and his friend Willie are serving you well in their mission.''

Sherman looked at her without response.

''I must admit we were surprised to have you ask that my son and his friend go South on this rather strange errand.'' She touched an artificial orchid on her hat, a little uncertainly. One wanted to say the right thing to this influential man. ''We wanted to serve you.''

''Madam, I have heard the goods I sent with them have arrived at my old friend, General Van Dorn's, southern camp. Your son Calhoun has not returned. It is, of course, of major concern, because I gave safe conduct to the two of them with the condition that they return promptly. Anything else would be a breach of trust.''

''I assure you, sir, that honor is a word every bit as important to Calhoun as it is to you.'' Althea frowned, but not too much. It took all one's patience dealing with Yankees. Honest but coarse this one was. He had seemed to want to go tit for tat, exchanging trading privileges for this odd, dangerous mission—taking a hearse filled with goods to Sherman's old army friend, now on the other side of the conflict.

''I am not as yet concerned,'' Sherman said. ''They have not really had time to pass through the lines and be back here. Perhaps by tomorrow.''

''Yes.'' Althea watched yellow poplar leaves drift down outside the window. They were falling early this year. It had been so dry, drier than she had ever seen. Creeks were tiny trickles. Even her mouth seemed desiccated.

She opened her bag and took out a lozenge, putting it primly under her tongue. "Sir, there is something else. You know that I am longing to get out to my papa and mama's property. They have flown south to Mississippi, and I am in constant worry about depredations on the premises."

"I know, madam. I do not believe your property has been damaged, but there have been so many corps, of both armies, through this area that I cannot be sure of anything at this moment."

"Why do you not let me go out there and check?"

Sherman sighed. "I have told you there are several reasons. The first is that I am still checking your credentials."

"You have letters of introduction from the commanding officer in Louisville who knows my sister—"

"Yes. But he does not know you personally. You are trading people—"

"You knew that," Althea said shortly. "We delivered some of the best hams and cornmeal that you have seen in a year, you said."

"So I did. Still, you are traders."

"What are you afraid of, sir?"

He stared soberly at her. "Frankly, madam, trading people from the north have made my life very difficult this last month or two. I trust no one now. Traders have been swarming about the city, contracting for cotton to sell to the Northern and Southern armies. Five thousands bales recently sold for a half a million dollars. There is very little cotton anywhere, and captains and even colonels in the Northern army are becoming cotton contractors."

"And what does this have to do with me?"

"I can't answer that, madam. Possibly nothing. But since many a woman who comes down to visit in 'dear Dixie' has money sewn into her petticoats to contract for cotton—"

Althea Dugger sat up stiffly in her chair. "Sir, I hope you don't imagine I am here to speculate in cotton. And I am shocked to think you are imagining anything about my petticoats."

Sherman looked tired. He ran his fingers through his lank, black locks. "There is no way to tell the black ewes from the white ones. I have given strict orders to all parties that cotton speculation is to cease. We cannot trade with Rebels at the same time we are fighting them. The cotton fortunes that are being made in the South are used to outfit new units to fight and kill our Northern soldiers."

Althea stood up from her chair. She looked squarely into Sherman's eyes. "Sir, on my honor as a lady and a citizen of Indiana I swear to you that I wish only to look at my family home, to see to it that it is guarded from harm. My father gave up his health to build our home, fought the wilderness for it. After this war is over, if there is nothing to return to, he will die. If I need to go out as a wayfarer, alone and dressed as a farmer, I shall go. I intend to protect my childhood home in any way that I must."

Sherman took a long look at the woman before him. "I miss my home, too," he murmured, standing to go to the window. "One of the worst things war does is destroy homes. Birds can't nest where muskets shoot. They leave their nests. Families can't live where the cannons are. So many innocent, beautiful things die. I do not like being a part of it. As a Christian, I deplore the killing. But worse would be to let my country be ripped apart like an old sheet." He returned to face her across the desk again.

Althea said nothing. She had heard that Sherman missed his wife terribly. Months ago he had grown so nervous about the war that he had some sort of a breakdown and had to leave his command. With a pang she realized they all must suffer, all these men who fought this war. "We all do what we must, sir," she said, more kindly. "May I go out to Fairchance?"

Sherman stood. He looked beyond her, at the door. "You may go out and see to your business. I will send Major Bachelder, one of my staff assistants, with you. For your own protection and to help you with the details of securing the plantation, of course."

"Of course, sir," Althea said rather coolly. Then, on impulse, she put out her hand to this good, decent man so aggrieved with the cares of war.

In the Mississippi camp of General Earl Van Dorn, Calhoun walked restlessly about, watching the activity of the cavalry camp this flamboyant officer commanded. Horses snorted in the woods where they were being fed, soldiers dressed in shabby Rebel gray came down the road bearing water buckets on tote sticks. The rivers of Mississippi were as dried up as those of Tennessee, and watering these horses was a matter of hours, not minutes.

Calhoun was waiting for Willie McClure to bring the horses and the hearse about; they were a day overdue on their return to Memphis. Van Dorn had welcomed them graciously, tried on the new gloves and boots sent him by his old pre-war friend Sherman, thrown a fairly fancy dinner in his tent and ended the evening, by getting drunk on peach brandy with them.

That was three days ago. Well, they couldn't go back; the two horses that had drawn the hearse were rubbed sore and needed to rest. In the meantime, Willie had fretted and chafed about his brother, Archie III. He had received no word since the letter that said Archie had been wounded east of them; indeed there was no way to get word to him.

Now Willie came up the road from the wagon ring. There was one horse attached to the hearse. "I'm takin' the bay and goin to see Archie," Willie said. "Don't tell me not to, Calhoun."

Calhoun looked at his friend, exasperated. "Willie, you know General

Sherman made us give our words of honor and sent us here on our personal recognizance, through the lines. If we both don't go back—"

"I don't give a damn, Calhoun. I cain't think of nothing else but Archie, lying there only fifty miles from us. If we had more time, I'd ask you to come with me to find him, but one of us has to go back."

"How you goin' to get through the lines, you fool? Your orders from General Sherman aren't goin' to be worth a bag of chickpeas down here in Rebel Mississippi."

"I asked General Van Dorn for a pass. I'll take m' chance. I got to see Archie, find out if he's dead or alive."

"An' leave me to face Sherman and Ma alone."

"You'd do the same thing in my place. Why, just picture if Delia was sick and needed you."

Calhoun's face didn't change and Willie knew he had chosen the wrong thing to say. Delia never seemed to need Calhoun.

"All right, Will. I'll come with you. No sense in our separatin'. I'll see if we can send a message to Sherman, and then we'll simply take our luck when we return."

The next day they were in Ruggles Command, Confederate Army of the Mississippi, at Jackson, Mississippi. And when Willie McClure discovered he had arrived too late to bury his brother Archie III, dead of dysentery and complications of a wound received in skirmish fighting the month before, he yelped like a coyote, with outrage and frustration and grief.

"I'm a-goin' to get these goddamned bastards that got Archie," he said. "Pa's gone and Ma's gone, and Archie and Ruby Jean and me were all that were left. I might as well die a hero as a shirker."

Sadly, Calhoun watched Willie head east to find a Confederate unit he had a particular yen to join.

Major Edward Bachelder drove a rented rig down a long lane lined with elder trees.

"The mistletoe is taking over the branches," Althea murmured beside him.

"There is no one to cut it down, I suppose, ma'am." Major Bachelder said, guiding the horses around holes in the rough road.

"Well, at least I suppose they are spending all their time seeing to my father's crops. Jonas is the colored overseer. Papa depended on him a good deal in the last few years. After all, my papa is in his late seventies—"

The house at the end of the lane was growing larger and larger as they approached it.

"Have you been here much, ma'am in the last few years?" the major asked.

"We have made yearly visits with the childrenin the spring, when the azaleas were in bloom. Mama had beautiful azaleas, put in the year I was married. They have had twenty years to grow."

"So long, ma'am?" Major Bachelder smiled. "That does not seem mathematically possible, unless you were joined in wedlock at thirteen."

Althea smiled. She was used to compliments of this sort from men. Her sister always told her she had one of those baby faces that never quite grows up (leave it to Addie to say it that way). Well, Adahlia had grown as plump as a pony, while her own figure was only five pounds heavier than before Calhoun was born.

"Sir, you flatter me," she said, almost automatically. She looked up into his eyes and saw it was a silly thing to say. She saw the honesty in his almost shy smile. There was not a line in his face, although under his black slouch hat was a head of the full gray hair which marks a man prematurely gray.

"Tell me, Mrs. Dugger, how long have your father and mother been gone?" Edward Bachelder asked. "Things seem a bit down at the heels." They had come to a stop by the porch, which had two boards sticking out of it. He helped her down from the rig, and she took his arm.

"They left eight months ago to go to my uncle's in Mississippi," she answered, looking around the yard as they walked toward the front porch. "But what can have happened here?" One of the hinges was off the screen door and the small, tidy yard inside the picket fence near the front porch was a bunch of lanky, dried up strings. Just then a young colored woman came to the door, drying her hands on her apron.

"Miss Althea, is you here?" she cried, from behind the door, almost as if she dreaded admitting the daughter of her master.

"Myrtle Jean, let us in," Althea said, and the slave woman, with distressed eyes, opened the door.

"The house is mussed beyond bearing," Althea said tiredly, dropping her gloves and pocketbook on a loveseat in the parlor. Major Bachelder set down her carpet bag and looked around at the fine hangings of damask, the embroidered firescreen, the tray with blue-etched venetian wine glasses.

"Miss Althea, don' blame me noways," Myrtle Jean burst out.

"Well, I don't see why you can't dust these tables and keep Papa's books in line on the shelves. It looks like a ghost mansion."

"Miss, things ain't goin' proper 'bout these parts," Myrtle Jean said in a nervous voice. "Jonas keeps us housefolks out in the fields pickin' crops."

"Crops? How many of the field people are left?"

"Six of us altogether. Well, acourse Saffronelley ain't able to pick or work atall no more. Only Jesse is here in the house now and she ain't doin' much."

Althea looked fixedly at the young woman. Myrtle Jean was a child when Althea left the plantation, but she did know her from her visits back home; her mother had always praised Myrtle Jean as a good servant. Lately, during her mother's more frequent ill spells, she had left a good deal of the plantation's care on Myrtle's shoulders.

Althea looked beyond the colored woman to Major Bachelder, who had walked to the mantel and picked up a small bird-cage music box. He was admiring the rosewood in its base. "My pa was a fine cabinet maker," he said. "The joining here is very fine, indeed."

"Yes," she said to him without releasing Myrtle Jean from her glance. "It came from a shop in the garden district in New Orleans."

A couple of slow, unwound notes from the music box clunked as the major handled it. Outside real birds sang in the bright, September sunlight. Althea was waiting for Myrtle Jean to say whatever needed to be said in way of explanation.

The girl looked as if she might cry. "Miss Althea, the Devil done grabbed hold of Jonas. He got us waitin' on him jes like quality folk and servin' him ham and eggs at your pa's good 'hogany table."

Althea stepped forward a pace. She felt her anger rising. She would let the girl go on with all her story. The major set the music box down and looked at Myrtle Jean with cold, wary interest.

"Worst though—oh, Miss Althea, they go at it night and day up in your ma and pa's bed. Unner they very own satin marriage cov'let."

Althea's voice came from between clenched teeth. "*Who* goes at what, Myrtle Jean?"

The girl glanced over her shoulder at Major Bachelder. She licked her lips nervously. "They—fornicatin'. Jonas and m' sister. You can hear 'em all over the house sometimes, and it can be in the afternoon or morning even and—"

"Never mind, Myrtle Jean. I think I had better go find Jonas. Where is he?"

"Why, he—" Her eyes went blank. "Why, I doan rightly know where he is." Althea exchanged glances with Major Bachedler; he gestured towards the door.

They left the girl alone and walked out onto the porch and down the steps again. The major strode silently beside Althea down the path. "What's in that big barn?" he asked, looking up a slight rise.

" 'Twas where Pa kept the cotton crop in the old days."

They came to the large, hinged double doors; one was open. Inside they could hear grunting and tugging; something was being shoved about. Althea pulled open the edge of the door and decisively swung it back to enter the barn. There, inside, were two young colored men she did not remember loading a wagon with cotton bales. Beside them was her father's colored overseer, Jonas.

"Selling off the crop, boy? General Sherman will not like that at all." Major Bachelder pulled a pistol and went to grab Jonas's arms.

The overseer shrugged. He was a young man in his twenties, with light brown skin and thin lips. His voice was smooth, oily. "Missus Althea, I was jest investin' a little for your pa's return." The two young boys stood sullenly.

"Well, Jonas, then you won't mind my taking any investment money you may have been making," Althea said, the calmness in her voice belying her pounding heart. She ordered the oldest of the two boys, a frizzled-haired, gawky boy of about fourteen, to search Jonas's pockets. He hesitated; the major gestured with the pistol and the boy went through Jonas's pockets and then turned to gesture helplessly; nothing was in the pockets. Jonas's eyes were inscrutable.

"You won't find Northern gold pieces in his pockets," the major said. "We'll have to search the house now." He placed Jonas under arrest and ordered him to wait.

Then Althea and Bachelder turned away from the colored men and strode towards the house.

"I intend to find out who that cotton shipment was meant for," Major Bachelder said. "There are so many men from the East, jewish merchants travelling about contracting for this illegal cotton. General Sherman is throwing them in jail. Maybe Jonas will talk."

They reached the porch. "Let me go up to my parents' bedroom myself," Althea said, turning towards the major.

"Mrs. Dugger, I am afraid I cannot let you do that," Bachelder answered, his pistol still in his hand. "For your own safety. We have found odd things afoot here, and we do not know what is upstairs."

They started up the mahogany staircase. "Of course you are right," Althea sighed. "I had wished to protect my parents' privacy. From what Myrtle Jean said—" She could not fully voice her apprehension.

It was fully as bad as she thought. There, in the corner of the room, Myrtle Jean was pulling on the arm of her very drunk sister, Jesse, who was sitting with her legs bare and crossed, Indian style, and her bodice open.

Whisky leeched onto the oriental carpet from a tipped-over jug; the bed linen had stains of all kinds on it. Jesse was singing a little song to herself.

Ole Dan Tucker was fine ole man
Washed his face in a fryin' pan.
Combed his hair with a wagon wheel
Died with a toothache in his heel.

"I ben tryin' to git her dressed, Miss Althea," Myrtle Jean said in a whining, morose voice.

"Well, you are not succeeding very well." Althea strode over to the collapsed heap of a woman slumped like a rag doll on the floor. She gave her a good, swift kick in the posterior. "Get up, you slut. How dare you profane my parents' bedchamber! I'll see you whipped."

The woman left off singing and said in drunken, taunting tones, "Cain't whup us no more, missus. We gone be freed any minute by Massa Lincoln."

"Is that so? Well, I'll show you that a determined woman may whup a slut any time it is necessary." She dragged the drunken girl into the middle of the room. "Help me set her on her feet," Althea ordered the frightened Myrtle Jean. Seeing that done, Althea delivered a scalding slap to Jesse's face, then another.

The major's voice came from the back of the room. "I can take her to Memphis to the pound if you—"

"Thank you, major, I will handle this myself," Althea said with effort. She had brought the girl to the top of the stairs. The girl sank again and Althea took her foot and rolled her down the stairs like a rug, where she lay moaning and trying to sit up.

The major peered down the stairway. "I hope no bone is broken," in a voice halfway between bewilderment and admiration.

"Don't waste pity on her," Althea said. And then, as an afterthought, she added, "I suppose as soon as these slaves are free people, from now on every person who justifiably kicks a colored slut will be accused of being anti-colored."

They descended the stairway. Jesse was moving slowly. She sat up. She was not injured, but her head was no clearer than it had been.

"I must search the house to see if money is hidden," Major Bachelder told her.

"You left Jonas unguarded," Althea said, looking out the window at a load of work clothing hanging out to dry between two ornamental trees, "I expect the woods has swallowed him up by now."

"We'll put a price on his head," Major Bachelder said. Althea turned from the window, glanced at the mumbling Negro woman, then came to stand near him.

"At least let me take the woman to town," he pleaded, looking at Althea with real concern in his eyes.

"I s'pose it is best," she sighed. They dragged the grumbling woman out and put her into the middle seat of the carriage and pushed her into the seat.

"I am not going back with you, major," Althea said as they walked back up the steps. "I have just decided I will stay here a day or two." Major

Bachelder raised his eyebrows in surprise, and Althea turned to reassure him. "I will be safe. If there is cotton money stashed, I will find it. I have the key to Papa's gun closet, and I know how to shoot. Not that that will be needed. Calhoun and Willie will be back at any moment and can join me out here."

"Well, I will search the barn and grounds again for Jonas. If I do not find him, I will send a patrol immediately. He will not go far, I assure you."

"He can live in the mistletoe till Christmas as far as I'm concerned," she said. "One thing—I will ask your indulgence in sending a letter to my daughter when you return to town." She went to the little Chippendale table which sat by the parlor door, dipped a pen in an almost dry inkwell and wrote out a message. "Delia is in Louisville right now. I think I will be required here for some time to come. She will have to continue to manage Rivertides as best she can." She handed him the note, written in her firm, decisive handwriting.

"Oh, and do not worry about me," Althea said brightly. "Papa bred me to be staunch, and I pride myself on solving problems. Above all I don't like unpleasantness and don't intend to tolerate it. Soon all will be set to rights around here."

Major Bachelder looked at her a long moment, either impressed or bewildered by her chipperness, and prepared to go look for the black man and depart. But before he did, he bent and kissed her hand in the old-fashioned way and then looked into her eyes with a small, wondering smile on his face.

A few mornings later, about nine o'clock, Delia and her cousin, Sophie Lavenham, sat in the parlor of the hotel in Louisville, hemming teatowels, casting tiny, almost invisible stitches and turning a quarter inch hem at the same time.

"A sojer come to the door and left this letter for you, miss," the rosy-cheeked hired girl, Annie, announced. She tried to put the calling-card tray on the small table between the young women, but, hearing an uproar in the street, dropped it on the floor with a cry.

"Whatever is the matter with you, girl?" Sophie asked, and after she had picked up the tray and left, told Delia, "She's as flittery as a dog in a thunderstorm."

"Everyone seems to be," Delia commented. "All these alarms about Bragg's army invading Louisville, about battles in the streets. Commanders unable to get the defenses going because they are arguing with each other." She smiled. "I have come at a fine time for a visit." Sophie nodded ruefully and handed her cousin the telegram.

"Mother says affairs are ruinous at the plantation," Delia said, reading the telegram. "A slave sold the plantation's cotton and escaped into the woods. She will be staying for a period of time. And your letter?" She raised her eyes to her cousin's in inquiry.

"Eightieth Indiana Regiment. U.S. Army." Sophie Lavenham took the letter from the small envelope with no stamp and unfolded the blue pages, about ten of them.

"Mr. Scott must have enjoyed his visit tremendously to write such a lengthy bread-and-butter letter, cousin," Delia said with a slight smile.

Sophie Lavenham gave Delia a lofty look and scanned the letter. "There is nothing in it, cousin, but military description. It seems interesting enough—but would you like to read it?"

Delia nodded and put aside her needle. She read the neat schoolteacher's script.

To: Miss Sophie Lavenham

October 1, near Bardstown

Dear Miss Lavenham:

I promised in my last "thank you" letter that I would relate to you the circumstances of life in our military camp, my first experience with such.

It all seems as if I am a newborn babe, with so much drill to master, so many commands and shooting instructions. But I have gone to school with good teachers, for the "veterans" have had a solid month of drilling and some skirmishing, and they keep me in line.

I am writing this by the light of a brilliant full moon in the camp of Major General Don Carlos Buell's army. All of us in this army corps are camped like spokes on a wagon wheel, on different roads coming into Bardstown. We are hoping to encounter Bragg's Southern army and drive them from the state of Kentucky! At least I am hoping so. I didn't leave behind a whole life of religion, and flaunt my dear father's wishes (alas, I cannot forget that sad truth) to sit idle in camp.

We took down rails of a farmer's worm fence and made head boards for our beds, as we say out here in camp. I have a blanket and I have spread it above the thistles. Some of the men are singing and drinking; several of them smuggled out whisky bottles from Louisville.

I do not feel like celebrating. I am here away from all family and friends, except for Tom Brooks. He has become my fast friend and asks to be remembered to you. He says his parents met you at the ball when the orphanage was dedicated. Right now he is writing a letter to his son and wife, whom he misses very much. But he is a stout fellow who wants to do his part. He believes in freedom for the Negro and is as strong a Union man as ever I saw. There are a few other men from the old neighborhood. Colonel Brooks is very kind to us and personally saw to my drilling lessons with one of the sergeants, a very humorous, joking sergeant named Keith Boucher who capers about and keeps all our spirits up.

Still, I feel odd under this moon tonight, almost as bright as day. The Kentucky countryside is barren from so many months of war; and its hills have an odd, forlorn cast to them. For some reason I keep thinking of my grandmother, Jenny McClure Scott, tonight, who died when I was young. Why should I be thinking of her? It is almost as if I can feel her presence in this place. She had lost her reason by the time I knew her, and I had to learn about her from those who knew her when she was a beautiful, intelligent young girl and woman.

My cousin, Catherine McClure Hogue, used to talk of Grandma Jenny and told me about the days when they all lived in Kentucky.

Odd, it was not far from here. When the McClure family first came to Caintuck, as they called it, it was in the days of Indian troubles. They lived in a stockade, could not even go out. Here in Kentucky, not thirty miles from here, the McClures built their fortunes, held slaves, had scores of children. But Cousin Catherine always told me that Grandma Jenny was unhappy in Kentucky, that she was haunted by the gloominess of the countryside near where they lived. The deep gorges of the Kentucky River, the swamps and cane breaks—she felt the spirits of the past in the "Dark and Bloody Land" all about her. Dark and bloody land. Pray God we may not find it so. The phrase haunts me tonight, beneath this elfin moon, with trees and hills casting long shadows on our campground, and the presence of my grandmother haunts my thinking too. There is the taps—

The next night—pardon me, Miss Lavenham, one of our men will soon be going into Louisville and I will send this with him in fifteen minutes. We marched all day in the hot sun. I did not have any water in my canteen and my throat was parched and dry. I cannot tell you how thirsty we are, and all the creeks are dry, with cows pawing at cracks and ooze to get a few drops of water. The Rebs are out there somewhere. Bragg's army is marching around, we think not far from us. Are they as hot and tired and THIRSTY as we are?

The men marched along singing "Billy Nelson's knapsack, strapped upon his back." Hundreds of voices made us step lighter, I can tell you that. I have forgotten about all the gloom of last night, about my strange thoughts of my grandmother.

I think I had those dark thoughts because I miss my family so. I am a simple body who has loved the homeplace and relatives as I think few do. I have no aspirations to anything but our dear acres with those I love about.

And now both Mother and Father are gone and Brother is estranged. My yearning for my family's love is strong, and so I think of parents, old days, my Grandmother Jenny.

Places cannot hold sad vibrations, pent up to be played out at a touch, like a music box plays tunes, though some think so. Some say that ghosts are only vibrations of the past, caught in time and held, to be played when a sympathetic heart is near. I do not think I believe that. That we are here within a few miles of where my mother and father lived so long is a coincidence. Pleasant and benign countryside it seems today! Farms that will be fertile soon as the touch of war leaves them.

It is not a dark and bloody ground. Such associations do not persist. What was it my father, John Robert Scott, used to say? "Only love persists through pain and death, through years to come." Come to think of it, I think he said Grandmother Jenny taught him that—I must close now. I am sorry to pour my heart out to you, but I found such a welcome in your home, felt such sweet concordances of feeling as we strolled through your garden and you kindly spoke to me of your interests—no more. I shall write later. Oh, give my greetings to Miss Dora, too.

Your friend (I can hope)
Jacob Joe Scott

Delia put the letter down and took up her sewing. She bit off a thread. "You should use the sewing scissors, Delia," Sophie said.

A moment passed. "Well, Mr. Scott is certainly a *belle ame*—what a sensitive heart he has," Delia said. And then she ventured. "You may recall seeing his twin brother. He has been often at Rivertides, seeing Calhoun. He and Jacob Joe are—very different."

"I do recall seeing—is it Zach?—at the ball," Sophie said without interest. "Mr. Jacob Joe seems full of silly superstition and folderol and silly speculations. I do not care for poetic language," she snapped a minute later, as if she were reviewing the contents of the letter in her mind and finding it unsatisfactory. "But he is uncommonly handsome and has a good fortune, so mother understands from Aunt Althea." She smiled like a contented pussycat and then tossed the letter on the table. Her sister Dora entered the room.

"Sister, did I hear there was a letter?" she asked. Her hands were folded in front of her, her face shone with anticipation.

"Yes. Mr. Scott writes from the wars. Hail the conquering hero," she said with a laugh. "Read it if you wish." Tossing her head, she returned to her sewing.

Two days later in Loogootee, Indiana, Thomas Jefferson Brooks walked along the main road from the Post Office. He was eating a large purple plum from a tree planted beside his store by Grandmother Poore, a slip from her old farm in Orange County. He was reading a letter that had been at the post office. It was from his son, Tommy.

To: Thomas Jefferson Brooks

October 3

Dear Pa and Ma, Gramma, Aunt Harriet and everyone else:

The Eightieth Indiana made its camp in the rain yesterday evening here about thirty miles from Louisville. My blanket was with the wagon train. I had only my fatigue coat, and I pulled it up around my ears and lay down in a corn shock.

Soon, though, the Pennsylvania cavalry came in and took all the corn in my shock and all the rest of the field as food for the horses. I lay in the rain all night and do not feel very well this morning; still, I am well enough to march I think. It is hard to go with no food; our crackers were spoiled with the rain in the haversack and we had to dump them out, so we all are very hungry.

General Terrill had turkeys for dinner, I suppose the general's right of conquest. One of the men in a Kentucky regiment had gone off on his own and found two ducks and a turkey, and Terrill found him out and made him cook the fowls for the general's pleasure. The smell almost made the men faint, they are so hungry.

Jacob Joe Scott is here near me and is a good friend. All he does is talk about some fine young lady he visited in Louisville. I think you met her, Sophie Lavenham, at a ball. Also Sergeant Keith Boucher is showing me the ropes. A good sergeant he is, too, and puts crawdads in our canteens and things like that. He keeps us laughing with his jests when our spirits get low, as mine do sometimes being far from home and my wife and baby. Sergeant Boucher has apple jack in his canteen, and it is good he does. There isn't much water as it has been so dry. The rain may make a difference, but I doubt it. The ground just soaks up the little that falls and there is no way to collect it.

Pa and Ma, in spite of all of these troubles, I am glad I came. Lewis has a fine regiment and it is an honor to be in it. He gives me no favors, no, instead treats me as if we had never grown up together, as if he had not held my hand and taken me to Mt. Pleasant school my first day. I think it must be right he treats me this way, so there is no favoritism. I try not to feel slighted, though it is odd to see your brother walk by and only nod. Lewis feels bound to act for honor and duty in all cases.

Tell my sister Emily that her husband Campbell is serving us well as regimental surgeon. I hope she will not miss her husband too much; Lewis depends on him. Campbell saw me and does not think my indisposition is much, perhaps a light ague.

As I see this huge corps spread out before the town of Taylorsville, I know I am in the right place. We must break the back of this traitorous Confederacy and see our nation united. It is just that simple. We cannot live as two powers. And I myself must fight to see the emancipation stick. Ever since I went to New Orleans and saw the shuffling, dull eyed slaves who I know God meant to be free people, I cannot let it rest.

Thomas Jefferson Brooks took the half-eaten plum from his mouth, and his mind went back to the trip he had taken with Lewis, Tommy and Will Houghton four years before to New Orleans on one of the last of the flatboats that travelled the Mississippi. They had eaten the old foods, sung the flatboat songs and sampled most of the exotic diversions of New Orleans. And Tommy had read *Uncle Tom's Cabin* to all of them. Tommy was an "Eliza and Uncle Tom" abolitionist, conceiving his dreams of colored servitude from the pages of a romantic novel. Ah, Tommy. The goodness of your heart! His father looked at the plum. They had brought slips for this plant from Massachusetts when they came in the covered wagon, he thought somewhat distractedly. Grandmother Poore, Susan and all the rest. He put the plum to his lips and began to walk and read again.

Many of the men here, as they get to know the slaves who are about, and see how it really is, are beginning to approve of the proclamation. Anyway, most do not oppose it. They say if it helps end the war, so be it.

The cavalry are looking for Bragg's troops nearby, and rumor has it that a huge army of Confederates is after us. It seems impossible we should not encounter them. Whatever may befall, you know of my undying love and devotion. Pa, I have placed Lewie and Lib under your management in my will.

His will. Here Thomas Jefferson Brooks stopped in his tracks. His heart turned cold and he stared straight ahead, into the yellow leaves of an enormous sycamore tree on Main Street, to calm himself. It was as if his troubled thoughts would lose themselves in the beauty and security of that old tree, as if it held all the mysteries of life and death in its deep, many-branched interior. Will. Well, of course a soldier must have a will. It only made sense. Tommy? Scenes tumbled over each other: of a baby, smiling up and taking his finger as if it were the only finger in the world, a little boy spending a rainy morning at the store playing hide and seek with a cat, a very young bridegroom with large, serious eyes, who asked his own father to be his best man. There it was, uncaring, the sycamore tree, turning gold because of the dry end of summer, beneath the calico-blue sky—the person he cared about as much as anyone in this life, was facing death on a bright October morning. This very morning, perhaps; it had been four days since the letter was written. The papers had said last night the armies were thought to be close enough to meet if fate decreed it; Bragg's army might number 75,000, some folks thought. His eyes went to the letter.

Well, I have the cussedness and courage you are always telling me the Brookses possess. I commend my earthly goods and dear ones to you and my soul to God, whom I ever trust for eternal life.

Your son
Tommy

To God, whom I trust for eternal life, Thomas Jefferson Brooks repeated, his eyes again lost within the rich foliage of the golden sycamore. Something my father the minister would have appreciated. Not I. Cussedness? Never, Tommy. Courage in unlimited measure, but you do not have a cussed bone in your body. Pure joyous goodness, like a spring in the wood. And that is why it would be such a ridiculous waste if—

In anger and disgust he crammed the letter into his pocket and started down the street again. As he passed the giant sycamore, he threw the half-eaten plum into the dust at the base of its trunk.

*   *   *   *

The soldiers of the Army of the Cumberland came near Perryville, their tongues cloven to the roofs of their mouths from thirst. Hot—it was unbearably hot for early October, even in Kentucky. As this march progressed, men faltered and died and were buried by the side of the road from heat exhaustion. Tension was high; with the army of Braxton Bragg so near, there were orders to shoot stragglers. Two of their graves marked the dusty road as the men advanced through clouds of fine, swirling dust which darkened their hair, clogged their nostrils, filtered into their mouths.

They stopped to rest and make camp; some of their soldiers drifted towards a stream to fill canteens and—God! There on the other side were soldiers of the Confederacy, equally hot, dirty and desperate. The all climbed trees or fell to the ground to load guns for a determined struggle to hold the creek. The Battle of Perryville had begun.

Through the afternoon there was skirmishing and then, at night, the moon lit the scene of preparation for battle; each man readying as much ammunition as he could carry, rolling blankets, fixing knapsacks which would have to be left behind. The exhausted men of both armies lay on the ground to sleep as best they could until five o'clock. The sky lightened and units formed to march into battle.

Bands played with almost feverish beat, the veteran units marched past new regiments so experience could lead the attack, the cannons boomed ominously and the units formed upon the hill, with Chaplin River in the distance.

About one o'clock in the afternoon, Jacob Joe Scott and Tommy Brooks advanced with their company, in support of a battery under Brigadier General James S. Jackson.

Keith Boucher, sergeant of what was mostly a Martin County company, had just helped his captain replenish the ammunition supply and was urging the men forward. Out of the corner of his eye Tom Brooks could see his brother Lewis on a horse, handsome, sword raised to direct movements of the troops.

"Can't think. God, those cannons fill your mind as if nothing but noise exists in the world," Tom thought. "Your brain turns to bread pudding." The line worked its way forward. Through deafening noise—shells bursting, round shot dropping, the whir of bullets—they passed the dead, lying on their stomachs, the wounded sprawled unconscious, their faces and uniforms covered with blood which flowed profusely from shrapnel wounds.

"Forward men, double quick. For God's sake, don't yield to the temptation to stop and shoot," Colonel Brooks shouted. Men in the line were falling; still, they were, somehow, reaching the crest of a hill overlooking all the fields. Loomis's Michigan batteries commanded the field, and the Eightieth and the other units would have to defend them. Bullets whined and the artillery action split the air and ears. "Hot going, here," Jacob Joe shouted, trying to make Tommy Brooks hear him.

"Snipers in the trees over there, and no place to shelter," Brooks called back. Colonel Lewis raised his sword and ordered them into column as skirmishers; they rushed to position. Out of the corner of his eye, as he worked to load and shoot, Tommy could see horses fly in the air, wounded from artillery fire, see men drop in front of him every few seconds. Nausea rose in his throat; he was terribly afraid. Tommy Brooks was throwing up a few feet from him, on his hands and knees over his vomit.

"Feel so God-awful," Brooks was screaming in frustration, wiping his mouth.

They had been ordered to shoot at will. Jacob Joe Scott was looking at

Sergeant Keith Boucher next to him, tearing cartridges with his teeth. "Odd," he thought irrelevantly, "Boucher is a dentist." The captain had kneeled and was firing beside him. "Not bad for new recruits, eh?" Jacob Joe yelled. "We're holding them."

"Keep trying to reassure us all," Boucher screamed. "And watch out for the shots in the trees to the right. Some of the goddamned traitors are coming within killing range, scrambling into the branches right now."

At that instant, just as he had finished speaking, Boucher jumped back, shot, and Jacob Joe turned to him. Boucher's eye socket became a fountain of blood, then a small stream. Fragments of his shattered eye flowed down his face. In shock—or was he dead?—he fell heavily and lay on the ground face up as yellow sycamore leaves from the trees dislodged by the battle fluttered down over his face.

"God in heaven," Jacob Joe articulated, then, realizing he must return to the battle, he looked up and loaded his gun. Tommy Brooks had stepped up, knelt, and was firing by his side; across the field the Confederate lines were inching forward. Brooks' hands were shaking so badly he could hardly handle his gun, but he was grimly determined.

Jacob Joe's emotions were a turmoil of rage, confusion and sick fear. The Rebs were coming at them, Cheatham's troops on the Confederate right flank, trying to take the position the Eightieth and other Northern regiments held with the battery behind them. Jacob Joe heard shouting and turned; there was Colonel Brooks, up the hill towards the batteries a little, hat on his sword, calling for the attack.

"Attack, attack," Jacob Joe's mind—or was it his lips?—screamed. All around him were whining shells, pops of musketry, calls of dying men, rallying cries of officers, neighing horses, curses, Rebel and Hoosier yells.

The scene seemed to swim before him, pulsating in little waves. Was the sickening smoke and turmoil beginning to cloud his reason? God! What was it—here—before him, not ten feet away? Couldn't be—a woman, the form of a woman, dressed in what? An odd, old-fashioned dress from George Washington's time. He stared at the apparition. Her face was beautiful, young, filled with love. Familiar in an odd way. She was, she was—God, it was Grandmother Jenny, as he had never known her.

Bullets screamed, Sergeant Boucher moaned.

"Do you see her—the woman?" Jacob Joe screamed at Tommy Brooks eight feet away.

"Her? Are you out of your mind," Brooks screamed hoarsely. "Nothing but goddamned Rebs here."

The vision woman pointed to the trees behind her, where the snipers were. Urgently, her lips moved in warning. Her message shot at him like a bolt of lightning, "Duck!" and he did. The vision disappeared and the man in the line behind him groaned, dropping from a sniper's bullet that had been intended for Jacob Joe Scott.

Towards sundown, as the Eightieth Indiana was changing fronts for the fourth time that day to meet renewed Rebel assault in this most savagely fought battle, Thomas Jefferson Brooks, Junior, was wounded seriously in the lower side. As he was carried by his friends from the battle to the tent of his brother-in-law, regimental surgeon Thomas Campbell, he passed his brother Lewis on horseback.

"Sir, your brother is dangerously wounded," Jacob Joe Scott cried to the man on the horse.

Lewis Brooks looked compassionately at his unconscious younger brother for a few seconds and then spurred his horse. "I know no one but my regiment," he said determinedly.

The telegram about Tommy Brooks' desperate condition reached his parents' home in Loogootee at eleven o'clock at night. Thomas Jefferson Brooks met the boy from the telegraph office at the door, read the message and turned, white-faced to meet the rest of the family. "Susan, Mother Poore—I—our boy is wounded, at a battle near a town called Perryville. Seymour, Eustace—your brother has been shot in the lower side, dangerously. They do not know if he will live." Here Susan Brooks cried out and ran to her husband and they clung to each other, both sobbing.

Grandmother Poore put her hand to her mouth and closed her eyes in prayer. When she opened them, she saw that Thomas Jefferson Brooks had recovered himself to read the rest of the telegram from his son-in-law, Emily's husband Thomas Campbell. "Lewis is safe. We are to tell Lib. It says the Rebels seem to be retreating into Tennessee. It was an accidental battle. They are vacating the state. A Rebel shell from a cannon—why Eustace, what is it?"

Young Eustace Brooks, with an oath, grabbed his coat from the coat tree and pushed past his parents and out into the cool night. His emotions were in awful conflict, and he wanted to be alone.

His father watched him disappear into the darkness and shook his head, not quite understanding. Then he headed towards the stairs.

"Are you going back to bed already?" his wife asked in surprise.

"No, I am going to pack my bag. I am going to the train station, to catch the five a.m. to Louisville. I must be with my boy."

"That is a battlefield area," Susan Brooks called out after him. "Are you, a sixty-two-year-old man, going to the wars?"

"Call it that if you want to. I am going to find my boy and see that he gets care. I will bring him home if he lives. If he dies, it will be with his father at his side."

Grandmother Poore went to her daughter and put her arm about her, but Susan turned from her mother and looked in the pocket of her nightgown for a handkerchief. "Seymour," she said through her tears, "you go to tell Lib and little Lewie that Tommy is wounded. Do not tell them how serious it is; we'll save that till tomorrow. And stop by Lewis's and Amanda's and tell the children that their father is safe. We will send word to Susie and Sandford in Wheatland tomorrow morning."

Seymour bounded up the stairs to pull on his trousers and shirt, and his mother followed slowly after him, putting her feet heavily on the risers. Grandmother Poore went to the door and looked out into the darkness. There was a shape, standing by the edge of the browning lawn. "Let him have his privacy," she told herself and turned away from the door.

In the shadows Eustace Brooks clenched his fist and swore bitterly to himself, as he fingered a Copperhead penny made into a pin, which was out of sight inside his coat. It was the badge of the Knights of the Golden Circle.

"Stop complaining," Thomas Jefferson Brooks said tiredly to his seventeen-year-old son as they bumped along in the day coach section of the train to Louisville. "I told you I needed someone to come with me. I can't understand why you wouldn't want to go find your brother."

"It isn't that," Eustace Brooks said. "Naturally, I want to know about Tommy. It's just the whole thing is so futile, so stupid."

"Of course it is. But what do you propose we do about it? The war is on, the slaves are being freed, the die was cast long ago. All this talk about reconciling the two warring parts of the nation sounds good until you stop to think what that really means. You can't put Humpty Dumpty back together again."

Eustace ran a finger over his face. Overnight, bumps had come out, ugly pimples. They always did that when he was emotionally distressed. They were so hard to shave over—"The North and the South should sit down and stop this war," he told his father emphatically. "The North is losing everywhere anyway. Just send a representative to Richmond, get President Jefferson Davis to sit down with Abraham Lincoln, have some coffee—"

"Which Mrs. Lincoln could serve. I can just hear it," the elder Brooks said sarcastically. "Mrs. Lincoln says to Mrs. Davis, 'Valera dear' " he mimicked in a high, little voice, " 'Will you have some cucumber sandwiches while the men talk about pardoning the 100,000 traitors in the army?' And Mrs. Lincoln would pass tea cakes, that is if she wasn't having one of her fits of pique or buying 100 pairs of gloves in the Washington stores.''

"Pa, you never understand what I say. You never even try," Eustace said. His voice was surprisingly menacing.

Thomas Jefferson Brooks looked out the window and let his mind stray for a while. None of the other boys ever would have dared to speak to him in that tone, he told himself. Not even Seymour, who was younger yet, did. Well, he had been busy while these younger ones were growing up. And it was a different age.

The towns they were passing through had tall buildings and telegraph wires and opera houses. Everyone was crazy for entertainment these days. Didn't have enough to do. Then there were those degenerate pictures of naked women you saw men looking at sometimes. They said there were almost naked women dancing in the Washington theatres. What was it all coming to? A young man in the store, a drummer from New York state, had whispered to him that there were things men were using—barriers made of sheep intestine and even rubber—to keep women from getting in the family way. Well, no decent man would ever think of using that. He shifted in his seat, feeling a little guilty for thinking about such things while his son was wounded, perhaps fatally, but in the perverse way the mind has when it most needs to concentrate, he could not stop thinking about the lurid things the younger generation was involved in. Could you just imagine? "Excuse me, please, my dear, while I—'' Unthinkable. God intended women to have children and that's the way it should be. Even if they died. Which they did.

They were passing the hilly "knobs" in eastern Indiana, beautiful in the first colors of autumn. Maple trees, just beginning to blush, like apples getting ripe, clad the sides of the hills outside the window. No, Eustace was just too feisty for his own good. Cussedness was admirable in small doses, but Eustace was so consarn cussed these days that his nostrils were snorting steam, like he was ready to toot down the track. Ought to put him to work on one of the old whipsaws they had used at Hindostan. My, time had jolted by! Wasn't it last Friday that he had come to forested, wilderness Indiana? Spent out the days of his youth, like pennies put across a counter, building a town that died and a fortune and family? Time was an accordion, and its folds crumpled back across themselves.

Yes, let Eustace stand in the pit and whipsaw for six straight hours, as he had done at almost the same age. Or help dig the dam they had built at the old town. He smiled. That would cure his cussedness, sure as hell. No good reason for the way Eustace was acting. Like a dog with turpentine under his tail.

Tommy wasn't like that. Tommy. Here it had been fifteen whole minutes and he had not thought of Tommy. Thinking of—other things. They would be there in an hour and a half, and then he would have to find Tommy. There had been a withdrawal now, Bragg's troops were moving off into Tennessee where they belonged, God knew where the Eightieth Indiana was. The ambulance trains were on the way, so the rumors went on this train. He would find his son, God willing.

No, he would not pray. He had done that a time or two in his life and had felt hypocritical. He had sworn off that sort of stuff years ago, when he was about Eustace's age, come to think of it. He had stood with his father by the ruins of the Brooks graveyard, where they had buried the old Puritan Brookses in the 1600s, when many of them died the first winter in America. He had told his father the minister that he was wrong, wrong to think the Puritan ancestors' souls lived on. They were just a bunch of bones, so he had asserted there, when he was sixteen or seventeen. His father believed so devoutly, so immovably in religion, in the God of the Puritans, in eternal life. Just as devoutly as he, Thomas Jefferson Brooks had come in this day and age to believe in the cause of the North. Two countries? Confederate States and United States of America? Didn't make a bit of sense at the practical level, no matter what Eustace thought.

Come to think of it, why did Eustace think that? Why was he arguing so much for peace right now? Like father, like son? Thomas Jefferson Brooks shifted his weight uncomfortably. Cussedness, probably just that same old Brooks cussedness.

Still, as he looked out at the southern Indiana countryside, where a railroad train was hurtling along what used to be the Buffalo Trace, (the accordion folding faster on itself now) his eyes were grim with concern about two of his sons.

Many hours later in a Louisville hotel, with Eustace already asleep on the bed, Thomas Jefferson Brooks sat down to write a letter to Lib, his daughter-in-law.

Dear Lib,

When I arrived here and saw the medical Doctor I saw I could do but little. It was uncertain who would come first. I learned 750 wounded would be in tonight. I went out to meet them. They came in wagons, and said Thomas would come in an ambulance. They did not appear to think him badly wounded. I did not get to see any from Company B, but they said some was along.

I could only talk to them as they drove through the streets. I shall tomorrow find the hospital all the wounded have been put in and go see them all until I find him. I am promised a list from the Sanitary Commission of all of the wounded that do come in tonight.

I have walked my feet sore going from one hospital to another and to the medical directory and Sanitary Commission and then out to meet the wagons, and I have still not found my boy!

Don't be uneasy. He will be well cared for. The papers speak well of the regiment, saying they fought them well for five hours. I am bushed tonight—

Yours truly
Thomas Jefferson Brooks

The next morning, amidst the confusion and welter of ambulance wagons coming into Louisville, troops hurrying through to march to other assignments and hearses with the dead under blankets, Thomas Jefferson Brooks and Eustace found Private Tommy Brooks, Company B, Eightieth Indiana Regiment, in one of the last ambulance wagons.

Running along the road, Thomas Jefferson Brooks begged the driver to stop. After the mules came to a halt, snorting and rearing their heads, Thomas Jefferson Brooks bolted into the wagon and cradled his son in his arms. Thomas Campbell, the husband of his daughter Emily, who served as the regimental surgeon, was by his side.

"Pa—we never gave. Not an inch," Tommy said. But his eyes were glazed and dull, his face red as blood and suddenly his mind rushed back to the battlefield, to the top of that brown, blood-drenched hill at Perryville. "Cheatham's—Cheatham's men and Rebel yell," he mumbled, trying to sit up.

"He went into the battle with a fever and fever has set in with the wound. He is dangerous, out of his head, but he may recover away from here. Take him home, Father Brooks," Thomas Campbell said.

"Yes, I will. Yes, Tommy," the old man said in a faltering voice. "How could they do this to you? Only a month ago—" He choked on the words. The accordion was folding tight. All the things he cherished most were inside the folds, he thought with anguish. "Eustace, help us get him out to the train station."

But his younger son did not move. He stood, his mouth open wide in horror as if he were an idiot, staring at the gaping wound, loosely bound, oozing blood and yellow liquid, that scarred his brother's side.

December, 1862

Chapter Eight

Two months later, Lettie Hogue sat in a chintz chair in the lobby of the Hotel Cincinnati. Near her, an aspidistra plant cascaded out of a Chinese pot from the table to the floor.

Women with the new, fashionable small hoop skirts swished across the Persian carpet, accompanied by the riverboat captains and shoe factory owners who were making Cincinnati rich. "An hour early," Lettie told herself. She picked up the *Cincinnati Enquirer* from the table beside her. "Yellow Fever Epidemic in Key West Dissipates," the headline said. She put the paper down. No sense in reading about misery if you could help it.

She took out a small mirror from her purse and, holding it in the palm of her hand, tried to look at herself without seeming vain to the women who were sitting nearby at the small desks writing letters on hotel stationery. Yes, her new hat was perfect. The pleated ruffles, not too many or too ostentatious, sitting there on top of her upswept hair, made her face look piquant. Her eyes fell on the front page of the paper. "Major Battle Looms in Fredericksburg. New Commander Burnside Promises Lincoln a Union Victory After Many Losses."

Reluctantly she picked the paper up again. Her nephew, John McClure, had written to say that he had come back from being sick to rejoin the troops just as Burnside replaced McClellan as commander. Henderson Simpson had gone home for good—couldn't take the army, but he, John, was well of his fever now and was putting on weight again. But now he would be in a major battle—that was bad news. Lettie's mother would worry about her grandson. Out there on the farm in that tiny cottage with Horace, Catherine had little to do and no one to talk to. So she sat around and worried.

But it had been her choice, hadn't it? To sacrifice for the McClure homestead? The old mansion had been saved. And it did give her mother a chance to be with her brother Billy and son Horace. Esther was in one of her "getting along" phases, and the gossip was flowing like a steady stream of sorghum over there. So Lettie didn't have to worry about her mother, at least for a while.

Lettie stretched her legs, looking at the new boots she had bought for the trip. Red morocco they were. One had to be dressed smartly for the academy. She had just finished the first week of a course in bookkeeping, and she had enjoyed it so much she had been up and dressed at six o'clock in the morning, ready to go.

She had seen the advertisement in Vincennes, in the *Enquirer* the ladies' library subscribed to. "Woman's course in bookkeeping given at the Cincinnati Academy for two weeks in December. Reserve a space now." No one had thought much of her going, not even in gossipy Vincennes. Fifteen years ago, even ten it would have been unheard of. But women went to academies and even colleges now. Women nurses were travelling about without chaperons—they had to. And after all, she was not a rosebud of an eighteen-year-old. She was a maiden lady in her mid-thirties.

Maiden lady. Old maid. Somehow those words hurt, even though she had been used to them for these ten or so years now. Anyone over twenty-five was an old maid. That was the way it was. And what did that mean, what was the real import of being an old maid?

It meant going to Christmas dinner with whoever in your family took pity and invited you, not cooking goose and mince pie yourself, though you might enjoy cooking and be very good at it. It meant experiencing motherhood through your sisters' and brothers' children, though you yearned to bear and cuddle a child yourself.

It meant doing, actually doing, very little. For many it meant getting up in the morning and paying especial attention to your toilette, drinking tea and eating toast sedately, sitting about with embroidery, eating lunch sedately, preferably served by a hired girl, sitting about again and eating dinner sedately. Thank heavens for the lyceums and Debate Society and Women's Shakespeare Club and Knox County War Relief committees. Maiden ladies (and married ones, too) would be bug-eyed with boredom otherwise. Forty years ago, in her mother's time, all that cooking over the fireplace, sweeping with birch brooms, slaughtering animals, whitewashing log walls—that kept the women busy. But now she had a cookstove in her apartment, rugs that were taken out once a year and beaten by men you hired, canned foods, meat from the butcher's.

"It's the aloneness I hate," she told herself. "Having nobody to talk to about what to fix for breakfast. I hate to make decisions on my own, most of all, because I don't trust myself to have a decent idea. Horace says I don't really have a will of my own. True. Used to get Papa to decide what bonnet I should wear, what books I should read. Then, after school, I moved in with Mother so she could make decisions for me. No will. Certainly I didn't for the last five years—I gave my will over to the dark things in the bottles."

The bitters in the bottles. She was not the only one. Those bottles of tonic, the spirits of laudanum and alcohol, those steamer cruises to exotic dream-worlds—how many women today in the new pampered world of leisure escaped with them? She did not know, but she knew she dreaded boarding that ship again, the deadening of pain and frustration at the price of surrendering your mind. The odd, half-shapes of imagination let loose to float in the mind like giant dolls, the too-loud bells ringing, the snatches of childhood mating in your mind with ugly street scenes in—what was it—Calcutta?

Then the long, long, opiate—sleep. She couldn't forget that night last spring, when, after tonicking herself to the tune of three bottles, she found herself by the river with the bottom of her dress wet. Had she lost such track of herself that she wandered into the river? Or did some part of her actually want to die? Scared, she swore off. She was determined not to pack her trunks for that long trip into narcotic confusion again. But how? She had made up her mind before, how many times? It was six months now without tonics, but how to assure that it would stay that way?

Lettie looked up at the German clock on the table, its round, golden wheels revolving under a glass dome. Not time yet for him to be here.

At first, the episodes with the bottles, which one of the members of the Ladies' Aid had made it a point to hint about, the drugged walk half into the Wabash, which some townsfolks had seen, made her realize she was a subject of conversation in the town. But after a while she grew inured to town opinion. She flaunted the town in taking employment, too, she told herself, and she liked it. She would like it even better when she was through with this course in bookkeeping. Her ledgers were too hit-and-guess. This first week at the institute, just finished, had taught her a good deal about double entry, account reconciling, and auditing as it should be done.

This new position released most of the energies which used to go into tonic-taking. But not all. No, not all. Lettie took from her pocketbook a little book, Mr. and Mrs. Evan Parsticle's *Cerebral Calisthenics* subtitled, the *Creative Release of Energy*. She turned to the chapter, "Place of the Sexual Act in Energy Release."

"I wonder if Mother knows what happened to her book during the move out to the farm?" Lettie wondered with a slight smile. "She reads this book for the mental exercises, one, two, bad thoughts go shoo. Ridiculous. I read it for—confess it, Letitia, titillation." To see these words in print, to think the thoughts her mind pictured, thoughts she had never been allowed to think.

Did her mother miss the book? Did she suspect Lettie might have it? Taking the book seemed stealthy, out of character for the babies' cradle roll teacher from Upper Indiana church. But then folks had never really known her true character. Letitia, the "booky" lady, secretary of the Shakespeare

Society, took a little too much tonic now and then and was lately odd and reclusive. Marched to her own fife and drum. Some of the old folks, Lettie knew, said she was too much like her Grandpa George McClure. Well, she'd never known him, so she couldn't comment. She knew she loved to read and was afraid of real life. Afraid to feel. Afraid to love.

Her eye fell on the page. "The marriage relationship, in which mutual partners, who are committed to each other's welfare, express their feelings by touch and step-by-step mutual sensation and release of feelings, channels energy in a way no other physical act can do."

"If the members of the Ladies Shakespeare Club knew what I think, what I have thought for years," she told herself ruefully, "they'd pop their buttons. They don't talk of it much, the marriage relationship. Performed with the 'organs of generation.' Those are the words that are used. No one ever talks about the exact process of joining of bodies, no one even says the word. You come upon it sometimes in medical textbooks or on walls written by boys before some prissy woman comes out and whitewashes over it. Intercourse. Mating. Copulation. Fornication, if you want to look in the Bible. Knowing."

She chided herself. "I am turning degenerate, falling from grace. I have not been to church now in two months, ever since Mother moved to the country again. On Sunday I think of Reverend Paden, see him in my mind at Upper Indiana Church announcing the hymns, see myself singing and listening to the sermons. And I also think of how good-looking he is, in spite of myself, of the way his chin juts out and his frame dominates the entire pulpit, and I wonder what he looks like under his coat. His chest—does it have hair on it? And then—the organs of generation. I never have allowed myself to speculate on that. You can carry all this too far."

Ever since she started the job and decided to stop taking her tonics, she hadn't felt right in church. She didn't know why. Must be these thoughts of hers. She couldn't seem to stop herself. She looked for books in bookstores that talked about—the marriage relationship. Well, she wanted to know what it was about. All the world but she and the other old maids were privy to secret knowledge. Not fair. In the Parsticle's book there was a strange thing. "Men practice self abuse and today we hear, even women"—She forgot the rest of it, but it didn't matter anyway. Touch themselves? She had never heard of that. She was shocked, but got up the courage there in her own bed. Nothing, nothing happened, only a feeling of shame and that same hot, outrageous longing.

Smells drifted out of the dining room, hot mutton and sage, she thought.

The truth was that all this wasn't only happening in marriage and never had been, although Mrs. Parsticle talked about it that way. Not at all. You just had to read the papers to know how many men, and women too, sought pleasure outside that bond.

Still there were such things as decency, morality. "What IS it you are after?" she demanded of herself. "What are you looking for, Letitia Hogue? Exactly what?"

She stood up and went to the window looking out on the Cincinnati street, continuing to berate herself. Why, exactly had she told Willis Mawkins, her employer, that she would meet him here for supper at this hotel? It could be logical, simply an employee-employer meeting. He knew she would be here, had encouraged her to come.

She would tell him what she was learning while he was in town, on whatever odd business it was he was about these days. He traveled a lot, it was true, especially in the East and even in the South, through the lines— none of her business. He had made it clear that if they were to be friends, she must not pry too much about his life outside the livery stable.

Friends. He had taken her to tea at the Vincennes hotels, walked her about in the park on Sunday afternoon, accompanied her to band concerts and lyceums. Nothing wrong with that in this day and age. Chaperones weren't required for people in their mid-thirties. Willis was divorced, and if he put his hand on her knee in the twilight darkness of a warm November night recently, awakening unforgettable wellsprings of emotion—he had never kissed her or offered offense. Did she want him to? That was the question.

She walked over to pick up the paper and suddenly Willis Mawkins came bounding around the aspidistra bush—that enigmatic smile, those sharp, bright black eyes, the same good smell of shaving pomade. "Hello, Mr. Mawkins," she said.

He bent to kiss her hand, then looked up, right into her eyes. "Miss McClure, I think it is time we called each other by our first names. After all, we are friends as well as business associates aren't we?" There was an odd fire in his eyes. Like a match, it struck something deep inside of her, caused it to leap to flame.

She put her arm through his and they strolled through the lobby, past palm trees in pots, towards the smell of roasted meat and brandied cherries.

*   *   *   *

John McClure sat with his head in his hands in the camp of the Fourteenth opposite Fredericksburg, Virginia. He had a headache. He had not quite recovered from the typhoid-like sickness which felled him in late August. All around him the sound of axes thwacking through logs made the river-bank woods ring; the men were building winter quarters at General Burnside's orders. Each resonating stroke of the axe seemed to strike a corresponding throb in his skull.

His cousin Henderson was gone, and certainly that added to his lowness of spirit. Henderson had contracted what the Washington surgeons called "social disease." It was gonorrhea, probably received those nights he was with the whores in the tents outside Pope's camp. The treatment with mercury pills had been so strong that two of his teeth had fallen out. But the Washington surgeon seemed to think that old-fashioned methods were the best.

Henderson was a moral lesson, sure enough, John McClure thought. Like the *Pilgrim's Progress* Grandma Catherine had sent with him. John spent a great deal of time lately reading it. It soothed him as he worked his way through what increasingly seemed a Slough of Despond.

Here, as he sat on this log awaiting his turn at the axe, he had the old book open. He saw again its odd writing from an earlier age. It had belonged to George McClure, well, not his great-grandfather who worked on the newspaper in Vincennes, no, not him but an earlier one. "This book given to George McClure, January 15, 1710 by his father, Alexander McClure, Physician Dunleigh, Ireland." Sure enough, 'twas a long spell back. There was another inscription here in faint writing, "Pilgrim, see page 36, G.M." George McClure the first?

The first time John had read it, he turned to page 36 right away. There was a lot on the page, and it was all so hard to read, seeing as how he had only been through the fifth grade, but there seemed to be a spot or blot beside a passage which read, "Pluck up a good heart, O Christian, for greater is He that is in thee, than he that is in the world." Beside it on the page was a scribbled note. "Saved my life once. J.M. 1818." His grandfather John, Dr. Jack McClure.

How had it saved his life? There was so much to know. Well, it was a good book with its stories of giants and fairs and beautiful, courageous people. And it passed the time. But it did not appear that he had anything to add to all these profound comments of the ancestors. People of faith they were, that was obvious. Probably they didn't have any troubles like he did. Although Grandma Catherine said something about his Grandfather Jack McClure being something of a wastrel as a youth, it was hard to picture. Somehow you always thought of your ancestors as being prissy and perfect.

He sighed and watched the men in G Company rolling logs for the houses. Once, on Cheat Mountain, he had been the one to push the men to build strong shelters, ditch their streets, take care of the chinks in the life of a soldier. Now, he lacked the heart, or maybe it was the strength, to do it. Anyway, they seemed to police themselves. The supplies were better. Lincoln was sending in good coats, plenty of shoes, decent food. And the states—at least his—kept supplementing the supply with extra things. They weren't hurting for shelter; after having built winter shelters fourteen times (or so it seemed), any corn-shock-head from the country got pretty good at it.

John coughed and spat onto wet leaves near the log where he sat. He sighed as he thought of G Company's officers. Brass Ass Van Dyke was supervising G Company. Assisted by Landon, the man who always wrote home to the Vincennes paper. Brass Ass made a good captain, just as Harrow, he had to admit, made a strong colonel. Except that Harrow was sick now, and Lije Cavins of Greene County was Acting Regimental Commander. The regiment changed officers faster than a maiden aunt changed bed linens. They were all waiting for Coons to return. Coons—well, Coons was at home in Indiana. Two months in a hospital after Antietam hadn't seem to heal his serious wounds, and the surgeons thought he should recuperate at least three months at home. So Walter McClure—Redskin, had taken him to southern Indiana.

Redskin McClure. Every time he heard that name John frowned. It felt like a lump was sitting on his gullet. It irritated the shit out of John to think they shared the same name, McClure, a name honored and remembered all over Kentucky and Indiana. Where in the hell did that Indian get the name McClure? Indians had names like Fat Dog and Ant Crap. Things like that. Somebody had told him that Indians went to court these days and just took a name, any name, to get more White-i-fied. Well, it wasn't anything to worry about these days in Indiana. They were talking about taking away the last of the Miami reservations in Indiana. About time. As if they deserved to have a reserve after the slaughters they had done on innocent people in cabins in his very own grandparents' time. He had listened to Uncle Archie and Aunt Jewell tell the stories. They hated Indians bad. Along with colored folks, niggers.

He put his hands to his head and began kneading the skin at the back of his neck. His sister Mary Jane used to always make his headaches go away this way. What was she doing now? He received a letter recently. She was courting with one of the McCord boys. Cousin of Keith McCord in Company B and the other McCord who had died at Antietam. And his own brother Bob was talking of coming out to the wars. He, John, had written a letter home that should have blistered their eyes off about that. War was not for a boy. He had found that out himself. There wasn't a man in the regiment that was living on the old recruiting-rally dreams any more. He coughed once more, searing his lungs. His back hurt with pleurisy. If he was home, Mary Jane would make a croup tent and rub his back. Like a mother she was and always had been to him and Bob and Annie.

He stood up, listening to the sound of angry voices inside one of the winter shelters. The men were arguing about something, again. Now, with all the failures, they complained and grumbled as much as the people at southern Indiana church meetings.

Still, there was a new confidence and dignity, you could call it, in the regiment. When he returned from the hospital, the regiment was different. They knew that they had won glory. General French had named the Fourteenth Indiana, the West Virginia and Ohio regiments that had fought with it the Gibraltar Brigade; it was said they were one of the strongest in the Northern army at Antietam.

But there was also bitterness, anger at the generals and Washington chessplayers for not pursuing Lee, frustrated rage at so much death and wounding. Some of them, tired of being "volunteers," had rushed to join the Regular army when a recruiter came into camp. The ones who stayed seemed unfulfilled. Clay Welch was an example; he was a corporal in I Company until Kimball busted him to private for drinking; he had been paraded about last July in a barrel. All he did these days was talk of redeeming his honor; he seemed morose and as nervous as a canary bird in a cage. And he wasn't the only one. The Fourteenth Indiana Regiment seemed to McClure, who had missed the terrible agony of Antietam, like an unlanced boil, and he wondered what treatment was needed to relieve the pressure on the unit.

John McClure looked over the river, at the spires of the town. An old town it was too, as old as that first George McClure, far away in Ireland. "Let's see—at the time the Irish minister (it said he was) was writing in this book up there by Londonderry, I guess, this town was building some of those mansions. Fine places they are." He wondered what Old Reverend George McClure's house was like in Ireland. Did it have dormers and pretty little panes of glass? Probably not. Grandma Catherine said the McClures were poor folk before they came to Indiana.

"The people have all left Fredericksburg," he told himself, squinting across the river. "Took carts and piled their silver sets and dogs and children in 'em and left. Good thing they did, too. We may have to stay here all winter, or we may march on the town tomorrow. But sooner or later, Burnside will level this Rebel hog heaven."

Every time he saw a house, though, he thought of the people in it. He began to walk towards the army's new shelters, but his eyes were on the river, and the buildings beyond it. "Jest think of the times the folks have in those houses," he told himself. "The fights the little ones have over toys. Talk the parents have, murmurin' under the eaves when it rains. Smells o' gingerbread, jolly teatimes before the fire. Christmas. Christ, you can't think of that in a war, McClure. Rebels, Indians, niggers—you have to whip up hatred for 'em or they'll take over." Captain Beem didn't think so. He thought you had to hate the idea, not the man. Well, maybe that was it, but anyways, it was true. Necessary hatred was a part of life. He pounded his chest, whooped like an Indian to clear his congested lungs, and headed into one of the G Company log cabins to offer his help again.

At four p.m. John McClure and all the rest put gum blankets and shelter tents over the logs walls to make the roofs of the winter quarters. And at that very moment Van Dyke, Landon, Houghton, Beem, Cavins and the other officers came around to say that they needed to be prepared to move across the river at 6 o'clock the next morning. Goddamn. Lee was entrenched on the hill on the other side, in the town. They were going to force him out of his position. If they could.

* * * *

Zach Scott was in the conservatory at Rivertides with Delia. The day was mild enough for December; the western sun came in weakly through the panes of glass on this late afternoon. Still, Delia was stoking a small stove and filling pots with water.

"At this time of the year, they need some moist heat to survive. The Florida plants can't freeze, not even a little bit," she said.

"And the sensitive plants? Can they freeze?" Zach asked with a smile on his face. Seeing the plants made him recall the first night they met, here in the conservatory at that long-ago ball when the world and the war were young. He had seen Delia very little lately. Her brother Calhoun had been away, and so there was no reason for him to visit. Calhoun had only just returned. Willie, they said, had not returned. He had joined a Confederate regiment in Ewell's corps.

Calhoun had experienced trouble with General Sherman and was suspected of being a Rebel spy. It took him over a month to clear himself, to convince the general that he was only visiting Archie McClure. When the general did confirm Archie's illness and then death, Sherman let Calhoun go. Calhoun returned and immediately wrote to Zach to come to Rivertides, and they had spent the last evening speaking of the war effort, and Southern sympathies in these states of the Northwest. It was Delia, however, that drew Zach to the plantation, fascinated him in spite of himself. He watched the sunlight, captured through the prisms of the conservatory glass, shine on her hair.

"That night at the ball," Delia said, as she put manure around the roots of a multi-colored coleus plant, "you spoke of your brother as a sensitive plant. I think perhaps you have been the one to cause him pain."

She was bringing up the very subject he needed to know about. "Miss Dugger, we have had our differences lately. Somehow we seem to irritate each other whenever we are together, like wool against skin. But I need your help now. I need to know where my brother is.''

"And you think that I know that. Well, you are right."

"The regiment has been in obscure places; some are in the hospital, and I do not want to spend weeks locating him. Our father's estate has been settled, and he stands to come into a considerable amount of money. I am executor and must notify him."

"You?" Delia looked up, a slightly sardonic smile on her face.

"Yes, well, my father set it up that way for some reason. And at any rate, someone in the military can hardly be executor. My older brother is not interested, and so it fell to me, the family black sheep."

"I did not mean that—"

"Well, you may not think you did, but so it is. Anyway, I must write him. You know that Jake and I do not communicate."

"He has been keeping in touch with my Aunt Addie's family," Delia said, putting small pieces of wood on the little fire. "My cousin wrote me just this week telling me with glowing words about what Jacob Joe was doing in the regiment, as he had just written."

"Your cousin Sophie?"

"Indeed not! She laughs at his letters, says they are full of silly stories. It is my cousin Dora who carefully reads them, and corresponds with him, too."

"I am interested in your comment that my brother writes silly stories. He was always so credulous."

"He has written that at the recent battle, there at Perryville, he believes his life was saved by some sort of vision."

"Oh? Some have said he was a psychic sensitive. That it runs in the family."

"Certainly not with you, Mr. Scott," Delia said, snipping off a couple of gardenia blossoms that had turned brown from insufficient water. "At any rate, he believes he saw the spirit of your grandmother, Jenny I think her name was, warning him of a sniper's shot. Do you believe such things can happen, Mr. Scott?"

"I should hope not. I do not want my ancestors coming to talk to me. One of them, my uncle Ish Scott, was supposed to be a real reprobate. The talk of Vincennes."

"His nephew is talked about, too," She turned to him, her eyes alight with mocking merriment. She was in one of the moods which came over her recently, really ever since she had been managing Rivershores. Restless, independent spirits would seize her. She felt she was capable of anything and especially wanted to bait the men. "The governor is suspicious of your traitorous activities, I am told. And then there are the barmaids seduced, the women who faint at the mention of your name. I am really quite afraid of you, Mr. Scott. You may be as bad as your Uncle Ish.'' She did not look afraid.

"You are bold, Miss Dugger. But my uncle Ish Scott was a lieutenant of the notorious Aaron Burr. And, so they say, a murderer as well as a spy for foreign governments. They say the Devil was in him. I do not know if I want him haunting me. Even the good ancestors,'' he said, contemplatively, "might have bones to pick with me about my conduct.''

Delia stooped to pick up dried leaves and bits of branches from the floor. "I do not know if such things run in families, do you? I am descended from slave traders and the men who beat up the Shakers on the roads outside Vincennes. Some people say heredity is everything.'' Delia turned to face Zach Scott fully, with a mocking smile on her lips. "If it is, then I had better protect myself when I'm around you.''

Zach was silent a moment, taking stock of the full-bodied, self-confident woman he saw before him. "You seem different to me, Miss Dugger, than when I last saw you. Certainly different from the aloof Southern belle of the ball the night we met.''

"Perhaps it is being my own woman, Mr. Scott. My mother has been gone months now seeing to the desperate state of her parents' home in Tennessee. She will return in the spring, I think, but in the meantime I've kept this huge farm going. I have hired and fired servants, brought in and sold crops, and made Rivertides a major supplier of Northern army goods. Mr. Thomas Jefferson Brooks has been my guide, and I have doubled our income this year.''

"Thomas Jefferson Brooks. It seems to me his son is out there with Jacob Joe.''

"Yes. Tommy Brooks was badly wounded at Perryville in October and has been out of his head intermittently with fever a good deal since. He is being nursed night and day, even now, and there is some hope he will recover. His father has been disconsolate a good deal lately, however, and cannot seem to work, so Mrs. Brooks tells me.''

"I am sorry to hear it, although sincerely, as a Southern sympathizer I'm not sad to see one of the best suppliers out of commission. So you are growing corn and sorghum and hams for the men near Vicksburg and in Kentucky? I thought you sympathized with the cause of the South.''

"My cause is taking care of Rivertides. I do not know which side I stand for, if any. But I now make up my own mind and do as I please.''

Zach moved a step closer, close enough to smell fresh soap and lavender. "And what is it you please, Miss Dugger?''

"That we shall see, as events dispose of themselves, Mr. Scott. But never again will anyone tell me what to do. I know that.''

He smiled and nodded. Then he took her arm, and they went downstairs to find Calhoun and take tea in the parlor. Delia read Jacob Joe's letter, sent by Dora Lavenham. Zach listened, nibbling on cinnamon biscuits.

"And so my brother and the Eightieth Indiana continue on duty in Kentucky, pursuing Morgan the Raider," he said, wiping white icing from his chin. "I doubt they can catch him. He is an exceptionally bright cavalry leader, with all the leadership ability that McClellan had and a penchant for action, too."

"Who exactly is Morgan?" Delia wanted to know.

"The terror of Tennessee and Kentucky," Calhoun said. He lit a cigar and leaned back in one of his mother's good chairs, tilting it on two legs.

"Put that down, Calhoun," Delia commanded. Her brother did as he was told.

Zach went on. "John Morgan owned a hemp mill in Kentucky. Organized a crack militia unit called the Lexington Rifles and went to war. He can slide into town, change horses, eat dinner, and be gone before the townsfolk even know he's been there."

"You sound like you know the man," Delia said, putting down her teacup and looking at him seriously.

"I do, a bit, from others," Zach said evasively. "And if the rest of Indiana gets to know him, it will be to their regret."

"Well, then, I hope none of us will ever make his acquaintance. I have enough to do without having a battle out in the middle of my cornfields."

"My?" Calhoun asked, tamping ashes off his cigar.

"Ours, of course is what I meant to say, Brother," Delia sweetly affirmed, and then, gathering her skirts about her, retired from the sitting room.

Zach Scott's eyes, coolly observant, followed her as she went.

*   *   *   *

Houghton and Van Dyke stood on the shores of the Rappahannock River near Fredericksburg watching long lines of overcoat-clad soldiers cross the river on pontoon bridges—boards nailed to the gunwales of broad, flat-bottomed boats. The thick, brown artillery smoke which hovered in the air the day before had blown away. Even the December mist, in which flecks of hoarfrost danced earlier in the day, had dissipated and the air was clear and crisp.

"Three weeks, three biting cold, frustrating weeks we've wasted while General Burnside tried to decide what to do with us and how to get us all across this river," Van Dyke said. Both he and Houghton were looking across the water to the blank eyes which were the windows of the houses of Fredericksburg, some still pouring smoke from the Union bombardment the day before from this side of the river. Picket fences covered with leafless climbing rose vines, a mill with bags of meal still sitting outside its door, boats by the side of a canal, all gave the town an innocent look which was belied by the presence of thousands of soldiers from Sumner's Grand Right Division, who were filtering into its streets preparing to fight a battle.

Houghton was dispirited. "It doesn't make any sense, Gus," he said. "We've let Lee occupy that hill behind the town while we waited on the wrong side of the river. I've never understood why we couldn't just ford it like General Sumner wanted to."

"Burnside had his plan. It was a pontoon plan. And even when the river rose and the mules had to pull the boats by land through mud up to their bellies, Burnside wasn't going to change. He's as venturesome as—an ox."

"Well, he didn't want to command. Give him that." Houghton was thinking of the day a few weeks ago when McClellan was ordered to give up command of the Army of the Potomac. He was wildly cheered, even then, but he patted Burnside on the back and introduced him, cordially enough. A true Napoleonic knight, that's what McClellan was.

Van Dyke was no admirer of McClellan's. "You know I approved of the sack of Little Mac, but now we have"—he gestured towards the headquarters house—"a quartermaster type. And not even a very good quartermaster. I think Burnside would bungle even the issuing of a ration of beans to the Army of the Potomac."

Major Lige Cavins, presently in command, had ridden up beside them. He surveyed the crossing troops a moment, then took off his hat and waved it in the air. "Gibraltar Brigade, to the bridge! General Kimball has given his orders to cross!" Houghton and Van Dyke nodded assent and went to direct their companies onto the swaying, creaking bridges above the gray-brown water of the Rappahannock. G Company, with Landon at its head, led the troops.

Later the men of Companies C and G sat together under a mountain ash tree, one of several which lined a street in Fredericksburg. " 'Bout time for dinner," Bushby Quillen said to John McClure.

"I s'pose so," John McClure said. "At least we have pork pieces. Let's build a fire and spear them on the old bayonet, toast 'em a bit over the fire—barbecue, hey?" He fished in his haversack for salt and an onion he had dug from a garden.

Quillen turned his head to watch soldiers from other units, also camped in the town. "The men of Wilcox's corps know what to do," he said, chuckling darkly. He gestured with his head towards the houses along the street, pock-marked from the artillery shelling. Some had broken windows or shattered doors, and men were beginning to drift with curiosity towards these century-old houses. Enlisted men from an Ohio regiment moved in front of one three-story town house, walking tentatively back and forth in front of it, like boys on Halloween deciding if they will upset a pumpkin on the porch.

"Let's see what our comrades are up to," Crim said, jumping up and leaving the campfire. Others followed.

"They're going into these houses. Where are the officers?" Quillen wondered.

"Ours, except for Lieutenant Landon and Lieutenant Harrold, are with the ambulance trains and Surgeon Burkhart. Organizin' them for tomorrow," Crim answered. They looked at Landon, sitting on his haunches by himself a few yards off, smoking a cigarette. Harrold was lounging about with the men. Hard to think of him as a lieutenant now, but that is what had happened after his bravery at Antietam.

"Look, some of the Ohio regiments are upstairs in that house." Quillen pointed at a stately two story house whose shutters were awry. "Yesterday artillery blasted holes in the brickwork by the winders."

Blue-capped faces looked out of the windows of the house. In a moment things began flying out of the window: a large ham, a wooden confectioner's box and a satin pillow. "Planning on a sweet repose t'night, m' friend?" Crim asked a soldier who had a mane like a blond buffalo. He was standing beside them, catching the loot as it clunked down from heaven.

"Shore thing, man, especially with this satin coverlet I borried me from the downstairs bedroom of that there house," the soldier answered.

Landon continued smoking, staring off in space, with his back turned to the men. John McClure and Tommy Thompson came up behind Crim and Quillen.

" 'Tain't stealin' exactly," McClure said, not sounding convinced.

"They intend to take the piller and coverlet and lots of other geegaws home. Spoils o' war," Quillen alleged. McClure noticed that soldiers were mounting the stairs of other houses.

"You couldn't get any treasures out of the town, anyways," Thompson said. "Burnie has set the provost by the bridge. Didn't you see that pile as we come over, with all them bureaus and fancy gilt mirrors? They're a-guardin' it."

"Hell, they're a-gonna need the provost elsewhere soon and then—watch out. I think I'm a-gonna see if there's anything in the eatin' line in that there inn, center of southern hospitality," Bushby Quillen said. He limped off favoring one leg which was injured at Antietam and never had healed right. "Hell, here come the real officers," he called back softly over his shoulder to the others.

Beem, returning from the ambulance detail, walked briskly over to the iron fence where the men of Company H sat roasting a chicken over a fire. He confronted Jess Harrold, who was lounging on his elbow watching the spit turn. "Lieutenant, what's going on here?" Beem demanded. Harrold jumped up and brushed off his uniform pants.

"I just saw Sam Bright going into a bombed-out house," Beem said angrily. "Two other men in this company are rolling a barrel down the street. I left you in charge, lieutenant."

"Aww, Davey—"

"How many times have I told you not to call me Davey? We're not in Spencer, Lieutenant Harrold."

"Well, Captain Beem, the men are just doin' a little appropriatin'. The damn Rebels deserve whatever they get. These ol' ladies that own these houses had the Stars and Bars a-flyin' out o' every window. And the flour in that there mill went to supply the cavalry that shoots our asses off."

Beem batted his eyes, unimpressed. "Tell every man in H that I expect him to honor the orders of Generals Sumner and Kimball," he said.

"Everbody's doin' it, Davey—"

"H company is not everybody, Jess, I mean Lieutenant Harrold. Never mind, I'll take care of this myself."

Later, as other units came into town and camped in the streets, and as the afternoon sky darkened, so did the mood of the Union army. Houghton, Van Dyke and Beem watched as men brought furniture out of the houses of Fredericksburg.

"I've given up," Houghton said. "Cavins doesn't seem to care, so how can we?" One man sat rocking madly in a walnut and needlepoint chair. Other men from an Ohio unit pulled grape-back upholstered chairs around the campfire.

"They couldn't use those chairs even in they got them out of this town," Van Dyke said.

"I thought there were padlocks on these stores when the Rebels left," Beem said, "but the men are walking around with rum and bourbon. Isn't that Crim?" he asked, astonished. Isaac Crim had a small handcart loaded with bottles of hair tonic from a barber's shop, biscuits, and glass jars of fruit.

"He's probably thinking of replenishing his sutler's supply," Houghton said dryly.

"I'm going to stop him," Beem said. Van Dyke put a restraining arm on Beem's.

"If you're going to stop them, then you're going to have to chase down half the regiment."

"I suppose you're right," Beem agreed, and went away shaking his head. Houghton caught up and walked by his side.

Along the road, in front of the inn, they saw some of the men from the brigade band. George Washington Lambert found a violin under a bed in a house and had tucked it under his chin.

> *Oh my darling, Nelly Gray,*
> *They have taken you away*
> *And I'll never see my darling, anymore,*

he sang.

Houghton and Beem leaned against an oak tree. Now that the sun had gone down, damp, cold Rappahannock valley mist was drifting in, chilling the bones. Campfires began to twinkle down the streets of Fredericksburg; Houghton and Van Dyke strolled towards one the Fourteenth was building beyond the inn. There, as some of the men from C lit tinder, Bushby Quillen was preparing to throw on wood. He bent and broke the legs of an antique end table over his knees.

"Stop that," Houghton cried, but his attention was diverted by shouts above him. Through the deepening twilight the men were pushing a piano down the stairs of a house. Others were running up side streets, looking for houses not yet looted.

"This is getting out of hand," Beem said.

Across the street Lieutenant Landon himself was leading a mock marriage. Tommy Thompson had found a wedding veil in some poor Southern woman's hope chest; he had put it on and was trailing about. Joe Sholts was playing the groom, forcibly trying to hold his "bride" in front of the "preacher." Landon's mocking voice was loud.

"Dearly beloved drunks and wastrels of the Army of the Potomac," he said to the hoarse shouts and laughs of all gathered about.

"We shouldn't have condoned it in the beginning—" Beem said irritatedly to Houghton.

"It's getting like the sack of Rome," Houghton said. "Sumner's Right— the Goths and Vandals."

Someone brought forward a Rebel flag to the mock marriage. The "bride" and "groom" waved it above their heads. Landon's voice was raucous. "So let anybody who has a gripe 'bout the marriage of this Rebel slut and this Yankee hero come forward or forever hold his piss—" The men gathered around in a circle to desecrate the Rebel flag.

Van Dyke came up, his arms akimbo.

"What is the matter with these men?" Beem demanded of him, looking all about him at the drinking of the "wedding party," and the looting, which had become rampant in the last half hour. "Landon is your lieutenant!"

"You can't be serious with that question, Davey?" Van Dyke said sourly, with an odd, half-insulting emphasis on Beem's name. He said it long and drawn out and affectionate, the way Harrold was heard to say it when he forgot rank. "What's the matter? The matter is that they have lost a series of battles they should have won—lost friends and brothers because of the bungling of commanders, gotten into a war that we can't seem to win. All the Copperheads and traitors back home say we should get out and come back to southern Indiana. Worst of all, look back there."

He pointed at the hill behind the town, and Beem turned with him. "See that house up there, Davey? Around it, beyond that field that anybody can potshot over, in the range of twenty-pound Parrott guns, are eighty thousand Rebels."

"It isn't that I don't know that—" Beem protested, with injured dignity.

Van Dyke went on. "And we have to run across that field and then straight up that hill tomorrow. And you ask what's the matter with the men."

Beem refused to be cowed. "That's still no excuse for soldiers in the Union army looting and running around like a herd of wild buffalos."

"Isn't it? Isn't it really?" Van Dyke was almost shouting. Some of the enlisted men eyed these arguing officers. "War isn't an elocution contest, Davey. This is a Confederate city. What's Rebel is Southern and what that means is bad. It's Chickahominy Swamp and gangrene and Antietam and one-third of the men in your company killed or wounded. Or don't you remember that?" Van Dyke shook his head in disgust, as if he were tired of explaining something that should be obvious. He turned on his heel and took off down the street. Beem and Houghton followed him.

"Why are you so angry?" Beem demanded. "I'm just saying it's poor discipline. Whatever we do tonight affects what we have to do tomorrow. Cavins is allowing a melee. Harrow wouldn't have allowed all this if he were here."

Van Dyke turned his head to look down at Beem, who was several inches shorter than he. "But he isn't. And looking at that hill that Robert E. Lee holds, I don't think it matters what happens tonight." He walked on, and this time the other two did not follow.

Houghton had been silent all this time. The December darkness was a black curtain, broken only by the glimmer of campfires in the streets and above, on the hill.

Beem turned to his friend. "Will, why did you let him say these things? You know he's wrong about it mattering. You're a different person when you're with him. Sometimes I think he almost hypnotizes you."

Houghton turned away. "I don't know. I'm like these men tonight. I don't know much of anything except that tomorrow we go up there. Nothing else seems to matter much."

Just then Private Clay Welch came bounding up. He had a huge overbite and a gawking, engaging smile. "Waal, captains, tomorrow you are going to see me strut my stuff. I'll be first to form in line, last to fall back. Southern Indiana will be proud of Clay Welch, yessiree. Redeem m'self a smidgen."

"Good, Clay," Houghton said and clapped him on the back without looking in his face.

John McClure, Isaac Crim, Tommy Thompson, and Joe Sholts stood before a jewelry store at the end of the street. A huge clock-watch in the window stood at five o'clock. Men from Ohio were taking watches out of the store.

"Five o'clock. What're the folks back home doin' at this very minute?" McClure wanted to know.

Crim was eating chocolates from a box he had "bought" by exchanging a cut-glass decanter for it. He stopped short at McClure's words and gestured with his half-eaten cream. "I don't want to know. Don't think about them."

"Aww, they're runnin' around opening up their lapels showin' the copper pennies." Thompson was sour on southern Indiana. His fiancée, Lina Everett, had sent him a letter saying she was not in love with him any more, was marrying a southern-sympathizing boot-maker in Vincennes. "Mockin' us with every step they take."

"Yep. Stompin' on our souls," Joe Sholts said, his bug-eyes bright with his own cleverness. Thompson looked at him darkly. Sholts was always showing him up. And yet, "stomping on our souls" was good. That was what Lina had done to him.

"Not my relatives," McClure said. "When I go up that godawful hill tomorrer, it'll be knowin' that my folks in Indianney are all cheerin' me on."

A shell screamed. They turned and McClure ducked; he had never quite overcome that instinctive reaction, even though it did no good. A live shell landed in a box where Brisbane of Company B was sitting, reading a novel. Without losing his place, Brisbane placed the toe of his shoe under the shell and heaved it out and across the road, where it lit without exploding.

McClure looked at Crim. "There's cool heads and then there's real cool heads," he said, shaking his head admiringly.

At that very moment, one of McClure's supporting relatives was in need of support herself. His aunt Lettie Hogue stood by the window of a lodging room looking out on a bleak Cincinnati street. Well, the first step of this defiant adventure was successfully completed, she told herself. She had passed herself off to the indifferent landlady as the sister of Willis Mawkins, Esq., of Vincennes. Now she waited for his return from some sort of business, he hadn't said what.

It was blustery, even for December. Evening was passing into night. The lamps were lit; their glow illuminated the frost corners in the window, turning them purple and gold. Men walking down the streets pulled their collars up around their necks and put hands on their heads in case a gust of wind should pick up their hats and send them rolling down the street.

Why hadn't he come? Lettie wondered, turning from the dirty window to stare at the interior of the room, the cheap oak bureau, the sagging bed covered with a machine-knit coverlet. Well, it was fairly clean anyway.

Was *she*? Did it matter? She had asked herself a lot recently if she loved Willis Mawkins. He was handsome in an enigmatic sort of way, and his looks and manner, quiet and insinuating, pulled her toward him on a current, as if a field of animal magnetism surrounded him. Animal magnetism. "Well said, Lettie," she told herself sardonically. Of course it was that, probably nothing more.

She did not know him well enough to know if they shared anything. If he would talk about himself, instead of going to all these meetings, she might think about it. He was a leader of the Democrat party in Knox County, everyone knew that. All the papers said that the leaders were meeting, the party leaders and the state officials, Democrats all, who had won the recent elections in a landslide. They were planning strategies to destroy Governor Morton, stop his financing of the war, force peace on the North. So the papers said, but Willis Mawkins did not affirm it.

No, she was not in love with him, she was in love with living. She had been ever since stopping the tonics. It was just that she did not know what to do with her new freedom. She loved it, yet she dreaded it, especially the decision-making.

Now Willis Mawkins made most of her decisions, had for a couple of months. He went to see the gas company about her lights and stove, paid her account at the store from the wages she earned. Did someone think this was odd? Too bad.

Mawkins had been here in Cincinnati, meeting with whoever it was, for three days now, and afterwards she and he had met at the hotel each day. Last night, when they parted in the lobby, he had touched her hand with his fingertip, just one finger, and it set something deep inside her rumbling, down at the core. It was happening frequently lately, every time he touched her, whether on purpose or not. It was as if she were a volcano, and he could set molten rock bubbling. She was experiencing a new reality, volcano reality, and it was probably because of these feelings she had allowed herself to be convinced she should visit him at his lodgings for a "friendly call."

She heard footsteps on the stair. Suddenly, her mind leapt inexplicably to a scene from her childhood. "Odd how the mind works at times of over-excitement," she thought quickly. She was in the barnyard of the farm-house, filling her pockets with ruffly hollyhocks. Soon, after she fed the chickens, she would make hollyhock dollies out of the flowers. She banished the scene and struggled for complete composure. Mawkins was at the door, showing large teeth when he smiled.

"Lettie, I am glad you found my little abode. Was Mrs. Archer accommodating?"

"She accepted me as your sister. I wish I were so close to you." Oddly, the child in the back of her mind refused to be banished. She was trotting into the chicken house now, as if in some other sort of reality, the scene which had actually happened so long ago, was being unwound step by step in her mind. "Go away child," she commanded, and took his hat. You were with your friends?"

"I—there are many Democrats in Cincinnati. We keep in touch with Kentucky men, too, here. We play our games with legislators in our states. They give us party men advice." He turned to her with finality. Subject closed. She looked into those black, banked-furnace eyes.

Willis Mawkins took off his coat, loosing the pomade smell she loved. It was odd that a man who ran a stable, who lived always among horses and grooms, smelled as good as a hay field. Hay field. Inside the chicken house in her mind, the child picked in the straw of the nest, moving the mother hen aside. There were one, two chicks coming out of their shells.

"You look charming, Lettie, in that coffee-colored silk." He took her hands in his. There was a moment of silence, too important to be embarrassing. The little girl stroked the new baby chicks' yellow fluff. She pressed them to her. Ominous clouds could be seen out of the windows there in the past; the wind was beginning to blow hard.

Willis kept her hand, pressed it a little. "I have so many things to show you—about love. Will you let me—teach you?" He unbuttoned her sleeve adroitly, ran one finger inside, tracing her wrist. The volcano at the core rumbled.

"I—yes. I guess I would like that," she answered, her voice a hoarse whisper. The little girl in the back of her mind gathered the chickens to her, covering them with her skirt. The sky was butterscotch yellow, the wind moaning and shaking the chicken house. The little girl began to cry in fright.

"Leave everything to me," Willis Mawkins said. He put his arm about her shoulders, gently, almost like the relative she was pretending he was.

He kissed her, long and deeply, then again. The pomade smell was spicy-sweet, his lips moist and warm. The volcano lava began rising, bubbling through the mountain, seeking channels to come to the surface.

"Love is like a dance, a wonderful dance," Willis Mawkins was crooning. His hands unbuttoned the bodice of her dress; soon his hand, those long, beautiful fingers, were roving inside it. (The child screamed in fright, her hand clenching the baby chicks, crushing the hollyhocks in her apron pocket. The door opened and there, framed in the doorway, against the background of the windstorm, was her father. The child ran to his protective arms—Be gone, ordered Lettie with finality to the memories!)

Lights very low, bodice off, skirt slipping to the floor, many, many kisses, man's trousers sliding down, she leaning back against the bed, consciousness of male flesh—

"Wait! I do not wish to have a child. Impossible to think of. You have said, hinted that there was something new—the only reason I—" He was kissing, touching, leaning all at the same time and the lava was exploding, spilling over the top.

"Yes, new," he whispered. "Something I can use. I have it here. Leave it to me."

"Yes, I'll leave everything to you," she breathed, moving back against the bed, feeling the mattress against the back of her knees. She lay down and clasped him to her. Then volcano reality was all that existed.

He left her at the hotel entrance, kissing her hand and looking into her eyes again before departing up the street. She bent to pick up something that had fallen out of his overcoat pocket. It was a calling card.

"Clement Vallandigham, Representative in Congress, State of Ohio," it said, and then, beneath that, in pencil, "Our cause awaits the uprising amidst the swelling tide of battlefield defeat!" Beneath that was the penciled form of a snake.

*   *   *   *

Lieutenant Colonel Lige Cavins spoke from horseback to the men of the Fourteenth as they formed in the streets of Fredericksburg the morning after the sack of the city. "We are to lead," he said. "Our regiment, of all of the Northern army, is to lead the assault on Lee on the heights. General Kimball will head the brigade; French, the Division; Couch, the Corps of Sumner's Grand Right. But we are first."

Thomas Gibson of Beem's company, who had joined the regiment just after Antietam, stood in the front line. He requested permission to speak. "Sir, I wish the honor of carrying the colors," he said.

Cavins leaned down. "It will be hot work, Gibson," he said. "Wingfield requested first, and since he fought at Bloody Lane—the honor is his. Next time, perhaps." He looked at Beem. "Some of the men were drunk last night. Are they fit?" he asked.

Beem did not meet his eye. It had not been his company in which the men were drunk. "Yes, sir. I believe so, sir." Heavy booms, cannon fire, had begun from the Northern artillery, across the river. That famous group of Lee's, the Washington Artillery, answered from the other side.

Beem turned to Lieutenant Harrold. "Do we have any more reporting sick?" he asked.

"Well, sir, we left Craig back across the river yesterday. Surgeon Burkhart will not certify him for duty. No one new today, though."

"Good." Beem turned to Houghton, who was checking the lines. Beem lowered his voice and spoke more casually. "I suppose Burkhart will be hard pressed today. He is to be at the field hospital. He will miss Walter McClure."

"We all miss Walter," Houghton said. "He should be back any time from Indiana. I just had a letter saying he is returning and Colonel Coons is improving enough to return by spring."

"If we are still an army," Beem said.

"Do you doubt that?" Houghton wondered.

"I take nothing for granted in this war," Beem answered.

Thick clouds of smoke from the artillery rose before them, on the plains they would soon be crossing, beyond the town.

"They can get us from three sides," Houghton mused, then turned to Beem. "Beem, I'm sorry about the melee yesterday in town. Maybe if I'd stood stronger, you and I together could have forced the issue with the brass. The men seemed possessed—"

"Well, as Van Dyke said, today has little to do with yesterday. Look at these men. Even Landon—especially Landon. He's exhorting all the rest. We're facing—suicide across this plain to that impregnable, sheer hill, and yet they seem to be ready."

"Each one says he'll go as far as another goes," Houghton said. "Crim and Quillen are helping Landon inspire them with idealism," he smiled a grim little smile, remembering the hams and broken chairs and the wedding party last night.

"Well, they are not without honor. Give the Fourteenth a moment of challenge, and they stand as well as anybody in the nation—who's this?"

A soldier with the build of an ox and a long, curling mustache came trotting up to the ranks. "Why, it's Craig," Beem shouted, clapping the young man on the back. "I thought you were with the surgeon." Then, more seriously, "Craig, you don't belong out here."

"Beg to differ sir, but 'tis here I do belong. We bulldogs of Owen County don't shun a fight, now, do we?"

"Join the ranks then," Beem told him, looking down line after line of blue overcoats, brass buttons and the glint of bayonets in the sun. "The fight has already begun on the left and we are to attack the hill soon."

Off to the left of the line forming in Fredericksburg, where General Franklin's Left Grand Division was already engaging the Confederates, Surgeon Burkhart reported to the area field hospital, just behind the lines. His eyes ranged over the field. Already a steady line of blue ambulances, wagons marked with red crosses on white Conestoga coverings, was winding its way towards the shake-roofed house which served as hospital headquarters.

The commanding surgeon was already doing amputations on a table to the left of the house. He raised his eyes to show that he saw Burkhart. "Roll up your sleeves, sir," he gestured with his head. He was poised, knife in hand, while his orderly cut a pant leg off an unconscious soldier whose lower leg had been smashed with flying shrapnel.

"This soldier is in shock," the commanding surgeon said to his orderly. "Keep him warm. Damn hard amputating in cold weather. Wish they'd only fight in July."

"Infection is worse then, sir," Burkhart said in his thick accent, watching blue-coated soldiers and ambulance bearers bring limp men to the tables.

"Do I know you?" the surgeon, who was from the Second Corps, said, looking Burkhart full in the face. "Are you from the German corps?"

"Ah, no, but formerly from Germany." There it was again, even at the height of battle. Meeting each new officer in the medical corps meant staking out some new sort of territory, encountering suspicion, especially of "Deutschies." Even though he had now been given a commission, now that he operated alone, and the other, politically appointed doctor had gone home—"Captain Jacob Burkhart, Gibraltar Brigade, Sumner's Grand Right Division," the Fourteenth's surgeon said with dignity.

"Well, I don't care where you're from, we will have our work here today as ne'er before. You're without an orderly—I can spare one of the soldiers to drop chloroform for you." He gestured towards a soldier carrying in a man who had just died, and the stretcher bearer came to Burkhart's side.

"You don't want me to assist you?" Burkhart asked the commanding officer.

"No, take that dining room table the men got from one of the mansions last night and use it. Put it to better use than it's seen in a while. Be sure to prop the leaves up some way. We don't want it to collapse as you're sawing.''

Burkhart and his assistant dragged the table to a stable place under a tree. As he rolled up his sleeves, Burkhart stood and looked to the right, towards the town of Fredericksburg where the rest of his regiment was preparing to advance. He knew that some of them would probably be under his knife soon, here, under this December sky in the cold air of the field hospital.

The men of the Fourteenth filed across the stringers of a railway bridge and into the fields in back of the town of Fredericksburg. They re-formed among a cluster of houses at the fork of a lane, ready to advance against the hill on what was known as Marye's Heights, where the Rebel army waited, firmly entrenched.

Private Clay Welch rushed by, rifle at the ready. His breath came in clouds as he said to Houghton, ''Well, sir, I know no fear. Today is the day I redeem m' reputation. If y' ain't got a reputation in Indianney, you ain't got nothin'.'' He joined the second tier of the line.

Ahead loomed the hill of Marye's Heights, tall, foreboding.

''I fear there's some sort of mistake, here, Beem, don't you?'' Houghton said sardonically as his fellow officer passed. ''Their position and strength are terrible to see. Someone has miscalculated.''

Beem sighed. ''I can't help thinking of the poem,

Forward the light brigade
Was there a man dismayed
Not though the soldiers knew,
Someone had blundered.''

The lines of blue began to inch forward, towards the inexorable heights, but Beem insisted on finishing—

''Theirs not to make reply,
Theirs but to do and die
Into the valley of death—''

A shell burst right in the midst of the advancing men of H Company. Beem rushed to where it had shattered; Private Craig, newly returned to the lines, collapsed in his arms, blood pouring from a gaping hole in his thigh.

''Here, Smart, come help Craig, poor fellow just returned to the ranks and then shot. Take him to the rear.'' A man pulled out of the line and began to drag Craig, shrieking in pain, to the rear. Then the line went on, through amber smoke.

General Kimball, commanding the Gibraltar Brigade, appeared on his mare like a ghost out of the mist. "On, men, and do not stop until you reach the top of the hill." He spurred his horse and disappeared into the smoke.

"Top of the hill." The words rattled about hollowly in Houghton's brain like a marble in a tin can, as he urged Company C forward.

The brigades fanned out, two hundred yards between the Fourteenth and the rest of the Gibraltar Brigade, then Andrew's, then Palmer's Brigades.

John McClure advanced with the rest, his bayonet before him. His copy of *Pilgrim's Progress* was safe in his blouse. "Greater is He that is in you, than he that is in the world." Maybe there was something in it, he told himself. He had never been much for religion, but in a battle like this, it couldn't hurt.

There, up there, was a house, McClure noted, or something, through the haze, and shadowy artillery. The oddest thing was a solid line of fire and musket smoke, coming from some sort of wall near the foot of the Rebel hill. You couldn't see faces, just bursts of fire. "A nightmare, a wall spewing fire and death, and we have almost no chance t' reach and stop it," he thought.

Men fell in all attitudes in front of John McClure, slumping, pitching backwards, raising arms and shrieking, crumpling with sighs, blood bubbling out of the corners of their mouths—

"God, worst we ever fought," McClure screamed at the man next to him—Lieutenant Landon.

"The flag has fallen," Landon shouted back. The regimental colors, held in the hands of Private Wingert, fluttered earthward as their bearer clutched his chest.

Before another moment passed, Gibson, who had begged to be color-bearer, surged forward, bullets flying over his head, and grabbed up the flag. Nearby, canister flew thick and deadly, sweeping away entire companies just a few yards ahead or behind them.

Then the ranks went forward a few feet, with men flying in the air, shells bursting, the line thinning inch by inch.

"I've taken it in the arm," Landon shouted and Van Dyke ran to him. "It's not that bad. I'm staying," Landon said firmly. Quillen was wounded in the knee and trying to get up to fire again. He mouth was moving in a stream of curses. Beem, watching, thought through his anguish, "It's as if last night never happened. All that ever matters when the Fourteenth is on the field is the bravery, the endurance. Southern Indiana has shaped us all."

Beem shouted at Van Dyke, "Hancock's men are coming behind us. Maybe with that power we can take the hill."

"Never!" Van Dyke yelled through the din. Houghton materialized through the smoke. "We're sure to lose half the regiment." He pointed towards the left. "There's General Kimball."

Through the lines, towards the brick houses where they had formed, two skirmishers were bearing General Nathan Kimball, wounded by a shell, obviously in excruciating pain.

"Captain Houghton. Find Adjutant Blinn," Kimball said in a still-strong voice. "He should notify Colonel Mason of the Ohio regiment to assume command for me." He raised his voice so all within range could hear, "On men, to the top of the hill, I say," and then was borne off, his eyes shut against the pain of a ragged shell wound.

"Where in God's name is the adjutant?" Houghton demanded, trying to get his bearings.

"There! Over on our left, towards Franklin's corps. I can just catch sight of his horse. I think he's headed towards us anyway," Van Dyke shouted.

Houghton stumbled towards the horseman, followed by Van Dyke. They raised their arms in a useless greeting in the melee that was the battlefield. The horse lurched within a few feet of them, panting and snorting, then reared in the air right before them.

"He's hit! The adjutant is hit," Houghton yelled as Blinn slid out of the saddle, senseless. "Van Dyke, find someone to take him to the rear!" Houghton took the reins of the frightened horse. "I'm going to find Colonel Mason as General Kimball ordered."

"No," Van Dyke shouted emphatically, as he began to drag the bleeding adjutant. "Shit, Will, those orders don't hold for you. Someone will get word to Mason and anyway we don't need anybody to command in hell! It's every poor sinner for himself. We need you here, Will." The first name rang forlornly in the maelstrom that was the Fredericksburg battlefield.

"It's my duty, I'm going," Houghton said, adjusting the stirrups.

"You're a target for those madmen behind the stone wall. Almost every officer astride has been hit. I tell you, it's madness."

Houghton galloped off, Van Dyke's voice, like that of a querulous old woman, following him.

Half of the seventy or so men who now constituted the Fourteenth huddled together, behind a breastwork of bodies of the men who had fallen before them.

"This is as far as this man's army goes," McClure shouted to Quillen. "The line is too thin to advance any further. Where's the officers?"

"Where all the rest of us are, lyin' on the field or flat on their faces tryin' not to get shot," Quillen answered. "Cavins has ridden for further orders."

They watched the rest of their regiment, who were still nearby, exposed on the field. D Company, Cavins' own men and men from H and a few other scattered units were still trying to make the stone wall one hundred yards ahead of them. One would break and run, raising his gun, then before he got three paces, be shot. Another would try the break away, run a couple of steps, then drop.

Then, a man emerged from the gloom and began a sustained run for the stone wall. He made three strides, then six as the men watched in amazement. The shattered line began to cheer.

"It's Welch! Clay Welch. He's heading for the wall. Make it Welch! Nobody else has!"

Finally, the lone man's advance halted within forty yards of the stone wall. He was close enough to see the eyeballs of the Rebels and hurl defiance in their teeth. Then, like a doll a child has stood on its feet he tottered, staggered, and fell, downed by scores of bullets.

Beem, kneeling near the exposed position, shook his head in amazement.

He turned to see the flagstaff, in the hands of Gibson, teeter, as Gibson was hit in the back. Cavins had galloped up, in time to see the bravery and slaughter of his own company, and he also watched the scene.

"Retire, Gibson," Beem ordered. "The flag will be recovered. You are wounded—"

"No, sir," Gibson countered, gasping a little. "This is what I left Owen county for." He dropped on one knee, his face white from loss of blood.

The voice of Major Cavins rang out, "Private Gibson, the United States does not need you to bleed out your life to save its flag. Report to the rear at once, and I personally will see that the flag is reassigned to another honor guard. You have my word." He gestured and Gibson put the flag into the hands of someone behind him.

Cavins again shouted above the din, "Captain Beem and officers of the Fourteenth still on the field: retire to that slight rise just behind us and remain there. You will be safe from the fire of the stone wall there. The Fourteenth has led the day and again covered itself with glory. My heart goes out to you in thanks!"

"To the top of the hill—" The impossible, gallant words echoed in Beem's mind as he dropped with the rest behind the slight rise facing the stone wall to await the disposal of events.

"General Kimball!" Surgeon Burkhart said in surprise. Stretcher bearers were carrying the general past a pile of arms and legs as high as Burkhart's knees as he stood beside the operating table. Kimball's hat was on his face; his body was covered in blankets.

"Met up with a shell fragment, captain," Kimball murmured as an orderly took the hat from his face. "Nothing to worry about"—he winced in
pain.

"Thigh wounds are often the worst, sir," Burkhart murmured as he pulled back the blanket and looked at the wound, full of dirt, congealing blood
and fragments of metal. "I think it best to give you a snort of chloroform as I
probe."

"Captain, I don't think that is necessary," Kimball said. His fists were
clenched.

"Sir, I outrank you at this moment." Burkhart motioned for the young
soldier with the chloroform bottle to begin dropping the fluid onto the cotton
wads which would be held above Kimball's nose.

"How is it going out there, sir?" Burkhart asked Kimball as he helped the
stretcher bearers ease the general onto the wooden table.

"Like hogs being driven up the hill to the lard pots," the general said, his
voice labored.

The orderly began dripping the fluid, Kimball sneezed and then groaned
at even that much exertion.

"Somebody's head should fall," he said, his voice beginning to ease into
comfort. "Put it right over there on top of that pile of arms and legs. Yes,
the head of Ambrose Burnside. . ." He was asleep.

"Odd how chloroform dulls the sensibilities and makes one say things
without restraint, things one would not otherwise say," Surgeon Burkhart
commented loudly, turning his head for an instant to see if any of the corps
surgeons were listening.

But all were involved with the cleanup of slaughter on a grand scale.
Slowly and carefully Burkhart began removing slivers of metal, some of
them three inches long, from the thigh of his brigade commander.

All that afternoon, ghost-like figures rose to retire from the lines at Fredericksburg, to leave the battle that could not be won, drifting to the brick
houses at the rear of the battlefield, or to the safety of the town. With the
continuing fire, it was almost as difficult to leave the little hill where they all
refuged as it had been to come.

Jess Harrold and John McClure made the largest house just before dark,
when the guns had ceased their activity and as an odd orange sun set through
the smoke of battle on Fredericksburg Battlefield.

John McClure stepped over two corpses by the door of the house. He
could hear voices within. Strange wayfarers, castaways of the battle, had
assembled in the battered walls of the house.

"The temperature has dropped," Harrold said in a sepulchral voice as he followed McClure in. " 'Tis bitterly cold. The wounded are dyin' and freezing stiff. Nobody to pick 'em up.''

A captain from the Eleventh U.S. Infantry muttered, "The ones left out there are using dead horses as bunkers.''

McClure, passing other corpses in the rooms, slipped towards the rear of the house. He passed an artilleryman with a completely blackened face drinking from a canteen, singing snatches of old lullabies softly to himself.

At the rear of the house, near an old fireplace, sat a woman. Her hair was wild and unkempt. She looked out the glassless window, but her eyes did not see.

"She stayed here, through all that?" Harrold asked. "Her lips are moving. What's that she's saying?"

McClure moved closer to her and watched. "She's saying 'These are the pearls that were his eyes.' ''

"Don't make no sense," Harrold said solemnly.

"No, none of it does. Not one goddamned bit of it," John McClure said. He stooped to pick up a ragged piece of cross-stitch that lay in a little hoop at her feet. "Home, Sweet Home," it said.

On their way out, they stopped beside the Regular army captain. "Do you think Burnside will send us out again, sir?" Harrold asked.

"In no way should we try another attack," the officer said dourly, staring into his now-empty canteen. Then he looked squarely at them through the gloom. "But a man insane enough to storm an impregnable hill could take up the same position tomorrow."

"Then I'd rather I'd died with my comrades out there today," Harrold said. They made their way through the living and the dead to the doorway of the brick house.

"You've been shot up five times, Harrold," McClure said to him. "And four of those times were at Antietam. Still, you're alive, while a lot of others we started with in Indianney are dead."

"Guess I beat the law of averages," Harrold said.

McClure thought about it as they made their way back through the edges of the town to try to find the Fourteenth. The law of averages did operate. In the middle of the battle, someway, it had come to him that there was a bullet out there for him. Thousands, millions of bullets the Rebels had, and one of them was for him, by the law of averages. He had been in a rear position at Kernstown, had not been at Antietam, had not been hit here at Fredericksburg. The war was not nearly over and the Fourteenth was getting front-line assignments everywhere it went. So, at some time, he now believed, one of those Minie balls had his name on it. Something just told him it did.

He touched the copy of *Pilgrim's Progress,* as some men touched the Bibles they carried during a battle. Maybe it was good luck, maybe something else. Not all bullets killed. Mostly they just wounded. Greater is He that is in thee? Could be true. If he had survived this hell today, he might yet beat the law of averages. What was it one of those old McClure geezers said way back when? "Do the very best you can each day, and things will generally swing round better than ye reckon." It was on a piece of paper in the little box they found after his father died.

Well, he would try that, best he could do in the circumstances anyways. The gunfire was stopping. Odd that Lee wasn't coming down, but he didn't seem to be following up his advantage. Maybe they were as bone-tired as we are. Rest, that's all I want, just to sleep even if it is on a rock.

There, there among the shattered buildings, were a campfire and familiar faces.

A few days later John McClure, Isaac Crim, Augustus Van Dyke, Jess Harrold, David Beem, Will Landon, Jess Harrold, William Houghton, Bushy Quillen, Surgeon Burkhart, the badly wounded General Nathan Kimball and all the rest of the Fourteenth who had not died at Fredericksburg moved with the Army of the Potomac back across the Rappahannock in defeat.

As for the dead, a few days after that, Rebel burial details stripped the bodies of all of the Yankees, including those of the gallant Fourteenth. One Georgia officer looked coldly down from his horse at the corpse of the soldier nearest the stone wall at the foot of Marye's Heights. He put a hook under the arm of the frozen body and pulled it thirty feet.

"Now you goddamned Yankee," he said to the corpse, "you was so eager to have the honor to get to our wall, now you have got yo' wish—and yo' honor."

And he left the naked body of Clay Welsh, Company I of the Fourteenth Indiana regiment, against the stone wall at the foot of the hill until such time as the Northern burial party should come and bury it.

Early March, 1863

Chapter Nine

Althea Dugger closed the door on the house of her girlhood home at Fairchance Plantation. She turned to Major Edward Bachelder, who stood on the first step, just below her, and took his hands. "I feel so right about leaving Fairchance in these good hands," she said with a smile.

"Not exactly in my hands," Major Bachelder told her with a self-deprecating grin. "Really, I think this new man from Memphis you have hired as overseer will do quite well. I will be out each week, even though it is not my duty any more, now that Sherman has gone and my assignments have changed. My pleasure now, for a friend."

Althea squeezed his hand and released it. "Well, I think Myrtle Jean is trained. I have spent enough time teaching her how rugs are beaten properly, how to supervise the smoking of the hams and bacons, the soap making—"

They headed down the steps to the waiting rig. "Should I infer something from the fact that you are paying her a salary?" Bachelder asked with an amused sideways glance. "A confirmation that slaves are free indeed and the Cause not what it was?"

She gave him her hand as he helped her into the rig. "Make no inferences. I want to pay the servants I have, whatever their status. I want no more cotton speculators on my father's land." She was seated next to him, and as he started the horses in a slow walk, she turned to him with a sudden question. "Jonas is in the Negro impoundment in Memphis? I was afraid they would never ferret him out of the swamps."

"Yes. I checked yesterday. He is surly, they say, and uncooperative."

"And making threats against me and my parents. I have not told them fully about how he ran amuck here—I did not think Father could stand it. His heart is weak, and Mother always was a wilting rose." Her expression was far away, as if she were remembering. "No staying power," she said firmly. Bachelder's face registered mild surprise at the disapproval in her tone. Her own mother? He always seemed surprised when she was unusually frank.

"No sense in beating around the currant bushes," she said, watching

Ananias, the new overseer, wave them goodbye at the end of the tree-lined lane. Not long ago, as they had sat in the deepening twilight in the parlor of the mansion sipping sherry, Edward Bachelder had told her that his original impression of her as a wilting Southern belle changed as he came to know her. "The belle has a steel edge," he said, amused.

"I call life as I see it," Althea had shrugged. "Yet," she had added, "sometimes I think I see only what I want to."

Now she said, "As to my politics, you are fully aware I still hold firmly to my belief that the Confederacy has a right to be a free nation and that it will prevail."

"We agree to disagree, as always, on that subject," the major said tactfully.

They had reached the town road, and he whipped the horses up a bit. "You will be in Louisville for a while?" he asked.

"Yes. I have decided to visit with my sister and nieces for a while. Delia and Calhoun will meet me there, and we will return to Rivertides together."

"I trust—I hope—you will have a peaceful visit."

"Well, we should, now that Braxton Bragg has taken his army out of the area there. But Louisville is never very peaceful these days. All the maiden ladies are a-twitter, afraid Morgan's cavalry will pounce down. Every third week there is an alarm."

"That is what Morgan wishes. Your fine Confederate cavalry rovers, raiders we call them, want to keep us all off balance, cut off major supply lines, divert attention from the areas of large battles."

His eyes were intense; she turned to look down the road ahead. "Well, they succeed, you must admit. Nathan Bedford Forrest and John Morgan ride into an area and troops are sent rushing in on the cars, the militia forms, mayors call for help."

"Yes. The last time Morgan threatened Louisville in the fall, one of the Union commanders grew so nervous he shot and killed another in the lobby of one of the hotels over defense procedures. Disgraceful." Althea watched the smoke rising from the Negro cottages along the road. It was good to see signs of domesticity there again, good to know that the "people" were staying to work, even if she was paying them from her own pocket. Ananias could be trusted, at least for a while. He had appeared on the doorstep recently, one of the wandering Negroes now roving the land, claiming experience in overseeing.

"You know, I did not hear of the murder in Louisville until fully a month afterwards," Major Bachelder went on.

They had left her parents' land behind; she craned her neck to steal one last glance at the house on the hill, through trees. "That violence in Louisville could have happened in my sister's hotel, though it didn't. She did know the murdered man. The military tried to cover it all up.''

Bachelder looked over at her quickly. ''Be careful, Althea. Louisville is a snake pit.'' He reached over and touched her on the arm. ''You are as good a friend as ever I have had.''

She squeezed his arm as they trotted along. She did not trust herself to speak. Through the winter months she had worked on putting the plantation back in shape, arranged for getting seed in these troubled times, hired servants on very small wages, dealt with the slaves who had been allowed to run wild and tried to arrange for loans to save the house and acres. Edward Bachelder had been her right hand. He had provided a guard, first, when renegade soldiers and freed slaves wandered about, foraging and looting. Then, he had come out weekly to advise and strengthen her. His presence, first ordered by Sherman, then condoned by the new commander General Hurlbut, kept the bank from calling in the mortgage and seemed to bring an implicit promise that this planation should not be ravaged during this protracted war. Recently the major had advised, even urged her to have her father deed the property to her. She, as a citizen of the state of Indiana, would not be subject to having the lands confiscated.

But the fact remained that Edward Bachelder was a Northerner from Massachusetts, born and bred an abolitionist. He was as far from her own background and beliefs as Massachusetts was from Tennessee. They could not talk about any of the politics of the war; and when they did, congeniality turned sour, like cream left in the sun, and they grew irritated with each other.

''You are the most determined woman I've ever known, Mrs. Dugger— Althea,'' Edward Bachelder had said to her exasperatedly last night in the newly-painted parlor, when they were discussing the war.

''That is because I believe in what I say. Lincoln is as much a tyrant as George III. He has freed the slaves by his own executive order, without the will of the people. And now, this very month, the Northwest will have to enforce this new, hated draft law he has ordered! I tell you there will be trouble back in my home when they try to force men to support the Union. The Revolutionary War was fought with volunteer militia. What kind of cause can it be when men are forced to leave their homes and fight!'' She clenched her fist in the lap of her blue dress.

Major Bachelder was leaning against the mantel in the parlor sipping berry wine, all the plantation could provide in these hard times. ''Well,'' he said, putting his crystal wine glass down on the mantel and watching her without smiling. ''As always, you have strong views. You could almost convince me you were right—if I did not know my own.''

''You can't prove that there is any real difference between the Confederacy in our own time and George Washington's new republic in 1776," Althea said decisively.

"Except that George Washington made his new idea stick by winning the war."

"As it appears the Confederacy will do now, after Shiloh, Antietam and Fredericksburg."

"Lee did *not* win at Antietam, though you Southerners keep saying so," Bachelder said with more emphasis than he probably intended. "It was just that McClellan let him get away. Kentucky is ours, and a good deal of the Mississippi River. Whoever controls the Mississippi wins the war." He frowned as he reached towards the decanter to pour more of the deep purple wine.

Althea had turned abruptly away from him. "Well, we shall see, Major Bachelder, Edward. We should not quarrel over it. There is so much that is good to talk about, really."

"Indeed, yes," he had said, raising his glass to her, his eyes catching her in his glance, as if she were a butterfly in a net. Sometimes, for just an instant, he sent a spark of longing at her, as if it were a tennis ball, and sometimes, against her will, she returned it. But not often. It was an impossible situation. He had a wife of several years back in Massachusetts, and she was not a giddy girl of sixteen. It was important that they stick to business, although surely a little courtesy, a little friendship could be allowed in this all too cruel war. Surely that was not too much to ask, even of adversaries.

They were driving towards Memphis now, through the countryside, past burned-out plantations, others that seemed to be plowing and planting on this greening March day. Now, Althea thought, her parents' fields were planted, and she was free to leave in peace. She had been careful to keep her father informed, there at his brother Bartie's in Mississippi, of plans, to consult him on which fields he wished sown in corn, which in beans, how to select stock in these days when cotton could not be grown. It was important he still feel in charge, though his health seemed to be failing and his mind was oddly troubled.

She could not control all things; she would have to trust to Providence in some matters. Providence, Yankee money-lenders and the Northern army, not a very reassuring thought. She sighed ruefully and closed her eyes.

When she opened them, Major Bachelder was driving onto the levee at Memphis. She had fallen asleep, and her head had ended up on his shoulder.

"Mr. Scott, do come in," Sophie Lavenham gushed as she brought Jacob Joe into the parlor of the hotel a week or so later. "We were so glad that

Colonel Morgan relaxed his frantic riding enough to let some of the regiment go on leave.''

Jacob Joe's eyes took the measure of the beautiful girl gently grasping his arm and ushering him through the etched glass door of the hotel into the hall. She was radiant in dotted Swiss with a pink velvet embroidered jacket—like a fashion plate from *Godey's Ladies' Book.* A matching pink ribbon held back masses of cascading, light brown curls.

"My aunt Althea and cousins Delia and Calhoun have awaited your coming. They are sure enough excited 'bout it all,'' Sophie said.

They entered the music parlor. Calhoun arose, laying his cigar carefully across a porcelain dish, and shook Jacob Joe's hand. "Sir, I am pleased to see you again.'' There was only a split second of oddness, fringed with pain, for Jacob Joe. Shaking the hand, he realized that it belonged to a man who saw his brother constantly in the nefarious Copperheading activities they pursued, a brother from whom he was sadly estranged. It was difficult for him to shake the hand of a Southern sympathizer, but he managed to do it.

Althea Dugger came forward and gave him her hand, too. "Mr. Scott, I believe your brother was trying to get in touch with you. I think my niece Delia was able to reach you, isn't that right?''

"My brother's lawyer did reach me.'' Sophie was still at Jacob Joe's elbow. "It seems I now own half of Father's acres. Our older brother wished us to buy his share of the property. I have a tidy inheritance also, though how I can use it in this Western army is hard to tell.'' Sophie gave him an admiring look.

Althea went on. "Please tell us of your battlefield experiences. You have been pursuing Morgan the Raider, I believe.''

Jacob Joe grinned politely, but did not begin immediately. He was among milk-and-cider patriots, as the boys in the Eightieth Indiana called them, weak sisters who leaned whichever way the boat tilted. Probably they favored the Confederacy. He was not going to tell them the details of the slap-dash, down-the-turnpike chase after Morgan through Tennessee.

"Well, we're back now, and we have been getting fat in camp, mostly, ma'am. Enjoyin' ourselves up hugely. But I suspect Colonel Morgan will give us some cause to put away the playin' cards and magazines and get on the road again.'' His eyes followed Sophie. She seemed to have tired of the conversation after it passed from his inheritance to the wars, and was walking through the arch to the large parlor that faced the street. Now she was absently patting her curls, using the window as a mirror. Over by the fireplace Dora Lavenham was emptying saucers filled with cigar ashes. The cloying, pungent odor of the ashes assailed Jacob Joe's nose; obviously guests had just left. Thankfully none were here now, and the hotel had put out a "fully engaged'' sign at the door.

Althea Dugger had not taken her sharp eyes from him, and her daughter Delia came up beside her mother to welcome the boy back from battle. "Mr. Scott, did I hear you say playing cards? Are you indulging in gambling?" Her eyes were merry. As he smiled and brushed aside the teasing with a wave of the hand, he looked at her wonderingly for a moment, struck by the contrast between her and her cousin Sophie, the one a dark mystery, the other a light-haired angel.

Delia's thick and luxurious hair was pulled up behind her head and caught with a wooden clasp; the dress she wore was sprigged cotton. Yet she was breathtakingly beautiful, aglow with a sort of inner composure and satisfaction. What a rare thing that is in a woman, he told himself. He had seen so little of that, or any other womanly quality lately. Most of the women he encountered in Tennessee were worn down, scraggly as jaybirds. Their men were off fighting. The fields were not producing as they should, and the strains and hunger had worn them into scarecrows.

Sophie reentered the small music room, followed by Dora. "I have an idea," Dora said, brightly. "Let's have our supper and go down and hear the lecture at Lyceum Hall."

Her mother, Addie Lavenham, had come from the kitchen and was putting small bowls of things to eat on the tables for the guests. She turned to Sophie. "I can't imagine what interest there would be in going to a lecture," she said, frowning.

"Why not, Mother?" Dora said spiritedly. " 'Tis the phrenologists, the husband and wife team."

"We've seen or read about phrenologists before," Mrs. Lavenham sniffed. "They've been around for twenty years or so."

Calhoun, on the settee, was thumbing through a circular on the small table in front of him. "These are the folks that tell a man's character by looking at the bumps on his head," he said

Dora went to Calhoun and put a pretty finger in rebuke right under his nose. "Now, cousin, that's not what it's about, although all the world thinks it is. It's really very scientific."

Jacob Joe looked interested. "I heard one lecturer on phrenology at Earlham College a few year ago. Somethin' about the brain being the site of the mind and being divided into parts: the organs of benevolence, mathematical ability, theft and mischief, and so forth, controlling actual character."

Dora brushed off cigar ashes that had drifted onto her apron. "The new phrenologists don't stop just by looking at the shape of the head. They teach about spiritualism, seances, mesmerism, too. And they write books to educate the public," she said.

"What are the names of these fine lecturers, cousin?" Delia asked. She was watching, fascinated, as Jacob Joe attacked the small bowls of refreshments on the table. He was trying not to be obvious, dipping his knees to scoop up salted pecans, popping Scotch shortbread into his cheeks. There was a kind of obsessional quality about his food-snatching.

"Mrs. and Mrs. Evan Parsticle, the authors of *Cerebral Calisthenics.*"

"Ah," said Althea softly, " 'One, two, one, two, bad thoughts go shoo.' It was all the talk a year or so ago." Then she turned to her niece with a scolding smile. "There was a chapter or two in there not designed for young maiden ladies, as I understand. I am surprised my niece is acquainted with it."

Dora did not lower her eyes; she certainly did not blush. "I always read as much that is instructive as I can," she said calmly. "Anyway, they have a traveling museum, with all sorts of oddities on display at these lectures, skulls of famous people with all the bumps in the right places, gorilla heads, and a crystal skull at least three thousand years old, made by Mayan Indians."

Delia continued to look at Jacob Joe. She noticed that during this speech he had quietly drifted away from the crowd and seemed to be backing into the kitchen.

"Bumps on people's heads, gorillas," Sophie said petulantly. "Who in the world would want to see that?"

"Well, I think I would," Calhoun said, popping pecans into his mouth one at a time.

"And I," Althea said. "How about you, sister? Will you come with us?"

Addie Lavenham sighed. "Someone has to stay here to be sure Morgan's raiders don't decide to raid us after all and come in and steal the few broken down nags we have left for the carriage and carry off the last three bags of flour to our name," she said. "No, you all just run along. I'll try to content myself with the cat and my chores."

Delia's eyes sought her mother's. Aunt Addie was at it again, her glance seemed to say. Playing martyr thrown to the lions.

"I'll bring the tray of sandwiches and peach tarts in now, and we can sup quickly," Dora said. "The lecture begins in an hour. We can walk quickly down the block."

Everyone scattered to wash hands and find hats and gloves and make one final walk down the path out back, bustling and scurrying in the way that people organizing to amuse themselves do. Sophie Lavenham was left alone in an empty room. "Well, I suppose if all these silly fools are going down and look at a skull made out of glass and a bunch of bones, I might as well go too." She flounced out of the room to find her bag.

Jacob Joe turned away from the oilcloth-covered table in the center of the kitchen. He looked embarrassed; pasty crumbs were at the corner of his mouth. Dora looked at the half-empty tray and smiled.

"Miss Dora, I am sorry," Jacob Joe said, wiping his mouth with his sleeve. "I can't seem to control myself. It's just like a magnet was pulling me. Real food! I wish all my company could just smell these tarts."

"I wish they could, too, Mr. Scott," Dora said, walking towards him. He was not a tall man, but she was like a diminutive doll beside him. "I think about them all the time, out there, so near to us here in Kentucky. I did some nursing, you know, after Perryville, and some of the men were from the Eightieth Indiana."

"No, I did not realize that, Miss Dora." He looked at her with admiration, really seeing her face for the first time clearly. He had not thought to notice it for looking at the others; she was a moon in the midst of the bright sunlight of beauty her sister and cousin radiated. It was a long face for such a small woman, the eyes were set a bit close, but it was the clearness of her gaze that he noted.

"I nursed your friend," she said, with a fond, remembering smile.

"Tommy Brooks? You nursed Tom?" Jacob Joe asked excitedly.

"No, I mean Sergeant Keith Boucher. With the awful eye wound."

"You did your job well. His socket is healed now and he has covered it with a patch. He's doing as satisfactorily as any one-eyed man could do." He paused a moment. "He should have mentioned that you had cared for him here in Louisville."

"I don't think we talked of knowing you. It was all so rushed, and we despaired of his life because of infection."

"He was eligible for release from the army, but he insisted on staying."

Dora took the damp tea towel off the sandwiches and picked up linen napkins. "You speak of Tommy Brooks. He did not come into our hospital, although I spoke to his father as he was searching the wagons. Pitiful it was, the old man, going from ambulance to ambulance, asking humbly if any had seen his son, his spirits lifted one minute, dashed the next—"

"Yes," Jacob Joe said. "I never saw Tom after his father found him and bore him to the train to go home. I hear regularly through Colonel Lewis Brooks that my friend Tommy is sitting up now, mending a bit each day." Jacob Joe sat down in a chair before the oilcloth-covered table. For some reason he did not want to be with the other people. Miss Dora was all very well; he liked watching her fuss about, readying the supper sandwich trays. That was comforting, homelike. But the others—he was too rusty from soldiering. He felt like a rooster who has walked into a church. If he could just see Sophie alone. He had written so often, poured out his heart, and she had had the courtesy to answer two of his letters. Did that mean anything?

Dora went on. "They are nursing Tommy Brooks at his parents' home because his wife has just had another babe and is worn with all the care she has. May they all find health soon," Dora murmured, taking the trays into the music room.

Soon she came in to put glasses and a pitcher of cold milk on the table. "You will come with us to see the phrenologist, Mr. Scott?"

He seemed to have hardly heard her. He was looking out the window at the pussy willow bushes. Fat, yellow blossomed fuzz had burst through the furry buds on their branches.

"Spring has come," Jacob Joe muttered. He had looked forward to this pass, fought to get it, and now he felt like Rip Van Winkle, coming out of the Catskills, the sounds of his long, dark enchantment roaring in his ears. In his case, it was the din of battle.

Jacob Joe turned to Dora, confusion in his eyes. "It is hard to think of sitting in an assembly hall with normal folk, allowing myself to be amused, chatting—all I keep thinking about is my friends. Sergeant Boucher, Tommy Brooks. Boucher's socket has about healed, but not his mind." He pointed to his head. "He lags in the march, sits without talking. Ever since Perryville."

"Are there many like him?" Dora wanted to know.

"Several in our regiment. They call it the blue-blacks. It is simply low spirits. The dreariness, the despair some feel over the way the war is going."

"I am sorry to hear that Sergeant Boucher is in low spirits. After the worst of his pain was past, he used to run about with his bandages flapping, as if he were a ghost. The others, even the ones with the dangerous wounds, would laugh."

"He was always ready with a joke. He trained us, Brooks and me and the other new recruits, and put sand in our beds and soap in the coffee. He made war passable for us."

"When joyful, joking men lose their spirits, it is the worst of all. They fall hard." She handed him two sandwiches. In some way, she understood his need to be away from the others in the music room.

Jacob Joe was biting dollar-size holes in the bread. "Well, but enough of Boucher," he said. "Colonel Brooks has a remedy for what ails him. He is sending him back to southern Indiana to recruit. And to serve notices under the new draft law."

"The conscription act. It is even stricter in the South," Dora murmured. "We have—well, you know we have acquaintances in the Confederate army." Jacob Joe did not look at her.

"That is no secret from you. Calhoun's friend, Willie McClure, has written from Ewell's army to say the Southern ranks are filling with conscriptions. Some of them are beardless, some almost old men. Every man who can walk is being drafted.''

Jacob Joe decided to ignore the implications of the conversation. "The draft is hated in southern Indiana. Keith will be heading into a hotbed of hostility, but at least he will be near home again. It may relieve his heart.''

"Is it a good idea?" Dora wondered. "Will he have enthusiasm to find new soldiers for the regiment?''

"Well, he'll be away from mud and marching. Away from the 'dulls.' Oh, yes, I think his spirits will lift like a balloon. When I left, he was already talking about a feather bed and hot milk toast. He's going to stop off and visit his sister in Madison.''

"Good, I am glad to hear that of my old patient. Now, Mr. Scott, we need to go. A trip to the phrenologist will banish your cares, if only for one night. Even Mr. Lincoln, with all his woes and worries, goes to the theatre on occasion, so I hear. One, two, bad thoughts go shoo.'' And with her apron, she laughingly hustled him out of the kitchen.

The auditorium was a panoply of bunting and gaslit splendor by the time the merry crowd from the Lavenham House arrived. Young women, some beautifully dressed, some in turned-out clothing from two years ago, were entering the theatre on the arms of older men who had to be their fathers. One young swain with a bright gold watch chain and elegant evening clothes bowed low to Sophie and backed through the theatre door still looking at her.

"Tucker Mahaffey," Dora said to Jacob Joe in an unimpressed voice. "One of sister's old beaus.''

Sophie had acclimated herself to the idea of the trip and was now laughing and teasing Jacob Joe. "Mr. Scott, I do declare you have been as serious and long-faced as a preacher at revival time. Now, I want you to read me this playbill. You know I have poor eyes, and I left my spectacles at home.''

Jacob Joe approached the theatre front and read from the gigantic poster that was the playbill. "Phrenology: The Science of the Mind. Mr. and Mrs. Evan Parsticle will lecture on the scientific application of the principles of physiognomy and show its practical application to all phases of life: religion, temperance, health, child-rearing, matrimony. See the oddities and curiosities in the museum show. Water cure, vegetarianism and homeopathic medicine also discussed.''

"I don't think we're goin' to get home by midnight," Calhoun Dugger snorted.

Jacob Joe looked at Calhoun. His beautiful sister shadowed the young man completely—a beautiful, deep-rooted oak above a spindly maple tree.

Calhoun seemed to defer to her in everything. And as far as Calhoun's attitude towards the striking, formidable woman who was his mother, Calhoun did not even approach her, except to take orders. This was a female household, indeed.

Sophie came and took his arm lightly. "Now, Mr. Scott, is there anything else on that playbill? We want to be sure we are gettin' our money's worth before we enter this house of entertainment. How much does a ticket cost?"

Jacob Joe looked down into her eyes, transfixed. The crook of his elbow, where her gloved hand rested, seemed electrified. "Ah, twenty-five cents adults, ten cents, children. Personal readings extra." His face was as red as a beet from her touch. "Can't you control your feelings?" he asked himself severely. "Rip Van Winkle. Emotions cascading like Niagara Falls. Sort of the opposite of the blue-black mood everybody talks about."

"Ten cents for children?" Sophie said as they walked towards the ticket window. "I don't know why anyone would pay to have the bumps on their seven-year-old's—" She stopped in the middle of a sentence, distracted by a commotion down the block from the theatre. People were milling about, chanting something. It had been going on for a few minutes, but now it was definitely loud, almost clamoring. Sophie and Delia turned quickly about and left the group, walking a few steps towards the source of the noise. The rest stared as the protesting group, whatever it was, began to press towards the theatre.

People clustering on the board walkway opened their ranks, drawing back with a little distaste. It was a sign-march; young men and a few women were carrying signs on stout sticks. "Society for the Protection of the Gospel Truth," some of the signs said.

"What is it they are chanting?" Jacob Joe whispered to Dora. They listened.

Atheism, madness reigns
Jesus never charted brains.

There were fiery-eyed young men wearing shabby, too-long topcoats and young women with serge dresses and homely faces, and a few surly, older-looking men with unkempt beards.

"The local churches have scurvy-lookin' congregations," Calhoun commented sarcastically.

"Landsakes, I never saw any of these people at the Episcopal Church," Sophie said.

"Some of them are from the Seventh Day Baptists. Others are just hooligans," Dora said. "Odd, I thought I saw some of these people listening to a 'free love' speaker in the park the other Sunday. I think they are like beetles in a log, coming out whenever the weather's decent to catch a little fresh air and march around.''

Althea Dugger spoke above the strident voices. "Let us go into the lobby of the hall,'' she said. ''This is my treat. I will purchase all the tickets.'' The marchers clustered around, obviously wishing attention from the lecture-goers. Pushing their way past a woman carrying a baby in one arm and a sign in the other, the Lavenham House group passed through the gilt-painted doors into the lyceum lobby.

The lights dimmed, and a man came to the lectern. "Evan Parsticle,'' Jacob Joe thought, settling in his plush seat, next to Sophie. But no, the tall, distinguished gentleman introduced himself as the President of the Society for the Dissemination of Useful Information in Louisville. He said that phrenology was a remarkable phenomenon, that it had come to the United States in the 1830s and was acknowledged on all sides as a new scientific miracle which was already changing the world. That such eminent men as the president of Harvard University and Mr. Henry Ward Beecher had been interested in it, and that it was in the head, and the configuration of the brain inside the skull, that all character lay, and if we could learn to read it we could bring in the millennium.

"I don't know why they are talking about Henry Ward Beecher as a judge of character,'' Althea Dugger said in an outraged whisper to nobody in particular. ''He was a philanderer, a man of the cloth and carrying on with his own best friend's wife for years. Of all things—''

Delia put a hand on her mother's arm.

The offshoot of this long introduction, the audience finally discovered, was that Mr. Evan Parsticle, author of numerous books, and his charming consort, Mrs. Clothilde Parsticle, would speak to them all about the new scientific marvels of his age, all stemming from the great discovery of phrenology.

"They claim a lot, don't they?'' Dora was saying. "Why, mesmerism and vegetarianism started up separately, and now these people are jumping on the train.''

Mr. Evan Parsticle, a little man with a bristly mustache like a hair brush and an oddly incongruous, cutaway suit, came striding across the stage. He was accompanied, not followed, by an emaciated-looking wife with a lor-gnette, the charming Mrs. Clothilde Parsticle. She was a good deal taller than he.

From out of the wings an assistant pushed an easel which bore a sign six feet tall, large enough to be seen from the back row of the hall. It was a chart of a man's head, bald as an egg, staring with a stupid expression. Like a jigsaw puzzle sections were marked off on the chart: "perceptive intellect" above the eyebrows, and behind them sections labelled "selfish propensities," "intellectual sentiments," "reason," "moral sentiments," "domestic interests," and so forth.

Mr. Evan Parsticle began speaking in a high-pitched voice. There was a sure, confidential tone to his speech, and it rose and fell in predictable cadences, as if he had practiced this spiel many times. Mrs. Parsticle pointed to the areas on the chart corresponding to his descriptions with a long, pointed stick.

"Alimentativeness, forwards of the top of the ear, desire for food."

"Well," Jacob Joe thought, "that area has gotten out of hand for me. Made a fool of myself at the party." He felt sleepy and his thought drifted in and out of attentiveness. Something about "Inhabitiveness, love of country and home, located in the middle of the back of the head. Men who have this area strongly developed are more likely to take up arms for home and country."

Suddenly, Jacob Joe's roving, unpredictable thought took a sudden lurch, and he stood again on the battlefield, next to Boucher and Brooks, with Cheatham's troops pressing down and the artillery rattling every birdnest, windowpane and ear within two square miles. The same over-riding fear of dying mixed with the firm resolve not to foul his pants, no he *would not no matter what they said about your first battle* enveloped him. In his theatre seat he began to sweat; simultaneously he smelled sulphur-acrid smoke, the smell of flowing blood, and saw again the gruesome, gut-wrenching look of the eye socket of his friend.

He loosened his shirt collar, and Delia looked at him curiously. This had happened before, in night dreams since the battle, five or six times. He wasn't the only one; they said it was common after a horrible carnage like Perryville, especially for fresh troops, and they had certainly been that. But to have it intrude on his leave—no! He would not stand for it. By sheer, sweating force, he banished the hallucination.

He sat back, sighed, and relaxed. Miss Sophie's scent floated through the comfortably warm air towards him. He shifted his weight ever so slightly towards her, till one of her ruffles touched his sleeve. Now Mrs. Parsticle had taken over the lectern. She was, really, a very tall, muscular woman. Would almost make two of her husband. How in the world did he—never mind, he rebuked himself firmly.

Well, now she was talking about Amatativeness. In the cerebellum, they were saying it was, at the base of the skull. "The faculty of physical love, which leads to the enjoyment of the company of the opposite sex and the desire to be united in wedlock. Overdevelopment leads to licentiousness," droned Mrs. Parsticle.

Oddly, at this very moment Sophie Lavenham's ungloved hand slipped a little in her lap and came to rest quite inadvertently next to Jacob Joe Scott's trouser leg.

He started, only a trifle, feeling her fingertips through the rough kersey army trousers. She was not taking her fingertips away. Ah, she was a free-spirited girl. Did it mean that she—that she favored him? It must. There were prickles of feeling going out from the fingertips into his leg, spreading upward. Stabs of fire began to spread through his groin. "Shame, Jake," he told himself. "To sit in a metaphysical meeting, with topics designed to exalt the spirit and feel—"

Mrs. P. was going on, as smiley as a rag doll, as cheerful and chipper as a treeful of cardinals. "The intensity of the amative side of the disposition is determined by the size of the area downwards and backwards, at the base of the skull."

He shifted his weight uncomfortably, overcome by the presence of Miss Sophie next to him. This was very embarrassing. Was there something the matter with him? He raised his hands surreptitiously to the base of his skull. Quite wide, really. "Wide development, showing licentiousness which is, of course to be avoided."

Naturally! Absolutely! Still, Miss Sophie was giving him modest encouragement. A token of affection, even acceptance as a suitor. He would speak to her later, this very evening.

Mrs. Parsticle was speaking of the benefits of this fine and sacred knowledge. "It leads on to the higher realms, peopled with spiritual ideas of the mind. To the Creator. Located between the ears is the organ of *sublimity*, which reaches beyond the material to contemplate the Divine in life. "My friends," she was saying, with regal elevation, "I may tell you that modern science, phrenology, psychology, mesmerism, all point to one thing: there is more to life than what we see. On this one fact—the Beyondness of Truth, rests successful living."

She went on to talk about psychical happenings, about the presence of "others" in our plane of existence, of angels, of sudden intuitions, of clairvoyance. "All of us have had some types of psychical experiences, and they prove the vast nature of the world of the spirit, beyond our ken."

Sophie removed her hand and was fidgeting around in her seat, humphing and sniffing. It was obvious she scorned talk of the "Beyond." Again, Jacob Joe's flighty thought launched off the branch, and he saw in his mind's eye the woman who had appeared on Perryville Battlefield, felt the sense of awe at her majestic presence, the need to follow her commands. He had told a few people of his experience, but had stopped doing so now; few seemed to even begin to understand what he was talking of. "Truly, there is more to life than what we see," he thought.

"Yes, Mr. Scott, you are right," Dora Lavenham, on his other side, murmured. He had said it aloud! Thank God it wasn't to Sophie; she had made it plain in her first letter that she did not wish to hear about such things.

He belched and sweated in remorse over the close call. His mind was turning over like a butter churn and his stomach, unaccustomed to ham sandwiches and fine shortbread, was also tumbling. What if he should pass gas right here? In the camp there were contests, with trophies, and he had grown callous to the customs of civilization. Unthinkable! "Excuse me, please," he said to Dora and bumped his way over all the row to get a breath of air in the lobby.

He passed through the doors to the street and felt better in a moment. Then he came in again to wander among the stalls of chocolates and pamphlets about the lecture. There was that fop, that Tucker Mahaffey, talking to a couple of other young wastrels. Money was being exchanged. Some sort of gambling debts? Why in God's name did they have time and money to waste on—whatever it was they were doing.

The fop squadron slipped back into the theatre and he drifted into a side salon, empty now. Along the walls, on tables, were exhibits in glass display cases. Ah, there were the skulls of the animals, small, elongated ones from raccoons and the short, larger ones looking like men's skulls. But what was this?

He had come to the far corner of the room. There, in a case by itself, was an object that made him pause and stare, a magnificent skull of pure, transparent glass. There was a card beneath the skull. "Found in the highlands of South America, this head was probably used by priests to forecast the future. Whatever its psychical powers were, it was also used with trickery, as the lower jaw is wired, so that the mouth can seem to give answers to petitioners' questions."

Jacob Joe looked again at the frighteningly beautiful skull. Light was shining through the prism of the eyes, an odd, mysterious light which seemed to transfix Jacob Joe. He looked deeply into it, and his eyes blurred. He blinked, and when he opened his eyes, there in the middle of the odd, white light from the center of the skull, stood the battlefield apparition. His grandmother, Jenny McClure Scott, he supposed, in the prime of her womanhood, dressed as of old. He squinted, frightened, fascinated. She was looking out, looking at him. Her hands were raised in the air, bent at the elbows with forefingers pointing. Slowly, as he watched, she moved the fingers together until they stood side by side, touching. Then, slowly, the vision receded into the enveloping light.

He turned from the skull. Must have been a function of this whole Rip Van Winkle dream he'd been involved with since he left camp. His mind was fuzzy. But no, he had seen what he had seen. Two fingers joined? He walked from the room rapidly and without looking back. In an instant, standing before a chocolates counter, he could not recall the vision distinctly, not even the way her face looked. All he could recall was a feeling, the immense, radiating affection in her eyes, the same love he had felt when he had seen her at Perryville, love his father had talked of as transcending time and destiny.

As he walked past the center doors to come to the aisle and re-take his seat, a commotion suddenly broke out. A crowd burst through the doors and headed for the auditorium. It was the marchers, their signs under their arms. They had evidently dispersed, according to the constable's orders, and then re-grouped for a foray into the depths of metaphysics.

Jacob Joe edged against the back wall of the theatre when the crowd burst in, then followed quickly in behind them to sit in one of the rear rows. Mr. Evan Parsticle was taking questions now, about the relationship of spiritualism and hypnotism to life. He seemed to bat his eyes, aware of the new auditors in the unused rows at the back of the auditorium, but had evidently decided to let the questions and answers continue as scheduled.

"As I have said, hypnotism suggests the freeing of the inner soul of man, just as learning about the modes of thought in the brain frees the character of man."

One of the hecklers, a homely woman with boots on, raised her hand. She seemed courteous enough, Jacob Joe thought. "Is it true, sir, that Oliver Wendell Holmes said phrenology was a pseudoscience?"

"He did, young woman, because he did not know of its application," Mr. Parsticle said stoically. "I have explained that in some detail, and, had you not arrived late, you could have profited from that discussion."

There was a ripple of laughter from people in the crowd, and they began turning their heads to see the questioners.

"And did not John Adams say that he did not see how two phrenologists could look each other in the face without laughing?" the woman continued.

"That was John Quincy Adams, young woman," Parsticle said, a little grimly.

He stopped recognizing the questioners in the back, but they continued to rise, one after another, and demand recognition.

"Does not all of this mumbo jumbo fly in the face of the Bible?"

"Have you not made hundreds of thousands of dollars off the sale of your salacious book?"

"Is not your mystical crystal skull made in Hoboken, New Jersey, by a gemologist from a piece of glass?" The crowd was gasping and tittering;

Mr. Parsticle was looking nervously at Mrs. Parsticle, whose flat bosom was heaving with consternation.

Finally, the youngest member of the group, a man with rumpled trousers, tobacco-darkened teeth and strong odor shouted: "Is there one shred of a reason, sir, why we should not tar and feather you as a charlatan and send you out of Louisville on the rail?"

All this time Jacob Joe's anger had been rising, and now he strode down the aisle. He had something to say, and he was not afraid to say it. Rip Van Winkle had no reason to stand on social conventions when he blew back into town. Jacob Joe's mind had finally cleared.

He walked down the aisle and gestured for permission to speak. Mr. Parsticle nodded, and Jacob Joe Scott went to the lectern, as the speaker stepped aside.

He looked out towards the dark, musky back of the hall. The hecklers were silent, more out of curiosity than anything else. "I am a volunteer," he said, "in the army which has just been protecting you from John Morgan's cavalry. I don't know what to think of any of this that has been going on tonight. Bumps on the head, mesmerism—you can believe it if you want to. I don't think I can. The only thing I really believe is that there is a lot more to life than what we see." The crowd had settled down and was listening intently. He could see, faintly, the faces of Sophie, and Delia and Dora and the rest, in the tenth row, surprised to see him there, but listening.

He looked towards the back rows, to the marchers, who had already begun to squirm and squawk again. "I want to ask you all back there something. I want to know if you believe we have the right to freedom of speech in this country."

There was a grumbling, discontented murmur from the marchers' seats, then, finally, the smelly young man said cockily, "Not since King Abraham put in his new laws, suspendin' it. And his draft laws, too."

"Ah, then you are showing your true tint, sir. You look copper-colored to me," Jacob Joe said, his voice ringing loud and clear. He went on. "And, sir, and all of you young gentlemen back there—coming to disrupt decent people's meetings—I want to know something else. Why aren't you in the army? Why are you not wearing Union blue?"

Again, the mumbling. Another man, the older one with the dishevelled beard arose. "Mebbe we like Butternut better," he said defiantly. The crowd buzzed; there were some hisses, some scattered, tentative applause. Probably that was Sophie's old beau, Tucker Mahaffey, and his crowd. After all, this was Kentucky.

Jacob Joe was unperturbed. "That is your choice. At least that would be fighting for a cause, however misguided. You have that right in this country.

And so does Mr. Parsticle have the right to speak without your rude interruptions.''

Somehow, what he said did not abate his anger. Perhaps it had been brewing for the whole day he had been in this city which didn't ever know that the war was outside its gates, which had the time to carry signs and argue about hypnotists while men were dying a few hundred miles away in Tennessee.

''Come on, you haven't answered me, why aren't you fighting? Cowering with the women and babies, tiptoeing around in lecture halls, while the real men are in the camps south of here!''

The grizzled older man and the small, younger one jumped from their seats and came down the aisle, making fists. Jacob Joe leapt from the podium and came down the aisle to meet whatever they might offer.

At that moment, as the crowd huzzaed and Mrs. Parsticle clapped her hands above her head for order, and her husband pounded the podium, the constable came through the doors of the auditorium and seized the marchers. In the melee that followed, they seized Jacob Joe, too.

An hour later, after an explanation at the constable's office, Jacob Joe was released and hurried to the hotel down the side street where the wisteria vines grew.

He was greeted by Addie Lavenham. ''Well, Mister Scott, we did not know if we should go testify for your character,'' she said, trying to take stock of the situation. Was this young man a hooligan? A hero? Her sister Althea had no question about which role Jacob Joe fit. She came up and squeezed his arm. ''Sir, your courage was admirable. It reminded me of my own papa fighting the Choctaws in an earlier time.''

Calhoun pounded the conquering hero on the back, Miss Dora and Delia laughed and offered him more sweetmeats. Even Sophie seemed impressed; she came to sit by him and purr a little into his ear. Mr. Tucker Mahaffey had offered to escort her to her dwelling, she confessed, but she had declined. Her interest was piqued by the mysterious, darkly romantic way he had acted tonight. The thought crossed Jacob Joe's mind that she saw him as Lord Byron defending the cause of freedom in Greece.

He raised his hand as they pressed him with salted pecans. ''No, thank you. My stomach is a little squeamish tonight,'' he allowed. ''Well,'' he told himself as he slumped into the settee in the music room, ''Rip doesn't have to eat up everything in the pantry to make up for twenty years in the mountains.''

Then he spoke with Miss Dora about the lecture, examining each point with her, listening to her opinions until she flushed, and her usually pale cheeks glowed with happiness. He told her the story of his Grandma Jenny and her appearance in a matter-of-fact way, and she nodded and said, quietly, so no one else could hear, that sometimes odd things like that happened to her, too.

And a little while later, when Dora had done up the dishes, humming a little tune to herself, she stepped out into the March garden, flooded with moonlight and cool, and her heart jumped as she saw shadows in the gazebo grape arbor. Creeping just a little closer, her mouth gaped in consternation. She discerned the shapes of Jacob Joe and her sister Sophie, embracing. And in the almost white light of the full moon, she could see Jacob Joe seizing kisses, devouring long, satisfying kisses, the way he had taken dollar-sized bites out of a sandwich earlier.

Mid-March, 1863

Chapter Ten

"It's a good thing I'm getting well, Grandmother," Tommy Brooks said. "It would be awful to die in the spring."

Forsythia bloomed brightly under the window where he sat in an invalid's chair; the heavy-laden branches were so near he could see individual blossoms opening tiny, jubilant yellow trumpets. Hannah Poore was spreading a white design quilt over his knees, and he smiled up at her. "All these things are greening up—I feel like a bulb myself. Something is pulling me up and out. I think I'll be able to put in garden in a couple of weeks at home."

"Well, but no need to rush," his grandmother said. "You have had quite a stint of it." That was hardly strong enough. First, the gaping wound to the side, which shocked her and brought tears to her eyes when she first saw it, and all those long nights of delirium after he had come home and infection set in, then the ague and mild lung fever that hung on like a burr in November and weakened him further. Months it had been, and only a couple of weeks ago could he really sit up in a chair.

Tommy's eyes strayed to the garden beyond the stretch of greening yard. "No, I need to put in garden. When I see those things come up, things of my planting, I'll know I'm alive."

His grandmother looked at him with mild reproof. Sometimes he spoke this way and had ever since they carried him in on a stretcher from the train station that dreadful day in October. Others of the thousands who had come home wounded to Indiana were the same way, so they said, morose, distant, some of them hearing noises in their heads, crying out to people who were dead. He felt he had a special dispensation, and because of that his life was precious, like a jewel returned to him for careful examination and special use. But he had to endure many painful times before he had seen, accepted the value of it.

"Well, in a way, when they brought me off the field at Perryville, I thought I was going to die. Everyone said I was mortally wounded. I think I just accepted it. The pain was so great I wanted to die to ease it. Then, later, they told pa I wasn't hurt to the death, and I couldn't believe it. It was as if I had accepted that I was touched by the finger of doom—''

His grandmother demurred but he went right on—''I had turned my soul over to God, had an odd peace with him, then I was called back to living. It was almost—unpleasant.'' An odd, twisted smile stood on his face.

Hannah Poore understood. She had felt that odd, unreasoning desire to give up living the day her husband suddenly died, in a cabin in the wilderness. Felt wrenched back to a life that she was not sure she could endure, but must—

Tommy's eyes were on the sweep of flower beds that bordered the yard. ''Over there, by the lilacs. There are solid spots of purple on the ground, like somebody spilled a paint pot. What are those flowers?''

''The grape hyacinths I carried with me from the East and transplanted for your mother and father when they came to this house.'' She picked up lint from the carpet, bending very slowly from the waist. ''These bulbs have travelled farther than I have. My mother always said the granddaddies of those grape hyacinths were in the fancy gardens of the Chute manor house in England in the time of Queen Elizabeth. Then they came with my ancestor Chute to America—Puritan bulbs they were. Hated the King I suppose.''

She chuckled and looked out the window. All her children, and their children, had some of the bulbs now. Susie Niblack had put them in her yard up the road in Wheatland, Johnny had planted them over by the Wabash in Duggerville; they were in Cincinnati and Iowa, and Kansas, and Missouri. Families did go a-journeying from home. Pulled up their roots, part of their lives. It was good to take some beauty with you, to remind you of the home, the love you left behind. Your relatives, your ancestors, too, with all their homes and gardens, were behind you, like clouds of witnesses. She felt their presence often lately. So many generations of rising to face the day, calling on God, joying and sorrowing and sending children forth, away from the home you've built for them, to dive into life and to pain, like Tommy's. And not a thing you could do for them, really, once they left that house.

''The flowers from those bulbs looked out of a garden near Plum Island not far from Boston for many years,'' she said, plumping his pillow. ''The wind blew free there, from all the way across the ocean.'' Turning from him, her eyes were far away. Even now, after eighty years, she had not forgotten the Plum Island wind on her face. She could not have left it, have come away from her home without her flowers. They were both seal and promise: love from the past, hope of the future.

''One day, poor things, they were uprooted and taken with nine children and a tabbycat across Pennsylvania in a Conestoga. Through the mountains, pushed about by thorny rose shoots, packages of seeds—''

Tom smiled at her, wanly. ''You brought plants and seeds all that way.''

"Yes. In 1818 the Shakers weren't coming around in their wagons to sell seeds, and Brooks store wasn't even thought of. Your grandfather and I were pushing back a big, black forest to make one little acre of light, fighting for every inch of civilization. Just see how it all has flourished!" She swept her hand across the stretch of grass. Rose canes four feet high stood in back of the beds of hyacinths. Yellow jonquils by the scores bobbed in the breeze.

"Those flower bulbs are like me," Tommy laughed, a little ruefully. "Carted around, almost died, and now have gone to sleep and wakened to life again. Yes, that's it! Glad of it, too!" His grandmother caught the sudden bright enthusiastic tone, and it surprised her. It was as if he had lifted a lid and let sunlight out of a cup. He must really be getting well. She rejoiced to hear it.

"I think I would like to learn to garden now. I'll put in lettuce, peas. Have I missed the planting season? Is it too late?" he looked up anxiously at his grandmother.

"No. You can plant late lettuce," she assured him. He turned from the window and moved his feet back and forth in his slippers. "I've never had time to garden before. I've been thinking a lot lately about what I really care about."

"I know. You've had a lot of time to think, haven't you?"

"More than I needed." He was silent for a moment, then frowned, his mood darkening suddenly again, like an April sky that has filled with sudden clouds. "It's bitter thinking of the Eightieth out there, defending Kentucky, with me like a rag doll in a baby chair. Sometimes when I was out of my head, I'd imagine I was there fighting with Keith Boucher and Jacob Joe Scott, we'd be charging up a hill, smoke all around, and when I woke up, I'd be sobbing. Sorry I wasn't with them." He coughed and spat into a handkerchief. "Anyway, I haven't been much of a husband to Libby, father to Lewie and the baby. I hardly know her—little one. It's terrible, Grandmother, to have your own baby born and you so delirious you don't even know it." Hannah Poore nodded. They had not been able to even show him the babe for nearly a month after she had been born for fear she would take the fever too.

Tommy went on. "I'm as impatient as a horse in a stall to be up. After a few weeks rest at home, I can take up my rifle with the strength of a man. I'll go to the wars again."

He was looking up at her, his bright black eyes earnest. "Grandmother, I learned to live out there." He said each word slowly, with emphasis, as if he were tasting it. "It was because I was with the regiment. It was something I was doing, on my own. Without Pa there, clucking over me, smoothing the way."

She looked at him, glad he wanted to talk. There were so many times he had sat silently brooding by this window. "Was it—did you mind that your own brother was the colonel?" she decided to ask. "Lewis can be—well, as distant as a stag out on the hillside. I've wondered about that, Tommy. Your pa thinks—"

"No. Pa doesn't understand. Lewis left me alone, and that was the way I wanted it. In fact, I liked having Lewis there, letting him see me that way, brave and wounded." He smiled and tossed his head a little, and she was again reminded of his charm, the boyishness that captivated everyone who knew him. "I never felt so proud in my life as the evening he finally came to me." His grandmother brought over a large blue pill and gave it to him with a glass of water.

"What was it—what did he say?" Hannah wondered. The entire family speculated about Lewis's doings a lot and always had. There was a sense of awe about Lewis's "just too good to be human" personality that sometimes bordered on scorn or humor.

"He was all I could have wanted—tender, solicitous. He brought me a bar of chocolate he had somehow gotten hold of. But he didn't hold my hand, or touch me. He knew I wouldn't want it. And he didn't quote the Bible once." He had been ignoring the blue pill; now he popped it into his mouth like a kernel of popcorn and followed up the action with a strong swig of water.

"They voted me captain, you know, after the battle. When I go back, I'll take up the position. B Company has an acting captain now, waiting my return." There was a flurry at the door. Both Tom and his grandmother turned towards it.

"Here's Susie—" Tommy said. He attempted to rise from the chair to greet his sister, but pushed himself up only a little way before his face turned white with effort.

Susie Niblack rushed to his side. "Tommy Brooks, you know your doctor told you not to push yourself up that way. Tom Campbell said you have to regain your strength." A small girl sucking on her finger toddled after Susie. Grandmother Poore patted the young woman on the arm, kissed little Emma on the top of her head and slipped through the door, leaving the sister to minister to her brother's needs and changeable moods.

Sweat stood on Tommy's forehead and he spoke through clenched teeth. Talking of the regiment had frustrated him again. "How am I supposed to regain my strength if I lie here like a dishcloth? Useless!"

His sister looked at him sharply. "Don't talk about yourself that way," she commanded.

"Why not?" her brother said, sinking back. "Lewis and the regiment are near Knoxville. I should be with them. I can't even walk well yet. And by the time I rejoin them, the Rebels will probably be occupying Washington.'' The screen door banged. Their grandmother had gone out to the yard.

"Lib will be over in a little while for her afternoon visit,'' Susie said. Little Emma had plumped herself down on the floor and was trying to get a drawer open in the chest of drawers in the corner. She had odd hair which was just coming in again after a mild case of scarlet fever.

Tommy sighed wearily. "Lib—my own wife doesn't want me home.''

"What do you mean? Of course she does.''

"Don't say nice things, Suse, when you know they're not true.''

Susie sighed. "All right. We've never lied to each other. She doesn't really want you home yet. But that's Lib.''

"She's relieved she doesn't have to have me to wait on and get under foot.''

"Well, she does have a baby and a small boy to care for. And she does suffer from various complaints herself.''

"Complaints is the right word.''

Susie was silent. The little girl was pulling knitting yarn out of the drawer, singing to herself. "Baa, baa back sheep, haveooenny wool—''

"I want to sit up on the side of this chair, Suse,'' Tommy Brooks said suddenly. Susie leaned over her brother, an exasperated look on her face, which faded as she saw the intensity of her brother's frustration. "Suse, don't you know what's been happening to me these last few months? I'm half a man, goddamn it.'' She leaned down to give him support; he clasped onto her arm.

"You don't need to curse,'' she said softly. "The infection is finally gone, and they say you don't need to be afraid of permanent damage.'' Little Emma was pulling out red sweater wool. She was examining a long, wooden needle which her mother eyed warily.

Tommy succeeded in sitting upright. "So they say,'' he said with a little difficulty. It was worst when he stretched his sitting-up muscles. He leaned over the rug, panting; and it seemed to make him bold, more like himself. "As for swearing—well, it isn't the first time I've cursed. You, if anyone, should know I'm no angel.'' He looked up at her, with something like the old Tom twinkle in his eyes. They exchanged a look and began laughing.

"Did you ever tell Pa about me and George Reilly and the fire in Old Man Cooper's shed?''

Little Emma was rolling balls around the room with the needle. Susan gently took them away and stood facing him in front of the bureau. "Me? Tell Pa his little darling and George Reilly shot off crackers inside a shed that didn't belong to either of them and caught the roof on fire so the whole place burned down?''

Tommy chuckled. "The crackers didn't belong to us either. We burnt down his shed with his own firecrackers.'' Laughing made lines in his thin face, lines his sister welcomed. ''Poor George, and Bo, too,'' he said, softly. Out the window she could see Grandmother Poore walking about the garden, bending over to see how many foxglove seedlings stood out against the brown dirt, peering inside tulips to see if they were ''blind'' or not.

''I've never told anyone about what I saw that night in the grape arbor, either,'' Susie said softly.

Her brother looked up her, his eyebrows lifted in a question. She continued looking out the window as her lips moved in just the suggestion of a smile. ''You and Lib. And the next day you told us you were marrying her—''

He expelled his breath in wonder. ''That was you? We heard rustlings, saw something move away. It was so dark. So it was you,'' he said again.

''It wasn't Lewis,'' Susie Niblack said, watching her grandmother bring a shovel out of the shed. ''Thank God.'' She laughed.

Tommy nodded his head and snorted. ''You distracted us and spoiled everything,'' he said. They both laughed harder. Finally Tommy began to cough and his sister left the window to come near to him, looking concerned. Little Emma was moving about under the huge crawlspace of the bed, which had long since lost its pioneer trundle. ''Star bright, how I wunner whut you are,'' she sang in a piping voice.

''Suse, that's the most I've laughed in two months. I can stand the pain. Shows I'm getting normal again. Back from the dead.'' He picked up a water glass, took a sip, then sat there staring into it. ''There were so many times during the last three months I've thought I was.''

''Was what?''

''Dead, really dead. In my mind I wandered among the tombstones at Hindostan and Mt. Pleasant. All our dead little brothers and sisters, there in the corner of the cemetery. An odd, lumbering purple squid chased me. And there was strange, ringing music, like an organ being played by the devil in a canyon. Delirium is frightening. I knew, though that Pa was in the room all the time, willing me to live. Somehow I didn't like it. Ah, so many odd things in my skull.'' He shook his head and held it in pain, as if memories were dragons, springing up with fire in his brain. Then, suddenly he looked up and out. ''What's grandmother doing?'' he asked.

Susie peered over him. ''Digging something in the garden.''

''Suse, help me stand,'' Tommy Brooks said. His sister turned to him, but she did not protest. She read the longing in his eyes.

Coming up beside him, she put her strong arms behind his back. With her help and some real effort, clinging to the bureau, he raised himself. He stood, leaning against the bureau. ''God, I want to walk, to dig in the earth, to take my boy for a ride in the wagon. To love my wife''—he laughed ruefully—''if I can. And then, go back and fight with my friends and finish this war.'' He turned his head. "I hear someone in the hall.''

Libby Brooks came in. She carried the squalling baby in her arm like a load of laundry. Her carrot-colored hair was hanging loose, frowzy about her freckled face. "I left Lewie with your mother,'' she said, giving her husband a rather cursory look. "You're out of your chair,'' she said, "That's good.''

Susie helped her brother sit back down on the edge of the chair again as Lib started talking, jiggling the baby to make it stop crying, rattling along like the 5:05 on the tracks outside town. "Lawcomercy honest. I just don't know how I'm ever goin' to get everything done. All the spring cleaning, and Belle was up ever couple hours last night.''

"Let me take her,'' Susie said, reaching for the child. She clucked and soothed and patted the baby, who soon began cooing and reaching for a cameo around Susie's neck. Lib Brooks gave her husband a peck on the cheek and turned away from him.

"I declare I have the worst case of toothache,'' she said. "I am a-goin' to have to go see Doc. I just don't have the courage. Even with the laughing gas. I've been chewing on cloves and even took some soothin' syrup—''
She was pacing up and down, not looking at her husband.

"Now that Tommy's standing, Lib, you'll probably be taking him home soon,'' Susie said, looking up encouragingly. She set the baby down next to Emma, who looked in awe at her small, kicking feet and clenched fists.

"Waal, we'll see,'' Libby said noncommittally. She walked over and sat down on the end of the invalid chair and looked at her husband. "We wouldn't want to rush things up—'' she said, smiling tightly and patting his hand absently.

Tommy turned away petulantly. "You've been so long without me you've lost the habit.'' She looked at him in surprise. "First, I was in Kentucky, then so ill and was tended here. It's like you were a widow.''

Susie lowered her eyes and knelt to play with the babies.

"No sech thing, Tom Brooks,'' Libby said, offended. "I jest want to be sure you'll have good care. Jest a-suppose I'm goin' to be able to run get you lemonade and blue pill ever time you call and me draggin' myself after these two little fellows day and night. I'd think you'd have more care o' me than to want to exhaust me!''

Tom hung his head. Through the silence they could hear the screen door creak in the back hall. They heard voices in the hall, and in a moment Hannah Poore came into the room carrying an ancient basket. "Hello, Lib. I saw little Lewie in the kitchen with his grandmother, Susan, and Eustace. Eustace said you were in here. Are you here to take your husband home?''

There was a strange, taut silence.

Tommy stood, straight and tall, his face white and cold as a stone. He smiled a little. "My wife has forgotten what it's like to have a husband in the parlor. I think it's time I got up and went. Suse, will you see that my things are put in the grip for me?" His sister nodded and, going to the wardrobe in the corner, began taking out shirts, sweaters.

"Well lawcommercy honest," Libby said hurrying to the wardrobe. " 'Twasn't that I don't want you home." She began taking things out. "I can do that. Guess I can do for my own." Susie nodded and stepped aside with an odd smile. The baby began to cry. Little Emma looked into her face with concern, then got up and ran to her mother and pulled on her dress.

Tom and Susie's brother Eustace appeared at the door. "Telegram just came for you, Tom," he said indifferently and sauntered out of the room without speaking to anyone in it.

Tommy looked after him for a long moment. "If I felt up to it, I would whop the pudding out of that young whelp. Always so arrogant lately," he said, opening and reading the telegram.

"What is it, Tommy?" Susie said, watching Libby pick up the baby with irritation.

Tom leaned heavily against the bureau, but he looked up with excitement. "Well, it's from Keith Boucher—my tentmate, the sergeant at Perryville. He was wounded in the eye there on the hill that same afternoon I was. He has been granted leave to enroll men for the new draft and will be here, in Loogootee, at the end of the week. By that time I'll be able to greet him like a man in my own home."

"Well, yes," Libby said, rising to the occasion. "I could kill a chicken, I guess, and maybe Ma could come over from Washington and help a bit with the young 'uns. We'll make do." The baby had gone to sleep; Libby wrapped her in a blanket, put her on the bed and went to look for little Lewie.

"Grandmother, would you ask Eustace if he could get the rig ready? You may have to beat him over the head," Tommy said, and Hannah Poore headed for the kitchen to call her other grandson.

Susie helped Tommy to the door, one slow step at a time.

As he went out the door, Grandmother Poore called after him, "I dug up some of the family grape hyacinths. They're in the basket, Tommy. Shall I put them in the rig?"

"I'll be back for them myself in two or three days," Tommy said. Then he turned with a bright smile on his face. "Grandmother, will you come over and help me?" he asked, his black eyes bright. "This Lazarus is going to put in a garden this spring or know the reason why!"

He hobbled down the hall, leaning heavily on his sister's arm, to say goodbye to his mother, who was cooking supper in the kitchen. Hannah

Poore shut the wardrobe door, then left the room. The clock chimed six as she returned, carrying a damp teatowel. From the kitchen she could hear the teapot whistling, her daughter Susan Brooks' voice low and steady, humming a little tune as she set supper on the table, the sound of the horses and rig disappearing down the lane. Lovingly, Hannah laid the bulbs, whose violet colored flowers were already beginning to droop, in the protective folds of the towel. It would be time enough, soon, for them to begin the next stage of the trip which had brought them so far from home in England, carrying beauty wherever they went.

Thomas Jefferson Brooks, Sr. was at that moment sitting by White River in Indianapolis. He and Governor Oliver P. Morton had decided to take advantage of the unusual warmth of the spring day to conduct their business on a bench overlooking the river, which was swollen by recent spring rains.

"Governor," Brooks said, pointing to a sheaf of papers in his hand, "your head of commissary wants me to contract in southern Indiana for commissary supplies in the hundreds of thousands of dollars."

The governor nodded. "Flour, dried and fresh fruit, molasses, pork and beef. You anticipate no difficulties I suppose. The United States government is doing increasingly better with supplying our Western army men near Vicksburg, but I will continue to supplement with state supplies. We have too many letters about scurvy and wasting illness due to poor health down there. I want them fed—"

"Yes," Brooks said, sighing. "But I have a question. If I may be frank." The governor offered a cigar, Brooks took it. Short, pungent puffs of smoke filtered into the spring air. "The way things are going politically in the state—how do I know I can pay the farmers I contract with? They are patriots, but they're not going to give their produce away the way the Southerners have to."

The governor crossed his legs comfortably. "Well, of course, I suppose I cannot be surprised that you wonder at our state's credibility. I wonder at it myself. If I had thought of the outrageous things that could happen in a nation fighting for its very existence"—he took his cigar out to gesture— "Democrats elected everywhere in the state last fall, conniving, supporting secret treasonous organizations. You and your son know about the Knights of the Golden Circle and helped me sniff them out in your home county." He stopped, suddenly, seeming to remember something. "I seem to have heard your son—fell at Perryville. Was he—"

"My son is recovering after a long siege. I am recovering, too." He was silent for a moment, then confided soberly, "I think we tie up too much in our children."

"Yes. I think of all of them out there as my sons," Morton said softly. Brooks looked at him, wondering if what he said was true, and to what degree. One could never tell at what point Morton the politician ended and Morton the man began.

The cigar began to point again. "As I said, the Democrats tied up the legislature, sent our Republican representatives in flight almost into Kentucky to keep the Democrats from re-districting the whole state to gain control of it. These men, and I tell you they are traitorous, Brooks, have taken the financing of the state out of my hands. Passed bills to force Indiana to stop supporting the war. The Democrats are determined to force a Southern peace on us."

"So the papers say," murmured Brooks. "They refuse to appropriate any money for the war. So how can the state survive?"

Morton looked at the river, which reached threatening fingers through the sapling swamps that stretched for fully two miles to the west. "I have not come so far to give in to traitors now, even if they sit in our own statehouse. I have taken over the arsenal here in Indianapolis and am issuing my own arms. I am taking the finances of the state into my own hands. Putting them under the military office here—in case of an uprising. I am raising, have already had pledged, hundreds of thousands of dollars from individuals, corporations, counties in Indiana to fund our part of the war from Indiana. And President Lincoln is backing us. He will send the monies to Indiana. And to hell with the Copperhead legislative Democrats!" He stood up and threw his cigar into the waters of the river. "You will be paid. sir. That I can promise you!"

Brooks nodded his head seriously, watching the churning waters carry the cigar downstream. "I hope so, sir. I have given two sons to the battlefields of Kentucky. A good deal of my personal fortune is going to clear up my children's financial distress caused by this war. I support my daughter Emily now that her husband is with the Eightieth, my son Lewis's and Tommy's families—I cannot give more."

"I know, sir. You have my word, the word of the State of Indiana."

He said it with solemnity and conviction. At that moment Thomas Jefferson Brooks was struck with a singular conviction. The voice he had heard spoke with real authority because Oliver P. Morton now *was* the State of Indiana.

Zach Scott and Willis Mawkins sat drinking whisky in a remote cafe down a backstreet in Cincinnati. Across the table from them was a man who had come in from Dayton to meet with them, a man who looked surprisingly like Abraham Lincoln, with a short, cropped chin beard and a shock of hair which stood up on his head. A close observer would not really mistake Clement Vallandigham for the President, however; Vallandigham's face was usually marked with a disillusioned smile that the rail-splitter from Illinois would have found cynical.

"So, gentlemen," he said in a low, easy voice, "have we finally arrived at the time to act? Our enemies seem to be playing into our hands."

Mawkins spoke quickly. "The Governor of the State of Indiana is acting like Ivan the Terrible. Taking the state coffers into his own hands, ignoring the elected representatives—"

"Ignoring our party, I believe you mean, Mr. Mawkins," Vallandigham said, looking into the depths of the glass before him.

"Ignoring the Constitution of the United States. Suspending habeas corpus, instituting the draft—" Zach Scott said.

"I see you are a man of principle, sir. I thought so when we first met, at that lovely ball on the Wabash." His eyes seemed far away. "Well, it is really the President of the United States who has suspended the Constitution of this land, although the governors have done their shares in the Northwest. Necessity, they call it." The cynical line that was his mouth grew taut as a string.

"There are enough Democrats to stop this war before it brings utter ruin on us. I can speak for southern Indiana," Mawkins said.

"And what can you promise, sir?" Vallandigham said. "I have made my speeches as a representative in Congress, and I am no longer there to speak. Nothing can be done there."

Zach Scott went on. "The President, the governors, have outraged the common people by pushing this unpopular war. Everywhere the Union army is losing, and the Easterners are getting rich while the middle states sit in poverty and loss."

Vallandigham cleared his throat impatiently. "And so—I ask, what can you promise to stop the war in your state? That is all that matters."

Willis Mawkins leaned across the table. "I can promise you control of the Indiana legislature. Democrats are in constant communication to keep Morton on the ropes. The Indiana Supreme Court will find ways to bind him. We will give him no money and we will defeat him and if not, impeach him."

"Good. And you, Mr. Scott?"

Zach drummed his finger thoughtfully on the edge of the table before answering. "Well, it is true that every week hundreds of new men come into the Knights of the Golden Circle in Indiana alone. Ten thousand now, hundreds of thousands in all these middle states, ready to act—"

"Act how? That is always what I ask myself. What can realistically be done?"

Mawkins tapped his finger emphatically on the table like a drum. "Take this citizen army we have raised for you and use it, Vallandigham. You have the national prestige to lead us all. If the Confederacy comes into Indiana and Ohio—"

Vallandigham set his glass down hard on the table. "Keep your voice down. These are friendly premises and Cincinnati a town friendly to what we believe, but—to Lincoln and his gang of usurpers, we are traitors. Treason. I do not like the idea. Anyway, I am not convinced bringing Southern troops in here would serve the purpose."

Mawkins' eyes were intent. "There would be an uprising. Wildfire in Indiana."

"More like a backfire, I think," Vallandigham snarled. "The citizens who are indifferent to the war, and that is a good many of them, would take it as a personal invasion, defend their lands—"

"No, we tell you," Mawkins insisted. "Get Colonel Morgan to lead thousands of cavalrymen into Indiana and Ohio and men will lay down their plows and join the Southern cause. They are sick to death of this war. Give them only the indication that the South can take the war into the North, that their strength is enough to win, and the Northern cause will be over in the Middle States."

Vallandigham was thoughtful. "How many did you say?"

Mawkins leaned towards him and whispered, "In our societies now, across five states, two hundred thousand men." He lowered his voice to a whisper, glanced around him and continued. "If the losses continue, three or four hundred thousand by summer. And if the Confederacy moves into the Old Northwest, I say half a million men would stand ready to throw off the yoke of King Abraham, rise up and demand peace. If we do not get peace, we may separate and join the South!"

Vallandigham was silent for a moment. Finally he said, "I cannot direct you further on this now. Clearly the time is ripe. I shall speak, write, organize from here. And I am thinking of running for governor of Ohio. From that position I could be most effective. But you will have to function in your own ways now for a while. I leave that part of the battlefield to you until it is right for us to be in touch again." He stood, bowed, and walked to the door of the cafe.

The two men sat for a long while, seeming to stare at the dark wood of the table. People were coming in for early luncheon. Zach had spoken but little to Vallandigham. "You will go south to see Colonel Morgan?" he said finally to Mawkins. "Tell him we are ripe for—invasion?"

"I'll find my ways to reach him," Mawkins said coolly. "Be sure the castles in southern Indiana and Illinois are ready, at fire-heat. We're only waiting for the biggest bonfire any of us have ever seen."

Zach looked thoughtfully at the other man. "King Abraham has instituted the draft," he said, almost musingly. "Army officers will begin enrolling every eligible man next week and when they come to Knox, Sullivan, Martin County—" He shrugged.

"The spark!" Mawkins said.

"Perhaps yes, perhaps not. I do not have a clear idea." Zach's face was inscrutable. "But nothing can prevent us from trying the strength of the fire."

They shook hands, pushed back their chairs and left the cafe, Zach to catch a steamboat down the river to Knox County, Mawkins to the hotel. There, another kind of fire awaited him in the arms of his companion, the woman who had given up life and reputation to follow wherever he went, his "slave of passion," Lettie Hogue.

Horace Hogue stood awkwardly on the braided rug in the parlor of the old farm built by George McClure after the Revolutionary War. Their was a look on his face that said he might be ready to report on the day's chores. His mother Catherine, Uncle Billy, and Aunt Esther sat with the windows wide open, breathing night air, and they did not pay him much attention.

"I always did like this time of year," Catherine was saying. "Spring. Frogs just wakin' up and croakin' and mosquitoes still in bed—wherever 'tis they sleep." She stopped to ponder that a little.

Billy tossed a dried-up apple he had been eating out the window. "Last o' the taters gone down in the root cellar and only a few worn out old carrots left," he said.

"I seen to the seed corn today," Horace said, clearing his throat. "Mice 'peared to 've left it alone." Nobody seemed to be listening.

"And the harness and plow blades seem to be in good condition." Billy picked up spectacles and put them on, fishing through a stack of papers from local towns that had come in the mail today.

Horace licked his lips. "I'm joinin' the Loyal Legion. Goin' to start trainin' in Vincennes tomorrow."

That did it. Everyone looked up in wonderment.

"Waal, you been seein' the papers," Horace said in explanation. "They're enrolling for the draft tomorrow here in the state. There's goin' to be trouble."

Esther stood up and shut one of the windows. "I should 'spect so. Forcin' people to take up arms against their own brothers—" Her husband gave her a warning look. One of the unwritten rules they had all tacitly agreed on when Catherine came out to the farm to live, savioress and guest at the same time, was that politics, denominationalism and the abolition of Negro slavery would never, never be discussed among them all. There were just too many differences. But now even Catherine had doubts.

"Son, will you be able to—that is, will you—is it right for you to go? We would—worry." She gave up, gamely shrugging her shoulders.

Horace looked at her, hands on his hips. "You mean is it right a thirty-seven-year-old cripple gets a gun and goes out to keep the Copperheads from risin' in revolt? Keeps the Southerners from pourin' crost the Ohio River and burning this house in the night, while we all sleep?"

"Said that way," his Uncle Billy said, "makes a mite of sense."

"Well, you won't see me supportin' this government. State or otherwise," Esther said and glided out of the room. Her voluminous skirt caught on the leg of the rocking chair and, with an irritated jerk, she pulled it free.

"Good luck, son," Billy McClure said, rising to shake his hand. "Hope there ain't as much trouble as you think from the draft."

Upstairs in the bedroom that her mother and father had lived in and her mother had died in, Catherine McClure sat down on the side of the small brass bed she slept in. She picked up a book from the bedside table. Mr. and Mrs. Evan Parsticle's *Cerebral Calisthenics: The Creative Release of Energy*. She had owned one copy before and it had disappeared, oddly. She bought another so she could have it with her, for strength of thought. Her grandson John was out of immediate danger; he wrote that the Fourteenth was drilling and biding its time with the rest of the Army of the Potomac. But soon they would be on the march and in danger again. And now draft troubles, and Horace in the militia. Absently she drummed a little tattoo on the book's lavender cover. "One, two, one two, bad thoughts go shoo—" she said to herself.

She opened the book and turned to the chapter, "Bastions of the Mind." She ran her finger down the page, seeking something, anything to relieve the uncertainty and distress that gnawed at her stomach. Her eye and finger lit. "What we can, must do, when negative energy forces attack us, and problems seem larger than life, is to decide we simply will not accept them. Raise a wall of creative thought-force energy and dwell behind it. Put hands on temples, which are the centers for reason and say aloud, 'Evil energies do not have power. I will rule them out. I will stay behind the bastion of the mind.' Thus, in reality, bad events do not have existence for us."

Then she set the book down. It was growing increasingly hard to read it here, in the room where her father George McClure had read Kant and Descartes. His books, left to her but hardly ever read, were over there on the shelf, and they seemed to mock her from their fine morocco covers, snicker at Mr. and Mrs. Evan Parsticle, call out that the couple were shallow and trivial. She reached inside the small drawer of the table and took out her

Bible. "Somehow, I think this mess'll be solved on the basis of what's in here rather than—that folderal in there," she told herself.

She ran her hand over the deep, black veins of its cover. Reassuring. She did not read, just sat there and held the Book as the noises and smells of awakening spring rose from the hollows, as night strengthened its hold on the riverbottom lands she loved.

The next day Horace Hogue took the train to Evansville. He went to a gun shop by the river; a bell on the door rang as he entered.

"Mr. Hogue, here, at your service," he said to the lank woman who stood behind a counter case full of rifles and pistols. "I've come for the mail order you sent me. You wrote it was in."

The woman leafed through a sheaf of papers. "Yes. Jest come in from Ft. Snelling area." She went into the back of the shop and came out again, bearing with some difficulty a wooden crate.

"Don't know what in the world you want with a cannon." Eagerly Horace worked his way through the sawdust in the crate. Finally he pulled out a small, three inch gun.

"Parrott cannon," he breathed in admiration.

"Ain't a Parrott. They don't make 'em like that. Don't know what the brand is," the woman said. She had a glass eye. Horace could not stand looking directly at her. "You carry it around and bolt it to a log and then fire. We done had the little balls made for you, like you said." She took out another box with balls the size of crabapples in it.

"Well, she looks like a baby Parrott to me," Horace said, unmollified. "I am a-goin' to call her Polly." Soon he was on his way to the train, the wooden boxes borne by a boy behind him on a pushcart. "Yankee Doodle went to town, a ridin' on a Parrott," he whistled, stepping lively. The music of martial fifes and military drums playing in his head accompanied him all the way to the train.

Shadows as dark as India ink lay over the ruins of Hindostan Falls, where 1500 people had lived in wild frontier days, and many had died in 1828, in the awful year the town sank in fatal yellow fever. The river, changing course, had some years ago claimed the street which bore its name; part of Thomas Jefferson Brook's inn rotted beneath its waters. The ruins of staved-in cabins lay on what used to be Church Street, and the cold, bright stars shone down on rusting nails, horseshoes, wagon wheels, halves of broken coffee cups and clock springs sticking out of the drift and humus of wet oak leaves.

Further down, on School Street, where Susan Poore Brooks had spent so many days drumming the continents and seas into the heads of frontier children, the school cabin had sunk down on its knees like a tired old man. Its roof had long-since fallen onto slateboards and carved-on desks. A picture of George Washington, with one eye gone, lay under the rusty debris of the old woodstove.

In the cemetery over the hill, beyond the barn of the man named Slicer, odd swamp gas lights flittered among the leaning, fallen stones. And on the hill above, equally odd lights glimmered inside the Slicers' barn.

Voices, low and measured, sounded within its walls. Or were they only the moaning, sad voices of the lost town? In spite of what the natives told each other, none of them liked to come here. That was the reason they never looted it, why things still remained. It was a place cursed, with only the pig-raising, half-outcast Slicers willing to live among the horrid, crumbling stones and debris of the past.

Inside the barn were the odd lights, odd voices.

"Swear. You will resist."

"We will resist."

"Come what may, resist the tyrant. Resist the war. With arms if need be. Though blood be spilled—"

"We swear."

The door finally opened. Then the lantern lights flickered and faded, snuffed out, and the sound of horses' hoofs clattered down the road. Soon, Hindostan Falls was left again to the rattling wind, the shadows, and the dark memory of the dead.

"Eustace wouldn't come tonight," Thomas Jefferson Brooks said bitterly the next afternoon, as he and Susan came through the door of their son Tommy's home on Church Street in Loogootee. "I don't know what happened to him this summer, but he seems like a stranger. He knew you particularly wanted him to meet Sergeant Boucher, to show our family's hospitality while he's here on the army's business."

"In my day, children didn't refuse to honor their parents' wishes," Susan Brooks said, kissing her mother. Hannah Poore had come over to Tommy and Libby's house earlier with Seymour Brooks, Tommy's youngest brother, to help with the supper.

"Ah, but you always complained about the youngest ones in our family, Amanda and Johnnie," Hannah smiled at her daughter. "Said I was spoiling them, letting them tell me what to do."

"And so you did. The babies of a family, the children of the parents' old age get just about what they want. Maybe we're just worn out, but I can't fight Eustace any more either. Sneaking off at night, God knows where, sitting like a stone at the supper table."

"I should thrash him," Thomas Jefferson Brooks said. "Believe me, Tom, I would have done that if you or your brother had acted this way."

"Pa, I wouldn't have thought to oppose you," Tommy said a little ruefully. "Maybe you've let him have too much, work too little." Tommy Brooks was standing by the door. Being up during the last few days had brought color to his face. He favored his wounded side, but he now walked freely about. He was master in his home, and his face shone with confidence.

Thomas Jefferson Brooks went on with his complaints about Eustace. "The boy won't write to his brother Lewis, doesn't want to hear his name mentioned."

Seymour Brooks was playing on the floor with young Lewie Brooks, Tommy and Lib's red-haired three-year-old. They were marching toy Napoleonic soldiers about.

"Eustace is a snake in the grass," Seymour said, smiling mysteriously to himself.

"What do you mean by that?" his mother demanded.

"Nothing, nothing at all," Seymour said. He was a near-sighted youth with large glasses who usually said very little, losing himself in books whenever he could. He had never gotten along very well with the unpredictable Eustace, who changed enthusiasms with every wind that blew down the road.

Hannah Poore went to the kitchen door to receive a bowl of corn relish from Libby Brooks. She glanced at the table. Cloth nicely ironed, set for seven. Lib had done well with the chicken, although it had sat now too long in the oven. The young man, Sergeant Keith Boucher, had sent word he would be an hour or so late—there, there was someone at the door now.

A tall, intense young man with a patch over one eye was ushered into the small parlor by Tommy. Lib was bobbing her head, shaking hands, turning nervously as she heard the baby cry in the back room.

Tommy came over, presenting his friend to his grandmother, and after a hubbub of exchanged questions and introductions, it was time to sit down to supper.

Lib was nursing the baby in the back room and called out for them to go ahead; Susan Brooks and her mother set the supper on the table. Dishes circulated about the table, stewed apples, green beans and onions, hot rolls (too hard, Hannah thought, should have risen longer, but never mind), ham she had brought over to stretch the chicken.

Susan Brooks gave a blessing. In the satisfied, expectant silence that succeeded her prayer, as everyone tucked napkins into their collars, Sergeant Boucher nodded deferentially to Thomas Jefferson Brooks. "Sir, I see you have much to be grateful for. My comrade here seems to be almost restored to health."

"Yes," Thomas Jefferson Brooks said, solemnly. "In Louisville I thought we had lost him. I must tell you, sir, that I have not been a church-going man. Really the contrary. But when I saw him, heard that his was a serious case indeed—I went into a church on the main street there and went on my knees. It was the second time in my life."

His eyes were watery, and to cover his emotion he laughed shakily. "It must be that since I had never drawn a check on the good Lord's bank, he felt I had a more than enough credit in the account unused, because he seems to have honored my request in full."

His wife leaned over and patted his knee. Sergeant Boucher smiled courteously and turned to his friend and comrade, who was eager to talk. Hannah Poore watched Tommy's eyes kindle as he and the sergeant spoke of the Eightieth Regiment, of its inactivity as action in Kentucky slowed, of the respect for Colonel Lewis Brooks, of his discipline and drilling, of how the boys awaited Tommy's return.

"Yes, Keith," Tommy said, animated by his joy in hearing about the beloved regiment. "Now tell me about Jacob Joe Scott. How is he doing? Did I not hear the love bug has bit him?"

"He is engaged. He came back from a leave with the promise of the maiden, who is known to you, I believe, a little." He briefly spoke of Sophie Lavenham; the group about the table nodded and smiled. Preserves were passed, butter requested. Tom Brooks asked more questions. The sergeant answered each of Tommy's questions respectfully, but volunteered little information. He seemed distracted, eating little, sometimes putting down his fork to gaze out the window with his one good eye.

Finally there was a silence. The wall clock ticked. Little Lewie, who was sitting on a pillow, clanked on the edge of his plate with a knife. From the bedroom came the noise of a baby being patted on the back, squeaking and bubbling from a full meal.

Thomas Jefferson Brooks looked steadily at the sergeant. Tommy had described him as the unit's japester—a laugh a minute--but he certainly was not that way tonight. He seemed almost morose, and his mouth kept flicking into a frown with a nervous tic. "Sir, I sense you are ill-at-ease," the older Brooks said softly. The others, not wishing to increase the discomfort the visitor was obviously feeling, looked at the food on their plates. Tommy Brooks looked distressed.

Sergeant Boucher sighed. "I have often been blue of late. I do not know why, except my outlook on life changed when I left the military hospital after the Battle of Perryville. I have had no zest for living. Enrolling others for the draft was not something I wished to do, but the officers in the regiment believed it would be good for me to get away. I did stop by my home east of here and had a restful day or two. But since coming here this morning, I have reason to be apprehensive."

"Keith, what went on?" Tommy asked quickly.

"When I first got off the train here, I felt ominously like I was expected. No one came up to greet me, no, but people were watching me. There was a small, bent man who looked like a weasel. He was wearing new blue jean trousers."

"That would be John Macaboy," Tommy Brooks said. "Anyone who keeps his eyes open around here knows he is the keeper of the seals of the KGC secret lodge. They say he even wears armor."

"He was only one of the men I saw staring at me with cold eyes, as I set up my table to enroll able-bodied men, there in a little nook by the station. The notice had been given that all should report today and tomorrow, and many did. It took several hours. But behind me, I saw some men giving some sorts of signs with the fingers against their wrists."

"Knights of the Golden Circle," Susan Brooks said. "I think they are dangerous."

"They're, not really. A lot of what's said about them is exaggerated," Thomas Jefferson Brooks said, as his mother-in-law Hannah Poore took away his plate. "I wouldn't be afraid of a lot of mumbo-jumbo secret signs. A good many of them are boys just out for the adventure, or disgruntled draft-dodgers or old geezers who don't understand what the war's about."

Sergeant Boucher still did not look up, but ran his finger on the tablecloth in circles. "That's what I thought. Although the papers and Governor Morton make out some kind of grand conspiracy, I pooh-poohed all the mystery. Rumor mill gone wild I thought. But then a man sauntered up to me and said, 'Some of the young ones here in the county aren't going to enroll. I just want you to know they are standin' on their rights'."

The shadows were deepening in the room and Boucher went on. "He made me angry. After all we sacrificed at Perryville, not to even want to enroll. I said I represented the law, and I'd just like to know who he was talking about.

" 'Don't mind if I do,' he said, and took a list out of his pocket. 'Defenders of the Constitution,' he said. 'You jest come on out and make a call on some of my friends, and we'll explain it to you.' He told me where he and the others lived; I wrote it down. I think I was business-like and I took care not to threaten. I guess they must be—Knights of the Golden Circle."

"Do you think you should court trouble like that?" Susan Brooks asked. "They might even rough you up."

"Everybody has to be enrolled. That's what the procedures call for. In some counties they're taking militiamen with them to reach everybody who doesn't come in. I don't think I need to do that. I've already been to one place on the list." He gestured to Hannah Poore that he was finished with his plate. Lib Brooks was setting down slices of angel food cake with lemon whipped cream icing. "It's a matter of principle," he said to no one in particular. "If they could die out there on that hill, surely I can get one Indiana county enrolled."

"Where did you go, Keith?" Tommy Brooks wanted to know. His eyes were like coals, and his grandmother thought gratefully that his vitality was flowing back, like a creek in early spring, finding its way through long-dry channels. Today he had taken the bandage off his wound.

"Well, I got a horse at the livery stable and went out the road to the south there—" Boucher pointed.

"Mt. Pleasant?" Susan Brooks wanted to know.

"No, the sign said something about a mill and a falls."

"Hindostan," Thomas Jefferson Brooks said decisively.

"The man gave me the name of Thornton Slicer, Jr."

"God, of course he would give you that one," Tommy Brooks breathed. "They say that the meetings of the Knights of the Golden Circle are in his father's barn. But it's so far out and the members so closed-mouthed that no one has ever known for sure what is going on out there."

Sergeant Boucher nodded, solemnly. "Well, I rode out there. I gave notices about the draft requirements to Thornton Slicer, and his father and brother came out from an old ramshackled house. The brother, Samuel, fixed me with his eye and said, 'We will see you later, Mr. Boucher.' He did not use my military title."

Around the table, activity ceased. Thomas Jefferson Brooks put down his fork and stared at the wall. "Sergeant, I believe one of us should ride with you. I will be honored to do that." Susan Brooks grasped his arm.

"No, sir, though I thank you. I would not take you from your family. Besides, it is best not to anticipate trouble. If it finds you, well then— thousands in the army are exposed to far worse every day."

He shrugged and stood. "I thank you for this fine supper and the chance to see my old comrade." Tommy rose slowly, his face troubled for his friend. Sergeant Boucher went on. "This evening I will take the papers to a man named Bartram Nash. Then I should finish the other ten names, all the resisters, tomorrow. Once they have been served the draft enrollment papers, I will sign their names and they will be recorded to serve in the army."

"Nash lives up a lane that takes off from the Shoals Road," Tommy muttered. "Do they know—did the Slicers know you are going there tonight?"

"I suppose so. They made up the list themselves, and they saw me looking at the name. They all seem to know each other." He watched Hannah Poore lift little Lewie off the pillow and set him on the floor, where he stood solemnly watching the man in military uniform.

Sergeant Boucher shook hands all around, beginning with Lewie. Susan and Thomas Jefferson Brooks took him to the door, Tommy Brooks following behind. Lib Brooks stood at the door of the bedroom, the baby cradled in her arms.

As they watched, he untied his horse from the hitching post and, waving his hat from the saddle, headed the horse down the street towards the Shoals Road.

Tommy Brooks turned from the door. "I should be with him," he murmured unhappily.

The sky was streaked with shafts of gold and orange from behind clouds as the sun prepared to set, and the fragrance of blossoms was borne on the spring air. "The magnolias must have opened just this afternoon. That is their heavy sweetness we smell," Hannah Poore told herself.

There was a crash. Little Lewie had pulled the corn relish dish off the table; his mother chided him in a strong voice. More scared than ashamed, he began to scream at the top of his lungs and all who were in the room began to gather round, arguing about the corn dish, comforting, picking up pieces of glass and corn.

Hannah Poore watched them, saw Tommy sitting heavily on the settee, his arms hanging limp like an ape's between his knees. Lewie refused to be comforted; the family's voices continued in their bickering way. Lewie was allowed too much freedom; Lewie was too restricted and showing off; Lewie was tired. "They are weary and strained by Tommy's illness and afraid for the friend who was here at supper tonight," Hannah Poore thought. "Pain and weariness and fear in families. At bottom, that is what war means."

Twilight deepened, yet Tommy Brooks still sat on the settee. His visiting family was gone; his exhausted wife was sunk on a daybed beside the children upstairs. The sounds of the village floated in through the open screen door: hound dogs yelping and baying at some raccoon on the edge of town, the sound of the 7:37 whuffling along past cows and fields towards Vincennes, sending back a mournful, distant whistle somewhere near the Martin County line, children's voices up the street, filling the April twilight with their piping voices, "Ring-around-the-Rosie."

He had played that game too, in Mt. Pleasant. That house where he was born stood out in his mind like a picture book scene. Red bricks, long, light windows which surveyed the valley from a small knoll. It was stately, like something in New England. But then his Uncle Lewis (dead now these ten years) had built it in the first days like the house of some Brooks ancestor in New England. Uncle Lewis had moved out when Hindostan died, and his father had moved his family in. The stagecoach, after crossing the river at the Houghton Mill, ran past that house and down the lane, north, twisting and turning west in its journey to St. Louis, snaking over a bumpy, difficult course. Like his life.

That lovely brick house, surrounded by cedars and hemlock trees, in gentle, gracious Mt. Pleasant was his home, always would be. For some reason his heart yearned for it at this very moment, for the peace it represented, before the war had come—there was a shape at the front door. He rose; his brother Eustace burst in, wild-eyed. He could hear a horse panting outside.

"Why didn't you come with the family, Eustace? What in the name of God have you been doing?"

Sweat was pouring off Eustace's streaked, dirty face. The road was dusty. "Tom, I can hardly face you, knowing what I've been, and done." His eyes were as scared as a rabbit's, and he turned away to look at the floor. "I thought it would be fun, dressing up, having secret brothers. I wanted to do something different, fly in the face of the family, 'specially Pa."

Tom looked at him sharply. "Secret—"

"The handshakes, the rituals. And I was angry at the trouble the war has caused—"

Tom's mouth flew open. "My God. My own brother. Knights of the Golden Circle. Why did I never know it when I spied on them all?" He put his hand against a table for support. Then, angrily, he lunged towards Eustace, collared him with a strength which suddenly poured into his arms.

"Tommy, I'm powerful sorry about it," Eustace protested squeakily. "Knew it was wrong for a long time, but couldn't cut the ties. You've got to listen to me. We don't have time for you to throttle me now." Tom let his brother go with a disgusted grunt.

"Go on," he ordered, "but keep your voice down. I don't want Lib and the babies awake."

"They are after Sergeant Boucher. Some of the worst of the knights. The Slicers—"

Tom's voice cut like a knife through the charged darkness. "What—where? Tell me now or I'll knock you down, so help me."

"He is to stay the night at the hotel, due to ride in after taking enrolling papers to the man that lives off the Shoals road."

"I know that—"

"Thornton, Sr., and Samuel Slicer have rifles. They are going to waylay and kill him and dispose of the body in the river!"

There was a moment of silence in the room. The smell of horse sweat and the sound of Eustace, expelling anguished breaths, filled the small parlor.

Tom Brooks turned deliberately and walked into the downstairs bedroom. He reached for a revolver he kept on the wardrobe shelf and then set it down on top of a chest of drawers. Then, pulling back the quilt on the bed, he ripped off a sheet, put in into his teeth and began tearing strips.

Eustace followed close behind. "What are you doing?" he demanded.

Tom did not answer, simply tore two wide strips from the sheet. "Help me here," he ordered, ripping off his vest and quickly slipping down his trouser braces. He gestured for Eustace to help him lift his shirt. There, beneath it was the bandage of the newly healed wound. Eustace had not seen it since it was made at Perryville; he gaped, wide-mouthed at the jagged edges, the pink flesh which had just completed the process of bridging the torn flesh and muscle. Tom had already started to wrap his stomach, tightly binding the wound. He indicated that Eustace should walk around him until the sheet strips bound him like a ceremonial sash.

His brother's eyes were filled with fear. "What will you—"

Tom pulled the shirt down over the bound scar and stood tall, looking out the window at the pink and mauve sky. "Now I can stand to mount a horse." He put on his blue Union jacket and belt, buckled as wide as it would go to accommodate the bandage, took the revolver from the top of the chest of drawers and slapped it into the holster.

"You're not—you can't—go after the Slicers. Please Tom. You're still too weak. Pa will kill me. It would break his heart—" Eustace was pleading, sobbing now as his brother walked carefully through the house. "Let me go."

Tom turned to straighten the belt. "This is my job, Brother, and I am going to do it."

Eustace's eyes narrowed and all the old hostility and confusion that had driven his spirit the last few months flamed into his eyes. "Why will you risk yourself? What does it matter if they drive him out of town, or even kill him? You never knew him before last August, and now you'll go galloping out—if anything happened to you, what about your wife? The little ones? *Pa*? Don't you or any of your Union soldiers ever think about anybody at home?"

Tom was out the door, striding to the hitching post. "You're a fine one to talk about Pa. You, take his heart and put it in a vise and squeeze all summer till it's dry without his even knowing what it was, and then you tell me this. A Copperhead is a snake, and ours has been in the bosom of the family." Slowly he swung himself onto the horse.

Crushed, Eustace looked up at the brother he had always adored. "You hate me. I don't blame you."

Tom Brooks, tall and strong in Union blue again, his eyes veiled with the pain that the binding of his wound could not stanch, looked down from the saddle at his brother. "I don't hate you. I don't think I hate anyone anymore, even the Rebels. But as for going after these scum—Eustace, God made me a male. But I'm the only one that can make myself a man. It is that way for you, too." Without waiting for an answer, he gritted his teeth and headed the horse at a gallop down the road towards Shoals.

He was just about fifteen minutes too late. His comrade had been surrounded by three of the Knights of the Golden Circle, the Slicer father and brother and the John Macaboy who had met him at the train station. The way-layers stopped Boucher near the Nash farm, down the road from where the captain had just presented information on the draft. As the front page story in the *Indianapolis Journal* said later that week:

The sergeant was shot by John Macaboy, who stood on a slight elevation of ground near a dead white oak tree and behind a thick clump of bushes, and was thus unperceived by his victim. The shooting was done with a rifle, the ball entering near the right shoulder and passing down obliquely through the lungs and severing the main artery of the heart.

Captain Thomas Jefferson Brooks, Jr., of B Company of the Eightieth Indiana Regiment arrived just after the shooting and succeeded in wounding Thornton Slicer, Sr, who was preparing to take the body to White River for disposal. The other two assassins fled into the woods north and east. Captain Brooks, who was on leave recovering from a severe wound at the Battle of Perryville, fell off his horse unconscious and was borne to his father's house in Loogootee—.

Where he lay while fever rapidly became pneumonia and other complications, sapping his strength hour by hour. His father, Thomas Jefferson Brooks, sat by his side, holding his hand. His wife Libby, little children, and the rest of his family came and went, shaking their heads, bearing Bibles and trying to get the old man away from the bedside, to come and at least take a bite of supper. To the father all of them except Tom seemed like shadow pictures thrown on the wall.

But he never left the side of his unconscious son, except for the briefest of moments, for three days, and he never said a word. When his daughters Emily and Suse told him that the Three-County Loyalty Guard, under the leadership of Sergeant Horace Hogue had apprehended the other two murderers, he did not bat an eye. When his wife Susan whispered that their other son Eustace was gone, leaving only a miserable short note behind, he did not ask where, but raised dull eyes to her until she thought it right to answer his unspoken question, "To the Eightieth Indiana, if they'll have him, to join and fight in his brother's place. He said something about manhood coming late."

Thomas Jefferson Brooks returned to his desperately ill son, watching him gasp through useless lungs for every breath, his skin as pale as a white violet's. And when, finally, Tommy Brooks slept serenely, almost as he had as a child in his cradle, his father brought to him the captain's bars that brother Lewis had just sent from the war camps of Kentucky. The old man placed them beside the hands of his son, now clasped in death, which lay on the coverlet Grandmother Poore made so long ago as a girl in Massachusetts.

Forsythia bushes shed their faded blossoms onto the dirt as the long funeral train of carriages and wagons following the flag-draped hearse made its way out the Mt. Pleasant Road. Thomas Jefferson and Susan and Libby Brooks headed the procession in a carriage driven by young Seymour, who from time to time took off his large glasses to wipe the mist from his eyes. Behind the front mourner's carriage rode other calashes and carriages draped in black carrying family members: Emily Campbell and her physician husband Thomas, who had tended Tommy Brooks at Perryville, and afterwards, Susie Niblack, her husband Sandford and their little children from Wheatland.

Grandmother Poore and her daughter Harriet Houghton and son-in-law John rode in a small black calash with a purple wreath on its side, driven by the undertaker's son.

"The redbuds are about to burst," Hannah Poore said absently, drawing back the curtain to look out. "They have that deep purple, about-to-bloom look." All of the hills near White River were clouded with the color of swelling buds, light green, pink, purple; willow, maple, poplar pulsating with the expectation of the coming flower and leaf time.

Harriet Houghton fingered the brooch at her throat. She was never quite comfortable watching the countryside go by in a closed carriage; still, she had mastered the early, frantic fears she used to have as a young mother about leaving her home. "Will so wanted to come to this. He and Tom were of an age."

"It is impossible for the Fourteenth to get leaves now," John Houghton said. Whenever he spoke of Will Houghton, the son who had recently been promoted to major for his bravery at Fredericksburg, and was thus the youngest field officer in the Army of the Potomac, his voice rang with undisguised pride. "General Hooker keeps drilling, drilling, preparing for a huge movement south soon. A major has constant duty."

"Let us hope the new movement gets further than the other ones have," Harriet Houghton sighed.

Then they were silent, watching squirrels and rabbits leap on the rills and hillocks at the side of the road. "Spring is a bad time to die, Tom said," thought Grandmother Poore in spite of herself. In times like these, she kept her little Presbyterian devotion book in her lap. *The Happy Christian.* Happy Christians did not think morbid thoughts. Still, it was an odd thing that the earth should be shouting for joy while all of their hearts mourned one of the finest, most inherently decent young men she had ever known. Nobly, beautifully dead trying to defend a friend and the cause of freedom, but still gone, never to see the redbuds of these Hoosier hills again.

Ahead, in the first mourners' carriage, Lib Brooks, tears streaming silently down her face, held little Lewie up to look out the window. Her mother had kept the babe, who was ill, at home. Susan Brooks, sitting beside Lib, handed Thomas Jefferson Brooks across from her a letter which had arrived just as they left the house. It was from Colonel Lewis Brooks of the Eightieth Indiana Regiment. His father opened it and read

Near Elizabethtown Kentucky

Dear Mother:

I received your affectionate letter yesterday and was truly glad of its reception; although it could but be sad, it comforted me in my troubles. Poor Brother, as you justly remarked, I can hardly realize that he has gone. May God have mercy on his soul. I sincerely hope and pray that I may live as to meet him where sorrow ceases. For although I know you will be kind to Lib and the children, I feel for them in their loneliness. Poor father, cares often fall on him.

I have been so busy with business since my return that I can scarcely think. My monthly reports and muster rolls are quite a task but I am getting along pretty well. I was yesterday the recipient of a magnificent sword with two scabbards, sash and belt enclosed in a rosewood case at the hands of my brother officers. We await orders for pursuit of our ever present foe Colonel Morgan. You know how I regret, in the press of all these duties and the exigency of time, being unable to be at Thomas's services.

Thomas Jefferson Brooks crumpled the letter. "I know of nothing but the regiment," he said aloud bitterly and threw the wadded-up ball of paper towards the window. His wife picked it up off the carriage floor, carefully straightened the wrinkles out, read it, and put it in her pocketbook.

The funeral procession was turning west, up the hill now, and into the sleepy village of Mt. Pleasant, past the mansion house where Susan and Thomas had been married, where Tommy himself had been born. Tommy had always thought of it as home, they all did, really. Home was where the happy reveries of unblemished childhood sleep under the stones of the walk, where deep, strongly colored associations lurk by cistern covers and beside rosebushes to jump out at you from another time, where bittersweet memories flutter about and come to rest about every chimney and doorpost. The burying grounds, Brooks Cemetery and Houghton churchyard, stood within full view of the houses of Mt. Pleasant, not far away as in some towns. The red brick mansion was only down a slope and over the hill from the fenced plot where Tom Brooks would have a final resting place. Home to Mt. Pleasant, today. Tommy Brooks was coming home.

The services were over, the last visitor's carriage, that of the minister, rolled its way out over the spongy lane to go back to Loogootee. New earth, strewn with crushed spring beauties and Dutchman's breeches lay in a rectangle towards the front of the Brooks plot. Hannah Poore stood looking at the grave sites, reading names chiselled in brown stone. "Lewis Brooks, born Lincoln, Massachusetts, his wife Agnes—Daniel Brooks, brother to T. J. Brooks—consorts, small children."

Here were her own Brooks grandchildren, who had died as babies or young people, sacrifices to diphtheria or typhoid or cholera, remembered in her life as bright swatches of light hair and toddling joy, like the pictures of angels in books. Hannah, Daniel, "Mary Chute Brooks—Asleep in Jesus," a small stone said of the ten-year-old girl who had lain under it for over a decade now.

"Asleep in Jesus. Truly they are. If I did not believe it, I would die right now," Hannah Chute Poore said to herself. She turned to go read from the devotion book she had brought and left in her old basket in the carriage. Her relatives would not go from this spot for a while. Each must make his own farewell, tear his heart from the plot of new earth behind the fence in whatever way he or she could.

Her daughter Susan was over the hill in the woods, sadly picking wildflower bouquets to leave on her babies' graves. They had dismissed the undertaker's driver; Sandford Niblack sat in his place reading a book, putting everything that had occurred out of his mind. He had not gone to the war, pleading the cares of a young family, and he did not wish to ponder the tragedies of those who had gone and died for it. It would have been a troubling conflict for him, and Sandford, a good sweet man, avoided troublesome conflict when he could. Hannah had noticed that.

His wife Susie and her father remained at the grave site; it was best that they be left alone. And she, Hannah, would fish in her old traipsin' basket, brought so far in the Conestoga in the old days, for the meditation book and whatever else she could find to give her comfort—the small comfort of familiar things.

"Cry, Pa. Or shout out or stamp your feet. Do anything but stand there like a lump of limestone," Susie Brooks said to her father. They both were facing the raw slash of earth, but neither was looking at it. Their eyes were on the far hills that rolled down to White River and Hindostan Falls.

"Why should I?" her father said blandly. He was holding the American flag, with two circles of stars on it, that had been taken off his son's casket before they set it in the ground.

"It was a nice service," Susie ventured. "I like to think that there are many mansions for us all. It is comforting."

"Well, it would be good if there were," her father said in that same contained, dull voice. "I have built a good many myself and seen them torn down on this earth. Almost everything I ever loved—"

"Pa—"

"Don't Pa me," he said with a hint of feeling. "And I don't see how the religion you and your mother keep pushing at me did a thing about it. I loved my sister Emily and watched a cruel, snivelling husband almost kill her with neglect." Susie patted his hand. She knew the story of her aunt Emily, whom no one in the family ever discussed, who had run away and "gone wrong." She never knew she had an Aunt Emily until word came the woman died in New Orleans, leaving small legacies to each of her nieces and nephews in Loogootee.

"My own father preached about God's goodness up in his church on the hill while the town ranted at Emily until she ran away. Then my friend was burnt up in a turpentine fire on a plantation, while all the Catholics around crossed themselves and called on Christ." His voice seemed to be gaining energy. "We built Hindostan and that was swept away in the epidemic, Methodist church and all. Your mother and I had to bury half the town ourselves. Whatever mansions had been built were—gone." His hand swept south, towards the forlorn ruins of the town.

Bloom bits from maple trees blew in the air, sifted down onto the grave.

"When I was a child, Emily and I used to build sand castles down at the seashore sometimes," Thomas Jefferson Brooks said in a far-away voice. "We would build them up with turrets and fine palisade walls, and the tide and waves would come in and wash over them in no time, melting our work to nothing." He sighed. "All for naught."

His daughter faced him squarely, her mouth set firmly. His sad heart roused. Susie looked to him, at that moment, much as her mother had looked in the first years he knew her. Same gray-blond hair pulled back from a face with sharp, angular features, same confident tilt to her head, same serenity of eye and heart.

"You have taught yourself the lesson you need to know, Pa," Susie said.

"And what is that?"

"We are not made of sand."

"No?"

"We are made of spirit and of love. Knowing how Tommy lived and died should have taught you that. That kind of courage, that self sacrifice doesn't spring from dust, from random chance."

"That sounds like something Lewis said once. 'Knowing one good man,' he said, 'should convince us of the existence of God.' "

"It is true. God lives and is eternal, and as He lives so does Tom."

Her father was silent. Then he said, "If I could know that. To believe that he does go on living, not snuffed out like a candle. You believe that, really?"

"I do not believe, I know."

"How?"

"There is knowledge deeper than our minds, older than these hills. It is the certainty of the deep-down goodness of this life," she said softly, and as he looked at her he felt a sense of wonder at her words. She spoke with such conviction, such wisdom, and the wisdom of his father and of all the wise people of the earth seemed to speak through her.

"Let Tommy go, Pa," she said. "Release him to God. Do not tie him to this earth. " She gestured towards the plot, the crushed flowers. "Give him his freedom at last. You have bound him too long—"

Her voice broke and she turned to him, to his arms. She wept and a tide of feeling flooded through him, finally, and he sobbed, silently, holding his daughter. "You have not seen the rest of us," she whispered. "Your sight was filled with Tom, though he did not wish it. Emily does not know you. Eustace has gone off, neglected, my children have needed their grandfather. And Lewis—"

"Lewis?" he managed to ask.

"You have done him the gravest injustice of all. You have measured him by his brother and found him failing. You have not seen the man he really was all along. We need you now.''

''I did not know, I did not know,'' her father murmured. Susan Brooks came up near them and knelt to place flowers on the little graves in the corner of the lot, then, at last, to the new slash of ground that held her son. Her husband and daughter turned from her, leaving the mother to make her own parting. They walked down the little rise from the burial plot and, arm in arm, went towards the funeral carriage.

Sandford Niblack looked up at them, coming with tear-stained faces, then glanced down again to mark the page he was reading.

And Hannah Poore climbed the hill as day was waning, carrying her old traipsin' basket. Slowly, she bent her knees, and tucking her mourning dress under her, she knelt by the new grave. Then she took a large wooden spoon out of the basket and dug a hole. Methodically and with a slight, remembering smile on her face, she put in the soft ground brown bulbs, the grape hyacinths, which bore in their genetic memory the salt marshes of Massachusetts and beyond that, the strong, enduring hills of western England.

April, 1863

Chapter Eleven

John McClure bent low, scanning the red mud in the Fourteenth's camp in Falmouth, Virginia. "Not a blade of grass. Not one tip of green in this gol-durned clay," he muttered to Tommy Thompson. "My sister Mary Jane writ that spring's a-bustin' out all over southern Indiana. The ground around here looks like a frozen turnpike in Feb'rary."

"What in the hell would you want to bloom for if you'd had the feet of fifteen thousand bored and DIS-couraged people stompin' all over you all winter?" Thompson demanded, hands on his hips. Then, in a more musing mood, "What else did Mary Jane say?"

Ever since Thompson's sweetheart Lina wrote him a sad little letter and marched down the aisle with someone else, he had pined and drooped at his lost fortunes. Lately, though, he was beginning to show interest in the possibility of new feminine conquests. A homely girl with a good disposition might be less fickle than some.

"Well," answered McClure, "she says that my uncle Horace is a hero. Three County militia rode like a posse all over the knobs and river valleys and rounded up the murderers that shot that poor sergeant that was a-notifyin' for the draft. Says Miz Poore's grandson Tommy Brooks, though, died on account of the whing-ding."

"Wasn't he the one shot up at Perryville?" Thompson pronounced it Purr-ville.

"Yes, and the wound was finally pretty well healed up. He re-caught the lung fever out there in the country the night of the assassination and died in a few days."

"Do tell. Sad." Thompson took out a plug of tobacco and rather affected-ly bit off a chaw. Chawing was one of the bad habits he had picked up in the army, "jest to keep up with the crowd." He was now the champion tobacco spitter in the unit. "I ain't heard from home in a month o' Sundays. What else did your sister say? Did she send any messages to anyone—'round here?"

"Waal, let's see. No, nothin' like that." McClure's face fell; he was obviously remembering something from the letter that was not pleasant.

Thompson drew near, his jaw working. "What is it you're thinkin' on? Tell me. Ain't we friends to the end?"

"Which ain't come yet, thank God," John McClure breathed, "although no credit's due for that to the generals of the Army of the Potomac. Anyways, I tole you I was worried about my aunt Lettie. Lettie Hogue."

"Yes, said she were actin' might strange."

"Mary Jane says she was spotted in Cincinnati by one of the ladies from Upper Indiana Church who happened to be in town. Comin' out o' the railroad hotel on the arm of Willis Mawkins."

Thompson's eyes narrowed. "The Vincennes livery stable owner?"

"The same," McClure said, turning his head. Musical notes floated into the clearing. A band was playing down by the river. A Northern brigade band giving a concert? Or maybe a Rebel unit tuning up on Dixie. The day was still; it would carry. They were not far from the other shore of the river.

"Sass Ass Van Dyke is back from Indianney," Thompson said, parking his posterior on a log that served as settee in the camp.

"I'll bet all the ladies wept a river when he left," McClure said coolly, surveying his fingernails.

"Saw Governor Oliver P. Morton, so they said."

"Begging for a colonelship, eh? Sass Ass goes right to the top, don't he?" McClure said, without much interest.

"Well, if he goes up, then Lieutenant Landon can shove right in, push everbody else off the rail and rule as captain."

"Which will be dandy dog," McClure countered, "if you don't mind a joke with each order and buckets of water on your head in the middle of a good night's sleep."

"I never have understood how he has held his own. He's as light weight as a banty rooster," Thompson said.

"Politics. Just politics. He knows everybody in Indiana. Besides he's not impossible. Neither is Van Dyke, for that matter."

Thompson shifted his weight to avoid a large knot on the log and McClure went on. "I don't know what Sass Ass saw the governor about, if it were 'bout the colonel thing or somethin' else. Anyways, he ain't goin' far now. Sass Ass thought when Harrow left durin' the time he was waitin' to be named general, and Kimball left because of the Fredericksburg wound, he'd have a chance for big brass. But Coons is finally healed up and back in the saddle, so to speak."

"And with Lige Cavins *ass*-isting, all of Van Dyke's *ass*umptions have landed him nothin' more than Quartermaster, which has been a dis*ass*ter."

"I wonder how Sass Ass has liked bein' quartermaster."

"I dont' know, but we have had awful food and not much o' that. Don't know if it's his fault, but what we get would make a hindoo puke."

They were quiet a moment. Overhead finches and warblers twittered and whistled in two octaves as if they were not in trees which had been blasted by cannon shell, near a town which had been shredded like a piece of lace in battle. "Anyways," Thompson offered finally, "Sass Ass brought back a load of shortbread sweet cakes from Indianney."

McClure looked suddenly interested. "Did you say sweet cakes?"

"I did, and they ain't stale, neither. I had me one. Sass Ass says there's more to come, some things comin' in camp soon in a special train."

The notes of "Lorena" floated over the camp, louder than before. McClure's mind formed the words as the song progressed:

The years creep slowly by, Lorena
The snow is on the grass again.
The sun's low down the sky, Lorena—

McClure and Thompson looked towards where the tootling and singing was coming from.

"Practicin' for an evening concert tonight," Thompson said, matter-of-factly.

"Appears to me the generals are hottin' the pot," McClure offered, pulling at a lone bloodroot blossom that had somehow survived the constant trampling to bloom. The generals. Joe Hooker, he meant. General of the Army after General Burnside got shoved aside, after General McClellan got shoved aside before that, after General Scott got shoved aside before that. This man's army was as bad for shovin' aside as the front row of a bulldog fight in Knox County.

Thompson looked blank. "Hottin' the pot?" he asked. He still found, even now that he was a wise and seasoned veteran, that he did not understand some things.

"All this drill General Hooker is pushin' twice a day, new uniforms, Father Abraham and Miz Lincoln comin' down last month to review us. Gettin' us ready for the big push."

"To Richmond," Thompson sighed. "I cain't hardly wait. I am so tired of sittin' around in the doldrums here. I'll march anywheres just to get away from Falmouth."

"Finally, I guess we may. Get us, the whole Army of the Potomac to break General Lee's lines and head past the railroad and south. Taint' far."

"Less than 100 miles."

"Sooo, they hot up the old teapot so the brew stays warm. Get the fire o' morale a-stokin' with new clothes and shortbread. Throw on lots o' band playin' and flag wavin' and then''—he shrugged—''we go out and get shot.''

Thompson thought about it and nodded a little mournfully. Then, sitting on their haunches, Indian style, they listened to the band practicing, the chorus singing. They couldn't seem to get one part quite right.

> *The story of the past, Lorena*
> *Alas! I care not to repeat*
> *The hopes that could not last—*

A rustling in the brush announced the arrival of Crim of C Company. He carried a journal book and pencil.

''How much you Tigertails in the pot for?'' he demanded, picking nettles off his pants. ''Pick you a winner in the greased pole contest and come in for winner take all.''

''How much is each chance?'' McClure wanted to know.

''One thin dime,'' Crim replied.

''Damned expensive,'' McClure grunted. He had been sending most of his paycheck home to Mary Jane. ''Which sportin' gentlemen are goin' to try to get to the top of the pole?''

Crim tamped his pencil on the writing tablet, looking like the calculating oddsman that he was. ''Well, George Washington Lambert of F, Joe Roseman—''

''The new recruit?'' McClure wanted to know.

''The same,'' Crim replied. ''Sergeant Mull of A and Redksin McClure will also test the game,'' he said.

McClure turned to Thompson. ''My money on Roseman. A recruit. He's as ornery as a sow in heat and wiry, too, with the wirin' we been givin' him. Not wore down by weevily biscuits and slimy meat like the rest of us.'' He dug in his pocket and came up with twenty cents. Crim wrote the wager down.

''The contests are at four this afternoon. Don't forget,'' Crim admonished. He started off a at dog trot down the lane to see to the wagering interests of the other units in the Gibraltar Brigade. He had worked hard as recreation head and wanted all his pet projects to go well.

''Tell 'em to use soap on the pole rather'n bacon grease,'' McClure shouted after him. ''Last time they greased it up so good nobody could get to the top.'' Then he settled back down on his haunches to dig with a stick in the dirt in front of him, like a small child who has an idle morning to fill and not much to fill it with.

Major Houghton and Captains Beem and Van Dyke watched the Rappahannock river from the shore. Its waters, fed by mountain streams and
spring runoff, licked at the toes of their boots.

"Better. Water level's lowering day by day," Beem remarked. 'In about
two weeks if we don't get more rains, we should be able to cross at least two
of the fords. Hooker's been in Washington. Surely this evening he will
return and give the orders to march—"

"Good. I'm more than ready," Houghton said. "Look—there's another
one of those miniature, ironclad Rebel boats coming in now." He was
eyeing a strange, makeshift little raft no more than two feet long, with a
metal bow and sides, which was lurching towards the Northern shore of the
river. It would tie up on driftwood, move towards shore a bit, be caught in
the current of the river and spin in circles, then move shoreward again.

Several men from a Pennsylvania regiment were trying to grab it with a
hooked pole. They ran along the shore, encouraging it along.

"C'mon, Maid of the South," they yelled. "Give us your virgin
pleasures. Bring us some of that good Virginia 'baccy. Don't linger, pet."

"I wonder what the original 'shipment' from our side was," Beem wondered.

"Probably coffee, as always," Van Dyke said. "The Rebs'd rather have
coffee than anything except shoes right now. What was this that went on
while I was gone, with our lads venturing into the very heart of the Rebel
stronghold?" he wanted to know.

"Oh, some bumptious men from a New York regiment," Houghton
began, "and a couple from the Eleventh Ohio, and one of the men from
Greene County, Cavins' Company D, I think it was, got a note in one of
these tobacco shipments to join a Virginia regiment for tea over across the
Rappahannock. Promised safe conduct to the other shore and safe return
when the tea party was over." A slight smile crossed his face.

"And?" Van Dyke wondered.

"Well, they all went over, had their tea, and then were discovered and
corralled by a Secesh colonel who happened to come into the Rebel tent. He
was on the point of capturing all the Yankees and shipping them to Castle
Lightning or Belle Isle prison when the Rebel soldiers pleaded with him,
saying they had given their word of honor, and so forth. So they were freed
but got a smart reprimand from the commanding officers. Coons was fit to
be tied."

Van Dkye stared at his friend. "It's a wonder Coons even knew it happened. Or that he knew the meaning of 'word of honor.' "

Houghton looked reproachfully at him. "Gus—"

Van Dyke refused to be mollified. "When I was back in Indiana I heard
how it was when Coons was home recuperating. Spent his time entertaining

the ladies with his war stories and telling Governor Morton just what a hero he was." Two soldiers were splashing around in the Rappahannock. They caught the "baccy boat" and pulled it ashore to the cheers of the others.

"And you didn't see Morton, I suppose," Beem offered, reentering the conversation. He was displeased at the open contempt Van Dyke expressed for the man who was once again colonel of the regiment.

"Of course I saw Morton. And because I had the gumption to go to the top, I've been able to do something for the regiment that Coons never even thought of."

"Did something for yourself, too, I expect?" Beem said, without rancor. They watched the soldiers who had caught the "baccy boat" running along the shore, passing out tobacco and Southern newspapers.

Van Dyke gave Beem a long look. "If you don't look out for yourself in this man's army, nobody else will. And as for the matter of honor—you certainly have plenty of that," he said, coolly eyeing Beem, "and I don't see anyone promoting you to colonel."

Beem, hackles raised like a feisty terrier's, took a step towards Van Dyke; Houghton stepped between them.

"Grand Parade in forty-five minutes," he said in a firm voice, then stood between the two officers who were his friends until both strode away in opposite directions.

When Van Dyke returned to the encampment of the thirty-five men who now constituted G Company, he headed for a clearing behind the canvas covered tents. There, working above a chair which he could tilt back and forth over some wooden cracker boxes was his old contraband Negro, Clem Smith. He was back; Van Dyke had seen to it that he was hired as the brigade barber. The colored man was stropping the bright razor vigorously along a leather strap. Then he took a towel from around the neck of his last customer. Bushy Quillen had finally got his odd goat beard shaved of.

"Can't bear to say goodbye to them kinks and curls. Like a friend of the family," Quillen said, getting out of the chair, his eye on the heap of hair on the ground. "Thanks to ye, boy," Quillen added, and took two pennies from his pocket for the colored man.

"Appreciate it, massa," the man said, gesturing to the next soldier in line.

"Hate havin' the army cut my hair," Joe Roseman muttered as he came up from the line. "Looks like hyena fur. But you all have made such a mess of it," he looked sourly at the men who were lounging about, smoking, in back of him. He was a small, bellicose man with a pug nose and a scar across his chin.

"A little bacon fat and skunk stink on the hair never hurt nobody," Isaac Crim laughed. "Besides, all you new recruits got to be inn-ish-ated. Hardened to the rigors of combat. We're toughenin' you up for your ath-a-letic pursuits this afternoon."

Joe Roseman sat down resignedly in the chair. The colored man took scissors and quickly trimmed off the worst of the greasy, matted locks.

"Now, massa, you go 'head and suds that head o' hair with some of that new white soap that come in, you be as good as new."

"That stuff floats," Crim mused. "Some of Van Dyke's ASSignment from some Ohio soap company. Boil the soap in the kettle way too long and it gets porous, they say."

Quillen lingered, looking at the colored man performing his job in a skillful manner. Smith stropped the razor on a leather strap to give Roseman a quick shave.

Quillen's eyes became slits as he spoke out of the corner of his mouth to the Negro. "So now you're paid wages—cash by the adjutant, just like a white man," he said in a slow, provoking voice.

"I gets my wages," Smith said. "And I need 'em. I got my wife and sons settled in New York City." The barber drew the blade rapidly along the length of the strop. "No work in the city for a freedman. So's I come back here to my friend, Captain Van Dyke."

"Better finish Roseman up, Clem. We have to get them all out for the brass to inspect," Van Dyke said, and glanced over his shoulder at Quillen. He was a little nervous at the implication that he was a friend of a black man. After all, he wasn't paying or sheltering this contraband himself; he had just arranged—

"Next thing we know, nigger, you'll be wantin' to pick up a rifle and carry it out into battle next to us," Quillen said, his voice like a rasping saw.

The colored man finished stropping the razor. The strop, hanging from a branch, swayed in the air. He put a brush in a cup of soap suds, pushed it around on the ivory colored cake of soap, slowly, tracing small circles. "Well, I jest may do that if push comes to shove. Some are fightin' for the Union and I 'spect I can man artillery good as many that now do 't, even though I got a few years on me. A colored man can mount and fire a gun as well as a white one."

"You and the orangutans and the apes from Africa," Quillen remarked and strode haughtily away.

Van Dyke watched him leave. There were still plenty of black-haters in the regiment. He wasn't one of them, really, any more. Room enough for all kinds of people in the country, if you thought about it. He might have to think about it more. He had asked Governor Oliver Perry Morton for a colonelship in one of the new Negro regiments that the Northern army was forming along the Mississippi. You had to change with the times if you wanted to get ahead, after all.

And there it was, Grand Parade, Second Corps, Army of the Potomac. Display of the tactics Maurice of Nassau had introduced in the 1600's, developed into a pageant show of power by Napoleon Bonaparte. Utilized by Fighting Joe Hooker to unify the failing and fragmented greatest army of the North. Across the fields of Falmouth men stepped smartly, presenting themselves for review in ranks like bullets in a box. Line after line after line of flashing silver and bright Union blue strode by in clean-cut order to the blare of the bands—"Yankee Doodle," "Hail Columbia," loud and clear under a bright spring sky. Then the lines halted and the men stood for inspection, as the big brass commanded by Darius Couch, General of the Corps, closely followed by the suavely smiling, handsome Colonel Coons and Lieutenant Colonel Cavins on big chestnut horses, rode by. They, like the other officers, wore their flamboyant colonels' hats with a jaunty confidence; ceremonial swords presented by their units flashed in the late afternoon sun.

Then, the final exercises: the men of the Fourteenth, already veterans of over a dozen battles, clicked forward under the watchful eyes of their officers, then wheeled to the left in file, presenting arms as if they were soldier machines instead of men. The other thousands of men of the Second Corps did the same.

From the heights of Fredericksburg, the Rebel pickets looking down saw the wheeling, writhing lines and were reminded of an awakening dragon, stretching, moving its limbs, pulling itself up and out of the cave. The newly reconstituted and armed Army of the Potomac was a recumbent monster, ready to be activated, awful in power and terrible in latent, mechanized strength.

The men of the Fourteenth remained in position, at rest, after the Grand Parade; Colonel Coons and Lieutenant Colonel Cavins had orders to keep them awaiting the arrival of an important guest.

Soon, straying eyes caught sight of a small train approaching; a blustery-looking, portly, handsome man in formal attire rode on the buckboard of the first of eight wagons, loaded with supplies. Oliver Perry Morton, Governor of Indiana, was coming to feed his "boys" with down-home food and words of cheer.

The men snapped to attention; the Brigade band, its cheeks already worn out with blaring and it arms weary with drumming, struck up "The Army of the Free,'' and Colonel Coons introduced the chief executive of the Hoosier state.

"Men, we are the recipients of a fine honor today. Governor Oliver P. Morton, whose care is always for the soldier in the field, has come bearing gifts, but not deceitful ones, like the Greeks, I hope." A chuckle went through the ranks; Coons was known for his polish, and an almost clubby, wry humor.

"We'll see about Greeks bearing gifts," John McClure standing stiffly in the ranks, told himself. "Morton's like Van Dyke. Two ravens on a branch, they are, keeping an eye on the worms below. Don't give something for nothin'."

"Our governor is himself a soldier," Coons went on. "He is tireless in running Indiana's war effort in the face of—well, we all know what that fire in the rear is back home. It does not need dignifying by description. To ease our hunger for both the food and the comfort of home, without further ado I give you—"

"That-son-of-a-bitch Coons," Van Dyke said angrily out of the side of his mouth to Houghton, who happened to be near. "He didn't even give me credit for setting up this food relief trek."

The governor took off his top hat and handed it to the driver of the second wagon, a grave old man with a gray beard, who held the hat stony-eyed as Morton faced the troops.

"Men, first things first," said the governor jovially. "And first things in this case are" (he gestured towards the wagons) "four hundred pullets in river ice brought on the cars all the way from Indiana; one hundred fine, huge hams from Brown County, berry and cherry pies and tins of fruit and soft white bread and even pickles." With great largess he swept his hand over the wagons. "For you and our other Hoosier regiments here at Falmouth. Few though they be in this Eastern theatre of war, they are the leaven of the loaf of President Lincoln's proud army."

At signals from their officers, the men gave three cheers and a tiger "grrr" for the governor, Mr. Lincoln's proud army and the pickles and pies.

"Men," Morton continued, his face growing increasingly scarlet, "our gallant soldiers from Indiana. My eyes, like a woman's, want to mist over when I see your ranks so stalwart and valiant before me. Many are the scars of battle on the limbs which bear arms here. The scars of Antietam, Fredericksburg, Kernstown, scarce healed, are the proud badges of loyalty and endeavor for the Union cause that you wear.

"You are not alone. We are defending our own state from the very hearths you have left. Indiana now has a Loyal Legion of thousands of men on the ready should the traitor or his cavalrymen of death come into our fair Hoosier State. Some of your relatives are serving in this honorable troop."

"Horace Hogue," John McClure thought, giving his uncle a mental tip of the hat, "you finally have your chance."

"But the soldiers of the Southern Confederacy are not the only traitors in our midsts. No, we all know the threat. Those loyal to the Southern cause, capable of meeting by night to plot and gather and even plan to overthrow the government of Indiana, these are the threat. I do not overestimate, I trust, the present danger of Copperhead disloyalty. Ten thousand men in Indiana alone are rising in perfidy to bite the heel of Freedom."

"That's a-gonna be one mighty sore heel if ten thousand men chaw on it," McClure thought. He knew Morton's florid, emotional speechifying from the Indiana papers his relatives sent to him.

"Men of the Fourteenth, these days in my office, as cares cluster about my head like a troop of harpies, as I try to protect the boys at the front and save the state from uprising and anarchy, my troubled thoughts fly away to the home of my birth—the charming rural village of Centerville.

"There in the spring, as the grass was growing green just as it always does at this time of the year, I used to wander as a boy on my way to the fishing stream. Carelessly, my jeans tucked up, I would go about my business through the fields until—unwarily I stepped close, or even into a hole of snakes, awakened by springtime, seething in an ugly way over each other, hissing to the skies.

"What a horrid sight that was and how I pulled back in disdain or even fled in my boyhood fear." There was a pause. Every man in the ranks knew he was talking of the Copperheads back home. He was fighting for his political life and the future of the military effort against the combination of Democratic political manipulation and secret society agitation which threatened an armed uprising to support the South.

"Our Copperheads at home are threatening to take our state by rotten politics or force of arms from the Union and join it to the Confederacy if we do not settle at once for peace," Morton said. His face, streaked with perspiration in the increasingly hot, late April sun, was a study in determination; he clenched his fist against the sky. "But I will not pull back now from the pits of vipers that attack our state and our very nation."

"I guess not," McClure thought, impressed in spite of himself. After all, somebody had to get pretty het up if this war was going to be won. His eyes sought those of Joe Roseman, newly clipped and spruce, standing beside him. Roseman barely moved his head to show his approval of the governor's strong stand.

"At this very moment from his home in Dayton, Ohio, that arch traitor, Clement Vallandigham, is making speeches deriding our President, disclaiming our war effort, and calling for insurrection! The Democrats will meet in a fortnight in Indianapolis to defy me and the war effort. They have called for all those loyal to their dastardly cause to join them in a giant anti-Union rally.'' There was grim mumbling in the ranks.

"Just let a few of us be in the midst of the meeting for fifteen minutes with loaded rifles,'' McClure said out of the corner of his mouth to Joe Roseman. ''There'd be a few less men and a few more high pitched ladies among 'em.''

"Men, your state has asked a great deal of you heretofore. We have expected you to leave your comfortable homes and villages, risk your very lives monthly, live in discomfort and disease, see your friends and relatives die before your eyes. Now we ask something more.

"The man who has come with me, whom you see before you, is living testament to the sacrifices this war is demanding. This is Mr. Thomas Jefferson Brooks of Martin County, who is my most reliable purveyor.'' Morton lowered his voice in deference and Brooks stood slowly up, his face unsmiling, impassive. ''Mr. Brooks's son has just given his life, within these last few weeks, for the cause of loyalty and freedom in the state. I believe you know the story; Mr. Brooks insisted on coming because he believed this is where his son would want him.'' The old man brought up a table and set it up. He laid sheets of papers on it, and the governor pointed to it.

"Your Colonel Coons has drafted a petition stating the absolute loyalty of the troops in the field, here at the seat of the war, facing a new strong offensive, under the wings of—''

"All right, shut up, get out the petition. I'll sign,'' McClure told himself. ''Don't mind if I do. If we can't send 'em a round of grapeshot, at least we can send 'em a message.'' Joe Roseman, Isaac Crim, Bushby Quillen, Walter McClure and the rest of the men, with varying but sincere degrees of eagerness, lined up to sign the petition to the people of Indiana.

Augustus Van Dyke came hastily to the side of the governor and walked beside him. Morton was hastening to catch a train back to Indiana.

"Sir,'' said Van Dyke, licking his lips nervously. ''Have you been able to do anything for me in the matter of—''

Morton looked about with a rather blank stare at the earnest young man beside him.

"The colonelship. In one of the new Negro regiments they're forming—''

"Oh. Yes. Captain—Van Dyke it is. No, I am sorry that will not be forthcoming. Perhaps we can do something about a staff position elsewhere.''

"Yes, sir. Thank you, sir,'' Van Dyke said with disappointment. His head hanging low, he went to find the men of Company G, who were beginning the greased pig contest on the field.

"Uncle, I share your grief," Will Houghton said emotionally as he embraced Thomas Jefferson Brooks. They clung for a few seconds, the memory of Tommy between them. Then they sat by the wagon, discussing the death and mourning, while the other men played field games through the last hour of the afternoon.

Grandmother Poore refused to see people and knelt in her garden day after day, Thomas Jefferson Brooks told his nephew. She insisted Will Houghton send her a long letter, and he promised to give one to his uncle before he left. Libby Brooks and little Lewie and the baby were doing surprisingly well; the babe was still ill. Lib's sister was staying with her, and sometimes when the old man passed the house he could hear laughing. "The hearts of the young, like their limbs, knit faster than those of us who are older," Thomas Jefferson Brooks told his nephew sadly, staring at the river.

"William, you have not written to your mother in over a month," he added in a moment.

"I know. I have so many duties—"

"She mourns and frets and conjures up awful woundings and dangers when you don't send her a letter."

"I know it pains her," Will Houghton answered, shaking his head. "And why I don't write, when I write to Lewis and my father, I don't know. I think I feel her presence too much and want less of it. Out here, for the first time, I have felt as if I were my own man. Is that awful, uncle?"

"No. I don't think so. I felt that way once when I was eighteen and came West to find my own manhood, leaving all the old folks behind. I cut the ties like the umbilical cord and threw the past away. But I regretted the completeness of it all, later."

"I know I still love her, but I need to pull away. Tell her I send my love." His uncle nodded, took out a cigar and lit it.

Will Houghton walked his uncle back to the officers' tents, pointing out the sights of the Falmouth camp along the way—long lines of supply wagons pulled by mules coming down muddy tracks, storage barns where hundreds of boxes were being unloaded, medical treatment and headquarters stations, and whole cities of tents. They spoke of Colonel Lewis Brooks.

"And so, uncle, my cousin Lewis is honored and advanced," Houghton said, cheerfully. There was an odd note in his uncle's voice when he spoke of his son's recent receipt of the ceremonial sword, of the praise he received for his leadership. Houghton wanted to determine just what the odd note was.

"Yes. I don't know why I begrudge him all that joy and appreciation. I guess it is because Tom has nothing, not even life."

"From what Lewis has written me, his mourning is deep and sincere," Will Houghton said, watching the men begin to cluster at huge mess pots for the evening meal. Here at Falmouth, cooks fixed decent meat meals with hot bread. Tonight there was even butter that Morton had brought.

"I have to believe he is mourning," his uncle said, studying the smoke that rose from the campfire. "He is occupied, that's sure—his brother Eustace has come into camp and he has had to listen to grumbles of men who don't wish to fight next to a confirmed Copperhead."

"My father wrote me of Sergeant Boucher's tragedy and Eustace's part in it."

"Well, Eustace says he's repentant and wishes to prove himself a loyal patriot to honor his brother's memory," Brooks said. "My mind on all that is frozen like a block of ice. If I had to think about it all—"

"Uncle, we can use all the loyal patriots we can find," Houghton said, thoughtfully, then with a brighter tone, "Uncle Thomas, tell—Colonel Brooks—" he used the term proudly, savoring the words that his cousin had earned with so much fortitude both in the Fourteenth and in the Eightieth—"that I wish—I wish I could see him. Just to talk for an hour."

"Of the war?" Thomas Jefferson Brooks wondered.

"Perhaps. I wonder what he thinks of Hooker's strategy, of our chances in the Army of the Potomac to break Lee's stronghold on the routes to Richmond," Will Houghton said. The smell of stew drifted over. He was silent for a long moment, then he said, almost plaintively, "But I would speak more of old times. Of play among the caves. Of White River now that the floods are filling the valley, and summer coming."

"You yearn for home."

"Yes, and the carefree times. Remind Lewis for me how we used to shoot the falls at Hindostan and almost drown ourselves."

"You did that?" Thomas Jefferson Brooks asked. "You young fools." And for the first time since Tommy died, he began to laugh.

When Houghton returned to his tent, Van Dyke was there, pacing about. "I suppose you've heard that Morton turned me down on the commission for the Negro regiment," he said glumly.

Houghton began to pull off his gloves. He had not had a chance to change out of his dress uniform. "No. I hadn't heard. I'm sorry Gus, but I know you'll keep trying." He unbuckled his belt and swung it off. "I thanked him for my own advancement," he said without looking at his friend.

"Oh, yes, your major's rank," Van Dyke turned to stare at him. His chagrined smirk, edged in obvious envy, made Houghton laugh. "I guess I haven't really congratulated you on all that very well, have I?" Van Dyke conceded.

"Well, you aren't the only hero of the Army of the Potomac. Lots of the rest of us like shoulder stripes too." He looked at his friend with admiration and affection. "Gus, in battle you're as brave—foolhardy—as a rhinoceros. You may win advancement on the field in a moment, as I did."

"I urged you not to ride on to honor, there at Fredericksburg."

"I know you did, but don't apologize."

Van Dyke looked uncomfortable, as if he'd been given a motive he didn't feel, but Houghton did not notice it. "Friends as close as we are don't keep scoring sheets," he said, offering his hand and warm smile to Van Dyke. "I think we may all have that chance for battle soon, don't you?"

Van Dyke nodded. "Hooker is back from seeing Lincoln. I think we may be moving out."

"God grant it," Houghton said. "And that we return. This is my third spring away from Indiana and I yearn for home." Van Dyke nodded sadly.

Slowly Houghton put his gloves on his small trunk. "Shall we ever see White River swell with the rains again? Does it even exist any more?" He sat down on the trunk with a sigh. "I suppose I should write home before this campaign begins," he said. "Settle up in case—. I should write to— well, I'll write to father. I don't feel like writing to mother." His mouth was a firm line in the gathering twilight.

Later that evening Walter McClure sat at a small desk in the surgeon's tent at Falmouth, Virginia. His bright, ruddy face was a study in concentration. Outside the men of the Fourteenth scuffled and pushed each other around in the May twilight. He lit a lantern to re-read what he had just written.

To: Dawn Yet To Come
Mishingomesia's Band
Miamis, Peru, Indiana

Dear Mother:

These are days of excitement here at Falmouth. Two weeks ago our President was here, and now Governor Morton has come. There are festivities almost every day. Late this afternoon we had a greased pole and pig contest. I, your son, won the pole contest, being good at shinnying up trees in Miami County from my youth! Money was bet on me; I was a "long shot" so am in good favor.

My thought, though, is serious tonight, Mother. Our general has just returned from Washington and rumor spreads that we will strike tents tomorrow and head out to find the enemy. We are being readied, like braves before the night of the war party raid, to go to battle. I think of my ances-

tors, the Miamis, and how they went through the ancient rites the Bird of Thunder taught, and spend a week of days doing it. So Mialanaqua, the Catfish, bandchief of the Miamis told me. Those from the tribes would come, gather round the campfire, and tell the justice of their war cause. The elders of the gathered tribes would listen, nod that the cause was just, and order feasting and dancing and war painting to last for days and nights to ready the warriors for their dangerous journey. The war axes and bows and arrows would be sharpened, faces were painted, and prayers made to the Manittos of the world for aid. As shadows fell in the night, the spirits of the men would soar towards the coming battle as Thunderbird the Brave soars on high. "Now," the drums would say, "now your cause is just, now you feel the enemy near, now you know your hatred of him. Feel it in your veins. Let it firm your will. You can go, soon, soon, soon to ride, to shoot, to die, if so the Manittos will it."

In a few moments there will be a prayer service at the Lacy House, conducted by the Sanitary Commission ladies, and though it is Protestant, I shall go. I need the praying. Lee's army is great, 60,000 men and though they are poor and dress in different colored uniforms their valor is every bit as great as ours. They have stopped us before. I pray their ruthless, brittle pride does not confront us, stare us in the eyes and o'erwhelm us. For, as Mialanaqua, Catfish of the Miamis, told me when he taught me battle skills as a child, it is the spirit which counts. Whoever has the greatest will as a man, and eye-to-eye defends his cause with raging spirit, will win.

Evening comes and I think of you as I saw you, sadly helping our relatives to live out their last days on the reservation of tribal peoples in the state of Indiana, there near the Mississinewa. Soon, the government says, there will be no more reservation. Promised, it was, to our people as long as water flows and·grass grows. All the other promises the U.S. Government made us are as a broken necklace of beads, scattered on the ground and trodden on. And so we Potawatomi and Miami, who claimed it all as free and open hunting grounds now can claim not a square foot. Do not be sad, Mother, you can live quietly and in peace in the little cottage we own, there by the river, and there is money for you to live on. The money of my grandfather Asondaki Caipawa of the Miamis, invested well, provides for you. And, if I return I shall hope to teach in Miami County, to keep traditions alive and take our children into the future as you have tried to do.

In our camp this week there is a freed slave, who has come north and brought his family. There are thousands of them in the land, and now they must make their journey to the stars like the rest of us. They have their freedom by the proclamation of Mr. Lincoln; now we all together must test the meaning of the word, as one tests the soundness of a stone or coin.

Equality cannot come with pen, or even with the sword. I have come to know that.

Surgeon Burkhart is treated unfairly; he should be high in the hospital department. Others less skilled than he have gained promotion. And my own relative, John McClure, hates me with a hot hatred because it rankles him that I have his name. If he knew I shared his blood and that the patriarch he so reveres—whose name all Knox County knows—was also my ancestor— but he does not. Still, it warms my heart to see the colored barber freely paid and beholden to no man. For this I came, against your counsel, to this war, and for this I stay. We are the brothers of the eagle, all of us the children of the Father, and under his wings are one race. For this I fight, for this I would die if God decrees.

Mother, should I fall in this great battle which is to come, I hope I can lie in the Godfroy Cemetery with my uncles. There, near the beautiful river that pours over smooth stones, near white rock cliffs, where the last chiefs of the Miami lie in peace, in Christian burial. Perhaps someone could carve the Bird of Thunder for courage and beside it put the cross of Christ above my head. I, as you, have loved them both so well. And near them, please, put the flag of the United States of America, which I have come to believe, in spite of all its flaws, is worth all I may give.

Little White Deer
Your Son Walter McClure

"There is a time at the end of April," John McClure thought, as he sat near the river in the twilight, just a day or two, when the world seems to reveal the meaning God meant for it. The best day of the year. If I were in southern Indiana I'd be seein' it–Leafin' out day.

"You go to bed with the bare branches, just like it's been all winter, 'cept some blossoms hangin' down and you wake up with birds singin' fit to burst, on branches spread with leaves, a feast for the eyes and heart. And all that day and the next, the leaves grow and spread like little umbrellas right before your eyes a'most, light, bright green so bright it wants to dazzle your eyes. And the beech and maple blossoms drift and pile up on the lanes and bluebells bob so pretty in the woods, beneath redbuds and dogwoods—

"Right now Mary Jane is a-seein' it. She's lookin' out the window at the sun settin' beyond the fields of the old McClure farm. At this hour, cows are a-comin' home with a boy switchin' them from behind, up the path to the barn, and Aunt Jewell is yoo-hooin' everybody in to sit down to the table and there are new onions and dandelion greens to go with the fresh pork roast.

"It's been two years. Just two years ago this week we left Knox County as spring came. Furrows are a-standin' in the fields I own, the fields Harrison gave to Dan'l McClure for servin' in the Revolution. And I may never put my hand to the plow again. Seems a waste, a sad waste.''

William Landon, the lieutenant correspondent for the Vincennes *Western Sun* was walking by. ''Hey, Landon,'' McClure asked, ''you read the paper all the time. How is it back in Vincennes?''

Landon stopped, his upper lip, with the small, tidy mustache on it, twitching a little in amusement. ''Same as always, John. Fires burning down houses, babies born, old people dying. And the river runs right by, yet, and it's still full of muddy water and poplar boughs that'll go all the way to New Orleans.''

Only we aren't there, John McClure thought, watching Landon join the rest. The band music had begun again. He sat for a while thinking and then, finally, he made his way nearer to the shore of the Rappahannock River to listen to the group of Northern bands serenade the troops.

Houghton had come down, too, and was sitting on his rubber blanket and thinking about the letters from home Morton had brought with him. His brothers Walter and Eugene wanted to join the army; he knew his mother could not stand that shock and worried his letter would not reach them in time. He was pleading with them not to join, and though he felt a little guilty about it, he still believed it was the right thing to do.

Isaac Crim was there, sitting on the ground too, along with most of the rest of C Company. He had distributed the winnings of the wagering pool and was thoughtfully reflecting that recreational activities would be suspended now as battle approached in the coming week.

And Captain David Beem and Jess Harrold his lieutenant were there, fresh from the evening vesper service at the old mansion that served as headquarters for the pickets, and assorted men from his company H and other companies, sat listening to the bands play, all of them on the grass or rubber blankets, serene and relaxed for at least a few moments.

Tommy Thompson was at the very edge of the river, alone. He could see the Rebels, as usual, across the river, the pickets, and also men in comradely groups, ''taking the breezes'' much as the men of Lincoln's army were on this warm night. The last strains of ''Yankee Doodle'' sounded behind him. Then in the silence that followed the end of the song, there was a call from across the river.

''Hey, Yank, play some of ours.''

''What?'' Thompson shouted back after a moment.

''How about ''Bonnie Blue Flag?'' the voice, calling from cupped hands, shouted.

Thompson turned and shouted at the band, which was standing under one of the few trees left within several hundred square yards. "Hey, George Lambert—'' he called to the drummer-conductor who had ingloriously lost the pole race earlier in the day. "Let's serenade the Rebs. In honor of May Day comin' up.''

The men in the band conferred and began with a spirited rendition of the "Yellow Rose of Texas.'' The Northern army men clapped their hands in time to the music and began to sing. On the other side of the river, the Southerners joined in.

> *She's the sweetest rose of color, this soldier ever knew*
> *Her eyes are bright as diamonds, they sparkle like the dew.*
> *You may talk about your dearest May and sing of Rosa Lee,*
> *But the Yellow Rose of Texas beats the belles of Tennessee.*

There was only a little lag to account for time as the sound crossed the Rappahannock. Clusters of men from both sides crept closer to the edge of the river, so they could become one chorus.

Houghton and Beem, though they were not singing, watched the scene from their blanket up the rise. John McClure, Sholts, Thompson, Roseman, Quillen, and others from the Fourteenth clustered with hands wrapped around their knees and sang softly, so as not to overwhelm the sound of the Rebel voices joining in from the other side. Darkness deepened. Picket watchfires leapt and crackled along both sides of the shore. The spires of Fredericksburg, fought over by both sides and sleeping a troubled sleep on this beautiful spring evening, were outlined against the pale-rose sky.

Walter McClure and Surgeon Burkhart came to the edge of the group and stood in the shadows of wagons that had been used to convey the goods earlier in the day to the regiment. "Hard, hard to muster the hatred we will need to kill them soon, when they are so near and so much like us,'' Walter McClure murmured to his older friend.

"It always seems so odd to me to be fighting to the death, with the earth so beautiful around us, and things so easy a few hundred miles back home,'' Burkhart said. He looked towards the wagoners from Indiana, who were smoking in the shadows, and to the businessman who had directed the wagoners there. Governor Morton had gone back to organize political campaigns in the state, but Thomas Jefferson Brooks stayed to see to the distributing of the goods.

John McClure saw the old man, who like everyone else was standing listening to the harmonies of hundreds of voices on both sides. McClure took off his cap and courteously shook hands with Thomas Jefferson Brooks.

"Sir, I was so sorry to hear 'bout your loss. I only knew Tommy slightly. Are you—have you found any comfort?"

"My children are my life, son," Brooks said. "And now my younger son has gone to join his older brother Colonel Lewis in the Eightieth Indiana."

"Seymour?"

"No, Eustace. He just turned eighteen." John McClure was silent and looked away, not knowing what to say. The river frogs chirruped, and Thomas Jefferson Brooks said something John could not quite make out.

"What did you say, sir?" John said, turning towards the other man.

"I said, 'They are all boys.' All of you out here, all across the land. All boys. Sixteen, seventeen, eighteen, twenty-year-olds. Should be catching river pike. Going to the academy."

"Yes, sir, and I for one wisht I was a growin' to manhood any place else but here," John McClure said ruefully. He looked into the older man's kind, blue eyes. "Will you be going back tomorrow?" he asked.

"Yes, I catch the train cars home. I have many interests to watch over. In some way the homefront goes on."

"So I notice, sir. So I notice," John McClure said courteously. "My best to Miz Poore. She wrote me the nicest letter a month or two back. And to all the folks in Martin County. Say my hellos to everbody for me. Wisht I was with 'em."

"I will, son. And I will take these signed petitions from all the boys from home to the governor."

"Yessir. Tell 'em not to forget what we're doing out here. To think of us some, when they can—"

The campfires along the shore blazed orange. Their smoke climbed, white and clean, towards the now black sky. George Washington Lambert, directing the Northern band, whispered to his flutists and buglers that it was time to close the concert. They nodded and raised their instruments. The Southerners on the other side waited. Sonorous, slow notes began—

Mid pleasures and palaces, though we may roam
Be it ever so humble, there's no place like home

By the second line the Southern chorus had joined in the singing again.

A charm from the heart seems to hallow it there
Which seek through the world, is ne'er met with elsewhere.

A rising, melodic tide swelled over the broad, separating expanse of the Rappahannock.

Home, home, sweet, sweet home.
Home, home, sweet, sweet home.

They began the second verse. Everyone seemed to know it.

I gaze on the moon as I tread the drear wild
And feel that my mother now thinks of her child,
As she looks on that moon from our own cottage door,
Through the woodbine whose fragrance shall cheer me no more.

The harmonies of the chorus reverberated solemnly.

Home, home, sweet, sweet home.
Home, home, sweet, sweet home.

Simple words—soldiers from both sides should have been able to articulate them easily. But as the band repeated the chorus one last time to end the evening, it played alone. Sweet, sweet home. Cliffs of Martin County, rolling fields of Knox. Cabins in the Michigan northwoods, fenced stone houses in the hills of Pennsylvania. And on the other side, the cloud-shrouded mountains of Tennessee, the red soil pine flats of Georgia. The eighteen and nineteen-year-old soldiers of both North and South were joined in one great, unsatisfiable longing. They were too choked up to finish the line.

That night, by the light of the lantern in his tent, William Houghton picked up the soldiers' petition and beckoned to his colonel, John Coons.

"Sir, come hear the final version my uncle will be carrying home tomorrow. I think it has spunk and will place some buckshot where it belongs."

Coons came over and picked up the paper, signed by every member of the regiment. He squinted in the dim light. A warm wind rippled the tent flap. Coons cleared his throat and read the petition: " 'From: The Fourteenth Indiana Regiment, in camp, Falmouth, Virginia. To: The Citizens of the State of Indiana. We, the Fourteenth Indiana, beginning our third year in the glorious effort to reunite our nation, do hereby state our unflinching loyalty to the government of the United States of America. As we commence what may be a decisive and dangerous campaign to regain the incentive in this war, we decry the disloyalty of the traitorous efforts of the secret societies and disloyal politicians in our state—' "

" 'Politicians who cannot have any feelings for the thousands of our state's sons willing and ready to spill their blood for the cause of our nation—' "

Horace Hogue read, a day or two later, from the Vincennes *Western Sun* to his mother and his Uncle Billy in the parlor of the old farm. Lately Billy listened to Northern sentiments and read newspaper arguments about the war when his wife was not about.

"Ma," Horace said, laying the paper down. "The soldiers in the Loyal Legion are going to Indianapolis, to join with some of the regulars guarding the meetings in Indianapolis this month. First the Union meetin', then the Democrats. Thousands of both parties are gettin' ready to go."

Catherine Hogue threaded a needle for a baby quilt she was piecing for a new baby in the Upper Indiana Church. "Did I read that Clement Vallandigham was going to be featured at the podium for that meeting? That it would be in front of the Statehouse?"

Horace's eyes were intent. "So they say."

Uncle Billy McClure stood and went to raise one of the old windows. The bubbled glass in the panes rattled. "I hear tell General Ambrose Burnside commanding the Army of the Ohio is angrier than a wild boar at Vallandigham."

"Yes, so it seems," Catherine Hogue murmured. "He issued an order against traitorous activities in the state of Ohio. But the Copperhead mobs have been meeting in the streets of Dayton, calling Abraham Lincoln a tyrant."

" 'Tis a powder keg," Horace said. He looked at a large pink cloud that was being appliqued to the white quilted pieces. On it in cross-stitch were the words, "Where did you come from, baby dear? Out of the everywhere into the here."

"Nice work, Ma," he said appreciatively.

"I miss my weaving. But my eyes—even with the spectacles, the work's too close."

There was a crisp knock at the door and all three heads turned. Billy McClure rose and lumbered over to the front door. "Well, Jewell. Hain't seen you for a spell around here," he said, inviting his large, formidable relative Jewell Simpson in. She came only a few paces from the door, as if keeping it within reaching distance for security.

Then she stood, silently, like a dark cloud waiting to pour rain. Billy

McClure asked, easily, "What can you tell us about your boy Henderson? Does he miss the boys in the Fourteenth since he left 'em?"

"Waal, he's better now. I'm a keepin' him fed up and rested." Her brows knit. " 'Ceptin that he's always off a-nights. And won't listen to a gol-durned thing I say any more. Ornerier than a mule in the mud. The wars spoilt him."

"I should think so," Billy nodded. There was silence again. Catherine continued her sewing, waiting patiently for whatever was to come.

"I thought best t' tell you my piece myself," Jewell finally said, addressing Catherine.

Catherine nodded slightly. She took a piece of embroidery cotton and separated two blue strands, pulling them out from the rest.

"I have just come from a Session meetin' at the church," Jewell said. "I want you to know what I did. Matthew 5. If you have anythin' 'gainst your brother, go and tell your brother first, afore you even appear at church again."

Catherine held up the needle. Through its eye she fixed her gaze on Jewell frigidly. "Speak your piece," she said.

" 'Tis about Lettie. I told the Session 'bout what Miz Fitzwater seen in Cincinnati. Lettie strutting about like a—well, like a married woman on the arm of Willis Mawkins. Outa some hotel. That she's been seen takin' tea with him at the hotel."

Catherine turned the needle to the light to thread it. "He is her employer."

Jewell exploded. "You been sayin' that, Catherine Hogue, for the longest time. Jest like you—all the McClures. Won't admit what's a-goin' on. Proud and lecherous. Jest as lustful as a troop o' young horses in a field in May. Always was that way. Guess I should know 'bout my own father and the rest of 'em. Anyways, it ain't for a Christian church to have a member that is fallen from grace. Church discipline says so."

Slowly Catherine pulled the two blue threads through the needle. She made a knot, deliberately. Then she said, slowly, "I know that as well as you do, Jewell. I am sure that Lettie can explain—"

Jewell interrupted her irately. "Well, Mrs. Pride-of-Knox-County, you jest tell me how she is goin' to explain that she got on the train to Indianapolis this mornin' jest a few people after Willis Mawkins did."

Catherine pursed her lips and set her fine work on her lap. Jewell had told her something about her own daughter she did not know. Still, she refused to be perturbed. "Well, and I suppose Willis was going to the Democratic meetin' in the big city. Lots of people are. Lettie may be goin' to that, too."

Jewell's voice had risen to a screech. "You an' ever other McClure that ever lived, 'ceptin' old George, are Whigs—Republicans that is. You can't tell me Lettie is goin' to the big Democratic meetin'."

"She better not be," Horace rumbled. "Still, mebbe she's a-goin' to the Union support meetin'." He said it uncertainly. Women didn't go to meetings alone. He and Billy were trying to look at the paper but could not, of course, resist the fascinating argument that was flaring before their eyes. Women's arguments were always good to watch. They fought like cats, with claws and "pffst"'s, instead of fists.

Catherine still did not look directly at Jewell. "I am glad you have come to tell us about your takin' the matter to the church, Jewell. Matthew 5 is surely a good verse. Since we're quotin' from the Bible, I'll just recollect you another one. 'Oh, hypocrites, remove the beam from thine own eye first then thou shalt see clearly to remove the mote from thy brother's.' That's Matthew, too. Can you see yourself to the door or shall I help?" With that she jabbed furiously at the taut cloth under the quilting hoop.

Jewell exited, fussing and puffing like a locomotive. "None of you McClures ever do a gol-durned thing about sin," she called back.

"I find it thrives very well without my doin' a thing atall," Catherine called to her. "Besides, you're a McClure."

"Don't claim it no more'n I claim the whoopin' cough," Jewell yelled back. "I had that onct, too." The door slammed and there was silence.

Billy watched her get into her rig. "She don't know her boy Henderson is a-squirin' the ladies about all over the county. He's like a young buck in the ruttin' season, since he came home from the wars." Catherine nodded listlessly. It was common knowledge. Henderson Simpson seemed like some sort of an over-heated cannon, spinning about the county. Mothers were beginning to hesitate when he asked to escort their girls to the socials, and yet he was a veteran—one couldn't say no. Floss Barger's pa was fuming, though.

Billy was still grumbling as puffs of dust issued down the lane after the departing Jewell. "And her over here talkin' 'bout Lettie."

"Well, she isn't the only one," Horace said without looking at his mother. Silence set in again.

Finally, Horace picked up the paper and calmly began to read the soldiers' petition aloud again:

"And so we, united in our fervid support of the Union as we are united when we advance into battle, do beseech and earnestly desire that the people of our state unite to stamp out treachery and opposition to this war. We call upon all Hoosiers to refuse to listen to calls for dishonorable peace—"

"To condemn secret societies and meetings which are being planned and executed at this very moment to divide our people in disunity—''

Calhoun Dugger listened with part of his concentration as his mother read the petition from the *Indianapolis Journal*. He held a letter from his friend Willie McClure, now a private in the Twenty First Georgia regiment.

Calhoun—we are plum swelled up to be transferred to the command of Stonewall Jackson. He is the greatest general there is. The Yankees seem to be makin some tipe of movement but we ain't goin to be caught with our pants down. Not Stonewall and Lee. The Yanks' ll never git past us.

I will stay till we win and never come home to Indianney. 'Tis a plain and simple fight. A man ought to be able to run his farm the way he wants and make his way without the government telling him nothin', no, not that he can't hold slaves. 'Tis a noble fight for freedom and I feel like a real man out here, like my great grandfather Will McClure fightin in the Revolution for free opportunity for all a us.

Althea Dugger put the *Indianapolis Journal* down firmly on the train seat beside her.

"Drat this petition from the soldiers in the Fourteenth Regiment. I had hoped there would be dissension among our Indiana troops and they would not have enough support to issue such a staunch proclamation. It does us no good," she said to Zach Scott, who was sitting with Delia across from her and Calhoun.

"I doubt it will hurt us much at this eddy in the river," Zach said unconcernedly. "We are on the rising tide. All of the Northern armies are stuck in the muck. Grant can't get up the hill or around the swamp at Vicksburg, Rosecrans is moping at Murfreesboro in Tennessee, and as for the army that claims the Fourteenth Indiana Regiment—" he gestured in a cocky way at the newspaper, as if the soldiers abode within its folds—"The Army of the Potomac can't outrun Stonewall Jackson."

"Sounds like they're goin' to try," Calhoun said, putting his letter away and taking up the picnic basket from the floor.

"There were stories in the paper of a great Northern movement beginning," Althea said, her eyes ranging past the two opposite her to a family of coal miners, a smudgy father, a well-scrubbed mother and two children who were barefoot even on this cool day. There was poverty in Indiana, no doubt about it, and the war had increased it.

"Can the soldiers not see how pitifully some in the state are suffering? How much better it would be to sue for peace and unite this nation before both sides have destroyed their own homelands" Althea demanded.

Delia was not looking at her mother. She was wool-gathering. Althea watched her. Delia often looked this way lately. When she returned from Tennessee, she found Delia exuberantly managing everything with nervous, staccato energy. Then, like a teapot cooling down, daily, hourly, Delia's joy seemed to ebb also. There was nothing for her to do. "What are you thinking of, dear?" Althea asked.

"Oh, nothing at all," Delia murmured, watching the pale and thin woman take out a carpet bag and fish around in it for lunch. The children clustered about her, eager, silent. Calhoun, meanwhile, unwrapped chicken breasts and slices of lemon pound cake.

"Do you look forward to these mass meetings we're going to, Miss Dugger?" Zach asked teasingly of Delia.

"You know I have no interest in politics," she said, turning indifferent eyes towards him.

"I've been wondering about that lately, Miss Dugger," he said, the same mocking tone in his voice. "In all of this posturing that we all are doing, what exactly are your sentiments? Are you the fence-straddler you seem to be? A milk and cider Democrat?"

Delia's face colored slightly. "I have never pretended to be as avid a supporter of the precious Cause as you all are. I don't know where I stand." She gestured with her hand slightly towards the poor family. "When I see the agony the war has brought, I think I am for the South. But other times—I don't know."

"Well, you'll have your chance to see politics first hand at this rally that is coming up," Zach said. "Half the people on this train are making a political trip. The Lincolnites are going to the big Union meeting at the end of this week. Then, they'll stay on for the Democratic rally in front of the state house. In the next week or so, people'll be pulling in from every county in Indiana—and from Illinois and Ohio too. Vallandigham draws them in like a magnet." He stopped talking and was silent a moment. Then, while he still had Delia's attention and her mother and brother were looking away, he smiled a half smile.

"Yes, a magnet," he breathed in a whisper, his eyes on Delia in a coaxing, tormenting way. She turned hot, evaded the eyes. Magnet. Had her mother noticed? It was his little game, lately. Since he had often been at the house in the past few weeks, he was growing familiar, really over-bold. It was his way, when her mother and Calhoun were not listening, to pick words with certain associations, to play with her emotions, to tease with unspoken hints about—about what? "Why does he do this," she wondered, "and why do I let him play with my feelings the way he does? Was it because I was too bold with him when mother was gone?" Mother and Aunt Addie always said there was a line of familiarity beyond which a lady did not go.

The coal miner's children had finished their lunch of bread with lard on it, picking up the crumbs from the paper in which it had been wrapped one at a time with their fingers and licking their fingers. Calhoun gave Zach a chicken leg and a piece of bread. Althea dug in the basket and picked out a fine apple and began munching on it. She looked up to see the two children watching her eagerly. She called them over and presented them with fruit and hermit cakes from the basket.

Then she looked sternly at Zach, prepared to broach a subject that had been on her mind for several days. "Mr. Scott, I received a letter from my sister. Her daughter Sophie and your brother Jacob Joe are planning a wedding."

Zach quickly averted his glance, refusing to acknowledge that he had any interest in the matter.

Althea continued. "My niece Sophie and your brother—we cannot refuse to speak of this any longer—are betrothed. You are Calhoun's friend, my political associate, so I am a concerned party. It is only proper that you be at the wedding. Can you not make up with your brother?"

"Yes, Zach," Calhoun said, pawing through what was left of the lunch. "You're going to have to be there. Wouldn't be kosher without you. Toast the bride and bridegroom with juleps—all that."

"Can you not write your brother, sir?" Althea wanted to know.

"It is his wish that we not communicate, not mine, madame," Zach growled.

"Well, that may be," Althea demurred. "But sometimes someone has to take a step." Her voice grew softer. "Besides, Jacob Joe is in daily danger. Every day he has to face going to fight with the knowledge that he's estranged from his family. He may die knowing that his brother does not speak his name, that his father opposed his going—"

"Not so," Zach said, shortly. Delia and Althea's faces registered their surprise.

"What do you mean?" Althea wanted to know.

"That—my brother Jake stormed away to war thinking that he was some sort of dramatic hero, flying in the face of our father's wishes." Zach seemed hesitant, then shrugged as if it were the least important subject on his mind.

But even Calhoun seemed confounded. He put down a chicken leg in mid-bite.

"Mr. Scott, what can you mean?" Delia demanded. "Jacob Joe has tortured himself endlessly, lain awake on the eve of battle—"

Zach shrugged. It wasn't even worth lying about. "Pa changed his mind. He believed the fight was a right one and said Jake could go if he wished with a clear conscience as far as he was concerned."

"When did he say this?" Delia asked earnestly.

"As he lay dying," Zach conceded. Then he looked out the window of the train. It was coming into the outskirts of Indianapolis. "What difference does it make anyway?" Zach demanded with a sneer. Calhoun shrugged and took out the scrap of a letter he had been reading off and on the whole trip. Althea rose in the aisle to greet a friend and when she returned, her face was flushed.

"What is it, mother?" Delia wondered.

"We have had awful news for the Cause," Althea said. "Our friend Mr. Clement Vallandigham was arrested. General Burnside ordered him seized as a traitor. Last night at 3 A.M., my friend said, the One Hundred Thirteenth Ohio Regiment arrested him."

"Drat," Zach mumbled.

"Poor Mr. Vallandigham. The soldiers stood outside his house with guns. He shouted, 'A-we, a-we,' from the window."

"Why did he do that?" Delia asked.

"Some sort of cry for help—" her mother offered, not really sure.

Calhoun grunted. "Secret signal to the supporters."

Delia looked incredulous, "A-we, a-we? Sounds like a—like a pig squealing," she laughed. Zach gave her a quick look.

"Hardly a joking matter," he said sharply.

"I think not," her mother said angrily. "One of the finest gentlemen I ever knew, a visitor in our home, treated like rabble. What will that horrid Burnside do with him now?"

"Try him," Calhoun snorted.

"That's illegal. Unconstitutional. To simply disagree—"

"Lots of things are changed, now," Calhoun said. "If he's found guilty of treason—" He pulled his hand across his neck as if he were slitting his throat.

"And you wonder why I hate the North," Althea Dugger said in a low, trembling voice. Then she stood to look out the window of the car. They had arrived at Indianapolis' Union Depot.

"Why," Delia whispered, "whoever is that?" She pointed at a determined-looking woman, large and handsome and carrying a carpetbag, who was walking down the aisle away from them and out the car. "That old lady must be nearly eighty, but she carries herself like a queen."

"I seem to know her, have seen her somewhere," Althea said. "Perhaps it was at the orphanage party at the beginning of the war?"

Zach smiled an odd smile. "That's my father's cousin Catherine Hogue. Never knew her to take a trip away from home by herself in her life. Must be something important." He lingered a little behind to get a bag. Catherine had not seen him.

Delia let her mother and brother go down the aisle. She had been raging inwardly since he let slip the story of the knowledge of his father's change of mind. She hissed at Zach, "You knew all these months that your father had changed his mind about the war. You kept it from your brother when he went into the battle at Perryville. What kind of man are you?"

"What kind of man indeed?" Zach asked. His eyes were neither troubled nor exultant. They contained a kind of dullness which was unreadable, and Delia gave up trying to plumb their depths and hurried onto the platform.

After hiring a hack to bring their baggage, they walked from the depot to the hotel. The streets of Indianapolis were alive with Yankee blue, soldiers heading to the depot, officers on leave from the western theatre. They were being called back rapidly, as Grant stepped up the campaign to take Vicksburg along the Mississippi River.

They walked towards the Circle in the central part of town. "Who are those young women out without chaperones? They seem brassy," Althea questioned.

"They work at the munitions factory, Mother," Delia told her. "Someone has to melt lead and make cartridges when no men are around. They look to me like decent women—grandmothers and sisters of fighting men."

"I haven't been to Indianapolis in two years," Althea said. "It's nothing but a big overgrown village." She looked around in disgust at pigs which were snorting around near their feet.

They crossed Washington Street and walked around the circular street which formed the center of the town. "They haven't even picked up all the rubbish when they tore down the governor's house. It's a mess!" Althea said. The Circle did look like a half-grown girl, part beautiful, part leggy and awkward.

"How can you say that, mother?" Delia cried. "Look at that new place of worship." Christ Church, still new enough that the flower garden and lawn in front of its entrance were just beginning to grow well, stood on the north side of the circle, as graceful and elegant as an English cathedral chapel. They came to a stop next to the church. "And this house—who does it belong to?" Delia wondered, pointing at a new mansion.

A soldier with one leg hobbled by on crutches. His face was sprightly in spite of what must have been a painful walk.

"William Morrison's home, ma'am," he offered courteously, taking off his Union forage cap. "He's a banker here in town and has made a bundle of greenbacks lately. There's a dining salon in there that seats twenty people at one table." They stood aside and let him pass.

"He cripples about for the rest of his life while Morrison, I suppose, makes money off war profiteering,'' Althea muttered. ''It makes me sad to see so many wounded.''

''All so useless, so much gone, so many killed. It all never needed to have happened,'' Calhoun said almost to himself, and Delia looked at him, surprised at the sincerity of his tone.

Althea was in high spirits by the time they reached Farmer's Hotel, near the Circle in Indianapolis. They checked into spacious rooms with silk hangings at the windows and ferns in dishes on the sills.

''Almost as good as the Gayoso House in Memphis,'' Althea said with a smile on her face. She led them down the wide walnut staircase for tea.

''Now, pets,'' she said to Calhoun, Delia and Zach Scott as they sat in the lobby. ''We are going to have a nice little visit while we wait for the meetings. Tomorrow we go to visit the Dugger relatives.'' A maid handed them steaming cups of tea drawn from a huge silver samovar that sat on a mahogany table. Iced petit fours, salted pecans, and Southern pralines sat in dishes on the end tables.

Calhoun poured whisky into his tea from a small silver flask he carried in his pocket, refusing to see the disapproving look on his mother's face.

''Ma, our Dugger kin are not people we'd receive back home,'' he said.

''Of course not, Calhoun,'' his mother said. ''But you don't give or take calling cards from your relatives. They come with the family you're born or marry into, like the furniture of the house. Except you can't throw them out like you can a chair. Your father's brother Addison and his wife Elba, and her mother Great Aunt Sadie came with your father when I married him. They're as coarse as burlap. Jay Byrd Dugger, your grandfather, and his old mother Delva were the same way.''

''Well at least Aunt Elba and Uncle Addison have got a decent house now,'' Delia allowed. ''Big enough for Great-aunt Sadie to have a smoking room to smoke her pipe in.''

''When we visited them last the old place was molderin' down. But now they have this''—Calhoun gestured vacantly northward—''three story mansion near the Circle,'' he said, sipping his tea julep in a satisfied way.

''Are these the cousins you spoke of who have come into a little fortune, Cal?'' Zach asked. He did not like tea and was tossing fondant mints into his mouth.

''Yes, and that's another thing,'' Delia said, stirring a lump of sugar in her tea, ''Aunt Elba and Uncle Addison have made their money in low ways—''

Zach stood and brushed nut crumbs from the trousers on his long legs. ''In this war there isn't any high way to make money,'' he said.

Because their backs were turned, they did not see the tall, dignified woman from the train come to the registration desk.

"I wish a small room with a window," she said and signed her name. "I will be here only one night and then I am returning on the cars. I have business to transact." The clerk looked at the firm, schoolteacher's signature in the book. "Catherine McClure Hogue," she had written. Then she paid for the room with a gold coin.

Catherine knocked briskly on the door of the small frame house on a quiet street east of the main part of town. A starchy, flushed, Irish-looking woman opened the door.

"Yes?" she asked curtly.

"You have a woman staying here?" Catherine asked after a moment of hesitation.

"Alone? No. I don't have none of these hussies that work at the ordnance factory here. Jest married folks and widows and bachelors. You can't be too careful I say, with all the unsavory women that trods the streets with the soldiers."

Catherine considered for a moment. She had shown Lettie's picture to the man at the hotel and livery stable, and the livery stable man without a word had written down this address. Why?

"Do you have a Mrs. Willis Mawkins staying here?" she asked, finally.

"I do indeed. Mr. *and* Mrs. Willis Mawkins." She opened the door and led her into the front hall. "Top o' the stairs and bear right to Room 8." She pointed.

The halls smelled of liver and onions. Still, it was clean and neat. That was something. Anything to give herself courage, she thought, her heart growing progressively more numb.

The door was ajar. There, leaning on her wrist as she lay on the bed reading a book was Lettie. She looked up, caught her mother's eyes and calmly shut the book.

Without looking at her daughter, Catherine walked through the door and over to the bed and picked up the book. *"A Woman's Full Place in the Marriage Vow* by Dr. Mildred Duddager Smith," Catherine read. "Well! A lady doctor. I hear they even have them in the army these days! And I suppose you must have borrowed my first copy of Mr. and Mrs. Evan Parsticle's book." She smiled a tight little "I'm completely casual about this," smile and then tears ran down her face.

"Mother," Lettie said, looking distressed.

"I just wanted to see for myself. I want you to tell me why this has happened, and I will accept what you say." She took a handkerchief out of her pocket and dabbed at her eyes. She had always hated crying women, and yet she did enough of it herself these days. It was one of the things that had happened to her after the change of life. She had put on seven pounds, no more, had one hot flash, and she cried now and again.

"Sit on the bed, here beside me," Lettie said, patting the bed. "There is no chair."

Catherine sat down with dignity, and Lettie took her mother's hand. Catherine looked at her daughter through misty eyes that kept shedding water. Lettie was beautiful, radiant as she had never been. Even her hair, worn up in soft curls, was shining.

"I needed someone," Lettie said simply.

"You had us, Horace and I."

"Mother, that's different. I needed my own man, to lean on, to be with. And—I needed the—physical closeness. These books say it isn't wrong to want that. You never thought it was," she looked at her mother imploringly.

"In the right circumstances it is a very fulfilling part of life. I never believed those old hens who said we should endure, stiff as boards. But in the right circumstances."

Lettie rose and began pacing about the small room. "Mother, I don't have the right circumstances. Maybe I never will. But I have this, before it's too late."

"But the shame if you should—"

Lettie interrupted her mother. "Don't fret about that. Willis has taken care of that."

After a moment, her mother asked "What do you mean?" trying to imagine if Lettie was talking about abortions—what?

"There are new things," Lettie said, whispering in embarrassment. "Made of sheep's intestine and of rubber. Men use them."

Catherine looked at her daughter in amazement, absorbing the information. "For heavens sake," she finally said. "My goodness."

"I don't think this will be forever and I don't care a teacup for what people in Vincennes say. I just know I am bound to him now."

Catherine had recovered from the shock of the sheep's intestines. "What about the Bible? What about purity? What about living your own life and not wiping the shoes of some man?"

That did it. Lettie rose angrily and confronted her mother. "It's my life, Mother. I'll think about those things some other time. I'm not ready for all that. Right now—I want him." Red spots were on her cheeks. She really did look pretty.

Catherine went to her daughter and kissed her gently. She smiled and took Lettie's hand, then closed it over the tiny miniature photograph she had brought to show people to find her fallen daughter.

"Give him this likeness you had taken for me last year. Maybe he'll look at it and find some way to value what he's got."

Lettie shook her head sadly and bade her mother goodbye.

Catherine went down the narrow stairs and out into the street. "Think of it," she said to herself. "Sheep's intestines and India rubber. That's going to change things quite a bit. Things may never be the same in the world again." She went to the hotel, got a fitful night's sleep, and the next morning took the train back to Vincennes.

May, 1863

Chapter Twelve

A few days later, May 2, a young girl named April Williams brought an envelope to Harriet Houghton as she stood in her mother's garden at Thomas Jefferson Brooks's house.

"My pa has just come back from the front with my brother, who was wounded by a shell," April said, handing it over to Harriet with a flourish. "Pa wanted you to have this." She bounded off.

Hannah Poore got up very slowly from the ground. "Is it from—"

"It's Will's handwriting," Harriet said. "Oh, Mother." There had not been a letter in so long. And now, with word the troops were starting on a great campaign, her heart was sick.

"It's to his father. To John," her mother said, looking over her daughter's shoulder, frowning.

"He won't mind if I open it. I'll read to you. She began in a charged, emotional voice: " 'Dear Father. I received your letter per Joe Williams and haste to send you a scrawl in receipt. You perceive we have moved and are now several miles in the rear of the Rebel works on the Rappahannock. Where the Rebels are I know not. On May 28 we struck camp and at six o'clock a.m. started by the River, our division leading the corps and our Brigade leading the division. We marched to United States Ford about 8 miles from Falmouth in right of the Rebel redoubts and awaited the pontoon trains—on the night of the 29th they came but a steady falling rain prevented them getting to the river's edge that night as was intended—it was expected we would have a desperate fight in crossing and of course OUR BRIGADE was selected to LEAD THE ADVANCE. There were not many unanxious hearts in our veterans' ranks when we knew we were ordered to take the first line in the morrow, and it was with a feeling more akin to anguish which the thought of the next day's slaughter would probably witness in our already shattered ranks—But the Rebels had flown—the guns were removed from the redoubts and at 4 p.m. yesterday evening the 8th Ohio, followed by the 14th Indiana and the rest of the Gibraltar Brigade took peaceable possession of the Rebel forts. The rest of the corps followed and we took the advance, pushed forward to join Mead at Chancellorsville, where we are now.

" 'Hooker sent a circular around yesterday that "the operations of the last three days have been glorious achievements. We have the enemy now in such a position that he will be compelled to come out and fight us on our own ground or save himself by an inglorious flight." It would be folly for me to prophecy now.

" 'Everybody is in glowing spirits and nature smiles on us for the first time in four days as if rejoicing at our success. We are lying still today, everybody seems to be taking the benefit of the glorious sun. The men are airing their blankets, rubbing and cleaning guns and drying ammunition. Some are reading, some writing, some sleeping. Bands are making all the old hills ring with splendid music. Birds are seen in every tree and we are again in a land of flowers. I am expecting a great battle soon and the sooner it comes the better it will be for us. We have eight days rations and can march to Richmond without further supply. All my love to Grandmother Poore. Your affectionate son, Will.' "

Tears came to Harriet's eyes. She let them course down her cheeks for a minute. "Nothing for me," she said and began to sob into her hands. Her mother watched her for a moment or two and then cleared her throat.

"When I was a young bride," she said, "and I took up gardening, neighbors gave me seeds. Marigolds, alyssum. That first year I put them in the ground and the next morning I started watching. I sat on my hunkers and I watched to see when they would be up. I poked the ground. I put on water twice a day. When they came up, I pulled every weed the minute it had the nerve to poke its head up. I chopped at the ground around the plants with my hoe. Then an experienced gardener came by—Mrs. Moseby, I think it was—old lady with a wen, as I recall." Hannah evaded her daughter's glance, rambling on innocently. " 'My dear,' " she said, 'you're smotherin' those plants with care. Let the sun and rain and the good Lord do their job. They don't need you every minute to supervise 'em.' "

Harriet looked up slowly into Hannah Poore's eyes. "And what does that mean, mother?"

Hannah Poore wiped her hands on her skirt. "Let Will go, Harriet. Let him go," she said.

That same afternoon in Indianapolis great-aunt Sadie Purdle ushered the clan from Rivertides into the salon of her son-in-law's new French-style home on Illinois Street. "Most woon'ful gas chan'leer," she said pointing to a hanging gas fixture. She had just bought new dentures at the dentist's and her teeth clacked.

"An' in the kitchen," her daughter Elba Dugger said in a little girl's voice, "is a six burner coal stove. We jest got it from the mail order store. Weighs so much I'm afeerd its a-gonna fall right straight through to the cellar."

They went out into the back kitchen and viewed the marvel with a shiny enamel hood. "Got a thingy-ma-jig tells whether 'tis a quick or slow oven." Elba's husband Addison was the little brother of Lucas Dugger. His wife was in her forties. She had never borne children and her hips were as wide as a pony's. Hoop skirts did not suit women with these wide figures, Delia told herself.

The group seated themselves in the parlor. A bouquet of velvet roses stood in a Chinese enameled pitcher on a small table.

"Chocolate cherry?" Elba asked, patting her frizzy hair. "They're Addison's favorites. He always insists on havin' 'em right cheer by his side."

"I love these," Delia said, biting one eagerly, letting the red juice go into the palm of her hand. Calhoun, Althea and even Zach, sampled the chocolate cherries. Delia asked, curiously, "And you say Uncle Addison is—in the South? On business?"

"Near, well—near *your* old home, Althea," Elba said. Sadie Purdle looked longingly at the dish of chocolates. She was afraid to bite for fear the teeth might fly out of her mouth and into the delicate, enamel dish in front of the company.

Elba went on. "He's doin' a little, well, a little buyin' and sellin' down there at Memphis. Lots of things the Yankees want. There's hardly anything for sale down there. So he's takin' Indiana merchandise to 'em. He's tradin'."

"In what?" Zach asked with just the barest fringe of insolence in his tone.

Elba laughed nervously. "Well—needles, sewin' machines, champagne, sides o' beef."

"Cotton?" Althea asked almost too casually, as she reached for another of the chocolates. Into her mind flashed the horrid money-making schemes of the overseer at Fairchance Plantation. She had not heard from Major Bachelder in over a month. Was he still keeping the Northern investigators away from the land? She signed and sent the deposition he had requested, saying she was a citizen of Indiana, a northerner, and the agent for her parents and she had asked them to deed the property to her.

"Just suppose I'm a-gonna tell you if he was," Elba said, tossing her head until the frizz shook. "Why, since Sherman left, Memphis is like a Northern prison. That new commanding general down there, General Hurlbut, has been meaner than a horned toad. He says that he is goin' to make the Rebels pay for all the trouble they've caused the North. And if anyone is found tradin' in cotton, why, he'll string him up sure.''

New commander, Althea thought. Edward Bachelder had written that a new commander, Hurlbut, had come in and Memphis was in mourning. Regulations to tell people how and when to go to church on Sunday and how to pay their servants. But from all she could tell, Fairchance was still unharmed. The new overseer had married Myrtle, and they were doing the best they could to keep things going, which was some consolation.

''You folks plann'n on goin to the Union meeting?'' Aunt Sadie said.

Delia looked at her. ''There's a Union meeting tonight?''

''No!'' Calhoun burst out. ''Bad enough that all the Yankees are heading' out against Lee, tens of thousands of 'em, all the papers pumpin' it up today. I'm not goin' to stand about while speakers praise Abraham Lincoln as the savior of his country. A tyrant who is suspendin' the Constitution—'' His vehemence astonished everyone in the room. Delia could not account for it. Calhoun had never said boo to a chicken, let alone a goose, in all the years she had known him. As flaccid in his character as a bag of laundry, and she had never been able to respect him because of it. What could be making him so—

''Well, I am going, and I suggest we all do,'' Zach Scott said. ''If we're enemies of this cause, we'd better scout the strength of spirit these home folks have while their boys are marching on towards Richmond.''

And scout they did. Ten thousand men and a surprising number of women took the breezes and stood together on a lawn of lushly springing, uncut grass, while a Union band played the old familiar patriotic airs from a small bandbox. Mostly wounded and older men in militia uniforms, which were rough approximations of the Union army's garb, circulated among the crowd to prevent trouble.

''Mother, there's that man that caused such a rumpus at the orphanage meeting outside Vincennes,'' Delia said, pulling on the sleeve of her mother's organdy dress.

''Horace Hogue. He's one of the captains of the Three County Militia. No trouble here tonight, I expect.''

''Isn't that his sister up there? Standing off to the side with that swarthy-looking man? Look, Zach Scott is talking to him. They're whispering.''

''I think Zach has much business with Mr. Willis Mawkins, as I understand,'' Althea said coolly, and then added. ''The Southern sympathizing meeting to be held later in the month will put this meeting to shame. Wait and see.''

Horace Hogue walked about, his hand on his pistol. He did not nod to the

Duggers when he passed their group; he did not want any more trouble with them of the sort they'd had at the orphanage party at the beginning of the war.

But there was no trouble that night. No, only several catcalls and several cheers for the Confederacy as the speaker, a state functionary who served Governor Morton, was introduced. Only bored yawns as he gave his pompous speech entitled, "The Flag of Freedom Must Prevail." Young women flirted with the militiamen and the few Union soldiers among them and surreptiously admiring the pistols on gunbelts at their sides. Paper dishes of ice cream were consumed with wooden spoons and sacks of popcorn were eaten as petitions from the soldiers in the field were read. Finally, the speechifying ended, as the moon began to rise over the old canal in back of the rickety Statehouse.

The last of the applause died down, and Calhoun, who had decided to come after all, shouted vigorously, "Down with dictatorship. Up with the Constitution and peace!"

As the crowd hushed, a Union soldier with a grizzled, brown-and-white beard shouldered his way through the crowd to where the Dugger group stood. "Two young men here are not in uniform," he said in an annunciatory voice, so that many could hear. "I call on them to say why they do not defend their cause—whatever it is—with their strong arms and lives."

Calhoun started towards the soldier; Zach held him back and said with calm hauteur, "Sometimes those with the most courage stay to defend their basic rights against usurpation."

"Cowards or Butternuts—which is it?" the soldier sneered as others in the crowd jeered. Calhoun pawed and snorted like a trapped steer in a pen. His mother and sister appealed to him.

Zach whispered in his ear as he restrained him, "You fool. We don't have to take up the gauntlet here in public. Save your strength."

But Calhoun was not mollified, and he had to be held back for several minutes until the small knot of a crowd that had formed around them dispersed.

Later that evening, as Delia and her mother sat at dressing tables in the hotel room brushing their hair and completing their bedtime toilettes, Delia asked her mother, "How do you muster enough hatred to keep fighting the battle among these people, Mother?"

Her mother stared in the mirror at her still beautiful, rather haughty face. "I remember what is happening at Fairchance. What could happen in Memphis," she said, then paused to listen to a bumping sound in the room next to them.

"Calhoun is drinking from his flask," she said with a sigh. "I cannot for the life of me imagine what is the matter with him." She set her brush down on the table.

Sparks were flying out of Delia's dark brown hair as she pulled the brush through it, holding the strands with her other hand. "I think I can explain it," she said.

Her mother looked at her inquiringly. "Before we left home," Delia said, "someone brought a letter from Willie McClure which had come through the lines. He is with General Ewell's forces at Falmouth. He is preparing to go to battle this very night to save the South. And Calhoun is here with us."

Althea's mouth was firmly set. "It does Calhoun credit," she said, "yet his place is here with us. Without a man, I have no one."

"You have me, Mother," Delia said quietly. Her mother turned to stare at her, uncomprehending.

"Well, of course, you have run the plantation but I can't count that, really." Then, to change the mood, Althea said brightly, "I have tickets for you three young folks. To see Laura Snead in *Octoroon*," she said.

She blew the oil lamp out, took off her peignoir and turned back the bed. Delia sat in an upholstered chair by the window. "You have it all planned, every move of it, don't you, Mother?" Delia said after a pause.

Her mother's eyes opened wide in surprise and then narrowed. "Don't you want to go to the theatre? After all, the mass meeting isn't for two weeks. I want to visit with Addison and Elba and Aunt Sadie—I thought you'd like it."

"Of course, mother," Delia muttered. Through the darkness she heard the sound of sheets rustling, a gentle sigh as her mother settled herself for the night, then, several minutes of silence.

Her mother's sleepy voice floated across the still room, finally, from the bed. "Why aren't you coming to bed, Delia?"

"I'm watching this bright moon and thinking. I'm wondering if it is shining on Willie, too—with Lee." And, after a pause, "And on Mr. Brooks' and Horace Hogue's relatives across the river on the Northern side—wherever they are tonight."

She sat for a long time listening to soft, comfortable breathing of her mother from the bed and watching the moon, bright as daylight, shining on the peaceful streets of Indianapolis on this beautiful May night.

*   *   *   *

The same moon was casting elongated shadows on Willie McClure, crouched among deep trees in a wooded clearing about a mile from a crossroads called Chancellorsville. His Twenty First Georgia regiment was sitting on cold ground, exhausted after a long march to catch Hooker's army unawares and attack their flank. They'd had a rare, wonderful success.

Exhaustion could not retard their elation. "Did you see how they ran? Upsetting their suppers, screaming in German?" Willie demanded of his friend Corporal Boone Epworth.

"Like coons in a shinin' party," Epworth agreed, nodding his head vigorously, joyously. It seemed as if they had been saying the same thing, singing the same litany of victory for the last hour with their fellow soldiers in George Doles' Brigade. It was a sweet, excruciatingly sweet military success after an all-day secret march through brushwoods. They clapped each other on the back, stamped on the hard ground, could not seem to speak of it enough, to rehearse what had happened, perhaps because they had been so apprehensive for so many hours about being detected by the Northern army.

Picking their way through the underbrush and woodlands, 30,000 troops trying a secret back roads march with wagons—they were walking, not sitting, ducks if the Northerners had only used their eyes or ears.

But no, the brilliant Stonewall Jackson had again pulled off a daring move. At 5 P.M. they had come around the enemy's right flank. Jackson had deployed them, with Willie's Georgia regiment in the last ranks. Astoundingly, they had surprised the Eleventh, or German, Corps of the Northern army and chased them into awful, hysterical flight.

"I can't forget it," Willie laughed, slapping his knees and reaching for a hunk of pork they had captured from the fleeing northern soldiers. "Goin' without noise through the woods into the lines. Then the bugles, all down the ranks—"

"Our Rebel yells, the poor, miserable token resistance before they started to run—"

"The mules screechin', the horses rearin' up and neighin' fit to kill, the cowarts layin' down their rifles, rushin' pell-mell. Bibles writ in German flyin'. And to think at first we s'posed it was a feigned retreat—"

His smile died. "But I think Jackson should 'a pushed on. Stoppin' to regroup we lost momentum. And the cannons fired too high."

His friend brushed the dirt off his ragged pants and took a drink from the Northerner's canteen he had picked up on the battlefield in Virginia. "Best damned thing that's happened in a year. Makin' Pope skedaddle at Second Bull Run was nothin' compared to this. At Winchester and all up and down the Shenandoah Valley we done won some battles, but Stonewall has rung the target this time."

Willie looked at his friend Boone Epworth admiringly. They had been together now since Willie had found this unit in Ewell's forces almost a year ago. When he and Calhoun found out about Archie's death, he burned to become a recruit for the Confederacy. He did not want to fight with Van

Dorn, and he knew the reputation of the Georgia regiments under Ewell. He had headed east to join them.

If you could choose—and he as a Northerner could—choose any unit in the Southern army, why not choose one with a glorious reputation, led by the indomitable General Ewell? Willie had learned to respect General George Doles, and was warily admiring of the eccentric, brilliant Ewell, who as a matter of fact was not commanding now: he had lost his leg at Second Manassas and was still recovering. Instead Willie had the opportunity to serve under A.P. Hill and the mighty Stonewall Jackson.

But most of all he had come to love this Georgia cracker Epworth, with his odd, old-fashioned speech, long, brittle fingernails and hard calloused feet that knew shoes only in the depths of winter. He was as brave a man as ever Willie had seen.

"Well, the Lord in his wisdom only knows what the morrow'll bring," Epworth said, putting the stopper in his canteen. "Jackson is ridin' forth to survey the scene."

"We're safe in his hands," Willie breathed and turned his eyes on the bright moon which lit the clearing in front of him. It was oddly quiet and still.

" 'Tis as quiet, now, just for a moment, as a Quaker testimony meetin' " Boone Epworth said. "Everthing looks haunted." The respite was short. Artillery began booming aimlessly, and across the way hot skirmishing began.

Across the grove the Fourteenth Indiana Regiment lay on their arms. John McClure warmed his hands over a campfire. "Hell of a position we got here, sittin' on our rumps while we should be attackin'," he said to Bushby Quillen.

"Hell of an army, if you ast me," Quillen retorted. "I thought we were goin' for glory, as always. When Hooker had us lead the whole army acrost the river—" Both men moodily remembered the glorious sally of the Army of the Potomac just a few days ago—the Fourteenth leading the division, which led the entire Second Corps. Then, after they crossed the river, no Rebels were there. Gone, aware that the Northern army was ready to take them on.

Well, no matter, the Northern army would go forth to meet them. In high spirits the Fourteenth and great chunks of the Army of the Potomac had marched to the crossroads near Mr. Chancellor's house. Finally, after months of waiting, they were going to have a chance to fight. They were ready.

At least the soldiers were. But their General Hooker was not sure. He shifted the corps about, and sent them on reconnaissance, and brought in reserves so many times that the veteran soldiers began to realize that the man did not quite know what to do with the 30,000 strong, well-equipped soldiers at his disposal.

As Hooker hesitated, shifting brigades and corps and sending letters of self-congratulation to Lincoln and his own troops on their fine position, Stonewall Jackson's men began a long, flanking movement and overtook the Union army right at sunset in the action John McClure's distant cousin Willie had just been a part of. As the Fourteenth and the other regiments were cooking dinner, first confused birds, then men burst out of the woods: the dismayed Eleventh "German" Corps, retreating before the advance of Stonewall Jackson, staggered into the clearing. Only a hard-fought relief effort by the Twelfth Corps stopped the rout. Both both sides rested and did a little skirmishing as the moon rose above Hazel Grove and Chancellorsville.

"Over there, as far as Upper Indiana Church is from the beechwoods, there is Robert E. Lee's army lyin' on its arms too. But they ain't goin' to stay there for long," John McClure mumbled grimly. "They could be on us at any minute."

Will Houghton and David Beem spoke in low tones. "Rations for eight days. Do you think we'll need them?" Beem said.

"If Fightin' Joe Hooker can get fit to fight," Houghton replied. Shadowy forms carrying rifles moved two hundred yards ahead like wraiths through the darkness. Sedgwick's Northern division, partially cut off from the rest of the army, was trying to rejoin the main body of troops. Sporadically the Rebels encountered them and fired; they fired back.

"It's an odd battle so far," Beem breathed. "Firing all day long from the big guns, then Jackson's little suppertime surprise. And now he lies to our west, ready for some sort of major action tomorrow. Not a good position."

"The Rebs are split, I think," Houghton said, pulling his hands apart. "If Hooker could send us in while the Rebels are still planning, we could round them up, overwhelm the parts."

"But he will not. His proclamation was as gassy as a spy balloon. Full of bumpkin," Beem said in an irritated way.

"Bumpkin? Do you mean—"

"Out in the hills of Owen County, bumpkin means foolishness. Hooker's letter to the President that the colonel read to us was pure bumpkin. Fightin' Joe Hooker is a handsome, red-faced, whisky-drinking mouth that prates of itself and cannot act. And so we lie in this clearing waiting for—what? More bumpkin," Beem snarled.

They lay silently, listening to the boom of artillery, the squealing of frightened mules.

"What are you thinking of, David?" Houghton asked his friend. He knew Beem went home recently for the funeral of his brother-in-law, who had been one of the recruits that came up after Fredericksburg. Mahala's brother Jack had died of fever, and they had not even been able to ship his corpse home properly, although Beem took it on the train with him. It had decomposed. It reminded Houghton of Bo Reilly, and the awful time they had getting him shipped back home.

"I am thinking of Hala," Beem said. "She's turned into such a staunch wife. Just a girl at the beginning of the war, afraid, unwilling to let go of me and stand alone. But now—"

"You know who I'm thinking of?" Houghton said, his eyes slits as he watched the firing and dying in the clearings ahead of them. "Ham Mitchell. And Bo Reilly. Remember Greenbrier?"

"Who could forget it? And yet it seems as if it happened in the time of King Arthur. So long ago, it was—several lifetimes," Beem said.

"I know," Houghton murmured. "I'm thinking that wherever we go, we take them—Bo, and Ham, and poor Horde with his rabies and Lunday—"

"Porter Lunday," Beem murmured. "I still think of him. I kept the picture of his family. I carry it into battle."

"That's good—but it's as if they are all in a giant family photograph. Our family. It's a strange fancy I have. Tomorrow, when we go up around that house to meet the Rebels, that crowd of witnesses goes with us. That we always do and always will carry each other, no matter what it takes to get to Richmond finally and stop all this."

"And if we should ever enter Richmond—" Somehow the words hung in the air, rich with pregnant, awful promise.

"They, Horde and Bo Reilly and Lunday and all the dead of the Fourteenth, are with us."

They watched the moon go under black, silken shreds of clouds and Beem said finally, "I've felt the same way, Will. And I'll take up the threads of your fancy. We're also carrying the people in Spencer, the farmers in Mt. Pleasant—all the home folks. As we climb the hill, they advance."

Houghton continued, after a moment, "None of it makes any sense unless you think—you really believe—that we're remaking the nation. You could say it that way—taking the broken clay and reforming it with our blood. Even the damned Butternuts who are probably dancing round the campfires and plotting to end the war right now in Indianapolis. They go with us against the Rebs tomorrow. What is happening is for them, traitorous bastards that they are."

"You're more generous than most of the regiment, Will. Almost any man here would grab them by the throats—'' He was interrupted. There was rifle fire, shouts, cries of satisfaction at some small triumph. They were far enough away so that it was impossible to tell if they were Northern or Southern huzzas.

"What's that? It sounds like the beginning of an engagement—or what?" Houghton jumped to his feet.

"Find Coons or Cavins. Something has happened," Beem said. "That's for certain." He rose to locate the men of Company H in case they were needed for action.

"You, there—who is your commanding officer?" an earnest voice demanded from the darkness in the Southern lines beyond the tree line from the Fourteenth.

"General Doles commands," Willie McClure answered. A shape emerged from the woods, a staff officer on horseback. "But Lieutenant Colonel John Mercer heads the regiment—"

The mounted officer interrupted him. "You two, both of you. Help us take the general through the lines. He is badly wounded."

Willie and Boone leapt to their feet. Through musket smoke and the flash of gunfire they scrambled to keep up with the man on horseback.

"We are in the Yankee lines," Epworth yelled.

"The big guns are startin' up again," Willie called back in a loud voice. Artillery fire flashed all about them; a shell whined overhead, narrowly missing them. The man on horseback stopped and beckoned Willie and Boone Epworth forward. A surgeon was leaning over the prostrate form of Stonewall Jackson, binding up his arm. There he was, with his black beard and mane of hair—anyone could recognize his countenance. His coatsleeve had been cut away to reveal a deep wound; blood flowed freely onto the dank earth. He moaned, half-conscious.

"Here, you two, we've got to find something we can use for a stretcher," the tall staff officer commanded. There, beside the general was a dead man with a gaping head wound. "Engineer—killed about five minutes ago from a Yankee shell. It may have been our own men who shot the general. There is such confusion on this field tonight," the staff officer said. He had dismounted to help them. There were other wounded; they were being dragged or assisted away.

"If you assist me, I can walk," Stonewall Jackson said. As gently as they could, several officers along with Willie and Boone picked up the dead weight of the best general in the Confederacy. The blood from his wounded arm poured over the arms of their coats as they helped him carefully out of the clearing and began picking their way along, through suddenly heavy and dangerous artillery, to find a litter to carry him.

With the dawn came the first shots over Hazel Grove. Stuart, now commanding in place of the mortally wounded Jackson, ordered the Southern troops including the Twenty First Georgia, to press their advantage. Hooker, a worried and beaten man, ordered the lines to reform and withdraw. He sent the Gibraltar Brigade, including the Fourteenth Indiana, forward to meet the Rebels' advance while the other troops withdrew. And so, amidst a maelstrom of rocketing and screeching shells, musket fire and awful noise in the thickets and clearings near Chancellorsville, soldiers of the North and South met again.

John and Walter McClure fought for their lives as the Rebels moved forward and around, tightening a noose on the advance brigade. Not fifty yards from them, ordered forward by the fortunes of war and Confederate General Stuart, Willie McClure pressed on, supported by devastating artillery support.

And ironically, in that hellish meadowland these cousins, descendants of brothers who fought to create the American dream of freedom and economic opportunity in the Revolutionary War, hurled death at each other to keep their own versions of the dream alive. As fate would have it they did not die, but in many places on that field of Chancellorsville, Midwestern and border state soldiers who were the great-grandchildren of Revolutionary War veterans, cousins and even brothers, fought on opposite sides, though many of the cousins did not realize they were related.

And when both sides had retired after the indecisive afternoon, leaving the field littered with the flower of the American frontierlands for the twentieth time that year, soldiers weary to the death pulled on knapsacks and sloshed canteen water over their smoke-blackened faces, having met but solved nothing—again.

"Withdrawal again for the Army of the Potomac," John McClure said disgustedly as the men in G Company finished pulling back. 'McClellan, Burnside and now Hooker. I wish I could line 'em up on a fence on my farm and shoot shit at 'em."

"Point blank range," said Joe Roseman. "Now I know what battle's like. Man looses a bunch of steers from the pen and runs 'em blind past the butchers."

"There'll be hell to pay for this back home amongst the Copperheads," McClure said. "They were prayin' we would fail, and I think we just did."

"He has pulled back when he could have won," Houghton said to Van Dyke and Beem in a voice hoarse from shouting commands. They were making camp on a field where battlefield smoke still hung.

"And we have left behind seven of the Fourteenth Indiana dead and sent sixty wounded to the hospitals," Van Dyke said. He looked at Beem. "Harrold was wounded again. So was Landon. He fought bravely," Houghton nodded. Though neither of them liked the wise-cracking correspondent, they respected his ardor for battle.

"But they'll make it and probably fight again," Beem said, "if we can ever find the will to win." He shook his fist. "God! I hope Lincoln removes this intolerable coward Hooker from command before the sun sets!" And then he added, slumping miserably on a log in the clearing where they were making camp, "Our boys. My men. Two years we've been together. Today some of them died for bumpkin. For pure, rotten bumpkin."

Walter McClure and Surgeon Burkhart walked among shadowy groves of second growth poplar as the men of the Fourteenth cooked a disconsolate supper.

"I have had hard work of it today, I tell you, with our own men," Burkhart said to Walter. "I could have used you."

"I know. But I still feel I want to fight, as my ancestors did, for the good cause."

"I *think* it is good," Burkhart countered. "Sometimes I even lose sight of what it is we are here for. I came from Germany to run from oppression and now even this government seems to be practicing it. Suspending the right to speedy trial. Drafting and shooting if a man leaves the war. And now I hear Mr. Vallandigham has been arrested in Ohio by Burnside. For opposing, he is called a traitor. It sounds like Germany. Still, I am glad I came to America even tonight."

They walked silently through the campfire circles. Comments drifted out. "Shell hit Hooker in the head". . . "Maybe knocked sense into it". . . "Hadn't been for those stinking Germans in the Eleventh we would have won". . . . "Damn Krauts ran. They always do. . ."

Walter McClure looked at the surgeon to see if he overheard. So many were blaming the Germans. The German men in the Fourteenth's E Company from Evansville were angry and chagrined over the talk. Burkhardt had heard this latest slur. "Well, not all Germans ran. Our Evansville German boys in E Company were first in the attacks. But the others—Howard's Corps—they did run," he said. "But there are many reasons to run. If you do not speak the language, you cannot always understand the commands or know if it is friend or enemy you face. Their new commander speaks only English. Confusion, not cowardice, may have caused their flight.''

They walked on and reached the pickets. As a surgeon Burkhart could wander and check the battlefield, and he chose to do so tonight with Walter. They walked over the fields to the west.

Dead horses, some with their heads blasted off, wounded, panting mules whom no one had found time to shoot yet, shattered artillery carriage, accoutrements, Bibles. This was the scene of the Eleventh Corps' debacle. The wounded had been removed in this well-organized Union army, but the dead lay in contorted or peaceful positions, without any reason for the looks on their faces except the random caprices of death.

They walked past several corpses and stopped at one very slightly-built young man without a hat. His soft, pretty face was almost girlish, it was a narrow face with prominent cheekbones and lank, blonde hair. His lips were pursed, prim and disapproving of the death which caught him as he cooked pork over a comradely fire.

"A German face. Probably from the Palatinate," Burkhart said softly. "Perhaps he came right off the boat. They recruited them, and the young men went to the wars because they didn't have a cent in their pockets, and they would be paid. They came to America to flee the wars.'' The young man's eyes were open in a wide stare; Burkhart bent to close them.

"We cannot blame these poor youths in a strange land for losing courage when their commander surrendered his," he murmured.

"The Miami Bird of Thunder says the battle goes to the man with the fiercest will," Walter said, looking at the watch fires of the Southern camps. And that man is there," he pointed at the Rebel lines. "We shall test to see if Robert E. Lee's will continues as the summer moon waxes and wanes.''

The surgeon took one last look at the young German. "*So weit von heim*!'' he said, almost to himself.

"Sir?" Walter asked.

"I said so far, so far from home."

Sadly the two walked back among the corpses of beasts and men to the Northern lines.

Zach read the second page of the *Indiana Sentinel* he'd bought from a bookstall outside the Indianapolis hotel. "God, look at this!" he roared to Calhoun. "Complete reports of Chancellorsville. It is as we suspected. A rout for Hooker. He has pulled back across the Rappahannock.''

He and Calhoun left the bookstall and walked rapidly to catch up with Althea and Delia Dugger, who were strolling towards the White River in

Indianapolis. "Hmm," Calhoun said to Zach, taking the paper off a cigar he had just purchased. "Any reports of casualties?"

"If you're thinking of Willie, it won't be in here. Seventeen thousand casualties for the North, though."

Althea folded a parasol she was carrying as protection from the hot noon sun. She spoke in a low voice so passersby on the streets could not hear. "It should strengthen us. Think of the meeting now. There cannot help but be twenty thousand people there cheering the cause of immediate peace!"

"Well, with the main speaker, the drawing card, not here—" Zach said cautiously.

Althea was not dissuaded. "It's true Mr. Vallandigham is under armed arrest. But Mr. Voorhees from Indiana is just as ardent. He will enflame everyone there—"

"If the meeting ever happens," Delia said idly. "It's still over a week away." She was getting tired of the rounds of visiting, strolling by the canal and buying candy and small gifts in the shops.

"Time will pass quickly, dear. Your brother and Mr. Scott have many meetings with the politicians, and you and I are getting a good rest. Besides, I like to be where all this activity is. I loved the Union meeting, with all the booing and shoving and firelight and speeches. I think half the people came just to see it all."

"Well, that was interesting," Delia conceded. Really, she did not care for the frivolities of this city visit. Her mind kept straying to the fine fields of Rivertides. She wondered how the final planting was coming. Of course that wasn't her responsibility any more. What really irritated, almost tormented her, was the constant association with Zach Scott. She hated being thrown with him. If others were present, most of the time he treated her like a younger sister, jesting, mocking her in a playful way. Her mother chuckled and treated his joshing in an indulgent manner, thinking there was no harm in sisterly teasing.

But other times, and they were too frequent, when they walked side by side, and her mother had strode ahead to see some sight or enter a store without them, Zach jostled her shoulder or elbow or touched her arm almost accidentally.

Or he kept up an odd war of words in her ear. Slightly suggestive, almost taunting words. "Bad women are in there," he whispered to her yesterday as they had walked past a building a block or so from the Statehouse. "The city had to build a refuge for them because the jail was getting over-crowded." Then he laughed in an odd way and walked up ahead to point out a blooming tree to her mother, as if he had said nothing.

Now today, he was raising his eyebrow and smiling sardonically at the painted girls who lounged about idly on the benches. "There are more of them," his gesture seemed to say. She lifted her head and refused to listen.

Of course she knew it was part of the teasing, mocking way he had. But some of it was beyond the line. He was rude, insulting, and she should tell him so. The trouble was, she had brought it all on herself, in the conservatory last fall. Why had she presumed to taunt him about his conquests in Vincennes? In an unguarded, high-spirited moment, she had loosed Pandora's box. What was it her mother always said? "If you allow familiarity, or heaven forbid, initiate it yourself, you have opened the floodgates for license."

She wondered if Calhoun heard some of the things his friend had whispered to her. Well, Calhoun couldn't pay heed to her; he was so caught up in his own morose thoughts. Her brother was getting worse; he hardly spoke. He just smoked and read the papers. Zach Scott was no gentleman, and clearly he had no feelings for her. She hated it that all of them were always being thrown together. In the name of politeness she was unable to escape the nearness of his tall form—the well-set shoulders, the striking, sensitive eyes in a face like one of the Greek statues in the Statehouse.

Being so near Zach made her lose her poise, pulled at her will, and if truth were told, did odd things to her body. If only he were not so strange, so darkly different. She could be attracted to him, she had to admit it, though she was ashamed of herself. She could care for him even, perhaps, but there was such a strange, almost despicable side to him at times. He was a bad man, that was all there was to it, and thinking anything else was impossible. She sighed and lagged behind the walkers in the Circle.

The parasol bobbed at her mother's side and the tiny heels on her trim pumps clacked along the wooden sidewalk. How could Mother not know what was going on with her own daughter and this dangerous, difficult man? Well, her mother only acknowledged what she wanted to, and often that was only the easy and proper action. She turned off anything she did not want to know like an oil lamp at bedtime. And, after all, as her mother mentioned casually one day, Zach had made her a promise, the promise of a gentleman. The problem was that Zach was not a gentleman.

Althea turned her head brightly around to speak to Delia. "Remember, we have tickets to the theatre tonight. At least you three children do. I'm going to supper with Addison and Elba."

"What's the play, madame?" Zach called to her.

"You are as suave and polite as Beau Brummel when you wish to be, aren't you?" Delia whispered loudly.

"Why of course, Miss Dugger," he turned to face her with a bright smile, his eyebrows arched in mock surprise.

"*The Octoroon,*" Althea called back. "by the famous Mr. Boucicault. It's a tragedy about Louisiana."

"Ah, octoroon beauties. More bad women, I suspect," Zach said in a low voice to Delia.

"I do not know if I wish to see scandalous behavior, Mr. Scott," Delia said coldly.

"Ah, we are all adults now, Miss Dugger, and after all, it is only art." Delia tossed her head and went to walk with Calhoun.

A couple of nights later, the curtain in the Metropolitan Theatre opened on a Southern dining room. The hour was obviously breakfast; dishes clattered and cozy conversation drifted easily out at the velvet and lace-clad audience. Minnie the Negro servant, was fanning Dora, a visiting heiress who had come to the Peyton plantation.

"Where's the yellow gal?" Calhoun said. "Didn't you say this was about an octoroon?"

"Shh," Delia said to her brother crossly. She was tired of his bad spirits. "The program says her name is Zoe. She'll be on soon." Delia was sitting between Zach and Calhoun, and neither of them would be quiet enough for her to hear the dialogue.

The plot began to thicken. Mrs. Peyton's nephew, the romantic hero, was attracted to the beauteous Zoe. When this lovely creature came on stage in the middle of Act I, Calhoun "humphed" and then sat silently for the rest of the act. Zoe, it seemed, was terrified of the plantation overseer, Jacob McCloskey.

McCloskey was the villain. He had a mustache, an unpleasant Yankee twang and an oily voice. "He looks like Simon Legree," Zach said. "Every second show these days is *Uncle Tom's Cabin*. Most of us real-life villains don't have curling mustaches and oily hair." He laughed so loudly a woman turned around to shush him.

McCloskey was pursuing the virtuous Zoe, that was clear. As he departed the stage, just before the end of Act I, the audience sighed and whispered in apprehension. With this sort of man anything was possible.

At the intermission, Zach joked and critiqued the play in a lively way.

"You're in good spirits, Mr. Scott," Delia said, amused in spite of herself at his interpretations of the old woman, her young girl visitor and the villain.

"And why not?" Zach said, leaning forward in his seat. "All my political plans are about to come to fruition." He lowered his voice. "Folks are coming in from Illinois, from Ohio and Michigan. They are angry as bees about Vallandigham's imprisonment. It has ignited the fuse—"

"Well, we shall see whether that fuse fizzles out at the meeting next week, shan't we?'' Delia said. She eyed Calhoun. He was obviously nervous, rubbing his hands together, sweating and wiping his forehead. The odd thing was that tonight he had not been drinking.

"Delia, come to the lobby. I want to talk to you,'' he said when the act ended. She excused herself as she walked past Zach.

Theatre goers were standing about under the gaslights, eating chocolate and drinking sarsaparilla. Calhoun found an out-of-the-way spot where no one would hear him and leaned against a Greek pillar in a dark corner near the Ladies' parlor. "Delia, I'm sick of being second fiddle. I sit around at these political meetings with Zach while they plot and plan how the Knights of the Golden Circle are going to rise up and demand peace. Take the state out of the Union maybe.''

"Hush, you fool. That's treason.''

"If they ever do anything. I'm gettin' tired of all the palaver. They been talking for two years. Bunch of farmers who'd rather talk than fight.''

"And so?'' She looked earnestly at Calhoun's florid face. Clearly, he was more distressed than she had ever seen him before, and her heart opened up to him, this stolid, inarticulate brother of hers. "Calhoun, what is it?''

"Oh—this bein' on holiday in war time gets to me. We flip around buying handkerchiefs and gloves. We eat good dinners at the hotel. Willie and his unit and the others are fighting for their lives and the life of the Confederacy!''

She answered him softly. "Yes, I know.'' Then he was silent, as if he could not easily say what he wanted to. She looked in his eyes. She had helped him do his sums in school and concealed his gambling from their mother. Now he was asking again. He needed her to help him be noble. She touched his arm and smiled encouragingly.

He breathed and said it. "I'm goin' to join Willie. Tonight. I'm leaving on the cars in an hour.''

"I suspected as much. I saw you reading and re-reading his letter.''

"Everybody thinks I'm nothin' but a mama's boy—an awkward puppy.''

She took his arm and they walked to the outside door.

"Tell Zach,'' he said. "I don't like being somebody's shadow. I'm not just a pampered rich beau.'' They went by the ticket booth, then outside onto Washington Street. Cool night air washed over their faces.

"Have you told Mother?'' Delia asked. A couple exiting early from the play brushed past them. The woman wore furs with little animal heads and paws on the end. She gave them a curious look.

"I'll write to her when I get to—wherever the army is.'' He had already turned from her, heading towards the Union Depot. He bumped the couple on the wooden sidewalk, and the animal heads flipped about.

"You don't know where you're going?" Delia called after him.

"I'll find them. Pass through the lines some way. They say it isn't that hard. Rappahannock River. Wherever Robert E. Lee camps, that's where the Twenty First Georgia is." He was shouting. The man and woman, and the few others on the street looked disapprovingly at him. This was still a Northern stronghold, no matter what the Copperheads might brag about.

She ran to him and kissed him on the cheek. "Don't hate Zach," Calhoun whispered in her ear as she clung to him. "He loves you."

Watching her brother lope off towards Union Depot, she put her hand to her cheek in astonishment, trying to understand what he had just said.

She decided she had neither time nor means to tell Zach that Calhoun had left when she came back into the theatre, but instead slipped quietly beside him just as Act II began. Somehow the play now seemed so unrealistic, with its jealousy between the overseer and the young hero over Zoe, the murder of a young black man on the plantation and the despair of the young octoroon girl.

And through it, Zach watched with occasional taunting comments. "Scandalous doings, eh, Miss Dugger," he laughed when the young woman and the hero went off together to a darkened arbor. She did not respond. Somehow, after what Calhoun had told her, she felt as if this strange man who treated her so scornfully, downright disrespectfully was now vulnerable. A secret, soft spot had appeared in his brittle armor. Could it be true? Did he actually love her?

He coughed and then coughed again. She'd heard him do it on this trip a few times and now wondered if he had caught cold. He responded to her unspoken question. "I have weak lungs, and in stuffy places with close air—" He shrugged in the darkness. On stage the overseer was acting dastardly, challenging the hero.

"I have something to tell you," Delia whispered. Gently she told him that her brother had gone to the wars, describing his earnest desire to fight for the Cause. He said nothing, but coughed again and shifted uncomfortably in his seat.

"Are you taken by surprise by his decision, Mr. Scott? Upset—" Delia asked him.

He stood on his feet. "No—there's smoke. Something's amiss—" Others in the audience began to murmur. There was the pungent smell of smoke, and gray-white wisps began to drift out from around the stage. Several people stood; then a woman screamed. Zach grabbed Delia's arm. The actors on the stage stopped in their spots as everyone in the three-story theatre watched orange tongues of flame lick around the corner of the peri-style arch.

The man playing the hero raised his hands, called for calm. There was milling about as people stood up, then some began pushing out into the aisles. Someone cried plaintively for an uncle in the rear, several women were calling to each other in frightened voices, asking where the exits were.

"Ladies and gentlemen, let us exit calmly—" the actor said, then exited himself. Delia watched smoke, now charcoal-colored and threatening, pour out from all but one of the doors which led to the stage. They were near the aisle; Zach pulled her into it. They had more than half a theatre of pushing, hysterical people to make their way through to get to the rear, as flames seemed to spread along one wall out from the stage.

People were jumping over seats; the smoke was so thick Zach could not speak for coughing. "There's hardly anyone heading for the stage exit. I think we'll be better off there. There's danger we'll be trampled otherwise," Delia suggested, trying to control her own rising sense of panic. Zach nod-ded and pulled her down the aisle. A few others, seeing them go for the east door to the stage, followed rapidly.

Through the clouds of evil-smelling blackness, and what was becoming searing heat, they found the door to the stage area and pushed through. The others turned back, confounded by the idea of being trapped in the flames which seemed to be everywhere backstage. "How fast it spreads," Delia murmured. Now, backstage, they were in darkness lit only by flames licking hungrily at the curtain, the floor of the stage, the very door they had come through. But there had to be a way out somewhere here—

Zach's coughing had become wracking. "I—can't—help you—can't breathe," he said. Behind them in the theatre was a chorus of screams. Some people were panicking. The fire was consuming the stage, the settee the actors had occupied only moments before, and the dining room table.

"Oh, God, help us find the street exit," Delia breathed, clutching Zach's arm. Suddenly she found herself staggering alone—he had slumped to the floor.

"Unconscious from the smoke," she thought, her own throat constrict-ing. She leaned to the floor, grabbing him under the arms. He was so muscular and solid she did not think she could budge him—but no, the floor was slick. Thank God! He was slipping along, lurching after her. As she began to pull him towards the back wall, amidst flames which were growing increasingly threatening and heat that sickened and sucked out her breath, she was aware that she could breathe better here near the floor. Bent over as far as she could go, pulling Zach like a huge bag of flour, she reached the back wall. She put her hand out; the wall was hot to the touch. It was made of stone. The flames were pressing. Must get out of here; was the door she had counted on here? It had to be. Dropping her burden momentarily and with her thoughts a-jumble, listening to the screams and the roar of flames, she ran her hand along the wall. There, some kind of break. A door jamb. Thank God. Now the knob—she drew back her hand and screamed in pain. The door knob was red hot.

By the light of the flames that now surrounded her, threatening, terrifying, she crawled on the floor back to Zach. Flames from the floor had caught the edge of her hoop skirt; in horror she gathered the skirt and dashed it against the floor. Then she bent and pulled strips off the bottom of her petticoat. She picked up the man under his armpits, dragged and pulled and coughed and almost fainted and then, using the cloth to diminish the heat of the knob, opened the door. By God's good grace it was not locked, and she felt the rush of cool air, the rush which meant she and Zach would live and not die.

Outside, in the din of horses neighing, bells clanging, men frantically aiming streams of water and children screaming, she stood up tall, and one incongruous thought ran through her mind: "Hoop skirts are useless and dangerous. I shall never wear one again."

No one saw her, there in the back alley behind the theatre. She would go for help in a moment, but first she paused to breathe. Her breath came in gasps from the exertion. Gasps turned to sobs, heaving sobs. Strange, she had not felt like crying; now she did. She looked down at Zach. His face was calm, almost too still. Suddenly alarmed, she knelt to listen for his heartbeat. No, there it was, rapid but even. She looked at his face. She had never seen it so calm, so unguarded. Usually there was either a glare of indifference or a scornful smile on Zach Scott's face. She pulled limp curls out of his eyes. Lying there, so still, he looked like a small child asleep. A small child, good and angelic.

But he was not coming to. She needed to move him at once, lest the building collapse on them, and she had not one iota of strength left. She pulled herself up and staggered to the front of the theatre, which was a seething mass of firemen pumping on large, cylindrical portable water tanks, ladders being raised up the sides, stretchers being carried back and forth, and frightened, fainting people coming out of the theatre in fancy boas and fur coats that smelled like smoke.

"Tell me how many are still inside," she asked a dashing fireman.

"Most are out, but the walls may go any minute and we still have a handful unaccounted for," he said and pulled firehose off the pumper cart to pour on the upper stories.

The firemen were all occupied. She turned to the crowd. "Can someone help me move my escort from the back of the building? I am afraid for his life back there.'' Suddenly a woman and man who were in the crowd watching the fire appeared at her side.

"We're from down home. Let us help, and among us, we can move him.''

They rushed back, talking breathlessly as they went. "I've seen you both, I think, in Vincennes, and, you, sir, at the Northern meeting,'' Delia said. "You're from the militia force.''

"Horace Hogue, ma'am, at your service,'' the gawky-looking man said. "This is my sister, Lettie.'' They hurried around the side of the burning building, trying to avoid hunks of flaming, falling debris, which trailed down from the roof like globular, descending fireworks.

"I know you are Delia Dugger,'' Lettie called up to her. They had arrived at the back of the building, and Lettie was kneeling by the fallen man's side.

"Why, it's our cousin Zach,'' Lettie exclaimed, looking into the face of the unconscious victim. Then she jumped up. All three pulled Zach away from his dangerous resting place just as the roof caved in, sending a shower of sparks and heavy, burning debris on the very spot Zach had been lying.

Delia and Lettie sat Zach up under a large oak tree. Water was pouring all over the building from huge hoses, and the flames seemed to be giving way.

"Smoke inhalation,'' Lettie said, concerned, looking into Zach's face. "It is poisonous. The cold air should revive him, but if he could drink something it would help.''

"Water everywhere and not a drop for him to drink,'' Horace muttered.

"I have coffee in a jar in my handbag,'' Lettie said. "Let's try to get some through his lips.''

As they dribbled coffee into Zach's mouth, he sputtered, opened his eyes, and came to immediate consciousness. His eyes lit on the fireman scrambling up ladders to complete the job of dousing the flames.

He barely moved his head and saw his relatives. "You saved my life,'' he said.

"Your companion did that, cousin,'' Lettie said kindly.

Zach coughed three or four times, drank coffee, stretched his legs and soon seemed fit enough to walk slowly down the street with them.

The half-hysterical scene, with all its rank smells, wild screeches and barking dogs receded behind them. "I did not know you were in Indianapolis, cousin,'' Zach said to Lettie.

Without blinking she said, "I have come to assist my employer. I know you are acquainted with him.''

"Oh, I see.'' Zach said without registering surprise. "You must be Willis Mawkins' bookkeeper. I have met with him several times. Odd he did not tell me you were here.''

"Well, I hope I can assist in record keeping and have a bit of a holiday with—my brother here at the same time," Lettie said. There was an odd strained moment, as if everyone did not quite believe the story.

Delia stopped to lean against a tree. She had not realized how exhausted she was. Her lungs felt as if they were on fire. She took a moment to recover her own strength, and as Zach took hold of the tree on the other side to steady himself, she went over and hugged Lettie. "Miss Hogue, I can't thank you enough for what you have done to help tonight. Please call on us at the hotel. And again at Rivertides when we return home."

Lettie's face broke into a pleased, grateful smile. Not everyone received her these days, and she was touched by Delia's genuine cordiality. They said goodbye to the Hogues on Washington Street, and Zach walked Delia back to the hotel. He was silent, thoughtful. Then he turned to her, his eyes anguished. "Thank you. Dragging me. Can't see how you did that. Look, what you did—I can't—" He did not go on. It was the first time she had ever heard him sincerely touched, at a loss for words. After all the emotion of the day she felt she might break down and cry.

But then in a moment he said in a forced jocular voice, "I regret we didn't get to hear how all those scandalous doings ended, Miss Dugger."

Delia smiled a small smile to herself. "It's time you called me Delia. After all, we have a special bond now, don't we? We are joined by pain." Her hand throbbed; she held it up for him to see. She would put some unguent on it at the hotel and bind it in bandages. He looked at the hand and then sent her a look that was as winsome and appealing as a child's. He was bewildered in the face of pain he had caused.

But only for an instant. Soon he was his chattering, insinuating self. But as she listened to him bandy her, looked at the mocking smile curling his lip, she rejected that picture and called to mind the angelic, gentle face of a small child with golden curls she had ministered to as he lay near the burning building. That was the face she saw, could not rid herself of. The next night, when he asked her to meet him for a walk in the grove of trees in the hotel's garden, she told her mother she was going for a breath of air alone and found Zach and they walked. And where the shadows were deepest, among sugar maple trees with wide, sheltering branches, he pulled her to him and kissed her hungrily and she kissed him, over and over and clung to him, and whispered his name sweetly, as she would a baby's.

The days flew by and Indianapolis prepared for the Democratic rally. The Indianapolis newspapers deplored the losses at Chancellorsville and printed Abraham Lincoln's despairing remarks. Where could the war possibly go from here? he asked. Only the news that Grant had gotten supply transports past the guns at Vicksburg and was preparing to strike in Mississippi cheered hearts a little. The rest of the news was dismal for the Yankees.

To sit in tea shops, to walk around the Circle, was to hear the alarmed rumors start like birds into the air. Twenty-thousand Copperheads would close in on the city in three days. Men and women alike were bringing weapons to prepare for armed takeover of the state government. Governor Morton had called out a company of Union soldiers to supplement the Loyalty Militia. Trainloads of Knights of the Golden Circle were arriving on excursion trains hired in Illinois and from all over Indiana. To do what? Even they weren't agreed. But they had robes and ritual manuals in their suitcases.

The day of the war protest meeting, Willis Mawkins and Zach Scott stood beside the old canal watching its gray-black waters, with odd little finger-nail-like ripples which were the only sign that water was moving through the ditch.

"Uck—what is that smell?" Mawkins said. He was smoking a cigarette.

"Must be the new meat-packing plant the Irishmen put up. Lard rendering," Zach answered. He was silent a moment, then said. "The canal stinks too. My relative, James McClure, was commissioner for this White River white elephant some thirty years ago, so they say. He saw it go bankrupt and then he went under this very bridge and died of cholera and humiliation. I can see why. Twelve miles of canal going nowhere with nobody on it."

Willis Mawkins casually dropped an ash into the water. "Your whole family must be as full of schemes as a bread pudding is of raisins."

"Well, we McClure kin have a lot of plans, good and bad. My uncle, Ish, they say, was the most malevolent reprobate in the West. Spied for the British in the War of 1812, went over to the Spanish. Even murdered someone. Maybe I have his blood. Sometimes I worry about myself." He laughed and leaned out over the canal to see if he could see his reflection.

Finally he spoke again. "I hope our present plans don't go as astray as the canal bust."

"I think not," Mawkins said, flicking an ash. "The call for peace has never been so strong as it is this very month. The northwestern states are as ripe for a rise-up as a summer squash in late September. They are going to make their voices heard. Outraged over the deaths, the battlefield losses."

"But will that outrage materialize into anything? That's the question," Zach said.

"The meeting will be a huge rallying. All the anti-Lincoln forces—the Knights in the castles, the county workers for the party, those who are worried about the Constitution and the arrest of Vallandigham, the frightened farmers—twenty thousand strong. At last they will be united, no matter what Morton says, no matter who he sends to strong-arm us."

"So you say," Zach said, frowning.

"I tell you it will be the first of many huge peace rallies. They will demand peace, and Abraham Lincoln will have to listen!"

"Some are bringing pistols."

"If there is shooting, it may show the strength of our cause."

"Well, there are a lot of one-issue people in this. A lot of these men from southern Indiana are enraged over the draft. Men like the Slicers."

Mawkins flipped his cigarette butt into the river. "The Slicers were stupid. They are going to be tried for murder and have accomplished nothing. We really do not need to murder to achieve an overthrow of this Northern government." He was silent a moment, and then went on, "I have had word from Colonel Morgan."

"A messenger?"

"One of his Confederate cavalry officers. His spies will be at the meeting. They are about in our towns, have been for several months. He is ready to ride through Indiana."

Zach turned sharply on him. "What did you tell the messenger? You know I don't favor Colonel Morgan's cavalry coming north. Counterproductive. It could unite opposition against us—"

"Well, you've been calling for action," Mawkins said darkly. "What will you do to end this war if the army doesn't come north?"

"Work through the party. Use public opinion to sue for peace. Time and tide are on our side. If they won't sue for peace, eventually the people will demand we get out of the Union and join the South. Unseat Morton and the other Lincoln governors. We already have the legislatures—"

Mawkins' voice was scornful. "We need more than just all this namby-pamby politicking. No, Colonel Morgan is ready to come in early summer. He is hoping to get permission from General Bragg. And then the whole state will rise with him, I say."

Zach shook his head, frowing. "Well, when is he coming?"

"Robert E. Lee and his army will move north. Lee is sure to invade the very heartland, bringing the war to a climax. Possibly Pennsylvania. And when he moves, Morgan will ride into the middle states, into Indiana and Ohio. Terrify the people to make them beg for peace on any terms. But that isn't all—men will come out of the farms and woods and follow him, swell the Southern army."

"When will all this happen?"

"Next month, or the month after that at the latest. We had better get ready."

"I suppose so, if it has gone this far," Zach conceded. "As soon as the meeting is over, we better meet with the state Castle heads and Colonel Morgan to coordinate all this."

Mawkins pondered a moment. "A courier can carry a private report to the colonel with that information. Morgan can name the place."

"Yes, you can have your secretary draft the message," Zach smiled a broad, taunting smile.

"My secretary?"

"Yes, my dear Mawkins. Why didn't you tell me my own cousin was your secretary. Or bookkeeper is it?"

"You didn't ask," Mawkins mumbled, turned on his heel and walked away, leaving Zach Scott alone with the murky miasma of the old canal and the pungent, rancid smell of lard rendering.

Althea Dugger sang along with the band playing "Tramp, Tramp, Tramp the Boys Are Marching" when the long-awaited political meeting finally began.

In the prison cell I lie
Thinking Mother dear of you
And our bright and happy home so far away
And the tears they fill my eyes
Spite of all that I can do
Though I try to cheer my comrades and be gay.
Tramp, tramp, tramp the boys are marching,
Cheer up, comrades, they will come—

Calhoun had gone, gone to be a soldier. She had been astonished when she found out he had left, and complex emotions followed on each other's heels like a train of dragons in her thought. Gone? Without asking her permission? He had done something that he had not even given her an inkling about. How could he have cut his own mother that way? Well, Delia had not been surprised, saying her mother should have seen the signs.

She was a little irritated that she had not been able to send him off, a little frustrated that he hadn't involved her one iota. Then, and only then, did she feel a twinge of fear that he would be involved in heavy fighting, that he might not return at all. Soon that had passed, however. It was an iron rule with her that one must be brave, put on a serene face no matter what. Feelings came to you to be controlled. Women had the right, the obligation to be as strong as men did.

The night was clear, the air calm for the Democratic meeting. Were there twenty thousand people there? At least fifteen. They were milling about on the lawn of the Statehouse, listening to bands, readying themselves for the speaker who was straightening his tie and taking a last drink of water near the podium.

Delia stood by her mother's side, fanning herself in the warm evening, only mildly interested in the proceedings. She was talking animatedly to Lettie Hogue, who had become her fast friend the last few days. Althea watched her daughter chatter to Lettie and thought, "Something a little odd about Lettie here in Indianapolis. She is supposed to be with her brother, but he is spending all his time drilling at Camp Morton with the others in the militia. Somewhere about here—" Her eyes sought the home guard men. You could pick them out in their almost bright blue, imitation Yankee uniforms. There they were, on the edge of the crowd.

But the regular Indiana regiments called out by Morton were not as conspicuous. No, they were circulating among the crowd in twos and threes, pistols at the ready.

Daniel Voorhees, the Hoosier politician known to Zach and Calhoun, was ascending the podium. "Nice-looking man," Althea murmured to Delia, and suddenly she thought of Major Bachelder. He had written to her again, the letter coming to the hotel forwarded from Rivertides, telling her of his visits out to the plantation. There were crops enough to feed the hands—no, the workers, as one should call them now. He was still on General Hurlbut's staff, but was not particularly happy with the general's harsh, unyielding, desire to break the spirit of the people of Memphis.

She saw Edward Bachelder in her mind, tall, with a rich, ringing laugh, and an odd little habit of rubbing his ring and third finger together when he was thinking. She recalled the way his lips quivered, rather sensually, when she said something he considered amusing. A Yankee, but decent and good as a sound apple. Perhaps she would see him again some time. The fortunes of war—if Vicksburg could not hold, things in Tennessee would get worse, not better.

Voorhees began speaking. She was so far back she had to strain to catch much of what he was saying. "Our leader Mr. Vallandigham has fallen, a little sooner than the rest of us, a victim of base usurpation."

True enough, Althea thought. The papers said Vallandigham had been quickly tried and given life imprisonment. It seemed unbelievable, beyond thought that such a thing could happen in the United States.

Lettie Hogue was fanning herself. Althea opened her pocketbook and took out a small handkerchief embroidered with weeping willow boughs and offered it to Lettie, and Lettie dabbed at her warm brow. What was Delia was looking at? Her eyes followed her daughter's line of view: there, near the podium and under a huge tree, Zach Scott and Willis Mawkins stood, silent and unsmiling, like dark sentinels in a stone monument. Vigilance personified. Why?

The speechifying went on, ardently witnessed by Althea, only half-attended by Delia and Lettie: outrage towards General Burnside in Ohio, General Milo Haskell, who commanded the Indiana forces, the Republicans in general and Abraham Lincoln in particular. Cheers broke out from rough farmers who had come in on the trains, proudly wearing their Copperhead signs in their lapels. Yelping taunts hurled at the Yankee soldiers by the Copperhead wives, who made fists and waved them at anything in Yankee blue. Grumbling hostility towards the farmers rose from the militia guard and Union soldiers, veterans of some of the recent battles, who were sprinkled through the crowd.

Voorhees, a compelling speaker, was holding his hands high in the air, reaching the climax of his fiery speech. "We will continue to struggle, though our leader Mr. Vallandigham is imprisoned. We will pay whatever price we must, even if it is the greatest of all. To prolong life at the expense of liberty is what a proud race cannot and will not do! We will fight and die if we must, to stop the senseless slaughter in the land!"

The urgency of his voice in the heavy air, the angry emotion it revealed, charged the atmosphere, polarized the crowd as if lightning had cleft a log in two. "Traitors," shouted a soldier near the front of the crowd. His neighbor turned to him with an oath and shoved him. A fistfight began. Horace Hogue, hand on the pistol at his side, signalled to his men, and they moved forward to surround the argument, smother and dissipate it as one would smother a white-smoking fire about to burst into flame.

But the crowd intended to be surly. Perhaps that was what they had come for. As Mr. Voorhees paused, Copperhead farmers turned to their northern neighbors and began to jeer, "Fredericksburg," "Chancellorsville!"

A Union soldier called for three cheers for the Union and half the crowd began to give them. The other half drowned them out with boos. More fistfights began; Horace Hogue and his militiamen could not control them; the size of the crowd overwhelmed even their numbers.

Voorhees called for quiet and calm, but no one was listening. Farmers took out pistols. Althea, Delia, and Lettie, from their vantage points near the rear of the crowd, watched in horror as men in the crowd clicked the hammers of their loaded pistols. The man who had called for three cheers for the Union began waving his pistol around threateningly. Then he shot it in the air. Other air shots followed, and scuffling and shouting increased. Then, Delia alone watched Zach step behind a tree, take aim at the Union man and fire his pistol. The man's pistol flew in the air; he clutched his wounded hand. He was surrounded by shouting, screaming Union men.

Then the small number of Union soldiers General Haskell and Governor Morton had called in took out their rifles. With looks of grim finality and outright loathing, they marched through the crowd, followed by Horace and the Loyal Legion. The shooting died down. As the military rifles stared them in the face, the crowd quieted down to a surly mumbling and finally allowed Mr. Voorhees to close his speech.

"They'll arrest all those people with the pistols, won't they?" Lettie wondered as the crowd dispersed.

"No," Althea answered. "Both sides had firearms and they are common enough these days. They may detain whoever shot the Union man's pistol from his hand—if they can find him. They will certainly be looking, but there were so many shots it will be difficult." She had not seen who fired the shot from out of the shadows.

"Terrible, terrible," Lettie murmured. Her eyes sought her brother, who with his Loyal Legion was helping move the crowds towards the Union depot and the excursion trains which would take them home. They used their guns like cattle prods on Southern-sympathizing farmers, who allowed themselves to be hurried along. Giving one's life for Constitutional liberty had a hollow ring to it when military rifles were at your back. Willis Mawkins was talking to Voorhees at the platform as the rest of the crowd drifted away. Althea looked at Lettie, who stood nervously twisting her handkerchief. Her employer, or whoever he was in her life, was a rabid peace Democrat, her brother an equally vehement supporter of the North. How could the woman stand these contraries? How could the nation?

A night mist, rank with the effluvia of the lard plant, was rising from White River. Delia stood alone not far from the tree where the shot was fired. Her mind still was fixed on the scene at the moment before the pistol had echoed, when she was close enough to see Zach's face as he shot the gun from the Northern agitator's hand. There was a look of cold calculation with just a fringe of indifference on his face, and it chilled Delia more than all the chilly vapors coming up from the river at this moment, when night was beginning to fall on the troubled capital city of Indiana.

"Herded like cattle," Althea mumbled indignantly as the soldiers stood beside the trains to be sure the Democratic supporters boarded peacefully. Their bags were loaded before the meeting; the excursion trains would go west to Crawfordsville, then south to Vincennes.

The train started up; Delia sat by the window and watched the station lights blur and retreat. The men of the Loyal Legion, with an odd assortment of rifles and homegrown muskets on their shoulders, grew smaller on the platform and became like toy soldiers. She sighed deeply. Thank God it was all over. She watched the crowd of Democrats around her take out whisky bottles and boxes of cakes and crackers to celebrate.

"Showed them what the force of freedom is like," one bald man said, upending a flask.

"Here's to peace at once," another man with a brown jug said, raising it high.

Her mother was in another car, taking lemonade and cakes at the small tables the Democratic party paid for when it had contracted for the excursion trains. She was planning things to do when they returned to Rivertides: call the overseer in to supervise the cultivation of the cotton crop, enlist house servants to air the rooms and beat the rugs—she would have a list a mile long. None of which included anything important for Delia to do. "Now that I'm back, you just enjoy being a lady. That's what you were bred to. I've been able to hire enough help for you to get out of the saddle and come back into the parlor. My thoroughbred—" Then Althea would smile her pretty, arranging smile. Delia did not know if she could stand that self-assured, well-bred smile that precluded any discussion about meaning in life.

Delia's eyes scanned the length of the aisle. Zach was—who knew where? Had he made the train? Been detained by the authorities? She did not know, and at this moment she did not care. The look on his face the moment he had fired that shot! How could she have thought she cared for someone who could shoot another man so coldly? And yet—she turned her face to the darkness of the countryside hurtling by the train window. Small chinks of light broke the blackness, oil lamps in the windows of farms just west of Indianapolis. Cinders glowed and fell all over the windows from the smoke-stack, like umbrellas of falling stars.

Over and over the feel of his mouth on hers, in the maple grove was a live fire in her mind, a searing memory. Now she knew that she had wanted what happened in that grove for months, years, ever since she had known him. It was as if all her life she had been waiting for that maple grove. And just as truly she knew she was in love with a man who was a mystery, an enigma. Ever since the theatre fire she had felt helpless. He'd been dependent on her, terribly dependent, for about an hour, and in that hour she let down her guard and fell in love. Now the future loomed, shadowy and uncertain, like the rushing darkness outside the window.

She turned from the window and watched the people in the car. The farmers and their wives were bumping about the aisles chatting, holding onto the seats as the cars swayed in the rough roadbed. There were laughter and coarse jokes, and then they began to take out the firearms they had brandished at the meeting. "Aww, let me see that Colt 45." "Land o'goshen whut's that thing you got there? Why 'tis a baby Dragoon—M' brother give it to me, got it in Cincinnati, newest thing in the army—"

Why is it men play with firearms, polish them, compare their size and capacity, Delia wondered. Firearms and carriages were the stuff men boasted of, joked about and lived for. Was it so in places other than this land of the free and home of bravado? No, these farmers swilling corn liquor and wearing Copperhead pennies under their lapels were not going to fight any-body. Calhoun was right. These Knights of the Golden Circle were talkers, not fighters. The guns gave them courage. But they left the real shooting and killing to the poor men at Chancellorsville.

A coarse woman whose face was pitted from smallpox leapt into the aisle. She had been tippling from the bottle and could hardly stand; still, leaning against one of the seats she began to pull up a hoop skirt which was very dirty around its flouncy edges. Other women, also rather drunk, pretended to hide their faces in shock; men clapped and whooped.

"If you want to see a gen-you-wine first class firearm to be used in the protection of our rights 'gainst tyranny, let me show you something—this!" The skirt was pulled up just enough to reveal, against the leg above the knee, a holster and in it a pistol.

" 'Melia, dance for us with the gun. Do a gun dance," the farmers shouted. The woman's husband, red-faced, with his sleeves rolled up, hopped into the aisle and began dancing with her there, a Virginia reel do-si-do. Just at that moment Zach burst into the car. He shoved the woman and man into a seat and commanded immediate attention.

"Now listen to me. You have just about two minutes to do what I say." The train was slowing down, grinding to a resistant, lurching halt. Delia peered out the window; lantern lights were swinging along the edge of the roadbed, carried by—whom?

"The Union troops of General Haskell have stopped the train," Zach growled. "They are in the back cars. Mr. Mawkins is trying to delay them. They were not able to arrest us at the rally; now they have us confined and cornered. If you do not wish to be detained and arrested as obstructors of the Union cause, as Mr. Vallandigham was, rid yourselves of your pistols."

"What?" "Where?" Frightened murmurs went through the car as men pulled pistols out of hidden holsters, valises. The woman with the hoop skirt was whimpering, pawing at the rolling hoops to get the holster off.

Delia went to her. "Let me take the pistol for you," she said, putting her hand to the woman's side to help her and then hiding the gun quickly in her own skirt.

"They have a matron to search the ladies—they've heard there are guns among the women." Zach reached over two frightened farmers to open the train window. "Quick," he said. "Open the windows. Throw your pistols outside into the stream over there."

"Pogue's Run?" the woman with the smallpox scars asked.

"Yes. It's high from spring freshets. If you can't reach—here. Give them to me. I'll dump them. I'm going outside." He began quickly collecting the assortment of guns. "Quickly," he said, glancing out the train window. "I can see them finishing with the back car."

For the first time, Zach turned to Delia. He leaned over to her. "I cannot be found on this train. They may connect me with the shot fired. I must not be known publicly. I'm going to slip away."

"I'm coming with you."

"You are?" The distrustful, half mocking look crossed his face. The windows were open; those nearest the stream were tossing their pistols out. The stack in Zach's arms was growing. "What about your mother?"

"Here comes Lettie up the aisle. I'll send a message to Mother." She moved forward a few feet and whispered to Lettie, who looked at them with frightened eyes.

Zach and Delia hastened for the door. There was a commotion as the searchers left one car, heading for the steps of the very car they were in—

"Come then," he said, arms loaded. She slipped after him out the door of the car just as the soldiers mounted the back steps of the car on the other side, to begin the search.

And so they went: down the hill in the darkness, the lights of the lanterns flickering beside the car they left. Around them were the shouts of the soldiers, rough and commanding. The guns, bright in the starlight, they placed noiselessly under clumps of huge mayapple umbrellas in a second-growth clearing out of sight of the train.

Then along the edge of the woods, hand in hand, they stumbled through thick grass across a field, towards the flickering candlelight in a window of a two-story frame farmhouse. Cattle lowed; there was a strong smell of pigs.

"If we knew this was a sympathizing farmer, we could seek shelter—as brother and sister," Zach said, holding her hand firmly to guide her. He suddenly looked at her, remembering something. "What did you tell Lettie?"

Delia laughed a little and pulled the small pistol from her dress pocket. "To tell mother that I had a concealed gun and no time to ditch it. That I fled and would find my way back to the Dugger relatives." They came to a plowed field with outbuildings; the farmhouse was up a rise. They stood under the May stars beside an old cabin. A huge lilac bush shed its fragrance by the rickety door.

"We can't risk it at the house. They can just as likely be Union—" he said finally. "If I were alone, I'd seek shelter in this cabin. It's far enough from the house that the farm people will not know anyone is here. Besides it's late. The lights have gone out."

He looked suddenly at the woman before him, his partner in this wild, dangerous adventure. She was breathing deeply, pulling the hair from off her damp forehead. The same pulsing energy that had electrified them in the maple grove flashed between them. Delia put her hands on his shoulders and looked into those large, deep eyes that hid so much, that she did not understand. Suddenly the fear of apprehension, the escape, their need for shelter for the night, everything was swept away before the power of passion. His arms went around her and he sought her lips. She held herself to him, opened her mouth, herself to him. The inexplicable, almost mystic tie, formed of interdependencies made in the poignant shadow of near-death, grew taut, pulling them into what was becoming a union of body and soul that defied reason, in fact was against reason, at least for Delia.

There were bundles of straw outside the cabin; they took some inside and spread it on the floor. She had given herself in unspoken vows of love and desire a moment ago and they had both understood they would be together for the night, in this place, and that was all that mattered. Zach shut the door and propped it with an old bench.

"Not much of a hotel," he said, looking at the sloping walls, the rocks which had tumbled from the fireplace onto the floor.

"This must have been the original settler's place," Delia said. "They have moved up the hill. Outside the cabin I saw lilies of the valley coming up. And flowering bushes. The lilacs have not abandoned it. They go on growing as if the children still tumble about the floor and folks still cook food in the fireplace. The lilac bushes do not know when we come and go."

They kissed again, hungrily, more than once. Then there was a moment when they stood in silence, listening to the faint sounds of the barnyard up the hill, half-embarrassed, half-desperate for each other. Zach gently put his hand on the bodice of her dress; she clasped it and held to her bosom as they kissed again.

Her dress was a simple morning frock; she had kept the promise she made the night of the fire to abandon hoops, and so it was easy to slip from it, to loose the hooks of the camisole, to lie beside the man she loved beyond all logic. Stars shone in the window; the lilacs filled the air with breathtaking sweetness. A dog barked; they raised their heads together until the cadence of its barks died away in the still night, then laughed a little and touched each other's faces. The air was chill and she trembled slightly as he leaned over her; she could feel the strangeness of his man's body as he spread her thick, black hair around her head on the straw and looked wonderingly into her shining eyes.

"I have wanted to caress this hair since I first saw you, so haughty and beautiful at the ball at Rivertides," he whispered. She shut her eyes so she could feel, feel, the blend of sensations: the movement of his hands, more gentle than she could ever have imagined, touching her body and making it spring to life, the smell of man's pomade, the foreign textures of man's skin and hair and muscle, the piercing pain of first surrender, then the rhythmic blending of bodies, inextricably sweet and oddly, poignantly sad. Finally, the earth seemed to pause in ecstasy, as the overpowering, beautiful scent of lilacs hung in the air in utter stillness. For her the universe stopped at that moment, and no matter what happened, no matter what battles were being fought or which debate politicians disputed in the world outside, that moment became the meaning of the universe, filled as it was with affection and the peace of still, calm, spring air, and the smell of lilacs.

"Perhaps you can make something out of me," Zach said finally, in a tight, controlled voice. She could not see his face. The dog barked a few more times, and then all was still.

June, July, 1863

Chapter Thirteen

"A wedding, Sergeant Scott? Well, July 3, 1863, has a good sound to it, doesn't it?" Colonel Lewis Brooks sat at his writing desk under the Kentucky magnolia trees looking into the boyishly round, hopeful face of Jacob Joe Scott. "Well, I know you made your request before and now you want final confirmation." He stood and clapped Jacob Joe on the shoulder. "We'll see what we can do. After all, what is a wedding unless the bridegroom cometh?" Then he gave a good imitation of a hearty laugh.

Colonel Brooks was trying to be more comradely, make a little jest now and then. It had come to him by the grapeshot grapevine that although his men respected him tremendously, they considered him a little aloof, a bit distant. It could enhance the trust they had in him to feel he was at heart one of the men, and trust was important if you were leading men in battle.

"Sir," Jacob Joe said, his fair cheeks as rosy as crabapples, "my dear Sophie is even now planning the nuptial festivities with her sister. It would be a great favor, since nothing major seems to be going on here in the Kentucky theatre, if I could have only three days to go and tie that knot."

"Say no more, sergeant," Colonel Brooks said. "You are right, of course about the military doldrums here. July will be as good a time as any to go. I think we have all given up on General Morgan as a serious threat. Alarms and excursions, that's all he's capable of. And with these heavy rains we've had, he will stay safely behind the Cumberland River." He signed the pass with a flourish. "You shall go to your Juliet. I was married at that time of year myself," he said, looking at the picture of his wife Amanda on the small table by his trunk, alongside that of his mother, Susan Brooks.

"Thank you, sir, thank you," Jacob Joe said, so happy that he wanted to bound like a rabbit around the clearing where the Eightieth Indiana was camped. Things were going so well. He had been made sergeant in his company, Sophie had given her consent to be his wife and now, finally, the date was set.

Lewis Brooks was unwilling to let his new sergeant depart just yet; he wanted someone to talk to. The colonel's mind stayed on the unsatisfactory situation his regiment was in. He had left the Fourteenth early in the war to find active command and now—"It pains me to say we are not likely to get called to active duty. The Western theatre's action is all at Vicksburg. Surely, surely soon Grant will break through there."

"We can all hope and pray so, sir," Jacob Joe said, folding the pass into the inside pocket of his coat.

After a little more conversation, his commanding officer let him go, and Jacob Joe sought out the company of the Vincennes men who were in the woods, out of sight of the eagle, puritanical eye of the commander. They were playing chuck-luck. They had cleared a section of ground of twigs and nettle weeds and traced squares with the point of a stick. In each stick was a number, made of small pebbles. Greenbacks rested on various numbers.

Eustace Brooks stood tall among them, wearing an odd hat with a feather on it. "And now, m' friends, I shall roll the dice. Will it be sevens or snake eyes?" He threw them into the circle in the middle of the numbers' grid. A private from the Vincennes company cheered and picked up several bills, giving Eustace one of them.

Ah, poor Eustace, Jacob Joe thought. The men had made him "banker" out of some sort of odd tribute to the colonel. Hope of favor from the colonel's brother? Or was it just a mockery of his youth and bounding, calf-like impetuosity? The poor young man was still trying to find some sort of recognition and expiation for the ignominious part he'd played in his own brother's death—murdered, really, by Copperheads he had known well. Perhaps he could make reparations, Jacob Joe mused. But not this way. He watched the bills go onto the squares. They were gambling a quarter of their wages in the game, and though Jacob Joe did not participate, he could understand it. Boredom and inactivity drove them to it, that and the depreciated value of the army salaries—worth no more than eight pre-war dollars a month.

How could the United States government put its soldiers into the field to bleed and die for eight dollars a month?

Jacob Joe raised his voice to attract Eustace's attention. "Take a banker's holiday," he called to Eustace from the edge of the circle. The boy looked up and gave his friend a bright, though chagrined smile. Sergeant Scott had taken an interest in Eustace Brooks when he was a recruit a couple of months ago, but after a while his mentorship had gone beyond tutoring to real friendship.

"You found us again, sergeant," Eustace said as he bounded up, pushing back the hank of hair on his forehead.

Jacob Joe was equally official. "Private Brooks, you know the colonel frowns on this game. So much money is lost."

"Just re-circulated, Sergeant. But we'll break up the game for your sake in a moment." He looked expectantly at his friend. "Was there something else?'

"I got my marryin' pass," Jacob Joe said with a shy smile.

Eustace began capering around among the trees. "Whoopee! Skee-bob-ble!" he shouted. "You'll be givin' up your freedom right when we're celebratin' Independence Day!'

Jacob Joe smiled. "My dear Sophie will make the most charming bride in the state of Kentucky." He thought a moment. "Private Brooks—Eustace— would you like to come to my tent to hear about the arrangements?'

"Sure would. Let me do one final banker's job and redistribute the mon-ey, scribble out the squares." Jacob Joe watched him tell the disappointed men the game was over. Then he began walking up the trail towards the non-com's tents. Eustace soon caught up.

"Tell me about your family," Jacob Joe said to the young man. "I did not wish to ask the colonel."

"Well, my brother Lewis doesn't often talk of home. Now and then he calls me in—" Eustace's eyes were strangely clouded for a moment. "We all spent our lives back home tryin' to please him, I think. Anyway, my sisters Emily and Susie are flutterin' about goin' to church suppers and washin' and starchin' children's pinafores. Keeps 'em busy. Susie also runs the Wheatland store. Well, her husband Sandford is s'posed to be doin' it, but he's as timid as a lady field mouse. Can't muster the courage to ask folks to pay their bills. So she does the dirty work. Anyway, my father is healin' up a bit after—it all." He stared at the gnarled, above-ground roots of a tree near the path.

"I hope so. I still miss him. But how about you? Are you healing up?"

A shadow crossed Eustace's face. "It's like an operation scar, always with you to remind you of awful pain. Especially my part. But I try not to think of it more'n fifteen minutes a day—if I did, I'd die. Bein' here helps." Then he brightened. "Pa's evaluatin' the Indiana troops' commissary distri-bution for the governor. Travellin' about in Mississippi and Virginia."

"How did this happen?" Jacob Joe wanted to know.

"The governor made a trip to take food to the Fourteenth in Falmouth a couple of months ago. There were complaints. And now that the U.S. government is supplying the food, Morton wants to be sure the boys eat decent. He wants Pa to inspect."

"I hope all the military brass there don't step on your father, or the speculating sharks eat him up," Jacob Joe said ruefully.

"I 'spect Father'll be all right," Eustace allowed. "He's seen a lot in his time as a yankee peddler."

They reached the non-coms' tent and went inside. Jacob Joe sat Eustace on the trunk and picked up a small bundle of letters tied in a ribbon.

"From Miss Sophie?" Eustace wondered.

"Well, one is. But the rest are from her sister, Dora. I'm making arrangements through her. The rest of the family, I think, isn't perfectly thrilled about the marriage."

"Well, I don't know why in God's green earth not," the young man staunchly asserted.

"They think I'm a trifle odd, I guess. 'Too sensitive,' is how they put it. That story about my seeing the vision of my grandmother at the Battle of Perryville, and then the way I acted when I was at the lecture in Louisville." He looked slightly crestfallen. "They'll get over that," he said. He picked up a blue, deckle-edged piece of paper. "This is the one Miss Dora sent me about the rings. Want to read it? I keep reading it over and over to be sure such a wonderful dream is really coming true." He handed the letter to Eustace, and Eustace scanned it.

May 20, 1863

Dear and respected Brother-to-be:

We are proceeding with our hurried plans on the belief that you will finally receive the official pass you've requested for the festivities.

As to the matter of the ring you wrote about—it is hard to locate a suitable gold band engraved with linked hands in these times in Louisville, but I have a friend journeying to Cincinnati and promise you one way or another we shall answer your request.

Your sister-to-be
In fondest affection, truly
Dora Lavenham

Eustace put down the letter, nodding his head in appreciative interest and Jacob Joe picked up another, this time to read aloud.

"Here's a later one—June 3." He skimmed through the salutation. " 'All is hubbub here. As usual, there are rumors that cavalry raids are heading towards us, but no one credits them anymore; still, they are unsettling, and then to have the wedding plans in the midst of it all. Mother is in bed with a sick headache. We are relieved to hear from our cousin Calhoun that he is happily settled in the Twenty First Georgia regiment. Odd if you should meet him as a foe! How the fortunes of this war go to split neighbors and family so, with people I care about on both sides! But General Ewell's Southern troops are in the Eastern theatre, so I do not believe you will have that odd opportunity. I took the train to Memphis to do some nursing there as the wounded came in from the battles near Vicksburg. The shelling wounds were awful. They do not let us women do anything but clean up dirty linen and feed the poor soldiers. I guess I have watched enough dressings changed to do it as well as some of the men nurses!

" 'Sophie sends her affection and devotion. I know she wrote last week, but is so busy with details she cannot think. She has been fitted by the dressmaker, who is trying to find cream-colored satin with rose lace to do the dress right. We will all pray, for my sister is determined to have the dress this way.

" 'Please let me know what sort of nosegay you wish to order, so I can tell the floral shop what to put together. Your loving sister-in-law.' "

Jacob Joe paused. "Well, I can't imagine that you'd want to hear these letters," he said, after a moment.

"Why ever not?" Eustace demanded.

"I always think nobody is interested in me, either at home or out here in camp. There are so few people I am close to, no real relatives to pour out all the things that crowd into my mind. Well, Eustace, I consider you almost a relative."

"And I you, Sergeant Scott. Maybe the brother I lost—" He turned his face away in confusion, and after a while they shook hands, and he left.

Jacob Joe sat alone in his tent. Outside, the leaves on the sycamore trees rustled in the heat of the day. So much idleness in this dreary sector of the war. He picked up the last letter from Dora, one which he had not shown Eustace, could not bear to share, really. Now he looked at it again, sadly.

June 15, 1863

Dear Brother (so I think of you now):

My Aunt Althea and Cousin Delia have arrived from Rivertides in Indiana to be with us until the wedding, to help mother out with the inn and the wedding parties. Only two more weeks—we are running about like elves who need to make shoes before the morning comes. Aunt Althea has made the inquiry you requested, and I have tried to be as tactful as possible, knowing your pride and fear your brother would not wish to come to your wedding.

Aunt Althea says that on the holiday they took to the Democratic rally they all attended, she told your brother Zach that his presence was desired at the nuptials. He did not seem attentive to the suggestion. Later he was involved in an incident at the rally and barely escaped when the excursion train was searched by Federal troops suspecting treasonous disloyalty. He fled the train into the countryside, and, oddly, my cousin Delia seemed to have been carrying arms also and had to flee, too, arriving only in the early morning at our relatives in Indianapolis. My aunt was worried half to death by all of this, although she pooh-poohs the suggestions she is upset. Although my aunt does not blame your brother for any of the confusion, thinking he acts in the just cause for the South, it is obvious your brother as an active Southern sympathizer cannot think of coming to the wedding of a Federal officer—even if he wished to, which he does not.

Jacob Joe put the letter down and stood up to fill his canteen. The day was warm; he walked to a water barrel in the middle of the circle of tents, immersed his canteen and watched the bubbles surface as water entered the neck. Where was this scapegrace brother of his at this moment? Serving the despicable cause he cared about in some way, somewhere. Jacob Joe pulled the canteen from the barrel and tilted it up to drink. He rinsed his mouth and spat on the ground, forcefully, before he drank deeply from the canteen.

* * * *

Zach Scott, as a matter of fact, was also in camp, a hidden Confederate camp in the Indiana countryside. He was sitting on a stump in the midst of the lushest grass he had ever seen, in Orange County, Indiana.

Captain Tom Hines, the chief lord-in-waiting on General John Morgan sat Indian-style on the ground.

"This is a dead horse camp you say," Zach said bemusedly, looking around at the cavalry horses which were grazing nearby. Some were spavined, their ribs showing through their hides like the ribs of some sunken ship, but many were good, fleshy stallions and mares.

"Half-dead would be more accurate," Hines answered musingly. "We rode these poor things from one end of Tennessee to another escaping the Yankees. Morgan told me to come north, through Kentucky to rest the horses in camps where lush grass grew, and I've extended his orders a bit to cross the Ohio River."

"How in the world have you escaped detection? I would think that a Rebel in God's Country would causes tremors."

"It would—if it were known." Zach took stock of the man who sat before him rubbing grease into a saddle harness, burnishing it with a cloth until it shone. Captain Tom Hines of General John Morgan's command was a small, intense man with bright, batting dark eyes and quick, articulate speech. He had read law before going with Morgan and was typical of the better sort of the cavalier's troops—idealistic and emotionally committed.

"I have been here several days, camping quietly in different places and exchanging horses. We pretend we are from the Union Army, District of Kentucky. I exchange 'dead' horses for healthy ones. I even give receipts for the difference in value on the quartermaster in Indianapolis." His mouth twitched in a small, sardonic smile, but he shifted his weight restlessly, put the harness aside. "I think I'm the dead horse, staying in this county at the end of the world while General Morgan perfects his plans. I yearn to get riding south again, to head back to Morgan's forces." Zach could make out the silhouettes of a few other men lounging about in a nearby orchard up the hill. They were roasting chickens over a campfire; applewood smoke rose into the sunset sky.

"When will you go back to join Morgan?" Zach asked.

"As soon as I think we can meet him directly, without detection. We are keeping to the hills and vales of the countryside. I don't want to hang around the villages either here or in Kentucky, to be seen by belles or old militiamen. We have pressed our luck this far." Hines stood. He had the wiry frame and bandy legs of one who is constantly in the saddle. "General Morgan loves the risk; he thrives on it," he went on. "He goes into dangerous places and poses and bows to applause from adoring women; just before the Northern troops arrive chasin' him, he dashes out of town, hat flying. The cheers and dust are still floating behind him when the Northern army comes in."

Hines picked up the saddle; Zach rose, and they headed up the hill towards supper. "General Morgan should have been an actor," Hines went on. "Not I. My face is known and I do not like it." He looked at Zach and smiled. "Still, you Hoosiers raise good fodder for horse and man. My men have been able to buy chickens and pies by the dozens. The people have been friendly. At least we now know it can be done. We will return."

"And when does he ride for these Northern states?"

"Soon, very soon. The Yankees believe he's in camp, but at this moment he is preparing to cross the Cumberland. I am awaiting a courier myself to tell me the exact day. The man will have to be wily, to slip through the lines, cross the river. The Yankees are beginning to get wind of what we are up to."

They entered the apple orchard that sat at the edge of the clearing where supper was being prepared over an open fire. Little green apples were ripening on the trees. After a long moment, Zach said, "I suppose you may have guessed that I am opposed to Morgan's coming into southern Indiana. I brought the message encouraging you from Mawkins, but I myself—" He shrugged his shoulders.

Hines was unfazed. "I know. You are not the only one. Vallandigham has been to see General Morgan."

"Has he?" Zach was surprised. He knew Clement Vallandigham, under orders from Lincoln, had been banished to the South "for life"; that was his "punishment" for speaking out in what Burnside considered treason during these dangerous times for the North. But had he been to see Morgan?

The other man began to walk with the harness to a broken-down shed up the hill from the campfire that served as his tackhouse. "Vallandigham's free to go about the South. He told Morgan he was afraid a raid into Indiana and Ohio would only rouse the Northwest against us."

"My opinion exactly."

"John—General Morgan does not think so. Nor do I."

"And what is your hope, then?" Zach wondered.

They had come in the door of the shed. Its walls leaned crazily, and they had to lift up the door to get it out of the dirt. "To act. At a crucial time. In the East you can be sure they are acting. At Vicksburg, the action will kill or cure us in the West." Hines walked in and deposited the harness on a long peg on the wall, and then began checking over the saddles and harness that would take them on the flying raid north, through these very farmlands. "And here in these borderlands, we need to show that the South is strong, ready to invade if we wish. To bring the North to their knees in all fields."

The sun was setting, looking oddly out of line through the shutter hole in the back of the crazy-walled shack. "Do you still believe the South can get the Northwest to rise?" Zach wanted to know. "After the rally at Indianapolis and the Pogue's Run incident, I'm not sure any more."

"Perhaps," Hines said. "It is worth a chance. Your message said there are 100,000 Knights of the Golden Circle ready to join us in these states—"

Zach's lip curled. "If they wish. But my experience last month in Indianapolis was that they were willing to hoot and whistle at the North but not fight." They turned to head outside.

"We'll see," Hines said. "We may have a gigantic uprising. If Lee succeeds and Vicksburg holds out, we all may be able to bring the North to beg for peace." He hitched up the door to the shed and shut it. "At the very least, we will have our horses in fresh grass like this—" he ran the tip of his cavalry boot over the grass at his feet, laying the lush, bright spears flat.

"And we may bring a little of the same treatment the Northern cavalry brought to our Southern villages," he went on, bitterly. "The sons-of-bitches have robbed our village stores and frightened and hurt our old men and women. My own brother was killed in Grierson's invasion of Mississippi." His face was dark, vindictive. "I won't have trouble at all burning barns and even houses."

They walked towards the smell of cornbread and chicken. Zach said to him, "Give us our instructions. I shall carry them to Mawkins and the others." The trace of a frown was on his face. "I may not agree, but I guess I have signed the muster roll for the entire campaign."

"Alert your castles of the Knights of the Golden Circle. Tell them to be ready to shelter us, give us fresh horses and food. And then find horses yourselves and join us near the Ohio River. Be ready in two weeks—we will send word to Mawkins in Vincennes. Lay low. Then we all ride—to hell if we have to!"

Zach nodded and they greeted the raiders and supper at the campfire.

Willis Mawkins made the rounds of the well-fed bays and chestnuts and dapple grays in the livery stable in Vincennes. They had not been exercised properly lately. He was neglecting his business for the party and Cause. It really wouldn't pay to do that. Sharpen your own hoe first, no matter who you serve. At least that was what his father had always told him. He said he had learned it from living with the Hogues. Willis spat scornfully into the cuspidor, thinking of the shame that old association always evoked, the anger of knowing your parents ate dirt for two generations as hired men for haughty village aristocrats.

Still, someday the war would be over, and he might need the business here in Vincennes. Perhaps not, though. Something else had occurred to him lately. The Cause was not merely all the folderol of the Bonnie Blue Flag and Southern glory and states' rights. There was money in this Cause. If things went for the best, he would be rewarded by the Confederacy. If the tide should turn strongly and the war be decisively won, land confiscated from Northerners in the South would be his. A pretty little estate near Natchez would be fine. Pillars and all, like the Duggers. Show these uppity Vincennes people what the son of a dirt-poor hired man could do.

Of course it would be necessary to win the war first.

Well, he was doing everything in his power to accomplish that. Scott had just brought the message from Hines' camp that Morgan would be moving through Indiana and Ohio within two weeks, raiding, raising troops. Unfortunately, today's paper had brought the news that Hines had been discovered as a Rebel and he and his party were being chased towards the river. No one suspected the secret invasion to come. Everything was coming to a climax at once.

He went into his office and looked through his mail. He was behind, thanks to all the delays caused by the Pogue's Run incident. They had made their show of strength, it was true. And other "Peace now" pow-wows were going well. But he had skirted the line, got into trouble. He was detained, questioned, but not held. No, he had always been sure to keep his coattails scrupulously clean, to be quiet, discreet. He would be no good at all to the party or the Cause if he were arrested. He had been sure that Scott, too, was out of the public notice.

Vallandigham, who opened his mouth and brayed like a jackass about his views, was banished, wandering around the South in disgrace. He was about as good as a third shoe to them all now. And these newspaper editors and speakers like Voorhees who constantly trumpeted their views—pshaw. Best to stay underground.

The screen door creaked as he entered the dusty office. His bookkeeper, Lettie, sat at the books. She, too, was behind because of the dratted trip. He spoke to her a little irritatedly, in a rusty whisper. None of the stable hands or wheelwrights were in the office, but they might be within hearing distance, under one of the windows.

"Will you be working late tonight to complete this month's balance, Miss Hogue?" he asked. She had insisted on the formalities here in the office, even though outside the office they were—close, and now he was glad.

"Yes, Mr. Mawkins." She looked up at him with soft, appealing eyes. "But I will be finished by eight o'clock. I can lock the office and be in the flat in a twinkling."

"Oh?" His voice was chilly. There was a reason. It was necessary to be very discreet here in southern Indiana now, to avoid any reason for talk now that the preparations were being made for Morgan's invasion, well—the raid. There had been some talk lately about him and Lettie, and it was putting him in the view of the town's collective eye. Besides, there was something cloying, unnerving about too much of a thing. As if you'd poured too much molasses on hot cakes and felt a little sick of the sweet.

She pursed her mouth and whispered, "Will you stop by?"

"No, Miss Hogue, not tonight." She was alarmed at the impersonality of his tone, reached to touch his hand. He did not pull it back. "I think," he said rather evenly, "we must not give cause for gossip in Vincennes for a while. My party work will come to a head in a few weeks. I cannot say more." Then he slowly pulled his hand away, as if there were something dangerous about keeping it under Lettie's.

"Your party work," she repeated, dully. She had been hearing this often lately. "I see," she said a little more crisply.

"Perhaps later in the summer—"

"Perhaps," she said, and turned her back on him. Gathering the small shreds of pride she had left around her, she returned to work.

She did not, however, stay to complete the month's balances. Instead, she left about an hour after the exchange, and as she walked down the street towards her lodgings, she fumed and charged like a dynamo, incensed at what had just happened. Something she sensed during the two weeks in Indianapolis had come to a head and burst like a boil. He was, or soon would be, through with her.

"Perhaps later." Perhaps not, if I have anything to say about it, and I do of course. For *this* I have put up with the odd looks of Mrs. Badollet and the ladies in the literary club. For *that man* the downright blistering venom of Jewell McClure. I have been brought before the board of the Upper Indiana Church, the place I love above all else. Faced the shame of having Reverend Paden think—know—I'm—.

She had reached home; now she put the key in the lock. "For love, I said. For lust, 'twas. I ignored my own dear mother when she came all the way to Indianapolis on the train at her age." She threw her pocketbook on the settee, pulled off her gloves and threw them on the pocketbook.

"Love. To be humiliated in that office that way. Well, he can't cast me aside as if he were scraping garbage off a plate. He thinks he can take it up again. We'll see about that, we'll just see."

She walked into the small closet that served as her kitchen, looked at the gas burner stove. She took out a pot and put it on the stove, then took it off again. She wasn't hungry, and anyway she had not been down to the butcher's to get a bone for soup.

She walked into the bedroom, stared at the bed. Here they had lain, ecstatic, while the rest of Vincennes slept, while children pressed their innocent faces against the quilts their mothers had made, while husbands and wives—of course. What else should she expect? She who had been raised a Christian.

She paused to let herself feel the pain, the shame, as if letting its burden press her flat might ease the guilt some. It wasn't only the—relationship, the bodies. That had been a revelation to her, but it was more than that. It was the closeness. The someone who was there to take care of her. The advice about the bills that sat on her little desk (not that she had ever taken money, heavens, heavens, no). She had savored the praise about the new hat she found in the milliner's shop or the dress she chose on a certain day; she had shared the worries she had about her mother's aging. She had depended on Willis Mawkins, and he had dashed her hopes as a housewife dashes a chicken's head against a stone wall.

She knew it was coming even in Indianapolis. He did not rush to her; he used her to relieve his tense feelings. No more courtly kissing of the hand, no whispered compliments. He tolerated her as he went about the thousand activities that were in his turbulent, confusing life right now. She was embarrassed, confounded that her own ardor began to exceed his.

She started to cry, painfully, wrenchingly, and she sobbed for over five minutues. It was unreasoning crying; in her heart she knew she did not love him, only desired him beyond reason, hated him for what he had done to her, but was tied with strings that were as hard to break as cat gut. Every day since she returned from Indianapolis she thought things would change; every day she slipped deeper into despair.

As the sobs subsided, she glanced at the brush on the oak vanity table, the ribbons laid out, the scent. Somehow seeing her own hair on the brush made her sad, as if something from her own body lay nakedly, sacrificially before her. She had worked so hard to appear comely to him. For naught. She went to the vanity and opened the deep but narrow drawer under the surface table. She pulled out a black bottle. "Miss Breddiger's Female Restorative. Contains morphia," the bottle said. She turned it over in her hand, slowly, almost wonderingly. Then, finally, she put it back in the drawer and closed it tight.

A week later Horace Hogue broke the silence in the parlor of the old McClure home where his mother Catherine, his uncle Billy McClure, Esther and Essie sat.

"June bugs fatter'n walnuts're hoppin' around on the stoop," Horace said. "Squished me a bunch when I went out to the cows."

"Waal, it's June," Billy allowed. He was reading the *Cincinnati Enquirer* as he did every night.

"Lightnin' bugs are thick, too," Esther said. "Strawberries're almost done bearing. Only the littlest ones are left to use for jam."

Silence hung comfortably in the room. The clock ticked.

"Lettie's case is coming up this month at the Session at Upper Indiana," Aunt Esther said. "Immoral behavior unbecoming a Christian is the charge. Jewell has done her work. Took 'em all spring."

"So much sinnin' in Knox County the deacons have to stay up nights reviewin'," Billy said. "Wonder if they have any fun with the details."

"Bill," Esther said reproachfully.

Catherine finally spoke. "Well, they are just too late in Lettie's case. She's decided she's had enough of sinning."

Horace looked up with a light in his eyes. Had his sister rid herself of that bounder that half the county knew she was paired with?

"Yes," her mother said. "She rode out to tell me. She informed him she was not going to see him again."

"And she has quit her job?" Esther said eagerly. It was not that she did not approve, down deep, or think women could work and do it well. It was that she was not free to do it. If her place was in the parlor, well then, every other woman's was, too.

"Nooo," Catherine said, in an uneven voice. "She says she likes the job and will find a way to work in spite of him being about all the time."

"What about the Session? They are already considering her."

"Well, Lettie's going out to see Reverend Paden before it meets. Goin' out quietly. No rush, sometime soon. She says she'll write him asking him to pray for her and help her ask forgiveness of God and the church. Maybe they'll withdraw the whole thing. She don't want, to go out, but she'll handle it privately."

"Good, good," Billy said, and Esther nodded.

"Ma, what's immortal 'havior becoming a Christian?" Essie asked. Her figure had just recently filled out, and she was full of questions she never could get answers to from anyone around the house.

"Hush, child," her father said. "Go out and squish you a few June bugs on the stoop. Better yet, set the cat to 'em. That'll give you both somethin' proper to do."

Silence again. The clock ticked.

"I'm leavin' again," Horace said with finality. "The Three County Militia is drillin' in Vincennes tomorrow and will wait there in tents."

"Whatever for now?" Catherine asked with surprise. "Things were bad enough in Indianapolis. Seems like there's a scare a minute around this state these days—a Confederate ghost ready to say boo around every corner. What do they need you for now?"

"General John Hunt Morgan has crossed the Cumberland River, and intelligence has it he may come into Indiana."

"They've said that before. We've hidden the horses and the silver teapot twice already," Esther said, her handsome face scornful.

"Well, hide them again, Esther," Catherine said calmly. "He probably won't come this time either. I'm not going to worry about you, Horace; my old worrier is worn out. Reminds me of the times in McClure Station when I was a little one. Indians were coming every second Tuesday. Well, it gives us all something to do." She rose, took her spectacles out of her pocket and picked up the paper her brother had put on the table. He gave her a surprised look. Newspaper reading was for men.

"I can read too, Billy," she said, and with a half smile pushed on the screen door. "Maybe you haven't noticed the abolition society papers that the mailman delivers me. Shoo, you June bugs—besides," she called back, "I hear General Morgan is a handsome devil. Charming smile and long, drooping mustache. I want to read what all the other ladies are talking about."

"Well I do declare," said Sophie Lavenham, twisting in front of the mirror of the large hotel parlor. The hotel was closed for two weeks for the coming wedding and the draperies were drawn. The dressmaker knelt before her, pins in mouth, taking up the hem of the satin wedding dress. "Only three days till the wedding and it's goin' to take you all three to stitch your stitches. Will you please hurry up? I feel like I'm goin' to faint in this awful heat."

Her sister Dora stood beside her, handing the dressmaker pins from a paper. Sophie twisted her shoulders impatiently. "All the trouble of gettin' this satin from Cincinnati," she said. "Pooh, what a bother a wartime weddin' is!"

"Not to mention that mother had to sell her sapphire brooch to get the satin," Dora said placidly.

"Well, who can imagine she'll ever use it again. A useless bauble—"

Her aunt Althea entered from the music room. "That sapphire pin was given your mother by our father on the day Adahlia turned eighteen. Poor Father. . ." Althea's voice drifted off. She had received a letter from Mississippi saying that her father had had another heart seizure. Undoubtedly he was driven by worry over the plantation near Memphis. Not that his worries were without cause; the Yankees in Memphis had ordered the fields sown with corn and wheat for northern commissary needs. Major Bachelder wrote urging her to come for a visit to stake the family claim in person. It was true she was a Northerner and her father was going to transfer the farm to her. Still, that had not happened yet. Absentee ownership invited confiscation. The overseer was weak, the major said, and they could not count on his management. She really must go check sometime soon, if for no other reason than to relieve her father's mind.

"Ouch!" Sophie yelled at the seamstress. "I declare you are the most careless woman I have ever seen. You have now poked my ankle with a pin. Whatever will you do next?" The frightened woman looked up miserably. This was the third fitting; for her making this hurried wedding dress had been a soul-rending experience: somewhere between an interrogation during the Reign of Terror and being left for a weekend with a two-year-old.

"Dora, it occurs to me that we have not yet turned the rose silk you will wear in the wedding," Sophie said. "Rose will complement my cream-colored satin."

"No, you have not thought of my old dress," her sister said.

"Dora does not have a new dress as maid of honor?" Althea asked.

"Of course not. We cannot afford two dresses, Aunt. And the rose will do perfectly well. Dora is content, aren't you dear?" Sophie demanded. She pulled at a satin rosette that had been sewn into a flounce.

"I—would be content," Dora said, flushing, refusing to look at her sister.

"Whatever does *that* mean?" Sophie asked. She really was not very interested. The dressmaker finished and gestured for the young woman to step out of the dress. Looking about quickly to be sure that none of the hotel's men workers were about, Sophie stepped out and stood in camisole and half slip, admiring her beautiful form in the mirror, while the dressmaker gratefully swooped up the satin dress and took it away.

"It means, sister," Dora told her calmly, "that I will not be here for your wedding."

"You *what*?" Sophie almost yelled. Even Althea was speechless.

"I have been accepted as a nurse in the Confederate Hospital Matrons' Corps. I leave tomorrow for the East."

Sophie stared, open-mouthed, then shrugged, as if to say that her sister, always odd, was beyond her comprehension. She went to slip into the calico day dress that lay across a chair on the other side of the room.

"You are not staying for your own sister's nuptials?" Althea said, uncomprehendingly.

Dora turned to her aunt, who was the most understanding person in her family, with an appealing look. They walked out of earshot of the bride. "Aunt, I have found real meaning in my life with nursing these poor young men. I cannot see everyone go off to war and stay at home just because I am a woman. It does not seem right."

"I have thought that sometimes, too," Althea murmured. "When Calhoun left, I wondered why it was only the men who went." She looked long and searchingly at Dora. There was more, there had to be more—

"I helped Mr. Scott, Jacob Joe, with all the details. I got his ring, advised him on the nosegay he will give my sister. But it pains me." Tears were in her eyes. "Great battles are coming up, so they say, the greatest of the war. It seems frivolous for me to stay and do these things while men are dying, men I can help."

"Ah," thought Althea. "He has made you his confidant and you love him. How sad for you."

She asked, "Have you told your mother?"

"No, but I will do so now."

"The news in the streets is that Morgan the Raider has crossed the Cumberland and is heading for us."

"That is always the news in Louisville," Dora said tiredly. "At least there will be action where I go, instead of the same old rumors and false alarms."

"Will that affect the wedding? Isn't Mr. Scott's regiment defending the border? What if he should be called to the field?"

"God help us," Dora said ruefully. "Save his life if he must go to arms and save all the folk around here if my sister's wedding is called off!" With that she went to find her mother and pack her small carpetbag to go to the front.

Zach Scott rode towards the Ohio River. A messenger had come to Mawkins saying General Morgan wished a guide north; Mawkins, maintaining his own "lay low" posture, had insisted Zach go. It was not an especially convenient time; Zach was trying to manage the estate his father left, to supervise the cultivating of the fields now, in the all-important farming month of June, to hay off fields resplendent with grass from the recent rains. And he needed time to go through the papers in the house. He had put all that off; family knickknacks and heirlooms and bits of sentimental paper were not at all interesting to him. Still, settling up must be done. Prudence must be served if the estate was to yield a fine return. He was being fair, putting his twin brother's share in escrow. No one could claim he hadn't handled it all well.

Now, Morgan's aide-de-camp, Hines, had sent for help. He was raiding through the border countryside, capturing horses to take to Morgan. Hines was in contact with the general, planning the invasion of Indiana, and he had specifically suggested that he, Zach Scott, to be the Indiana scout and guide once Morgan's force crossed the river. Well, he did know every road in southern Indiana, had ridden them all organizing the castles.

The castles. They were meeting openly now in spite of Governor Morton, bonfires burning bright in front of barns, with the expectation that if there was an invasion of the North, the state would rise to join the invaders. Zach was not at all sure of that. The signs he saw were different. Where would it all end? Dispatches said Robert E. Lee and the Army of Virginia had begun the long-feared swing north, had crossed the Rappahannock and were somewhere—where? In Pennsylvania so the papers said. The Northern army was in pursuit, as they were also on the Mississippi. At the other end of the Confederacy, could the Southern defenders of Vicksburg hold their siege? Their food and water was running low.

Zach's horse came to the cliffs near the Ohio, west of Madison. A road cut through them, and he took it, passing under a shady overhang of maples and sycamores.

Should the South lose—but he would not allow himself to even consider that possibility. Each man in the border country, in southern Indiana, had to choose at the beginning of the war. From the first he staked his bet on the South's winning, and he could not think of any other possibility. After all, you must play with what you have been dealt. And if you have a few good cards, you can build them into a winning hand, by keeping cool and awaiting your advantage. The South had disadvantages all along—not as many men, only a few factories—but with high spirit, bravery and cunning they could win.

That was his personal stance, too. He glimpsed the Ohio river ahead of him, wide as a highway, sparkling through trees, and hurried his horse a bit. You could go a long way if you did not have to worry about a moral code. He chuckled ruefully, thinking that never was a problem for him. Cunning was especially important. So many men had meringue brains and never used what they had. It was all so easy to use everyone for what you wanted—or it used to be, he thought in spite of himself, until Delia.

He stood in the saddle, forcing himself not to think of her, but the associations crowded in. Try as he would to resist, he was soon awash in sensations: the warmth of her body, the smell of her hair as she lay on the straw, his own total surrender in the height of the moment of love.

That was the thing that troubled him, the loss of control. No woman, of all the several shop girls and farm maids he had possessed, ever drew anything but physical release from him. Pure physical release. But Delia. For just a moment, one uncomfortable moment with her, something else poured out of him and he had a raw glimpse of a force he did not know he possessed—a soul. It had best not happen again. He would make sure it did not. They parted in Indianapolis with passionate promises to meet again. He would have her body, let her have his. That was fair. But he would make sure he did not surrender anything else. Too much was at stake.

He reached the edge of the river. Debris floated by, chunks of logs and chicken coops. The other side looked far away. There was a ferry here; he could cross as a Northern citizen with no trouble and ride to rendezvous with Hines. Hidden on his body was a pass from Colonel John Morgan himself for safe conduct behind the Southern lines. It was not dated and was therefore the most useful pass he could have. Well, here was the river, the point of no return. In Indiana he could do as he wished and be a Copperhead agitator. Once across the Ohio and behind the lines with Morgan, he was a traitor. With a sigh he headed his horse to the ferryboat dock.

"Sergeant Scott, Jacob Joe, I am sorry about the wedding, terribly sorry. I have not had a chance to tell you personally in all this hurried rush to put the regiment onto the roads to meet Morgan." Colonel Lewis Brooks was riding at the head of the regiment; Jacob Joe was beside him, also astride today. Two of the lieutenants were on sick call with malaria, and so he was pressed to assume the duties of his own lieutenant." This malaria epidemic has peaked at the worst possible time," Colonel Brooks said, as if to steer the young man's thoughts from the personal disappointment that had overtaken him. "I myself am not at my best. Caught the ague with the Fourteenth in the Shenandoah Valley for the first time and have been battling it ever since. But I am able to do my duty today, thank God.'' The horse snorted and heaved. Brooks had ridden ahead of the marching troops to do his own reconnaissance.

"You have that admirable habit of always doing your duty, sir,'' said Jacob Joe with real respect. "And I shall do my duty, too.'' A telegram sent to Louisville, a hurried, passionate note from him after that, as the troops broke camp and the bugles blew—and thus was the moment of a lifetime shattered, at least temporarily. He could not think of the folk at the hotel in Louisville—of his beautiful bride, weeping, looking at the likeness he had sent her. An odd note, though; sister Dora, as he now thought of her, was gone. Mail call that arrived just as the Vincennes Company went into ranks had brought a letter from his adored Sophie before she knew there was to be no wedding. It said Dora had gone to be a nurse—and the dress finally fit. Odd irony.

He would not think of what might have been. Here the discipline of the army would serve him; he would simply banish it from his mind. Something rang in his mind that he didn't really like—the thing that silly Mrs. Parsticle wrote about in her books—"bad thoughts, go shoo.'' Ridiculous. Instead, Army discipline.

He enjoyed being astride, for once, helping supervise the hurried march. He turned his horse to check on stragglers who were drifting into the copses along the wooded road. It was a hot day again, and the men in his company would be panting under trees, fainting, even. Like Perryville.

Perryville had been in October; now it was late June and the regiment was in action again. It could be a spirited engagement; the Northern troops under General Henry M. Judah had the job of stopping Morgan before he got north—if they could. Locating this wily, hit-and-run cavalry officer and his almost 3,000 men was like locating a running group of wild hogs, greased at that, in a second-growth woods.

Jacob Joe had, as a matter of fact, reached a fringe of woods through which the end of the column was filing. He dismounted. There, as he had suspected, were four of the men in the Vincennes Company. "Oswald, Brucker—you other two, get up. We can't afford to rest. General Hobson has told Colonel Brooks we may meet Morgan around any bend.'' Reluctantly, they rose, brushing twigs and moss from their army blues and began to trot listlessly down the road. "Thank God Eustace Brooks wasn't straggling,'' Jacob Joe told himself. "He must be managing to hold his own in the march. Perhaps he's growing up, just a bit.'' There was that satisfaction, at least, on a day that had precious few moments of light.

Jacob Joe galloped up to Colonel Brooks at the head of the column. "Sir, may I suggest you not do your own reconnaissance? And our captains are also too valuable to spare at this moment. As all others are engaged, I volunteer to ride ahead. Morgan may be heading for Columbia, up ahead of us by any of several roads.''

"You are right, Sergeant Scott," Brooks conceded. "In the confusion of this morning, we have no idea where he is." He was understating the case. It was one of those unfortunate but typical situations in which two Northern generals were sparring for turf with the Yankee troops under their commands, and the men had been ordered out, ordered back and had changed roads twice already. John Morgan could easily slip through the sparse, quickly drawn net they had concocted on these roads near the Cumberland River.

"Ride ahead, Scott. Stay to the side of the road when you can, seek out paths. Find a high hill and use the concealing underbrush or a grove of trees to hide yourself as you look below."

"Yes, sir," Jacob Joe said, and saluting, rode ahead.

He proceeded cautiously straight ahead for about three miles. As he trotted, paced, and looked about, his thoughts idled. The situation was dangerous; he had been taught to pray, and yet he could not. His heart was cold lately, numbed, as if ice water had been poured on it. Uncalled for, day after day, thoughts of Zach had been coming to him. Zach at his father's grave, Zach organizing Copperheads, Zach hating him, now, finally Zach actively supporting a Northern rising against the war in Indiana, riding the hot winds of Southern sympathy.

"And I, and my unit, reap the whirlwind. Never, never, after this, can we be reconciled. I should never have asked, have even thought, I wanted him at the wedding." Anger, hatred of his brother, coursed through his veins.

He came to a crossroads. There, sure enough, was a path going up a hill. He urged his mount upwards along the fairly wide path, past scrub oak and clumps of sassafras. Up and up—he would be able to see quite a distance when he reached the top of this winding path. Finally it seemed to level off. He rode to the edge of the hill to catch a glimpse of the town of Columbia below. What was this? There was some sort of skirmish down below. Cavalry officers dressed in Union blue and Southerners in hand-to-hand combat, across the main road leading into the town and in the woods.

He had better return at once and tell Colonel Brooks. He took one final look and a sudden, personal pang hit him. At this very moment, if John Morgan had not crossed the Cumberland, he would have been entering his bride's home in Louisville. Preparing for the bridal dinner. What a beautiful, bright day it is, portending fair weather tomorrow, too, promising a perfect day for a wedding. Zach was urging Indiana to rise with Morgan; Morgan, encouraged, was heading towards the state. In a way, it was his brother's fault he could not marry his love. "Zach, Zach, if I had you here—" he clenched his fist, so eager was he to push it in his brother's face.

Still, he was not dismayed about his own future. Had he not seen in that skull the vision of his grandmother, raising two fingers which were joined together? It must inevitably mean that he and Sophie would be joined someday. He turned his horse to descend the trail and give his message. "Some sun shall rise on my wedding day, in spite of you, Zach, and all you traitors," he told himself. It was the last thought he had before running almost directly into a scouting party dressed in a variety of shades of Butternut gray. They captured and held him in the name of General John Morgan and Jefferson Davis's Confederate States of America.

"This has been an ill day. From bridegroom to bondman," Jacob Joe told himself as he was brought, arms tied in front of him, with only the reins hand free, into Morgan's camp in Columbia. "Still, there isn't anything to be really afraid of. They will parole me. They are paroling everyone."

As he came into town, he saw more men and much more equipment than he would have suspected for a hit-and-run cavalry unit. The scouts who captured him brought back the news that his brigade had seen the Confederate strength here and turned back. Well they should; this was no ordinary raid shaping up in this securely held town. An invasion was being mounted into the heartland of Indiana and Ohio. The ramifications of it all—the artillery he saw, the supply wagons, the thousands of eager, bright troops, made his heart sink.

The Rebel scouting party, secure in the knowledge that the Northern troops had turned back, dawdled after capturing him along the road, letting their horses graze and eating lunch from saddlebags. They offered him green apples and fried chicken prepared by the adoring women in a town last night; at first he declined the Rebel food, then smelling the chicken drumsticks, he asked for some and ate greedily. "You're already compromised, Jacob Joe," he told himself sadly.

Now in the late afternoon, he was escorted to the headquarters of General John Morgan. Guarded by a young man about his own age, who wore an odd, ragged uniform which could have been a Zouave's from early in the war, Jacob Joe waited, then waited some more in the hall of some sort of public building.

Finally, after sunset, the soldiers received word that General Morgan had left the building he had commandeered by a back door and was out at the cavalry camp on the edge of the city, among his own men, where he loved to be.

Twilight was settling over the camp when Jacob Joe was ushered into

Morgan's camp under guard. Around campfires, eating good food, were hundreds of cavalrymen in a variety of "uniforms," some in blue homespun, some in frock coats, some in farmers' overalls, some in the bright, new gray of home-outfitted Confederate infantry units. All were singing "The Sun Shines Bright on My Old Kentucky Home."

> *'Tis summer, the darkies are gay.*
> *The corn tops ripe and the meadow's in the bloom*
> *While the birds make music all the day.*

Surely it was this time of year that Foster had written that song, Jacob Joe thought dispassionately. At the end of each verse, the men gave a "hip hip, hooray" for General John Morgan. Well they should. He had brought over 2,000 men from Tennessee and Kentucky right into the bluegrass state, eluding the entire Union border army, and he would probably continue to do so, considering the disarray of the Northern generals and the size of the countryside. Yes, it was clear to Jacob Joe that this army was probably going to go wherever it wanted.

"A fine bay, nourished on Yankee oats," said a booming voice over by a smithy's fire. Jacob Joe cursed inwardly and watched the man who was advancing, sizing up his fine Northern mount. Morgan obviously, from all the fame they had of him: dapperly dressed in fine gray with gold braid, flashing good teeth in a smile six inches long. A real cavalier, with his eye on a fine horse. But this was his lieutenant's horse; how could Jacob Joe ever explain if Morgan took it? He would never go back to the regiment, of course, that was the promise he would make to get the standard military pardon, he thought sadly, but this fine horse—Colonel Brooks and Lieutenant Jophrey deserved it back.

"Sir, your name and rank?" Morgan demanded, standing before him with supreme confidence.

"Jacob Joe Scott, sir, Sergeant, Eightieth Indiana Regiment, serving under General Harmon, General Ambrose Burnside's command."

Morgan pulled on his mustachios. "Eightieth Indiana, you say. Scott is your name?" Jacob Joe nodded assent.

"What is your home neighborhood, sergeant?"

"From around Vincennes, sir."

"Ah. I have a new scout named Scott." Jacob Joe's heart froze, and Morgan continued, "I have not had the pleasure of meeting him, but from Tom Hines' description, I have it that he is blonde, curly haired, taller than you, but of an age. Have you relatives? A cousin, perhaps?"

"What is the given name of your scout, sir," Jacob Joe asked hesitantly. God in heaven, could it be—

"Zachary Scott of Vincennes. Do you know him?"

"He is my brother, sir," Jacob Joe said in a voice as dull as dust.

Morgan was silent for a moment, distracted by men handing him a plate heaped high with food brought in hampers and wagon loads by friendly Kentuckians. Someone pushed a plate at Jacob Joe; he gestured it away.

"Why then, sir," Morgan said, picking with his fork through watermelon pickles and short ribs, "you must also be a wealthy landowner with over a thousand acres, the recent heir to your father's fortune."

Jacob Joe was silent. How much did he have to tell this cavalier?

"You must also be from one of the most prominent families in both the Quaker church and southern Indiana." He looked at Jacob Joe with eyes like a woman's, the color of dusty mint. "Yes? You do not answer, but I think you are he. Interesting." He questioned Jacob Joe for a few moments, but easily discovered he had no knowledge past his own of the confused military state. "Eat your supper, sergeant. I command it."

Listlessly Jacob Joe picked at the fried chicken and pork barbecue, the baked beans and canned peaches. Any other time, he would have eaten this plate in six gulps, but now food choked him.

General Morgan walked about the circle of cavalrymen, laughing and clapping his officers on the back. Soon he returned, the crowd of jovial officers behind him, all carrying plates. "Sir, you are a valuable commodity for the Confederacy. We cannot let a fish like you get away." Jacob Joe's mouth fell open in disbelief. What was this? He had to be pardoned; it was the protocol these days. It couldn't be otherwise—

"We have another prisoner in camp. He is a lieutenant colonel we captured in the cavalry skirmish outside this town today. You will travel with him, and your party will pick up a third prisoner, this one a Confederate—an obnoxious Quaker—pardon, sir—" (he bent low and swept his feathered hat off into a ludicrous mock bow) "—a member of the Friends Church who refuses to serve in any capacity in the Confederate army, though we have tried him at several. He, too, is rich and prominent. Winslow"—here he gestured to a barrel of a man who was managing to out-eat all the rest— "that good horse of yours has been bearing too much weight with you on its back. I want to use it for one of the scouts." The officer looked crestfallen.

"Pick up one of the Indiana nags and take this—victim of the ill fortunes of war, this prisoner, under your command. You will escort him, the lieutenant colonel over there and the Quaker you meet later, to General Buckner in east Tennessee with my direction that they be taken on to Richmond."

"God, no, not to prison," Jacob Joe thought with an agonizing heart.

"I suggest they be put in Libby Prison or at the best, Castle Thunder, with the other prime plums we mean to exchange. Let them rot until that happens, or as far as I care, through the rest of the war there."

Jacob Joe could not suppress his outrage. "I should have a military pardon, I demand—"

"You will miss your dear relative by about forty-eight hours. He will be having a rendezvous near the Indiana border with Captain Hines right about now, and they will ride to meet us at the Ohio when we cross. Too bad your brother is not here to plead for you," Morgan said with narrowed eyes. "If he would. My own brother was killed not long ago by a bunch of Yankee bastards near Lebanon in this state, gallantly leading a charge. I have no sympathy for anyone who is a Yankee, brother or not. Prepare yourself to depart at dawn. Take him away, Winslow." He turned his back on Jacob Joe, and the portly captain came out of the crowd brandishing a pistol at him.

"So much for the cavalier spirit," Jacob Joe thought. "So much for my war career. So much for my wedding eve." He tossed the food the Southern belles and matrons had cooked into the fire. As he lay on the cool ground on a miserable blanket that night next to the other prisoner, whom he had barely spoken to, his only hope was that the reports they heard on the march were true. At this very moment troops were heading to encounter each other in central Pennsylvania, the great armies of Robert E. Lee and George Meade, now commanding the North. A great, awful battle could be looming, and even though he would not be in it or any other battle now, perhaps the cause he had joined to save would begin to prevail finally, after all the defeats.

And Harriet Houghton, at her home in Loogootee, all alone because her children were scattered to the winds on this beautiful summer evening, was visited by her niece Susie Niblack, who brought a letter. Mailed several days ago by Harriet's son Major Will Houghton, it said that the Fourteenth Indiana, the Army of the Potomac, was hurrying after Robert E. Lee, marching northeast of Lee to protect Washington from invasion, and that surely a terrible battle would ensue. Harriet sat down heavily and took from the mantel the little branch of laurel Will had sent her from Cheat Mountain early in the war. She did not really hear her niece as Susie told her that Will had been all right before and would be all right again and that they should pray for him, along with Lewis and Eustace and the rest in Kentucky with Morgan. Harriet continued to turn the little piece of laurel over and over as if it were a rosary, feeling its dry, rough leaves against her soft hand.

Catherine Hogue received a letter at her father's sixty-year old Revolutionary War land grant farm and took it out to the far hill to read. Her grandson John wrote in his hurried scrawl during the last week that the

Fourteenth was marching through horrible, hot dust and men were dropping of heat prostration, and he did not think he could go on because he was ill with fever, but he must. They all must endure, because this was the largest battle of the war and Lee must be stopped, no matter what it took.

Catherine Hogue looked out from the hill south towards the rise where her own farm, owned by strangers now, had been, and her eyes sought the site where John Hogue, her husband, had reared a log fort during the time of the Battle of Tippecanoe as her young brother marched off to fight, and she wondered why those she loved were always fighting in wars and how long men would go on killing each other in America.

Dawn Yet To Come of the Potawatomi, mother of Walter McClure, whom she called Little White Deer, was rehearsing for the Fourth of July parade in Peru, Indiana, when a newspaper was handed to her by a Miami from the riverside band. She took it in her hand, but did not glance up. She was responsible for getting "The Injeeans" together to march as a group, and she was irritated and despondent. The town had invited the remaining Miamis to march for the Fourth, and most of the Indian nation had been pleased. After all, had they not been left out before? Were they not living in America too? Did not their children speak English better than Miami dialect and go now to the free schools?

"Do not march like fools in their parade," Dawn, who was a member of the council now, and its first woman, said. "They have stolen our lands, forced our relatives to go west, broken all their treaties and now they want to be friends. But their friendship means treating us like slaves, hiring us only to clean out their barns, mocking us in this town and seeking us only when they want to know the best fishing holes or game snares. Besides, they want us to dress as Western Indians. Sioux! Wear the long feather headdress and leather skirts! They do not know or understand our embroidery or fine quill work."

But to no avail, and since she loved this band of "left behind" Miamis, she was helping them organize for their "performance." She looked down, finally, at the copy of the *Miami County Sentinel* that someone had placed in her hand. "Great Battle Looming in Pennsylvania," it said. "Indiana Regiments Are Marching to Certain Bloodshed." "Oh, my son, Little White Deer, in the Fourteenth Indiana troops," his mother thought fervently. "Take out the cross of your ancestress, Mulberry Blossom of the Ohio Band, that I gave you when you went to war. Put your hand on it and pray that the God who protected and saved you and me in the awful March of Death to the West and brought us here will save you now again to return to me."

Then to occupy her mind, she turned and put streaks of "play" war paint on a pretty four-year-old Indian girl who chattered happily of the band that would play soon and who did not know a word in the original tongue of her ancestors. "And may he may return to teach the people," she concluded "their birthright heritage."

Althea and Delia Dugger, travelling home on the train after the fiasco of cancelled wedding plans, heard travellers excitedly talking about Morgan the Raider's eluding the Federal troops and coming towards the Ohio, and about the telegraph reports that first shots had just been fired at a small village called Gettysburg.

Althea told herself not to worry about Calhoun. Put worries in the cedar chest and smile no matter what, that was what she had always done. In spite of all her brave sermonizing to herself, of course worries did creep in, especially when her guard was down. He had left without a word to her, and she had received only one letter from him since he had left to join the Twenty First Georgia. That was sent from Virginia, after a battle at Winchester, where the southern troops prevailed against northerners trying to stop the Confederate advance north. Calhoun emerged without a scratch. More she had not heard. Where was he? With Willie McClure and someone named General Doles, serving under General Rodes. Names only to her. The commanding general was Ewell, the crazy man people talked about, who looked like a goat. "Do you suppose they are in danger?" she asked aloud.

"Who?" Delia answered, absently watching the countryside in southeastern Indiana rush by the train windows.

"Are you woolgathering? There is a battle beginning in Pennsylvania. I mean your brother, of course, and Willie."

"I expect so. We are all in danger, mother," she said softly. "Some more than others."

Her mother looked at her curiously for a moment. Something in her tone—she really did not want to know what that was about, and so she did not ask. Put the questions in the cedar chest. She brushed cinders off her skirt and looked out the window.

*　　*　　*　　*

If Althea Dugger had wished to answer her questions about her son, she would have needed to go back a few days. As General Morgan had crossed the Cumberland, as Jacob Joe Scott had left with his regiment to chase him, and as Zach Scott had gone to meet the cavalry scout unit, Willie McClure and Calhoun Dugger were coming into Middletown, Pennsylvania, marching with Rodes' Division of Ewell's Confederate Army corps.

It seemed to Calhoun that he had been marching all his life, that he could not remember when he did not have blood blisters plastered with unguent and rags on his feet, when he was not sweating and swearing along a dust-choked road. He had lost twenty pounds and taken up tobacco chawin'.

He and Willie had a joke. It started when Calhoun came out in the first place to join the army, simply appeared, after much searching around among units in Lee's army who were returning after Chancellorsville to settle in the same place they'd occupied all winter. When he had been mustered in, and seen all the different kinds of uniforms and shoeless soldiers, he said, "Well, this isn't a real army, is it?'

"Waal, now what in the hell are you expectin', Sir Galahad, Napoleon Bonaparte and his Eagle flag?" Willie had laughed, and every time Calhoun encountered something new, Willie would joke, "Well, is this real hard-tack? Is this a real privy pit? Is this a real Northern holster?"

When they fought at Winchester on the way into Pennsylvania recently, Calhoun had taken it up again. "This don't appear to be a real battle," he had said, as shells rocketed about and horses reared and died to belie his words.

When they retired with a victory in their pockets Willie, in high spirits, had said "Naw, that weren't a real battle."

But the Twenty First Georgia was a real marching unit. That much was obvious to Calhoun now. On June 22, after they cleared out the Shenandoah Valley so Lee could start marching north, Ewell led his troops across the Potomac. Then they had marched through Pennsylvania to the stares and rude comments of the rustics along the old road from Chambersburg to Harrisburg. "We're going to harvest Harrisburg," Ewell had said, thinking of the rich farmlands in the northern city, ripe with food for both men and animals.

"My grandpa, Archie McClure, used to talk about this neck of the woods," Willie told Calhoun as they marched into Carlisle. "Said his pa, William, had grown up here, outside Carlisle. Somewhere called Conodoguinet Creek. Funny how we go in circles, ain't it? Here I am comin' back to the old stompin' grounds."

Not for long. As the refreshed, eager troops prepared to take Harrisburg, word came from Lee that Yankees were somewhere in the vicinity and they must be prepared to go find them. The trouble was no one knew exactly where the Northerners would show, not even Robert E. Lee. Now, as they marched into Middleburg in the early morning of July 1, 1863, they still did not know where they were going.

"I don't think Ewell knows a tad more'n we do," Willie said, wiping dust from his mouth, off his very teeth. "He has his heart set on fightin'

Yankees whenever they appear, but he's so crazy you don't know whether he's a-gonna do it with spy balloons droppin' cannon balls from the sky or come up the Susquehanny in canoes.''

"I don't know why I couldn't have served under Stonewall," Calhoun murmured. "When I came out, I hoped for glory."

"Wall, it must be around here someers," Willie answered. He looked at Calhoun shrewdly. They had been friends since they were three years old, and there was very little about Calhoun Dugger that Willie did not sense. "Tain't like you to fight, I know that well enough. Who you takin' the glory back to?" he asked.

Calhoun took off his wide felt hat and wiped his forehead. "Delia," he said. "Sure not Ma. She don't know what I'm doin.' But I want Delia to think well o' me. That's why I wanted to fight with Stonewall. But this new man, Ewell—"

"Waal, this 'un has character, you go to admit. Drinks buttermilk all the time for his stomach, stumps around on his wooden leg till he rubs the stump raw, cusses worse'n an old whore."

Ewell was riding with their corps, with his favorite general Rodes. Ewell travelled in a buggy, back in the van, since he lost his leg. Calhoun turned his head and reported, "Hey, that's a courier from headquarters," he said, noting a rider approaching Ewell's buggy. "Rodes is stoppin' the column."

The long line of troops which had started down the road slowly braked to a stop and stood while the courier delivered his message. Minutes passed. There seemed to be some sort of hubbub. Turning their heads to the rear, Willie and Calhoun could see the general reading the dispatch, looking up to talk to the courier, reading it again.

Soon orders were barked up and down the line. Couriers began to scurry. A.P. Hill had found the Yankees west of Gettysburg. The van took up its line of march to rush to his aid. Soon the general was riding past on a sorrel mare, his wooden leg jutting awkwardly out of the stirrup.

"Well, at least he ain't goin' by balloon or in a canoe," Willie said dryly, as he watched Ewell take his position at the head of Rodes' Division.

With the sound of their own pounding feet all around them the troops advanced. Then, as they neared the town of Gettysburg, they halted. In the stillness of apprehension they stood panting, trying to wipe sweat from their faces with sleeves. They murmured to each other, hearing the boom of cannons to the front. Rodes turned his division off the road, onto a ridge and deployed Doles' brigade on the left. The brigade spread out, surged forward and came over a small rise.

"Damn," said Willie. There, lying before them was the army of Confederate General A.P. Hill, already fully engaged with thousands of Yankees across a series of rises near the town of Gettysburg. Artillery roared; men in butternut fired at men in blue, and some were so close they were engaged in hand-to-hand combat.

Ewell's men had unexpectedly come up on the flank of the Union army and were in an excellent spot to turn the battle for the Rebels. The Twenty First Georgia listened, nerves pulled taut, for General George Doles' commands to their colonel to rush into action.

"I think we may have a real battle on our hands, Calhoun," Willie said.

"A real battle, Willie," his friend murmured, and held his rifle at the ready.

July, 1863

Chapter Fourteen

Forced march! The Union Army command spread the word to its advancing units in the Army of the Potomac that Reynolds' First Corps was desperately engaged with Hill's forces on the edge of a small town called Gettysburg. Lige Cavins and Colonel John Coons urged the exhausted veterans of the Fourteenth Indiana forward through the sweltering heat towards the town.

They came to Harney, Pennsylvania, their long lines marching at a brisk pace through the village street. Major William Houghton, astride his slate-gray horse, watched women in long bonnets pointing up and down the road. "La," said one, "Lincoln's men are a-comin' at us from both sides."

Sure enough, a small Federal train was retreating, coming into Harney from the other side of the town nearest Gettysburg. Colonel Coons called to Houghton, "Major, ride to see what that train of wagons is about."

Houghton rode forward and found an ambulance van. "Who's inside?" he inquired of a grim-faced adjutant accompanying the van.

"Major General John Reynolds, commander of the First Corps," the man told him.

"He—is—wounded?" Houghton asked apprehensively.

"Dead. Killed in the battle. The First Corps is still bravely holding the position, with only 5,000 men or so. You must hurry."

Houghton nodded his thanks and guided his horse back to the Fourteenth.

It was mid-afternoon when the Gibraltar Brigade arrived at Gettysburg.

"We're here, wherever here is," John McClure said tiredly to Joe Roseman. "I thought I was going to have to get into the ambulance wagon the last five miles."

Roseman wiped his face with the rough rag he called a pocket handkerchief. "It's shit having to get ready to fight when you're sick."

"Well, I'm not going to go on report," McClure countered. He was breathing deeply, trying to ignore the cramping in his stomach. He'd been to the woods several times on the march and then hurried to catch up, adding to the pain in his gut. "I don't care what anybody says. I've spent half the war ridin' sick with the baggage wagons," he said defiantly.

"Surgeon Burkhart has been watching you," Roseman told McClure. "He saw you puke in the woods. The Sanitary Commission's been on the generals. You know he can't allow you to be in the ranks sick."

"When they send the Fourteenth in, I'll be there. Don't look for me to be the last possum out of the woods," McClure said. Abruptly he ran behind a tree.

"Thank God Hancock is here. He is making a splendid show in force with the first part of our corps," Van Dyke told Houghton and Beem. The Gibraltar Brigade was standing in the road, waiting for the generals to deploy them. Van Dyke was acting as adjutant. He had just taken a message to headquarters for Colonel Coons. "General Hancock has chosen a hill in front of the town," he pointed, "beyond those woods there. You can't see it. He's beginning to deploy the corps."

"Why are the Rebel generals hesitant?" Houghton wondered. 'They have just won the first phases of this battle, yet they are not pressing us—"

"God only knows. If I were commanding I'd have taken those two hills in back of the town an hour ago even if it meant losing half my men. Whoever has that high ground has the battle," Van Dyke said. Then he added, "By the way, Beem, Coons wants your company battle flag. Do you still have it?"

"Yes. 'Tis folded away and I've carried it ever since the ladies presented it in Spencer the first week of the war," Beem said, with a slightly ironic smile, remembering. "We all thought we'd need a flag for each company— among other delusions."

"Well, our regimental flag is in tatters, and Coons wants to use H Company's for the advance tomorrow."

"All right. On the condition that Norris can carry it. He's the worthiest man I know, and his mother worked to make the flag. I'll send it up in a little while. Meanwhile, Coons' orders are for us to hold here until orders arrive for specific deployment, right?"

Van Dyke nodded assent and galloped off on his courier duties.

It was so swelteringly hot that the tar which had been put on the road to stay the dust was melting; men were upending canteens and swatting flies which lit and clustered thick in this cow country.

Houghton dismounted to allow his horse to nuzzle the rich, emerald grass of Pennsylvania. "We've been heading for Richmond for three years," Houghton mused. "Now we have finally decided to go for the Confederate army instead. And I think we've found them," he murmured.

"Yes," Beem said, turning his head to look at the long line of troops coming down the road behind them. "What do you suppose the plan will be?"

"It depends on what the Johnnies do," Houghton said. "There's a strange sort of lull here that I don't understand. But then I've never understood a lot of what the Rebels do," he sighed. "I'm to ride up on an observation hill to take a look, with Coons. We'll be with General Harrow."

"Harrow! It's been many a month since we've seen his snarling face," Beem said with a slight smile. "Odd to think he's commanding another brigade in our own corps."

"It's a good thing they didn't put him in command of our brigade when Kimball went home. I think the men would have mutinied. He's a good soldier, but—"

"Much too harsh," Beem finished. "And he has about as much sense of honor as a woodchuck."

"Maybe. Colonel Carroll does have honor. I'm glad they advanced him out of our ranks to that spot. Even if he was from the Ohio regiment. I trust him almost as much as I did Kimball."

"Van Dyke's been hanging about, finding means to speak to Harrow," Beem said. "Currying favor again, right in the midst of all of this."

"Of course. The sun still shines, doesn't it?" Houghton asked wryly. He was silent a moment. All thoughts these hours led to the battle ahead. "The army seems to be knit together, anyway. We are better led than we were at Chancellorsville. With Hooker gone, and General Meade in the saddle commanding—anyway, I'll know more of the lay of the land for what's coming here when I return from the officers' reconnaissance."

The group of Northern officers and staff dismounted and stood looking down over a valley which separated Rebels from Yankees. "There—there the sons-of-bitches are," Harrow said. "We are seeing the men of General Richard Ewell and General A.P. Hill. Fresh from victory, the bastardish swine."

He pointed down to the distant, milling mass of butternut-clad soldiers, some hauling artillery around and pitching tents, some standing as if awaiting orders, others grouping for some type of action. There was scattered sniper fire in the air. From this eminence, just behind the Rebel forces, Houghton could make out a battlefield strewn with the bodies of horsemen, officers, and enlisted men in blue and gray, death having shown no partiality.

"We are investing that large hill over there," Coons said.

"Yes. Thank God Hancock had the fortitude to snatch it with the few men he had. Why Ewell didn't order it seized—'' Harrow did not finish. Bullets began to whistle through the clearing.

"My God, sir, step back," Coons said in a loud voice.

"There's some sort of attack beginning again in that wheatfield down there," Houghton shouted. At that instant a ball whistled by Harrow's ear. He laughed and led his horse back a few paces into the trees.

"Did you see what that goddamned sniper did to me?" he asked Coons. "Advanced all the way from a captain to a brigadier-general, and now the motherfucker wants to end me with a bullet before I get to command here. We'll see about that."

Quickly the officers re-mounted. Houghton looked down at the wheat field one more time, at Rebels hotly pressing retreating Northern soldiers. "Some of the Secesh down there don't seem to be giving up," Houghton said to Harrow, "even if their officers are."

When they reached the foot of the hill Harrow handed a folded sheet of paper to Houghton. "By the way," he said, "this is the promotion Captain Van Dyke has been pressing me for. Pushy and as obnoxious as the Devil's hind end, that young man is. If he wasn't such a fine officer—well, I've put him on my staff. Reckon there'll be two of us. Tell him he doesn't have to report immediately; if he prefers to stay with his company, I'm certain they can use him more than I can tomorrow."

They swung into their saddles and rode off the observation hill and out of immediate danger from southern bullets.

"Christamighty, looks like we're stuck up to the axle," shouted Willie McClure. His face was as begrimed as a coal miner's, and he was temporarily half deaf. General Ewell's forces had crashed down on the Yankees just north of Gettysburg, pushing through confusion, awful fire and artillery shelling. Finally Doles' Brigade had turned the tide and sent the Yankees fleeing. They pursued them almost through the town. After all the action, though, the Southerners were now stalled amidst Gettysburg's stone and frame buildings awaiting further orders.

"Epworth, why doesn't that bald-headed bastard Ewell order us forward?" Willie demanded. He was sitting on a stump, hunched over, exhausted.

"There aren't many of the Yanks arrived yet," Calhoun added. He was standing by in the street, turning a plug of tobacco over and over in his hand to relieve his anxiety. He was still panting deeply from the exertions of the last hour and a half, and he, too, looked up at Epworth with outrage.

"Our brigade already killed more'n a thousand of the Yankee reserves as they came out from Gettysburg and we can kill more," Willie insisted hoarsely. "Just let us loose. I've advanced and loaded and aimed and run over these God-damned hills until I can't hardly move, but I'll still go forward if it means we can take the heights." Willie pointed past the town at the ridge of bumpy hills.

"I don't rightly know why we're stuck here, boys," Boone Epworth, now a sergeant, said. "Maybe Ewell's afraid, maybe he's jest obeyin' Lee's orders. As usual, Marse Robert's orders are as polite as a ball invite and jest as indirect. Still, this afternoon General Ewell is like a skittery raccoon. Been that way ever since Second Manassas. Can't seem to make up his mind and has odd impulses since he lost his leg. So they say."

"Well, we're all goin' to lose our legs and everything else if he doesn't buy back some of his courage," Willie maintained. "Jackson would have been lookin' down at the Yankees from the top of that cemetery hill by now."

"Stonewall," Calhoun said, reverently savoring the word while he tamped his finger on the tobacco.

"This ain't Jackson by a long shoot," Epworth said. "Still, we have another day to fight."

"Right," Willie retorted. "An' I don't want to do it straight up those hills with Yankees potshootin' from the top."

At that moment General Richard Ewell himself rode into town, and Calhoun and Willie and Boone Epworth found themselves caught up in a victory celebration, as men from different Southern regiments who had chased the Yankees back crowded around their leader's horse. Strong voices rang around Calhoun and Willie:

"Sir, we sent 'em skedaddelin'."

"Sir, did you see us turn and change fronts? General Doles was riled and rarin'."

"Sir, we found this wine in a basement over there—" the soldier pointed across the town square. "Have a swig on us."

"They weren't supposed to loot," Willie murmured from back in the crowd. "What'll he do?"

"Nothin'," Calhoun grunted. "He's not goin' to spoil a golden moment like this." He was right; Ewell demurred, smiling a little. There was noise from the right and the crowd parted to let someone pass. A brigadier general was shouldering his way through the milling Rebel soldiers.

"Who's that?" Calhoun wanted to know.

"Someone from Early's Division," Epworth said. "I've seen him—" he leaned to ask other soldiers. "It's General Haynes, sho' nuff. His face is red as a boiled beet."

The brigadier's voice was angry as he spoke to General Ewell. "General, when are you going to attack the Federals on the hill south of town?"

The crowd of jubilant soldiers calmed down to listen to what their chief would say. They were wondering the same thing. The rumor had been circulating that Lee had ordered them to stop advancing. Perhaps Ewell would talk about those orders now. He raised his hand in a conciliatory manner.

"Won't you Louisianans ever have your bellyful of fighting? Can't you let even a day—"

Haynes hardly let him finish. "I want to attack now! To prevent the slaughter of my men tomorrow."

Ewell looked somewhere between resigned and perplexed. He seemed about to speak again, but an aide approached him and said something urgently.

Epworth leaned towards Calhoun and Willie. "Probably tellin' him it ain't safe in this town. Sniper's bullets are flying in some parts like hail. There—they're a-leading' Ewell off. They got a house for his headquarters. But he still didn't answer the question. Why ain't we up there and the Yankees down here?"

Calhoun took a chaw. "The answer to that is with Mad Dick Ewell himself. But I 'spect we'll get a real battle tomorrow," he said sardonically, "if the general can find his balls somewhere over there in the headquarters house."

A strange, discontented quiet settled over the two armies. The Northern army's General George Meade used the evening and nighttime hours to secure the high line of rises called Cemetery Ridge. Southern generals fumed and argued and tried to develop a fail-proof plan. Finally each and every one of them understood and agreed upon the plan of Robert E. Lee: a two-pronged attack to split the army, seize the artillery and break the lines.

And so daybreak came, and the front thundered into action, action so dramatic and poignantly intense that the simple rural places around Gettysburg where the battle raged became touched with tragic greatness. Ever afterwards the names of those simple meadows and hills and the men who led the struggles on them were intoned with the reverence of an epic: Hood sweeps through Devil's Den to Little Round Top to be repulsed; McLaws sweeps through Peach Orchard and Wheat Field; Rebels almost break through the middle of the Northern line and the First Minnesota captures the colors in a brave, doomed, counterattack and finally, Ewell fails to take Culp's Hill.

In none of the drama of the second day did Willie and Calhoun and the Twenty First Georgia, or John McClure, Beem, Houghton and Van Dyke and the boys of the Fourteenth take part. Their part of the drama, or was it their destiny, awaited in the hot, smoke-filled dusk of the evening, when the unbelievable day reached its climax.

Tension began to mount earlier in the day for the Fourteenth. They had stood about, on reserve, as the troops clashed.

There was a sense that they were involved in the grandest event of the war so far, and they spoke not of trivial, but of philosophical things as they lounged behind the lines. "What is the most difficult part of honor?" Beem asked, as a part of the eternal discussion the unit had on the subject.

"To keep your legs from running when everyone else is high-tailing in a retreat," Isaac Crim offered. He was now a corporal and more likely to speak to officers than he had been.

"Well, that is difficult," Beem conceded. His eyes were flicking about, taking stock of the different geological formations in the odd out-croppings around him. Granite—even some basalt. The round-topped hills they had secured—could they be ancient volcanos? It had sounded like volcanos exploding earlier in the day. The crack-crack of gunfire split the air from time to time, but now the big cannons were silent.

"Honor is doing a duty off somewhere where nobody sees but God, just because it is a duty and helps the cause," Houghton said. He was leaning against a tree. He had been thinking that he had not said goodbye to his mother. If it was goodbye.

"What do you think, Captain Beem?" Crim asked. "Honor is your strong suit."

"Well, I think it must be to look an individual man in the eye, or at least to see him, and then decide to kill him because it is your duty."

"Nobody has to do that in this war."

"Not usually. We line up, the bands play, we shoot half a mile and somebody drops. Or the cannon-stuffers jam in a ball, ignite and wham-mo—some mother's son out of sight gets his head severed right off."

"Out there right now they are so close that the gun barrels almost touch," Houghton said, looking quietly over the brown fields. "So close their bullets fuse, if they're fired at exactly the same instant."

"Yes," Beem answered, looking up quickly into his friend's eyes. "Today has been different, so the men coming in from the lines say. I don't think I could muster the anger to kill a man I could see. Then, instead of him being the enemy, and I an avenger in a righteous cause, he would be a man, and I a Christian faced with disobeying the murder commandment."

"Pshaw, sir," Crim told him, "a Rebel is a Rebel. Put you face to face with a Rebel and you'll remember Fredericksburg and Chancellorsville and the Copperheads back home. And you're the one who's always tellin' us 'bout rememberin' Bo Reilly and Ham Mitchell and the rest. You could kill face to face if you had to."

"Do you think so, Crim? Do you think I could get angry enough?"

"For honor's sake, sir, you could."

"Perhaps. I wonder."

Van Dyke rode up on his horse. He had been afoot, as an officer of G, helping ready his company for reinforcing the line if they were called. Houghton looked up. Van Dyke was brushed up. He had trimmed his beard and washed. What—

"I have received a promotion to General Harrow's staff."

"I know," Houghton nodded. He had, of course, been the one to bring the letter, although they had not until now discussed its contents.

"I am going to ask Colonel Coons to replace me as officer today as of now."

Houghton was dismayed. "Now, Gus?"

Van Dyke swung out of the saddle and tied his horse to talk to Beem and Houghton. He kept his voice low. "Nothing's happening here, and I don't want to hold a reserve position in one of the great battles of this war. I will be with Harrow, in a command position, seeing it all, in the midst of glory. You can surely understand that," he said earnestly eyeing his fellow officers.

Houghton was not satisfied. "All I understand is that you are leaving your company at the moment they need you most. You are to command G today and nobody else can do it. Landon is still in the hospital in Washington. The other lieutenants are weak sisters."

"Coons will find someone to cover my spot," Van Dyke said coolly. "That's his job."

Beem frowned and shook his head in disapproval, but then he usually disapproved of Van Dyke. It was Houghton who always mollycoddled him—but no, here was Houghton surging forward, right into Van Dyke's face, confronting him as he had never dared before.

"Gus, G Company is one of the keystones of this whole brigade. They have been our finest company since the Fourteenth left Vincennes. General Carroll will depend on them, and the men in G depend on you. You know how reduced they are with sickness. The surgeon has ordered McClure and Thompson and I don't know how many more to stay back with the wagons—G's morale is precarious."

"You're blowing this all out of proportion, Will," Van Dyke said in an uncertain, high voice. He was looking towards the horizon, where the sun was moving lower in the sky. Sunset would be in a couple of hours. He needed to mount and ride for Harrow's nearby command soon if he was going to see some of the action today.

"Gus," Houghton went on, his voice like coarse sandpaper, "the Rebels are going to have to try to seize that cemetery hill. Our guns are there, and if they can destroy those guns, they can destroy our strength. Like as not our generals will call on the brigade to go in, as they always do, to pull the fat out of the fire.''

"And?'' Van Dyke climbed back into the saddle. He swung his leg over, showing handsome boots he had managed to secure, someway, out here in the midst of a battle.

Suddenly a tremendous shock wave of artillery rent the air. The Rebel guns above the field had begun a bombardment.

Houghton went to Gus Van Dyke, looking up into the strikingly handsome face that was as cold as that of an equestrian statue's. Houghton had to raise his voice to be heard over the cannons. "Each officer is needed at this crucial juncture of the battle, and the war. You must know that.''

The artillery din increased. The Northern guns on Cemetery Hill answered the Southern cannons. Beem had been silent, watching the emotional scene play itself out.

"What about honor, Van Dyke?'' he now asked, his mouth an enigmatic line.

Van Dyke looked across Houghton at David Beem. "Honor!'' he snarled. "There is more to life than honor. You both live for this miserable unit, as if it were all the world. The Fourteenth. Its glory! Its esprit de corps. As if it were some sort of living, breathing animal. Well, I say I have a life to lead and after three years of existing through this war, I tell you it's an empty word. I've seen too many men die stupidly for officers that have their brains in their hind ends. Honor is just five letters that spell futility! Go to hell, with your honor.''

Houghton put his hand on the stirrup. "Gus, stay just until tomorrow's action is over. See the men through this. In the name of friendship. I don't usually beg—''

Van Dyke did not look at him. "Don't beg, Will. It mars your good-looking smile.'' He turned his horse and rode off.

Ewell called up Doles' brigade as soon as the Southern bombardment began. Willie and Calhoun moved out, slinging canteen straps over their shoulders.

"We have to bend our asses,'' Epworth told the men. "They're trying to dislodge the Yankees from the top-most spot. Being in this goddamned town has put us on the far edge of the advance. We'll have to dogtrot to even get to the battle. They'll be storming the cemetery hill, maybe the others—''

"Glory,'' Calhoun breathed, grasping his musket tightly.

"C'mon. We'll give 'em what we gave 'em at Chancellorsville,'' Willie said and advanced, rushing like a steam engine down the road towards the battle.

The sun had set; the heavy air was humid, almost suffocating, and heat seemed to radiate from every rock the Fourteenth passed. The regiment advanced through the smoky, leaden twilight, led by Corporal Isaac Norris of H Company, bearing the Stars and Stripes of Spencer, Indiana. To the right were the sister regiments of the Gibraltar Brigade, Eighth and Eleventh Ohios and Seventh West Virginia.

"The Rebels are taking the guns on Cemetery Hill now," Coons had told the Fourteenth ten minutes ago. "We are the unit chosen by Hancock to go in and stop them!"

Bursts of musket fire all around lit each face. No one said a word; the grim, determined veterans of the workhorse regiment were on cleanup duty again, and if they had emotions, they kept them to themselves. The men advanced on the double quick, the new, experimental, breech-loading rifles French had given them after Chancellorsville at the ready, and began crossing an old cemetery.

Beem's mind caught at flimsy fragments as it always did when he entered these battles. "Those bursts of fire on the hill, like Spencer on the evening before the Fourth of July," he thought. They were passing through a peaceful churchyard with small children's graves. Would he ever father, know his child? There was a gravestone, with dim writing but he could see—Jacob Heidenreich, Revolutionary War soldier, "Born Homburg, 1740, died Battle of Trenton, 1776." So, had he also fought his own countrymen from Hesse? His cousins, as they were? It was hard. But his schoolteacher in Spencer had said the Battle of Trenton saved the Revolution. We all owed these sleeping bones some thanks. Would anybody ever thank him and the others in the regiment?

They approached the Rebel Hill. General Sprigg Carroll's voice, guiding them, boomed out of the darkness ahead.

Rebel gray was thick at the top of the hill, among Ricketts' Northern batteries. The Rebs were taking the crucial guns of the entire Northern defense at Gettysburg. There was hand-to-hand fighting over the gun carriages. Musketry was a solid blaze in the advancing Fourteenth's faces.

"The Johnnies'll sweep around to the rear and take the whole Northern line! Who's defending?" Beem shouted to Houghton several yards to his side.

"The Eleventh—the Germans," Houghton called to him. Visions of the frightened dash of the Eleventh at Chancellorsville flashed into Beem's head. Forward, forward, gunfire, artillery shells, men falling, screams, horses neighing—but there was something down in front! It was the colors!

Beem rushed forward. Norris, brave, confident Norris from the outskirts of Spencer, was bleeding profusely from a Minie ball in the head. Blood poured over his hand, onto the flag his mother had made. The flagstaff was shattered. Someone else came forward for the flag; Beem lay the young man down. Nothing he could do here; they must advance. He looked up to see the artillery horses' heads being turned to be taken down the hill by Southerners. Was no infantry regiment staying to defend these guns?

Suddenly men began rushing past again, coming down off the hill, with strange galloping strides. The Eleventh Corps was retreating, again.

Immediately, intense anger flooded through Beem. Norris dead and these bastards retreating. He hated, hated them. Sweat coursed down his face, and his nostrils were filled with the smell of powder and the fresh blood he could not wipe entirely off his hand. He hated this unspeakable war that sent some young men he cared about out to die in the name of honor and others to retreat and live in ignominy. He cursed, for the first time in his life, a string of oaths at the outrage of the war. His hatred was strong and vital, a living presence, and, strangely, he savored it. At that moment a captain of the Eleventh came in sight.

Beem collared the man and looked into his blanched, thin face. "Now you listen to me," Beem said drawing his sword. "You are going back to the line, right up there, or I will run you through with this sword. Do you hear me? I will kill you on the spot."

The officer saw the rage and determination in this odd little man's eyes and nodded. He turned and began to stride wearily up the hill again. The men of G Company had stopped in their tracks, watching the Eleventh. Some of the Gibraltar Brigade were new recruits; they hesitated at the peril directly above them. One of G's weak-sister lieutenants had fallen, wounded; the sergeant behind him was immobilized.

Damn Van Dyke; he was probably riding his horse around looking at the action with a spy glass while his men faltered. "Men of G, remember the honor of the regiment!" Beem urged; soon Houghton came forward to aid in getting them up the hill. Forward, forward through the blistering gunfire— the Hoosier yell—

Answered! A cheer from above! Beem could make out Northern cannoneers—men staunchly defending their own guns with clubs and captured rifles. They were cheering the Fourteenth on. Ricketts, their own commander charged up on horseback, "Hold my guns, men, don't let these bastards have the cannon!"

And now the Fourteenth and its sister regiments were near the crest, near the guns—Carroll's voice ordering a volley, Coons ordering a charge—

Rebels, finally seeing they could not hold the position turning and retreating, in the very face of the Northern muskets. How they loathed giving up the fight!

"Brave Confederates," Beem shouted to Houghton.

"The men of Jubal Early, I think," Houghton called to him and turned to receive a Rebel captain who almost bumped into him.

"Men, we have some candidates for our Indiana prisons," Colonel Coons shouted from his snorting bay horse and ordered the men to seize the colors and round up the remnants of the Twenty First North Carolina, which in honor's name had waited just too long to retreat.

"Captain, I told you that you could hate enough to kill on the spot," Crim said a few moments later, as they dipped their canteens in the spring they had just captured. "I saw you with the German."

Beem upended his canteen, wiped his mouth and answered, "Yes, I can hate enough. All of these men could—" He gestured about at the artillerymen splashing their completely blackened faces with water from the spring, the stretcher-bearers trying to get a drink of water into wounded men's mouths.

The smoke was thick enough that they could not see more than three or four feet around them, but from somewhere behind a tree nearby they could still hear the booming voice of their brigadier-general, Sprigg Carroll. He seemed to be talking to a staff officer from headquarters.

"The line is secure, but why in the name of God doesn't Howard get his troops back up here and protect these guns? We could lose the whole line and with it the battle and war—"

"General," the staff officer said, "our troops are very much demoralized, and General Howard doesn't believe they can be depended upon."

"Why doesn't he come up here and inspire them? Don't let them cower like a flock of sheep up there behind the batteries!"

The officer tried to lower his voice a little, aware that their voices were carrying "—ran like sheep, and so he has no confidence in them."

"God damn a commander who says he has no confidence in his men!" Carroll's voice rose, wrathful and ringing. "Hancock ordered me in here to secure this line and I have done so. But I have no real authority in this corps. Tell your commander to either support me or relinquish his command. If I had authority here, I'd resurrect things faster than hell could scorch a feather. And if I had him here, I'd kill him. I hate such cowardice, I tell you!"

The voices faded and Beem and Crim turned from the spring. "Yes, the war has made us all hate machines," Beem said, ruefully. "And what is more, I think that is just about what it will take to win it. Nothing else will do.''

They made their way down to Norris. "We will bury him where he fell," Beem said to the men of H. "Perhaps some day we will come again and mark his grave. I do not think we will forget where he lies."

"Shit, we got to the party after the cake was et up," Willie said disappointedly as the Twenty First Georgia finally reached the battlefield. All kind of action had taken place on Cemetery Hill; as they rushed up they could see the musket fire and hear the shouts. But all was still now, and General Doles was halting the panting, sweating lines.

"Well, there's sure to be somethin' big tomorry," Epworth told his two comrades. "They'll plan another party, that's for certain."

"Glory Day," Calhoun said and watched far-away sniper fire, like the luminescent burst of fireflies, on the hills beyond them.

Glory Day was slow in getting started the next morning, July 3, 1863, and the Gibraltar Brigade waited apprehensively for the sound of cannon or signs of a Rebel advance. Still stationed with Howard's corps near the cemetery, the regiments in the brigade worried that they were not near enough to the rest of the army to be involved in the main action. Still, almost all day long, like the rest of the Federal troops, they played cards, they joked nervously, they sat and hugged their knees in the sweltering, oppressive heat. What would Lee do? Surely some great attack was imminent.

As the armies awaited battle, John McClure and Walter McClure idled with the wagons behind the lines in a village near Gettysburg. Because they had been taken ill late in the march, the surgeon wished them to remain one or two more days off duty so their recuperation from a bout with the fever would be complete. Tommy Thompson was in one of the wagons across the clearing, sleeping.

The two McClures had hardly spoken a word to each other in the several months the army was at Falmouth. But now they found themselves together here, under the same elm tree about two o'clock in the afternoon. The concern they shared for the regiment made them break their mutual silence.

"What have you heard about the fight?" John said, scratching his initials with a stick in the ground.

"A corporal from the Eighth Ohio came in with broken wagons this morning," Walter said, without looking at the other man. "He said the

Secesh tried to storm Culp's Hill for three hours this morning but finally withdrew. He said their bravery surprised everyone.''

''I don't know why they were surprised,'' McClure mumbled. 'They have as much, or more bravery than we do. They just don't have any shoes or food. Now what will they do?''

''Storm the hills with all their army. Truly a brave plan. And a foolhardy one.'' Walter McClure shifted his weight. His bones hurt from the fever he'd had. But he was better, really he was. Surgeon Burkhart should at least have let him be a stretcher bearer—

''I s'pose it is a bad plan,'' John McClure said. He stood and, a little weak-kneed, leaned against the tree. ''It was at Fredericksburg, anyways.''

''There is a saying. 'If your enemy is on the hill, you must use brains, not weapons to get him off.' ''

John McClure gave Walter a withering look. ''Injeean saying, I s'pose.''

''Potawatomi. I learned it from my mother.''

''I thought so,'' McClure said scornfully. He bent down and picked up his customary stalk of timothy to chew on.

Normally, Walter McClure would have said nothing in reply to the strident, insulting tone in the other McClure's voice. But his bout with the fever had left him testy, weakened, not so much in body as in spirit. It was as if his rational spirit had hidden itself somewhere deep inside of him and now all that was left was his childish, emotional self. ''I do not like your tone,'' he said, standing and staring defiantly into John McClure's eyes. ''I am proud of being a tribesman.''

''I s'pose you are. But I don't know why,'' John McClure was as testy as Walter. ''Some people say Injeeans are a lower form of man. Ain't got developed like the rest of us.'' He spat green juice.

''Who are you to say? Have you known the tribal religion, which reveres decency and fairness and honesty? Have you known the gentleness, the peace, of people who have an ear for all the kinds of rain, who know the moods of clouds?''

''What in the hell is that supposed to mean?'' John McClure said. He had begun crushing the stalk of timothy, and now he threw it angrily to the ground.

''Never mind, you would not understand,'' Walter said darkly. Both men were silent, chewing on all the rancor of three years' standing between them, as if it were some kind of jointly-shared cud. Finally Walter spoke.

''Perhaps the saying about dislodging your enemy through cleverness comes from hard experience,'' he said in a oddly taunting voice. ''The whites in Piqua in Ohio in the 1780's knocked the Shawnees off their hill in a very clever way.'' John McClure did not answer.

Walter went on, ''They sneaked around in back and shot at women and children hidden in the rocks so the Indian men had to stop to defend their families.''

"That ain't the way I heerd it. My great-grandfather Dan'l McClure jest happened to be there,'' John McClure said, pounding his fist to emphasize his point. "Somethin' 'bout Injeeans burnin' the Caintuckians, homes and massacreein' innocent settlers. They were out for revenge on the Shawnees.''

Walter McClure paused, cleared his throat and continued his narrative. "Finally the Shawnee and a few Miami came out and stood in lines beneath their hill to make a last stand to protect their women and children. The white men shot them down like hogs.''

"Which was jest about right, as I figure it,'' John McClure said and spat into the weeds. "They stink like hogs and eat garbage—''

"God allow me to remain patient,'' Walter McClure prayed inwardly. "His attitude is really no worse than half the men brought up in Indiana.''

He continued: "After the battle, the white men mutilated the bodies of the brave fighters on the other side.''

"Well, that at least showed them that the Injeeans did have balls after all.'' John McClure chuckled unremorsefully, and Walter left off praying for patience. He looked at John with a sharp, bitter hatred that was as foreign to him as being ill this last week had been. Perhaps it was connected in some way, he thought in passing.

"Then the white men burned all the wheat fields that would have fed the women and children and so the Indians starved.''

"If more of 'em had of done that we wouldn't have had half the problems we had in Indianney later—say,'' John said, then, suddenly wondering, "How come you know so much about that battle anyways? Piqua?''

"Well, how do *you* know so much about it?''

"I told you, Redskin,'' John said pointing his finger at Walter, "My great-grandpa Dan'l McClure, who was one of the finest men ever to have trod the earth and don't you forget it, was there. His brother was leadin' the Pennsylvanian Caintuckians and they won that battle.''

"Yes, they did.''

"I ast you how you knew all about this. You shore didn't read it in no McGuffey reader, if you can read.''

"I can read probably better than you, but that is not where I learned about the battle of Piqua. My great-grandfather was there, and the story has been passed down through my family, too, as a clan tale.''

Perhaps it was the heat of the day, and the disappointment of not being with the regiment. Perhaps it was the nature of the ague, which was supposed to make people irritable, or maybe it was just three years of having to get along with a bunch of men with their stinks and squeaks and oddities day and night. Whatever the cause, John McClure felt particularly ornery, like a thistle waiting for someone's legs to brush it. He yearned to provoke. "So at the Battle of Piqua, your stinking, heathen, son-of-a-bitch Indian great-grandfather—"

Walter, quietly simmering to a boil, answered crisply, "No, my stinking, heathen, son-of-a-bitch white great-grandfather—"

"Wait a minute. You got that wrong."

"I *got* that right. I am part white," Walter said.

John McClure was astonished. He stopped to consider this. Well, that could explain some things. Perhaps that was why this Redskin was so smart, why many people liked him so much. He had white blood.

"What was his name? Tell me," John McClure demanded, turning to face Walter squarely.

"Oh, Lord," Walter prayed silently, fingering Mulberry Blossom's crucifix, "Do not let me profane the ancestor of both of us by shouting his name for revenge, in anger," but his blood did not cool, because he did not really want it to, and he went on: "Shall I tell you the clan tale? Yes, I think so."

"How long is it?" John McClure asked impatiently. "I ain't got time to listen to some crapped-up Injeean hoo-haw about the Spirit of the Cootie or whatever."

"Oh, it won't take long." Walter rolled his eyes. He had decided to act the part of the cliché Indian of the travelling shows. He sat down, crossed his legs, and gestured for John McClure to do the same. Since John was tired, he complied. Walter patted his hand against his mouth. "Wa, wa, wa," he entwined. The power of revenge coursed through his veins; he was having a wonderful time.

"Once, many moons ago, in the hunting grounds of Ohio lived a band of Miami Indians. They were blessed by the Great Spirit, yes blessed with many quail and fine venison deer for their pots." John McClure was yawning.

"Outside their wigwam village, the Revolutionary War raged. The Miami Indians helped the British. But this particular band was pledged to support the Americans, and they went against the will of their tribe." John McClure looked over at Walter, mildly interested in spite of himself.

"Rising Star, bandchief, son of many bandchiefs, was the wise one of the tribe. His son, Hidden Panther, Kinozawia, welcomed American long hunters now and again."

"Get on with it, Redskin," John McClure said, shifting his weight in his sitting position on the ground. Flies were buzzing and biting. Perhaps it would rain tonight. What in God's name was going on at the battlefield?

"Hidden Panther had a sister, kin-close, beloved by all as a weaver of baskets. M'takwapiminji—"

"That's not a real name."

"Yes, John McClure. Mulberry Blossom in Miami. This lovely maiden, blessed by Manitto spirits, was very young. Still, she was not too young to love my white great-grandfather, when he came on the long hunt to Ohio. She loved him and of their union was born my grandfather, Asondaki Caipawa, Shining Morning Sun."

"Now there your story breaks down. No self respectin' white man would go into a strange camp and sleep with a Injeean girl. Everone knows they had the clap—I'm tired of this story, and I'm tired of you, Redskin." His attention had flagged, replaced by boredom, like a man who was throwing a stick for a dog and was now tired of it. It was as if he were talking to a sub-human, or a child. Walter saw bright red again.

"And so, this Revolutionary War hero who was my great-grandfather—"

"Revolutionary War hero, is it?" John McClure growled, leaning closer, his arms akimbo. "This Indian-screwing, butt-headed, flea-bitten asshole who was your great-grandfather—name of George Q. Washington—"

"This Indian-screwing, butt-headed, flea-bitten, asshole great-grandfather of mine, name of Dan'l McClure—"

John McClure was absolutely thunder-struck. His mouth flew open. Forgetting his bodily weakness, he got up from the ground and pulled Walter McClure to his feet. Walter did not resist. "Why you goddamned, lying, insulting crab. Use the name of my great-grandfather, one of the most respected names in the state. Mock me that way—you've been after me since rendezvous camp, taking my name, mocking me and why I don't know."

He began shaking Walter, who pulled away and trembling with anger, said in a low voice, "Tell me, John McClure, if you know what your great-grandfather's first, treasured hunting rifle was like. Do you know that?"

"What's it to you, Redskin?" John McClure said cautiously. "Maybe I do."

"It had a goose in flight on it. Made in Pennsylvania for Dan'l McClure's father, he gave it to my great-uncle Kinozawia in friendship. Does that sound like the rifle you have heard of?"

"Why you goddamned sneak, how did you know about that rifle? I'll teach you to insult the name of one of the finest men who ever lived—" He pushed Walter McClure to the ground and began pummeling him. Walter pummeled back and flipped John on the ground, delivering several blows to his face.

He held him down and spat in his face. "We had the same great-grandfather, Dan'l McClure. Your blood is in my veins, mine in yours. I have as much right to the name as you. So hate me, and hate yourself!''

John McClure grunted, pushed with his feet and flipped Walter over, and the two men crashed about amidst the underbrush, yelling and socking and cursing at each other, as Thompson and other sick men from the Union army arose from their pallets and struggled into the woods to try to stop them.

And as the two cousins fought, fifteen thousand Confederates under the command of General George Pickett roared the Rebel yell and advanced toward Federal positions at Gettysburg. They charged into walls of musketry and seas of artillery fire in an attack that shook the very ground. Thirty thousand men on both sides were fighting and dying that awful afternoon because, in the final analysis, they could not live peaceably. They had grown to hate each other so much they could think of nothing else to do but fight, though they shared common blood and heritage. And so, the sad fight between the two McClures, and Pickett's unutterably tragic charge and its repulse on the afternoon of July 3, were really in that way much alike.

Calhoun Dugger and Willie McClure were not at Pickett's charge; the Twenty First Georgia was not engaged. That night, in the aftermath of the awful battle, Willie and Calhoun were part of a detail which removed the wounded from the field, and from there to Oak Ridge, the scene of the first day's fighting, where the Confederate army would bivouac.

Calhoun stood on a little rise and surveyed the desolation. He drew in his breath. "No glory here," he said. "Only dead bodies and men shot to pieces. No glory at all." Sadly he and Willie began to walk towards those gray-clad men crying for help, as the drizzling rain began to fall on friend and foe alike.

*   *   *   *

Hoofbeats clattered down the dry-baked mud road leading north from the Ohio River in Indiana. Two thousand of John Morgan's Kentucky cavalrymen had just finished an early breakfast and were heading at a brisk pace towards the prosperous villages of the river valley.

Zach Scott rode beside Chief Scout Winder Monroe. They had not spoken much; Monroe was a man of few words, a Tennessee hill man, whose hands on the reins were as black as untanned leather. All last night at the conference Morgan had held with his odd assortment of officers Monroe had said little; he stood with one foot up on a cracker box, chewing tobacco and spitting it through the gaps in his teeth. The cavalry troops that had crossed the Ohio, including his own, were bivouacked all along this road. He was riding with Zach to collect his men, as the sun cast elongated shadows on the misty fields of tasseling corn and sorghum.

"Hoosier hospitality ain't much, is it?" Winder finally said.

"That miller was a fool," Zach said. "There was no good reason he shouldn't have accepted Confederate money for the barrels of flour the men took. Silly pride—"

"Well, pride goeth before a downfall, don't it? I hated to see the men torch them mill buildings. Must have taken a generation to raise sech quarters. But he rubbed their fur the wrong way. They were willing to pay justly for what they got, and he treated them like raiders."

"Aren't they?" Zach wanted to know. "They should have paid for the stuff with the money they took out of the Northern soldiers' letters." Along the river, Hines' company had found and opened bags of U.S. mail. Zach had not seen much of Hines himself; he was supervising the rear guard and baggage trains.

"Sure as hell don't like the word raider," Monroe said. "We have the Fourteenth Kentucky Regiment and other top drawer units."

"As well as reprobates out of prisons and fifteen-year-old boys who have run off from home."

"Well, all are joined in one cause—to take the war t' the North," Monroe sighed. "These Hoosiers don't know nothin' of what we've been through. This is the land of plenty, garden o' Eden. Every house we go by has a pot bubblin' on the stove. Fat hens stewin'. Light bread and apple pie on the windersills. The war is only a dream for these folks, made up out of newspaper stories they read while they eat hot biscuits and strawberry preserves and ask for more cream for their coffee. My men hain't had a taste of coffee for the best part of a year. They're hell bent on giving these fat farmers a smidgen of the trouble we've had."

"Well, it's happening in two places, then," Zach mused. "The people in Pennsylvania are getting to know the Rebel army in person, too, right at this moment."

Troops were coming in from side roads as the sun rose higher. "Maybe in one of these villages we're goin' to hit we can get a feel for how Lee is farin'," Monroe said. "The first word we had on the other side o' the river wasn't good, but the tide may have turned."

"Perhaps."

"We'll see how m' friends in Quirks' Scouts passed the night here," Monroe said, heading into the yard of one of the prosperous farms. "The Dean family, I seem to recollect their name was, hosted the pride of Tennessee." When he smiled the gaps in his teeth showed. Zach dismounted and headed for a rain barrel with a tin dipper to get a drink.

Young cavalrymen in the odd assortment of homespun and bluejeans that constituted scout "uniforms" were preparing to ride out with their chief.

Several were carrying crocks of preserves and hams from a smokehouse, as the enormous lady of the house waddled after them in distress. Zach took a drink from the dipper and then looked down at it. It had a fermented, whisky sort of a tang around its edges. He put it back on the lid of the barrel.

"Hurry up and get the victuals in the wagon," Monroe told the men, gesturing towards a baggage wagon with a long fingernail that looked more like a claw. The wagon was already piled high with sacks of flour, crocks of eggs, and tin milk cans. The men tossed ten huge hams on the top as the large woman shook her head a little. It had been a trying night, and there was hardly anything left in the house that could be eaten, worn or read.

Some men chased squawking chickens and turkeys about. "Whooee, got me some brandied peaches," one man with spectacles sang out as he capered about drinking from an open can. He was only one of several. Zach raised one eyebrow. The fruit cellar had been raided; that would explain the fruity dipper.

"Did you change the nags for better mounts?" Monroe wanted to know.

"Yessir," the peach man said, putting down his can. He pointed to eight horses just in the final stages of being resaddled with Confederate equipment. Then he gestured towards the barn. "We got a winner for you."

A beautiful roan stallion, resisting and pawing the ground, was being brought from the barn by two men in filthy leather clothing and slouch hats. "Sir, Mr. Scout," the red-faced woman said, looking apprehensively over her shoulder. "Don't let them take Pickaninny."

The fat woman dabbed at her face, lips, forearms, with a wet tea towel. Zach watched her as he remounted. He was afraid in this growing heat she might have apoplexy; her face was the color of a beet-dyed easter egg. "My man's not here, more's the pity. He got Pickaninny in Caintuck a month ago. Intends to run him at the Harrison County fair. Don't take him—" She began folding the tea towel, first in half, then in ever tighter squares, like a flag at sunset. Then she dabbed again, this time at her hairline.

"Thank you kindly, ma'am, Monroe said, tipping his hat to her. "We'll be right proud to have Pickaninny. We're leavin' you some fine full-blooded mounts, the pride of the Lexington bluegrass, I can tell you, for these Hoosier plow nags we got from you. Most of 'em will fall on their bellies two hours out of here." He gestured for the men to take the roan horse into line, and left the woman, weeping and dabbing, in a cloud of dust.

Zach picked his way into the cavalry line which was passing by the house. Harness jangled, Kentucky riding horses and Indiana farm horses neighed and snorted, and joyful men laughingly rode on their way to adventure and retribution.

In a few minutes Monroe craned his head to see through the dust ahead. "General Morgan's stickin' his head out of his carriage," the scout said. "Ride up and see what he's after."

Zach complied without much enthusiasm. He was fulfilling a job Willis Mawkins had assigned him, serving the Cause. Although he had come to like Hines and even Monroe, he could not stand John Morgan, whom he found as egotistical and posturing a man as he had ever seen. General Morgan's bravery he did not question, nor his leadership. He seemed to mesmerize his men, and some men from southern Indiana had already joined his grand sweep of the southern counties. Morgan was one of those men for whom life is a great drama, and he the leading actor. For men like this, supporting players are only necessary evils, backup people to the great performances of their lives.

Then, too, Zach could not forgive Morgan for the way in which he announced the news of Jake's capture. When Zach had come into the Ohio River camp, Morgan let Zach sit for over an hour before saying, casually, "Oh, by the way Scott, someone you know was in our camp a few days ago. You just missed him, I regret to tell you." Then he had gone on, without looking at Zach, about the "necessities of war" and "unfortunate need to provide exchange prisoners."

It wasn't that he thought Morgan did the wrong thing; after all, this was war, not a Sunday School picnic. Besides, he cut his ties with Jake long ago, even before they had argued in the cemetery. He pulled away from his brother when they were children, and his parents always viewed Jake as the Angel Gabriel and him as Beelzebub.

But he was insulted by Morgan, by his insolence, giving the news almost as an afterthought. Probably intended to put him in his place immediately. Morgan had a way of doing that to men of stature around him.

These thoughts had taken him to Morgan's carriage. "Sir?" Zach said, as Morgan again put his head out of the side curtains. Drat! John Hunt Morgan did have an inordinately ruddy, handsome face with drooping mustachios and the soulful eyes of a doe. Women all over the South and Indiana called for smelling salts when they saw this visage on the broadsheets.

"Are we approaching Corydon, Scott?" Morgan raised a ringed finger, showing the cuff of a clean shirt he always wore. His gray Rebel coat was brushed lintless each morning by doting sycophants who followed in his dust.

"Yes, sir. The first capital of Indiana. Now a sleepy village."

"Rich farmland?"

"Yes, general. You see it around you—" his hand swept past rolling fields with fat hogs feeding on corn, the stubble of newly harvested winter wheat and brown cows.

"Good, good." He looked past Zach. "They have a barricade up across the field which commands the town," he said, pulling on one of his long mustachios.

"So we hear." Zach had received the information from Kentuckians who were travelling with the corps now. These young sparks, cousins of the girls of Corydon, had recently "made visits" to get the lay of the land and reported back on the "arming" of southeastern Indiana.

"The men are all back on the road now," Morgan drawled. "I have ordered a scouting party out. Advance guard—the best men from several companies." Zach nodded, knowing it already, of course. He could see them pulling out of line, riding ahead. "They will scout for us. Winder Monroe will lead the party. I want to know how many old gaffers and wet-behind-the-ears boys are out behind those logs and brush piles, there at the entrance to their town."

"Yes, sir," Zach said. "My people at the local Knights castle say they've been sending out the alarum all over southern Indiana for militia volunteers. But most of the militia have gone to Indianapolis."

"And we won't be within a hundred miles of it," Morgan chuckled in a self-satisfied way. "I'm going to swing like a scythe and do as much damage as I can and then, cut through Ohio to—who knows? Pennsylvania? West Virginia?" Then he looked directly at Zach. "Speaking of your Knights of the Golden Circle, where are all these thousands of boys so eager to ride out of Hoosier barns and rally round the Bonnie Blue Flag?"

Zach avoided his eyes. "Seem to be as scarce as turtle hair, don't they?" he said. "But I never promised—"

"Never mind," Morgan growled. "I wouldn't respect them much anyway, even if they came in droves. They're disloyal to their own cause."

"What do you want with me, sir?" Zach wanted to know.

"You know these roads, Scott. Direct this advance guard. Choose some likely farmhouses and get information. Then ride back to me."

With a wave of his hand, he dismissed Zach, and the train wound its way down the narrow road as the sun rose higher and hotter every moment.

"The Mill Road takes a sharp bend up here and joins another road into Corydon," Zach said, pointing with his hat through maple and elder trees which obscured the view ahead. "There's a good mansion house. It's only three miles into Corydon. A minister lives in the house, I think, with his family. They can give us information, if they want to."

"If they want to," Captain Winder Monroe said, wiping his grimy face with his sleeve. "We'll ride into the side lot in full force, with the colors flying. Give 'em a little display of Southern valor."

Zach swung out of the saddle as the twenty or so cavalrymen thundered into the yard. The yard was silent, hung with the dusty oppressive heat. A lone hen clucked ominously somewhere behind the barn.

As the horses snorted, Monroe shouted in the yard at the inhabitants. "Throw out your guns and come out. We are many and armed."

The smell of manure rose steamily from the trampled yard; flies lit and crawled up horses' manes and the arms of the men waiting, astride, in the yard and along the road. Finally the answer to the shouted demand came; a sharp, whizzing shot that caught one of Hines's cavalrymen in the head.

"Take your traitorous riders and go to the Devil," a young voice shouted from in the house.

The cavalryman had been shot from his horse; he was bleeding profusely and was not moving. "Kilt dead. Shoot at the house," the head scout, Monroe, said coldly, and the men in the yard obeyed. Zach, behind his sycamore tree, watched the skirmish develop. Bullets flew into the shutters, broke a window, hit a piano key inside the parlor.

"Hutty, take three men inside and get those snipers," Monroe ordered one of the men from Quirk's scouts. Zach watched; from his observation point not ten feet from the window he could see inside the house.

Soon, an overweight, middle-aged man with a frizzy, gray beard came down the stairs, bearing a handkerchief on a fire poker. He opened the door.

"I am Pastor Glenn," he said, waving the fire poker from the door. "I tried to get Johnny to stop a-shootin'." The handkerchief fell off; nervously he bent to pick it up, never taking his eyes off the Southern troops.

"And so you surrender, now, after you have shot my man," Monroe sneered. Someone seized the minister's arms and started to drag him outside.

The cavalryman whom Zach had only heard referred to as "Hutty" charged down the stairs of the house and out the door to report on his bedroom inspection. "This man's son did the shootin'. He was wounded slightly," he said "He's in the upstairs bedroom, with his cousin takin' care of him. What should we do with 'em?" Hutty had salt-and-pepper gray hair, a mouth that was continually open, and a leering, eager face.

"They shouldn't cause no more trouble now, I reckon. We'll deal with 'em in a minute," Monroe said, biting into a plug of tobacco. A fluttery-looking woman with hair piled high on her head came out of the back room. The door was open; she stepped out and over to the scout captain, walking in tiny steps as if she had a foot problem, or as if her stays were too tight.

"Bring her over by her husband," Monroe commanded. The rest of the search party charged out of the mansion. "Sir, let's fire the house," Hutty said. Monroe shook his head. Hutty came up and spoke in the face of the minister. "I'm a-gonna get the captain to fire your house in just a minute." There was pleasure and jubiliation in his tone.

"Who is he?" Zach whispered to Monroe.

"Georgia cracker thinks every Yankee is Satan. His brother-in-law was at Fredericksburg and don't talk of nothing else but the burnin' of the mansions in the town."

The wife trundled over to stand beside her husband. "Pa, recollect your heart pain." She addressed the soldiers who held him. "Don't tax him too much now. He has spells."

Pastor Glenn looked at Pickaninny, the tethered roan thoroughbred who was now grazing with the other horses on thick grass under an oak tree. The pastor began to mutter and raised a hand in front of him, like a Biblical prophet. "And there went out another horse that was red, and power was given unto him that sat thereon to take peace from the earth, and that they should kill one another; and there was given unto him a great sword." Captain Monroe glared at him.

Zach watched one of the advance guard men he knew from Hines' company rush up to the scouting party leader. "Sir, Dobbs has died," the young man confirmed, his eyes wide with the meaning of it all.

"So that son-of-a-bitch that shot him is a Yankee executioner," Monroe said.

"Ain't give himself up yet. He's inside still, with his cousin," Hutty said in an ominous voice.

"That's our boy Johnny." the thin, nervous woman pleaded. "He don't mean nothing. He's been in the militia and don't take it kindly that—"

"Fire the place," Monroe said. Several men ran into the house and took fire from the stove on pieces of newspaper and began touching it to draperies, bed pillows, books in bookcases, anything that would burn. The pastor ran in and began smothering flames with his coat, but the cavalrymen dragged him outside again.

"Recollect his heart pain," the woman called out and made her husband sit down under a tree. Then she turned to Monroe. "My good settee, my ma's grandmother clock, will go up in the flames. Leave us somethin' in the name of the good Lord," the woman cried and went back in to drag some of her furniture out.

"Sir, can we help her?" some of the younger men from Hines company asked. "After all, she didn't start all this and we're supposed to remember honor, especially to helpless women, General Morgan says."

"Why, shore thing. Get the honorable son-of-a-bitch settee and the helpless grandmother clock out," Monroe affirmed, nodding his head and spitting tobacco juice on the larkspur by the door.

Zach stayed with the horses, watching the young men from Hines company haul a large settee with a Chinese pattern out the door. Other pieces of furniture came out, but then the furniture moving had to be suspended. The fire had taken hold with a vengeance; tongues of flame and billowing smoke were pouring out the windows.

"Now you tell us what you know, ma'am," Monroe said, and listened as she described what she had heard of the preparations of the town of Corydon. Her husband sat sullenly by on the settee, mumbling verses from the Bible and watching anxiously to see if his son and nephew were coming out. Suddenly the sniper shooting began again from behind the house. The young men had evidently come down the stairs and sneaked out the back door.

"Oh, Pa, Johnny and Armistead won't give up," the woman cried.

"They can do a lot of damage afore that house falls on 'em," Monroe said. "Take cover, men, and fire from behind the trees out at the road," he shouted.

Zach stepped out of the crossfire and retreated to the springhouse, where he looked out from behind Rose of Sharon bushes. "Not my war, after all," he muttered.

Hutty, the man with the salt-and-pepper hair and the Hoosier-hating temperament, pulled out a carbine and, standing behind the tree where Zach had just been, took careful aim as the two young men stuck their heads out. "Enough, enough, tools of iniquity," the minister shouted at the raiders. He struggled to get his huge bulk off the settee and lunged at Hutty. In spite of the continuing crossfire, Zach came out of the door of the springhouse. He watched the minister grapple with Hutty, saw them struggle over the carbine, heard the cursing and shouting of the Southerner and the ranting of the minister.

"Shoot him, shoot him," someone called out to Hutty. The carbine rang out; Hutty had held the gun against the thigh of the old man and pulled the trigger. Still Pastor Glenn contended for the gun; then a comrade came and aimed a pistol at the minister's side.

"I give up," the minister said, blood pouring from his wounded thigh.

The shooting stopped. With flames pouring out of the windows in back of her, his wife streaked across the clearing.

"Now, now you see, you awful Rebels what all your ridin' about so brave has caused. My husband is bleedin' bad." The wounded bushwhacker son and the cousin were still behind the house, shouting imprecations. Nobody seemed to want to go back there after them.

It took three men to hoist the minister onto the settee. Monroe stepped forward. "Where in the hell is a knife? We need to cut these overalls off," he said. Zach ran out of the springhouse with his pocket knife and they quickly cut off the overalls at the thigh as blood spurted out, making a pool all over the ground.

"Thigh shot to pieces," Monroe said.

The minister groaned. He opened his eyes and looked at his son, then at Monroe. "The great day of his wrath is come, and who shall be able to stand?" he said and sank into unconsciousness.

It was over in a matter of minutes. The blood saturated every cloth they could bring, and while they tried to make tourniquets around the huge thigh, blood saturated the boots and trousers of Southern cavalry men and Northern wife. The fire roared like a furnace in back of them. Finally the son and cousin came out, hands in the air to be placed under guard. The man's life flickered, then faded, then went out.

"Come back, Pa, come back," the miserable wife cried, shaking her husband's limp shoulders. "You was fine jest ten minutes ago and now you're gone."

"Main artery," said Hutty, who was standing by looking into the barrel of his pistol. "Severed." The shake roof of the house caught fire; it popped and snapped like dry tinder; fifteen foot flames, feeding on the sun-baked boards, leapt into the sky. The flames, and the memories they brought of the fire in Indianapolis that had almost killed him, made Zach break out in a sweat.

"It's war, you know," Hutty said, with a slightly defensive tone in his voice as he walked towards the road. "They said the Yankee sons-of-bitches peed in the church in Fredericksburg," he called out over his shoulder.

The cavalry scouts, most of whom had grazed their horses through this entire happening, came out of the meadows around the house and began to form a line again. The two young men from Hines' company who had spoken about honor hoisted the dead Rebel soldier up on top of the hams in the wagon.

The wife, the cousin, the son, whom they had decided to leave behind, all sobbed inconsolably while the wind fanned the flames onto trees around the house.

Zach Scott watched the dust and airborne ashes slowly coat the blue, ragged-robin flowers at the side of the road, listened to the sobs and the roar of flames behind him, and turned his horse towards the Buffalo Trace. It was mustering-out time. Monroe and Hutty, for God's sake, could give whatever information they had to Morgan. His mouth was impassive; his expression as inscrutable as if shades had been pulled down over his eyes.

Horace Hogue had his five volunteers from the militia tether their horses behind the bulwark at the edge of Corydon. Horace's face was dead sober; this was war, after all. Morgan and his men were threatening life and limb in the greatest stretch of country God every gave to man. "Bolt that gun to a stump," he said to one of the men from his Three County unit. They had carried Little Polly across the Buffalo Trace, as they came in answer to the frantic call from the southeastern counties in the state. Most of the militiamen had gone to Indianapolis, where Governor Morton was amassing thousands of troops to guard the capital, but Horace calculated that Morgan would cross near Corydon and ride east.

"Thank God you're here," Colonel Lewis Jordan of the local militia said when Horace quickly explained what his tiny contingent was. "Hardly any of these men have experience under fire. I called to New Albany for officers but nobody came. These Corydon men are shooting with squirrel rifles. Rebels seem to be heading for our left. Take your gun over there, sergeant, and prepare to fight."

A frightening cloud of dust was nearing from the south accompanied by the sound of galloping horses' hoofs and Rebel yells. Horace and his men rushed over a lane and a couple of hills to the left of the half-mile wide fortifications. They took out the four-inch cannon and secured a huge bolt through the top of it.

Men all around were putting guns over the breastworks, and firing began as the Rebels came within range.

"Start firing, Bosgrow," Horace said. Bosgrow, a cattle farmer from near the old McClure homestead, shoved small shot into the mouth of the gun, added powder and attempted to light the fuse.

"Tain't workin', sergeant," he said to Horace.

"Let me try," Horace said, limping up. He took a piece of felt from his pocket and twisted it, sticking it in the small fuse hole. "Wet fuse, Bosgrow," he said and the stolid farmer nodded. Horace struck a match and lit his fuse, then stepped back as the little shell shot out, over the Rebels, exploding among them and blackening their faces. The Rebels, hit from intense fire from behind the barricades, fell back a moment, then mounted another attack on the left. Horace and his men continued to load and fire until their faces were pitch black.

A very few tense minutes passed as the Rebels fought their way nearer. "Hell, this'll be knowed as the Battle of Corydon," Bosgrow said. "We're a-gonna be winners and heroes."

"Don't count your medals until you get 'em," Horace muttered. He was watching the original Rebels regroup and other Rebels, over a thousand of them, ride over the crest to the south. They were gathering under the Confederate flag for a charge—no, for several charges. As he worked with the gun, he watched them split up and come towards the entire line, not just the left. He leaned over the stump and looked into the mouth of the tiny cannon.

"Swabbing—we need to swab," he told Bosgrow's young son, a boy of sixteen who had left young ladies at a Wheatland picnic party to come to the wars.

"Swabbing—what'll I get, sergeant?" The boy's eyes were enormous with awed fright.

"Flannel—from my pack. Oh, never mind, I'll get it myself," Horace said and hobbled off as fast as he could go.

Colonel Jordan was riding the line and spied him. "Sergeant Hogue, I want to commend you. I've seen what that small cannon has been doing." He shook his head and quickly turned his mount to return to the right of his line. "Not that any of what we're trying is of much avail. Hold out as best you can," he shouted over his shoulder.

As the colonel rode off, Morgan's cavalry reached the left and Horace's "contingent" at a furious gallop and began storming the trenches. Some even leapt over the forward parts of the barricade. Horses and men were falling into barricades, the Rebels were yippeeing and brandishing swords.

As Horace, back among the trees with his pack, turned about with the flannel in his hand, many townsmen at the barricade left their defensive positions and began to flee. He took a few steps forward. His sight was partially blocked. Where were his men? Still among the trees, he could see the spot where they had stood, just a moment ago. Rebel soldiers, some afoot, were at the first level of the barricade, not a hundred yards out. They were shouting encouragement at each other; he could hear their drawl, smooth and rich as chicken gravy. Skirmishing had died down.

"Bosgrow and the others left Li'l Pol," Horace thought with a sinking heart. "And my horse must have been ridden off." No sense in sacrificing himself and the gun, too. If he stayed here in this grove, perhaps squatted down here behind these huge thistle bushes and stayed quiet, the Rebels might not detect him.

He sank down, favoring his game leg, and drank from his canteen. The local defenders were withdrawing from this left part of the militia line, anyway, it seemed. Probably the Rebels had flanked the line on the right; they would be pursuing the fleeing soldiers to capture them. Ah, poor Bosgrow and his son and the others might be prisoners at this very moment.

A thistle brushed his hand and set it smarting; he put it to his mouth and ground the plant with his heel. A slow, steady smile spread across his plain face. "Commended by a colonel," Horace thought. "He noticed our men and my Pol." Well, there were probably 3,000 of Morgan's cavalry, and the Corydon farmers had defended their town stoutly. None of them needed to be ashamed. They would parole them, make them promise not to fight again and then ride on. Morgan's raiders were in the barricades now, talking about a few dead Indiana militiamen that were left on the field, picking up equipment they wanted. "Don't find Li'l Pol," he prayed and shrank himself into a tight ball, even trying to bend the game leg.

Soon their voices died away. They were not spending much time here; they had business down the road; that was clear. Moments passed, an hour. Not one voice was left at the barricades and he raised his body, slowly, painfully from behind the nettles. He went to the line and surveyed the scene. Down below there were dead horses among the brush, and a couple of Confederates who were not moving. Along this line, as far as he could see, only one dead man. There must have been wounded; the Rebels probably took them into town.

But Li'l Pol was gone. Suddenly, he felt his eyes mist. After so much, his gun gone away, kidnapped by the Rebels. She was now riding with Morgan's men into slaughter and rapine and a particular brand of hell. Then a comforting thought came. Commended by the colonel. Horace Hot Foot praised for his action in the battle. He held his head up and smirked. Then he went to get the reins of one of the poor old nags Morgan's men had abandoned, exchanged for a better (probably his). He would see if a Southern nag would bear the weight of a man, an honored survivor of the Battle of Corydon, someone proud to fight for his home state as duty, however limited, had called.

Near sunset Horace came slowly to a house on a small byway to the southwest of Corydon. His bones ached and his sooty face was streaming sweat. The horse had given out and collapsed, snorting and foaming by the side of the road and refusing to go another pace. Surely Morgan's men had ridden on by now. Which direction would they go? North to Indianapolis? He thought not. It was too far from the Ohio and they were, after all, too few to meet the thousands and thousands of militiamen and regulars Governor Oliver P. Morton had called to the capital city. Morton had even ordered multiple rounds of shells in from Cincinnati, Horace thought a little enviously. How they could have used those men and that ammunition here today! But then Morton was as flustered and hysterical as everyone else in Indiana, Ohio and Illinois today. The riders of the Apocalypse were loose, and brimstone and destruction were reigning in the minds and hearts of the folks of the middle states as well as with the Southern cavalry.

"Must rest," he told himself, limping more markedly than he usually did. His leg was as stiff and sore as it had ever been since that day when his friend shot him by mistake in the hunting accident. The pain had marked his days and hours, though he had never tried to ease it with narcotics, as his sister Lettie had eased her own unique pain with morphine.

A farmhouse, small but comfortable, loomed ahead beyond a woodlot.

Neat curtains were at the windows, flowers in boxes under them. The thought of Lettie added an extra fringe to his sadness. "Lettie," he thought, "you in your little apartment at this very moment, behind your own neat curtains? Are you hidin' from the eyes of the world?" The Upper Indiana Board was supposed to review Lettie's case yesterday, at the request of that obnoxious, meat-eatin' female animal, Cousin Jewell Simpson.

Probably last night Lettie would have been escorted by two elders from her home to hear and give testimony, and Jewell with all her fangs bared, would have been uncaged. No doubt about that. Lickin' grievances of fifty years like a bobcat licks its paws."

Now he was at the front door of this house near Corydon, which was guarded by white hollyhock sentinels. He looked about to see if he could find any of the signs of Copperheads about—southeastern Indiana was almost as ripe with them as the western part of the state. "No, there's a flag inside, draping the pi-anner," he told himself. "Patriot family, and brave, too. If Morgan the Raider had happened by here, he might have axed that pi-anner for 'em."

The door opened. Had he knocked? A gun was stuck cautiously through the opening. "Hello, ma'am," (it seemed to be a ma'am rather than a sir back there in the gloom). "Sergeant Horace Hogue of the Tri County militia, havin' escaped the Rebels, would beg from you a little water and perhaps a bit of bread."

The door opened wide as a woman with a round, piquant face and a pretty pug nose opened it. "The widow Limeberry, sir. I was afraid you were a traitor come to rob the smokehouse. But I see by your blue uniform and brass buttons—but come in here, dear sir, come in." He was ushered into a charming parlor, with a stuffed settee covered with a bright floral pattern. In the corner was a boy of about ten reading a book, *The Baptist Youth's Companion*, by the declining light at the window. A bird in a cage hopped about and twittered a welcome.

"One of them canary birds, I presume," Horace said.

"Yes. It belonged to my dear husband, now gone a year. Birds of the heavens, harbingers of truth and spring," she said with a flourish. Horace nodded his approval of the poetic sentiment, and they stood looking at each other.

"Sir," she said, suddenly remembering herself, "I can't think what's got in my head. Mama would be turnin' over in her grave to see how ill-mannered I am. And I genteelly brought up. You will be wantin' to wash up." She took him to a small back room where a washstand, soap and towels were placed. When he emerged, delicious smells were floating through the parlor.

"I was just preparin' to set a meal before m' boy and m'self. We would take it kindly if you would share our repast. We are havin' pot roast and onions—"Horace advanced to the table—"last o' the lettuce, wilted with onions and bacon, first o' the pole beans"—Horace pulled out a chair and sat down—"and a black raspberry pie, picked fresh today"—Horace shook out a large napkin as she set silverware in front of him, nodding his head in delighted approval.

Horace and the boy ate the meal through its several delightful parts, urged on when they flagged and set their forks down on the checkered tablecloth, by a magically replenishing plate of fried biscuits and apple butter. Mrs. Clarissa Limeberry came and sat with them towards the end of the meal, eating delicately, mincing each bite.

The three of them talked to each other, as people do who don't know each other but want to impress their new friends, giving little summarizing soliloquies which showed them at their best and revealed their situations and characters. Horace said he was a hard-working farmer who helped his uncle on rolling acres in Knox County, that he did go to church but he blushed to say not as often as he should, Presbyterian persuasion, though he hadn't nothin' against the Baptists, had been a widower for many years now and was a-courtin' no one, havin' give his time to his ma and now *his country*.

Mrs. Clarissa Limeberry said she was a widow woman, who lived for this fine boy, the only child of a short but happy marriage which had left her comfortably well off, and she just loved to putter about her little cottage puttin' curios here and there and crocheting little doilies and makin' dresses for bisque dolls—and for outside interest was, yes, well, she shouldn't say so but did, a lady novel writer who was just completin' a three hundred page work, oh, no, she can't say how its story went, Mr. Hogue, that would spile it should you wish to peruse it at any time—but its theme was *love*.

And the boy, who seemed to have more capacity for food than anyone Horace had seen in a long time, told of how he had gone into Corydon, which was really only a mile or two away, this afternoon. He had seen all the captives in the streets, lined up by Rebels, looking forlorn. They were all pardoned and had to promise they wouldn't fight against the Confederacy again, which wasn't hard considering the circumstances.

Then he had seen the raiders go into stores and order up all the merchandise, paying for it in Confederate money or nothing at all. They had emerged from the Bon-ton of Corydon carrying armloads of useless stuff, silk scarves and ice skates and high-topped ladies' shoes. While this was going on, the boy said, General Morgan was having lunch in the Kintner House Hotel. A local woman told Morgan the news of the final, awful defeat of Lee at Gettysburg, and he looked awful sad, said the boy. Then he and the men, loaded with their ice skates and other frim-frams, got on their steeds and rode out of town fast as they could.

And Horace Hogue got his pack and took out a spent bullet, and a photograph of a bunch of Southerners sitting on a veranda someplace where moss hung off trees, and a carbine, all of which he had picked up from the battlefield. And the boy marvelled and thought it was much finer than the *Baptist Youth's Companion* book and would look at little else that night.

So they all sat and smirked at each other with utter satisfaction in the parlor that sultry night, and after an hour or two Mrs. Clarissa Limeberry served lemonade and read a little of her latest story, "The Queen of the Congo" and Horace, finally told of the battle, in jerking phrases, with an odd, sad face.

Mrs. Clarissa Limeberry insisted he stay the night on the settee and he agreed and as she came near, he smelled a nice scent and felt a strange yearning to tell her about what it was really like, at the core, so to speak.

"Worst thing was I don't know if m' men got away all right," Horace said. "I brought them there, took them from picnics and what-not, and they might be dead for all I know tonight. An officer's responsibility is to his men."

"Yes, I understand," she said reassuringly, and he thought she meant it.

"I thought I always wanted it, and I got commended," he went on, "but still 'twas a dirty, hot, ugly dangerous slice o' stupidity," he ended in a bitter voice.

The boy had gone to bed, carrying the carbine with him. The window had grown dark, a little at a time, and now they could see the moon shining as cool as frosted glass itself, through it. "Still," Clarissa Limeberry said, from the darkness, " 'tis an ill wind that blows no good."

"That's true," said Horace. "That's true enough."

July, August, 1863

Chapter Fifteen

Four elders huddled about a table in a Sunday School room of the Upper Indiana Church on a hot night in late July. On the steps outside the church sat Lettie Hogue, waiting for her trial by the minister and the Board of Elders on fornication charges. She had appealed for private dismissal; that had failed. She had refused to appear, then tried to beg off without success three weeks ago, and this meeting of the Session was her last chance to explain herself to her church.

Because of the distance, she had come out to stay with her mother, who thought the whole thing a tom-fool hypocritical farce. "Callin' people up there for dancin' and card playin' and all the rest. Not that what you did wasn't wrong, but you are workin' that out with God. Nosin' into everybody's business and listenin' to gossip! Why, some of those people have been seducing the hired girls for years and tearin' up their villages gettin' drunk on Saturday nights. Then they sit in judgment!"

Horace, Lettie's brother, had brought her over in the rig. "My," she thought as she sat on the steps, "whatever has gotten into Horace?" On the way over to the church he was as playful as an eleven-year-old, making the horse trot and dust fly all over her skirt. Dust even got under the dust cover she'd worn over her dress. Ever since he'd returned from chasing Morgan the Raider, he'd been like a boy, full of stories. And now the army and militia were chasing Morgan all over Ohio, about to close in, and Horace had been whooping all over the pasture lot. He had had a fine time, no doubt about that, at the wars. Nice of him to carry her over here. But he couldn't bring her home, said the elders had promised they would take care of that. He "had letters to write to friends." Whatever that meant.

She turned her head impassively to the cemetery. There, standing beside the Emison monument was Jewell Simpson, her accuser, who had also been called in. Well, she would not think of her. Her business was with the men inside—and with God.

Mary Jane McClure, who had come with her aunt Jewell, paced about at the edge of the churchyard, watching the evening sun filter through oak and tulip trees past the McClure graves on the far edge of the churchyard.

Mary Jane had been stealing glances at Lettie as the poor woman sat there on the steps of the church, smoothing her dress. "What must she be feeling?" Mary Jane asked herself mournfully.

"They said eight o'clock," Jewell Simpson announced, consulting a watch she carried on a little velvet ribbon in the pocket of her dress. "The elders will come'n get us after they bring her in. So be ready."

"What else can I be?" Mary Jane demanded a little testily. She did not know why she was involved. Of course she had been with Aunt Jewell when they saw Lettie with Mr. Mawkins, looking out the window of Lettie's lodgings in Vincennes. But they certainly didn't need *two* witnesses to prove poor Lettie's shame.

Jewell saw her discomfort at the situation, but did not intend to take notice of it. " 'Tis all according to Scripture. We are jest followin' scriptural command. Efn you have somethin' 'gainst your brother, or sister in this case, call together the elders and spit it out."

Mary Jane turned her face away from her aunt and watched Lettie stand up from the step, reach for her pocketbook and pop some sort of candy in her mouth. There was pride even in that simple gesture. Or was it defiance? Most people never came when they were accused of unchastity; they were too ashamed, and let the church just excommunicate them. She needed to present her case this time, or she would be excommunicated. That would be awful in this county, where to be "unchurched" was to be outcast.

"Pay me mind, Missy Big Heart," Aunt Jewell said. " 'Tis a strong matter with me that you testify, too, to this sinnin'. All those years I tole you about how lecherous the McClures were, amongst their other faults, and now you can see that I was exactly right. We are goin' in there and root out the sinnin', we are—"

"*You* are, Aunt Jewell," Mary Jane said in a low voice.

"What say?" her aunt said, peering into her face.

"Lettie is a dear relative of mine. I have jest decided I will not go in there and testify 'gainst her, even if you do."

"Why, young woman, what do you mean, defyin' your aunt, that took your pa and ma's orphants when they was drownded dead in the river and treated 'em like her own—"

Mary Jane turned and took her hands. "Auntie, I know you did all that, and I'm grateful. But I'm not goin' to testify against my Grandma Catherine's daughter. Actually, she's my aunt, too, just as you are, though she doesn't like us to call her that.''

Jewell Simpson opened her mouth, then popped it closed again.

"And I'm goin' to say somethin' more, too, Auntie,'' Mary Jane went on, red spots appearing on her cheeks. " 'Tis time this stupid breach in the family was healed up. 'Tis about some score that wasn't settled by people that are dead long time past. It makes me want to weep. Sometimes I wake up in the night and think on it. I keep wonderin' what would happen if John got hurt or even—'' she lowered her voice and head "—killed over there in the wars and all of his family a-squabblin' so?'' She pointed at the graves on the other side of the churchyard. "See all them graves, Aunt? Way far side, there, Jane McClure and the brothers who came after the Revolution and their wives and kin and all the Emisons and Bairds and everybody else is out there.'' Jewell Simpson looked, taken aback by the vehemence in the young girl's voice.

Mary Jane went on. "Some of them didn't ever speak to each other. They argued over politics and whether you was a Baptist or a Shaker. But they're all gone now, and they ought to have spent their time in lovin' and livin' not squabblin'.'' She dabbed at the tears that had come to her eyes.

Jewell Simpson batted her eyelashes. "Seems like some folks is big for their britches over things they don't know much about,'' she said rather mildly.

An elder leaned out of the church door like a figure in a Swiss cuckoo clock and beckoned to Jewell. "Well, the fallen woman's gone in and I 'spect they want me, too,'' Jewell said and frumped towards the church door.

Lettie Hogue took a seat at the head of the table. Reverend Paden was already seated, his long legs awkwardly folded under the table. He smiled a beatific minister's smile at Lettie. "Oh,'' she thought, "it's good he noticed me in a friendly way. That may mean something.''

He had always been kind and friendly. He would understand that this was a silly call. The sinning was already over. She had left it behind, told Willis Mawkins she never wanted to see him again and then made it stick. They were getting the horse out after the barn had burned down.

She saw that Mr. Samuel Thompson, Jr. was presiding. His grandson Tommy was away with John and the boys in the Fourteenth. And Mr. Jabal MacMahon, the town postmaster, with his balding head with combed-over hairs plastered over the signs of aging, had an I-wish-I-wasn't-in-this-embarrassing-situation look on his face.

She wondered how much they knew. Probably very little. Jewell had saved her bullets for the big scene she was going to make before the elders. Well, Jewell was just too late, Lettie told herself primly. She herself had taken care of it all and would redeem her reputation with them. Not many people in the town really knew or cared anyway. She would say the truth, that she was no longer "carryin' on." Now she was working in a dress shop and trying to hold her head up again. When you showed signs of sincere repentance, they wouldn't deny you fellowship.

Out of the corner of her eye she saw Jewell Simpson edge into the room and sit in a small chair from the Sunday school. Her posterior protruded over the sides.

"Let us open this meeting with prayer," Mr. Samuel Thompson, Jr. said. He was sixty years old and had gnarled, arthritic hands. Lettie could not take her hands off them as they lay folded and bumpy on the table. "*Oooh Lorrd*, give us the light of Thy truth, give us the light to open up the dark places of the soul. If there is sin, bring it to light and let us all seek the consolation of repentance in the Spirit. *Aamen.*"

"Now let us have examination of the matter before the Session," he said. He presented the process. Lettie was cited for immorality; the witness who had brought the citation was to tell her side of the matter with Lettie out of the room. Then Lettie would present her testimony and leave the room, while the elders and minister deliberated, and Lettie would return for the final judgment to be announced.

Lettie sat in the church sanctuary, at the other end of the building from where the sound of Jewell Simpson's testimony was proceeding in a low grumble. She looked up at the sturdy frame walls, the stained glass window, not portraying Jesus carrying a lamb, like in the Methodist church, but just glass. On the wall was a plaque. It said, "This church, the First Protestant Church in Indiana, was organized by Mrs. William Henry Harrison, Daniel McClure—" Oh yes. The ancestors. There was some family story that old Dan'l had come across the Buffalo Trace with Mr. Samuel Thompson. Was that this board member's father? Her mother Catherine was always talking about all this cobwebby stuff and she only listened with half an ear. She tossed her head; she didn't care about 'em. Live for today. She didn't want to hear about those old flusterpates.

Then a new idea came to her, filtering into her consciousness like the rays of the sun through these blessed stained glass windows of a Sunday morning. Maybe she was angry at the ancestors, and even her own family a lot of the time now, because she felt she had let everybody down. Really, she felt so dirty, like a handkerchief dragged in the mud. She had wanted bliss—and she found disgust. Finally, that was what it had all got her. Thinking of the ancestors made her ashamed, as if she let everyone down who had ever sat in a church pew at Upper Indiana from 1800, or whenever it was, on. What pillars of virtue! They probably never did anything wrong.

They were all out there in that churchyard, and if the dead could think, they were thinking, "So that's George McClure's granddaughter. The Revolutionary War veteran? He was always so upright. Weren't you, George?" Maybe the old man, whom she'd never known, was standing about, listening to this testimony. How embarrassing! That your grandfather would hear what you did in bed, against the law of God and man. It was like saying a prayer in the privy, 'twas unseemly and odd.

This whole ridiculous thing was beginning to get to her. She had fought against despondency ever since she forced Willis out of her life, and here it came again, that low-in-the-stomach, deep-down awful feeling. It pulled at your heart and strength. Blue-black despair was always hiding out there, behind the bayberry bushes in the woods, cheerful as you wanted to be. "Give up," it said.

She sighed deeply, and gave in a bit to the bayberry bush voice. What was the sense of trying to redeem your life anyway? She was foolish thinking she could leave it all behind, redeem herself in the eyes of the community. Of course people knew. They must. What was her life worth anyway? No one cared if she lived or died. She heard a rustling at the side door. Someone was coming in. She turned her head.

Why, it was Mary Jane McClure. "Hello, Lettie," she said, smiling that sort of homely, buck-toothed smile.

"I thought you were coming into the meeting, Mary Jane."

"Not on your life," Mary Jane said, slipping into the pew beside her.

"Should be interesting," Lettie said ironically. "You're missing stories that are better than a modern novel."

"Not to me. Are you guilty, Lettie? We saw you with Mr. Mawkins late at night, but—"

"I was guilty, Mary Jane," Lettie sighed. "But I've given Mr. Mawkins up. I had the silly idea he might marry me, and I've always thought I needed a man. I guess I was willing to do anything to get one."

"I know. Nobody seems to want me, either," Mary Jane said a little sadly. "The McCord boy only took me to church onct. And nobody else—"

"They will. You're young yet." Lettie looked at Mary Jane full in the face. "And as pure and pretty as a lavender pink rose in June." They both sat silently, at peace with each other.

"What do you hear from John and the Fourteenth Indiana?" Lettie finally asked.

"His last letter said the Yankees and Lee's army were near each other again and they were playing hide-and-go-seek with each other. Quiet now, I guess.'' They sat, smelling the musty, hymn-book smell, hearing the insect noises outside the windows.

The low voices in the other room ceased. Chairs were scraping. Evidently the testimony was over. Mary Jane turned to Lettie and took her hand, as if there were something she needed to say before the others came.

"How do you feel about all this, Lettie?"

Lettie smiled a sad little smile. "I just want Christian forgiveness. If I can feel right with God again I can face the town. For so many weeks I yearned to be in church, to feel clean but I couldn't face the price. Redemption and forgiveness, isn't that what the church discipline says? I'll tell the truth and ask them to forgive me, and then I will feel pure again.''

Mary Jane nodded and smiled as Lettie returned to the hearing room.

Inside, she glanced around. Mr. Jabal MacMahon, the postmaster, looked like he was about to go to sleep. An owl hooted in the darkness outside the window, and a chilly mist was rising from the bottomlands. Jewell Simpson was gone, thank goodness.

"We have heard serious allegations, Letitia, made against you,'' the minister said. He had his spectacles off, was rapping the table with them. "Your cousin reported seeing you in compromising situations more than one time. She says she heard you were in Indianapolis, too, with Mr. Mawkins.''

Lettie drew in her breath. So they knew of that.

"Tell your own story in this matter,'' Mr. Samuel Thompson said.

So Lettie told them of her seduction (albeit in modest language), her fall from grace, her immersion in sin and her final awakening. Proudly she held her head up and said she had turned from her former association and repented.

The men nodded, cleared their throats, scraped their shoes, and asked her to leave. She walked out the door. Jewell and Mary Jane were on the way to their home nearby; she could see the lantern they carried swinging through the trees.

Reverend Paden beckoned her in. He had a smile on his face. The news must be good. She came in and seated herself with her hands primly in her lap.

"Letitia,'' Mr. Samuel Thompson said, "we want to accept you back to Christian fellowship. You told us you have turned from your former— umm—folly. There's lots of different kinds of sinnin' in this church and everwhere, for that matter. There's sins of pride and of covetousness and bearing false witness, and these don't get noticed like the ones you can see when a man and woman who aren't married keep company on the street. That doesn't alter the wrongness of what you did, but the Lord said it all when he caught the adulterous woman. He told everbody to keep watch on their own sins and told the woman to, 'Go and sin no more.' We wish you to go and sin no more.''

Lettie breathed a long sigh. It was as she had hoped, prayed.

Mr. Samuel Thompson went on. ''There will be certain conditions, which we have all voted on, for your return to the congregation. Reverend Paden will take you home, as your brother requested, and speak of your readmission to the sacraments of our church. Let us close with a prayer—*Dearrr Gawd*—''

Lettie's bad spirits left as quickly as they came, slinking off to the bayberry bush lair. Reverend Paden gallantly helped her into the covered rig. Now she would start over. They understood and forgave. She was redeemed.

It was wonderful to be with Reverend Paden, to see him sitting, tall and firm beside her, not speaking, just nodding encouragingly. She could depend on him! She knew he must be eager to get home to his wife and children up near Bruceville, but here he was taking time to drive her home. He pulled into a little lane, blocked by trees from sight of the main road. Now he would talk about her full return to communion, to faith! She looked up towards him. In the light of a half-moon his eyes shone.

"Lettie," he said in a low voice.

"Yes, Reverend," she answered, her whole soul throbbing with the joy of rejuvenation.

"We want you to feel thoroughly welcome. Let there be no reservations among anyone. Let love be without dissimulation for you. I will tell your aunt, Jewell Simpson, that."

"Thank you, Reverend."

"I do love you, Lettie. I want you to think of me as your pastor, your teacher, your brother in love."

"I do, Reverend Paden. I have always revered you more than any other man, I think, admired—"

"I am glad to hear you say that, Lettie," he continued in a low voice, looking at the odd moon and not at her, "because I have revered you too, felt drawn to you. Tonight at the meeting I was strangely *stirred* by you and, I must admit, by your tale of sin."

Lettie did not respond. She did not know what to say. The minister put his hand lightly on her shoulder and turned towards her but did not look at her. He took off his spectacles and then gazed into her eyes. "I want to get to know you better. I may be able to teach you things about love that you do not know."

"Teach you things," she thought, blankly, odd echoes of Willis Mawkins reverberating in her mind, like a window shade that had run up suddenly and was going flap, flap, flap.

Suddenly he took her hand and spoke, oh, so softly, so blandishingly. "My wife does not respond to me, Lettie. Can you believe that? After seven children she does not wish me to share love with her, spurns my natural husbandly advances—forgive my frank speech, but you are an experienced woman—" An experienced woman? Blankness became apprehension.

"I am a warm-natured man. It comes with my calling, I suppose, and I have been shrivelling up, dying on the vine. You say you admire me more than other men—" he put his arms around her. She could not speak. Her mouth was dry as cotton.

"We can meet and learn love together. No one need know of our arrangement. I am only half a man. You can help to make me a full man, a better minister. You are beautiful and your heart is ardent. I could feel it tonight, pulsating out at me as you spoke to us." His hand went to her breast.

She still could not speak; her mind and emotions were in turmoil. She felt as if she would break apart from within and fly in pieces, like a Dresden doll set on a hot stove.

"I know I do not offend you," he went on. "You know what I mean when I speak of the joys of joining bodies and souls. I need that—you, so—" He was leaning over her, moving to kiss her.

"No!" she said in a strangled voice. Gently he pulled back his hand, leaned back a little, startled. He had not expected resistance? "You seem to think of me still as a—fallen woman. Ready to do anything for a man."

"And you aren't?" the minister said in a smug, slightly sarcastic voice.

"No. You said I was forgiven, redeemed in everyone's eyes. Now you are acting like a lecherous—"

He leaned again. "What I feel is not lechery, my dear, attraction. You fire my senses, and I am a man like any other." He grabbed and kissed her.

"Go—a-away. Let me out," Lettie screamed and fought him. She found the handle on the door of the rig and worked it up and down.

There was an instant of silence, then the minister's voice, chilly and patronizingly gentle. "You have misunderstood my natural concern for you, I am afraid," he said.

"Just—let—me out of here," Lettie said, panting. The door handle gave.

"Yes, misunderstood. And if you should say anything otherwise, no one will believe you. You are the fallen woman." Lettie turned to him, eyes wide. Betrayal! It was an icy waterfall and she had plunged down it in a barrel twice this summer.

"A fallen woman is what you are, miss," he said coldly. She clambered down and his voice followed her into the chilly mist of night. "What made you think you could buy redemption simply by asking for it, like chocolates at a store counter?'' She was running down the lane; still he was calling after her, once again the raging Old Testament Prophet, hiding in the robes of religion. ''To be redeemed you must do a redeeming deed, slut.''

She ran, stumbling on roots in the old lane, and reached the road. Soon the horse and buggy came by her, clattering like the carriage of doom. Tears and perspiration coursed down her face; and she walked along with her hand on her shoulder where he, a minister of the gospel, had touched her with lust. She could still hear the horse's hoofs thumping fast as he whipped the poor beast to get away from her as fast as he could.

''Slut, slut, slut, slut,'' the clattering hoofs seemed to say as they echoed down the hard dirt road.

''Lost, lost Lettie,'' she said to herself. ''Foulest of all! Your heart leapt when he put his hand on your breast. All the while your soul and mind were condemning him, your body wanted him near you.'' She scrubbed at her lips to remove his disgrace and her disgusting thrill. Then she pulled up her skirts to avoid the dust and made her way through moon-cast shadows and the night-time damps of these bottomlands to the ancestral farmhouse around the bend.

The sun blistered down on southern Indiana the first week in August, baking the dirt roads to rock, drying the last of the blackberries into small pellets on the vines. The rivers ran sluggish and foul, and typhoid fever lurked in their depths.

About all there was to do was sit on porches and watch the corn roots lift from the soil in the garden, the dogs pant in the dusty shade. Harriet Houghton brought her twelve-year-old son Hilary over to her sister Susan Brook's house and they plumped into the wicker chairs on the porch. Their mother brought out a pitcher of lemonade and joined them.

''Thomas Jefferson has just brought the mail in. There is a letter from Eustace for you,'' Hannah Poore said to her daughter Susan.

''Read it to us, mother,'' Susan said. Hannah Poore took out spectacles and put them on.

'' 'Dear Mother,' '' Hannah began to read, shooing away a small fly that wanted to crawl over the paper. '' 'I want to tell you how the Eightieth Indiana helped capture Morgan the raider. He went through Ohio lickety-split and frightened everybody and took horses, just as he did in our state, but General Hobson and our troops caught up with him at Buffington Island. We trapped him (well, they did; we were in reserve) and captured some of his finest officers. Still, Morgan himself managed to get away and rode on across the state for three more days, trying to cross the river into West Virginia till he was captured, finally, to end this terrible raid. Lewis led us well, but is ill again, his old complaint of ague and lung fever, agitated by all the rush and heat as we chased Morgan. You know that my friend and yours, Jacob Joe Scott, was captured by Morgan in Kentucky and sent to prison camp. We have not heard word from him, which makes all the unit sad. But we are glad Morgan is captured and himself on the way to prison.' " Hannah Poore put the letter down and reached for a glass of the mint lemonade.

"Well! Finally captured! Think of that!" Susan Brooks said. "And only a few of the Copperheads rose to join him here, not half of the state as the Rebels expected."

"I should say not," Hannah Poore snorted. "He riled folk so, riding about burning barns and stealing horses, that Indiana people finally united— in despising the raid."

"Governor Morton has written Thomas a letter, now that the excitement has finally passed."

"Morton. He should have a little bit of jelly roll on his face, I think," Hannah said with a frown. "Calling up thousands of troops and ordering guns and ammunition as if Morgan was Robert E. Lee and the Army of Virginia. All over two thousand men who never even came near the capital. War hysteria, if you ask me."

"Political hysteria," Harriet opined. "It discredited the Democrats, and Morton will do anything to fuel the fire of hatred towards the opposition party." She looked at her sister, who was fanning herself with a fan printed with Bible verses and an advertisement from the local funeral home. Susan did look well. Age had been kind to her, Harriet had to concede. Even if she had not been a beautiful girl, she was a handsome woman. Susan still had her figure, Harriet told herself a little ruefully, looking down at her own broad lap and thick ankles.

"What was in this letter Thomas got from the governor?" Hannah asked. She watched young Hilary Houghton push a croquet ball around with a stick in the yard; he was walking around the edge of the house towards the back door. His brothers Walter and John were preparing to go to war; he would be the only one at home soon.

"You remember last spring? When Thomas inspected the sutlers who serviced Indiana regiments?" Susan Brooks smiled with pride. "Well, President Lincoln has asked him to serve as one of three men on a committee to do a general investigation of sutlers in the Federal army. He—we, actually, I am to go too, is to leave in a couple of weeks."

Hilary had gone looking for his cousin, Seymour Brooks, and now they were putting up wickets for croquet. The dirt was so hard in the yard they had to pound the wickets with mallets to get them into the ground.

Harriet set her glass of lemonade down on the porch rail. She twirled her finger about in the cool mist that had formed on the outside of the glass. "I wonder—would you want anyone—I mean, is it something I could go along on, too?"

Susan looked at her sister in surprise. "Go to Washington, Sister? You have never been on a train."

"I know. I have hardly been out of Loogootee since I came here. I thought I might go." Perspiration wet her starched blouse; she unbuttoned the top button of her collar. "Not for the sights, really." She looked across the yard at the croquet game. The balls were bumping across the ground lickety-split as the two young men, bored with the summer heat, shot them like cannon balls along the sun-parched ground.

"Why would you go, Harriet?" Hannah Poore wanted to know.

"Well, the Fourteenth Regiment is not far from Washington. They are in camp on the Rapidan River, so Will wrote to us all last week, and I thought I might go to see him."

"Would you now?" Susan Brooks said with a little irritation. Seymour and Hilary had taken off their shirts.

"Boys, the neighbor girls might happen by and see you," Susan called to them.

"For heavens sake, Susan, what is the matter with seeing a man's chest?" her mother demanded, rising in her chair. "Sometimes I think you get too finicky reading those ladies' magazines about Queen Victoria. Everyone so modest. I guess you've forgotten how much of each other we saw in that one-room cabin out in Orange County in bygone days." Her daughters looked at her with condescending smiles.

"It's so hot," Hannah continued, "I think I'm breathing in a Pittsburgh coal furnace. If only the breeze would blow."

Susan sighed, considering her sister Harriet's request. "Well, I suppose it would be all right for you to go with us to Washington. I'm sure Thomas wouldn't mind. Seems a bit odd, a mother going out to camp, but fathers do go out—"

"Odd, indeed," Hannah Poore muttered and stood up. "Seymour and Hilary," she shouted across the lawn, "let's get a bucket from the well and I'll slosh you with water. Then I'll put on my day dress and you can slosh me—" Her daughters looked at her with mild disapproval.

"Pish and pother, even Queen Victoria would want to stand in a showerbath on a day like this," she said and went to get the bucket. As she passed Harriet she said, almost casually, "Once the croquet ball is through the wicket, it's gone. And if you try to call it back, you break the rules. No good to chase it halfway across the nation, either."

After she had removed her soaking wet dress, towelled herself and changed into a cool gingham, she sat before her old Chute writing desk. It came all the way from Massachusetts, survived the lean-to living in the wilderness and the flood that had nearly washed them all away, and still it stood proudly, with relatively few scratches. "Like me," she thought. "I need to be needed. They are starting to treat me as if I were senile. Those tight, patient smiles, I hate 'em. When I was forty, my idiosyncracies were part of my 'rugged frontier individualism.' Now I'm just a tiny bit dotty."

She picked up a letter that lay on the desk. "Nobody thought to ask if I had a letter, too." She reopened the letter, which was from Eustace also and read it again. The last paragraph said, "Grandmother, my friend Jacob Joe Scott has been gone now over a month. We have no word but think he has been tranferred among cavalry units, in various Rebel camps on the way to Richmond and prison. Will you pray for him? I fear the worst."

"Of course," she thought, opening her Bible. "It comes as naturally as breathing for me to pray for this son of my old, dear friend. Companion in spiriting Negroes across the state to freedom, Friend John Robert. I pray for your son, for both your sons, because I know that they both are swimming in troubled waters." She opened the Bible at random and saw the verse, "Whom the Lord loveth, he chasteneth." Then she sighed and bowed her head in reverie as much as prayer.

Delia Dugger stood on the hill above Rivertides, her back against a catalpa tree. The wind blew her skirt about her legs and pushed fretfully against the picnic cloth where Zach still sat, smoking a cigar after a huge lunch. They had tethered their horses a half mile back and walked through the woods on a barely perceptible trail to this spot above the Wabash where Delia's father had brought her when she was a child.

"And so they captured him, after all," Delia said, scanning the waters. A steamboat passed slowly by on its way to Vincennes. It would have trouble, maybe go aground in these low waters. Like the people in her life.

"Ironic, isn't it?" Zach said. "Hardly a month after his men captured Jacob Joe and sent him God knows where, Morgan ends up on the way to prison himself."

"More than ironic," Delia said coldly. "Tragic is a better word, at least in the case of your brother. You are quite cavalier sometimes, aren't you, Mr. Scott, about others' lives?"

"I couldn't have done anything to stop Jake's capture. I've told you that."

"I know. You arrived just too late. But what if you had been there? That's what I want to know. Would you have spoken?"

Zach was silent, stubbing out the cigar with his boot heel against the brown dirt by the picnic cloth.

"No," Delia said, her eyes still on the Wabash. "You would not have lifted a finger to save your own brother because you hate him, have been jealous of him ever since you were small children, and grudge him everything he ever had."

Zach did not disagree, but frowned at her defiantly.

"Just as you stood by, as you have told me yourself, as a preacher of the Gospel was shot through the thigh by a bunch of adventurers and thieves. As you yourself shot a man, in cold blood and without flinching at the rally in Indianapolis."

Zach rose and brushed himself off indifferently while Delia watched him. "React to what I say, I tell you," she said, banging her fist against the tree.

"Why should I? I am who I am." He came to her. "You must have known that for quite a while. Why didn't you say that I am deceiving your mother? That the only reason she lets us go about alone is that I gave her my word as a gentleman that I would treat you like a sister." She looked up into his eyes, anger battling with the magnetism that seemed to radiate from him, like heat from the August sun.

"That while your brother marches with Ewell and Lee, I take his place for you and her. And I do, except that your brother cannot love you like this." He reached inside her bodice, put his hand on her breast.

Delia showed no sign that the touch aroused her and took his hand from her bodice. She looked at him fixedly. "Why did I save you in that theatre?" she said in a low voice, filled with hatred—really loathing of herself. She had met him more than once around her own home in the last few weeks for desperate, passionate encounters, all of which had left her both fulfilled and confused. She loved him; she despised herself for the secret, sinful nature of that love.

"You saved me to adore you," Zach said, pulling her to him.

"You are bad—just bad," Delia said, struggling a little. He put his parted lips slowly on hers, held her closer. She ceased her struggling. He kissed her again, unbuttoning his shirt so his heart could beat close to hers. She clung to him, savoring in spite of herself the nipping, moist kisses he was giving her, the feel of his chest against her bodice. "And I am hopelessly caught by my own despised love for you," she finally said. They clung, and finally sank to the earth near the picnic cloth, above the smooth, earth-brown waters of the river.

Afterwards they lay watching the sky through a canopy of catalpa leaves and the long seed pods which hung among them. Delia's head was pillowed on Zach's muscular arm. The passion which had swept through her left her mind passive and her will temporarily suspended.

"Marry me, Delia," Zach whispered in a voice so faint she was not sure she heard it.

She sat straight up and turned to give him a look in which scorn and love were equally mixed. "Marry you? I've given you my body and part of my soul, but my own name, my life, never! You are a scoundrel! It is my misfortune that our lives are twined, that I love you and perhaps always shall, but I will not marry you."

Without a word Zach slowly stood and, with a small bow and an enigmatic smile, helped his lady love to her feet.

Jacob Joe Scott sat despondently outside the courthouse in Orange County, Virginia, now a holding place for prisoners on their way to the camps which were spread all over the Confederacy. His cavalry guard was grazing his horse, his gun pointed at him from a distance. He had been alone for this last leg of the journey; the lieutenant whom Morgan had sent with him under guard had been transferred to a prison in Georgia.

"Don't go in there, friend, if it isn't forced," a voice said behind him. "Thee would not stable animals there, let alone a man."

"I can smell it from over here," Jacob Joe said and turned to face the man who had spoken. He was a small man with a rather too-large head and huge spectacles.

"Thee has just joined us," the man said, shaking Jacob Joe's hand. "'Tis a long road to take to Richmond and we are not there yet, friend."

"You are right to call me friend, sir, for I see you use the Friends' speech which I have given up, though my rearing and calling are as a Quaker."

"Good, good," the man said, wringing Jacob Joe's hand in congratulation. "Sit thee down and tell me how thee happen to be in the hands of the Devil."

And so Jacob Joe told the man, whose name was Tilghman Vistal, how as he was scouting for the Eightieth Indiana of Lincoln's army and how he had come upon Morgan's Raiders, or rather they had come upon him, and how he was taken to Morgan's camp, had met the famous general and was sent away.

"And thee hast wandered about Tennessee and western Virginia for a month, waiting for a guard party able to take thee to Richmond."

"Yes. I have one guard from Morgan's troops. Lucky for this man he did not ride north into Indiana and Ohio, for most of his cavalry was taken, thank God, but he still feels bound by his orders and now half the Confederate army knows about them. I am to be put in Castle Thunder and used as exchange bait."

"Ah, yes. If we can survive to get there."

"Tell me your story, sir."

"We shall have time for that. I and my guard have been added to thy party and we will be travelling together. Let it be said, friend, that I am an objector in my conscience to fighting in any form."

"I was that way at the beginning of the war but changed," Jacob Joe murmured a little sadly.

The man looked at him not unkindly. "We shall talk later. Let me show thee the quarters we have tonight."

The two men stood and Jacob Joe's guard followed, a few paces behind.

"Who is thy guard?" Vistal whispered.

"A Louisiana rice planter who joined the war late. He never lets me out of his sight," Jacob Joe told him in a low voice. "Perhaps it gives him something to do now that Morgan's cavalry is destroyed. Perhaps it's interesting to him to see the sights of the Confederate army as it tries to right itself after what I think are awful blows—the losses of Vicksburg and Gettysburg."

"Has he been humane to thee? My guard is sarcastic and mean-spirited," Vistal said a little sadly.

"Mine has said little and offered fewer opinions. What he does is guard me like a hawk. I cannot believe I am so important. My family is well-connected in Republican circles, it is true, in Indiana—"

"Then that is why thee are being held. There are many Southerners that Richmond wishes returned, and you will be bait."

They had drawn near the steps of the huge, looming three-story Georgian building. "I think I have heard of the Orange County Courthouse," Jacob Joe murmured. "I should have known it by its smell."

"Half the world has heard of it by now," Vistal said. "Its infamous squalor could only have been dreamed up by the Confederacy at its dregs."

"I don't rightly see how it could be any worse than the spot we stayed last night," Jacob Joe said. "My guard arranged to have us stop at Lynchburg. We were in a leaky old farmhouse which seemed to have a spring in the cellar. Water kept creeping up over the floorboards. And the heat and flies and mosquitoes were beyond bearing."

"Yes. But it will be heaven compared to this—" Vistal took out a hand-kerchief and covered his mouth. They climbed the steps into the interior of the building. Jacob Joe felt his stomach turn. The smell of human defecation and sour vomit was so strong it was difficult to breathe without retching.

They turned, hesitant, but Vistal's guard, wearing the uniform of a Confederate Tennessee regiment prodded them forward. "Go on in, draft dodger," he said to Vistal. "Ah've been given the privilege of seein' that you get to stay in the Orange County Courthouse for one night. Then we join this Yankee's party and take you on to Richmond. You've caused us all a mess of trouble with your beliefs, whilst we're looking for men to win this war.

So we'll see how you like a night in the Hotel Orange." He brandished his pistol and Vistal, shrugging, went in.

"You don't have to go in yet, Scott," his guard said in his Louisiana drawl.

"If my friend goes, I go," Jacob Joe stated flatly.

They went through the door, into what was originally a house parlor, later a public court house chamber. It was now serving as the quarters for scores of men on their way to one prison or another in the South. Boards were ripped up, insects crawled on the walls. There were no chairs and only a few filthy blankets for cover.

"Abandon hope all ye who enter here," said a man cooking strips of raw pork fat over the fireplace. Others coughed and spat in the corner.

"There's consumption in all these places," Vistal whispered.

Smoke filled the room, and it wasn't only from the cooking fire. Other men had fires going along the sides, under the windows, anywhere they could. The smoke filtered all over, leaving eyes smarting and making the coughing men hack harder.

"This is impossible. And that stench—"

"The worst yet. There is no privy. Only a back room with no outlet."

"Don't they let the men go outside?"

"The guards here are the lowest specimens the human, or ape race, can dredge up. No one else would take the duty. That back room is beyond any human description."

"I'll find a way to hold myself till morning."

"Thee will be one of the lucky ones. Here, I have a scheme for surviving the smoke. There's a little office, used to be the court clerk's, here off the big one. If we sit near the floor we can hold these wet scarves over our faces and manage to breathe and talk."

"Well, there's no chance of eating in this reek," Jacob Joe said.

"It don't matter. I don't get rations anyway. I have to beg or buy what I eat."

Jacob Joe looked at him in horror. "They don't feed you?"

"No. They have punished me from the moment they met me. They hate all prisoners at this point in the war, but Quakers who won't work in the army get the worst treatment." His eyes were implacable. "In the beginning they all had their honor—the honor of the Southern gentlemen. They dined with prisoners of war, treated them as honored guests. But now they have lost too many battles. They steep in their own bile and take it out on us."

"I see," Jacob Joe said quietly. He had noticed it too, all along the path. The strident remarks, the lack of concern for his shelter. But he had learned to take care of himself in the army anyway, and above all else, he told himself, his spirits would stay high. That was the only way to survive.

Somehow it worked. Though he lost so much weight he was like a ghost, he had not been seriously ill, and he was still able to walk and ride a horse.

They made their way past the men cooking their miserable suppers. As they went, some yelled sardonic greetings at them, "Hail and farewell, fellow passengers on the ship of fools," or "Welcome to the Excretion Inn." Some gave them surly curses, as if they expected newcomers would be vying for spots at the meager fires.

"Being a prisoner makes a good many men selfish," Vistal said. He led Jacob Joe to the small clerk's office and they sat down. Their guards sat outside the window under a tree. The smell was not as bad here off the main room, and the two of them could breathe and talk.

"What circumstances could have made them hate you so that they glory in putting you in this sewer hold," Jacob Joe wanted to know after they had settled themselves.

"I am a reproach because I insist on following my own inner voice. I came from Tennessee. I was conscripted at eighteen by the Confederate army, and I refused to go for conscience's sake until I was arrested last Second Month."

"You would not pay the fine?" Jacob Joe wanted to know. It had been a debate at his Quaker college, Earlham, when the war broke out. Which was the most Christian way: go to free the slaves, stay and pay the fine, or stay back, refuse to do anything at all and face consequences?

"I was not at liberty to pay the fine. To do so would have been to support the killing. We are taught that paying money to soldiers is just as bad as firing the rifle."

"I know. I went through the same quandary and finally went to free those in bondage. It seemed the greater call."

"For some it is. For me, I could not serve the god of war in any guise. I was assigned to the Fourth Tennessee Regiment. They tried to swear me in, but I told them I was not at liberty to be sworn. They took me to camp and wanted me to clean the jakes if I would not clean a gun, but I said I was not at liberty to clean the privy. I would not cook, I would not serve as an officer's assistant. I would do nothing."

"They didn't let that pass."

"No. They were not at liberty to do so, I guess. My case went on through the ranks upward, and finally I went to see General Polk. His adjutant was kindly, but he asked me what I would do if men came to my house to kill all within."

"What did you say?"

"I told him I would try to follow the Savior as closely as I could in my actions then. He let me go to my home, then, for a while, but soon they called me again. Even my father thought I should pay out now, but I was—"

"You were not at liberty to do so," Jacob Joe said with a wan smile.

"Exactly. I was with the Fourth Tennessee again, and again I refused to help the war, even when they gave me hospital duty."

"Well, many Friends have felt they could humanely work in the wards with the wounded."

"Not I. Finally the soldiers began to grow surly. They tried everything but I would not serve, and they could not accept my conscience. I grew ill and they left me outside, exposed to the elements without care. Finally a surgeon took pity on me and brought me inside. When I was better, they took me out to a brush pile, determined I should at least clear land for camp. Some of the men were drinking. They took me bodily to the pile of brush and pointed their guns at me."

"And?"

"I would not move. Then a man took a sickle and put it in my hand and began to chop with me. I stayed like a rag doll. Then they began to curse at me. 'Damn you, you molly-coddled Quaker, we are fighting for the life of our land, seeing comrades die, and you refuse to even cut the brambles.' "

" 'This war is wrong! Wrong in the eye of the Savior, wrong in the word of God. We are commanded not to kill. Thee asks me to endanger my soul's salvation?' I asked one, looking him in the eye. He took out his bayonet and stabbed me in the thigh. They all took their bayonets—"

He could not go on. He looked out the door, where loud shouts were coming as men doused the fires, throwing coals and water on each other in their frustration and wild energy. Vistal rolled up his sleeve. There were scars, not fully healed, many of them, on his upper arm.

"My God," Jacob Joe breathed. "How many wounds—"

"They stabbed me eighteen times, with wounds from a half an inch to an inch deep. They hit me on the head with the butts of their rifles and sat me in the sun. Finally I collapsed, and they called for medical aid. But after that they demanded a court martial for me and I was tried and sentenced to Castle Thunder, where I go now."

The noise in the other room was like horses thundering as the men began to fight each other. Finally guards with guns came in and circulated, and dusk settled over the camp.

"What will Castle Thunder be like?" Jacob Joe wondered. "I have found no one who will tell me. It cannot be worse than this."

"No. It is for 'valuable' prisoners of the Rebels. Rebellious or criminal officers, prisoners of conscience like me, mostly from the South. Lately they have been admitting a few choice plums from among the captured Northern ranks. But there is one awful thing that tortures them all, even when there is food and the floors are swept."

"That is?"

"Loss of liberty." Jacob Joe nodded and finally, through the rosy twilight that filtered in through the one window in the office, Vistal asked, "Now, my friend, how did thee lose thy liberty? Thee are not a prisoner of conscience."

"No," Jacob Joe exhaled carefully through his mouth, as he was wont to do in this place. "And yet, in a way, I probably gave up my liberty, too. I am not at peace, friend, because I hate my brother. I was about to be married and my leave was cancelled, and I hold him for part of the blame."

"A sad fortune of war," the other man said.

"Yes. My poor love Sophie has not heard a word from me. The hardest thing of this confinement is I haven't been able to write letters. She must be pining, wondering if I am dead. I pine for her. But I was not without fault, sir. I was angry at the world, and particularly at my brother. Zach has always done me wrong and he finally supported the South openly. I did not obey the Biblical command we grew up knowing."

"If your brother hath aught against thee, go to him and speak."

"Or bless those that curse thee, pray for those that despitefully use thee. Instead I chose to hate, inwardly, where no one could see. Such a state of mind is not good in the eyes of God. I rode into trouble, and here I am. I am more a prisoner of myself than of the Confederacy."

Vistal looked at Jacob Joe sharply. "Ah, perhaps we have been put in each other's ways for a reason. We shall see."

"We shall see. I am going to find my guard, and then I'll return and stay this night with you."

He went through the door, through growling, surly men in groups about the room. "We will have many more nights together, my friend," Vistal said to himself. "Many a long road to traverse before we find the meaning of the word liberty." He took out his Testament and began to read.

Sophie bustled in and out of the shops along Fourth Street in Louisville. Her Aunt Althea was more or less willingly carrying her packages. In spite of herself, Althea was fond of this niece of hers, who wore frivolity as charmingly as any of the other garments she put on. They stopped before a window of a hat shop.

"Well, I guess we should give thanks for the war in Louisville, anyway," Sophie remarked.

Her aunt looked at her questioningly.

"Oh, I don't really mean all the killing and all that. Of course that's dreadful. I guess I should know, with my own dear one gone off to God knows where. But if we have to have a war, and be home, I think we might as well do it prosperously. And our hotel is just a-swarm with paying Yankees again.''

Althea looked at a delicious straw bonnet with clusters of fruit on its brim. ''Some folk say we should be sacrificing too. Sewing bandages, having bazaars.''

''Oh, they're doin' that too, Auntie. Or they were at the beginnin' of the war. But I can't really get excited 'bout makin' bandages for Yankee hospitals. And after so many bazaars, even if you go just for the sociability, it gets tiresome. It does to me, without anyone to dance with.''

''What have you heard from Jacob Joe? I asked his brother Zach last week before I left and he said he had heard nothing. You'd think they'd at least inform his next of kin.''

''Well, *he* wouldn't tell you if he had heard. He's about as forthcoming as the Old Man of the Sea, if what Jacob Joe tells me is true.''

''Zach has been a fine help to me on the farm. There are so many things I can't do. Delia wants to be in full charge, flaunting herself like a field hand, I say, and I can't let a young lady of breeding do that forever. While I was gone there was no choice. Anyway, I don't have time to think on it too much. Keeping accounts for my father and mother's plantation, writing to Calhoun—''

''And how is my dashing cousin? Lawdamercy, dashin' off to war like that right in the middle of the drama. I didn't know he had the courage to say tat to a turkey.''

Althea looked at her with a frown. ''None of us may have known him very well. He and Willie are near the Virginia rivers with Doles' Brigade, still. And though he writes once a month, I write every week. I didn't know I'd miss him so. He never seemed to do much, and I don't think I paid him much mind.'' Pensively she pulled back from the shop window. ''Anyway, I don't have a minute to worry about deep things.''

''I need a bonnet for the vested fall corduroy. To think, finding a dress that fits in a shop. Ready to wear. That'll soon be the rage. Why, every dressmaker in the county will be out of business.''

A tiny bell tinkled as they entered the shop. A summer storm had blown through in the morning, cooling the sizzling streets and rooftops, and it was comfortable in the store. The shop clerk, a child of a girl with thin arms and bright, intelligent eyes. who looked as if she would be happier behind the borrowing desk at the ladies' library, brought out new plaids and checked cottons.

''Just think,'' Sophie said as the girl went to the back to get the newest thing from New York that Sophie had demanded, ''that friend of Delia's is working in one of these places. What did you say her name was?''

"Lettie McClure. A distant relative of Jacob Joe's. Her grandfather and his grandmother were brother and sister. They came up from Kentucky—"

"Posh and piffle, don't tell me all that pother," Sophie said with a tinkling laugh. She was pulling out yard goods, holding them over her hands. "Everybody in southern Indiana and Kentucky is related to each other. We're just a hotbed of incest—well, figuratively speakin'." She put down the cloth bolts and picked up a hat—a spoon bonnet with larger-than-life pansies around its brim. "Anyway, I don't want to be related—if I ever am—to a shopgirl." Althea looked about to see if the poor shop clerk had heard, but she seemed to be fussing with tissue paper in the rear of the store. Sophie smiled at herself in the mirror. "Just tell me if I look winning in this bonnet."

"Depending on whom you want to win," her aunt said with a slow smile.

"Well, whoever takes me to wear the corduroy to the Fall Mummers' Ball," Sophie answered with a cat-like grin.

"Who would take an engaged girl?"

Sophie set the bonnet down forcefully on the table and came to stand before her aunt, her hands on her hips. "Now, Aunt," she said with a broad, strident smirk, "we can't sit around and pine away because Lee and Burnside no, Hooker, Meade"—she threw up her hands in exasperation, trying to remember—"whoever the silly Yankee is, are sitting facing it off somewhere out on a river. The soldiers don't want us to mope about till we get sick. After all, they're fightin' this war for us, aren't they?"

"Well, among other reasons, I 'spose."

Sophie tied the bonnet ribbons with a flourish. "Well, then—let's dance—to celebrate the coming end of the war, whenever that may be!"

Althea looked at her bemusedly. "And who will we dance with?"

"How about Tucker Mahaffey? Will he do?" Sophie asked, grinning brightly.

"Do I know him?"

"You remember—he was at that silly lecture at Lyceum Hall," Sophie answered.

Althea thought a moment, then said, her brows knitting, "Wait a moment, didn't his brother ride with Morgan the Raider?"

"Well, yes. He was one of the ones got acrost the river there in Ohio and is home on leave."

"But Morgan captured Jacob Joe. How can you—"

"Aunt, why are you so fussy? I thought you were a Southern supporter. Besides, Tucker is charmin'. He persisted in callin' on me even though he knew I was spoken for. Mama admitted him. I didn't plan it that way." Her eyes grew tender, and Althea believed her. "You know I try to favor Mama's whims. She's had so many disappointments."

Althea nodded. Sophie had always been a devoted daughter, first to her father, whom she had nursed through dropsy, then to her often difficult mother. But that did not answer the question she had asked. "I repeat," Althea insisted, "does Mr. Tucker Mahaffey take engaged girls to dances?" The shopgirl had come over timidly and was standing about to see if they liked anything, like a dog waiting at a table for a tidbit to be tossed. Sophie put her finger to her lips. "Shoosh, Auntie dear," she said to Althea.

They paid for the fruit bonnet for Althea and the straw hat for Sophie and the shopgirl went to put them into bags. Sophie said in a low voice, "Aunt, how can I be engaged to someone who is in a prison camp? If he is even alive. I've thought about it a lot, and I think our vows were broken when he was taken prisoner."

"Were they now?" Althea asked coolly. The girl returned with the bag, and Sophie waited until they had exited the shop to take up her explanation.

"I'm not sayin' I don't love Jacob Joe. It's just that now that time has passed, I'm confused. I don't know if I could wait two years, be the type of girl who sits faithfully, lookin' at his likeness on the bedside table. I was born for fun!"

Althea nodded. There was something to be said for knowing oneself, after all. "And what about Jacob Joe?"

"Well, I'm just goin' to a few parties and gettin' about the town a little. When he comes back, we'll take up where we left off. After all, I'm not a widow woman, am I?" They walked along the streets which emitted wisps of steam from the drenching rain of the morning.

"Who have you told this to?"

"Well, Mama, of course, and I wrote to Dora at the hospital in Georgia. She wrote back a very chidin' letter, I must say. Preached at me just like Parson Pribble."

"Trust Dora to do that," Althea murmured. "Well, perhaps she's worn out from all the nursing she's doing. The wounded from Gettysburg fill up the wards even down there, they say. And there isn't enough chloroform or medicine."

"Piffle, Aunt, there you go again. Always talkin' about tragedy. Tragedy, tragedy! I get so sick of it. I feel like I'm livin' in the middle of a play with William Booth in it. I can't help it if I'm twenty when this awful war is goin' on, and I intend to live in spite of it. Now let's go into the confectioners' for cakes and tea."

Her aunt nodded, more out of weariness than assent, and they proceeded down the street.

"The war is not at all over," Willis Mawkins said, tilting back the chair in his office. An oil lamp dimly illuminated the face of Zach Scott, hunched over a newspaper on the other side of the desk.

"With the surrender at Vicksburg, the Mississippi is gone. And Lee was smashed at Gettysburg, to say nothing of the miserable mess General Morgan made of his raid," Zach said disconsolately. He looked down at the newspaper. "Morgan taken to prison in Columbus, Ohio after capture," he read aloud.

"Well, 'tis true it didn't succeed, but that was because the gallant general dallied too much in villages and didn't recross the Ohio soon enough. But it did accomplish the purpose I thought it would have." His voice emerged blurred through the cough drop he was sucking on.

"What purpose do you think we served?" Zach said, staring into the wick of the lamp. "All the work we put into the castles of the Knights of the Golden Circle. They didn't lift a finger to help the South."

"No, but they still may. They exist; they meet, even more now that the Negro is freed and filterin' into the North." Mawkins chuckled grimly and reached in his pocket for another cough drop. "That, of course, is the kernel of the nut, isn't it? The men of the Northwest won't accept Negro equality. I say they never will. It knocks them off their own perches."

"But how can we channel that hatred, that disgust with Lincoln and the war?" Zach wanted to know. "Not even a raid right into the heartland jarred their complacency."

The chair Mawkins was leaning in came down with a thump. "It takes a good share o' trouble to get a man to put up his fists. If the war keeps on goin', if Lincoln keeps on suspendin' civil rights, if the farmers see more hard times—"

"If. You have built a house of cards made of 'ifs.' I think we don't have the power in the state to keep anti-war fervor going. We need something else." He had folded up the newspaper; now he thumped it against the edge of the desk to make his point.

"Yes. Something else. It just may come. Something a good deal bigger."

Zach raised his eyebrows. What did Mawkins know?

The other man was not going to go beyond that. "We must bide our time now, wait out events. Keep the castles going—"

"They don't need us. With all the rigmarole and back-slapping and whisky drinking they do, they'll continue no matter what happens to the war."

"As long as hatred fuels their cause."

"I thought you believed it was states' rights and the independence of the South." Zach put the paper on the table again and unfolded it. He opened it and thumbed to the second page, as if to indicate that he was finished with the discussion.

Mawkins put his hand on the paper and pulled it down. He looked briefly at it. "See this?" he said stridently, pointing to the headline "Seventy thousand persons protested the draft in New York City. Burned Lincoln in effigy. Negroes were killed, the draft halted." He looked Zach in the eye. "Slogans may start the wood in the engine, but hatred is the coal in any war. There is fuel everywhere now, even in New York City."

Zach stood up. "Even New York can have pie in the sky. If something really important comes up, let me know. In the meantime I have personal concerns and my farm to look to—"

"Personal concerns," Mawkins said, in an insinuating voice.

Zach narrowed his eyes. "What do you know of them?"

Mawkins took a small, pearl-topped box from his pocket. It appeared new. He took the cough drops from his pocket and put them in it, lining them up carefully with one jewelled finger. "I keep tabs on my old secretary." he told Zach. "In fact, I visited Lettie today. I know she has a friend who seems close to your heart."

Zach rose and put a finger under the other man's nose. "Mawkins, leave her out of our dealings."

Mawkins backed away a bit and snorted scornfully. "I do not intend to mix business with pleasure. See that you don't. We both stand to have more than idealism left when the war is done. I think you may look for fine rewards, if my contacts beyond the state are true to us."

"Contacts?" Zach looked at him, interested. Mawkins had always been very vague about who he talked to in the larger Southern cause. Now that Vallandigham was out of the picture, fled from his confinement in the South and headed on a ship for Canada, who was Mawkins contacting?

"When the time is ripe, you will know," Mawkins said evasively. "Look for something bigger," he added. Then he turned the lamp down and slowly watched the flame go out, as Zach turned on his heel and left the shop, leaving the newspaper on the table.

Lettie stood in the darkness looking at the Wabash River. Mist made pulsating haloes around the few lights on the levee, on steamboats and barges. The warehouses and factories were ugly scars on the shores of what had been a beautiful river shore. She knew that somewhere to the north was the beautiful mansion of William Henry Harrison, now a shadow of its former self, with leaky windows and warped floorboards.

Horace and her mother had talked about this lately. Harrison had been governor of a territory all the way to Louisiana and President of the United States, but he was gone now, along with the forests and the Indians, and his house was sinking into disrepair, used for this or that purpose, surrounded by factories.

If you lived in Vincennes, her mother said, you could see what change meant, maybe more than any other city in the old Northwest. Catherine McClure Hogue had come in 1803, when Vincennes was still a French village and the memory of the Revolution and its heroes was new. But everything changes, and heroes die. There, near the spot where they said Clark had conquered the British were tanning plants and a steam mill. The old French houses stood, repainted and lived in now by painters and shoe factory workers. The French themselves, who had built these houses, had disappeared from the city they founded—or married, long ago, so their identity was lost.

Vincennes was an ugly place now. The bankers and lawyers who were building three-story homes with ballrooms over on Sixth Street, trying to pretend they were People of Importance in the New Era, didn't care.

It didn't matter. Whatever dwelt among the shadows in the bayberry bushes was waiting, Lettie told herself firmly. She was thirty-eight and had no one except a mother and a brother to love her. And the brother himself was going a-courting. That was what he was doing, writing to a plump widow with a son over in Corydon. This weekend he had gone to Corydon, in a new suit and tie, with a fancy haircut. He was like a young fox, gone looking for a vixen, all proud and prancy and bushy-tailed.

There was no one to love her and no chance now. Half the town talking, still, and there was no way to tell them about Reverend Paden's outrage.

She began to walk back to the flat. Willis had come over in the afternoon, oily-voiced and solicitous. He wondered how she was getting along, how her affairs were progressing, had missed her sound head at the books. What he wanted was another surrender in her bed, gratification without any commitment. This was what she was reduced to. She was the woman a man could go to for gratification. It hadn't come to that but it might. A woman on a back street, with a daintily engraved card she could give out to a few discreet men. Not really a whore, but—

She turned the skeleton key in the lock. She had brought the whole mess on herself by wanting to live, to feel. Oh, it wasn't remorse she was feeling, or pain, or shame. None of those. Just deadness. The emotional carousel she had been riding for the past few weeks had stopped. Her heart was still, dead still, like a dynamo that had thrown its fan belt. *Slut, slut, slut.* That was it, that was all. The words no longer pierced like daggers, they fell like lead. It was never going to be any different. She took off her hat, threw down her gloves on the settee.

She went to the desk drawer and reached far to the back for the brown glass morphine bottle. Then she drank a very large amount of it and took her chair to the window to wait.

The lights above the river swam. The room became smaller, objects receded and began to murmur to her like benign friends. Even fear no longer had an edge, but was dull and comforting, like an old bed quilt. After a few moments, the shape that lived in the bayberry bush came out of the shadows. It was as big as all the universe, and it moved to swallow her pain.

Late August, September, October, 1863

Chapter Sixteen

William Houghton looked out from his perch under a tree on Governor's Island in New York Harbor and saw the crowded New York City shoreline, with barges bobbing at piers, and the masts of schooners etched against the sky. Across the water as he turned his head a bit in a different direction, he could trace a skyline of the sturdy factory buildings of Jersey City and Brooklyn.

The wind was blowing strongly. It never seemed to stop out here on Governor's Island, and he could not help but be impressed by the power of the ocean and the wind, proudly, relentlessly, pushing at what man had created in this greatest city in North America.

It was a rare moment of calm in a round of unceasing administrational duties for Houghton. The Fourteenth and other veterans of Gettysburg had been called up to enforce the draft in New York City after rioting swept the city in July. Initial order was restored by the first troops to arrive. Now, before the next drawing of draftees, the Gibraltar Brigade was awaiting assignment to camp somewhere near the city. Colonel John Coons was away on a general court martial and Lige Cavins, who was in command—well, Cavins was having a good time, representing the regiment in a social way, was what he called it.

Houghton had a lonely job as major, seeing to the safe quartering of the men, the gathering of daily reports which had to be submitted to Division Headquarters, the superintending of the quartermaster. Quartermastering supervision had, as a matter of fact, suddenly grown easy. Beem had been appointed acting quartermaster, and things were actually getting done in the food and supply line. But there were the sick and injured, too. Yokum, one of the recruits, had fallen into the hold and broke his leg just as they came in on the steamer into New York Harbor. And some were just returning from long-term care of wounds after Gettysburg. From what he knew of general hospitals, he was surprised any of them had returned. The cynicism of the thought embarrassed him. Anyway, someone had to arrange for beds, provide meals for those who were recuperating, and get them pills. The surgeons like Doctor Burkhart had been taken away from regiments, sent to Division Headquarters. Walter McClure, his assistant, was now on regular duty with the regiment, so somebody had to hold the sick men's hands. He was making arrangements for all this nursing care.

Houghton watched the great schooners come into the harbor, their sails tugging at the rigging and the colorful, painted prows cutting the water like plowshares. As a middle-state man who had rarely seen even a pleasure sailboat, Houghton could never get enough of watching them, these mistresses of the seas. "There will come a time," he thought, "when there will be no more of these fine clippers and working schooners, and the world will have lost a piece of its beauty."

There was little of beauty in his own life. Certainly of companionship. If it wasn't for Beem, he would be bereft. All respected him, none sought him out for talk. Well, he was a major, after all, now. There was a slim, paper-thin line of deference now drawn between him and the old friends of his youth—those that were left.

Sometimes, not always, he was tormented by the memories of those left behind. In his dreams he still saw the grave of Bo Reilly and all the others of C Company, his own friends. There was a chain of graves like road signs marking the way back over three years. Gettysburg, Chancellorsvile, Fredericksburg, Antietam, Kernstown, Greenbrier, Cheat Mountain—all had deprived the folk of Martin County, Indiana, of sons, and deprived him of priceless companionship. Bo and Ham and all the rest had been snatched away.

Oddly enough, he thought of the regiment itself as his friend. Every man, now, of the two-hundred fifty who still marched together was his friend, at least in enduring the ordeal. One in soul, forged and amalgamated by trial.

He turned from the water. Cavins came out of the officers' quarters, buttoning his coat. "The orders have come through, Will. We're to camp tomorrow in Brooklyn. Some of the other brigades are going to Washington Park. General Carroll wants us to go over and parade in the streets. No sign of a riot, but you never know with the people of New York," he said. Houghton stood to meet his superior officer, who was freshly bathed, his mustache trimmed. Cavins was handsome, even if his eyes were a little crossed.

"Fine new uniform," Houghton murmured, eyeing the double-breasted frock coat, the dark blue trousers, the sword belt and narrow band of gold braid on his hat.

Cavins turned to be admired. "I'm to meet with the council of women's clubs of New York. They want to honor us, while we're here, with parties and a ball, and we're to perform dress parade for them. I'm jumping out of my skin to go. New York ladies are very forward and flirt even with old married men like me. Harmlessly, of course. I miss the company of ladies, don't you?''

Without an answer to his question, he was off, and Houghton walked back to the officers' tent to arrange for the march and new quartering in Brooklyn tomorrow. He would have to meet again with Beem, but they had already discussed the food and tenting arrangement. Cavins had told him that he wanted the men fully armed and prepared as they marched through the streets. The riots a couple of weeks ago, the papers were saying, were the worst in American history. The mobs murdered two men they thought were unfairly drawing the draft numbers and burned a number of buildings, and President Lincoln wanted the people of the city to understand there was to be no repeat of the wanton disorder. The seasoned troops needed to make a big show as they marched to their new quarters. The bands, he supposed, would be expected to play their most martial airs on the way, and he wanted to be sure the band director, George Washington Lambert, was ready.

He sat at his small desk, determined to do a few personal things before he finished the official papers. He reached into his trunk for a couple of letters needing to be answered. One was from his mother, loaded with details of the trivial lives of people he felt increasingly distanced from as the months passed. He put his pen down and stared at the signature, as heavy with emotion as an exclamation point, then picked up a letter from Augustus Van Dyke, at the Second Corps, Second Division Headquarters.

I am bored with the trivial life among the big brass. Aide de Camp is interesting only when battle is imminent, which is not our situation in the Army of the Potomac now. Brigadier-General Harrow, the shooting star of our regiment, is contemplating resigning. He is bored, too, I guess. When he does, I will be nowhere. You were right at Gettysburg, I suppose, Will, as you usually are. I left at the wrong moment, and I know that now. I miss your chiding.

Houghton was unable to put pen to paper because his thoughts were churning, blown to spume, as the waters he could still see through the tent flap. It was the question Cavins had asked in passing as he left for the meeting with the New York matrons. He had not been able to forget it— something he had asked himself many times in this war. Did he miss the company of women?

Certainly others did. Some of the men visited shady backstreet neighborhoods; he heard Lambert talking about getting away in New York to some of the flats that women kept who paraded the streets, twirling parasols and passing out "calling cards." So people said. It was nothing new of course. The army chased the men out of brothels in every town it camped near. And some of the officers near the towns had even resorted to bigamy to answer the need for female companionship.

He could not say how he felt about all that. Certainly he felt no desire to go to prostitutes as they did, despised that in fact. And he experienced no longings for the girls back home, who had caused him a great deal of trouble in the past.

He started thinking about it after his only real and deep friend, Van Dyke, had left. Left, that afternoon at Gettysburg, ignominiously as far as Houghton was concerned. Houghton pined for the long conversations with Gus, the joking, the confiding he, not Gus had done. Houghton had loved Gus more than a brother and that made him vulnerable to pain more than once when Gus had let him down.

More than a brother. What, exactly, did that mean? And what did it mean that he could not develop any lasting affection for the women he knew? He turned to look through the tent flap at the harbor waters, whitecapped with a stiff breeze from the west, and he wondered if there was something wrong with him.

Wrong? What could be wrong?

As he sat holding the letters, the emotional trauma that enveloped him off and on like miasma since Gus's departure tugged at him. He could not allow himself to even form the words to describe what he was talking about, was not even sure he knew them. There was talk of mules and capons—he had never even paid it enough heed to think about. Of course there were males, men, who did not like women, but he didn't think it was quite that with him. Or was it?

He sat for a long moment, then wadded up the piece of paper he had before him. Mother! All this had something to do with mother! She always covered him, cloaked him with her fluttering attentions. She had sewn him to her skirt with steel ribbons of anxious affection. He'd fought for years to escape. Now, as he continued to watch the power of the wind and the ocean, as he felt their relentless strength, determination awoke in him to free himself once and for all.

And as far as Gus went, if the truth was known, he had been Gus's dog, following him about, listening to his often pompous opinions, which had as much meaning in them as a half-baked potato. Gus had hypnotized him, became his Mesmer. And he let it happen, encouraged it.

Whatever was the matter with his emotions, whatever was going on, one thing was clear to him, and the realization poured over his soul like cold ice-water. In the world as he knew it, the world of Loogootee, Indiana, to which he would be returning should God grant him the ability to live through this war, he must, and would be, married to a good and decent woman. Anything else was unthinkable, and that was what he wanted anyway.

And when the orderly delivered the mail with word in it that his mother was coming to New York City with Uncle Thomas Jefferson Brooks and Aunt Susan, the ice-water in his soul spread throughout his veins and mind, also.

John McClure had been sorting through his gear looking for cash, so that he'd be ready to buy food when he was loosed upon the big city. He looked up to see Lieutenant Landon, who had picked up mail from the orderly for him.

"Lieutenant, you survived the horsepistol?" John McClure said, smiling.

"So they tell me." Landon was occupied shuffling the letters.

"I know there were two for you here somewhere—"

"Survived the nurses and doctors?"

"They were not hard to live through. It was the visitors."

"Came in droves, did they, to see you?"

"Me and all the other poor souls who had the misfortune to be in that Washington hospital." Landon put a foot on a log and continued sorting mail. "They came in, crinolines flying, young ladies and preachers mostly, holding their noses against the awful smells. 'Ah, Lordy, Alice, how dreadful,' " he mimicked in his best Washington belle accent. " 'Do any of you poor soldiers need the Bible or a novel read? No? Well, we'll just be meandering on through. Whew, Alice.' "

"Must've been bothersome talkin' to 'em all," McClure opined.

"Couldn't get a bit of rest. And if it wasn't the local belles, it was the relatives of the sick men. Came and camped out. A woman extremely large with child came to see her wounded husband, a Gettysburg veteran, and ended up having a baby in the bed next to me. The nurse had to leave some artillery victims to deliver the baby."

"Do tell," McClure said. He chuckled and came over and patted the lieutenant on the back to encourage him to quit talking and finish sorting.

"Mackintosh, McBain, McClure. There it is." Landon finally came to his letters, gave them to him, and walked, still a little painfully, down the road.

Tommy Thompson, who had no letter, looked vaguely over his friend's shoulder longingly, as if some of southern Indiana could ooze through the postage stamp and the paper and give him the comfort of home.

"Gawdamighty," John McClure yelled, reading the first few paragraphs. "This is from Mary Jane. Lettie Hogue took morphia."

"What?" Tommy asked blankly.

"Morphia, spirits of morphine in a bottle. She's done it before."

"Did she—was it an overdose?" Tommy asked anxiously, as he quit looking over John's shoulder.

"No. But she almost did herself in. Listen to this. 'Dear John: You will be shocked to hear that our Aunt Lettie a'most died from taking morfia. She was saved at death's door when her friend Delia Dugger came to her place—found her on the floor with the bottle still cluched in her hand. She pulled Lettie up and screeched at her and Lettie mumbled something bout men—Delia said don't you want to live and Lettie said I guess so and Delia went to the horse trawf and threw water on her face and walked her round and woke her up—someway she lived. Oh, John this is a result of that stupid quarel our parents all had over religion and politics and nobody should argue bout neither of them. But it is also because Willis Mawkins shamed her. He ruined her and then dropped her like a hotcake. Then the church tryed her, John. I was there and she wanted to do better but something happened. Miz Dugger was in town to see about a shipment to the army from their farm and had a appryhention. I can see twas God's hand in it caint you? Your sister.' "

Tommy Thompson sat pulling his chin. "Goldurned glad Miss Dugger got there." Finally, he said, "You got another letter, too. What more could there be?"

John McClure, tired of his friend's curiosity, turned his back and opened a small blue letter. " 'Tis from my grandmother, Catherine," he murmured. He read it to himself.

August 16, 1863

Dearest Grandson John:

Just a short note to let you know we are having dark times here but it could have been worse. I have Letitia out here at the farm now. She was despondent and tried to take her life. Willis Mawkins has a lot to answer for, although Lettie can take blame too. And Jewell Simpson put Letitia's name up before the Session at church, so she was almost a murderer. And if there is enough blame to go around, we will give some to Upper Indiana Church for the way they handled it all.

She seems to genuinely regret that she got so desperate and won't try it again, she says. She's reading her Bible but doesn't want to go to or talk to Reverend Paden. I guess she's still shamed. Trifle odd since they re-admitted her to fellowship.

I sent you socks, did you get them?

If I see Jewell Simpson I am going to hit her with my fist. We will see if an

angry, almost eighty-year-old woman can inflict real harm on a fat, flabby
sourpuss of a face.

Your Grandmother
Catherine McClure Hogue

John McClure stood and shook his fist and told Thompson what was in the
letter.

"John," Tommy said guiltily, "I did know that they were trying Lettie at
the Session. My grandpa wrote me. But 'tis odd, he said he sympathized
with her and was glad she was back in the church."

"I don't know about that," John McClure said, "and there ain't nothin' I
can do about Aunt Jewell, but I know that if I ever see that snake-bellied,
rotten-hearted, fornicatin', son-of-a-bitch Mawkins I'll knock his copper
head right into the Wabash."

Thomas Jefferson Brooks, his wife, and his sister-in-law Harriet Houghton, on a business and holiday trip to New York City, came out to see the
Fourteenth Indiana on Sunday parade. Now nicely established in their camp
in Brooklyn, ten of these veteran regiments had marched out and were
preparing to form a parade march in front of over three thousand people.

"Crowds, crowds, I have never seen so many people," Susan Brooks
murmured. "Look how they press the boys, Harriet."

Harriet nodded glumly, looking in apprehension at the crowds pushing
towards the troops, ringing them about with curiosity.

Susan was trying to raise her sister's spirits. Since they had arrived, Will
steadfastly refused to spend time with his mother, or any of them, for that
matter, pleading the cares and duties that had devolved on him. He even
refused to go tomorrow with them to Barnum's Museum, though with the
quiet in the town he could get off from duty, so his friend David Beem said.
Beem and a soldier from Martin County, Isaac Crim, were going with them.

The brigade band was playing "General Meade's March," and the men in
new blue uniforms began to step out and form in regiments. Suddenly, the
crowd surged forward, pressing from behind to see the veterans of Gettysburg. George Washington Lambert, the leader of the band and today its
drummer, was shoved, and his drum fell to the ground. The fife and horn
players and the rest attempted to continue, but the crowd continued to push
forward.

Harriet Houghton screamed as she was shoved forward.

"Sister-in-law, don't panic," Thomas Jefferson Brooks cried. Mounted officers from the Fourteenth urged their horses towards the crowd, which fell back, murmuring for a moment.

"Let us see you, Yanks," men's voices cried.

"We have a right to see, too," women called out, holding up children. But those in back refused to quit pushing. There was danger some in the front would be crushed. Thomas Jefferson Brooks stood like a bulwark before the women.

Houghton, on his bay mare, raised his sword above his head. "Fourteenth, Battalion, charge bayonets," he called. The men in the Fourteenth turned towards the crowd and, brandishing their rifles, moved forward in an ever-widening ring to clear the area.

Thomas Jefferson Brooks mopped his brow. The crowd was only temporarily pushed back. It seemed to be forming in back of them again. His sister-in-law Harriet, always afraid of the company of folk in unfamiliar places, was in a state of near panic; he and Susan both were holding her hands.

Will Houghton rode to them. "Put mother up in back of me," he shouted, and Harriet Houghton somehow climbed into the saddle. Will Houghton moved outward, clearing a path for the civilians to exit. Gently he put his mother down. "I don't intend to let a bunch of impolite aunties and uncles and pushy upstart youngsters beat us in this battle after all we've been through," he said without smiling, then returned to post guards so the parade could finish.

Later, the visiting relatives sat on camp stools in Houghton's tent.

"Mother, why are you so afraid of crowds? Fearful of going about?" Will Houghton asked in a matter-of-fact voice. "I want to know."

His mother, now composed, looked at her sister and brother-in-law. Odd how no one had asked, she thought, through all these years. Of all those close to her, only her husband, sensitive and patiently quiet, talked to her of her fears. That Harriet was a little odd, that she had been so fearful she could never go out, no one mentioned. That she was better when Will went to war, but still felt fear akin to panic when she was in crowd, the whole town accepted as they did Cousin Ozro's goiter and Miss Mapleton's "fits." Perhaps they did not wish to open up the subject, in fear that the nightcrawlers might pour out over their feet. Or perhaps they were embarrassed.

"I don't know exactly. I've been that way since I was about twelve. I only know that when I was a child in the wilderness I had a friend who was an Indian, a Delaware who was left behind when the other Indians went west, and he frightened me badly one day." Her eyes went to the dirt near the front flap of the tent, where Will's boots were neatly placed.

"He was so sad he went insane. One day when I was with him, he went wild and hung himself. I was the only one there."

Will blanched. No one had ever told him anything about this.

"Oh, you don't know it all to hear Grandmother Poore talk. At times it was awful out there in the wilderness—the snakes, the dirt in your very teeth, the cold through the chinks in the cabin. We lost the crops, grubbed out the stumps with our own hands and were yellow and sickly most of the time from poor food."

Her sister looked at her, a responsive memory in her face, and they were silent. For a split instant Will Houghton felt that a cold draft had come into the tent and he saw a side of the "fine old frontier" nobody talked about—a squalid, terror-filled side.

Thomas Jefferson Brooks rose and lit a cigar. "There were good things about it," he said. "We survived and made money, and when we were done, we were as tough as a callous on the bottom of my foot."

Harriet found the strength to go on. "For years I couldn't even remember, or wouldn't face, what made me so afraid of the world. But when you were going off to the war, I wanted to say goodbye. So, I made myself look the past in the eye, and after that I found I could go out."

"I suppose we are all shaped by our childhoods," Will said softly.

"Shaped, but not bound," his mother said with dignity. "We all have to pick up the pieces and try to build a whole picture out of the puzzle," she said. "Nobody in the world stops us from doing that. I am better, you know."

The Brooklyn street lights shone on maple trees outside the tent, casting odd, dancing shadows on the canvas. For the first time in his life, Will looked at his mother and aunt and saw people, as flawed and vulnerable as he was. He surveyed the wrinkles which creased Aunt Susan's face. The sun had burnt her year after year, even when she had the patience to use sun bonnets. She had cultivated, even plowed the fields when she was young. And his mother. The dewlaps and soft arms and piteous, questioning look in the eyes. He forced himself to look into them, distasteful as it was to him in his present, antagonistic state of mind. "Does anybody love me, warped though I am?" they seemed to say. Startled, he turned away.

"Maybe I will go with you tomorrow after all," he said, finally.

"This is some breakfast soirée," Thomas Jefferson Brooks said to the soldiers he sat facing around the Fourteenth's campfire the next morning. While the ladies were having their tea, toast and marmalade at the hotel, he had come to have breakfast with "our boys." An odd campfire it was. Women from the city stood around watching bacon frying in the pans and coffee bubbling out of the spouts of huge pots over the coals, while pointing and chatting about the "heroes."

"They look at us like we're giant snakes at the museum," Isaac Crim grumbled.

"You're going to Barnum's with us, I hear, Isaac," Thomas Jefferson Brooks said. "Quite a reputation, from the stories we read. In the old days my brother had an oddities museum in Hindostan Falls, but it fell down due to poor construction. Like the rest of the town, in a way." His voice was dreamy, far away, then strong again as he looked at the eager young men around him. "Have any of you been to see the sights at Barnum's palace? They say they'll stand your hair on end."

"I can hardly wait, sir!" Crim said enthusiastically. "Wisht I had half the brains Barnum has. He's turned odd things into money, like some kind of elf. Why, I hear tell he's got white whales floatin' in seawater, and sharks, and the first hippopotamus seen on the North American continent."

"Probably the South American too," Thomas Jefferson Brooks nodded seriously.

"What say?"

"Never mind. We'll see all the marvels this afternoon." He turned and called out to someone at the next campfire. "John, John McClure. Can you come over here?"

Brooks shook hands with the young man he'd gotten to know well during the visit just before Chancellorsville.

"Miz Poore in health, sir?" John wanted to know.

"Yes. My daughter Susie and her children have moved in while we're gone and the two of them are in charge of the house. Mother Poore's busy anyway. She has been asked to teach the Young People's Sunday School class at the Presbyterian Church, and she's boning up."

"Shouldn't think she'd need to do that," John opined, smiling broadly. "I 'spect she was born with a Bible in her hand. How'd your sons with the Eightieth Indiana survive Morgan's raid?"

"Tuckered out, plum tuckered out," Brooks said. "They're at Knoxville in Tennessee."

"Not much action for any of us now," John told him. "Some kind of calm, I guess, while the Rebels lick their wounds and try to decide how to proceed. Won't do 'em much good, I opine."

Thomas Jefferson Brooks took a cup of coffee someone handed him. "John, I need your help. I'm commissioned to do a study for the government on sutlers."

"Son of a—a gun, sir. They strip us and rip us of our paychecks and then when we're lyin' on the ground without a cent, come and bring dollar pieces o' cake before our noses so we can borry enough to buy their wares."

"Dog meat cut up into sausage, is what it has been," Crim called out and others, grumbling, threw in comments: "A dollar for a pie that ain't fit for a possum." "The women are worse'n the men."

But when he pressed for names and dates, Thomas Jefferson Brooks ran into vague answers, and the men drifted away. Soon the clatter of metal plates and cups being washed in dishpans, and the acrid smell of drowned campfires announced that breakfast was over. Before the men took up morning duties and drill, however, Brooks invited John McClure to go with the group to Barnum's Museum in the afternoon and noted the young man's pleased acceptance. Still, not a word more about the sutlers.

Puzzled, Thomas Jefferson Brooks walked down the road towards his nephew Will Hougton's tent. An earnest young man with a shock of brown-black hair caught up with him. "Sir, I'm Walter McClure."

"McClure. Any relation to—"

Walter, resigned to answering what was a frequent, or perhaps unpleasant question, interrupted him. "There are several McClures in the Brigade. Anyway, I think I may be able to help you with your assignment."

"Oh?" Brooks said, lifting his eyebrows. They walked past the tents a bit and sat on a bench in a nearby park.

"The reason the men aren't helping you is because they're nervous. The sutlers supply whisky, and for many in the field whisky has become a necessity. That's one of the problems with the whole sutler system."

Thomas Jefferson Brooks nodded assent, wondering why he hadn't thought of it sooner. Then Walter McClure began to talk of the sutlers, of their corruption, high prices, and especially their sale of contraband whisky.

"There are syndicates, sir, in the Eastern theatre. They go up the ladder from selling supplies to speculating in illegal goods for both North and South, but the main part of it is whisky. Some men who started out with carts have made millions."

"Well, I can understand the men's wanting to keep their own supply coming, but why protect this scum? The men obviously hate the sutlers."

Walter was silent for a minute, as if deciding something, as they moved away from the bench and back towards the camp. Finally he said, "Some of the men are low-level parts of the syndicate. Maybe some people back home are involved. The others don't want to rat on them."

They had reached Will Houghton's tent. "Thank you, Walter. I'll consider this confidential. I see I have some real nosing about to do. If you can find out anything more, let me know. I assure you it's appreciated—all the way to the top of our government."

At the last minute, David Beem decided not to go to the museum. "I don't want to pay money to look at all the misery and mistakes of humanity. I've seen enough of that in the war," he said.

"Goodbye, then, oh regimental philosopher," Houghton said, bowing low and taking off his hat.

A hack took the festive group from Brooklyn to the very door of Barnum's American Museum. Carriages were dropping folk off from several different approach streets. "My, just look at that," Susan Brooks said, stepping back to look at the imposing structure—four stories, with a multitude of windows and flags of many nations flying from the roof.

"Come, I'm treating. I'll get the tickets if you gentlemen will escort the ladies in," Thomas Jefferson Brooks said. Will Houghton, Isaac Crim and John McClure helped Will's mother Harriet and Susan Brooks into the crowded, bustling portico of the museum.

Inside, crowds of fashionably dressed women with skirts so big they took up space enough for five soldiers perused the catalogue, looking for the exhibits they wished to see.

"I'll get one of those," Susan Brooks said, paying a man in a stall for an illustrated guide. "Frank Leslie did these pictures. I saw one of them in Loogootee," she murmured, looking with great interest at the aquarium pictures. "They keep great sea beasts here and provide the water temperature and salinity they need," she said.

"Till they die," Thomas Jefferson Brooks said, chomping on a cigar. "In the last few years no less than ten whales have died. Barnum gets 'em off the coast of Nova Scotia and then carts 'em back in big tanks, poor beasts, on the train. Two thousand people come to see 'em in two weeks, and then it doesn't matter if they die. Another two are caught and shipped up."

"Well, they're only beasts, I suppose," Isaac Crim said. His head was turning like a top; he had never seen so many bright, inviting and intriguing sights. There were posters of Jenny Lind, the Swedish Nightingale, whom Barnum had introduced to America in a lengthy, fabulously successful tour and the Siamese twins who fought and tormented each other, even while he was exhibiting them, and a variety of exotic animals.

"Are there any live ones?" John McClure wanted to know.

"Yes, according to this," Susan Brooks said. "One of Grizzly Adams' famous bears, Baby Bea, is on the lower level."

"Let's see that first," Thomas Jefferson Brooks said, and everybody nodded enthusiastically.

They traipsed down a wide staircase to see a huge bear in a large cage, just to the right of the stairs. A keeper, on the job all the time, was baiting the brown, huge-jawed creature, which was kept at least twenty feet away from the crowds by chains held by sawhorses.

"Hey, that's some b'ar. M' grandpa Hogue used to fight them in the woods of Indianney when it was wild," John McClure said. "I think they were black, though."

"Well, soldier," the keeper said, "Grizzly Adams used to fight all different kinds of bears. He was one of the few men alive who could break a grizzly hug. Why, he could make 'em as docile as pussycats. Had a whole troupe that went around the country, and he would march 'em across the towns, even had one of 'em carry his gear like a pack animal."

"And they never hurt him?" Harriet Houghton wanted to know.

"Of course they did," the grizzled woodsman said. He chawed tobacco and spat every minute. "They clouted him, whenever he wasn't looking. Took those huge claws and tore flesh outa him. When he was younger, it didn't matter. But the last two years o' his life 'twas terrible. One big old booger bear batted him so hard it took the top o' his skull off and you could see his brains. He wore a cap. But he jest kept on a-workin' for Mr. Barnum."

"My goodness, you'd think Mr. Barnum would have been concerned that he was responsible for working a man to his death," Susan Brooks said with outrage.

"Wall, to give P.T. his due, he did try to get him to stop. But Grizzly needed the money for his wife. Worked until he dropped. And this here is the last bruin of his bunch."

"Still looks mean," Will Houghton said. The bear chose that moment to growl, baring his teeth and rattling his cage, and both women pulled back and wanted to go upstairs.

They wandered about, breaking into twos and threes or just meandering about alone on the first and second floors, seeing the giant hornets' nests, the chain mail and armour exhibit, the orangutan, the odd, blue baboon, the mummy case from Egypt, the Indian artifacts from the Ute tribe out west.

"What're you doing, Crim?" John McClure wanted to know. Isaac was jotting things down on a pad of paper. As he walked about, licking his upper lip and pushing back the blond shock of hair from his forehead, he was reading the posters, seeing the engravings and portraits of Napoleon Bonaparte and the panorama of the Battle of Tippecanoe.

"I'm learnin' from Barnum. Tryin' to extract the juice of his method."

"For what?"

"For making a million dollars off of a bunch of baboons and beehives. I admire him, everybody does. I'm going to see if I can find out what his first principles were, and then mebbe I can apply them back home, if and when I get there."

"Barnum in Indianney?" John McClure wanted to know.

"Why not? He must know something to get people to pay him to see all this."

Crim caught up with John McClure in about half an hour, as John was viewing a strange chair. "Siamese throne with real gold," the sign in front of it said.

"Want to know what I found?" Crim demanded. John nodded without turning away from the ornate, jade-encrusted monarch's chair, and Crim said, "Reading all the posters about Barnum and looking at all this, here's what I think makes the old man a success. First, he don't leave nothin' to chance. Plans ahead. It says when Jenny Lind came to America he had everthing planned, even to what sweet cakes she would eat at what time, what her private railroad car would look like. And when he was a-bringin' the whales up here, why—"

"Don't mention the whales." Thomas Jefferson Brooks had come up behind him. "They make me hot under the collar. Take these beautiful beasts, just swimming along with their families, put them in big boxes and pour water on their blow-holes while they ride past Poughkeepsie, New York—"

"Sir, I thought you was a free market capitalist," Crim said.

"I am, but it peeves me to see how we use everybody in the name of the dollar. Did the same thing with the Indians. I saw it with my own eyes when they rounded them up to go west. Like herds of cows."

"Injeeans, did you say?" Crim asked, surprised.

"Never mind. You're too young. Go on with your list of Barnum's first principles."

"Let's see," Crim said, consulting his list. "Well, he ain't afraid to blab about his product. He advertises, as they say. Well in advance of the next attraction, he's cultivatin' newspaper people, puttin' out circulars, lettin' people have sneak looks."

"I understand that," Brooks said. "Used to do some of the same myself when we were building the towns in Indiana."

"Lastly," Crim announced to anybody within hearing distance, "P. T. Barnum never despairs. He sees the good in life, not the bad and looks down the turnpike at the goal, instead of at his tired feet. So it says. He lost a fortune, but look at where he is today!"

"Good question," John McClure said, coming away from the Siamese throne. "Where in tunket is the man?"

"Restin' in his pleasure dome." Crim pointed at a huge lithograph of Iranistan, Barnum's palace, with its Arabian domes and many wings, the pride of Bridgeport, Connecticut.

"That says it all. Restin' comfortably well off, and havin' somebody else do the work is the ul-time-et of all labor," John McClure said.

"Well, the big thing seems to be," Crim said, folding his papers into his pocket, "that with Barnum it's do or die. Full out on the organ. Don't stop until you have done it right."

"We should've had him runnin' this here war," John McClure said as they headed on down the hall.

Finally, as the afternoon sun shone low through the windows, they came to the freaks. There was Fat Boy Floyd, an enormous, bloated youth of about eleven, who sat in an overstuffed chair behind a screen. He weighed three hundred pounds, a sign said. Houghton noticed that his eyes, which had almost vanished in the rolls of flesh which were his face, were listless and cold. He seemed not to have anything to do.

The Human Stump was behind curtains. You paid a dime extra to see her. She had no arms and no legs and rolled around on a little trolley. She was as talkative as the Fat Boy had been silent, and when the crowd assembled, declaimed "The Boy Stood on the Burning Deck." She was very eloquent, her voice supplying all the gestures she could not execute.

After she had rolled away, a pock-faced man came out on the little stage (the customers were sitting on half of it) and said, "Ladies and Gentlemen. We have a rare and unexpected treat today. Mr. P. T. Barnum is willing to let this select group see one of his all-time best exhibits for no extra price and for this one day only!"

Susan and Harriet talked excitedly to each other. Thomas Jefferson Brooks, whose brother had been a showman himself, tilted his chair back and looked skeptical. John McClure said "Hogbath."

"Patrons of the American Museum," the former smallpox victim went on, "we have with us today one of the most famous dwarfs in the world."

"Is it Tom Thumb?" Crim asked, jabbing McClure.

"Seems to me he's in Europe," McClure answered

"Presenting, Commodore Nutt!" the man shouted in a showman's fortissimo.

A tiny man with a round, appealing face came out from the wings of the little stage to strong applause from the forty people who witnessed him.

"Why are we being allowed to see this famous dwarf when nobody else can?" Susan Brooks whispered to the pock-man.

"Well, madam," he said, in a lordly way, "Mr. Barnum is considering another European tour for him, and he wishes to get attention in the papers for him here at the Museum. Commodore Nutt has been out of the public eye for a while after a disappointment in love." He smiled a tight-lipped, know-it-all smile.

"That means," John McClure said in an equally lordly way to Crim, "that Tom Thumb married *his* gal."

"I knew that," Crim retorted. "I read the papers too, y' know."

"I didn't," Will Houghton said, leaning over towards John McClure. "Tom Thumb was married last year wasn't he? But I didn't know this other little man was in love with Tom Thumb's fiance?"

The little man was standing on a box. He was almost three feet tall and he wore a little riding habit, with jodhpurs and a hunting cap.

"Good day, ladies and gentlemen," he said in a voice that sounded like a twelve-year-old's. "I use this riding habit to ride my pony. Sometimes we go hunting, sometimes take a fence or two. I rode my pony for the Queen of England," he said.

"Isn't he cunning?" Susan Brooks said.

"Humph," Thomas Jefferson Brooks answered.

The pony was brought out, and to the delight of the audience, Commodore Nutt rode him about quite nicely in the tiny arena of the little stage. After two or three circles, he doffed the cap to the crowd and departed, and the crowd filed out.

Will Houghton stayed in the freak room. There were pictures of Barnum's other freaks, the Siamese twins who hated each other so much, and had to eat breakfast and even visit women, as a duo. There was a woman with hair all over her face and arms, people with bizarre arms and legs in the wrong places. After staring at them for quite a while, Houghton felt as if he wanted to weep, and he did not know why. No one else felt that way. He heard John McClure say, as he left the room, that P.T. Barnum treated his freaks well. He divided profits with them so that they were now wealthy. He arranged for Tom Thumb's marriage and even made out the invitations himself to all the Crown Heads of Europe and Barons of Industry in America.

But this room, and the performance of the little man, made Houghton almost physically sick. Later, when he tried to tell the others about it in the hack, all he could say about his anguish was, "When people asked Commodore Nutt a few questions, they weren't any of the right ones. They wanted to know, 'How big were you when you were born?' and, 'Are your brothers and sisters normal?' "

"What are the right questions?" Thomas Jefferson Brooks asked him.

"Well, how about 'How did you come to sell your soul to a man with a ticket booth? Was it all that was left for you in life?' or 'Is it anguishing to have everyone treat you like a six-year-old boy dolly?' Or even, 'Lying awake in the night, do you ever curse God?' "

"What makes you sure those are the right questions, major?" John McClure asked.

But Houghton shook his head and would not speak. He only thought the answer. "I am a freak, too, so I know. We all are."

"Corporal," Thomas Jefferson Brooks said to Walter McClure, "I'd like you to accompany me as I visit the camps of the Army of the Potomac on this sutling investigation. I've asked Governor Morton to see to your release for a couple of months. I need someone in the army to help me with protocol. I think having a soldier with me will ease my entry and possibly open people's mouths. Will you come? I assure you, you will not be compromising anyone in your regiment."

"Well," Walter said, a little surprised, "it's certain nothing much is happening here. I hate to leave without telling Surgeon Burkhart. He's back in camp with the Division in Virginia. But I guess I can write him a letter."

"Good. Let's be off. We're packing up tomorrow morning at the hotel. We can put the women on the train for Indiana and then begin touring. We'll put our ears to the ground, listen to the drums and come up with the report the President needs."

When Will Houghton went to the station with his mother, he resisted her attempt to hug him to her bosom. He pecked her on the cheek instead, and then he put a letter in her hand.

"Mother, I want you to hand deliver this letter. It is to Miss Lizzie Kelso, there on Elm Street."

"I know where Lizzie Kelso lives," Harriet said shortly.

Houghton weighed each word carefully. "She is—a special friend of mine."

Harriet Houghton gave one brief nod and boarded the train without another word. But Susan Brooks smiled and gave her favorite nephew a big hug, whether he wanted it or not. Will Houghton stood and watched as the train left the busy New York station. After it became tiny in the distance, and finally disappeared completely, he stood smelling the surphuric smoke. Then he brushed cinders off the blue sleeve of his coat and slowly walked back to the ferry to cross over to camp in Brooklyn.

*   *   *   *

"I feel as if we should be arriving at Castle Thunder in a rainstorm," Jacob Joe Scott said.

"Well, if there was rain," his fellow prisoner Tilghman Vistal replied, "it might cool down this prison yard." It had been a particularly trying ride. They had come on railroad cars into Richmond and walked up to the huge, old tobacco factory where the South confined political prisoners and those who could be used as trade goods, should the complicated accords the North and South had on prisoners ever be fully reinstated.

"It could be worse," Vistal told his friend. "We could be in Castle

Lightning, across the street. That's where they keep the hard-core roustabout prisoners. We are supposed to be living in the plush in here.''

They mounted the steps. The ever-present armed guard which had taken them from the Orange County Courthouse had dwindled to only Jacob Joe's Louisiana officer, who pushed hard at their heels. Inside, they signed into an entry journal kept by a Confederate guard, loaded down with two pistols. Then they mounted two flights of steps, slowly, for their legs and spirits were weakened by the long, roundabout trip which seemed designed solely to torture them, but was really a result of changing Confederate fortunes and camps.

On the third floor, the main one confining prisoners, there were several cells to the right and left of the stairs, and a small ante-room, like a cloak room, sweltering in the September heat.

Jacob Joe's Louisiana guard prodded them to a table in the small lockup entry room. "Empty your pockets," the guard sitting behind the table said. An effeminate man with an insignificant mustache, he was repairing a military belt.

"Leave your loot on the table," he commanded. Vistal counted out seventy dollars in Confederate money and ten dollars, sixty-five cents in gold. Jacob Joe had no money, but took out his watch when the man asked for it.

"Dangle the bait over this way, fish," said wheedling voices from behind the bars. Several men with perspiration streaming down dirty faces and long, unkempt hair reached through the bars.

"Discipline cases," the ladylike man said, poking holes with a huge awl in the leather of the belt. "We don't have many of them. Thank God the worst are over across the street."

"Fishee, fishee," the voices said, as hands waved.

"They'll steal you blind in there, if you let them. Best let us have the valuables," the guard said with a smirking smile. Somehow Jacob Joe did not feel reassured, especially since the guard took the fine pearl-handled pen knife Sophie had given him as an engagement present and began using its finely honed steel to jab the leather instead of the blunt awl.

There was a voice from behind them. "Goodbye forever or until the duration," said the diffident sergeant from Louisiana, who had brought them across three states. They turned to see him tip his hat and depart. The lockup attendant gestured with his pistol and they went to the door of the barracks, where the attendant was opening the door into the central quarters with his huge loop of keys.

"Fresh fish," was the cry as the door rang shut behind them, and soon they were surrounded by scraggly men who crowded around as if they had never seen a fellow human before. One, wearing blue fatigue trousers, taller than the rest and barrel-chested, sauntered up.

He grabbed Jacob Joe under the armpits and lifted him high into the air.

"Who might thee be, sir?" Vistal asked with a stony face as his friends' legs hung in the air.

"They call me Carlo the Corsican, stranger. Lieutenant from Kansas in my former incarnation. I'm in charge of all who come in here." Then, harshly, "Salt these here fish, men," he said and a pummelling session followed in which the two new men's pockets were searched.

"Wait a minute," Jacob Joe cried as a man gleefully held up a picture of Sophie in a gilt frame. "That's all I have of my Love."

Vistal cried his protest, too. "I beg thee, sir, leave that token."

"You are the Quakers that we were told were a-comin' eh?" the robbing soldier said, looking quickly between Vistal and Jacob Joe. "Waal, if I recall the Good Book it saith that a man's life don't consist of the number o' his possessions. So I am helpin' your immortal soul, friend." He sauntered away, chuckling over his shoulder at Jacob Joe. Carlo the Corsican ordered a reserved, spare man of about forty to give the new fish a tour of the prisoner barracks with its huge bunk/living rooms, cooking room, and two small yards.

"Well, it's relatively clean," Jacob Joe said, as they passed from room to room. The man told him his name was Abner Duchin.

"They try to keep it safe," he explained. "They have their sanitary commission too, and anyway, if they are ever to exchange those of us in here from Lincoln's army for their top dogs, we have to be in health."

The tour finished in the sleeping room. Duchin stood silently, and Jacob Joe sat down tiredly on his bunk. It seemed like he was always tired these days. They watched Vistal put his few possessions under his own cot. "Exchange—when will that be?" Jacob Joe wondered aloud.

"Whenever the Yanks and Johnnies get together about conditions," Duchin said, coming to his side. "All the exchange commission does these days is strut around and send insulting letters across the lines. They're hardly speakin'. They don't worry much about us anyway. There are only a handful of us Yankees in Castle Thunder, almost all commissioned and non-commissioned officers. It was set up for the political prisoners of the South. We're strangers in a strange land."

"What are the duties for us all?" Jacob Joe wanted to know.

Duchin's bunk was across from his; he sat on it now, taking off his shoes. "We don't even have to scrub the floors. Something about not making officers do menial jobs. Conventions of war. They have an army party that comes in every morning. Only trouble is they come in before we're awake. They also whitewash the walls regularly."

"There are—how many men here?" Jacob Joe asked, looking about.

Duchin looked at him with calm, blue eyes. He had been a teacher in a college in Ohio before he became an adjutant in a Northern company from Cleveland. He kept touching a huge birthmark that started on his cheek and ran down his neck into his collar. "One hundred twenty, more or less, are usually quartered here."

"And the food?"

"A piece of cornbread and a cup of bad cabbage soup a day right now. But it will get better."

"Why do you say that?"

"There are six thousand of us in and around Richmond. Without meat we may get surly." He had an odd, twisted smile on his face.

"Riot?"

"It's been talked of before."

Jacob Joe punched the mattress. Straw in it slid over to one side, leaving bare ticking.

"What does Carlo the Corsican have to do with all of this?" Vistal asked.

"Who is he, anyway?" Jacob Joe wanted to know.

"He was originally from Alabama. Went to Kansas as a pro-slavery man and became the lieutenant of an early regiment captured at Bull Run."

"My God," Jacob Joe said. "He's been here all this time?"

"Yes," Duchin replied, lowering his voice. "It turns out he was one of the John Brown murderers back in Kansas. He joined the Northern army to get out of town. The Rebels know he's important and think they can do something with him, but they don't quite know what. He's taller and meaner than anybody else"—he looked around—"and so he commands here."

"Commands?" Vistal asked with distaste.

"He took over, claiming he was from both the North and South and so should lead. The guards let him organize the daily routine, working with the prison guards. He assigns details, slop buckets, food cleanup, medical exams—"

"Is there much sickness?"

Duchin shined his shoes with a piece of filthy towel and then lined them up, heels exactly even with the edge of the cot. "It goes through the ranks when new fish come in, then subsides. If only we can avoid typhoid and smallpox this winter."

"Why do the men obey such a degenerate specimen of humanity as Carlo the Corsican?" Tilghman Vistal wanted to know.

Duchin offered the smallest of smiles. "Among the sewer rats, the one with the largest tail and sharpest fangs rules. Carlo has spent this war in prison. He knows nothing else, and he feeds on his powers here so that he doesn't really want to leave, I think. He has rubbed up to the guards like a fat tabbycat and he offers bribes to his subordinates."

"Are there not a few officers in here from the United States Army?

Gentlemen of the Confederacy?'' Jacob Joe asked, sitting very still on the bunk.

"In prison there are no gentlemen. Just as there are no Yanks or Rebs. All there is is miserable men turning worse. Even men who are decent on the outside will sneak and lie to survive. If you do not, my commendations to you. Carlo the Corsican commands among thieves. And it is he who bargains for the food. With that kind of power, who will say him nay?''

After Duchin and Vistal had left, Jacob Joe sat for a long time, staring at the wall, listening to the rumpus in the room below them. A man on a nearby cot told them that another new man had just come in and was being tossed in the air so the few pennies in his pockets would shower down on Carlo the Corsican's followers.

His mind formed bitter words. "Grandma Jenny, you saved my life at Perryville. Was it for this?'' He reached into what he supposed were his empty pockets and found the only thing the ransacking fish-salters had missed: the small pocket Bible. He took it out and looked at its worn cover wonderingly. Then there was a commotion as the "fish salters'' clambered upstairs and entered the sleeping room, looking for him.

Within ten minutes he was nursing badly bruised legs. He had been tossed in the blanket just on general principles until he hurt, and in the process, his Bible had been torn to pieces.

*   *   *   *

It was mid-September when Lettie Hogue decided to tell her mother why under no circumstances would she return to the church she loved. They were sitting on the porch of the old farm on a cool night. Rain had washed the dry fields; its good smell rose from the earth like a benediction. When she finished her degrading tale of the minister that night in the moonlight, her mother stared straight ahead.

"My pa George McClure had a theory. He said that ministers could be the most lecherous of all folk if let loose.''

"Why is that?'' Lettie wanted to know.

"They het themselves up like little wind-up toys when they sermonize. Haven't you seen that? Get a minister going on a hell-fire subject and he pours out feeling like a hot stove. Radiates. You can't sit in the front row or you get burnt.''

Lettie gave her mother a half doubting look and Catherine went on. "Then there is the power. Ministers have a special kind of power. When they get to giving us God's word, forced through the sieve of their own imaginations, some folks, them included, get confused about just who it is that is speakin'. So that red-hot heat and too much power makes them very dangerous. Pa thought they were the most dangerous people on earth. We have to do something.''

''What is there to do?'' Lettie said wearily. ''He has written me a preachy, harsh letter about the love of the Lord and between the lines I can still feel him hankering for me.''

''We'll just use his own sin to catch him. The harvest festival at church is in just about a month, isn't it?''

''Yes, but what does that—''

''We're going to catch him with his pants down.''

Lettie looked highly skeptical, yet interested. They began to talk, and finally Catherine won the day. The conversation drifted into how they could wreak the vengeance of the Lord on one of his called ministers who was committing the sin of the Holy Spirit by leading His little ones astray.

Dora Lavenham stood beside what she imagined was the smokiest stove in the state of Georgia. ''If there is such a thing as a moveable feast,'' she told herself, ''then a Confederate hospital is a moveable fast.'' Well, it was certain that they had moved twice since she joined the Ladies' Hospital Attendants Corps last June. They were first at Mobile, Alabama, in a well-constructed new hospital with airy, open rooms and separate wards for ''catching things'' like the infectious erysipelas. The surgeons were very forward-thinking, believing in special diets for each patient and individual treatments, which were recorded by the nurses and female attendants on the end of each bed. They served milk and eggs there, too, and chicken soup, and Dora had been happy, in spite of seeing the death litters coming down the stairs in the deep stillness of night, broken only by the groans of men with thigh and gut wounds. So many were dying that there was no time to help the men in the litters die, and sometimes their names were hardly known.

But the war came too close, and there were defeats instead of victories as both armies struggled for control of the lower South. When Northern cavalry came into Alabama, as Bragg and Rosecrans maneuvered around Chattanooga and seemed determined to take everything south, too, they had to leave the lovely hospital.

She stirred soup, trying to move aside as the acrid wood smoke poured out in white clouds at her, remembering the agony of taking a hospital of sick men on the road.

A moveable fast—or a fast move to Dalton, Georgia. Ambulance trains, bearing groaning men for whom the slightest shift was agony and who must now jolt over muddy, chuckholed roads with furniture, cooking equipment and nurses, sped towards the cars to evacuate before the warring Northerners and Southerners clashed in earnest.

Some of the ladies who served in the hospitals (they were not called nurses, only men could have that title) and their children piled into the cars assigned to them, behind the wounded, and sat in the midst of huge heaps of desks and operating tables and cooking tables and hospital linen and washing boilers.

And so they had come here to Georgia, and stayed to hear that a huge battle would be fought for control of the routes to the deep South. Reinforcements were pouring into the area from Virginia, and their surgeons were called to the place it seemed the armies would clash: Chicamauga near Chattanooga.

The word came, first filtering in with messengers, then confirmed with restored telegraph service. Victory! Really and truly a Southern victory. But at this moveable fast that only meant deprivation, men coming in on carts from the battlefield crying out for water, and a shortage of food to fend off even basic hunger. They were living in a Confederacy which could not provide for its own any more, and they had to endure shortages of bandages and medicines and blankets in the increasingly cool weather in this small field hospital, where she was tending the worst wounded.

And the men themselves after Chicamauga, black as Negroes from the cannon and musket smoke, drearily plodded in for amputations. The surgery was performed beneath trees whose leaves were coated with the red dust of autumn, and it filtered onto the open wounds.

The hospital authorities would not allow the women assistants to help nurse here. No, a woman's place was to wrap bandages, and so they had wrapped as fast as their fingers would allow, and cooked, and here she was doing that on this smoky stove now.

And those very surgeons, who had only whisky in some cases to set broken bones and do serious surgical repairs, drank the whisky themselves so they worked in a stupor, and she cried until tears fell on her dusty hands to see young men who had won the day on the battlefield losing their battle with death. They bled to death from unsewn arteries; they died of shock, because their surgeons were blind drunk.

She sat with first one young boy and then another, whose faces were like the faces around the punch bowls at the balls in Louisville, the "chivalry" of a whole new nation called the Confederate States of America, and she watched the red liquid draining, sometimes spurting out of the bandages, and saw them look up with pleading eyes, asking her to write to their mothers or wives, take out a likeness of a child from a pocket for them to see one last time, pray with them to the Mother of God or the Savior, and then bubble at the lips and die.

She cried to see their spirits sinking as the days after the battle passed, even though it had been a "victory." Eighteen thousand men fell, and Bragg refused to pursue the beaten Northern army. As word filtered into the wards, the wounded moaned that their sacrifice had been in vain. Gettysburg, Vicksburg, Chattanooga—all lost, and now Bragg let Rosecrans go.

Dora pushed the hair out of her eyes and peered inside the kettle. Yes, this might be decent soup. There were some beef bones, part of the army's rations, and they had found turnips and onions and carrots.

It was difficult to keep up spirits these days in the Confederacy, and a hospital after a battle was the worst place to do it anyway. Hot soup was about all she could offer, and she took a generous bowl of it herself before she served the rest.

She needed to have a care for her own spirits, too. She had never been a die-hard advocate of "the Cause" anyway. She believed the South had the right to be independent, that the politicians of the North were tyrants, and she supported her friends, the young men of Kentucky who joined the Confederate Army. Dora was not there because of political reasoning, though, but because she pined to nurse—and because she could not face the wedding of her sister and the man she herself loved.

In her apron pocket was a letter from her sister Sophie that she had carried for weeks. It described an endless round of parties, mentioning Tucker Mahaffey in every other line. There was a passing mention of her "beloved in the horrible prison camps," next to a line about a horse race. Dora's numbed brain could not even allow her to formulate the criticism of her sister that was beating at her breast. Sophie, and the women of Louisville, the South in general—she hated them.

Where were they all, anyway, as these men were suffering and dying? Tying bonnet ribbons and listening for the strains of the violin to dance with the "local chivalry" who had stayed home. Whatever would become of them all if the women of the South waltzed the war away while the brave men fainted and died for want of water and basic care in the hospitals?

"I never go to hospitals. They smell!" a sturdy Christian lady had sniffingly told her at church last Sunday when she begged for help, food and bandages. That wrapped up the devotion of most of the women she encountered. And if self-denial and sacrifice were the only way to get the war won, then they had all better be afraid, because half of the Confederacy wasn't going to be inconvenienced by a dismal old war, thank you.

She reached for soup plates and a ladle to give what comfort she could.

That night, in the small house which served as a resting place for the women at this field hospital, a message reached her from the surgeon general of her section. "You are hereby appointed Matron in the Medical Department of the Army of Tennessee. Be prepared to to move tomorrow."

Move. Again. To take the fast behind the retreating lines once more.

Retreat! Defeat! The words so close in sound they were almost echoes of each other, resounded off the mountain slopes around Chattanooga, the stone cliffs near Atlanta, the ranges of Virginia, bringing with them dismal discouragement. The subtle threads of a faltering war effort wove themselves into the fabric of life in the South, affecting to greater and lesser degrees almost everyone, even the twenty-year-old waltzers who never seemed to stop dancing, though trumpets sounded withdrawal and newspapers deplored the situation and exhorted increased efforts.

For some, the defeats only meant increased activity towards the goal, deeper faith in the mission. Doles' Brigade of Confederates, with General Ewell and Robert E. Lee, defied the growing army on the other side of the Rappahannock, skirmishing, settling in for the winter. They had ample faith that the area around Chattanooga and Atlanta would be held firmly for the South, and when that area was secured by Bragg and his Southern army, their own Army of Northern Virginia would again move out. This time they would decisively defeat the troops which had beaten them at Gettysburg.

"Jest give us one more chance to whip 'em. We almost had 'em at Chancellorsville. If we hadn't been too tired to pound 'em to the ground after we beat 'em. Almost had 'em at Gettysburg, if our general had acted on time." Boone Epworth was cleaning his rifle, drying his ammunition in the October sunshine.

"Almost ain't good enough," Willie McClure said. He and Calhoun Dugger were washing clothes, boiling them in a big mess kettle. Their hair was cropped short since they were living in these complicated trenches, more like rabbit warrens, that Robert E. Lee had ordered the men to dig. The trenches were complete enough to have food supplies, shelves for books to pass the time away with, and of course, lice and fleas.

"Jest give us one good chance," Epworth went on. "One good chance. Our spirit is stronger now than when the first recruitin' meetings marched us off to war. Even Old Bug Eyes" (he looked towards Ewell's headquarters) "seems better. He don't let a raw stump of a game leg stop him."

"Well, we'll all have our chance. And I 'spect this time 'tis kill or cure," Calhoun said.

There was a silence. Somewhere in back of them a cow was bellowing; beeves had been coming into camp and the men were preparing to butcher. Beef stew would be a welcome respite in what had increasingly become a diet of cornbread and fatback. The southern troops were as lean as the steers they were bringing in, some of them from as far away as Texas.

"What d'ye suppose the folks in southern Indiana are up to today?" Calhoun wondered.

"Well, whatever it is, it has sumpthin' to do with eatin'," Willie said wistfully. "It is the gol-durned eatin'est place on the face of the earth. I guess I had everything a pig could ever want t' home. Never knew it till I come out here, though."

Upper Indiana Church, at any rate, was celebrating eating in a big way with the Pumpkin Pageant and Festival. It was a Presbyterian undertaking, celebrated each year to commemorate the Pilgrim's early survival by the hand of God and the subsequent harvest feast. The elders tried to give the annual pageant a spiritual side by having two church services, one to start the festivities, the other, billed as a "Giving of Harvest Thanks" service, the morning after.

Now, just before the festivities were to begin, ladies from the church puttered around the food tables set up all over the grounds, spilling over onto the adjacent Dan'l McClure property and up the road, too. After the afternoon service, there would be a supper, with huge pumpkins in the center of each table, which had been carefully set by the ladies' Dorcas Society. Families in the church would carry in dishes of hot bergoo stew, roasted veal and onion, fried and smothered and fricasseed and roasted chicken, pork pie and chicken pie swimming in gravy. Neatly displayed in their own sections would be yeast biscuits and apple butter, beaten biscuits and strawberry preserves, German coffee cake and strudel, hominy in three forms and cornsticks with buttery brown lacy edges. Not to mention relishes in crocks: watermelon and cauliflower and hot corn and piccalilli from green tomatoes and four kinds of dill and bread-and-butter pickles, four kinds of slaw, sauerkraut and stewed and brandied fruits in several varieties.

The best table was reserved for the pumpkin dishes: pumpkin custard, everyone's favorite made into bowls and pies, and pumpkin fluff pie made with egg whites, with flaky lard crusts, and pumpkin spice cake and pumpkin delight pudding made with dates. There was also angelfood cake and pumpkin cookies with black walnuts and even pumpkin waffles dusted with powdered sugar. And sitting beside them, as jaunty little accompaniments, whipped cream, in bowls on ice and a freezer of pumpkin ice cream.

Oh, pilgrims, thank God you made it through that first year. Thank God you brought those pumpkin seeds from the midlands and Kent, or wherever it was you came from. Thank God for this land that loads these tables so that some of us can't even waddle after this church supper. Thank God for our church and church suppers and harvest. Even our President Abraham Lincoln had an official day of Thanksgiving last year with talk of making these harvest festivals permanent. Thanks that we're all here after Morgan the Raider tried to take this very state, thanks that we can give you thanks at the Pumpkin Festival, was a thanksgiving prayer that redounded, or at least should have redounded off every wall of the church.

Jewell Simpson, who had been appointed by Reverend Paden and the Session as head of the 1863 Pumpkin Pageant and Harvest Thanksgiving, bustled about being sure there was plenty of hot coffee for adults, plenty of cold milk for the children.

"Well!" she said to herself, as she stood surveying the tables. "It's a good thing we don't check the church register to see who is of our flock. I see the Bridgeford brothers and—isn't that Jack Spagle and his family? Yes, I thought so, there's the clubfoot daughter. And they are from *lower* Indiana church. Some of James Emison's family—from Mariah Creek Baptist, and I see people from the churches of Vincennes. Well, as long as they all brought their covered dishes and the table space holds out—"

Jewell was in a mellow October mood. It was a good day for the pageant. Leaves as gold as the sun crowned the trees, and they had not yet fallen. Clouds were in the far skies, slatey-looking omens of the fact that all the leaves would go down in a blaze of thunder and cloudburst at some point. But not yet, and it seemed as if the children's bag games and races could be held without mud or rain—pshaw, that would ruin everything.

Jewell plumped around, checking the sugar bowls on the tables, watching over her shoulder as buggies began arriving for the three o'clock starting hymn sing. She smiled more benignly than usual, and in the smile was the satisfaction that her little world was "jest uncommon fine right now, thank you kindly."

Even her marital mood was a mite blissful, for a change. Her husband Archie had agreed to come for the festival, even to the service. Usually Upper Indiana Church was foreign territory populated with Hottentots for Archie, so this was something new indeed. Annie McClure, her young ward and John's youngest sister, had unsquinched her prune face to act in the pageant, and hours had been spent on her costume. Young Bob would be in charge of rigs and wagon parking. And Henderson, her beloved boy returned from the Fourteenth Regiment, would be in the pageant in one of the major scenes.

Dust coated the ragweeds and dry grass at the edge of the road leading into the church grounds, and buggies were stirring it into small particle-filled clouds. Was Henderson there? She turned her head. No, the darling was probably combing his hair and looking for his Bible back home. He'd be here, just you wait. She had worried so much about Henderson, though she would not tell anyone, lest uppity relatives, name of Hogue, might hear of it. She knew things were whispered about him as a ladies' man. When he first came around after returning as a hero—well, a victim of what seemed to be some sort of odd dysentery if we must be truthful—he had seen the young girls a bit too much. Finally one or two of the fathers, Floss Barger's in particular, had mentioned it with stern looks. He complained about late-night spooning in the parlor, long walks from which people returned blushing—well Henderson had an ardent spirit, didn't he? "Well, it was the McClure in him, drat and dog-nab it, anyways," Jewell justified to herself.

But jest think! Miracle bigger'n the weddin' at Cana. Henderson had got religion. "Thanks a bushel, God, and no time to say more now, 'cause here they all come."

More and more people were coming in, and Jewell took stock of them as the buggies arrived and tied up, as women took rags to their leather slippers and folded the dust lap covers under the seats and pushed at the pins in their hair, and men took drinks of water from bottles and spat dustily into the grass.

Jewell smiled a smile as broad as the edge of a saucer. She had just surveyed the crowd and couldn't find Catherine Hogue, Lettie or Horace. Couldn't show their faces. I guess not! After being reprimanded by the Session, the slut. So shame-faced—and she shouda been—that she couldn't even come back to sit in church! She lifted her chin with smug satisfaction. Sin uncovered. Devils and unclean spirits rebuked. Pride chastened in the name of the Lord!

People drifted towards the chairs where the hymn sing would begin and Jewell went to see if copies of the new "Protestant Hymn Favorite" booklet that had been printed at the Vincennes print shop for this occasion was in place on every seat.

The pageant began right after supper. People tottered from the stumps of trees, chairs and hillocks where they had taken their loaded plates, refilled for the fourth time and deposited them in the huge tubs of soapy water for the Mary and Martha Society, the church's group for young teenaged girls, to wash. The Bruceville brass quintet was tuning up, blatting and tweeting around near the woods at the edge of the church lawn. They were preparing to march in.

Jewell Simpson bustled about in front of the stage made of wagon beds and old barn boards, lining everyone up in proper order, being sure costumes didn't need last minute tacking together, calming stage fright.

They began supper at 4:30 so they would have an hour and a half to honor the pumpkin—the bountiful harvest of the land.

Tad Thompson, Tommy's fifteen-year-old brother, was ready in his pilgrim suit. Jewell patted him on the arm, took a deep breath herself and looked out at the seated audience. Then she gasped and her hand went to her bosom. There in the front row, looking as normal as anybody else (the effrontery!) were Catherine Hogue and Lettie. They were sitting with Horace, and next to him was a red-cheeked, pretty matron and a bored-looking boy of about nine, neither of whom she had ever seen before.

The band marched in to the tune of "The Church's One Foundation," their trademark number, and Jewell slowly sat down with the prompting script, determined to put sluts, sinning and outrageous effrontery out of her mind.

After seating itself rather stiffly on the chairs, the band blazed forth with a trumpet flourish. "Let the 1863 pageant in honor of our native American pumpkin begin," the leader said.

Tad walked out on the stage, his shoes creaking oddly from the black oilcloth flaps and sides that had been glued on them. Under his pilgrim hat, also decorated with black oilcloth, his round face was perspiring in the October sunlight. "I am John Alden," he said. "I'm no ordinary John Smith, but I have to be told how to act around the ladies," and Jewell smirked when the audience laughed at her—well, actually Henderson's—witticism in the script.

Tad cleared his throat and went on. "When your forefathers came to America, to the rock-bound coast in the 1630s, they brought with them packets of seeds. Of all the seeds, apple and pumpkins seeds from the orchards of England were the favorites. But the Indians also had their own varieties of the toothsome delicacy we enjoy in so many ways, the pumpkin." He stood, his speech completed. The band began to play something that could be identified as an Indian war dance from the popular Indian stage shows. Necks in the audience stretched a little bit. Was there supposed to be an Indian?

Jewell moved quickly to the head of the line, where young Bob Roy Esenwalder, who seemed to be garbed as a Sioux, was dreaming in his place, unaware of his cue. "Bob Roy, git yourself up there," Jewell hissed and the young man scooted so quickly he tripped on the steps.

"I am Squanto," he announced in a squeaky voice. "I bring food to the white men. I bring corn and show them how to plant. I bring also seeds of squash and pumpkin and make hills. Put in fish." He reached into his pocket and pulled out a small bluegill which he waved around the stage with a mischievous smile.

"He wasn't supposed to do that," Jewell whispered to the line waiting to appear. "That fish smells awful." But Bob Roy was soon gone to the other side of the stage, and John Alden went on.

"There were starving times for the Pilgrims through the first grim winters, but somehow they survived. When fall came and the harvest was a good one, they sat tables in the fields and invited their Indian friends." (Here Squanto rubbed his belly and grinned and bowed a little. Jewell tried to signal him to quit ad-libbing.)

Tad went smoothly on, and Jewell thought, "The Thompsons always could talk smooth as cream. Well, 'cept for Tommy, and he's as tongue-tied as a giraffe." She frowned, recalling that she thought Samuel Thompson, chairman of the Session, had been too lenient with Lettie. And furthermore, she did not appreciate the little "Christian toleration" speech he gave her the Sunday after the Session meeting. Didn't seem to matter because Lettie never did show up in church, oddly enough.

"The Pilgrims gave thanks for the foods the American continent produced, as we do today," Tad continued. "Will the foods please step forward?" He bowed and extended his hand towards the steps. A giant yellow squash came forward as Squanto went down the exit steps at the other side.

"You say this happens every year?" Clarissa Limeberry asked, speaking in a gentile whisper behind her fan.

"Yes," Catherine Hogue said confidentially. "For twenty years now. I remember when Horace was seventeen, he was a cream separator. The theme that year was Fruits of Industry. They always talk about the Pilgrims, then they go into the theme for the year." The corners of her mouth turned up with just the hint of merriment. "I remember Horace got all agitated when a threshing machine bumped into him and he forgot his lines."

"No such thing, Ma," Lettie countered, on Horace's behalf. She was sitting to her mother's left, and she smiled around Catherine, encouragingly, at Horace.

He looked at Clarissa apologetically. "Ma don't really approve of the Pumpkin Pageant. Says it's silly."

"Well, I do wonder what John Calvin would have thought of such folderol for good Presbyterians," Catherine admitted with a sardonic smile.

"He ain't here," Horace said, and Clarissa gave both of them a nod and smile, as if there were merit to each of these portentous positions on the Pumpkin Festival.

Catherine decided not to tease her son in front of his spark, and anyway, all this leaning around over people and whispering was causing glares from the second row. She sat back, contemplating the turn of events that had brought these visitors here with them tonight.

After Horace presented her with the astonishing news that he was courting a ladyfriend with serious intentions, Catherine found the news had grown on her. Imagine! Horace, serious about a woman! After all these years of being odd! Not that being married again would alter that, but this was such a genial, pleasant *well-off* woman. The boy, Clarissa's son, of course, was as congenial and well-mannered as an alligator, but he had been deprived of a father's love and discipline. That could change—

The giant squash lumbered across the stage. "Indians grew squash like me in hills near beans," it said in a rather muffled voice. "They cooked me chunked in with venison or boiled up with 'lasses."

"With venison," young Montmorency Limeberry down the row, sneered. "That sounds hideous. Pukey."

"Now, Monty," Clarissa said indulgently. She reached out to pat his hand, but he scooted away, sitting as far from her as he could without bumping into the generous posterior of Mrs. Almeady Beckwith of the Bruceville musicale.

The squash left and the audience next viewed a turkey, played by Annie McClure in full regalia of velveteen feathers and multicolored felt wattles. She strode proudly around the stage, majestic in her full-blown turkeyhood, while John Alden recited statistics from *Farm Journal* about the number of turkey farms now in America.

"This ain't jest old-fashioned stuff, you know," Horace said, leaning towards Clarissa. "We have high tone too. One year we had a Shakespeare theme." He turned to his mother. "Clarissa, Mrs. Limeberry that is, writes beautiful stories," he said.

"I'm looking forward to hearing them," Catherine said, her eyes on the stage. There, coming up the stairs with Jewell Simpson proudly standing by, was Henderson Simpson, dressed in the black gown of a Puritan minister.

"What's *he* doin' up there?" Horace wanted to know. "Henderson playin' the minister? That's like Vallandigham playin' Abraham Lincoln." He began to mumble as he thought of Vallandigham. It was said he had reached Canada and might be intriguing up there some way for the Southern cause.

"Henderson's got religion," Catherine said, staring curiously at the stage. "It's a good thing, before all the whisky in the township was drunk up. All the fathers around here are breathing sighs of relief. Hope they aren't premature."

The minister, clasping his Bible and looking up towards heaven as if he expected to see Elijah and his chariot, smiled like a saint. John Alden introduced him. "Most important to the early people of our nation as they gave thanks was the place of religious thought. They had fled from persecution into the wilderness, and now they went in small groups into the wilder-

ness. Puritans, and soon Baptists and Quakers, founded their own congregations'' the black-clad preacher intoned.

Floss Barger, a tousle-headed fluffball of a girl who had been one of the
recipients of Henderson's attentions, applauded stoutly, then looked around
when she saw no one else was applauding and sat down abruptly.

"Who wrote this play, Ma?" Horace wanted to know. "Jewell Simpson
can't hardly write her own name."

"Well, she did put some things in, they say. But Reverend Paden always
writes it," Catherine answered. She watched the man standing moodily, his
large frame hunched over, by the now-empty tables on the little knoll where
the church stood. Then she looked at Lettie with a smug smile. Tonight was
the night. Comeuppance time. Somehow the spirit of her father, who had
scorned hypocrisy among the clergy, seemed with her tonight, and she
hoped and prayed that Lettie would have the strength to do what George
McClure would have done in the circumstances, what Lettie herself must do
before the evening passed away.

Finally, "Eight great Presbyterian clergymen" and "heaven-inspired
religious efforts on the frontier," including the founding of Upper Indiana
Church itself by the venerable patriots, were all portrayed. The last round of
applause was accepted by the cast. As quick as field mice, the squashes and
pumpkins and Mrs. William Henry Harrison and Dan'l McClure himself
retreated into the clapboard dressing rooms in the bushes to take off their
costumes.

Jewell Simpson, breathing a sigh of relief, signalled to Mrs. Almeady
Beckwith and the band to close the pageant by rendering "Battle Hymn of
the Republic," the stirring song by Mrs. Harriet Beecher Stowe. The song
was catching on even out here in the backwaters of the nation. Jewell looked
out at the enrapt audience. The pageant was a success. Only the fact that her
upstart relatives had the nerve to come and sit in the front row edged the
brightness of her evening with gray. Mrs. Almeady Beckwith's round tones
rolled over the band's measured tones.

> Mine eyes have seen the glory of the coming of the Lord
> He is trampling out the vintage where the grapes of wrath
> are stored
> He hath loosed the fateful lightning of his terrible swift sword—

Almost all of the people had somebody out there in the war, Jewell
thought. Maybe the pageant had made 'em feel better. Lots of 'em here had

lost a loved one, at—what were the names of those odd places, Shiloh, around Chattanooga, now Chickamauga.

> *I have seen Him in the watch fires of a hundred circling camps*
> *They have builded him an altar in the evening dews and damps*

Somehow Jewell's thoughts fled involuntarily to John McClure, her ward, whom she loved, always in the camps. Waal, at least Henderson was home, never to go again.

The band changed keys, solemnly beginning the third verse. "Downright pretty song, that is," Jewell mused. Sort of made you want to cry, though she didn't know why. Made you feel the sadness of it all, the thousands of young ones away from their own churches and pumpkin festivals, shot up, dyin'. Sometimes she wondered, why, why?

> *He has sounded forth the trumpet that shall never call*
> *retreat;*
> *He is sifting out the hearts of man before His judgment seat*
> *Be swift my soul to answer Him; be jubilant my feet;*
> *Our God is marching on!*

Jewell surveyed the faces of her neighbors in the October gloaming, as babies cried afar off where their older sisters had taken them, as men lit torches and put them on sticks to light the way of the soon-to-depart pageant-goers. There was that front row. There were the new people, the bratty little boy who was leaning almost to the ground in boredom, the pert woman sitting close to Horace Hogue—whatever in the world for? There was Catherine, with her haughty face listening to the song as if it had been written for her. Abolitionist she was, and her face lit like one of the torches.

> *In the beauty of the lilies, Christ was born across the sea*
> *With a glory in his bosom that transfigures you and me*
> *As he died to make men holy, let us die to make men free*
> *While God is marching on!*
> *Glory, glory hallelujah! Glory, glory hallelujah!*
> *Glory, glory hallelujah! His truth is marching on. Amen! Amen!*

And, as the song ended, its last amens sounding plaintively against the background of the shrouded woods, Jewell noticed that it was not Lettie McClure she was looking at next to Catherine. There, with her face shining too, with the sadness and exaltation the song produced, was her niece Mary Jane McClure. The young girl had walked over and come in late during the pageant and her arm was twined lovingly through her grandmother's. She was sharing a deeply-felt experience in a way she never had with Jewell.

Mary Jane had taken Lettie's place and there, on the edge of the crowd, to add to Jewell's discomfiture, was the fallen woman talking earnestly to Reverend Paden. They walked down the path behind the church and out of sight, and the look on his face did not for a moment show reproof of a fallen woman.

A little bench for quiet meditation after Sunday services had been built down the path in a clump of young beech and poplar trees. The gee-hawing and goodbye-ing and clattering of hoofs and wheels behind them indicated the wagons' departure. Torchlight and a half moon lit the bench as Reverend Paden and Lettie approached.

"I must do as mother said. I must free myself for all time from these men who hold my life on a string," Lettie told herself. Reverend Paden's arm almost touched hers. He was surprised when she asked him for a word late in the pageant, and they said little while walking the path to the meditation seat. What was there to say?

The plot had been carefully drawn by her mother, and it was worthy of all the astute, conniving and strong-willed George branch of the McClure family, from which they both were descended. Lettie had sent Reverend Paden's last letter to Samuel Thompson of the Session, told him when she would be meeting with the minister and asked Mr. Thompson to come and witness the sordid tryst—

She was being sweet and confidential to disarm him and now touched his arm innocently with her own. He smiled and touched back. The man thought she was coming around! To learn about religion in his bed, oh sacrilege! His face was a study in pure, raw, physical yearning as he sat down and took her hand. She should know what that was, she sighed. But he was a rotten shepherd, a whited sepulchre. Her mother had told her to keep reminding herself, lest she lack courage to confront him.

"Lettie, dear, I knew you would seek me again. I knew that my own love would conquer your reticence and we could seek communion together—"

"Reverend Paden," she said, withdrawing her hand, (Get to the point. Whited sepulchre). "I've sent your last letter to Mr. Samuel Thompson of the Session."

The man's face went as white as the moon. "You have what?"

"I sent him the letter, the one in which you said you wished me to know the real warmth of love of fellowship, that you were reaching out to the fallen one whose lips you had known. . ."

Reverend Paden stood suddenly and leaned back against a young maple, shaking its red-gold leaves to the ground, where they lay fresh and untrampled in the moonlight. "You couldn't have. You know it casts you in a bad light."

Lettie did not rise but stared straight ahead, not looking at him. "I don't care. I have the other three letters. They are worse. Have you forgotten? You quote the Song of Solomon, comment on my bosoms."

His voice was unsteady. "And you will—"

She took out three pieces of paper, waved them without enthusiasm. "My plan is to present them to Mr. Samuel Thompson. He will be here in a short while."

He came again to her at the bench and looked down with a mixture of deep anxiety and fear into her face. She did not flinch. His look softened, seemed touched with—was it perplexity? He breathed, "You know I think I really love you. My God, I don't know why."

Lettie was silent. She held a waxen maple leaf in her hand, tracing its veins with a fingertip.

"There is such a thing as divorce, you know," David Paden whispered.

"You don't love me," Lettie said, watching a few other leaves drift off the tree. "You lust for me. I know what lust is."

He stepped back again into the shadows. "Dante told of the seven deadly sins," he said in a low voice. "The least horrible, the one God forgives first, is lust because it is a corruption of His love," he said, sadly.

"It is not the least awful, it is the worst," Lettie breathed. "It snorts and fires and frightens everyone before it like a steam engine." She could not see his face now. He was in silhouette; he put a hand out behind him to hold onto the maple.

"This is not the first time it has driven me," he said bitterly. "In divinity school, there in the very heart of our religion, I was a secret visitor to the back streets of Boston. I was consumed at times, helpless. From time to time it is the same, as if something else takes over my very being."

"And yet you would pull me into the same stinks of corruption you lived in. I a member of your flock."

"I know," he said, pounding his fist against the tree agitatedly. "And yet," he said in a moment, more coolly, "you stayed many months in your corruption before you repented. Perhaps it was when your passion was spent. A deathbed baptism." His voice was bitter. She did not answer, could not disagree.

He stepped nearer again, put his hands on the vertical edge of the upright bench, looked over at her. "What will you do with me?" he asked, with hopeless eyes. "When is Mr. Thompson coming for this confrontation—" His head was low. He was ready for whatever fate decreed. Reputation lost, wife humiliated, family cast upon poverty. What church could he go to?

"Yes," Lettie said in a whisper, watching his hands tightly clench the boards of the bench near her line of sight. "You have asked for the worst I can give you, and in the name of honesty, which I must seek if I can ever hope to find peace, I must turn you over to our Session."

He gazed at her, accepting that punishment must come eventually. A soft breeze stirred, loosing more leaves to fall on their shoulders, the bench and the ground. Rain was coming. David Paden sighed softly, painfully.

"And yet," Lettie continued, with tears filling her eyes, "we are of the same ilk, and the blistering shame you've put on me I put on myself earlier." She rose from the bench, and as he closely watched, reached into the pocket of her frock and held out her hand to him. "Here are the rest of the letters. I give them to you. I shall speak to Mr. Thompson in general terms and tell the truth, but without the letters. I will not damn you specifically. I leave you to make your way to the Throne of Grace alone, in the same footsteps I leave behind me. Singed, smoking. Unbridled passion is awful." She handed him the letters and turned away.

He emitted a long breath and put the letters inside his coat. They stood there a long moment, looking past each other, not speaking. "Thank you," he finally said. "Perhaps I may be able to repent and change. Be God's angel, truly, as I have at my best. I do want to, though you may not believe it. I cannot keep living in this fiery hell."

"I know you can't. Nor can I. I need to return to the church."

"Of course. Perhaps tomorrow could be a beginning," the minister said. He laughed ruefully. "The subject of the sermon is 'True Meaning of Harvest: Conquered Sin." Branches rustled. Someone was coming down the path.

Lettie looked into the minister's troubled face. "Did you hear the band and the singer?" she whispered fervently. " 'With a glory in His bosom that transfigures you and me.' Perhaps it can happen."

"Perhaps," he said. "Only something that wonderful could do it. I have tried everything else." He went into the woods quickly, up a tiny path that led back to the church another way. Samuel Thompson came into the clearing, and Lettie spoke to him quickly for a few moments. Then they both returned to the near-empty church grounds. She would have to explain to her mother that she had changed the plan. Catherine wanted ironic retribution— the chairman of the Session discovering the minister in the act of forcing his affections on Lettie.

No, that was not the way it needed to be. You could not ask for forgiveness and compassion for sin and then refuse to grant them to your fellow sinner. Besides, Lettie had struggled for all she was worth to become free of domination by two men, and she did not intend to surrender her freedom now to a woman, not even her own mother.

Annie McClure stood beside the wagon, waiting for her aunt to finish cleaning up and ready the churchyard for prayer service tomorrow morning. She had just seen Reverend Paden depart, and her aunt Lettie Hogue had gotten into the wagon with Uncle Horace and his crowd and gone.

The fine day had cooled down visibly now that it was evening; the wind was rising and the stars looked frosty, remote, as rain clouds began to drift over them. Something about falling leaves, that ominous rising of the late October wind that promised winter, always put Annie McClure on edge. It was winter when her parents had died, they said, the dead of winter, and she always feared to see it come.

Annie opened her mouth, puffed air out, "Huh, huh." She tried to make a little cloud of mist. "Can't see your breath yet," she said aloud, as if it reassure herself.

Her cousin Henderson Simpson came by, carrying a bushel basket of pumpkins that had been on a table. On top of them was a Bible. Floss Barger was trailing after him, pointing her toes as she daintily minced about in the dust.

"Stay right here," Henderson ordered Annie, pointing at the wagon. "Ma's jest about ready. Pa's lockin' the church up." He put the pumpkins in the wagon and carefully placed the Bible he had carried in the pageant where he would be sitting. "See you don't touch the Good Book with your greasy fingers," he admonished Annie.

His lofty tone irritated Annie. Mischief flared in her contrary heart. "That revival you went to shore did ruin you. Never saw anything like the snivellin' and simperin' you do. You're as prissy as a pouter pigeon."

Henderson looked above her head. "I can't expect the likes of you, child, to understand how I found Grace."

"Grace? Is she the one I saw you lyin' next to by the stream when you tole your ma you was fishin'? Some fishin' you was doin'."

Henderson shot his cousin a decidedly un-Christian look. Floss Barger opened her mouth in astonishment. She had thought she was the only one.

Annie clambered into the wagon and pushed the Bible aside purposefully. "Come to think of it, I never did tell your ma 'bout that fishin' expotition. Jest plumb slipped my mind. Guess I will now." Henderson started to mumble something, but at that moment young Montmorency Limeberry appeared on his way to Horace McClure's wagon.

He was all gawky, doing a sort of mocking leap, his arms in the air, the sort of thing boys do when they have sat too long and cannot restrain themselves one instant longer. "So," he called to Annie, "I hear we are to be cousins."

"That so?" Annie called back. Her introduction to the young man tonight had left her singularly unimpressed with him.

"Your uncle is marryin' my mother," he smirked.

Annie stared at him. For once she did not know what to say.

"Imagine me," Montmorency continued in a tormenting voice, "cousin to a turkey. Or is it a monkey from the jungle?" He stood snickering and pointing.

Without any consideration Annie picked up one of the smallest and softest pumpkins and hurled it at him. It all happened so quickly; Montmorency ducked and the pumpkin hit a tree in back of Henderson, splattering its seeds and stringy pulp all over him and Floss Barger.

Both Annie and Montmorency, suddenly on the same side, began picking up other pumpkins and tossing them at the tree. They whooped with laughter, pointing at Henderson and Floss and throwing pumpkin seeds at them. Floss took off irately down the lane, and when Jewell Simpson arrived a minute later, she saw the new convert chasing two children around, swearing at the top of his lungs.

"Waal," his father said, seeing to the horses. "I always did say there couldn't be much to it if you can get, and unget, religion all in one week's time.

In less than a week Old Man Barger had run off Henderson Simpson with a shotgun as he was "trying to explain himself" to Floss at three o'clock in the morning in the barn of the Barger farm, and the next morning Henderson went to join the army again—this time the One Hundred Twentieth Indiana Regiment.

November, 1863

Chapter Seventeen

Carlo the Corsican stalked into the courtyard of Castle Thunder, where Jacob Joe Scott worked raking leaves with Abner Duchin on a "light chore" detail.

"You there, Scott, someone to see Vistal wants to see you, too."

The "Corsican's" manner was less insulting than it had been earlier in the fall when Vistal and Jacob Joe had arrived as "new fish" in the prison camp. Then Carlo had assigned Jacob Joe to the most rugged duties in the kitchen, carrying pots of boiling water off the stove, disposing of garbage, washing dishes. And not only had Scott done them well and without complaint, much to Carlo's surprise, he asked to cook and began turning out excellent dishes for the "Napoleon mess"—Carlo and his friends. He created "Brunswick stew" from an ancient chicken and a few onions and turnips, "hot cakes" from half-stale flour and some smuggled sorghum. Since food was the obsession of all the prisoners, second only to the subject of freedom in their thought and conversation, Jacob Joe was buying toleration for himself and Vistal in the prison with his culinary abilities.

So when Carlo summoned him to the office for a conference, it was with grudging acceptance, if not respect.

A handsome woman of about forty, dressed in a Quaker gray, man-tailored suit, was chatting in the room with Vistal as Jacob Joe Scott entered. Early November sunlight streaked weakly through the tall, dirty window at the top of the little visitors' office; a battered desk, three chairs and a spittoon were the only furniture.

"Nephew Vistal, we are taking thy case to the Secretary of War," the woman said. "Friend Crenshaw has spoken to all thy relatives and meeting folk at home and they all believe we should pay the fine for thee and let thee go free."

"I thank thee, Aunt Judith. I know Father thinks the same, but I have not felt free to do so. I cannot pay the $500, and I do not know what I think about thy paying it. I have been a sign unto the people of our state of the error of war. It may be that I am supposed to continue, even in prison."

"Foolish pride is keeping thee from thy freedom," Vistal's aunt said, pulling off her gloves a finger at a time. The woman appeared weary to Jacob Joe; she told them she had travelled from Tennessee and had already made an appointment with the Secretary of War of the Confederacy. "Why make this needless sacrifice when it sufficeth nothing? These people are not improved by thy example. Thou has tried everything with them, refusing to fight, refusing to work, appealing to the courts."

"How can I support the killing process, Aunt?" Vistal wanted to know. The room was frigid; Jacob Joe pulled his blanket-cloak about him. Blankets were coming in to the prison in an experiment with the Northern prison authority. They had sent wool bedcovers in, and the prison guards let Carlo the Corsican distribute them among the prisoners. The men on Jacob Joe and Vistal's floor had obtained thread and needles and stitched the very comfortable blankets into double-thick cloaks.

Vistal's aunt pulled out a new Bible and put it under Vistal's nose. "Thee has asked me to bring a new book of Scripture for thee. Thee has worn the old one out reading it. Now where, Tilgh, in this Bible does it say thee may not pay the tax and must die in this foul prison? What Scripture can thee quote?" Vistal shook his head. "As to specific passages, none. But 'Thou shalt not kill,' is one."

"That is not enough, Tilghman. We are told to resist evil, and thee has done that. But after all that has been done to and for thee, thou has paid and may be let out. Even the saints Paul and Peter went out of prison when they could. Where does witness end and stubbornness begin?"

"The Lord sent his angels to Peter and Paul."

"Yes. That was their sign. After they had it, they left in due time. Consider the home folks thy angels and respond when the Lord sends aid. To stay on forever seems to show overweening pride, the desire to trumpet forth thy righteousness. It does the Friends discredit. I am saddened to say it." She put the Bible in his hands emphatically.

Tilghman took it and sank in his chair with a deep sigh. "It is hard when even the Friends back home cannot agree with me—I do not know. I sit and think for hours. Some Quakers in old times did stay in prison in England and other places for the faith. Now the home folks think I am courting death to please myself. They may be right. I trust their light. Still, to have been kicked, incarcerated, tried, bayonetted, left in the cold, ill, to die for my faith and now, to leave this place and go free—I do not know."

"Find me the Scripture that says we must stay in jail forever for our beliefs. Find it."

"I cannot."

"Then we shall take thy case to the Secretary of War. I shall take him the

$500 the home meeting has raised.'' With that she stood, gravely pecked her nephew on the cheek and turned to Jacob Joe.

"Friend Scott, I hear thou hast need of faith, too. I have brought thee tracts to read." She took out pamphlets and pressed them in Jacob Joe's hands. "And in the case that thou does not have a book of Holy Scripture, I have brought a Bible, just like the new one I have given to Tilgh. I have inscribed it.''

He took the Bible and looked inside, read the name and brief message and thanked her. He had not really read Scripture since before Perryville; then the Napoleon Mess had tossed his book to pieces in the "fish fry" ceremonies when they first came.

"You have my prayers, both of thee.'' Her eyes were filled with sympathy, and she added, after a moment of reflection, "Each of thee has his own separate ordeal.'' She patted Jacob Joe's hand and left.

Jacob Joe and Tilghman Vistal lay on their rough cots in the huge sleeping room in the darkness of the November afternoon. In the two hours before supper, most men returned to their cots to restore wasted strength, and because there was little else to do in a place that provided few lights. Carlo the Corsican and his assistant bandits had the only light; they were sitting on the floor at one end of the barracks playing cards. "Will you go, Tilgh?'' Jacob Joe wanted to know.

"I do not know. Sometimes I think I can go out as the home meeting wants, other times, I am determined to stay until they free me on principle. But if it is the Lord's will that I leave and go elsewhere to witness—I must listen and respond to His will only, and that is hard to know.''

"Well, you will soon have to decide. The $500 fine is going to the Secretary of War.'' Jacob Joe turned on his stomach, lifted his head up like a turtle, and smiled a little. "Maybe he could have a two-for-one-sale,'' he said.

"Do not despair, my friend,'' Vistal said, turning his head on the cot towards his friend. He was suddenly aware that Jacob Joe was as thin and sallow-faced and despairing as he was, and that they had not talked of his friend's concerns in a long while.

"If only I had some word from home,'' Jacob Joe said, tracing an initial on the blanket absently. "It is hard that they keep the mail from us and do not let our letters go home. My people, my dear Sophie, don't know where I am.''

"It is part of the torment our jailers inflict on us. My letters to my family in the South sometimes get through, sometimes not. Yours are supposed to be taken to the lines and carried by the Federal mail service, but now our jailers will not allow it. They do it in retribution for what the North is now doing to flatten the South.''

"I know. The North wishes to keep 14,000 prisoners here in the heart of the Confederacy for the overspent government to feed and clothe and give medical care to. And to use as a bargaining chip.''

"Or to cause an uprising.''

"It may come to that, if they can't feed us. When we came, we at least had a little bad beef, rice and beans. But this week—are they trying to starve us?'' He swung his feet over the bunk and addressed his question to Wilson, a prisoner who had been an assistant surgeon in an Illinois regiment. Wilson was just in from a stint at the nearby hospital, where he was allowed to assist the Southern surgeons, and was pulling off bloody, foul civilian clothing to take to the clothes boiler.

He was a brisk, breezy man with a high forehead and giant mustachios, which he managed to keep trimmed even in prison. Probably used the hospital scissors, Jacob Joe thought.

"Trying to starve us all, Scott?'' Wilson repeated. He did not look at the other two men, but pulled on worn army blue trousers. "Quite the contrary. These Southerners are so steeped in chivalry they hate to be accused of being inhuman. And they are afraid of our storming the city—no doubt about that.''

"That wouldn't end the war,'' Jacob Joe mumbled.

"No, but the citizens of Richmond are panicked over the fear we may revolt.'' The doctor took off the gloves he wore against the cold even indoors and opened his surgical case. He searched for a small vial and pulled it out.

"There is smallpox across the street in Castle Lightning. Have you two been vaccinated?'' he asked the two men.

"I don't know,'' Jacob Joe said, eyeing the small scraping scalpel the surgeon was wiping on his handkerchief.

"Nor I,'' Vistal said.

"Well, gentlemen, 'tis time you bared your arm for the serum. We can't have you breaking out with the pox—''

Jacob Joe did not move to take off his cloak. "How did you get serum?'' he asked cautiously. He was not impressed with Wilson; the doctor talked of the patients in the Southern hospital up the street as if they were cases in a medical textbook.

"Oh, from a case in the hospital. An older gent. Quite a fit specimen for the serum. There was a slight difficulty in that we had to use the pus instead of the lymph, but I suspect it should work anyway.'' He reached for Jacob Joe's arm, which he defiantly pulled back.

"Well, we don't have much choice now, do we?'' the surgeon said emphatically, as if he were talking to a balky child. "I can't force you of course, but smallpox which develops in a constitution that is already weakened from hardship and poor diet is—a ticket to the graveyard." He stared at Jacob Joe.

"So be it," Jacob Joe retorted. "At least I'll ride there myself. I've heard these pus vaccinations are worse than the disease. Besides, who knows what other illnesses the patient has? People are saying more and more that all these contagions are passed about by the blood itself. I think I may have been vaccinated as a baby, but if not—no, thank you. I'll risk it."

"Smallpox is nothing to toy with," the surgeon breathed. Others in the sleeping dormitory raised up from their cots and listened to the conversation. Carlo came over from a card-playing session and bared his arm; he indicated to Duchin and his other followers to roll up their sleeves. There would be no shortage of takers for the small amount of serum, and Wilson set up his supplies on a small table by his bed and motioned the men into line.

"And you, Vistal?" the surgeon demanded.

"I thank thee, surgeon, but I will not even be exposed. I will be leaving within the week. I'm going home." The surgeon arched his eyebrows in surprise and moved on to scratch the upper arm of the first soldier in line.

"So, you have decided you will go out when your aunt pays the tax," Jacob Joe said to Vistal as they went to the commissary for cooking supplies. They were on the detail which helped with meals.

"I have prayed over what Aunt Judith says, and I feel free now to go. So many at home have prayed and worked for me. I have fought the good fight, kept the faith and now my conscience tells me I may go."

Jacob Joe turned to his friend and offered his hand. "Vistal, you are the most amazing person I think I've ever known. You seem like one of the apostles or disciples to me. I wish you well. Pray for me to get out of here alive, too."

"I think thou should pray for thyself, Jacob Scott," Vistal said, fixing fierce eyes on him.

"I can't seem to pray any more," Jacob Joe mumbled. "It's as if there is a Chinese screen between me and God. It's been that way ever since, well, since I was supposed to get married."

"An impediment to prayer means there is a hatred somewhere within."

"Probably more than one," Jacob Joe sighed. They reached the commissary window. A new system had just been implemented; Jacob Joe was cooking on a small stove just for his own floor. Carlo, Duchin and the Southern commissary supplier stood behind the window handing out supplies.

"Two ounces of beef per man is what there is tonight," the Southerner who manned the commissary bellowed out at them, as if he took some pleasure in the bad news.

"Two ounces? That isn't enough to keep a cat alive," Jacob Joe complained.

"Well, it's enough to keep the army of Robert E. Lee alive," the man informed them, gesturing for Duchin to hand out a bumpy package of oxtail and rib meat. "That's the army ration this week." He began wiping greasy hands on a blood-stained apron. "Show me the shit-head who thinks you jailbirds should eat better than the flower of the Confederacy," he said. Then he poked Carlo in the ribs and the "Corsican" scrabbled in a nearly empty barrel, and with his filthy hands tossed a meager bag of rice after the meat.

The next morning at eleven o'clock Vistal's aunt reappeared and asked the commander of the prison for an interview with both of the young Quaker men. When they came into the tiny receiving office, she was crying.

"I took the money, Tilgh, but the Secretary of War refused it. He said the Confederacy has had enough of prating Quakers and passed a new law which does not allow them to pay the fine and be exempt." She paused to wipe her eyes with a handkerchief. Tilghman remained impassive, and she continued, "He also said thou were the most obstructionist, difficult man he had seen in his entire career in the army. He wants to make an example of thee. Thou are to be sent to Salisbury Prison instead of released."

Tilghman Vistal was quiet for a moment. His lips moved, but nothing came out.

Finally, with his voice ringing with an odd sound, as if weak metal were trying to forge itself into steel, he said, "I had finally come to believe that perhaps my call was—outside." Then, in a stronger voice, "I am glad for the new Testament thou has brought, Aunt Judith. The binding on mine was so loose, and I hear that Salisbury Prison is wet and dank."

"As well as brutal and dirty," Jacob Joe whispered.

Tilghman Vistal did not go to Salisbury prison the next week. By that time he had a terrible sore throat, next a high fever, and then he broke out in swollen sores all over his upper body. Jacob Joe watched a stretcher-bearer come get him to take him to the Richmond hospital, out of his head with high fever and smallpox. He called to the stretcher bearer to halt half a moment; then he grabbed up Vistal's spectacles and Bible and a few other things from the floor and put them on the stretcher for his friend. It was a forlorn gesture of hope that Vistal would survive the next week to use the things he was sending.

That night, Jacob Joe tossed about on his cot, shivering under his thin blankets. All around him men coughed and gasped for breath; the temperature had gone down to thirty degrees and there was no heat except for a fireplace in one end of the sleeping room. The air was dank and foul; his head hurt. The Rebel authorities had set up what was supposed to be a model water closet in one end of the prison room; a long trough where the men sat to relieve themselves was sloshed with water at regular intervals which flushed the trough through a gravity flow system to the sewer below the building. Supposedly. What really happened was that the drain pipe had been clogged for some time, so nothing left the trough, and it was now a festering sewer that fouled the entire end of the room.

Finally, breathing in short gasps through his mouth and covering his face with the blanket, he fell asleep. After a while, he dreamed.

With vibrant reality he stood in the music room of the hotel in Louisville, and his heart leapt and pounded with joy as he saw his beautiful Love coming in from the parlor on the arm of a man whose face he could not see. Ah, it was his own wedding! A small part of the rational mind in the bed knew he was experiencing what he had been deprived of. The immense distorted emotion of dreams, like watercolor paint running over a wet canvas, flooded his dream self with happiness.

His Love, he could not remember her name, only her presence, wore a creamy satin bridal gown. Encircling her veil were pink rosebuds, entwined with baby's breath. He could see the flowers in perfect detail. He recognized Cousin Delia, standing as her maid of honor, bearing a small bouquet of yellow buds. Aunt Althea played a wedding hymn, quietly, sedately on the piano. He could almost recognize the tune, but his rational mind pulled back from the task of identifying it to immerse itself in the bliss of the bride's presence.

Then all eyes turned towards the hall, from which the groom's party was emerging. First came the best man, a teenager in a frock coat that was too big for him, then the groom. His observing self, on the edge of wakefulness from the cold and bad food, could hardly wait, filled with the thrill of realization that he would be married. But no, what was this? The groom was someone else! Pain and shock engulfed the dream as he saw the face of a small-statured, almost effeminate fop, someone he seemed to remember seeing in Louisville. His sensing ability faded as it reached out to touch the identity.

Delia took the bouquet from the bride—what was her name? She and whoever the fop was stood, hand in hand, listening to the minister in the robes of the Episcopal church as he gave the vows. The dream proceeded, and he could hear every poignant word clearly. He could sense the calm serenity of the bridal ceremony,—a serenity which, strangely, came to permeate him, as the dream observer, calming all agitation.

He looked at the faces, was vaguely aware someone important was not there, but he could not tell who. He focused on the mother of the bride who stood looking more tired than anything else. Then he sensed an odd ambiguity in Delia's eyes and saw there, behind Delia in the crowd, who—why it was Zach, his own brother. "At this wedding," the rational corner of his mind thought with anger, "could that be?" His troubled sleeping self thrashed around in pain. Yet, as he looked and felt the old hatred, some sort of bubble broke. That same cloak of love and serenity from the wedding wrapped round him, and now there was no feeling of hatred in his sleeping self but a yearning overcoming everything else. He wanted to linger on his brother's face, to shake his hand, to speak.

Suddenly the viewpoint shifted oddly to the man on the other side of the bride, to the unknown man giving her away. The face came into focus. Familiar—why, it was he! He was giving away this bride. And there was a smile of beneficent acceptance, a rightness that fought with the reality of the sleeper's own pressing, agonizing turmoil—he woke up in a cold sweat with his blankets kicked off.

For almost an hour he tossed and sobbed uncontrollably on his cot in that befouled, frigid prison room, and then he fell asleep exhausted. When he awoke at the chilly hour of dawn, he found he could pray again.

In the days to come he became convinced that what had happened to him, most of it, was not a dream but the unaccountable reexperiencing of what had really occurred. Had the second sight returned? He believed so. And he tried hard to recapture the profound, cleansing feeling of forgiveness and comfort he experienced in that dream. He sensed that only that feeling would enable him to face the truth he was now convinced of: that his Love had married someone else while he was gone to prison.

"Matron, assist us in placing these new patients from the prison in the quarantine wing," Surgeon Wilson commanded. Dora Lavenham looked at this officer and told herself, firmly, that she must obey him, even though she was the Matron Superintendent of a Southern hospital and he was a Northerner. The health of men transcended politics, even war, she thought. After all, they cared for more Northern than Southern men at this pavilion hospital in Richmond, as she found out when she arrived a few weeks ago. And they were all terribly short-handed.

"Doctor Wilson, what services do you require?" she asked. He was supervising the arrival of about twenty men from the tobacco factory prisons, almost all of whom had smallpox. All were on stretchers, and some looked as if they could not last the night.

"The usual: clean beds, fever cloths. Be sure to spray the air with boric acid before the men come in. We don't want the flying effluvia to get into the air and be carried to the rest of the hospital. Then we'll want stimulants—eggnog and toddies. Study the charts; you have not been reading them well enough."

His tone was so peremptory it was almost insulting, but Dora and the four matron assistants who worked under her were used to it from him, and from the Southern surgeons he assisted. No one in the Confederate military really wanted women about in the hospital wards except as housekeepers and food-cookers. But as the war plodded on, the women's roles expanded. In the North their counterparts were doing actual nursing; here, in this long third year of the war in the South, with severe manpower shortages, women were beginning to be allowed to do a few dressings and to care for the men. Still, most of the surgeons were not pleased with the necessities the shortages of trained male nurses forced on them, and they showed it in their attitudes.

Dora walked through the general ward to get to the linen closet, where the sheets taken off the beds and boiled clean only yesterday were stored. As she went through this ward, her mind repeated a little litany, one she would not allow herself to forget. As she walked, she reviewed the medical history of each patient, so he became alive to her as a human being.

"Crossing the aisle back and forth, as I walk, Sergeant Sheets from Mississippi, shrapnel wound, Ensign Roadhammel from Baton Rouge, internal injuries from blast percussion while he was in the water after iron-clad battle. (Nice youth with no relatives. Must try to read to him, he hurts so badly his lip is bitten sore.) Then, quiet and withdrawn, Jackson Billings, eastern Mississippi, leg ulcers; Captain Block, bone infection (he has never cried out in pain, not once). Here, in the middle, behind a separating screen, eight typhoid patients, sweating, suffering from intense pain in the joints, two deranged. "May they not be deranged if they must die," she prayed, "for they need to meet their God in their right minds if they can."

She completed the row, identifying each man she could remember, and came to the central hub of the building. Off the middle wing, like the spokes of a wheel, wings for commissary and housekeeping, serious erysipelas cases, and hospital gangrene, the infectious diseases that made surgery con- valescence a nightmare. At this late date in the war the surgeons were realizing that all these things were transmitted among the patients, either by flying through the air or some other way. They debated about it a lot but one thing they knew: the "catching" diseases must be isolated.

Dora continued the litany. Off to the left was the smallpox quarantine wing—already the men from Castles Thunder and Lightning had disap- peared through the door and into that wing. She must hurry with sheets. Betsy Pickering, assistant matron, a tall, capable woman from Williams- burg, appeared, and Dora gave her the task of getting the keys to the closet and the linen, while she hurried into the smallpox quarantine ward.

Dora had grown accustomed to awful sights, to stiff, bloodied dressings that had to be cut away from the wounds of suffering men, of brains and viscera coming out of wounds, of maggots in the southern climates crawling on beds and the wounds themselves, but the sight of a score of men with smallpox sores still distracted her. They were so weak and pitiful, so swol- len and unlike themselves, calling out through their fever in grunting or yelping voices, as if some awful devil had come in with heat and fire and stolen their bodies and very souls to replace them with unhappy trolls. No wonder in Biblical times it was believed the diseased were "possessed with demons." Seeing men with the smallpox, she understood.

Betsy Pickering came in with the sheets, and she and Dora began dressing four of the beds which had been left to air after the last catching cases, men with mumps, had returned to camp or prison or died.

One of the new smallpox cases, a lanky, homely man with spectacles which he seemed to need even flat on his back, clasped a Bible to his chest. He was trying to read it, even though his hands kept shaking with high fever. She went to him and put her hand on his forehead (Thank goodness she had been inoculated by someone who knew what they were doing in Mississip- pi.)

"Soldier, how are you doing?" She asked the perfunctory question that gave her something to talk about with the men. Obviously, his face swollen and red as a beet, his whole body trembling, he was not doing very well, though Wilson's chart did not say his case was extremely critical.

But his answer surprised her. "I am not a soldier, thankee, ma'am."

She scanned the record. "Ah, yes. An objector because of conscience. A Friend, perhaps." She paused a fraction of a second and let her voice cherish the word, as she thought with pleasure and sadness of Jacob Joe. God grant he was still alive, somewhere! It was her constant prayer.

"Yes. I have been in Castle Thunder, but I am due to go to Salisbury Prison as soon as I am well." She did not know what to say. It was harder to say which would be worse: having a case of the smallpox, or going to Salisbury Prison, where anarchy and brutality ruled.

"Do you need anything? A cool compress? Water?"

"Not now, thankee, ma'am. I am at peace and give thee thanks for the clean bed and quiet of this ward."

"It is called New Hospital and is an enlightened facility, built recently. Anything else?"

"I wonder if thee could read my Bible to me. I have been delirious and I still cannot focus on the words."

"Yes, certainly." She glanced over her shoulder. Betsy had seen her speaking to the man and was finishing the bed making. There would be time to read; they did not need to start supper for a few moments.

"The Ninety-first Psalm, please ma'am." The young man's voice shook. His chart said his name was Vistal. Tilghman Vistal.

She picked up the book and began to read:

He that dwelleth in the secret place of the Most High
Shall abide under the shadow of the Almighty.
He shall give his angels charge over thee
To keep thee in all thy ways.

Her gentle, confident voice read on, until he fell asleep. She lay the Bible down and pulled the blanket up around him, straightening the bed.

She decided that later she would return to this unusual man, who asked only for the comfort of Scripture and a clean place to heal. She started to lay the Bible, along with the spectacles, by his hand on the bed. The Bible's imitation leather cover fell open, and her eyes lit on the handwriting: "November 8, 1863. From Judith Mendenhall to Mr. Jacob Joe Scott, ever a Friend." She gasped. Jacob, Jacob Joe. The date was only two weeks ago. This man had the Bible. Jacob Joe must be in Castle Thunder, now!

She stood, pondering the meaning of the revelation. She tried to sort the situation out as the sky darkened and she went to supervise the preparation of the patients' supper, meager as it was in these hard times in Richmond.

She hadn't received a letter since leaving the deep South, over a month ago, and at that time the folks in Louisville did not know where Jacob Joe was. There was even a rumor, brought by another captive, that he was dead.

But he was alive and only a few blocks away! Thank God! He must have been committed there by the Rebel government after John Morgan fell. Morgan was in prison in Columbus, Ohio and out of touch, and his prisoner had ended up in the Castle. She reached the small kitchen. She must know more. Anything she did would be for Sophie's sake, of course.

"What are the prisoners in Castle Thunder held for, Betsy?" she asked Miss Pickering as they put bread and cheese on plates for the supper.

"Oh, there are Southern conscientious objectors, disciplinary offenders of a non-violent sort, and a few officers of the Northern army who are being held as bait when the exchange finally starts up again. What makes you ask? Do you know someone there?" Betsy Pickering's eyes were curious. In these days of rancor towards the Yankees, it was strictly forbidden for hospital staff to have personal contacts in the tobacco prisons, let alone Belle Isle, the awful enlisted men's holding pen. Women had been accused of being traitors. These were awful times.

"No, of course I don't know anyone." Dora was uncomfortable lying, but she must not reveal what she knew until she determined what to do next. Would she be able to see him? Did he need help? She would have to spin her plans very carefully or she might ruin any chance of seeing or helping him. Alive and nearby! She could not stop thinking of it. "They've sent dried apples tonight for a change. Let's sprinkle sugar on them," she said, joyously.

Practical, homely Betsy Pickering was a good friend, a collaborator in the plan to beat all the distress and ridiculousness of hospital routine. A young widow whose husband had been killed early, at Shiloh, she wore her hair pinned back in a severe bun, sponged glycerine lotion on her aching feet each night, and knew no life but nursing. Each day she and Dora confronted indifferent, overworked and underrewarded surgeons and male nurses, reams of paperwork and regulations, and chronic shortages which only worsened. They determined to detour around the troubles which they met in managing this hospital and find a way to help the patients get well, if they could.

"Dessert for the men? There aren't but a couple of cups of white sugar." Betsy turned widely set, inquiring eyes towards her friend. Then she caught her friend's mood and smiled broadly. "There is a little cinnamon. Shall we be naughty and use the stuff tonight?"

"I feel like being festive."

"I don't know why, Dora," Betsy Pickering said wryly, reaching for the wooden boxes where the apples were stored. "The government is almost bankrupt, and Confederate money isn't worth enough to start this cookstove."

She banged the box down on the old monster of an iron cookstove resurrected from the cellar and went on. 'No foreign powers recognize us, we are losing battles and territory all the time, and now 14,000 men in the prisons may just decide to strike down the bars and come after us all tomorrow."

"What do you mean?" Dora wondered, looking at her friend in alarm.

"There is no meat ration today, and there will be none at all tomorrow.

There is none for the troops in the field.'' She spread out the apples in a warming pan. Then she reached onto the top shelf, opened the cinnamon tin and began sprinkling the spice on the apples. As the warm, inviting smell began to drift through the room, the women grinned.

"Where there are cinnamon apples for supper, all is not lost," Dora said, putting her finger in the few grains of sugar left from the sprinkling and popping it into her mouth. She never was political about the war, anyway. She joined this army because it was where her family and friends' sympathy lay, and to take care of wounded men. And to forget. Now, it seemed, she did not need to. Well, if Jacob Joe survived the prison camps he would go home and marry her sister, but at least he would live. If she could help.

"Where there are cinnamon apples," her friend sang it as a little song.

"And where Jacob Joe is," Dora told herself, "in the same city and still, I pray God, well, all is definitely not lost. I will do what I can, in Sophie's name, of course." She popped the apple tray into the oven and slammed the door shut with vigor, as if she were slamming the door on the whole war, if only for ten minutes.

Later that evening, as they undressed by lamplight in the small cabin which served as the matrons' quarters, she found a letter that had been delivered. She picked it up eagerly and sat down on her narrow army cot to read. Finally, word from home! Her eyes, squinting in the dim light, scanned the round hand—her mother's handwriting. She read it, then she frowned and crumpling the letter, turned to throw it on her small travelling trunk.

"Why, Dora, whatever is it?" Betsy Pickering asked, her bright eyes curious in the shadowy lamplight. She was neatly folding her chemise and skirt on the top of the trunk.

"My sister—has married. Sophie was engaged to someone, I think I mentioned—to someone captured—whose whereabouts are unknown—and she gave him up for dead and cobbled up a marriage to a local beaux. In two week's time she called all the family and friends in and married herself to a silly, prattling man whose whole life is his drinking club."

"I am sorry, dear," Betsy said, putting down the clothing and coming to her, taking her hand. She looked into Dora's eyes and Dora lowered them. "And, yet I see," Betsy went on, "you are bearing the news without too much sadness."

"I did not think the match with the Northern soldier well made for Sophie," Dora finally said. "So I have confused feelings. I am angry at her disloyalty, yet it is so like her." She smoothed the already smooth blanket, her oval nails, now chipped and discolored from scrubbing with harsh soap, delicately touching its roughness. Betsy sat down on her own cot. As the lamp flickered over its spent wick, Dora said, "Yet it may all be for the best. We shall have to wait and see."

It was not the cold that made her shiver so violently as she climbed beneath the covers in a few moments. It was the knowledge that even though her sister had given her love to another, Sophie could not disengage herself from Jacob Joe's heart no matter how hard she tried. In the many letters he sent to Dora before he was captured, with open hearted candor, Jacob Joe had stoutly pledged to love Sophie until the day he died.

Back at Castle Thunder two weeks from the day he was vaccinated, Carlo the Corsican broke out with fever which was not smallpox. The man Dr. Wilson had taken pus from in the hospital to make serum for inoculations at the prison was desperately ill, not only with smallpox, but with pneumonia. Carlo the Corsican, one of several who contracted the disease but the only man who seemed to take a virulent case, died of complications in the hospital, and the atmosphere at Castle Thunder changed considerably for the better within a short time.

Thomas Jefferson Brooks stood by a pond not far from a small creek named Mine Run, where the Army of the Potomac was camped. A half mile or so down the gully and all along the other side of the creek was the army of Robert E. Lee.

Brooks had walked out of camp to stretch his legs for a moment. He gazed into the pool rather absently, glad to have something to do that did not have all the cares and complications of the war connected with it. This pond had been dug as a cow drinking hole by a local farmer, he thought. Not unlike ponds which drained Martin County. But unlike the Martin County cattle, cows in this area had long since been moved away or slaughtered by foraging parties from both sides of the war. There it was again. You couldn't escape it.

As the broad sun of this Indian Summer day lit the waters of the pool, Brooks looked at his mirrored image. He turned a bit (It was all right, nobody was around. And at his age he could be allowed one-and-a-half minutes of vanity). Trim figure—well almost trim. There was a sort of round watermelon on his stomach.

It was odd how people took on weight as they aged. Most did in these affluent days where you didn't need to worry about food on the table—well, on the home front, anyway. For sixty-four years he had been enjoying the ample viands of the gustatory table spreads of various women who had served meals to him, and it was taking its toll.

Some men just fleshed up and out all over their bodies. But Brookses had always had pot bellies. He chuckled to himself as he remembered the visit he made to his home in Lincoln, Massachusetts, when—well, when Tommy was a baby. Everyone came off the porch to welcome him and Susan and the baby as they got off the stagecoach. There was his father, the Reverend Daniel Brooks, and there were his sisters, all standing with their Yankee uprightness and sternness of countenance, all looking like they were holding small balloons on their stomachs.

He took note of his attire in the pond-mirror. Not exactly how he prided himself on dressing as the Yankee Trader, manager of big stores and supplier to the Union Army, one of the commercial lords of southern Indiana. Baggy old trousers, none too clean, a wool jacket and a slouch hat. But this was the only proper garb for travelling among the camps of the Army of the Potomac on his investigative mission. Fancy duds would have been silly, even though the mission was an important one, from the President of the United States himself.

He turned from the pond. He had better return; he might have inadvertently passed out of the Northern army's picket lines. He headed back towards the clatter of camp noises. The Fourteenth and other selected units of Meade's army were trying to flank Robert E. Lee's lines, and they did it in such a leisurely, or was it confused manner, that the Rebels had had time to come out and spread themselves along this Mine Run Creek, blocking the way.

General Gouveneur Warren, the hero of Gettysburg, was perfecting dignified plans for whatever was coming about, and the veteran units waiting for action were in no hurry either. From ahead, up a little rise, Thomas Jefferson Brooks could hear mules braying and laughter float out of the camp.

As he slowly climbed the final hill towards the Fourteenth's encampment, he thought about his nearly completed mission.

After the visit in September to New York, Susan and Harriet Houghton left him to return to Indiana. He and Walter McClure, whom he had asked to assist him, went to Washington, and he, Thomas Jefferson Brooks, actually met with Abraham Lincoln! He had written letters about it to everybody he could think of and tried to sound casual as he described every detail, and now he pored over it again in his mind.

He was seated in a handsome, walnut-paneled office at the White House when Lincoln strode in with a small group of men, two of whom were provost guards. The President dismissed the guards with a wave of his hand and came to shake Brooks's hand.

"Well, sir, you've come with a breath of fresh Hoosier air to the stinks of the Potomac,'' the President said. He was rumpled-looking, like a man who had slept on the settee for several hours, and his hair stood up in spite of pomade.

The President did not wait for an answer from him. ''I've been shooting, practicing my hunting style out by the armory. People say I shouldn't walk around Washington like any average citizen. They tell me I have to take a pack of coon dogs at my heels.'' He gestured in the direction of the provost guards and sycophants who were standing in the hall. There was a candid quality about the president, Thomas Jefferson Brooks thought, that one did not find in many people in Washington. Lincoln went to a table and poured tumblers of cider.

''How is it now in southern Indiana, Mr. Brooks?'' the President had said, putting the small glass in his visitor's hand.

''First killing frost, Mr. President, I hear in my last letter from Martin County. The pumpkins that haven't been picked up are starting to cave in out in the fields, and the shocks are white 'till the sun hits 'em.''

Lincoln nodded. ''I never will forget the way southern Indiana smells in late November. In the early morning.'' His eyes seemed far away. ''Smoke, from sugar trees being burnt in the clearings, coming to your nose, and bacon from up a ways at the cabin, drifting down. Lots of cabins and town houses too, are empty of their men these days.'' He seemed to be saying it to no one in particular, but then he turned to his visitor, ready to get down to business.

''We are doing a much better job of equipping our army these days, Mr. Brooks. The quartermasters are getting just a mite efficient. Honest people like you have replaced the rotten purveyors, and supply lines are functioning about three quarters of the time.''

Thomas Jefferson Brooks nodded, glad to be able to affirm it all.

Lincoln emptied his cider glass at one gulp. ''But we have several weevils to get off the potato plants. One of them is the sutler question. Ever since the first men went to camp at Rich Mountain in that first battle, these men with carts have angered them. Inferior goods, outrageous prices, whisky under the coats.''

''That doesn't always anger them, Mr. President.''

''No,'' he murmured. ''You have me there. They claim this is a drinking war for officers, a fighting war for enlisted men. But that's the way it has to be. We can't issue whisky with a free hand for all.''

''And the sutlers fill in the gaps, in spite of all the commanders and regulations try to do.''

''True. A year ago we passed the Wilson Bill to regulate sutlers. What they sold, how they sold it. All the provisions of licensing were regulated. I want you to find out how widespread the evasion of the regulations is in the Army of the Potomac.''

Brooks moved his chair forward a few inches, eager to respond. ''When I was with the Fourteenth Regiment in New York, they told me they all are spending too much at the sutler stores, even yet. Their pay goes too fast there.''

''Well,'' the President said, ''we think we have controlled the credit problem with the sutlers anyway. At the beginning of the war the cartmen came in just at payday and took everyone's money, then put whatever else was wanted on the tab.''

''Ah,'' Brooks said to his President, ''I used to watch the Indian agents get the Miami and Potawatomi Indians to sign up for credit in just that way.'' He had looked out the window of the office, thinking of that time.

''Yes, Mr. Brooks. Times don't change. The carts are gone and the log huts with the armies look like mercantiles. But greed only goes under a log for a time to reappear with a new skin. The sutlers arrive with the paymaster and leave in a day or so after all the cash is gone.'' Lincoln looked at him with interest. ''But you're talking about a fair spell ago. The 1820s. You were in Indiana in Indian times.''

''Since 1818. My brothers and I were some of the first settlers in Martin County.''

The President nodded heartily. ''As a man who pioneered with my father in that area, I can trust you even more than I knew.'' He seemed delighted at his choice for the sutler project. ''Go about General Meade's camps of the Army of the Potomac near the Rapidan and Rappahannock. Do you think the men will be honest with you about the sutlers?''

''Some will. But most will talk to the soldier that has been released to accompany me.''

''Who is that?'' the Commander-in-Chief asked.

''A private named Walter McClure. He's a mixed Potawatomi and Miami Indian. He's earned the respect of a good many of the men.''

Lincoln looked surprised. ''I knew our army was made up of as many different vegetables as a stew, but I had not heard of this kind of 'improved variety.' '' He smiled a wry smile, and wrinkles creased his face. ''Well, send my regards to Private McClure and the best to both of you. You must think him wise indeed to take him with you. I could use some wisdom in the Indian affairs out west.'' He offered his hand to signify the interview was coming to a close.

''Come back in a month,'' he said, ''to make your report. I have two other reliable reporters in the other armies. If you should have anything ready, any kind of preliminary report we can tell people, telegraph it on. The soldier discontents like the sutler affair remind me of fleas, biting the political animal right now. We must win the congressional elections and rid ourselves of these Democrats who want to give up on the war.''

''Yes, Mr. President. But I don't think you will need my report to do that, nor will it help much in any case.''

A secretary appeared and ushered him from the room.

Now, as he recalled it, walking along in the woods near the camp of the Army of the Potomac, he was aware that he felt a little disappointed that Lincoln did not tell a funny story. They said that he did this to illustrate points, and that only men from the northwest frontier states could understand the jokes. Perhaps he did not have anything to joke about. At that time he was receiving news from Chicamauga; thousands of Northern soldiers had been killed or wounded in a smashing Confederate victory in Georgia.

''And now,'' Brooks thought, as he finally reached the Fourteenth's Camp, ''Three months later I think we have succeeded a little in what President Lincoln asked, though it took longer than I had anticipated.'' After his visit to the White House, he had not been able to start immediately; some of his affairs back home needed to be set in order with telegrams and long waits for replies. Then he and Walter needed to stay in Washington for two weeks, to be sure they understood the laws and military regulations and to talk to the commissary and other departments that dealt with sutlers.

Then, after they began the visits and interviewing, there were times when they could not be with the army, when it appeared Lee might start some new offensive. Finally they got permission to go no matter what, on their own responsibility, and they asked the questions and got some of the answers they needed. And now he was here, finishing up.

''What did you find out, Uncle?'' Will Houghton asked later sitting with Beem, Walter McClure and Thomas Jefferson Brooks outside Houghton's officer's tent in the northern camp.

''Well, I visited sutlers' tents and cabins and wagons. I found out there are a few very good men selling things to soldiers, several of the middling sort, and one thousand too many scoundrels.''

His nephew smiled. Now and then Uncle Thomas did exaggerate. ''There are all kinds of scoundrels out here,'' Houghton added, spreading his hands to indicate the Army of the Potomac.

''Yes. And as far as the sutlers go, there are regulations under the Wilson Act to keep them in line, but they aren't being enforced.''

''I can tell you why that is,'' David Beem said. He looked up from his travelling desk, where he was checking through the morning reports prepared by his subordinates. ''I served as quartermaster and I saw it all. Individual units have to enforce the regulations and colonels and generals don't want to bother with it. Besides," he lowered his head and voice, "some are on the take themselves."

"Yes, that's true," Brooks said. "Especially with the whisky. Only officers are allowed to buy whisky, and sutlers are strictly forbidden to sell it to enlisted men. But when the sutlers deliver the officers' ration, they just bring a little more for the officers to sell to the men on the side."

The wind was blowing, and Beem held the papers down with his elbow. "Did you—was the Fourteenth involved in this?" he wondered apprehensively.

"Walter can better tell you that," Thomas Jefferson Brooks said, deferring to the young man who remained in the tree shadows beside the tent, listening quietly.

"I asked in the other regiments of the Brigade. I didn't want to investigate or betray my own comrades. I think many of us have suspected, had our ideas." Walter McClure looked at Houghton and Beem and, reluctantly, they nodded.

"Colonel Coons would never allow shenanigans if he knew about them. He may have his faults but he sticks to the book," Walter said candidly. Houghton nodded. Coons had a hot temper and a slick, superficial manner, but he was a soldier through and through.

Walter McClure went on. "One of the Ohio regiments up the way has a complicated graft system going, with the sutler bringing in the whisky in false-bottom boxes and middle men quietly dispensing it after dark. Our regimental whisky 'agent' is"—he looked up at Houghton—"Do you know?"

"Lieutenant Harpring of I?" Houghton asked quickly. "I've wondered— he's often where he doesn't belong."

"Yes. We'll be reporting it to Colonel Coons and Lieutenant Colonel Cavins tomorrow and let them act. But there are others, in many of the units."

"These sutlers are getting rich as Midas," Thomas Jefferson Brooks said, stubbing out his cigar in the mud outside the tent. "Now that most represent larger units than just a regiment, they do hundreds, even thousands of dollars worth of business a day. I've calculated the sales these people make— all the pies and shoes and hats and popcorn and stationery and raincoats. Can you guess how much sutlers will make in the Army of the Potomac this year?"

Houghton and Beem shook their heads.

"They will gross ten million this year and half of that is clear profit."

Beem gave a long whistle of surprise.

"It's outrageous," Houghton said. "I've seen them interfere with advances and slow down retreats. We have it right under our noses this very moment. Here we are, trying to force Lee out of his lines, advancing like a cumbersome rhinoceros,''—Houghton was all but snarling—"and now the enemy is facing us off on the other side of that creek, with real battle possible, and there is a sutler's tent.'' He gestured towards the back of the encampment, where a fancy, clean new tent stood alone, near the wagons. "They find us out even in the jaws of battle to separate us from our money.''

David Beem closed the brown, morning report book and looked at Thomas Jefferson Brooks. "Well, besides the fact that human nature is what it has always been, what else have you learned?''

Brooks laughed and jabbed Walter McClure in the arm. "Well, one of the best things that's happened is that I've come to know this young whelp.'' Walter smiled in acknowledgment. "He's as fine a man as you have in the regiment.''

"I can testify to that, uncle,'' Will Houghton said, bringing up camp stools for all of them. "Even if he isn't from Martin County, we've adopted him.''

Walter looked grateful. "It's been a privilege to be with Mr. Brooks. And I found out he knew me once before.'' Beem and Houghton looked surprised, and Walter quickly added, "Well—I wasn't born yet, but I was there, riding with mother.'' His face grew serious. "Mr. Brooks watched my tribe's roundup when the Potawatomi went west.''

"Worst thing I ever saw, in '38,'' Thomas Jefferson Brooks said. "His father was put in a travelling jail and his mother was kicked. I've told him how I felt about all that, that we all have a lot to answer for.''

Houghton asked about the story of the Indians' trip west and Walter told briefly about the broken treaty in northern Indiana and Michigan, the settlers' thirst for the last remaining land in the state, the governors' panic that there would be bloodshed, and the forced trip west through blazing heat to Kansas.

"Many died, but there were births too. Little White Deer was born to Chief Paukooshuck and Dawn Yet to Come.''

He paused, as if expecting some reaction, and they looked at him inquiringly.

"That's me,'' he said, smilingly.

"White Deer,'' Beem said wonderingly. "So that is your Indian name. A wonderful one. I'm glad you told us.''

"Not everyone would understand,'' Walter added, hesitatingly.

"Well, we do,'' Houghton said, giving him a smile that seemed to imply he felt privileged to know the name and would keep it confidential.

"Mr. Lincoln even knows about this young man, and I will introduce him when we get back to the White House next week,' Thomas Jefferson Brooks said heartily, clapping Walter on the back.

Beem looked at the older man. "What will you tell the President, sir?" he wanted to know.

"Well, I've been telling Walter is what a shrewd Yankee trader I am," Brooks replied. "And have been for forty years." Walter nodded eagerly. It had been rewarding being a captive audience for this wise, witty older man. He'd learned things they never taught in the Catholic Indian School, that was certain.

"I'm going to General Meade, then to the President and I'm going to tell them to deal with the sutlers like a Yankee trader would," Brooks said with a self-satisfied smile.

"And how is that, Uncle?" Will Houghton asked bemusedly, as he stooped to pickup one of Beem's papers which had blow away.

Brooks leaned confidentially towards his nephew. "Hit them where it hurts," he said.

Beem looked questioningly at him.

"Use their prosperity and their weakness. Let me put it another way." He took out a cigar, looked in his pockets for something to light it with without success, then went to the campfire the men were just beginning to build a few yards away and took a flaming stick to the cigar.

"As I was saying," he told them, puffing at the cigar when he returned, "there's a country story from our parts. A neighbor of mine, living out in the hills upriver from Hindostan, owns a stand of timber that still has game in it." White smoke rose in puffs and hovered over the heads of the party sitting on the little stools.

He cleared his throat to go on and everyone settled back, anticipating one of the frontier tales like the President told. "The farmer was a happy man to have game, because we don't have many deer in Martin County anymore." Beem nodded his head. He was not surprised. His home county, Owen in the hilly country south of Indianapolis, did have all kinds of game, although it was not as plentiful as it had been.

"But this man had some, and he loved the taste of venison and wild turkey, especially." He put the cigar between two stained fingers and watched the cooking tripod go up above the campfire. "Every now and then this man would hear shooting, and he'd see men going by with deer on poles or wagons full of wild turkeys."

Beem was folding his camp table up, but he continued to listen to the shrewd old man tell his story. "If the man watched," Brooks continued, "he could pretty well spot when the poachers went into his woods, and the next time he saw them, he stood by the path. 'Well and good you poach in my woods,' he said. 'Guess I cain't stop you. But half them turkeys is mine from now on in. Call it a turkey toll.' "

Houghton looked at his uncle, waiting for the point.

"If you can't stop the sutlers, and they're getting rich, as we've seen, tax 'em. Let the government share the profits. Use the tax for hospitals, good vegetables for our wounded, and for the prisoners. We can have the common humanity to take care of the Confederates in our jails even if they're starving ours."

Houghton and Beem nodded, impressed with the reasonableness of the plan for a turkey toll.

"Hit 'em in the potbelly," Brooks concluded smiling and pointed at his, while all the men laughed.

Later that night, while the men cleaned their guns for action tomorrow, Thomas Jefferson Brooks packed his small carpet valise, putting in the socks with too many holes, the linen drawers, a mildewy shirt, and his long account book with notes from the several camps he had visited. On top of the other things, he placed three letters that had reached him just yesterday. He sat on the camp bed. Walter was saying goodbye to Company C; he would be back momentarily, and they both would be taken to the rear, out of battle range.

A head popped in the tent flap, and the smiling face of John McClure beamed at Brooks.

When the young man was seated on the floor, cross-legged, Brooks said to him, "Well, I wish we could tour Barnum's again, don't you?"

"Waal, we're expectin' a circus tomorrow around here. If it comes to town. Lately the whole Army of the Potomac's been in the doldrums."

"Winter isn't a time to fight."

"Guess not." McClure looked thoughtful. "Sir, I was wonderin' how Miz Poore and the rest are."

Thomas Jefferson Brooks unbuckled the portmanteau and took out the letters. He handed the first one to John, who held it up to the smoky lamp to read.

"Hmm, Miz Poore says she has the sore eye. Cain't see, eyes swole shut. That's bad, but it does pass. They're butcherin'. Colonel Lewis is home recuperating' from intermittent fever. Has resigned his commission. Hmm."

He put the letter down. "What about Eustace, sir?"

The older man picked up another letter, one with a soldier on its corner proudly holding a flag. "Eustace has been promoted to corporal and has started into real action now. They've been with Burnside, in East Tennessee and at Knoxville. They're moving into the deep South where there's some hard fighting."

"Well, we ain't had much of that lately," John McClure said, brushing dirt from his trousers and pushing himself off the ground. "We been so out of practice lately, we prob'ly forgot how to play the tune when it comes to fightin' tomorrow."

Brooks rose to shake hands, and as he did so Walter McClure came through the door, talking as he came.

"I saw my old friend Surgeon Burkhart. He is with the Corps medical service now but—" He stopped, his eyes on John McClure. "Hello, McClure," he said, in a strained, hesitant manner.

John dropped Thomas Jefferson Brooks's hand and saluted him in fare-well. Then he left, passing Walter McClure in the door of the tent without looking at him. "Not hello, goodbye," he said in tones that were as cold as any Brooks had heard in a while.

Walter passed to his bunk to get his gear without meeting the older man's questioning eyes. "What was all that about?" Thomas Jefferson Brooks thought. He hauled his valise on the bed and looked with dismay at the folding cot which had been prepared for him, then snorted and lay down on it to rest. Within a minute he was snoring.

And so on November 30 at Mine Run, John McClure and Isaac Crim and Bushby Quillen and Tommy Thompson and Joe Rosecrans and Jess Harrold and Beem and Houghton and the rest of the Gibraltar Brigade came out with their generals to see if these units of the Army of the Potomac wished to resume fighting with the Army of Northern Virginia, and decided not to. And Willie McClure and Calhoun Dugger and Boone Epworth and the rest of Doles' Brigade, and the Southern troops on the other side of the creek, looked at the situation and decided not to provoke the North, and everybody went back to the lines and went into winter quarters. Things had not grown desperate enough in Virginia for anyone to try to end the war.

The situation was getting fairly desperate, however, for Southern sympa-thizers in the Middle States. Castles of the Knights of the Golden Circle still met, their chants muted, their disappointment over the falling fortunes of the Confederacy bitter and deep. In spite of discouragement, numbers continued strong and new men joined. The freeing of the slaves and the formation of Negro regiments unsettled Southern sympathizers, and they gathered, and changed the names of their organizations, and ranted and hated, though still without action.

John Morgan escaped from the Northern prison where he had been con-fined and returned to cavalry service, but he tried no more Indiana raids. And in Indiana and Illinois, a desperate plot was being formulated to pull victory like a rug, in spite of everything, out from under the feet of Lincoln's army.

"Canada? They're talking of making a headquarters for secret actions against the North in Canada?" Zach Scott looked with mild surprise across the table at Willis Mawkins. They were dining at the American Hotel in Vincennes.

"This war has always been a balancing act on a tightrope. Tip the wire, let the wind come up, and the balance can shift again. The Northern home front is bitterly sick of the war." Mawkins reached for a long dish with radishes and celery in it. These Chicago hothouses could send anything down on the cars these days, even in late November, the dead of winter.

"But Canada?"

Mawkins crunched a piece of celery. "There is support for us, and some fortunes have been put at our disposal. Canada is free of spies and near Southern sympathizing areas in the Old Northwest. A good place to operate actions for peace, whatever their nature."

"Well, the folks are desperate for peace," Zach conceded. 'What the terms would be, I don't know. They can't unfree the slaves."

"No, but the North can let the South have its own independent nation, quit fighting and set up peace on its own terms. That they can and will do *if* they are under enough pressure."

He popped a canned black olive in his mouth. Zach noticed he was well enough fed; his brocaded vest was stretching its buttons over an expanding middle. Mawkins was no longer young, but the war had made him prosperous. There was a garnet pin in his tie, a large ruby ring on his finger.

"You stand to win both ways, don't you, Mawkins?" Zach said with a darkly amused smile. "You're profiteering."

Mawkins, in an exceptionally good mood, looked around quickly to see if anyone could hear. "The travelling I have done for the Southern cause has opened doors, put it that way. I am seeing that the North gets Southern cotton and that certain important families along the Mississippi don't starve." The waiter brought roast goose and dressing; Mawkins helped himself from the plate, served Zach, and waited until the waiter was well out of hearing before he spoke in his slow, wheedling voice.

"Matter of fact, I'm conducting my transactions with relatives of your friends."

Zach took a forkful of cornbread stuffing and raised his eyes inquisitively.

"Duggers from Indianapolis. They travel to Memphis and the South now every month as my agents. As Northerners, with relatives there, they can find supplies, discover Federal officials who need forbidden luxuries and necessities and bring them in from the neighborhood. They take back cotton when they can evade the Memphis commander.''

He picked up a piece of white bread. ''The Duggers are stupid as hogs and smart as foxes, all at the same time. Relatives of your fiancée—is it?''

Zach put his fork down and wiped his mouth on a napkin. ''I met them in Indianapolis. Delia is not my fiancée, though I wish she were. I am a friend and confidant of the family and—she won't have me. You know that.''

''Confidant, are you? Cat as captain of the canaries,'' Mawkins said, curling his lip in a sardonic grin. Zach gave him a scathing look.

''You were talking about a change in the Confederate fortunes,' he said in a measured voice.

Mawkins lowered his voice. ''The North is worn out. If something big were to happen, people in the Northwest could easily turn against Lincoln in the presidential election in the fall, and if they do—'' He snapped a piece of celery right in two.

''*If* the South wins a big battle,'' Zach said in a low voice.

''That can happen,'' Mawkins answered insistently. ''Or, more likely, things will get worse here at home. Much worse. If something desperate were to happen right here in Indiana and Illinois—''

''Desperate? We got desperate and tried Morgan's raid and it failed,'' Zach said frowning.

Mawkins leaned across the table. His voice was almost a whisper. ''I cannot speak of this matter yet. Suffice it to say that Canada is a good spot for activities at this point in the war. Vigorous, even clandestine actions which could tip the balance and cause peace. Vallandigham is in Canada even now, talking. If Southern leaders were to go there, they would be among friends in some parts. There is money, lots of it, for the Cause there, and if the time is right—something big could change the course of the war.''

''How do you know this?'' Zach demanded intently.

''I have my contacts in Richmond. In a month or two the moment will be right. I'll need you when the time comes. They will be ready in Richmond.''

A long moment passed. Zach continued eating and then put down his fork in a moment of realization. ''You are the Northern Mask,'' he said.

''Our romantic friends in the Knights of the Golden Circle—''

''Sons of Liberty,'' Zach corrected him. The lodges had decided to change their names to foil the secret agents who were constantly around.

''Ah, yes, of course, the Sons of Liberty, thought up that name—the Northern Mask. I had to keep my relationships with the Confederate capital secret. But since the beginning of the war I have been the contact with Richmond about the anti-war movements and yes, I admit it, with agents of Jefferson Davis, at certain points.''

"Real treason!" Zach said softly. There was talk of treason trials in Indiana; many things were dangerous these days.

"I have covered my trail. I'm proud of my part in Colonel Morgan's invasion. I still am in contact with Captain Hines. He's a part of what will be happening in Canada."

"What use is it all now? Vallandigham has lost contact and effectiveness, and the Knights refused to act and still would not fight, I think."

"I have told you. We want to end the war on our terms. So decisive action—"

"Desperate action—"

"Desperate action is indicated. Be ready."

"What makes you think I will still be here to help you?" Zach asked insistently. "You have your own reasons—you've been promised rewards in the new Confederacy, and you like to plot and scheme. It gives your brain occupation."

The waiter cleared the plates. "Why should I mark myself for treason in what looks more and more like a lost cause?" Zach demanded.

"Because you are part of the McClure family. My father worked for them for years, until they—unfairly—drove him out. Incurable idealists, fools. You can't resist." Mawkins eyes seemed far away. "I can see them now, your Cousin Catherine and her family, in that big house, while we slopped their hogs, with her rich uncles down the road. All of them had been poor as dirt, and then they were lords over us. I hated them all, with their airs and pianos and easy chairs."

Zach did not need to be told that Mawkins hated the McClures. He'd sensed it ever since he got to know him and could hear it in his voice now. This could explain, at least in part, what happened to Lettie Hogue, his cousin, Delia's friend. At least Delia said so, that Mawkins was getting even. Well, Delia was satisfied now because Lettie seemed happy enough without Mawkins, working in town and sitting in the pews at church again.

"Bunch of Scotch-Irish princes, at least they thought they were," Mawkins went on darkly. "Fighting with each other, drinking, ruining the King's English, evading the laws, and all the time sitting under framed war records from the Revolution and Tippecanoe. But they were bulldogs. Get hold of some cause and they never let it go. That's your clan. You won't give it up."

"You forget I'm the black sheep," Zach said. "I may turn traitor on you, too."

"I don't forget it, Scott. Your evil nature is written in every line of your face. That's why you're compromising the Dugger girl and deceiving her family. Why you secretly rejoiced and went to the wedding when your brother's fiancée married someone else, there in Louisville."

Zach frowned. He never should have told Mawkins about the wedding.

"Black sheep don't bleach out. I should know. We're two in the same flock." Mawkins wiped his mustache a final time and motioned to the waiter to bring the bill. "You'll be with me when the time comes."

"Don't be too certain of that," Zach thought as they pushed open the big carved oak door of the hotel and went into the street. But as he drove the calash back to Rivertides, where Althea Dugger was waiting for him to help her go over account books and Delia was waiting as always as his reluctant, clandestine love, he could not think of anything that would stop him from participating in whatever Mawkins was hatching. The idea of a desperate war-saving scheme, whatever it was, involving Morgan's Captain Hines, Jefferson Davis, and secret support in Canada would probably be fascinating enough to lure him into cooperation.

Winter, 1863

Chapter Eighteen

A strange quiet settled over the land in those last days of 1863. The war was neither won nor lost, and the troops pulled into winter camps in most places and waited in discontented silence for spring to open up the roads so cannon and horses could pass to renewed conflict.

Christmas arrived but brought small cheer. January and a dismal new year came to the White House in Washington, Richmond's "President's Palace," and small cabins and mansions from Florida to Minnesota. Winter darkness circled over the warring land, like a strident, flying crow, and its wingspan covered both North and South, bringing gloom and distress. The boys were gone, the land was yet torn. Would it never, never end?

When February came, and the first crocuses tentatively spiked through last fall's leaves, Althea Dugger stood by the fireplace at Rivertides, watching the Wabash River cut a wide swath into the bottomlands near Duggerville.

"Floodwaters are heavy this year," Delia said, coming up behind her, pinning a camellia from the conservatory in her hair.

"I was thinking of Calhoun and Willie, out there by the—is it the Rappahannock River? I wonder if it is as broad as the Wabash."

"The papers say it is like the White River, smaller than the Wabash, and that it, too, is flooding. The last letter Calhoun sent said camp was dull and muddy."

Delia looked at the waters below them with the eye of an expert farmer. "If the waters recede early, as they should, we can plant the lower forty with corn. Corn sucks up the muck and acts like nothing ever happened. And then, with the hundred new peach trees, we should have a fine profit. Mr. Brooks has arranged to sell them to someone who will can peaches to send to the Yankee boys on a government purchasing contract."

"We raise crops to keep the Yankees fit and fed, and our own brave boys dine on rancid bacon and crackers, when they can get them," Althea said gloomily.

"Well, but you always say the South has the spirit."

Althea drew herself up and sighed a long, determined sigh. "If noble spirit won wars, Calhoun and Willie and all the rest would long since have come home victors."

There was a knock at the door and the colored servant, Trotter, came in with Ruby Jean McClure, Willie's gangly, twelve-year-old sister.

"Miz Dugger, telegram come into Duggerville, guess it was by mistake and Ma sent me up with it," Ruby Jean said.

"And how is your mother, Ruby?" Althea asked.

"Uh, she's got the pleurisy from all this cold, but she's fat and sassy." The girl paused a moment. "She ast after you."

"That's good of her," Althea replied, taking the telegram and sending Delia a look. It wasn't true, the girl just said it to be polite. Willie's stepmother Margery did not like the "uppity" people on the hill. She was especially cutting about the "rich folks" among all the neighboring folk now that Willie's dad was gone. Perhaps it was because Delia and Althea and Calhoun had become Willie's real family.

Althea read the telegram, while Ruby waited and shifted her weight from foot to foot and longingly looked at the bisque doll under a glass cover on the piano.

When Althea finished, she stared into space for just an instant and then said briskly to the colored servant, "Trotter, take Miss Ruby into the kitchen and give her some hot chocolate and some of that orange cake."

"When you're done, I'll take out my old doll and show her to you," Delia said, putting her hand on the girl's thin shoulders.

Ruby hopped away after Trotter, her face alight with excitement.

"What's in it, Mama?" Delia wanted to know the minute the pair was out of hearing distance. "Is it Cal?"

"Bad news, but not from the boys at the front. No, from Tennessee, from my friend Edward Bachelder. That Yankee General Hurlbut has arrested your Uncle Addison and Aunt Elba Dugger."

Delia breathed a sigh of relief. "Only that. I thought it was something awful."

"Well, it's bad enough. They are being held for war profiteering."

"Caught the pirates with their smuggled goods?" Delia said. She could not pretend to be unhappy. She never could stand Uncle Addison and Aunt Elba.

"They have been smuggling contraband goods, things taken from confiscated estates in Mississippi and Tennessee and bringing them up here."

Delia could hear Ruby Jean in the kitchen telling the colored help some long-winded story about a groundhog in the spring house. "I knew Aunt Elba and Uncle Addison were involved in something shady. But how did they get by with smuggling Southern goods out?"

"They had wagons. Said they were transferring all the stuff from *my* property, from Fairchance, here. For us." Althea stretched her hands out and looked at her long fingernails. "Well, I did ask them to stop by and bring up the canopy bed Papa said I was to have, but I never expected—"

"Miss Delia, can I look at the doll baby now?" Ruby bounded into the room, wiping her mouth with her sleeve.

Delia went to the piano and took the dome off the doll, whose bright blue eyes seemed to look far off, into the mysteries of the universe. Her filmy pink dress was hardly rumpled; Delia had preferred to play with toy soldiers and wagons when she was little.

"Waal, will you look at them li'l pumps on her cute li'l feet. Isn't that cunning?" Ruby tentatively touched the doll's eyelids; they went up and down, brushing her cool, china cheeks. "I guess this here is about the prettiest little doll in the whole *You*nited States of 'merica."

"Do you have dolls at home?" Delia wanted to know. She had not been to the McClure house in a long time. It was curious how inextricably bound these families around Duggerville had grown through the years. Cut off from the rest of southern Indiana by two rivers, thoroughly Southern, holding slaves for as long as they possibly could, Duggerville was almost like an embassy on foreign soil, so different were its people from their neighbors. Yet, since Willie was gone and his father and brother Archie had died, there was little to compel interest down on the levee. They hadn't been down in a long while.

"No, Step-ma don't 'low me to have many toys," Ruby said, more embarrassed than sad at having to make her family out in a poor light. She was staunchly loyal to everything McClure. "Well, we ain't rich since Pa and Archie died, I guess, an' everthing we have goes for Midgie." Delia nodded, understanding. Midgie was the five-year-old who was the mother's darling, her "real" child.

"I sure do wish Willie would get home," Ruby said. "He's the only one who pays me any mind. Sometimes I feel like I'm a wash stand or claw-foot table or somethin' around there."

"You know," Delia said, putting her arm around the child, "I think my poor old doll feels just the same way. There's nobody to play with her any more and she is getting so dusty. Ruby, I wonder if you would mind taking her over, adopting her now. She needs a mother."

Ruby looked into Delia's eyes to see if she really understood what she had just heard. "Miss Delia, I couldn't—"

"No, now I insist," Delia said. "It's not right to have beautiful things and just put them up for show. Dolls need to be loved."

"Ooh, my," was all Ruby could say as she accepted the doll and hugged it to her breast. "Oh, I'll love her always and make her m' best friend."

"At least until Willie comes home," Delia smiled. As the young girl left, Delia told herself she would look into the matter of Archie III's estate. Zach had read law. He could advise her. If he would. One never knew if Zach would ever do anything to benefit another human besides himself. And lately of course— well, that was another matter.

Althea stood before her daughter, the letter in her hand. "We must go to Memphis tonight. Aunt Sadie is too old to help, and apparently their financial affairs are in a dither. Someone up north seems to have been supplying money, but now they are without funds. Your Uncle Addison and Aunt Elba have no other relatives. Your father would have wanted, expected us to do our duty and bring bond money."

"Yes, of course," Delia said, absently.

"We'll pack our things, have Trotter drive us into Vincennes this very afternoon. We can spend the night there and then board the cars for Memphis. We must try to contact Mr. Scott. I hope he can go with us."

"Mother," Delia said, suddenly alert, "do you really want Zach to come?"

"We cannot travel in that dangerous area without a man, and I respect his advice." And then, almost to herself, "He is ruthless, but he is rational." She looked up, suddenly aware of what Delia had said. "Why do you not wish him to accompany us? He has been a fine companion to you, almost like a brother."

"Almost," Delia said wearily. How could her mother not see their love under her own nose all these weeks and months? She had been half-frantic that Ruby's busybody mother down the hill would get wind of it. Apparently she had not, but her own mother asked no questions. Delia had concluded that Althea must want to delude herself—that was the only answer for it.

"Still, we will not be under his protection much longer," her mother said with tired eyes. She added, almost by way of an explanation, "It is only because Calhoun is gone and I have no one else."

Delia nodded wearily and went to take the empty doll dome to the attic.

Althea took off her flower-bedecked, black felt hat and placed it on the imitation Italian credenza in the room in the American Hotel in Vincennes. "We do not have much time," she said to her daughter. "Take the carriage. Trotter will drive for you. Go to Mr. Scott's place, there out on the river road north. Ask, beg him to come with us. He can meet us tomorrow morning at the train station, or come in to the hotel as he likes. Didn't he say last month when he was with us, that he'd be sorting out papers this week? Pray that he is there!'' It was more of a command than a statement.

Delia turned towards her mother, suddenly understanding the tone in her voice. ''Mother, you are afraid to go south, aren't you?''

Althea's mouth was a firm line, but her eyes were large. ''You know I never allow myself to be afraid.''

''At least you never admit you are fearful of anything. Perhaps that is because we all depend on you so much.''

Althea sat down wearily on the bed. ''Everything seems to be falling apart, everything I care about. I try not to notice, to smile and be brave, but it is getting increasingly difficult. The Cause is ebbing. I do not allow myself to think of the plantation. If I ever had to tell father that it was seriously damaged, I do not think I could do it.''

''You will have to tell him the truth, if that happens.''

''I have *never* told my father the full truth. I was brought up to be a lady, and if you tell the truth, at least in the South, people won't like you. They'll think you're common—.'' Then she put on a forced smile. ''There now, this won't do. We don't know anything really awful yet. Things will turn out well—what is that Willie always says his McClure grandfather said?''

''Do the best you can and things will turn out better than you think,'' Delia said resignedly. She did not really believe it.

''Pity that McClure confidence hasn't rubbed off on us, too!'' Althea said. ''Now, shoo! The river road may be muddy and impassable and you must be back before dark. That gives you three hours.'' She went to the wash basin for water and put a cold compress on her forehead.

The river road was not muddy and impassable. The February mild spell seemed over, and cold was settling into the riverbottoms again. The ground was firm and full of hoarfrost. As the horses stepped smartly along, and the bare trees and river views of the Wabash north of Vincennes went by, Delia realized they would be at Zach's in less than an hour.

''And what will that mean?'' Delia thought. Last month, when Zach had come for a New Year's visit and to help his mother go over their accounts, he and she fought bitterly over everything they talked of. They had been irritated, taut, ready to pounce on each other, so much so that Althea commented that they were as testy as two children arguing over a hobby horse.

Was it because their physical relationship dominated them when they were together? That its demands and torments always hovered above them like a gargoyle, grinning and feeding on their need for each other? Shall we be able to slip away? Would twenty minutes in the barn at twilight be enough when the groom is up at the house having his supper and we want to see the horses? Will mother hear if we slip to the third floor ballroom at midnight?

There were other strains. Their love was stretched, like a piece of taffy candy when it is pulled, attenuated and weakened by the pressure of his brother's imprisonment, the odd marriage of Delia's cousin Sophie that he'd attended, the secretive duties which took him riding about to lodges all over three states. And their love was stretched by Delia's own pride and guilt. Every time she kissed his lips she lied to people she loved, and it made her cross and desperate.

This said nothing of what the gloomy news from the war front wrought on Southern supporters in the Midwest. No one who loved the Confederacy could be happy these days. Its sad fortunes spilled over everything.

And so, the last month or so, Delia had come to the point at which she did not want physical love from Zach, in some way could not stand it. The price was too high and there was no ending to the road. So what to do? She finally knew. She had to detach her love. Harden up the thin, sweet line of taffy that bound them and then break it, snap it in two. Somehow she had found this resolve, on his last visit. She had told Zach she would not be intimate with him again, that she had completely lost her head and now wished to find it. And, nodding, with that eternal, cynical smile that seemed to say, "I knew no one could really give themselves to me, life is like that," he accepted what she said and they now played in reality the "brother and sister" role they had so long feigned.

So, when the carriage pulled up to the two-story Scott farmhouse built sixty years before, Delia's feelings were as shaky and clattery as the branches of trees in the February wind. Putting her feet on the carriage step, she vowed to continue her resolve. This would put the final stamp on what she had said at Rivertides last month. Again she would be friendly but business-like. It was so odd, so difficult. Once you have gone down that road, known the hidden secrets of the other, to keep apart seemed artificial. But she had decided. Telling Trotter to wait, she knocked briskly at the door. Yes, she would have the courage to detach today. She wanted to. Her love had been only weak, despicable passion, she could not allow it, he was unworthy—

His face, surprised, shown like a light as he opened the door. "Delia— why what brings you to this lonely house?"

"My mother sent me for you," she said, and he brought her into a dark hall, its late afternoon gloom broken by the halo of one lamp on a table.

Standing there in the dusky hall, she told him of her mission in a few words; he considered it absently and nodded, saying that he would be able to go. He nervously ran his fingers through his blond hair and looked into her eyes.

"What is it?" Delia asked. "You seem unsettled." It was infrequently that his mask of controlled amusement was down. She was not used to seeing him this way.

"Well, I have been so busy. As fortunes in the South fall, we find more are joining the organizations. I have to keep the records, give them investment materials, coordinate—well, enough of that." He licked his lips. "Today I've been going through our family papers."

"And?"

"They are—odd. Really just trash, I suppose. And yet, they interest me." He looked at her with a slight smile. It was odd, Delia thought, seeing him here in his own home. He seemed different. She had caught him off guard. The picture of the boyish, peaceful face she saw at the time of the fire flashed into her mind.

"Can you stay for a while?" Zach asked, going to the window. Trotter was stomping about on the half-frozen ground, his breath clouded, mingling with that of the horse. "Tell Trotter to go to the out-kitchen. Old Frank is there, spending the winter before the fire, and the hired girl can serve them both tea. She's always trying to get me to eat some of the things she bakes. If you could stay an hour, I'd show you the papers."

Delia considered. All had been business-like so far. Perhaps it could go on. It must, because this trip they were about to take together must be—impersonal. Yes, it was surely all over. She had detached, broken the thin, sweet line between them, taken her emotions and put them away on ice. Now she and Zach could spend some time together in a civilized way, as acquaintances. Not friends, really, he was too cynical for that, but—

She went to tell Trotter that he should wait an hour in the old summer kitchen with the hired girl, Ella, and Old Frank, that she needed to go over papers with Mr. Scott.

"Yes ma'am," Trotter said, nodding and unhitching the horse as she went into the house again.

"That's a handsome black coat," Zach said, looking at the Persian lamb collar around smart, brushed wool, as she hung it on a coat-tree in the hall.

"Thank you. Mr. Thomas Jefferson Brooks sent it to me from New York to celebrate some new contracts we have for supplying the troops. He sent mother a mink-trimmed hat."

"Did I hear he saw Lincoln? It was in the Vincennes paper."

"Not once but twice. His report was accepted and they placed a tax on the sutlers in the Northern army." She turned to see Zach watching her expectantly, almost wonderingly, as if he were seeing her for the first time. Perhaps now that there was no longer "carnal knowledge," another kind of knowing might be seeping in—the knowing of who she really was. Then she spoke to him about Ruby Jean McClure and he agreed, with little nods of the head, to see to the matter of her inheritance as soon as possible in Vincennes. There was a silence between them, poignant and odd.

"And now, you wish to show me the papers?" she said with a small smile.

He indicated she needed to precede him on the stairway.

"Upstairs? The papers are above stairs?"

"Yes, of course, in the old attic. It's a bit dusty, but I want you to see the trunks."

Well, that should be all right. If she were detached, then she should be able to look at papers, wherever they might be. "Better get your coat again. It's chilly up there," Zach suggested.

As she ascended the old staircase, fashioned by the same master carpenters who had built the house of William Henry Harrison, she could not help but notice the rooms beneath them, the parlor with its old-fashioned, cherry wood deacons' benches and Windsor chairs and, in the corner, an odd, old loom. On the wall in the hall she passed two portraits, one a soldier in a Revolutionary War uniform, the other a woman of about thirty-five in a high-waisted gown from the French Empire period.

"My grandparents," Zach said, answering her unspoken question. "James and Jenny McClure Scott, who built this house. It's full of memories. Harrison started for the Battle of Tippecanoe from across the way, there. Earlier my father talked of being forced to shelter a murderer through an awful night. He had escaped after killing a fellow soldier at Ft. Knox."

Delia shuddered. It was cold and dark in this house, and now that she thought about it, she was not sure all the darkness was caused by the decay of the years. There was something strange about this house; it was suffused with an atmosphere that made her afraid.

They stood now at the top of the stairs, in a hall which led to the bedrooms, with a worn, oriental carpet as its runner. A door stood before them and Zach gently lifted its old-fashioned latch. Without a word they ascended the stairs, the lamp he carried casting long, blade-like shadows on the unfinished boards of a large attic.

And there he was, with that same unguarded look on his face, showing her old trunks with maps of Pennsylvania in 1770, trappers' maps of the Mississippi valley, and a casket of letters in French.

"My great-grandmother, who was my grandfather, James Scott's, mother, was a Frenchwoman from New Orleans named Marguerite. I can't read French, can you?"

"Well, I studied for several years. Cal and I had a French dancing master who read with us." She picked up the papers, old, brown parchment with neat, slanting handwriting on them.

She picked up one with the date 1738 and tried to make it out.

"It's to—to Marguerite's father."

"Yes? I think her mother died of the Yellow Fever there in the swamps."

Delia began reading. " 'Dear Papa, I miss you terribly. I do not know why you think it dangerous for me to be there when the voodoo nights are going on. I promise not to go out again. Truly I was frightened when I did disobey you.' " Delia put the letter down and said, softly, "A child's round hand. She must have been about nine or ten."

"Voodoo?" Zach said, puzzled. "Ancient mumbo-jumbo from Africa? They had it on plantations in the South, I guess."

Delia picked up another. "Let's see if I can figure this one out. I have read many of these letters. The dancing teacher used to take me to Vincennes, to the church vaults to read the letters. Thought I was bright—this seems to be from the plantation, written to New Orleans. There, on the back, with the sealing wax, is an address." Zach looked over and as he did the lamp tipped over briefly, almost dousing its light. Delia gasped. There was only one small, dirty window and the darkness in the attic was deep and unnerving.

Zach quickly restored the light and it cast its shadows again, on the old trunks, swords, tintypes, rocking chairs and straw ticking mattresses which cluttered the attic.

Delia looked at the letter two full minutes, then translated in only a slightly stumbling fashion: " 'March 12, 1739'? Yes, '39. 'My Dear Sister. You must keep Marguerite there a little longer. The blacks are still—threatening to rise up and are passing the news among the plantations all along the river and bayous. There is no doubt but that Big Emile is prominent in it. What an evil man he is, almost evil incarnate. The voodoo drums beat constantly in the swamps. They are dipping people in the'— something, mud I guess—'in that awful rite they do, and Emile is their leader. I do not understand the power he has over the slaves, and to tell you the truth, I am afraid of him myself. I intend to sell him as soon as all this passes and it is safe to be a master of slaves again. Little—Joe—is fine, staying with me constantly. I will send for Marguerite at the very first moment I think it safe. I know she is—lonely and needs her father, poor little poppin, now that her mama is in heaven. Yours, Joseph LaFrenier.' "

"Voodoo! Slave uprising! I wonder what ever happened?" Delia breathed.

"Strange," Zach answered without looking at her. "I also read my father's diary—yesterday. Written when he was eleven or twelve."

"Did you?" Delia asked.

"Yes." His face was turned towards the shadows. "John Robert Scott— odd, I never knew how much he lived through, his mother going insane when he was just a child, his brother a murderer, the Battle of Tippecanoe on his doorstep. He had to comfort his aging father—" Suddenly he seemed to be aware of his words and the mood they created, and after a slight pause, said, "Well, life is not a bowl of cherries, hey?" He laughed, and it was the same old strident, mocking laugh she knew so well.

"Anyway, there was this—drivel I guess—about when Grandmother Jenny, his mother, had gone off the edge and was raving, one day." He scrambled in a box of papers. "I think I can find the damn thing here."

"Zach—" Delia remonstrated mildly.

"Oh, yes. Ladies present. Well, here it is." He handed a small, worn book to her to her and she read, holding it up to the lamp.

November 15, 1813. News of the war with the English and Indians on every lip, and none of it very good. Mother scribbling on a pad of paper, wildly, as I have never seen her do before, about swamps and terror and evil. She wrote one odd, chilling thing. "Migrated! His evil spirit migrated and I could not stop it! Oh, no, no, no! This kind comes not out but by prayer and fasting!" She put down her pencil and then she sobbed for Ish, so long lost in the mires of murder and treason and every other sort of evil.

The wind blew branches against the roof of the attic. Would there be snow? There was only about an hour or so of daylight left. She would need to leave in a few minutes.

"There was more, about me," Zach said in an odd, pained voice. "About how much trouble I was to mother, my naughtinesses driving my parents to distraction." His voice was bitter and pained. "Pshaw, I knew all that. But there was one entry, when I was about three. I'll show it to you."

Delia watched his eyes, straining in the poor light. He was frantically flipping through the pages of an old book of his father John Robert Scott, dead in such a painful way on the eve of this terrible war that was now raging, written when that father was young. He pointed and she read:

This day a terrible one with young Zach. He tormented the animals, teased his brother Jacob Joe with coals from the fire, poured spirits of ipecac on the carpet. Worst is when he runs from us and poor Mahalia, with her slowing step of late, cannot catch him. It makes her cry in frustration. He mocks and pulls faces from the other side of the room.

So, we collapsed on our bed after dinner, with Jake asleep by our side. Zach must have come in and seen us, for he ran jealously screaming from the room. We were so tired we did not pursue him, bad parents that we are! What a cross to have a constantly mischievous, mocking child.

Later I awoke and realized I had not sought Zach for many minutes, possibly an hour. The house was still. Was he in the stove, dead? Had he run outside, laughing and taken a boat onto the river?

No, surprise of all surprises, there he was in Grandmother Jenny's arms, asleep. Odd, usually his presence distresses her. But the poor old mad woman had such a look of love and tenderness on her face that it had calmed him completely. I think it was the most complete look of love I have ever seen on any face.

Odd, but I love him too, and it is my secret that my heart yearns to him more than to our dear, good Jake. Father said it was so with mother and my brother Ish. She loved him beyond all bearing. When did this cycle of Zach's ugly behavior begin? Do we rage at him because he is bad or is he bad because we rage at him? I do not know, I only know I lie awake at night loving him, worrying, and then I get up the next day and spank him again.

Delia halted her reading. She was deeply moved. Then she began to read aloud, as if she could not bear these poignant thoughts unless they were shared with the person they concerned," 'I suppose we love the fallen, errant ones more, though they do not know it. I think it is the way of nature where mothers yearn for the runt of the litter, protect the bird with a broken wing, take back the black sheep. It is the way the Savior taught. I love Zach! May I live to see him in strong, free manhood.' "

Zach took the book and looked at Delia, and in that look was all the pain and frustration of a troubled child who feels unloved, and who rages with evil behavior, he knows not why. It was the look of the child Delia had dragged from the theatre and bound to her heart at that moment.

"I did not know," he said, and his eyes looked deeply into hers and met understanding.

And then he reached for her hand, and took her in his arms. He sat there holding her, leaning against a trunk. She nestled under his arm, touched his face; he stroked her hair, tentatively, gently. When, finally, they lay back on the mattress of some Scott ancestor in the dim days of the far frontier, she opened her heart to him as she had said she never would again, and loved with all her soul and body the boy who thought no one could ever really love him.

"And so I am not free of the hold he has on me," Delia said to her friend Lettie Hogue. "It is more than a taffy wire of sweet passion. I thought it was only physical, but it is more. I do not understand it." Her voice was strong and determined. "Perhaps I cannot stop loving him—for a while. But I will not go to his arms again, no matter what. I will not deceive my mother on this trip. That part I can control, and will."

Delia had walked over to Lettie's flat above a Vincennes store after supper.

"I never knew what standing up straight was until I quit leaning," Lettie said. "On my father, first, then on the husband I could never find, my lover, then the minister."

"What about Reverend Paden?" Delia asked. "He is still in the pulpit."

"Until summer. Presbytery is sending him and his family to Iowa."

"Is the congregation talking about—you and his affront to you?"

"No, for once. They do not know, of course. There are vague rumors about his—ardent disposition—but no one knows for sure except Mr. Samuel Thompson and whoever makes the decision to change his call."

" 'Tis best, I think."

"I suppose so," Lettie said. "I know that I can look him in the eye. I think when I forgave him that night at the festival, it freed me. I'm not afraid of anyone in the church or town. Not even Willis Mawkins. Odd, he has been gone a lot lately, they say to Canada. But when I see him on the street he speaks and sends hot looks at me, although they bounce off me as if I were a frosty window. I almost think Willis loves me a bit."

"What odd strings of love we all tie about each other," Delia said. "Strings that knot about in hundreds of loops. Hard to cut." She made her fingers like scissors, and Lettie laughed and poured tea from a pot into one of her mother's wedding teacups.

Then she opened a tin and handed her friend a sweet biscuit. "Speaking of knots, Horace is married," Lettie said, with some merriment.

"No!" Delia said, wonderingly.

"He has married the sweet, rich lady with the chiming voice."

"And the bratling son you told me about."

"Horace is a father now to the boy. He and Clarissa were married in Corydon. Mother went over. Then guess what she did?"

"I can't. To hear you talk of your mother, she is not to be predicted."

"She volunteered to keep Montmorency so the couple could have a honeymoon."

Delia laughed. "Your mother is seventy-six."

"Seventy-seven, but vigorous as someone ten years younger. Still—" Lettie picked up the teacups and headed towards her little sink. "Well, she said Montmorency could be a playmate for Annie."

"Annie McClure?"

"Yes, John and Mary Jane's sister, who lives out with Cousin Jewell." She put the teacups in a pail of soapy water. "You remember me telling you all about them. Annie's a little pickle puss. This is the week that she stays with her grandmother."

"I thought your cousin Jewell did not allow the girls to see your mother any more."

"Not if she can help it. But she can't help it this time. The court has set up a week for them to visit at Grandmother Catherine's every other summer.

Mary Jane had her week last summer—well, she's old enough to set her own visits, but they still go through the form. Now it's Annie's turn."

Delia rose and picked up her wraps from the settee. She had walked through swirling snowflakes from the hotel to say goodbye to her friend. Now her mother would be pacing about, worrying that they would retire too late and miss the early train in the morning.

"Where is the happy couple honeymooning?" Delia asked. She picked up the brown fur muff her father had given her long ago and buttoned up her coat for the walk she must take through the chilly night.

"They're going to Niagara Falls."

"In February?" Delia asked in surprise.

Lettie brushed a piece of lint off her friend's collar. "Well, Horace always did do things a little differently. And with Mrs. Clarissa's money, they can hire the best, warmest hotel suite in the whole resort and be cozy and alone together, man and wife."

Delia followed Lettie to the door. There was a sad edge to her friend's voice as she spoke of the nuptial scene. Employment and independence she now had, yet her odd brother had found more. Delia stepped out into the brisk night air, hugged her friend goodbye and turned to watch the door shut behind Lettie. Then she raised her muff to her face and stood, pensive for a moment, feeling the softness of the warm fur on her cheek as the wind blew off the Wabash river and snowflakes fell upon her eyelashes.

When she returned to the hotel, Althea met her with a telegram in her hand. Cousin Addison's and Aunt Elba's cases would not be heard until April, and they could not see them until then, orders of the military commander. They would have to defer the trip a few weeks.

As Delia crawled between the chilly sheets of the hotel bed, she sighed with relief. She would not need to face Zach, could use these weeks to heal, to distance herself. The thought was a reassuring, comforting blanket, dulling her sensibilities. No need to see him—

"First thing tomorrow we shall send a message to Mr. Scott telling him we will require his kind services still, in April. I know he will reserve the time for our trip."

Her mother's voice seemed to hang in the chilly air, and Delia turned over and pulled the cover up around her shoulders. No need to see the love who tortured her—for a while, anyway.

*   *   *   *

Jacob Joe Scott watched the Sanitary Commission whitewash the walls of the sleeping room at Castle Thunder prison with a satisfied smile. There, before his eyes, slapping whitewash on the walls to prevent the spread of disease, was his dear friend, the sister of the girl he had almost married (and still yearned for). There was Dora Lavenham!

He could still hardly believe it, though it was two months since she first appeared in this God-awful place. She turned now to move a table back with her knee, but her eyes did not meet his. That did not surprise him. Above all, they agreed after that first meeting that they must not show they knew each other.

What a Christmas gift it was! The hospital commission was visiting during that gloomy, cheerless week before the birthday of Christ. He had been reading his, no, it was Vistal's, Bible on his cot. His had disappeared. The commission was bringing back the smallpox patients who had survived, Vistal among them, and after they placed the recuperating prisoners on their pallets, they distributed a few things to raise the spirits of the prisoners of war.

He helped to tuck Tilgh into his covers, patted him on the shoulder heartily to show his joy at how much better his friend was, and sat back down on his own rude cot, hands around his knees, Indian-style.

A tall, dark-haired matron-attendant had come to him and, after giving him a few dried peaches, a meat pie and two novels, had remained, looking about in an odd way. Was she seeing if she was observed? He looked up with interest when he saw she held his Bible, the missing one. She leaned down and placed a note in the Bible and left. Curiously he opened the Bible.

My Dear Friend:

I have had my friend bring this note to you; I dare not risk directly coming to you. Please do not show any surprise when you read this. I, your friend Dora, am a matron in the hospital which has just released Tilghman Vistal and I have discovered you are at Castle Thunder.

I want to do all I can for you, and especially I want to show you friendship in this discouraging time. Times are chaotic in Richmond now as you must know and we are on different sides of this war. But I yearn to be of service to you. I will be watching you read this note and will come by. We are forbidden, with serious consequences, to consort or know Northern prisoners, so above all do not recognize me. I will find ways to contact you.

Your sister, as you used to say, Dora

He looked up to see Dora coming towards him like an angel of mercy, her slight form swathed in a great, gray cloak. A Christmas angel. He was overcome and tears came to his eyes in spite of all the admonitions in the letter.

She touched his hand as she set a bag on Tilghman's bed. The touch said, "I know what you are feeling. I am here, from a happier time, your friend."

"Well, gentlemen, we of the hospital have put together something for you. We made several of these—"

She took a very small Christmas tree out of the bag. It was a real evergreen, sea pine, a baby sprout of a tree, yet it glowed with color and cheer. Bright buttons had been strung together instead of the popcorn that was as scarce as everything else. Little blobs of seeded cotton, rare indeed but not impossible to secure, were snow drifts on the tree. Tiny paper chains festooned the branches.

As she arranged the tree on the box which served as a table between the two rude bunks, she said in a loud voice, "We will return to sing some carols for you."

Then, looking straight ahead with a fixed nurse's cheerup smile on her face for anyone who chanced to pass, she whispered to Jacob Joe, "I have let my family and yours know where you are. They were never notified. Just nod."

He did. Tilgh turned over and went to sleep. He was better, but he was still weak as a chick just out of the shell.

"Now, Mr. Scott, I am going to leave medicine for Mr. Vistal. You will need to be his nurse," the strong public voice continued.

He nodded and she whispered. "How is your health?"

"Nothing is sure here. Men have had typhoid, camp fever, smallpox— one day they are well and the next sick, from cold, poor food, slops, contagion. I had a fever, now I have a wracking cough that will not go away, but past that—I am surviving."

She studied his face from the corner of her eye. "Sophie—" she said, but did not say more.

Jacob Joe raised pained eyes to hers. "She is married. I know."

"How—"

"I had a dream. Remember how we spoke of things beyond heaven and earth one night—long ago?"

"Yes. I still believe there is so much beyond. I see you are reading your Bible."

"I have again become a Quaker. I was separated from God, from my faith by my own pride and—hatred."

She touched his sleeve, gently, in affirmation. Again, the louder nurse voice. "Now this bottle has elixir in it to stimulate his vital energy. Give it every two hours."

"I will," Jacob Joe said audibly, then whispered, "How is my brother?"

"Delia wrote that she has seen him a few times and he is well. Though I do not think my aunt Althea knows it and I hope she does not, I know they are in love. It shines in Delia's eyes."

"Ah, good fortune for my brother."

"It is a doomed thing, I fear. Your brother—" she searched for words— "seems tormented by a troubled, evil frame of mind. Some men are like that, but they ruin the women they love." She turned to smooth Tilghman Vistal's pillow.

He was seized with a coughing spell and then, when it quieted, said, "Yes, you are right. He has almost ruined me. I've forgiven him, though. But I am still tormented myself. I know my father damned war and could not bear to have me in its midst. He could have forecast all these evils that have happened to me."

She spoke again in the loud voice, for the benefit of a passing surgeon. "See that he gets up and walks about at least twice a day, for half an hour," then the whisper, this time intense and determined. "Your father would have been proud of you."

He coughed again. "He did not wish me to go to war. He choked and died with a seizure because I was traitor to the Quakers. I killed him."

"Nonsense," she said so loudly that one of the men in the wash-water detail slopped his pail in surprise.

"Your friend will get better, Mr. Scott," she said loudly to cover the outburst. "Don't fret so, but do your nursing job."

Between clenched teeth and the eternal, fixed smile, she whispered, "You deceive yourself, surely. Long captivity has made you maudlin. Your service in the war was a result of conscience and for you, God's direction. We all hear the voice of God in different ways, and surely this is true in war, particularly."

He looked up into her face, marvelling at her wisdom. She might be almost as small as a child, but Dora Lavenham was no child.

She picked up the tote bag. "I will return as soon as I properly can."

Panic rose in his chest. He had found a good friend, she was like a shaft of sunlight in a cave, and he could not let her go. "Tell me of the war. We do not hear accurately."

"The troops from the Fourteenth Indiana are along the Rappahannock still, awaiting a quiet Christmas. I think the letters from home said your home regiment, the Eightieth Indiana, is near Chattanooga and Knoxville. They are firmly in Union hands," Dora told him, as she brushed past the pallet, her oval hoop touching his arm. Barely turning her head she whispered. "I do not think the war can last long. You will be free in God's good time."

"If I am still alive," he muttered watching her small form make its way through the squalor and stench of the Confederate prison.

She came every week since that Christmastide, and now he was watching her whitewash the walls. She and Betsy Pickering, her friend, were on tiptoe on chairs, reaching high. What was that noise? She turned for just a moment towards him. He shook his head, smiling. His angel of mercy was whistling. A message for him. The words of the song she was whistling echoed in his head:

Tramp, tramp, tramp, the boys are marching!
Cheer up, comrades, they will come,
And beneath the starry sky
We will breathe the air again
Of the free land of our own beloved home.

*   *   *   *

Tinkling laughter blended with sounds of torrents of water pouring onto rocks. A small touring party of two people and a guide, all dressed from head to toe in oilcloth greatcoats and hats was making its way under Niagara Falls.

"My heavens, aren't we daring? This is like the worst downpour I ever did see," Clarissa Hogue, formerly Mrs. Limeberry, laughed, holding onto her new husband's hand. "I thought every minute I was going to slip on the stairway in that tower coming down."

"I can hardly hear you," Horace shouted over the noise of roaring water. Clarissa had climbed a lighthouse by herself for the view, then they both had descended a stairway tower, what seemed to him 150 feet down to the level of the falls, and now stepped out into cold, fuming spray from the descending water.

It was a warm day for late February. His game leg bothered him, and ice made their steps treacherous, but here they were!

"And now, sir and madam," the guide shouted, "You may follow me along the solid rock under the falls, should you not mind a cool drenching this morning."

"Ah, no, I shan't walk. I don't want to get my little pink feet wet," Clarissa yelled, holding onto Horace's arm.

He disengaged himself and marched stoutly along, following in the guide's soggy footsteps and getting completely drenched every step. When he returned, spitting water and wiping his eyes, Clarissa took his arm in hers.

"What a bold dog you are," she shouted.

"Well, all the Hogues, and McClures, too, are bold dogs," he said proudly, guiding her toward the bottom step of the descent tower. "And anyway, I was a commended hero wasn't I, when you met me at the Battle of Corydon?''

"What'd you say?" she screamed over the tumbling torrent.

"Never mind."

"Yes, a bold dog," he thought as he panted up the steps. He had hired a special winter guide for this dangerous descent that not many people wanted to make. "And a cold dog," he told himself as the wind howled through his saturated slicker.

"Are we going back to the Clifton House now?" Clarissa wanted to know, speaking of the good hotel they were staying in on the Canadian side of the falls. "I want to write to Montmorency. I miss him so. I'm sure your mother and he are just getting along swimmingly." Her eyes showed she was not at all sure whether Catherine Hogue was getting along swimmingly or going under for the third time with her little dear.

"Yes, honey pot, we'll soon be as warm as a tea cozy," he said watching her take off the oilcloth coat and hand it to the guide, seeing her figure, as round and vigorous as a little pony's.

"An old dog," he thought, reminding himself of the fine farm he would be managing when they returned from their honeymoon and the various duties incumbent upon him now as a husband.

He gave the guide a bill from the draft he had cashed on their new banking account. She took his hand, interlocking the fingers with hers. They were both completely wet and would have to change clothes immediately.

He looked fondly at the woman beside him. "An old dog, but it's good to know you can teach an old dog new tricks. Or anyway, tricks he had forgotten for a very long while."

*   *   *   *

"Pa, I am not going to take Annie and Montmorency to Sabbath School," Effie said petulantly. She was talking in an exasperated voice, looking up the stairs at the old McClure homestead, almost defying anybody in the bedrooms to avoid hearing her.

"Now, pet, you know your cousin Annie is about your age and she's an orphant," Billy McClure said to his daughter. His wife Esther was upstairs primping; he was in charge of getting the party ready to go to Upper Indiana Church, of warming the bricks to put at their feet in the old wagon, and, most of all, being sure that each person took his place in the wagon on time. With all the freezing and thawing in the last week, it could be a hard trip to the church, and he could not afford trouble at the last minute.

"Annie is thirteen and I am thirteen, but she is *very odd*. Acts like she's nine." Effie came over to him, the skirts her mother had made her from a magazine pattern flouncing after her. "Pa, let me explain this to you. I'm glad Aunt Catherine has not come up from her cottage yet, so I don't hurt her none."

Her father stared at her, as he often had lately, as if she were from Siam, an exotic stranger who had arrived a few days prior and he could not get used to. Since getting her growth last year, she'd shot up like a walnut tree almost overnight and become a young woman. Now she talked to him as if he were a three-year-old. Perhaps it was hard because he was rather grandfatherly for a father. His older children had long since left the house, and he sometimes still felt rusty at parenting.

"Pa, these last few days have been very hard. Montmorency is *ten years old* and you expect me to *play* with him! I have tried everything." Effie was a methodical girl who squared the corners of her sheets when she made her bed and polished the silverware before she ate.

"Well, your Aunt Catherine is a little along in years t' have these active children here, and I thought we could help," Billy told her. "She lent us the money to pay for the farm and I have only half paid her back. I don't know why she sprung for the honeymoon caretakin' anyways, but she did. I've tried to take Montmorency and Annie into the barn to help me ready the tools and gear for spring plowing. I thought you could help with nursemaidin'."

"*Help*, I need help after bein' with them for all this time. I gave them my dolls to play school with and they took off all their clothes and took to 'em with switches. I gave them the dollhouse, my favorite dollhouse Uncle Horace made for me, and they got into a fracas and turned it upside down and broke the gran' pianny and the cupboard and three of the li'l teacups."

"Waal, I know it's hard, but—"

"The only thing they liked was the Mystic Egyptian Oil-on-Water Box. They played that into the wee hours back in the press."

Her dad gaped at her with open mouthed. "The mystic—what did you say?"

"Oil-on-Water Box. It's a spiritualist flim-flam Montmorency brought with him. If you tilt it a little and watch the oil float around, it makes shapes and letters. But mostly it's s'posed to give you messages from the Great Beyond. Annie and Montmorency love it."

"I thought I heard clunkin' in the eaves," her father murmured. "When was this?"

"Night before last. They were a-tryin' to levitate it."

"Levitate the Mystic Oil-on-Water Box," he said slowly, trying to understand.

"Yes. An' callin' on the ectoplasmic spirits to materialize and give their messages direct."

"Waal, what do you know. I hope to hell the spirits don't do that. They's probably a plenty of 'em about. Anyways, your ma will be down in jest the shake of a lamb's tail an'—''

Effie took a small embroidered handkerchief out of the drawer. "Well, I can tell you I am not a-goin' to take them to my class. Puss Warren will just throw a fit when she sees the way Annie dresses, and Elmer Eubanks, well, I'd just be shamed and humiliated to let Elmer Eubanks see 'em.'' Billy nodded, trying to picture Elmer Eubanks. He could hear Esther walking around above him, in a square with little mincing steps. She was making the bed. Soon she would start down the stairs.

Effie placed the handkerchief in her velvet pocketbook and closed it with a snap. "Jest-a-suppose they got talkin' bout the Bible at Sabbath School. That girl knows everything vulgar and mean in the Bible.''

"Vulgar and mean?'' Billy seemed perplexed.

"You know, 'bout the slaughter of the Assyrians for God to get even and John the Baptist's head cut off by a dancing girl and the daughters of Lot looking on his nakedness.''

Her mother had reached the bottom of the stairs. "Whoever told you about that business, Effie?'' she demanded, but not too threateningly. She was a member of the new school of thought that believed children should be dealt with some frankness—not too much, of course.

"Why, Annie, Mama. She says it's all in the Bible, 'bout King David's concubines and taking all the foreskins—''

Grandma Catherine came up from her cottage, carrying a lap rug. "My, my, my,'' she said. "It sounds like Annie is an education in herself.'' It had been a bit difficult at times this week having two exploding cannons with short fuses in the parlor. But it made her feel wanted. Particularly when Annie had spilt the beans about her homelife, about Mary Jane's sadness this winter, her yearning for her brother John, away at the wars, and Catherine's and the family's rift to be healed. Annie saw a lot and understood more, and she had rattled along like a freight train, when she wasn't plotting the kind of malicious mischief that set the household in a pother.

"Where are my little darlings?'' Catherine asked.

"They are behind the door in the press,'' Effie said primly. "They was playin' Egyptian medium the last time I looked in on them. Said they *wasn't* goin' to no Sabbath School.''

"Why, I'll show them who's goin' where,'' Billy McClure said, starting towards the staircase.

"Never mind, Billy,'' Catherine said. "They seem to be able to take care of themselves quite well. I think we ought to let them do just that while we go have a breather for the rest of the day. There's a George Washington Birthday picnic up at the Crullers' barn, and we are invited, I think.''

"Waal, is it all right?'' Billy looked hesitant.

"After all, Annie is thirteen. They're not goin' to set the house on fire and bring the rafters down round their heads," Catherine said. "They're too selfish for that. Let 'em fend." She went upstairs to the rafters closet to tell her charges.

"All the ghosts better look out," Effie said, sniffing. "They will have raised ever kind o' ectoplasm in the neighborhood by the time we get back."

"Well, I don't know why we ain't able to raise any spirits direct," Annie said discontentedly. The sounds of the wagon, first on the drive and then on the road, had died away and they were alone. "We tried everything you said to do. I don't think you know as much as you allow."

"Smarty pants," she thought. He had been lording it over her that he had a carriage and was going to the academy. And that he had a new father. Even at his age he had learned the fine lines of his society; he did not let her forget that she was "ignorant," he the product of a learned, affluent home, a member of the village gentility. And, she was an "orphant," that lost race of unfortunates who occupied a place in society somewhere between the village idiot and the penniless old maids.

She did not think of herself as an orphant, refused to talk about it, to even acknowledge that there were two parents, not even remembered, who had drowned long ago. Sometimes she even lied about it, and told casual strangers Aunt Jewell was her "mama."

"Candle lit, fingertips pumiced, all light removed," Montmorency Limeberry said, mulling over the requirements for successful seancing. The box, with its rosewood and metal frame and glass top was just a tool—a spot for the spirits to light. They hadn't seemed too eager today to do that, to materialize. His round boy's face shone in the light of the taper. A shock of hair, squared off on the end, hung down towards his nose. "Perhaps the spirits in this house want to be spoken to. Who are they? Do you know? Maybe we could call them by name." He had a diffident, correct speech pattern honed by years of solitary reading and could be what was called a "little gentleman," when he wanted to be.

"Waal, the ancestors," Annie answered. "Let's see whoall that was. Grandma Catherine was just puttin' me in remembrance of 'em, but I didn't pay her no never mind. There was the old lady, first come on a buffalo or somethin' 'crost a track with George Washington, I think it was. Name of Grandma Jane McClure."

Montmorency held the candle and looked into its flame. "Oh, Grandma Jane McClure, if you hear our voice there in the world beyond our sight, please give a sign. Give us a sign."

"Hoo ha," Annie said, after a moment.

"What's the matter?" Montmorency demanded.

Annie looked at him scornfully. "I don't know what to think about all this stuff. Sometimes I still think this is stupid like I tole you from the beginning. Sometimes I'm kinda scared."

"Well, everybody's tryin' it all over the place. I got the box—well, all of this from Mort Moseby in Corydon, kid about fifteen. His ma's a spiritualist. Let's try again. It would be better if we had something of Jane McClure's, some possession. Do you have something?"

"Waal, Grandma Catherine tole me the old lady's spinnin' wheel was up here. Say, I think it's there, in the eaves. See?" She pointed at an old wool wheel, its spindle broken.

"Spinning wheel?" Montmorency strained his eyes through the gloom. "How'd they work 'em, anyway in the olden days?"

"Ain't you never seen one, Monty? They just spin 'em around like a top and the flax turns into gold. Haa haa!" She pounded him on the head and tried to spin him around and laughed and laughed.

"I've told you a thousand times not to call me Monty. It makes me sound like a riverboat gambler," Montmorency said, his face flushing.

But Annie could barely stand to desist and pounded him a few more times before she sat down. One of the few pleasures of this week with her grandmother, along with having someone actually speak to her as a person instead of a giant blue pill, was tormenting this boy. He spoke with his snoot in the air, he talked about magazines and books and he thought he was Little Lord Pooh Pooh. It had been necessary for her to put ice balls in his shoes, set the terrier on him and lock him in the barn. Put him in his place, I guess so!

"Well, if you're done now," Montmorency said, calming himself forcefully, "go touch the spinning wheel while I call for the old lady." Annie got up and, suddenly serious, went into the forest of dust balls where the spinning wheel stood. She looked at its giant spokes, like a wagon wheel, its worn spindle. She put her hand up. Crash. The spindle fell down, echoing strangely. "Hell's bells, and green crap," she blurted out, running back to where the boy sat.

"Well," Montmorency said, slightly shaken himself at the noise, "are there other family members?"

Annie thought for a moment. Mary Jane had told her the family stories when she thought Aunt Jewell wasn't about. Her sister had secret albums of miniatures and daguerreotypes, each likeness written on for identification, and some letters she kept in a locked trunk. "We mustn't lose our birthright, Annie," Mary Jane sometimes said. "Aunt doesn't want us to know we're McClures, but she can't deny our birth and blood. Fambly's everything, and because we've missed out on it, it should mean that much more." Sometimes her eyes filled when she said it. Pshaw. The only emotion Annie felt when Mary Jane carried on this way was anger. Long ago she had turned all other emotions way down low, as a lamp is lowered. Feelings turned down, almost off, did not hurt too much.

"There were, lessee, Grandfather George and Grandmother Jean. They built this house. And some of their children—" She named the ones she could think of, and Montmorency called them. But try as the Mystic Egyptian Oil-on-Water Box would, it could not rouse a single ectoplasmic manifestation from the ancestral walls.

"Their spirits are probably at peace," Montmorency said. "All the experts say it's only the unhappy spirits that wander and haunt. That's what Mort said. He had a book on it."

Annie shook her head.

"Wasn't there any unhappy ghost in the neighborhood?"

"Oh, wait a minute," Annie said, pounding her fist in remembrance against the floor. "There's Buzzard Woman."

This was another tale of Mary Jane's, told solemnly to show how unkind and intolerant people could sometimes be. Annie ignored that part. "Waal, everybody round these farms knows about Buzzard Woman. Her and the witch master." The candle flickered. It was getting close in the press.

Annie went on, her voice rising and falling with the epic cadences of once-upon-a-time. "'Bout the time that the Old Lady come to Indiana on a buffalo with George Washington or whoever it was, well, they was lots of Injeeans 'round here. One of 'em was called Buzzard Woman and she lived in Vincennes. Seemed my Grandpa John Hogue took a notion that she was witchin' him."

"Doing what?"

"Witchin'. Causin' bad things to happen to him. Unlucky things. Anyways he went and hired a witch master out in the country to undo the spells. But people found out about it and started to get scared of Buzzard Woman. They did bad things to her and the church finally told my Grandpa, and all of 'em to stop 'cause she was a Christian herself. Finally she was so sad she drown-ded herself in the river."

Montmorency's eyes were solemn and a little frightened. "And her spirit walks abroad today?"

Annie's voice was barely a whisper. "They say she walks, looking for the witch master and my grandpa."

Montmorency grabbed her arm. "Where's she walk?"

"Oh, she's been seen over by Grandma's old place, where Aunt Lettie and Horace, your new pa, grew up. Some Germans live there now. An' by the old fort Grandpa built in Injeean times, that's just a couple mounds of dirt now."

Candle wax was dripping on the floor. The taper was about out. "An unhappy spirit,'' Montmorency said, nodding his head up and down wisely. ''I don't think we could call her back now in this house. There's too much church-goin' always happening here and people bustlin' about. Ectoplasmic manifestations want lonely, deserted places.''

''I know just the spot!'' Annie shouted. ''The old Mifflin place down the ways a bit from here. The place they're usin' as the orphantage now.''

Montmorency picked a mound of candlewax with his fingernail, molding it into strange shapes. ''That big old place? But it's occupied. Fifteen orphants and their matrons, didn't somebody tell me?''

''Ha'nts don't go away just because people come in. That place was empty for years before they got the idea to use it for the kids. There was always strange lights about, so everyone says.'' She lowered her voice. The candle flame shrunk in on itself, using up the last of the wick, burning its wax in the saucer.

''Do you suppose,'' she whispered, ''that the old Indian witch is wanderin' about in that big old attic above the orphantage, looking for those who did her wrong? Wanting revenge, walkin', janglin' her joo-ry,''—soft, soft voice. Montmorency leaned lower to hear what she was saying.

''Some poor orphant is goin' to be sent up to that attic to get somethin' and—then—she'll *GRAB 'EM, LIKE THIS MONTY!*'' She pounced on him. The light went out. The poor boy jumped out of his skin and cruel Annie rolled on the floor with laughter.

''I'll get you yet, I will,'' Montmorency said, his heart bounding frantically, but she paid him no attention whatsoever.

The offshoot of it was that they came down from the press and went into the kitchen and poked around and found some nutmeg pound cake and bread pudding with caramel sauce and piccalilli and blackberry wine, and had that for Sunday dinner, and when they had finished, they picked up the Mystic Egyptian Oil-on-Water Box and several beeswax tapers and matches. Then they put on their coats and went out the door to go over to the ''orphantage'' to raise the ectoplasmic manifestation of the poor old Buzzard Woman, who had drowned so tragically in the Wabash River in 1808, and who deserved to rest in peace.

And after a walk across hills and fields, they stood in the kitchen of the orphanage. Annie was known to the German cook who was stirring pots on the top of the cookstove, and she nodded briefly at the children through clouds of potroast steam. She was trying to make everything come out hot at the same time for the fifteen orphan children and three matrons who would soon be eating Sunday dinner. She did not even have time to think why Annie and her friend would be visiting her now. Annie was odd, after all.

The cook knew her Aunt Jewell, who was in charge of "unchurched visitors" at Upper Indiana. Jewell Simpson had asked her to bend her needle to make costumes for the pumpkin pageant.

The cook was preoccupied because the dumplings were getting heavy and soggy and would give people indigestion. When she went into the dining room to be sure the girls' chore party set the table properly, she found that they had put on the scorched tablecloth and six chipped glasses. And the dried money plants in the pitcher in the center of the table had shed their coins all over. And all this, ach, with the superintendent of poor relief, Mr. Benson Beckwith and his wife Almeady coming to dinner this very day! By the time she got done resetting it and returned to the kitchen, she never even noticed that the two children were gone, nor that the key to the locked attic stairway was not on the nail beside the door where it should be.

"There's a full floor betwixt us and the people," Annie said as they lit the candle in the dim attic. "The sleepin' floor part of it is below us, and Sunday mornin' nobody is there." They looked around. A broken butter churn, trunks with the leather straps askew, pots and fireplace apparatus from an earlier time, and mouse-chewed paper shards were everywhere.

"Same ole stuff," Annie said. "Me and Bob used to slip away and come over here and explore."

"Who's Bob?" Montmorency wondered.

"My brother, younger'n John and older'n me, don'tcha know?"

"Where is he?"

"He's talkin' 'bout goin' west. Says it's better'n the army now for excitement."

Montmorency was circulating around, poking among the debris and memorabilia. "What's on this table? Looks like a camera," Montmorency said.

"Ole Mr. Mifflin useta take pitchers of folks. Sometimes he made the people come up here. I think they sat in those chairs." She pointed at two dilapidated thumb chairs, covered with sooty dirt. "So they say. I don't know, I wasn't there. He had chemicals." She bent over and picked up bottles. One was marked "magnesium," another "silver nitrate."

"Yes, I've read about it in *Baptist Boy's Magazine*." Montmorency puttered around with interest in the pile of photographic debris, the glass plates, the black photographer's hood, the paper.

"Well, let's get on with it, Monty," Annie said. "I sure as hell hope the Injeean don't whoop it up when she comes back from the dead. Don't want the orphants' head matron hearing us down below."

"The matron?"

"Mrs. Paden, the wife of the minister. She is sickly, but they need the money and she is acting until they get a full-time matron."

"Oh. Missing the services, is she?" Montmorency wanted to know.

"Yes. They have their own out here. Sit in straight chairs, listen to sermons."

"You ought to be glad you don't have to be put in here," Monty said, shrewdly watching her. He had discovered it was a sore point with her.

"Well, I'm not really a orphant, not hardly at all," Annie said loftily. The mention of services had rattled Annie's hinges a little; she thought of her Grandmother Catherine, who was the one fixed star in her firmament and for whom she had some decent shreds of respect. Grandma Catherine was probably just now singing, "Sweet hour of prayer" before the benediction, and she, Annie, was raisin' the dead. Consultin' familiar spirits. When Saul did it, it was as much trouble as the dog pound let loose. That was one of the "good parts" of the Bible she poured over when sent to her room by Aunt Jewell to get "spiritual eddy-fig-ashunt."

Well, nothin' to stop this callin' up now. She took the Mystic Egyptian Oil-on-Water Box out from under her coat, brought the two rickety chairs over and, after sitting Montmorency in one of them, promptly watched the chair collapse and dissolved in silent laughter, pointing and hee-hawing all over the attic.

Down below Mrs. Paden, the acting head matron of the orphanage, was ushering Mr. Benson Beckwith and his wife Almeady into the dining room. "You see, we've set you right at the head, together, because you are our honored guests," Mrs. Paden said. Then she coughed discreetly. The orphans, all fifteen of them, stood behind their chairs, looking clean-scrubbed and Christian. The cook set pitchers of ice water on the table and brought in the biscuits.

Mrs. Paden looked at Mr. Beckwith, a small man with a rather stooped back, who was almost totally bald. "Will you honor us with grace, Mr. Beckwith?"

Looking a trifle unprepared, he gestured that all should bow their heads and began mumbling and stumbling a grace of his own invention, invoking blessings on these orphans, and all the generous folk who had donated this fine wing and re-done the old house, and yes, on the pickled beets and mashed potatoes, and finally, Father, on our boys at the front. Then chairs scraped on the still-new oak floor and the cook went out to bring in the dinner.

"Hope it ain't hock and beans again," said one of the older orphan boys, whose head emerged from his stiff collar like a bluejay's.

"It won't be," the boy next to him said out of the corner of his mouth. "They always trot out the delicacies when the top brass blows in."

As they all put big linen napkins squares under their chins, Mrs. Paden coughed, this time harder.

"My dear," Mrs. Almeady Beckwith said with concern, looking at the matron's thin body, her complexion as translucent as Haviland china. "I hope you aren't seriously ailin'." There was talk that she had consumption and the board certainly hoped that was not so.

"No, no, I am better, really I am," said the minister's wife with a weary smile.

"Oh, Buzzard Woman, come out of the great beyond, whether it be heaven or hell or you dwell here on earth," Montmorency intoned, holding just the tips of his fingers on the glass top of the Oil-on-Water Box.

Annie's eyes were shut, but she had left a slit open to see out of. The candle's flame blew flat and then rose again. There was a draft somewhere; maybe it was from that stove pipe coming up from the kitchen. Might have a hole or two in it. They didn't replace the old stove when the orphantage took over.

"You were mistreated by the county people, now come back and let us feel your presence, Buzzard Woman," Montmorency said, his voice smooth as oiled paper. "Are you angry at us?" he asked of the gloomy, stuffy silence in the chilly attic. "Angry at Grandfather—" he looked for direction at Annie.

"Hogue," she said.

"Hogue," Montmorency interned.

Suddenly there was a loud crack.

"Oh shit, she's madder'n hell at Grandpa," Annie said. For the first time, she began to take the ritual seriously.

"That was a crack of thunder. Odd, though, at the end of February," Montmorency murmured.

Annie closed her eyes again and watched his face through the eye-slit, which was feathered by her lashes. She had to tilt her nose up to keep his face in view. He looked serious, almost worried, and he kept shaking the hank of black hair out of his eyes. "I am going to be sure the candle is straight in the holder," he said. "We don't want to set the attic on fire."

While he was gone, Annie shut her eyes completely. "I lit another and brought this one here," he said, returning to sit on the edge of the broken-down chair. "Perhaps her spirit will be attracted to the flame."

"I feel you here, Buzzard Woman. I feel your presence," he said. The way his voice moved made the hair on the back of Annie's neck raise. Was that just a hint of cold air brushing by her? Maybe, just maybe, there was something to it. After all, there had been that odd crack of thunder.

"I think she is with us. Now take your fingers off the Oil-on-Water Box," Montmorency commanded, as if he were Emmanuel Swedenborg himself. "Oh, Buzzard Woman, we wait your appearance. Come as a voice, come as a wind, come as ectoplasm. We shall sit in silence."

Annie shut her eyes completely.

In the kitchen the cook opened the oven door. Perspiration streamed down her face, a strand of her red hair was in her mouth. She was German, from Evansville, and she had taken on service to support her aged parents. She didn't like going to the Presbyterian church and cooking dumplings the Hoosier way. Lutheran church and potato dumpling, that was better, ya. And these wise-mouthed, impudent boys and girls in America—give them the rod at home.

The oven door was stuck. Cursed, effeminate son-of-a-burgermaster oven. Was that the bell ringing from the dining room? The serving girls were standing with bowls in their hands, waiting for more green beans. There— the oven door had finally come open. She bent down to stare in its depths and saw—that it had burnt the custard pies.

Too much. She kicked the stove with her ample shoe. Then she kicked it again, three times. On the third kick, the stovepipe shook and re-arranged itself a trifle, sending a little soot into the green bean pot. Quickly she dabbed away the soot and dished up the green bean seconds, took the pies out of the oven, and scraped the tops completely off, leaving the surfaces as bumpy as a sixteen-year-old's face. "I hope I did not dislodge the pipe somewhere up above," she thought.

"What was that?" Annie said opening her eyes. A strange clunk had interrupted the seance.

"Buzzard Woman, are you here?" Montmorency said in a controlled voice.

The one candle before them had burnt out. There was only the one over by the table. Odd little teeth of fright began nibbling at Annie's stomach. "Light the other candle, Monty," Annie said in a shaky voice. The clunk- ing, or was it flapping, noise continued as Montmorency got up to go over to the candle.

"I will light the candle," he said, fumbling around over by the table, "and bring—it—(coming increasingly nearer)—right over here to *YOU*." There was the light of a match on a little pile of powder he held in a paper, and it illuminated Annie's frightened face. After that a minor but very definite boom, a magnesium flash, bright as day right before her eyes. Then, a loud, fiendish, laugh, then darkness. Finally, there was the sound of a few steps and the slamming of the door, then the turning of a key in the lock.

"Monty—where?" Annie's voice, rising in panic, finally overcame the astonishment which had reduced her to silence. Little white suns were everywhere in the attic, shining in her eyeballs.

"Have fun with the Buzzard Woman, you bratty witch," said a voice from behind the door. "I'll teach you to squelch me day and night." Steps went quietly but rapidly down the stairs.

Annie fumbled around in almost complete darkness. The pungent fumes of magnesium filled the air, but the suns were growing small, receding in intensity in her eyes. Her face was not hurt, but as black as coal. Wisps of smoke drifted about, the clunking continued. But wait—what was that smoke? Not just from whatever had exploded. No, there was real smoke in here. Wasn't there? The place must be on fire. It was smoking and soon would break into flames. She must get out.

"Well, I suppose I must go up the stairs to see if the stovepipe is out of whack," said the cook to herself as she returned from the dining room. "There are clunks and bangs all over the house and I suppose, ya, that the stupid thing is pressurizing the old soot and knocking itself loose at the joints. If one section gets loose it affects the others. I'll have to see that the seams go together, ya, as best I can or the house will be full of smoke." She did not really understand the way a stovepipe worked, but something was the matter, she knew that. "Where is that key?" she asked herself. Not finding it on its nail beside the attic entrance, she rattled the door in desperation and found it open. When she opened it wide, there were the keys on the floor. Odd, some trick of these rotten spoiled American bastardy, ya. Slowly she began to ascend.

"Oh my gawd I'm gonna fry up here and pay for my sins of calling up the dead." Annie whimpered. She was like a simmering pot sending up a few effervescences as it approached boiling, then more. Fear of the smoke and ghostly Piankashaw Indian presences, confusion in the darkness, and especially anger at Montmorency bubbled in her blood.

"Ooh, if I just had him here. Ten-year-old shit-head asshole, I'd explode his butt. I'd like to see the pieces flying all over this attic. What chemical did he use to do that to me? Oohh." She bumped around in the dark, trying to find the door, or the matches, or anything.

Down below, Mrs. Almeady Beckwith sipped her ice water and tentatively poked at her dessert. It was an odd meal. They had waited for food as smoke floated through the dining room. There was, unusually, whipped cream on the custard pie and it was plastered on the whole top, like a toupee on a bald man. Now there were odd bumps going on, somewhere.

The tall orphan boy nudged his next-door neighbor in the ribs. "Is Rover after a rat?" he asked out of the corner of his mouth. "That dog's too big to keep in a house, anyways. Even a asylum."

"Maybe we got a ghost. Somebody said this place is haunted," the other boy replied, screening his talking with his hand.

Mrs. Paden rang her bell. "I don't know where the coffee is. Cook— cook—where is that woman? Ophelia, go see if you can find her," she said to the oldest orphan girl.

When the cook reached the top step, she found the door to the attic locked. Carefully she reached into her apron pocket and took out the key. It was then that she realized she had not brought a lamp. She did have a match. Well, maybe she could take a quick look anyway, joggle the pipe a little.

Something flew through the just-opened door. It brushed past. Gasping for breath, the cook clung to the wall and watched what seemed to be a young girl in a coat and scarf storm down the stairs to the kitchen, yelling and cursing all the way.

By the time Annie reached the bottom step a small, curious crowd had formed in the kitchen. Anger, outrage, all the emotions that had been turned down like lamps for years burst out of Annie's overheated system. She did not even notice Mr. and Mrs. Benson Beckwith, Reverend Paden's wife, or any of the orphans who stood gazing in amazement at her black face and dishevelled hair.

"Where is he?" she stormed, looking in the dining room. Then she realized that, of course, Montmorency had gone home. "Ooh,' she cried, hitting her head with her hand at her own stupidity in underestimating the enemy. He had got the best of her. That had never happened before! Her rage became a thing not to be contained. She took dishrags out of the sink and slopped them on the floor, then stomped on them, calling her adversary's name over and over. She poured whipped cream on the floor. She upset Rover's dish. Then she stopped, panting, to get her breath. She looked around at everyone staring wide-eyed at her.

Mrs. Paden was the only one in the kitchen who knew her and she was speechless. "Who—what—" Mrs. Almeady Beckwith asked. She did not recognize her because of the soot. "Who are you? Are you an orphan?"

The question seemed to stop Annie in her tracks. All the anger and desire for revenge suddenly drained out of her. "Well, yes, but what's it to you?" she said, finally, in a grownup voice. "Lots of respectable people are orphants." Then slowly she flipped her scarf about her neck and exited with dignity, being careful to avoid the dishrags and whipped cream on the floor.

April, 1864

Chapter Nineteen

Edward Bachelder met Althea, Zach and Delia as they came down the gangplank of the steamboat. He kissed Althea's hands, bowed courteously to Delia, and then shook hands gravely with Zach. The group stood, waiting for baggage, facing the broad Memphis levee, with its assortment of brothels, gaming houses, new Union receiving terminals and trade houses.

Major Bachelder seemed to be fumbling for words. His news was evidently not going to be very welcome. "I will take you to see your relatives. The hearing was held last week. There's a new man in charge now. All you need to do is pay the fines for them and they can go. The real problem is not them."

Althea raised her eyebrows. He hesitated, then said, "Your parents' plantation has been confiscated by the Federal Government."

Althea's face was as impassive as stone. She shut her eyes, the only sign that she was reacting to the news. "Poor old Confederate veteran," she breathed, finally. "After all these months of somehow hanging on, I guess I thought Fairchance would survive the war. What happened?"

"I think General Washburne was angry at your cousins' behavior. They took advantage of their relatives' position and moved out contraband goods. You are a Northern citizen and it should have been safe, but after all, you are only the daughter in the case—" He sighed wearily.

Zach picked up bags the stevedores had set down while Delia checked the baggage, leaving Althea and Major Bachelder to talk alone.

"Your cousins are in jail, but more of the real criminals walk the streets looking for trading deals," Edward Bachelder said, looking back over his shoulder towards the city. "Memphis has been a sink of corruption since it was occupied. Commander replaces commander, the bribery and illegal trading continues, and I stay on." He stooped, picked up a stone, and tossed it into the river.

Althea studied his broad, handsome face, felt a rush of warmth as he turned to smile a little sadly at her. Momentarily, her anguish over the mansion house was put aside as she turned to this loved, respected friend who had done so much for her family.

"The only reason that the house has not been seized before," she said, "was that you took care to be sure that I, as manager of the house and a Northern citizen, was represented as lawful, and loyal. You had to hedge on that, of course. We are not model Northern loyalists."

"It was the one positive thing I may have done in this awful place," he assured her, keeping his voice low. After all, he was part of the military machine that ran Memphis. "General Hurlbut, who served after Sherman, was as bad as Bluebeard. He connived in the graft; he built the bastiles we put our political prisoners in. I asked to be transferred, to see action, anywhere, but they seem to think that since I have been here almost from the beginning, I supply 'continuity.' " He and Zach led the way carrying the bags, and they all walked across the broad levee and up to the street to catch a carriage. When they were settled in it, Althea spoke again.

"Well, I expect Elba and Addison deserved their medicine," she said.

"Your cousins, dishonest though their undertaking is, are only part of a giant sideshow," Bachelder said, "with every sort of disgusting, deformed creature performing."

"Aunt and Uncle were buying furniture and cloth and luxury goods and taking them far south in wagons?" Delia said, trying to understand. "They said they were taking it all to Grandpa and Grandma in Mississippi?"

"North, South—contraband traders are selling illegal goods for exorbitant prices everywhere. Some Southern agents connive with the Northern officials and strip the confiscated homes. They sell 'Southern treasures' like tapestries and paintings in Illinois and Pennsylvania. Your relatives went both ways."

"The charges said they went south, behind Confederate lines," Delia said.

"Yes. There's a long list of things, almost everything, really, that cannot be taken or sold to the Confederacy. Your aunt and uncle had a permit to transport goods, supposedly for emergency purposes, to a sick and distressed old man, your grandfather. Their greed trapped them. They kept returning to get more furniture 'to take to our poor, dear cousin.' Those wagons were loaded so often your father would have to need twenty beds and sixty sideboards. Odd to say, there are plenty of people in Mississippi who still have the money to buy luxury goods. I hear they had been taking them north, too." Delia and Zach, sitting facing them, listened closely.

"How did they catch Elba and Addison, Major Bachelder?" Delia wanted to know.

"Even though many officers in our own army are conniving at all this trade, times are changing. Under pressure from Washington, the top brass is now beginning to arrest people. But there's graft even in that. Suspicious detectives are everywhere, paid by the government for every arrest they make. One reason is, that they want to confiscate all this rich property. When your relatives' cart was finally stopped, going out of town, there was a bag of gold under the seat—thousands and thousands of dollars. That is quite serious. Gold is one of the things the Confederacy needs to win the war.''

"How could they get that kind of money?'' Althea wanted to know. They were well off, but I don't see—''

"There are people in the North who are investing in smuggled goods,'' Bachelder affirmed. ''They deal in the lowest kind of human misery.''

"When the sun comes out, the lizards crawl from beneath rocks to bask a bit,'' Zach said. He smiled a twisted, knowing smile and the odd way he said it made both women stare at him. He offered no further explanation.

Edward Bachelder went on. ''Your relatives gave the Office of Military Detective and the Abandoned Property Division the pretext they need. They were able to connect you and Fairchance plantation to the crime and decided to take the house. It wasn't hard, because you do not own the house; it is in your father's name.''

Zach stared out the window as they passed the tall post office and the new theatre. Delia sat silently, her eyes inscrutable, wondering if a new theatre had been built in Indianapolis, feeling in a flash the pain of the night last spring.

Althea wanted to know every detail of the house's seizure. ''What will happen, Major?'' she asked, looking into his eyes. ''Shall we be able move the furniture out?''

"The government will continue to farm the plantation for the complete benefit of the Union army. Your overseer works for the Yanks, now. All possessions within the house are subject to seizure. Your father will have nothing from it, perhaps forever.'' There, he had said the worst.

Althea sank into the seat. ''No. It cannot be possible. My parents will die if they have nothing to return to. Can we go out there? Take a few things with us, a few valuable family keepsakes.''

"Nothing can be taken now. Besides, it will not be safe for you on the roads. Now, here we are at the Gayoso Hotel,'' he said, with relief. Edward Bachelder was glad he did not have to be the bearer of any more ill tidings to this woman that the war had made his friend. Courteously he tipped his hat and bade the party goodbye.

"Mama, I suggest we go to the blockhouse where they are confined, and

Zach can go out tomorrow to the plantation and see what is happening there,'' Delia said, entwining her mother's arm in her own.

They were in their rooms, and Althea had collapsed, exhausted in a chair. She fished listlessly in the pocketbook that lay in her lap. "Delia, take this bank draft down to Uncle Addison. Ask Mr. Scott to attend you. I do not think I can stand to see them now. I might claw their eyes out. To focus attention on us now, to anger General Washburne so—'' She waved her daughter away.

The streets were a melange of sights and sounds, most of them rather coarse, as Delia and Zach walked to the prisoners' blockhouse. Army officers' wives, twirling parasols and wearing new gowns with the popular checked vests, veteran enlisted men in Yankee blue on crutches or wooden legs, neatly brushed captains and majors laughed and jostled each other. Scores of the notorious Memphis "low women,'' with exposed arms and veiled, cynical eyes clustered on the corners. They cast their unsmiling glances both at military men and scruffy-bearded teamsters drinking from whisky bottles. But Memphis was not all wartime driftwood, washed ashore by the surge of the Northern Army through Tennessee. Southern women with ragged ruffles and defiant, high-held heads, brushed by on the arms of the stooped old men who were the only local males over forty left in town.

Everywhere people were selling things in plenty—china and silver and napkins, radishes and the first lettuce of the spring, buttons and lace and men's pipes. If you had signed the loyalty oath, you could buy or sell anything that came to your hand. Thus it was in this city of the South which had been occupied almost from the beginning of the war, and was not suffering now, at least on the streets.

But behind closed doors, where arbitrary Northern might ruled, that was another story. They came to a tall building known as Irving Block. "The bastille,'' Zach said. He had heard of Irving Block; it fanned Copperhead hatred, along with the shocking stories of Southern military prisons.

Inside they ask the military attendant if they could see Addison and Elba Dugger. They were led down a dank, hideous hallway, loaded with the miserable human effluvia of the war in Memphis. The Dugger kin were confined in a section on the first floor. Two other married couples and a young girl ill with tuberculosis were in the same small room. The attendant opened the door with a key from a large ring, and the Duggers rose from the boxes which served as their chairs.

"Oooh, Lawcamercy honest,'tis you, Delia,'' Elba said, coming to her niece, grabbing her in a tight hug. The smell of unwashed bodies was strong; Delia tried not to notice.

"Aunt Elba, mother has come to try to aid you. We brought a bank note for your fine.''

"Fine or payoff," Addison Dugger growled. He was a small, meaty man with a nose so turned up you could see into his nostrils. "You have to have a thousand dollars to pay the fine and five hundred more for the bribe."

Delia was only a little surprised. "Can the military governor be allowing bribes?"

"Allow? You know Bachelder said they were encouraging every type of graft and corruption," Zach said, seating himself on the box. The other two couples retired as far back as they could on their own boxes. One of the women's hair fell long and uncombed over her skirt as she leaned in discouragement on her husband. No one was introducing anyone; the despair and squalor of the situation would make such social formalities ludicrous.

"Why are they here?" Zach asked.

"The girl there insisted on goin' to find her sweetheart behind the Southern lines," Addison said. "She didn't obey the military order the general gave her and was caught outside the lines. Some people have defied the government. Mr. Whithead, there, is a newspaper editor. Most of 'em are here on trumped-up charges."

" 'Tis true," Elba said. "Anybody who has any money 'tall gets arrested and slapped with false charges. Then they have t' buy their way out."

Zach offered Addison a cigar and he seized it eagerly. "Or they have their property confiscated." He looked at Delia. "Like your ma. Only sometimes they don't wait for an excuse. They take the property right from under the nose of the mansion owners. Or if they go away—" he pulled a finger across his throat. "U.S. Government issue."

"It does not say much for the Federal justice system," Delia murmured.

"Or for the general in charge. He's the gov'ment, the president, the judge and the jury in Memphis today," Addison said.

"Still, you folks cannot really complain, can you?" Zach said scornfully to the Duggers. "Your actions were about as sordid as theirs on a different side, weren't they?"

Delia sent him a warning look that said, "I'm the only one who can offend my relatives," and sighed to think that this was another example of how strained their relationship now was. They had managed, through precarious distancing and polite friendliness, to make the first part of the trip bearable for Althea and to allow themselves to survive the pain of shattered love. Eat politely, dab at your lips with your napkin in the salon of the steamboat, talk about the children with their nursemaids on the steamboat deck, cluster at the rail and be alarmed when you go aground, retire early and read a book—it could work.

Especially if you did not think past the courtesies of the moment, if you shoved the deep, springing remembrances and attachments that tried to rise, ever deeper down. They could be acquaintances, it appeared, if not friends.

But it was all a balance act, a walk on a rope over the roaring falls of emotion. Sometimes, when Zach did something courteous for her mother, or when, unaware he got "that look" on his face, love, or was it attraction, jumped up out of its jack-in-the-box and Delia had to push it down. On the other hand, whenever Zach reverted to his obnoxiously cynical flippancies, it was almost too much for Delia to bear; she hated him at that moment. Detach, detach, pull at the taffy-iron ropes. It wasn't easy to unwind these ties; two months ago she had hoped it would be definitely over by now.

The Duggers looked at the banknote with relief; the others were trying not to eye it. The young woman on the shelf bunk coughed dryly, pitiably. "Is it this way all over the prison?" Delia asked in a low voice.

"Worse, much worse upstairs," Elba said, shaking her head as if she were unable to say more, "than anything I ever seen."

Delia nodded her goodbyes to her aunt and uncle and the guard came to rattle the cage with his keys and let them out. Zach stayed behind a moment, on the pretense of having lost a button under a bunk. When Delia was out of earshot, he eyed Addison Dugger coldly. "Don't expect help from your charitable organization back home," he said.

"Whatever do you mean, sir?" Addison Dugger asked, licking his lips uncomfortably.

"I mean Mawkins. I know of your arrangement with him."

Addison Dugger stood stock still, saying nothing, and Zach went on. "I know him all too well. When the weather's fair, he's aboard the ship, smiling. But come the gale—well, all rats overboard." the Duggers were speechless. That this friend of Delia's knew about their affairs confounded him.

Zach looked at the filthy floor of the cell as the guard came to let him out. "Rats overboard. Come to think of it, that's not a bad comparison."

Althea finally forced herself to go to that same Irving Block prison the next day. She had arranged to meet Edward Bachelder, and she was on his arm as they came through the door of the converted building. The attendant sergeant ushered them to the "High-toned" cell as the minimum security room was called. Elba and Addison were packing up; General Washburne's Head of Abandoned Property Division had pulled the proper strings, deposited his ill-gotten gains, and scheduled the criminals for release. They chirruped and strutted around like banty roosters and seemingly had no idea they had irritated, inconvenienced, and completely outraged their relative by causing her property to be seized.

"Jest apply for reconsideration, dearie," Elba advised, tying her bonnet strings under her chin. "And cross their palms with coin. Greenbacks are gettin' to be as bad as Confederate dollars in these here parts.'' She picked up a carpetbag loaded with novels and candy the guard had gotten for her, then put her hand briefly on Althea's sleeve. ''Oh, an' obliged to you for steppin' in. Toodleoo.''

''Some people seem to believe the world is their pasture,'' Edward Bachelder whispered as the Dugger kin bustled out of the cell and the door clanged behind them. ''A thoughtful somebody takes care of everything and they never need to worry.'' He smiled at Althea.

''Well, I'm going to write them a letter of the terms for my *loan*. And I'm not going to just accept the seizure. Take it like a shorn lamb—'' she looked up at him for confirmation; he nodded. They walked down the hall, giving passing glances to several awful confinement rooms, at the same time trying to avert their eyes so they would not embarrass the gentile prisoners within. ''It is more awful up above,'' Bachelder said. ''On the women's floor, young girls and silver-haired grandmas sleep on straw in the cold and vermin. And at the blockhouse at Ft. Pickering— that is the worst yet. There they keep the hardened criminals. It is there that your plantation foreman, Jonas, remains.''

Althea stopped in surprise. ''What? Is Jonas here? I thought he was kept in the freed blackmen's compound in the middle of town.''

''He was let out of there, but was picked up again for trouble-making. Inciting blacks to demand better conditions. Then he got drunk and robbed and stabbed someone down in the—'' he halted, hesitating to offend the ears of a modest woman.

''The brothel district?''

''Yes.'' Bachelder was trying to usher Althea out of the building.

She went through the door but halted dead still on the street. ''I must see Jonas.''

He stopped and looked at her. Her eyes were filled with sadness, anxiety. What in the world for? For the times of sweet summer in a golden past, when darkies sat on their porches and supper was served in the twilight? Perhaps these prisons—Irving Block, that they had just left, with ''Southern chivalry'' lying in the straw, the other just down the street here, where their former slaves were kept in compounds, fed and clothed like children—drove home the reality that the South was dying forever. If so, it was an awful reality. And the military prison was the worst of all.

''Surely you do not mean to visit the Negro. The quarters at the Fort are unspeakably filthy and disreputable. Even if I could get a pass for you.''

''He is one of our people.''

Bachelder shook his head. Never, never, would he understand Southerners.

Three hundred prisoners slept on the floor where rats and mice ran during the night. Their food was thrown in through heavy bars to lie on the filth-covered floor. There, sitting on a chair, staring out with eyes that glared hatred at the world as it now sat upon his shoulders, was Jonas. He looked up to see Althea staring in at him, as a visitor views an animal in a zoo. Instantly she knew she had made a mistake in coming. The Negro rose to grasp the bars of the cage.

"You! Missus. What do you want?" he demanded coldly.

"Jonas, I've come to see if there is anything you need, if—"

"Anything I need. I need to be out of here, missus." His voice was strong, velvety, with an almost insolent authority. She did not like it.

"Well, but you did put yourself in here, I think. Still, I thought if you needed food or—" Bachelder pulled back on her arm and she did step back a pace. The Negro's powerful body, taut with repressed rage and some sort of latent, hostile energy, was intimidating. He said nothing; she went on, almost to fill the odd, frightening vacuum between them. "After all, we have cared for your folks for so many years."

He looked her up and down, her new, clean corduroy dress, the hat that matched it, her sleek good health. "We ain't on the plantation, missus. You cain't come to the cabin and give me fatback and beans cause I'm doin' poorly. That's all over the hills and faraway. Ain't it, missus?" The tone in his voice was mock-deferential. He was being insulting.

Althea tilted her chin. Her eyes flashed.

"Ah, missus," he said, smiling a mocking smile, "you don't like the slave boy tellin' you things. Well, you reap the whirlwind, don't you, missus? You always said I was a smart boy, taught me my ABC's when I was still toddlin'. But somethin' in you made me think you was talkin' to your pet *dog*!" As he spat out the word, Bachelder pulled Althea forcibly back three full feet from the lockup cage. The black man's knuckles fastened hard on the bars.

"You brought me up to think and live like I and all your family's niggers was half-human, and when I acted just as you learned me, you turned on me. When all you white folks left us to our own scrabblin', and it got to be a dog-eat-dog world, I did what any dog would do to live." His voice was scathing. " 'Twas you, then, pretty missus, you turned me in. That rubbed salt in the wounds."

He lowered his voice to a threatening whisper. "When I get out of here, you got to be real careful, pretty missus." He roared and rattled the bars in what seemed to be a calculated demonstration, until the blue-clad prison guards came to threaten him with guns. Althea retreated, gathering the skirts of the plaid corduroy dress above her ankles.

"You are angry, not fearful, as I expected," Edward Bachelder said as he drove her to the hotel. "Why?"

"He was a clever boy. Now he is a clever, vicious charlatan. Playing a part I can only think he enjoys. Still—the place is utterly revolting. That it has come to this! I helped rock his cradle when I was a young wife, back on my visits. I brought medicine to his mammy when he was ill, and he has made it sound so wrong. Twisted it all. You say they are free. Downtown we walked by that compound where hundreds of 'freedmen' and women are being kept like monkeys in a pen. They can't even find cornbread for themselves; the government has to build their tents so the rain won't soak them. And it's this way all over Dixie. The slaves we kept in comfort are dying of yellow fever and cholera. Is it better than before?"

Bachelder was silent. He did not know the answer to her question.

All of the ugliness of the previous day was forgotten, or at least put aside the next morning, as Althea and Delia sat at tea and toast and marmalade in the sunny dining salon of the Gayoso House. Zach had rented a rig and gone out to the plantation with Major Bachelder. Althea poured oolong and told Delia that she was appealing the confiscation. She would officially petition the general to cancel the Bureau of Confiscation decision. Since she was a Northern citizen, and since Elba's and Addison's fine had been paid, there was a fifty-fifty chance of getting the house back.

"I had the deeds drawn today here in Memphis for me to own the house. I had taken the first steps to have it deeded late last year, but I did not have the heart to take it from Papa and Mama." Her eyes were troubled, like a little child who has sassed its parents and expected punishment. "We must take steps—well, I have written to Papa and Mama and told them not to worry." Althea said. "If the decision should go our way, if Fairchance is returned, why, when the war is over I as a Yankee and owner will simply deed it back to them, as I had planned earlier. But it all depends on the infinite mercy and goodness of Abraham Lincoln's government." The last words were said with deep scorn.

Delia picked up a spoon to eat a dish of stewed cinnamon apples. "How much hope is there for the house to be returned?" she asked.

"Edward—Major Bachelder—thinks we may have a chance. The President himself has investigated the situation in Memphis. The commander may try to show he can be fair and due process does exist. We can hope."

"When will they make their decision, Mother?" Delia wanted to know. She was anxious to get back to Rivertides before spring planting, to see to the whitewashing and trimming of the fruit trees, to plan the rotation of the fields with the hands. Her mother was again letting her manage a few of the acres. And she did not want to stay where Zach was.

"At least two weeks. Maybe a month. These things take time."

Delia put the beautifully filigreed spoon beside the dish of apples. She was not really very hungry. A month. That long. This situation with her former lover really was impossible. She had not seen him since that night in the Scott house. For one night there, she had forgotten herself, but then she remembered. The six weeks they'd been apart had helped. She was succeeding in cutting ties, that most dangerous and painful of all the games of love. Yet now, when this trip had finally happened, the sight of him, day after day, was like having a burnt match head put on soft skin. Sometimes walking with him, talking to him, seemed normal and she almost forgot the past; many other times the sight of him was intolerable, knowing what she had known, feeling what she felt.

"Can you stand it, love?" her mother wondered. Delia looked inquiringly at her. Stand it? Stand Zach? Did she, was she finally aware—

"I mean being away from Rivertides. I know how you've grown to love managing those fields."

No. She was still as dense as a fencepost. "We can write Osco and Sammy. And Trotter, though he's good for little but housework. Tell them what to do," Delia said resignedly. "I am sure I can stand whatever I have to."

When Zach came in that afternoon, he said the plantation was quiet and that Major Bachelder had placed two men on guard again. While the life or death decision for the house was being made, justice would seem to be done. Zach also said he was going to take a boat north and then return as soon as he could. He had received a telegram from Willis Mawkins and through its vague, veiled language he'd determined that time was ripening in their affairs, and his advice was needed immediately. Delia nodded and did not even wave to him as he bounded up the stairs to pack his suitcase.

*   *   *   *

Dora Lavenham sat in the small sleeping room she shared with Betsy Pickering, reading a letter from Tilghman Vistal, from Salisbury Prison in North Carolina. Since she was in a Confederate hospital, she could receive mail from the South. She would pass it on to Jacob Joe when she saw him next.

She turned up the light on the oil lamp. She should husband the lamp light; it was difficult to get oil these days and many people were using cheap candles, but the hospital still had a little oil.

Second of Second Month
Eighteen Sixty Four

Dear Miss Lavenham:

I hope thee are in health, going about on the Lord's business there at the hospital. I have been here now two weeks. If thee are ever over at the Castle Thunder, I hope and pray thee can find a way to convey my greetings to Jacob Joe Scott my friend and tell him I am recovered in body, but still sorely beset for my faith.

This prison was formerly a large cotton factory. It is enclosed by two plank fences. The grounds contain several acres, a hospital and officers' dwelling house which is known as Headquarters. There is an inner fence. This is surrounded on the outside by a platform built near the top, on which are placed guards, who regularly walk their beats to prevent the escape of prisoners.

There are small cottages in which the prisoner blacksmiths and carpenters stay. We are allowed the privileges of the yard during the day, but at night are confined in two buildings.

The first floor of our structure is empty, the second is occupied by northern citizens, the third by Confederate soldiers who are convicts and the top by prisoners of war. I am on the convicts' floor, where there is much roguery.

Mischief is done in this room almost every night. On the first of this month it was my turn to be imposed on. I was considerably beaten with a stick but not deeply injured. I started to report this to the commander, but before I reached the steps I thought better of it. It is customary for some of the rude clan to make the man imposed on promise not to report the incident. A man came toward me, carrying the club I had been beat with. He looked at me a short time but turned aside without telling me his business. I knew it was meant to be a warning.

But later the clerk of the prison saw blood on my clothes and decided to take me from these bad men. He put me in the workmen's quarters. I want to go to school, and one of the reporters here Junius H. Brown has been graciously correcting my writing, both grammatically and rhetorically.

My Aunt Judith is still working to free me, and I will go if freed. My loving best to my friend Jake.

Your friend
Tilghman Vistal

Dora gently folded the letter. "Jake. The name his brother calls him—intimate name," Dora thought. "I shall take the letter to him soon. I shall go in and see his form—so lean now, like a little boy's, his face like an angel's, with his golden hair long and waving and his beard about his mouth and I will want to—bold thought—kiss him. But of course I shall pass by as I always do, and when I have the chance and no one is looking, I shall say a few words. I shall tell him of home, shall say the hotel is prospering back in Louisville, and Mama has hired girls to do our work and has redecorated the parlors, so I think she will not need me when we return home.

"Return home. When? Ah, faint hope revives. It is spring and the men are stirring in the camps. The great Northern army, so strong and well-equipped, will come out of its lair and try to march around the barrier of our soldiers. Our Marse Robert, as the soldiers call him, General Lee, great man that he is, will go out and do battle. Perhaps he will win a mighty victory, and the North, pressed by its dissenters, will sue for peace on favorable terms.

"Just perhaps. Or—like Behemoth, they will lunge and surge toward us here and if they get momentum they will come to crush and ravage, and we will be no more. But either way, it will stop, stop. Oh, God, let it stop!

"And, while I am praying, Dear Lord, let me have the courage to tell this dearest man on earth what I do not want of all things to tell him, but I must." She bowed her head and turned the lamp off to conserve the fuel that every day, as the North destroyed railroads and strangled the supply lines, became harder to come by.

When Dora did go with the hospital Sanitary Committee for inspection of the quarters at Castle Thunder, when she did find a time when the rest of the committee was absent, she left the letter from Tilghman Vistal under Jacob Joe's pillow. Later, when she passed him in the hall, ostensibly stopping to give him a bottle of molasses tonic to strengthen his wasted form, she whispered her messages. And when she was done, she gave him the real one she dreaded.

"Sophie's husband has left her. After only these few short months. He had gambling debts and has fled to Texas. She is bereft." The light in his eyes, the light of long-dead hope kindled unexpectedly to bright flame, gave her the answer she had expected, but hoped against hope she would not find.

"Waal, I never in all my born days heard the county a-talkin' so much about anything," Jewell Simpson said, two weeks later, her hands on her broad hips. She had just come home from her Dorcas Circle meeting, the first of the spring, and was supervising her husband and nephew Bob as they cleaned the smokehouse. Annie sat in the midst of a bed of spring beauty flowers. New duck chicks had hatched, and she put a newly born baby duck in the palm of her hand and was letting it walk around.

"Now jest cut down those two hams that are left, yes, check for mold. We can scrape it off—" Jewell instructed, then turned towards Annie. "Anyways, everbody at the circle was click-clackin' with talk of your she-nanigans at the orphants' home. Made me want to slip under the rug." Annie refused to look at her.

"The cook has quit over there and the minister's wife, Mrs. Paden, has took to her bed over it."

"Cheep, cheep—" Annie said, fluffing the duckling's yoke-yellow fur with one finger tip and talking to it.

"Get the renderin' pots out and let's scrub 'em in the yard," Jewell said, pointing Bob towards two big iron kettles in the corner. "Almeady Beck-with was the worst."

"Quack, quack, quack," Annie said again, raising one eyebrow to her aunt, who continued her barnyard soliloquy.

"That whiny voice a-sayin' 'Waal, I know you did your best Jewell, but poor thing, deprived of her ma and pa when she was so young—sometimes no matter what you do, they turn out bad.' Take those corn shucks and the lye soap." Jewell pointed as the kettles went out the door. "Draw a little water to start the suds." Her husband gave her a taciturn look as he reached for the bucket.

"Seems like you stored up a lot of directin' in you at the circle meetin'. You got a whole watch-spring of bossin' wound up in you today." Archie Simpson chucked the pot under a big oak tree. "I got a letter from Hender-son, from the One Hundred Twentieth regiment. It just came. Don't you want to hear what it says? He don't write much."

"You know we ain't suppose to put water in these iron pots, but the trouble is they go rank," she shouted, her attention on her younger nephew Bob. "We just got to chance the rust—" She turned away from Bob as he began the pot scrubbing. "What'd Henderson say?"

"He says the One Hundred Twentieth Indiana ain't as good as the Four-teenth and there are lots of lazy soldiers there, but it's good for him. Says he's finally learnin' a mite of discipline, and this time around he's goin' to do better in the army. Says again, like he did in the Christmas letter, that he's sorry he left so sudden, but the neighborhood was gettin' a little con-finin' for him."

"Do tell. Yes," Jewell said, distracted. Annie was down on the grass, kicking her heels and showing her frilly underlinen. She had not been listen-ing. She was watching the duck chick walk and squawk in the wildflowers and new grass.

Jewell walked across the yard, dragging the rest of the butchering equipment out of the smoke house as she talked. "I shoulda whopped the stuffin' outa you and efn you weren't so big I'd still do it. I know it was the influence of those people of yours, so-called relatives over there in that house. I tole the court when they called us in for that hearin' five years ago that it was terrible bad for you and John to always be tore apart and havin' to go over to those strange folks. Spiritualism medium boards! What kinda people keep that sort of ha'nt stuff right in their own parlors? Not to mention all those nigger equality tracts back in your grandmother's quarters. I tell you I don't want to see you over there any more, and come to think of it, young lady, why don't you come with me to the Dorcas meetin's? Almeady Beckwith's youngest, Lila June, was there and—"

"Aunt, I'm goin' to Oregon," Bob said. He stopped scrubbing the lard pot and sat back on his heels.

"Whaat?" Jewell demanded. It was as if he had said something in Chinese.

"I'm a-goin' for adventure to the West. May settle there. Reverend Paden is reassigned in a Oregon town and is goin' in June. I've talked to him and I'm a-goin as teamster for him and his fambly's wagon."

A moment passed while Jewell shifted her gears. "An' who gives you leave to decide you're goin' anywhere?" she demanded.

"I don't know, but I'm nineteen and I'm a-goin' to do it," he said firmly, returning to his pot scrubbing.

She threw up her hands. "Waal, this has been the most gol-durned, whip-crackin', pig snorter of a day," she said.

It got worse. At dinner that night, as they finished off the last of the canned succotash and ate some of the fried smokehouse ham, minus mold, Mary Jane said, timidly, "Aunt, I want the money that is in trust for us."

Jewell was caught off guard again. "You want *what*?" she roared, leaving the slice of ham she had just speared in the air on the end of the fork. Even Archie looked at his niece in surprise.

"I'm of age now, and John is, too," she said, timidly. "We own the land that was our Great-Grandfather Dan'l's, and I know Uncle Arch has been leasin' it out for our benefit. There must be a tidy sum by now in the bank."

"Well, an' what if there is?" Jewell had the piece of ham on the plate now and was spooning red gravy on it. "You're not s'posed to get that till you're twenty-five."

"Jewell, it can mature when they are twenty-one. You know that," Arch Simpson said sharply.

"What will you do with it, anyways?" her aunt wanted to know. "It's s'posed to be your dowry. Annie's too."

"I'm never gettin' married," Annie mumbled, eating the pile of straw-berry preserves that she had spooned onto her plate, and which represented the sum total of her dinner fare.

"I've written to John," Mary Jane continued, looking guilty in spite of herself. "Well, since our piece is the tail end of the Dan'l property and they ain't a house there, we want to build a little farm cottage, go to farming there together. Take Annie."

"Yes!" Annie said, animated for the first time in the conversation. Jewell shut her mouth and shook her head strongly, as if the ideas were too prepos-terous to even consider.

"I, uhh, I thought we could go into town next week and talk to the bank," Mary Jane said in a small but hopeful voice. It had taken her tremendous courage to broach the subject. Her aunt grunted noncommittally.

Mary Jane persisted. "Uncle, won't John be coming in soon?"

"He—all of 'em in the Fourteenth'll be mustered out in June, if he don't reenlist. He'd have to be dumber'n a gourd to do that," Arch Simpson said.

"Next week! You want to go next week?" Jewell had seized on some-thing. "We're s'posed to do the spring butcherin'. What do you think we cleaned the smoke house out for? Jest-a s'pose you're a going to be flittin' about doin' your *Fi*-nanshall investigatin' and cottage plannin' and leave me with the scaldin' and renderin'."

Mary Jane looked flustered. "No, I forgot about that. Of course. We could go into the bank the week after—"

Her aunt sat stiffly, not eating. It was all too much for her.

Mary Jane looked at the biscuit on her plate. "Aunt Jewell," she began, tentatively, "you have been so good to us. It's just that John, and Annie and Bob and I—"

"Don't count me in," Bob said, raising his hand. "I'm a-goin' to Ore-gon."

"Well, yes. But maybe you'll come back. Lots o' folks do. We are a fambly ourselves. I've dreamed of it so often." Her eyes grew misty, far-away. "I can jest see us, sitting by our own fireplace. I'll be knitting. There'll be a Bible, and flowers on the table. And in my dream—" she stopped, hesitant.

"Go on, Janie," Arch Simpson encouraged, looking at her with affec-tion.

"In my dream *both* my aunt and my grandmother, the two I love so much are there, side by side. They're smilin' at each other jest ever so nice." She expelled her breath and stared again at the biscuit, now growing cold. It had cost her a pretty penny to get this far.

"Waal, that will never happen," her aunt began. "If you think I'm going to ever sit down by that woman's side after what happened with Annie over at that house—'' and so on.

It was too much. Mary Jane burst into tears, jumped up and ran from the table.

"You have money, actual gold in your pockets for this expedition to perdition?" Zach Scott asked sceptically. He sat across from Willis Mawkins in the Heidelberg Tavern in south Indianapolis.

"Not perdition. Just to victory, for the Confederacy." Mawkins took out a handkerchief and dabbed at a square inch of ale suds that had spilled off his beer. "Doubting Thomas," he sneered, tilting his captain's chair back a little and stretching out his legs. "Have I not told you the Confederacy made $90,000 available to us? Some of it is in Morgan's captain—Hines' hands—"

"And how is my old friend Tom Hines?" Zach asked with a good deal of sardonic relish. He had enjoyed the Rebel captain's company on the Morgan escapade, both in Indiana when he visited him on the "sick horse" raid and later, in the few contacts he'd had with him during the fiasco at the Battle of Corydon.

"He was at the bottom of Morgan's escape from prison in Ohio. Hines dug through the cement floor and the men passed through a hole into the air space beneath and then out to Kentucky. Now, he's the circus master in this grand scheme with Vallandigham and the Canadian Confederates."

"Circus is the right word. Now let me have it again, step by step." Zach called the waitress over to order food. He was hungry. When the girl, dressed in red-and-white-checked gingham covered by a full white apron came, he had her read the menu in English. Brokenly she was able to point out sausage and kraut, which he ordered, with plenty of white bread.

The Heidelberg was a good spot to plan intrigues; most of the men were from the German section of south Indianapolis and could not have understood the complicated and definitely treasonous plot that Zach was listening to.

After the waitress left, Mawkins leaned close. "I met with Hines in Canada. The Confederate government through its agent has delivered money to help the South win the war through the Great Northwest. For a giant conspiracy, through the back door."

"Fire in the rear, they have always called us," Zach murmured.

"Yes, well but that was just brushfire. If this fire gets going—this conspiracy—it will reverse the trend in the war, raise the support we've always known was waiting in the Northwest, and give the South the manpower it needs to turn the tide. And it comes right from President Jefferson Davis himself. I know, I saw him.''

"You were at Richmond?"

"I have been more than once. Somehow I am still alive, although there have been several scrapes where I thought I was all played out.'' He stared at the bubbles in his ale with a certain degree of satisfaction. ''But to plant this—I don't want to call it a conspiracy—a *plan* to save the South—this time I went from Washington and from there to Suffolk and the Blackwater country to Petersburg. Thence to Richmond.''

The waitress brought the kraut and sausage. Zach watched her put the plate down. She was well formed, with a small waist and a beautifully rounded behind, like the globe on a glass lamp. In the old days—his thought died. He supposed he would have to find his way back to the old days again. His true love had shoved him aside. He pushed it from his mind, reaching for the mustard.

"What sorts of papers did you have?" he asked Mawkins.

"Well, my Southern papers were no trouble. I had magic names on the passes I carried and they transported me like a flying carpet. But I kept drifting into the Northern lines. Here I used sutler trading permits I got in Nashville. You know I've done some contrabanding along with everyone else. I had saddlebags full of chloroform and surgical clamps for sale to field hospitals.''

Zach ate his sausage, cutting it into one small slice at a time and dipping it in the hot mustard.

"And I did sell some," Mawkins admitted. "Actually made several hundred dollars. After all, what's a war for but to make money? And since it doesn't look like the war will end on terms favorable enough for me to get an estate—'' he shrugged.

"Of course not," Zach could not argue with him. All around them in the North, fortunes were being built in one way or another on people's misery. He thought of the prison in Memphis, and he thought of the people he had left behind there.

"Let us hope your trading in intrigue turns out better than your contraband enterprise with the Duggers in Memphis,'' he said.

"The fools," Mawkins said, without letting it spoil his good humor. "Going back time after time for more loot. They are as simple as children. But then, children always want one more lollipop and that's the one that makes 'em sick.''

Mawkins ordered another glass of ale. He was feeling expansive. "Yes, I even bought some sapphires that had come in through the blockade. There's a lot of strange things in Richmond today. Rich wines, jewels, but almost nobody has enough food.'' His smile faded. "I got the sapphires to give to—somebody. Thought it might—thaw the ice again. But no go." He frowned.

Zach recognized the would-be recipient of the blockade sapphires as Lettie Hogue, Delia's friend, but he let it pass. "What's Jefferson Davis like?" he asked.

"Well, I saw him in a receiving line. I really met with the Secretary of War. Davis can only support The Plan from a distance. But rest assured, he does. It may be the only way to win the war."

"Treason," Zach told himself with a small start of realization. "What you're listening to is rank treason." Well, listening was not doing. He had done so many ignominious things in his life, but treason? His stint with Morgan was bad enough. His part in the affair had never come out. But this would be different. This was spying.

Uncle Ish Scott had not batted an eye. He went to the British, then the Spanish. Naughty old Uncle Ish. They said he really believed the United States deserved to fall. Or was that just part of the pose? Evil old Uncle Ish. He himself—well, he didn't know. How much did he believe in the Cause? Enough to risk getting his neck stretched? He thought not. Lately—

Mawkins was going on. "Now, to The Plan. I will go through it step by step. I will not tell you all the details, because only three people on earth know them, and you are not one. All of us in who support the South in the North will meet very, very quietly. Hines will be travelling to Illinois to prepare agents of the prisoners at Camp Douglas. We will eventually arm them for revolt. They will finally be joined by a general uprising in these states. A civil war against the Civil War." He took out a silver toothpick and began to pick his teeth.

"How many knights do you now think we have?"

"Forty thousand in Ohio, eighty-five thousand in Illinois, and in Indiana fifty thousand."

Zach put down his fork. "I know those castles and I can tell you there aren't two thirds that number. Still, there are a good many. How many prisoners are there?"

Suddenly Mawkins constricted his eyes, cautiously. "The total number you do not need to know. Enough to bring Lee's army to full strength. If they get loose, think of the terror in the Northwest, the pressure to end the war."

"No doubt about that. And my part?"

"The money in gold I have at the hotel. It is for you to take to New York. You will go first to Richmond to take the sealed version of The Plan in person. You will be our liaison. I cannot go again. My face is getting familiar in that neck of the woods."

"In person? What the hell makes you think I want to go into the Southern lines."

"Every month brings more confusion in the South. It gets easier to pass about down there. You will have the same supplies as I, carry easy passes into the Southern lines."

Zach considered for a moment. "Well, and I do have my own passes. I still have Morgan's. And I have my own traders' pass from Memphis. We are delivering boatloads of fresh fruit this summer to the city. I am going back to complete the details of the sales."

"Our? We?"

"I—well, from my farm but also the Duggers'. And others. Something new—I represent with military permission Mr. Thomas Jefferson Brooks the food purveyor for the area south of Memphis. I can just as well sell surgical supplies with it as anything, at least until I get out of the Northern lines. Althea—Mrs. Dugger—has managed to make friends with General Washburne at Memphis and he signed my permit himself. I wrote to Mr. Brooks and he organized the territory for me."

"Oh," Mawkins said, uninterested. "Well, those western army passes won't do much good in the eastern lines. I'll give you my forged passes, but they're just for an emergency. You'll have to depend on sneaking through, really. When you have delivered your message in Richmond, provided you get there, you must pass back through the Southern lines to New York City. I'll meet you there. We will go to the headquarters in New York and receive the guns for the uprising. They will be in crates marked "Religious books for Sabbath School: Southern Indiana.""

"You'll meet me there?"

"Or even go with you," Mawkins said, licking a drop of suds from his lips.

"You do not trust me?"

"Two conspirators are better than one. We counter-check each other. We'll accompany the guns on the train back and bring them to the livery stable in Vincennes." He pulled out a cigarette. He had been using them, along with the silver toothpick and instead of cigars to show his important status. He could not be open about the halls of power he now trod, but he had his subtle ways of asserting it.

"And when will the guns be needed?"

"They will stay hidden at the livery stable until—a certain time. This summer. When the time is ripe and the final orders given, the troops Hines commands will enter secretly and free the Southern prisoners at Camp Douglas in Chicago. It will be the signal for other uprisings and then—but enough of the details." He took out a match and struck it against the rough table. Zach thought it was probably intended as a symbol, but—it did not light.

"Well, I hope things go better for us as we try to fan the Northwest into flame," Zach said with a half-indifferent frown. Ridiculous scheme, desperate. And yet the Confederate government believed in it enough to back it with $90,000 in gold. It might be their last, best chance. It had some elements of risk, of adventure. He had always liked risk and adventure. Probably that was why he was attracted to the Southern cause in the first place. Defiant, spit-in-the-eye support of the underdog. Support the South because everyone around him was supporting the North. It struck him as an insight, almost a revelation. Was that the only real reason he was willing to risk trial for treason?

Mawkins kept striking the match, finally successfully, against his shoe. Treason? Perhaps, perhaps not, Zach told himself. It depended on who your loyalty was to. Unless you got caught. He had always been good at subterfuge, even lying, when he had to. If nothing mattered, then why not risk everything in a wild, romantic plot? Yes, why not?

He pushed his plate back and watched Mawkins blow cigarette smoke.

"Be ready to go by May 5. Come to Indianapolis and I will have money, tickets and supplies ready for your—our—trip East. I will give you the sealed plans for conspiracy, which you are to keep on your body at all times." He called for the waitress to bring the bill.

When they left the restaurant, they went into a dark, Germantown lane whose only inhabitants were thin cats and slinking dogs. Mawkins reached inside his coat. He took out a pistol and gave it to Zach.

Zach examined it, turned it over, admiring the octagonal barrel.

"Square dragoon pistol. 1857, Colt's," Mawkins said proudly. "I got that in New York. The arms capital of the world, now. It's yours."

"The proud recipient of the gift of the sapphires refused them," Zach said with a mocking grin. "Perhaps she has more sense than I do." He took the pistol and put it in the overnight satchel he was carrying. Then, with a dismissing wave of the hand to Mawkins, he turned to walk to the railroad station. He was catching the cars to the Ohio River and the steamboat south.

Two weeks later a rented rig jolted down a muddy road outside Memphis. Althea Dugger, at the reins, trotted the horse on the brief stretch of dried road and fumed and fretted when the potholes and sloughs forced her to let the horse pick his way through. Mist rose from the road and the April night was warm and breathless.

"You're going so fast you're making me sick with your jolting, Mama," Delia complained. She had had a touch of what her mother insisted must be the "epizootic" influenza, and this was the first day she'd been up. "Why do we have to rush so? The house will still be there."

"Ah, Delia, I can't wait to cast my eyes on it. I spent so many hours in General Washburne's office trying to get it back."

"You could charm a cat off a roof or a king off his throne, Mama," Delia said, smiling. She looked out the side curtains. "It's beautiful tonight with the mist rising from the hollows. The sun will be setting in a few minutes."

"Yes, I used to love to take my horse out at this time of night. I'd put on Pa's trousers, saddle the mare myself and ride, ride to who knows where on this very road. Then I'd thunder back, trying to beat the darkness.

"The darkness is hard to beat," Delia said a little sadly. Lately, since Zach had returned and with this "epizootic" sickness, her spirits were down. Her mother nagged, begged and wheedled until the general had revoked the confiscation order on Fairchance. The lawyers arranged the deeds her father had sent, and the plantation belonged to her, Althea Dugger!

Zach had been busy, meeting merchants to whom Mr. Thomas Jefferson Brooks had given him introductions, being sure the Yankee authorities knew he intended to sell the southern Indiana peaches and pears for consumption right in Memphis, not further down in the Confederate held-territory. Delia had only seen him at suppers, where they managed civility.

Now, today, the order had come through and her mother had rented a rig. Fairchance! Now it was Althea Dugger's and, of course, eventually her father's, again. "I have the key right here," Althea said, like a child in her excitement. "We'll go in and look at it this very night. Of course you saw it as a child, but it has been years—oh, it will be dusty. Myrtle Jean has not been allowed up there since the confiscation, but she is in the neighborhood. We'll call round to get her after we get through checking it, dust the piano, sweep those beautiful floors. The fields will grow for the Northern army, but when the war is done, it will be ours! Get up there, you lazy mare!"

Delia tried to hold on. Trees flashed by with streaks of clouds and the setting sun between them. When the horse tired, they slowed the pace, and her mother began to speak again in that same excited voice. "We will all get on the steamboat and go to Uncle's house in Mississippi and I will say, 'Papa, here is the key to Fairchance. I have saved it for you, through all this awful war. You can go back home.' "

Delia looked at her mother's determined face. "Why is it always 'Papa' you speak of, Mama? Why not your mother?" Delia asked curiously.

"Well, she is there, of course, and I do speak of her." The question seemed to irritate her mother a trifle. "Mother is sickly, has been for many years. In fact," she let the worry in her voice show, "the last letter from papa in Mississippi said she is failing. They are seriously worried. Now, what was I saying? Oh, yes. I will take the key and tell Papa that I have saved the house for him.''

They were passing a field with the traces of last year's sorghum crop. Across it they could see the sun, a giant, orange ball floating on the edge of the horizon in the late April evening.

Althea continued. ''I have always thought, all through this, that if we could just save the house, no matter what happened, everything would be all right. Even if—God forbid—the war was lost, if Fairchance was here for them, all would not be lost.''

Delia did not answer. The numbness of spirit she had felt lately dulled her responses, like the heavy mist that was coming at them in clouds from ahead, in the low parts of the bottomland.

''The North was factories and railroads and lots else,'' Althea went on. ''But the South never was more than farms, wonderful farms with lovely homes on them. The plantations. If these houses remain when it is all over, then the South will be alive, but if not—''

Then something happened, and as Delia remembered it later, her heart jumped into her very throat. From around the bend ahead of them came a thundering horseback rider wrapped in a great mantle and heavy felt hat. He galloped past, startling their own horse by the fury of his pace, then reined. Her mother uneasily began to trot the horse again, into the clouds of mist. The rider turned, and his horse began to keep pace with them, exact pace, so that they had an odd feeling of being suspended in some sort of frightening, tandem dream-ride. Into Delia's mind flashed the vision of the horse of the Apocalypse with its grim rider. The weakness and sickness of the last few days gripped her stomach, sending waves of nausea through her, and she tried not to look at the man; her mother whipped their horse but the rider only whipped his beast forward, too. Gradually curiosity overcame fear; Delia wheeled about to look at the man, but found his face was turned from them, the hat and the deepening mist obscuring a full view. He was black, that she could see, a frantic, frightening black man galloping with them into—what? For what horrible purpose? When he started to turn towards her, Delia screamed.

Then, without warning, he stopped, letting them go racing on through the increasing obscurity.

''God in heaven! How awful that was! There, there, girl,'' her mother shouted, trying to calm the horse and slow her a bit. ''We are almost home.'' She turned her head. There were hoofbeats, again, on the road behind. ''It must be that same black demon!'' Althea screamed. Now both of them were deeply frightened. She leaned forward to apply the whip to the horse.

The rider came alongside. But this face was not black; in the dying light, through the mist, Delia could see Zach's face, intense, waving at them to slow and stop. They reined the horse; he brought his own around.

"Major Bachelder sent me. Jonas, the slave from Fairchance"— He was panting, his chest heaving, and he had to gulp for air. "He's escaped, with two others."

"Jonas! Of course," her mother said. Delia put her hand on her mother's arm in frightful recognition. The horseman of the Apocalypse had been her mother's former slave.

"Did you see a black man on the road? We encountered him; he frightened us! It must have been Jonas!" Althea shouted.

"No, no one," Zach told them. "He must have taken one of the side roads into the swamp."

"We'll tell them to send a search party when we return. This evening mist is as thick as cotton." They all looked into it, then their eyes went skyward, at a trail mounting from over the next hill.

"Mother, that's not mist, it's smoke! If the wind had been right, we would have smelled it before!"

"My God, no!" Althea screamed, looking at the direction of the smoke. "He's set fire to Fairchance!"

It took over an hour for a plantation house that had been standing thirty years to burn to the ground. Flames were licking out windows when they came up and it seemed only minutes before the roof caved in. The sounds were awful, torture in themselves: the blended roar of wind and flame, one giant, orgiastic, continuing rush; the ominous crackling as finishes on fine mahogany took flame, the thunder of a floor giving way, taking all the bedroom furniture of a lifetime down into a maelstrom—even the bizarre music of the piano strings crashing and banging into the cellar.

"Tinder dry," Althea murmured, her mind frozen, her hand clutching Zach's arm.

"Mama, I'm scared that that insane Negro will return," Delia said finally, after the flames had assuaged the worst of their voracious appetite and subsided into a quiet, smoky licking of what was left.

"Yes. She is right. We must go," Zach murmured.

"Back to the hotel." Althea spoke like an automaton.

"No, from this town. As soon as possible," Zach said. "With this man loose, your life is in danger." Althea turned her head and looked dully at him as if she did not comprehend.

"Bachelder says the Negro threatened you," Zach said. "I will see you to your uncle in Mississippi. I have that much time. Your father is there.''

"Yes. We must go. Go—'' Slowly they led her away, through choking smoke she did not even seem to be aware of.

Late that night on the deck of the steamboat going downriver, Zach and Delia spoke together, really talked to each other for the first time in weeks.

"She is asleep. I wonder she didn't cry,'' Zach said.

"She never cries. It's a rule with her. I have never seen her weep. Yet, she is shaken even more than she was at my father's death.''

"I brought her a letter from the front, from Cal. What did he say?'' Zach wanted to know.

"That they are preparing to meet a great offensive from the North. General Lee is calling in troops from far-flung places. Any day now. Perhaps at this moment, they may be marching. Calhoun said he would not write until he could cover himself with glory. For me.''

"For you. Quite an obligation,'' Zach said.

Silently they stood at the rail, watching the dark waters. On them the moon traced reflections of hooded trees from the shore and shadows of the fire-breathing smokestacks above them.

"You haven't told me what you were doing back in Indiana,'' Delia said.

Zach looked at her warily, shrugged, and told of the meeting with Mawkins.

"And I suppose none of that gold will get into pockets of the conspirators,'' Delia said skeptically. Zach shrugged again, this time slightly, with one shoulder.

"And that not a cent of it will get into your pocket.''

"What of it? As Mawkins says, what is war for but to profit from?'' The steamship's warning horn sounded hollowly across the darkened waters, and a flare went up, fanning into a falling umbrella of fireworks. They were rounding a bend.

"Do you believe that?'' Delia wanted to know.

"What else is there to think?'' She stared into his face, so familiar, so contradictory, and knew at that moment that she loved him deeply and always would, and that the love had little to do with bodies. She had been lying to herself about it, and now it felt as good as this crisp, night air to tell herself the truth.

A long moment went by as another steamboat, sparks flying from three chimneys, passed them, sending waves against their side. In the illumination from the chimneys you could see the wheelhouse, with its picture of a jaunty General McClellan.

"Zach, I'm expecting a child,'' she said, simply.

He stood very still, almost as if he had not heard her correctly.

"Yes, it is true. I had to wait to be sure, and now I am." There, she had told him. The suspicion, then finally the certainty, that had been chewing on her for these past weeks was out and shared by the person who needed to know it.

His reaction was unexpected. He pounded his hand on the railing and shook his head like a horse.

"You're happy," she said, without smiling.

"Of course," he said, breathlessly. "I have asked you to marry me so often."

She laughed comfortably. The events of the day had wearied her so that all that remained was a little reason and humor. "I'm not going to marry you."

"Of course you will," he said quickly.

"No," she said, again with easiness. "What made you think I would?"

Confusion had replaced the usual cynicism in his eyes. "Well, everything. What else would I think? You are having our child. Conceived, I suppose, among my ancestors' papers. Surely—you wouldn't—do anything else—would you?" He looked in her in complete puzzlement. "Find somebody else? Have a—bastard?" He could hardly get the word out. It was mildly satisfying to see him so ill at ease, she told herself. She had wondered a hundred times what he would do when she told him.

"Oh, I see," he said, some of the old ease returning to his manner. "You want me to do it properly. Get down on my knee." He did. "Miss Delia, will you marry me? As soon as possible? So our child will have a name and you will be spared the ignominy of bearing a child out of wedlock—oh, guess I shouldn't have said that." He rose, nervously took a cigar out of his pocket, played with the seal, but did not attempt to light it.

"Relax, Zach. I said I would never marry you and I mean it."

"You'll—do what with the child?" he asked, beginning to be a little piqued. She was probably playing some sort of game.

This time it was Delia who was confused. It was easy enough up to now, but at this point—"I'll probably stay in Mississippi. Keep the child and claim a soldier husband was killed in the war. Or give it up." She turned away. Tears were coming to her eyes, even though she had sworn they would not. "No, I could never give up the child of my body." She began to sob.

"Delia, I love you," Zach said, all pretension aside. "You are the only good thing in my life. I would die for you." He took her in his arms and she did not resist. He gently covered her face with kisses. Finally, though, she pulled back, her face wet with unwelcome tears, and held him at arms' length. "Zach, one final time. I shall never, never, marry you. Not if you were the last person on earth."

"Why?" was all he whispered.

She breathed deeply, once, and then she said, determinedly, "Because you are bad. Selfish. You are not at all a good person." He turned his head away, looking down angrily at the deck.

She continued, with intensity. "I have seen you send your brother off to die with a lie on your lips, shoot a man in cold blood, break an oath of honor to my mother, take up with the greatest scoundrels on this earth—" He did not look at her but neither did he protest. Finger-shaped clouds spread themselves across the moon, throwing the boat into dimness.

Delia shook her head. "And this latest thing—the Great Conspiracy." She laughed ruefully. "Riding about in disguise, evading soldiers with guns, all so you can loose thousands of rabid, hateful prisoners to wreak revenge on the farms of the Northwest."

Zach did protest now. "It's not going to—"

She interrupted. "Say no more. I've had over a month to think about this, and I am absolutely sure. We will take my mother to Mississippi, I will decide what to do with this child, and you will leave and go on your escapade. Then, I never want to see you again as long as I live."

The moon came out from under its tent of clouds.

"You hate me," Zach said finally. "I never knew that."

"No," she said, turning her head to the water. "I love you. Many women fall in love with bounders and even live their lives with them, but I am not going to marry mine. I will not have my child brought up with Zach Scott as its father!"

"You would rather bear a bastard than be my wife?"

"That's right. And now I am going to bed. I am ill a lot these days." Gathering her skirts, she made her way to her stateroom. She desperately needed a couple of hours of rest.

For a long time, Zach Scott stood watching the steamboat cut the still waters, sending ripples from the prow and stern which washed the shore with small, silent waves.

*   *   *   *

John McClure readied his haversack for the Spring offensive which was about to begin for the Northern army.

"Letter for you, Whiteskin," a voice said. Sergeant Walter McClure delivered the mail, flipping a letter in the direction of his distant cousin.

John McClure let the letter fall onto his shoe and then picked it up when Walter had gone whistling down the lane. He did not even want to be on the other end of a piece of paper this pretended, or possibly even real relative of his held. They only managed to avoid outright conflict by not speaking or having anything to do with each other.

McClure called Tommy Thompson over. "It's a letter from Mary Jane," he said. "I'll read it to you."

Thompson was eating peanut brittle his mother had sent him. "I have been meanin' to write to her. When we get home, I sure am goin' to come a-callin'." He looked over McClure's shoulder and read as his friend read.

Dear John

As alwuz excuse the printin. We are gettin ready to do the hog killin. It is a dirty greazy job but it must be done. When it is Aunt Jewell is goin to take me and Bob into the bank. He is goin to get some of his inheritans out to go on the Oregun Trale. I am goin to get us a little house started, like you and I have talked about. I have talked to Mr. Ephremson the carpenter and he can have it done by fall. I am glad all this is out in the open now, not just in yours and my letters.

John, I yearn to be a little fambly, just us. Well, you will get married some day but until then we will have it. I can remmber Pa and Ma so well in our house in Orange County that used to be Miz Poore's. They was so in love. I remember Papa Alfred puttin my head on his knee, Mama nursin' Annie in a big chair and you and Bob playin in the old potato hole. Papa had a nice big book he was showin' me pitchers in. One was of a collie dog.

I am gettin' things for the house. Not exactly like goin' to housekeepin but almost. I have in mind a good cookstove and a copper teapot. A big chair with chintz on it. I am piecin comforters and Aunt Jewell even says she will give us sheets. She don't seem to mind as much as I thought or maybe she cares a lot for us. I guess I never doubted that. I tole Grandma Catherine and she is givin us the McClure grandfather clock. Was Great-grandpa George's. Maybe I can even find a book with a collie dog in it.

I am only joshin you. Now, John, we read in the Vincennes Western Sun that you are goin for a big battle to get to Richmond. Grant is your new general and they call him "United States Grant never fails." If that is so, you will fight hard. Now John, please, please, take care of yourself so you can come home and we can have the fambly and the nice new house on the Dan'l McClure acers that are ours. We have all waited so long. And when you do I promise we will have a reyounion party and Both Grandma Catherine and Aunt Jewell will be there. No spoofin. It is not impossible, though it seems so. After all, they are both McClures. So come home safe to us no matter what! I can hardly wait.

P.S. Miz Paden the wife of the minister is very ill. She has got consumption and some folks say Annie has put her in her death bed by the shenannigans I wrote you of. But that is ridickulous.

Your loving sister
Mary Jane McClure

P.P.S. I am sorry to say that word has just come that Miz Paden has passed from this life. Be so, so careful John. You have made it this far.

John McClure finished reading the letter and cleared his throat. Then he turned his head and walked away. Thompson watched him go, embarrassed. Sometimes, he told himself, it was best to read letters before you shared 'em with your friends. Sometimes they said too much and made you too upset before your friends.

Still, when he got home, was it about a month now? he would look up Mary Jane first thing out. A tender-hearted girl like that would make a good wife. One that was as tender-hearted as that would love you all your life.

"We cross the Rapidan tomorrow," Beem said to Houghton. They were looking closely at a map of the area around Culpeper Court House and the valleys of the Rapidan.

"Eight A.M., Colonel Coons said."

"We will miss Lieutenant Colonel Cavins," Beem answered, looking up from the map. "But the prison authority needed him to command, I guess."

"Yes, Cavins," Houghton agreed. "Not to mention the rest. Van Dyke and Harrow are at Chattanooga, Kimball in Arkansas, Brooks back home from the Eightieth Indiana, and of course Bo Reilly, Ham Mitchell, Lunday, Norris—and all the rest of the dead—you name them, and the wounded in five or six hospitals. We have two hundred people left in the Fourteenth."

"Two-hundred good people. A skeleton regiment."

"Odd name, skeleton regiment. At least they are still brigading us as the Gibraltar Brigade, with Carroll. Eighth and Fourth Ohio, Seventh West Virginia. McClellan's, Burnside's, Hookers, Meade's—now Grant's workhorse unit."

"And Landon is back. He's turning into a pretty fair soldier," Beem conceded grudgingly.

Houghton's pencil roved around the map. "Landon and lots of others. War is a giant blast furnace. You throw in the crudest raw materials and after a good deal of heat, steel comes and the slag goes out the bottom." He touched spots in Virginia on the map. "Where will we light?"

Beem was not listening. He was thinking of their chances in battle. "Brigaded with six other veteran regiments. It should still work. They will probably still give us the workhorse duty. Worn-out nag, but it'll still run." Beem smiled a little grimly.

Houghton put his pencil down on a dot. Beem looked over his shoulder. "Across to Chancellorsville. Again?" he wanted to know.

"Well, that's what lies in the path. And beyond it, Jordan," Houghton commented, in a quiet, dry voice.

"The Wilderness. We could not fight there. It is a giant bramble patch."

"We may have to. I still call it Jordan." Houghton's look was pained. "I pray we may all cross it and come back, one more time. Just one more time."

Beem looked at Houghton, into the eyes of a man he had shared more with than anyone on earth could ever share over four long, agonizing years, and he said, "Will, I thank God for the opportunity of knowing you, and pray I may for years to come. When this is done, we will meet and toast the victory as veterans."

Houghton nodded, smiling a little. "In water, in your case, David."

"Do you still think," Beem continued, "that we still carry them, all of the dead, with us in a way when we go into the middle of it all?"

"Mitchell, Reilly, Lunday, McCord, Craig, Welch, Norris," Houghton said, folding up the map. "Say it like a litany. And the names of all the rest you can remember. Say it when you order the men to drop their shelter tents and overcoats tomorrow and advance with only guns and ammunition. Say it when we come to Chancellorsville again and see the battlefield there. Cross Jordan with their names on your lips. Never, never forget."

"I won't, Will, I won't," David Beem promised. "Never."

Late April, Early May, 1864

Chapter Twenty

Althea Dugger sat on the porch of her uncle's long veranda in Amite County, Mississippi. Spanish moss hung from live oak trees, and the air was hot and oppressive. Looking at the limbs around the porch, she thought, "Like me. Something hanging on my limbs, too, this last month. But I will not be choked out. No, not at all."

First there was the fire, then, when they finally got to Mississippi, the news that her mother had taken a turn for the worst, and died of apoplectic stroke two days before she arrived. She had even been too late for the burial. She visited the tomb in the family burial plot down by the bayou, looked at its stone scrolls and rusty iron grate. Mama had been lain in a tomb with people she did not know, her husband's brother's family, in an exotic land where everything seemed too rank, too lush, and where strange animals lurked.

Althea sighed. Everyone in the Mississippi plantation house had acted odd, strangely off-key when they spoke about the funeral. Delia had asked why they seemed distant about the death, and Althea could say nothing, except that she had loved Mama, and Mama had been sickly and had her problems for a long time.

Zach Scott hung about, strangely dispirited, saying every day he would be going back up north soon and yet not leaving. And then there was Papa. What to do about him?

Frank Fryerson was despondent, of course, about Mama, but there was an edge of relief, or was it resignation, to his mourning. She had been ill a long time and there was no longer anything to take her home to now, anyway. And, though it shamed and bothered Althea to think of it, Mama had required nursing care for over a year and much of the measuring out of spoons of medicine and going to get cups of beef tea had fallen on Papa, who, of course, was not well either. He was sad, but freer than he had been in a while.

Neither was her father devastated by the loss of Fairchance, not helpless and old in the face of irreversible disaster. It was not as she had expected, had visualized in these years since she had been unable to see him. No, he wasn't a helpless invalid, waiting for his brave little daughter to save Fairchance. He was fine—well, enduring, anyway. The old, rugged, red-haired man did walk with a cane, slowly, work for breath now and then, and take foxglove infusion for pain in his heart, but he was the same old sturdy stump of a frontier gentleman. He seemed to pride himself on being stalwart, intrepid in the face of the devastation of his wife's death. He was, of course, personally distant from her, his own daughter, Althea. But then, the Fryersons never were the sort of family who hugged and kissed each other. Leave that to Addie and her kin, all that smothering billing and cooing.

And Fairchance? Her father had accepted the news she brought, nodding, seemingly without emotion. "We still have the land?" was all that he asked.

"Yes," she told him.

"Then that is enough," he said, and did not bring it up again.

Had she imagined his attachment? Not really known her father after all these years of separation? Or was he dulled, inured, by the problems of old age and the war. She decided it was probably that.

So she visited with her uncle Bartie Fryerson, a frailer, more indecisive version of her father. Bartie had made his fortune by coming west a few years earlier than her father, grown cotton on thousands of acres and recently had grown rice to feed Confederate troops until after Vicksburg, when the area finally fell to the Yankees.

And Althea watched, as she had years before on an earlier visit, the quiet household management of the old Negro woman who really ran the premises, Mavety.

Mavety was one of the most unusual women Althea had ever known. She stood almost six feet tall, had an oil-black complexion, completely unwrinkled, with short, fuzzy hair she cut to make a halo around her face. Her fierce eyes fixed themselves on you as if to know your soul, and she had a rare, wide smile.

"Where did she come from?" Delia wanted to know the second day they were there, as they were all trying to rebound from their grief over Althea's mother's passing. They were sitting in the parlor, sipping cool drinks. Frank Fryerson was upstairs, resting in the mid-day heat.

"Mavety's from the West Indies, I believe," Althea answered. "I think Uncle Bartie bought her when she was a young woman. He was a relatively young man at the time, had just come from North Carolina and decided to live in the Mississippi country."

"She has an accent. Is it French?"

"Yes. They speak French in Haiti."

"Isn't that where they practice black arts? Voodoo?" Delia pretended to be intrigued. It gave her something to talk about, anyway. She needed now, badly, to tell her mother about the child that was growing inside her, but she had promised Zach that she would not do so until he went north. And that, it seemed, he was not quite ready to do. Perhaps he thought she would change her mind as time passed. Well, she was not going to. No, not at all, and she needed to speak to him tonight, this very night. He must leave, tomorrow. She must make plans. She put her hand to her head and sighed, wearily.

Her mother was talking about voodoo. Some of the slaves here practiced it when her uncle was not around, although they thought of themselves as good Catholics. She had read up on it some after her last visit—on and on her mother rattled.

Mother did talk a lot, rarely about really important things in people's lives. She steered clear of how people felt, about how things went wrong and people hurt. She was always as chipper as a canary. It was going to be hard to tell her about the baby.

Her mother stopped in mid-sentence. "Are you still feeling ill from that epizootic? We will have to ask Mavety to give you some tonic. She's very good with herbs." Then, without even seeming to care for an answer, she went in to see about dinner.

A hundred aromatic smells drifted in the air. First roses were in bloom in the garden outside the house, and their sweet odor filled the night. Zach and Delia sat in a gazebo on a hill where a breeze refreshed the air and was supposed to keep off mosquitoes. Still, at this time of year, mosquitoes were awful in the bayou country, and there was cloth netting tacked up around the gazebo.

"Tomorrow. You will go tomorrow," Delia said. It was a command.

"I can't leave you like this," Zach insisted. "I feel like my future is on a chopping block, like a turkey's head. The axe hasn't fallen, but my head is just lying there, waiting." He was smoking one of the cigarettes Mawkins had introduced him to.

"I am telling Mama tomorrow. You had better be gone when I do."

"You do not need to tell me that." He looked up, breathing smoke coolly out of his nose. He had been drinking rum drinks since supper, and now held one in his hand. "What is that noise?"

Delia listened. "Drums. Off there in the lowlands. Do you smell smoke?"

"Yes. There's a bonfire down there. I can hear voices, singing."

"Ugh," Delia shivered. "Do you suppose the workers are having a voodoo ceremony? While my uncle is gone to Natchez on business?"

Zach rose and put down his drink, looking deeper into the darkness. "I don't know, but I am going to find out."

Delia put her hand on his sleeve. "No, Zach, no. We have had enough trouble as it is around here. And anyway—" She did not finish.

"You don't want me to get hurt? Is it that, my dear love?" His tone was strident. She opened the door of the gazebo and indignantly began to walk to the mansion house.

"Nothing," he thought. "Not even an answer to my torment. She is so indifferent to me now she will not even argue." He threw the cigarette on the floor of the gazebo, then ground it out, cursing a string of oaths. He went to the doorpost and hung on it, swaying, pushing on it as if he would uproot it until his immediate anger was spent. Sweat began to trickle down his face. He pulled up his shirt collar against the insects and began to walk towards the eerie noise he heard coming from deep in the woods.

Insects crowded his face, his neck; he hiked up his collar and let them swarm on his hair. Here was a path of some sort, going in the right direction. Earlier it had rained but now, under huge trees and by the light of a half moon, he stumbled down the path, tripping on vines that almost blocked the way every few feet. It was difficult going, partly because, as he conceded, he was about half-drunk. He stepped over fallen logs, was startled by miniature spots of lights in a tree and found them to be a possum with her children. He was drawing nearer the voices.

"Why are you going down this path to whatever this stupid ceremony is?" he asked himself. Nothing, nothing, mattered and so why should this? "Well," he answered, "it may pass an hour." What they were doing could not be as bad, as evil, as what was passing in his life, had passed since he was a child. All, all of his own doing. And without hope.

The drums beat louder, intensifying. Whatever was going on was reaching a crescendo. Then, suddenly he came into the edge of the circle. Black families from the plantation were standing about, talking and laughing. Two men were beating a rhythm with the palms of their hands on tin nail drums turned upside down. He looked at familiar faces he had seen waiting the table, working in the rice fields. They saw him and raised hands in salute. Nothing ominous here. Some sort of Halloween breakdown party, it seemed to be. It had the same spirit. There were children here, and mothers, wearing red dresses and red bandannas. Rum bottles were going around, and apparently had been for quite a while. Many were tipsy. He took out another cigarette and lit it.

There was Ephraim, a wiry, middle-aged man who was one of the field-hands he had seen before. "O-goo, O-goo, come to me," he was yelling. Several men picked Ephraim up. They carried him to a sort of mud pit, a trough that had evidently been beaten by many bare feet at the side of the clearing where the fire was and dumped him down. He fell into the mud, but instead of getting up, he wallowed around, calling "O-goo, O-goo." Then he stood up straight, covered with mud. His eyes were glazed.

"Oh, O-goo, ride the horse," the others cried, some laughing, some half-fearful. The bottle continued to make its way around. Women brought their children into the circle and Ephraim began to walk around, touching them with a muddy finger.

There was a feverish, demented look in Ephraim's eyes as he walked around that circle. He looked like—he must have thought he was possessed. By who? O-goo, whoever in the hell that was. Zach took the cigarette out of his mouth and stared at him. "Touch me, St. James," the cook of the house called, pulling at a crucifix around her neck. "I have the goiter and it no go way." Ephraim-O-goo, put a muddy finger on the small lump on the woman's neck.

Others murmured, "St. James, my father is far away. I want to see him." "O-goo, I love a man on the next plantation. He go with Yankees to Natchez when they raid these parts. Bring him back." Ephriam-O-goo touched. Soon he began touching harder, smearing. People began to laugh in a rum-soaked way, pulling back. He reached for them, began to hug, to yell in a funny way that made them laugh. "It's like pin the tail on the donkey now. Nothing forbidding about these rites," Zach thought. "Not at all what people think."

Then, laughing, the mothers began to drop their children in the mud, rolling them about, praying for blessing. "Ah, St. James, pray for us, O-goo, come to us." "O-goo from Voodoo, and St. James, the Catholic saint. They've covered themselves on both fronts," Zach thought coolly. The children ran around like muddy wraiths, laughing, trying to touch people. Some of the more drunk staggered around, their friends pulling them back from the fire.

Then a group of three or four who knew the visitor standing at the back of the group began whispering among themselves. They slapped their knees, screamed with laughter and before Zach knew it they had upended him and were carrying him to the mud. A gasp went up from some of the women. "Ah, to take the white massa that way, to disrespect the massa's friend—" But it was too late. Zach was in the mud.

"Goddamned nigger breakdown. Whoever thought they were smarter than apes was wrong." He lay in the mud, trying to wipe his eyes, but failed. "Can't see, can't smell—son-of-a-bitch." The fire, there, he could see but it was spinning around. He felt terrible. Mud in his mouth, nausea. He pulled himself to a sitting position, felt terrible pain in all his joints, rubbed his eyes again.

Then, panting, looking into the fire as all watched, his vision began to clear. Only what he saw wasn't the same scene, it was something else. What in the name of God, or the Devil—he tried to stand but could not move an inch. He had to look at what was before him, reading it as one looked at a play on the stage.

An eerie moon rode the sky. Bitterns made their odd cries somewhere far off. He seemed to be seeing another voodoo ceremony, but down by the river, and in another time. The women's clothes were from a period at least a hundred years ago. But it was similar—the same songs, chants, circle dances went on. But then, from up the river, canoes seemed to be landing. He watched red men, Choctaws from somewhere north get out, walk toward the circle. They spoke, and a Frenchman with them translated.

Zach sat transfixed. He had no option. His limbs were bound to the earth. In some way he could understand the French they spoke. There was to be an Indian uprising, and they were asking the slaves on this plantation to join with them, to murder all the whites, move with them and take—was it New Orleans?

One of the slaves seemed to go into a trance. He pranced about in affirmation, while all the rest sang a weird song. But his trance was not complete; as this slave leader came near Zach, the moon came out full bright and caught the glitter of Zach's eyes.

The huge man came to Zach and Zach could see him as clearly as day. He reached over and grabbed Zach's shoulders, and Zach looked deeply into his eyes. Lusts, blood hates and hideous ecstasies of dark evil seemed to swim there. His lips made words Zach could understand, though there was no sound. "You are mine," he said, and the sepulchral words resounded in Zach's brain, petrifying him.

But suddenly he grew angry. "You are mine"—what in hell did the son-of-a-bitch in this stupid delirium hallucination or whatever it was mean? Mine, as evil as he was, as black and depraved and ugly as sin? "I'm not yours. I'm nobody's. Never have been, except my own. Get away, get away, you bastard!" He pushed against the hands on his shoulders with a might he never knew he had and then he screamed, loud, willing all the anguish and pain deep in his soul to the surface in protest.

He opened his eyes to the jovial, tipsy scene he was in at first. The woman Mavety stood before him, staring into his eyes with deep curiosity. She gave him a hand and he stood unsteadily and stalked out of the mud.

"Two more days, Delia, just two more. I must get back but—something is happening and I don't understand it." Zach had been up all night, cleaning himself, sweating in the heat of the night, pacing about smoking, and now he had found her wandering in a dressing gown on the veranda as the first rays of dawn came. When she wanted to know what he meant about things happening, he could not tell her, except that he had gone to the voodoo ceremony, that he was upset, and that he could not leave without putting himself back together.

"I am going out of your life. I ask two more days. Is that too much to ask? After all," he said in a low voice, "the child is half mine, too."

"You are right," Delia finally said, watching the pink dawn streak the sky above the flower beds and camellia bushes. "Today and tonight. That much I'll give you. But if you ask for more, so help me, Zach, I'll have you carted away. I've got to plan my own life."

Breathing a sigh of relief, Zach finally threw himself on his bed as the sun rose, and slept till noon. When he came down, dishevelled and hollow-eyed, Althea looked at him coolly. "You keep odd hours," she said. She was reading to her uncle and her father from *Harper's Magazine*.

Then, in a kinder tone. "I have some news for you, and I'm afraid, like all the rest we have had in the last month, it is not good."

Zach's head ached. He did not think he could stand any piece of news, let alone bad. Althea put down the magazine and reached into her pocketbook. The black woman Mavety moved noiselessly around the room with glasses of port wine on a little tray. Where did they get that? Zach wondered in spite of himself. Uncle Addison and Aunt Elba must have made it here at least once in reality. Probably sold them the wine at twice the value, even in Natchez.

"My sister Addie writes us from Louisville. She is hoping to locate you. You know that Dora, my niece, is a nurse in the Confederate army at Richmond." Zach accepted a glass of the port wine from Mavety, looking up at her with a pain in his eyes that he did not try to conceal. The black woman did not give any sign she even knew who he was.

"Dora has been able to bring some comfort to your brother in the prison there," Althea went on, putting on her spectacles so she could read the letter better.

"His brother is in the prison, Althy?" her father wanted to know.

"Yes, Papa. Castle Thunder they call it. For political prisoners. They are keeping him to exchange for an important Yankee officer."

"But the papers say the North is no longer exchanging any prisoners at all. It is a part of their starvation policy, to bring us to our knees," the old man said.

Althea looked at her uncle; he nodded affirmation. "Ah, then I understand her fear," said Althea, perusing the letter. "Dora says Jacob Joe is poorly. His health is bad."

Zach set his glass on a little table and listened in spite of himself.

"He weighs little more than a hundred pounds and has had a series of complaints through the winter. Now varioloid is sweeping the prisons—"

"Varioloid," asked Althea's father, "Now, is that like scarlatina?"

"No, Frank," his brother said in his rather quaky voice. "Varioloid is a mild form of smallpox. But if Mr. Scott has been poorly, it would not do him well to catch it. I have seen fatalities in weak constitutions."

"Bartie, did you know that Jenner did not discover the smallpox vaccination?" Althea's father asked. He and his brother were antiquarians, collectors of often insignificant bits of information about history. They used it to amuse themselves and taunt each other when they were bored or irritated.

"No? Who then? May I have more wine, please Mavety?"

"Cotton Mather's slave. A black person. It is in *Harper's*. The slave said in Africa they pricked the arms of children and gave them a little smallpox."

"Do tell! A nigra. What do you think of that?" Bartie Fryerson remarked wonderingly. Althea looked at them, as if awaiting permission to go on with the letter.

"Go on, please, Mrs. Dugger," Zach said, sipping his wine.

"The long and short of it is that Dora is terribly worried. She is taking him to the hospital, but he can only stay a week. Then by the new rules of the Confederate prison service, he must return and stay in the prison except for emergencies. She is afraid that with his weakened constitution, he will—"

"Yes, Mrs. Dugger," Zach said, leaning forward.

"He will be unable to ward off disease and will die within the month. He begs us to try everything we know to have him freed from the Northern side. Do anything, she says." Althea looked up and took off her spectacles.

"It would appear, Althy, that not only is my granddaughter Dora a good nurse, but she has also gone sweet on a Yankee prisoner," Frank Fryerson chuckled.

"It would appear so," Althea said, pondering. Her mind returned to the time in Louisville, when Dora read a letter from Jacob Joe and for an instant pure love had flashed in her eyes.

"Is there any way to get him traded and out of there?" Frank Fryerson wanted to know.

"I don't know," Althea murmured. "We are probably not the people to know that, Southern sympathizers that we are."

"Jake. Failing fast," Zach said hollowly from his chair. He went to Althea and wordlessly took the letter, then excused himself to take it to his room, where he read it twice and then fell asleep again in deeper despair than he had been the night before.

He rose with the moon coming through his window and staggered out to the slave quarters. He did not know why, but he must find Mavety. Three or four cabins were near the house, cabins for the house "hands," not the slaves. Not any more. He poked his head through the door of the first one. No, not this one. There was Ephraim, lying on a pallet, his wife cooking cabbage in a pot over the fireplace. He had as much of a mud hangover as Zach did. What in the hell was in that mud, anyway?

"Hallucination, that's what it was," he thought, stumbling and falling, then picking himself up. Yes, it could have been that. He had heard of people lying in poppy fields and going out of their heads. And there were things Mexicans ate, mushrooms, that made them hear bells and see saints. Perhaps there had been something in the mud. It certainly hadn't been the rum; he had been clear-headed enough when he hit the goddamned mud. Perhaps Mavety would tell him something about it. He reached the next cabin and looked inside.

Not this one. There were young children chasing each other in front of it, nor the next one, with a lone old man in it, washing stockings in a washtub. But the fourth cabin, there, back of the rest, was on the edge of a ravine. Its door was shut, and sweet-smelling smoke rose from the chimney. He knocked. In a moment Mavety's eyes looked out at him. She waved him inside.

The cabin was neat, whitewashed clean. Its only furnishings were a trunk, a fresh-scrubbed table with two chairs, a bed with a beautiful star-patterned quilt on it and a picture of Jesus on the wall. It might be the cabin of any back-country old woman in Indiana.

There was a blazing fire in the fireplace, and yet it did not seem to be hot. Mavety pulled the two chairs in front of it. "Sit down, massa," she said.

"Mavety, I—you saw me last night." He ran his fingers through his hair. "I am trying to understand what went on."

"Put me in mind of what happened in the slough." Her eyes were heavy-lidded, inscrutable.

"It was a vision, I guess. Something in the mud must have drugged me. I saw Indians in canoes and a terrible, huge slave from the olden days who seemed to want to harm me."

"Big slave you say?"

"Yes. But I forget the details." He put his head in his hands. It ached so. From inside him, his voice dragged forth, and it began to say words he didn't feel responsible for. It was as if someone else were saying them. "Mavety, my life is ruined. I am awful, horrible. I have fathered a child, and the mother does not wish to marry me because she says I am an evil man. I think she is right. But I love her more than life itself. Now I hear my brother is in mortal danger, and I am afraid for him. Then there is the matter of this terrible dream, or whatever it was last night. It frightened me, awfully." Am I saying this, Zach wondered? Is this me?

Mavety moved to him. She took his hands with her wrinkled ones, blue veins on black parchment skin. She looked deeply into his eyes for thirty seconds. He did not blanch.

"Massa, you are in pain of the spirit. I reads it in your eyes, and it touches me down in my heart." She went to the picture of Jesus and fell on her knees in prayer. Her lips moved; her hands were folded in front of her.

When she rose she went to the fireplace, to a copper pot.

"The vision may be a wisdom vision. I shall try to see as you saw last night, feel as you felt." She took herbs from the pot and threw them onto the fire, where they blazed with a green flame. She sat on the chair, staring into the fire.

One, two minutes passed. The shouts of children outside, the humming of insects, hammered dully in the back of Zach's mind. What was she doing? The fire burned, certainly nothing unusual in that—

"I see as you saw last night a time a hundred years ago or more," she said in an odd voice, as if she were wondering at, considering what she saw. "Not far from here, perchance downriver, but not far. There are two women standing looking at you."

"At me? You mean now?" Zach wondered.

"Do not speak. It vex the spell. I will interpret for you. Guardians stood at the fire last night. First guardian is a young maid, golden-haired, with a crucifix she holds always. The other a missus, long brown locks she has, and a plaintive look."

Zach scarcely breathed. What could it mean?

"The little maid you saw last night came upon the voodoo as you did, but a long spell ago, when it really happen. She is— blood kin—to you, great-grandmother. While she watch, right long time ago, evil man come from the slough, ridden, ridden hard by the spirit from across the sea. The people think he is good spirit, but he is not St. James, he is demon spirit." Her words were drawn out at this point, as if to see was painful.

"Big Emile. That man's name who carry strong spirit." Zach moved forward in interest. Big Emile, wasn't that the name in that letter in the attic? The one from his great-grandmother Marguerite Scott's father, on the plantation near New Orleans? Yes, great-grandmother, that was what Mavety was saying. They were afraid of the voodoo rites then, and the slave insurrection!

"Yes. As girl stands at the slaves' circle at night, Big Emile come that time to her with hate, bad hate. He will kill, kill all those who sleep in the house above, but little maid is not afraid. She call on Christ for help and run. Rouse the house and they chase and get Big Emile, finally he die. But not really, spirit who ride him, evilest spirit of blood and treachery from Africa, he go on and migrate.''

Migrate? Wasn't that what Grandma Jenny had written in his father's diary?

"Spirit go through someone else, I cannot see who, someone bad, and when he dead, come now" she twisted and turned, as if in physical pain, put her hands on her head and shook it as if to be free of something awful— "Come to you."

Suddenly she was herself again, but stared still at the fire. "Massa, the evilest spirit kill your great-grandmother. Possess your uncle, drive your grandma mad. Then it come to you."

"What did it mean," Zach whispered, "last night when that awful hallucination said—in that terrible voice, sounding like it had come from the crypts, 'You are mine.' ''

"Spirit has many parts, like arms, legs, can go from Africa, come from West Indies, still be spirit. Part of the spirit ride you all this while. Part sleep in the mud. When you come there, it see its mirror self and claim its own.''

Zach looked at her in astonishment. He could hardly fathom what was being said to him and the absurdity of it all struck him. That he, unflappable Zach Scott, should be in this Negro cabin, talking to this old woman about voodoo. Still, it had all been so strange—his head began to hurt, and he put it down on his knees.

The woman rose and knelt by him. "Massa, the witnesses of the old time help you for a reason. Stood by your side last night for just a moment. Great grandmother and grandmother, Scott. You shout something last night, important I think. What was it?''

Zach looked up, and he began to laugh, in spite of his splitting headache. "I called O-goo a son-of-a-bitch and told him to get the hell out of there. I said I wasn't his or anybody else's. Never have been.'' He threw his head back and laughed and, surprisingly, so did Mavety, joining him with her own ringing laughter.

Finally, they sat, chuckling. "Massa,'' she said. "You done did the right thing. The very right thing, massa. The spirits ride men but they do not like to be talked back to. It vexes them and justly robs them of their power, too.''

"Does it? Does it, Mavety? Well, if I'm possessed at least I'm a bastard enough to fight back. It takes one to know one.''

"Massa,'' Mavety said, moving to stir the fire, "you have been a very bad man.''

Zach sat a moment without answering. His head felt as if it were floating. He felt as though Mavety was inside his head reading his brain the way some people read handwriting. And she was right; he might as well admit it. The events of the last week or so had peeled off the topmost, superficial layers of his personality and what was left underneath—well, it was just too much trouble to cover it up any more. "Yes, Mavety. I have just about ruined my life. I told myself it doesn't matter, that there is no meaning to anything. And I was right. Right now I might as well be dead or lying in the mud with—whoever that black-hearted ghoul is."

"Would you be better there, massa? Then why did you tell him you weren't his?" She went to the door, opened it, and returned with an armful of logs.

"Here, let me help you," Zach said, rising and carefully criss-crossing logs on the fire. They both sat down and a moment of silence, almost peace, passed between them.

"Massa, you can be free."

"Free? You mean I don't have to—always live like this? Hurting those I love? Betraying my own kin, lying to others and myself? Respected by no one, rejected by the very people I would please?" The fire sputtered and licked about the edges of the new logs. "No, I don't think so, Mavety. I don't think I believe your little ghost tale. I was born bad. So they say."

"No one is born completely bad, Massa," Mavety said. "You have said you loved. Miss Delia, I think"—her eyes were sharp—"and your brother." He gave no sign of affirmation, but neither did he deny.

"Whoever has one grain of love, say voodoo wise men, has the seed of God in him. And whoever has that grain of good can throw off any spirit if he wish." She smiled fully, a wide smile with lips that stretched half across the face.

"Throw off the rottenness? Well, maybe not. It may be permanent. Where does badness come from?" Zach demanded. "Do we inherit it? Does a drunk father spawn drunken sons? Is it in the blood? Or do the homes we come from, the jealousy"— here he stopped—" or mistreatment if it is there, cause the ill? Does God, if he exists, send badness to try us? Does the Devil? Is it to punish our parents? Or did it really jump from all the accumulation of evil in Africa, through the swamps near New Orleans, through my uncle Ish to me? Tell me, Mavety."

"Do it matter, massa?" Mavety asked. "Call it spirit or devil throwin' a man, as Jesus did in his time, call it in the blood or homeplace as the men of science do, call it the bad spirit ridin' us around, to be his horse so he can see the world, like voodoo say. Whatever it is, it don't help you. It hurt you bad."

"That's true. Very true," Zach said, shaking his head, unsettled at the nerves this bizarre conversation was exposing. Or was it amused? Yes, that was it. Hallucination, all of it. All a game of dream-world. If you could just play this game, accept the propositions, you could go one step further. "And how do I get free, then?"

Standing up straight, the Negro woman raised her hands in the air as if receiving, or giving, revelation. She laughed that ringing, joyous laugh. "You a horse, and you don't like who is on your back, what you do?"

"Ahh, throw him?" Zach answered like a pupil in a school.

She clapped her hands, once. "Throw him, massa. Right off your back. And leave him behind in his own mud. You already start to buck last night, I think."

He nodded. Could there be any sense to this? Any sense at all? Because if there was—

"Lots of folk don't know horse is in control, not rider. Horse allow rider on his back."

Zach sat still, considering this.

"But, massa, if you decide to do this, you must swallow your words."

"How so, Mavety?" he wondered, finally rising, straightening himself.

"You have said nothing matters, there is no meaning, good or evil."

"Yes, I have said that, often, as a matter of fact."

"Well, massa," she said, clapping one more time, "if you choose to be better, to throw your evil rider, then it must mean that it do matter. Good is best. There is a meaning to all we see."

"Yes?"

She took his hands in hers and he felt the power, the warmth of the woman's goodness. And he relaxed in that broad, broad, smile which seemed to encompass all on the earth. "*All* is meaning," in a voice as rich as honey. "Every blade of grass, every cloud that hides the moon. All is meaning, massa." The children's voices had stilled outside. Cool mist began to rise from the hollow beneath them, came in through the netting at the window.

"Do you feel it, massa?" she asked, in a whisper. "Do you feel the meaning?"

He looked into her dark, kind eyes. "No, Mavety, not yet. But maybe I will." She released his hands, and he turned, heading for the cabin door.

"Maybe I will, maybe I just will," he said, his voice filled with feeling.

"Massa, run free," Mavety called, laughing heartily. "Run free, I say. But use your freedom well, lest another spirit come from the mud and jump on your back!"

"I'll try, Mavety, indeed I will," he shouted back, laughing a little, directing his comments back at the door, which was slowly closing.

He began trotting up the path. As he did, he passed Ephriam, staggering out of this cabin door. The black man looked in astonishment as the white man broke out of a trot into a sort of gallop, then began running up the path towards the big house. "Jest like a chile," the black man said out loud, "jest like a little chile."

"Epizootic," Althea said as she and Delia sat in the small sitting area in the bedroom at the head of the stairs. "How could I have thought it was epizootic? Still, it came on in the morning and was always gone by evening. So—"

Fog from the bayous was filtering into the bedroom. Delia rose to shut the French doors. "Mother, that isn't the point. I am expecting a child in the late fall. Have you heard me?"

Althea rose and unhooked the back of her dress. It had been a long day, taking tea and talking to the old men, and she wanted to get into her dressing gown. "I heard you. I don't want to hear you but—here, please get the hook and eye for me, dear."

Delia went to her mother and undid the hook and eye and then sat her down forcibly on the Josephine bench at the foot of the bed. "Mother, you must listen for once. I am having a baby and I will not be married. I cannot marry Zach Scott."

"Zach Scott!" her mother said in anger. "I'll have him horsewhipped. Send him here to me—"

"No, mother. I have spoken before he has gone, although I promised him I would not speak. I couldn't bear my load another moment. You will let Zach go his way. Now look at me. Look squarely into my eyes. Don't turn away."

Althea did as she was commanded. Finally, she spoke. "Delia, how did this happen? How could I not know? My poor child." She took Delia in her arms and Delia began to weep silently.

"Mother, you have turned your back on everything you did not wish to see for years. Calhoun grew up timid and unsure of himself and you kept telling him he was a knight and a scholar without really getting to know him. Zach and I loved in that very house and you threw us together and made it impossible for me. Not that I don't blame myself." She pushed back and sat on the bed, facing her mother.

Althea raised her finger in admonition. "Now, Mr. Scott promised me on his word that he would treat you as a gentleman would."

Delia began to laugh, a little desperately. "Mother, you live in your own world, one full of imaginary people and idealistic situations. It's deception! I have hated that the worst of anything. Epizootic—you kept the truth from yourself, and that's the way it's always been. I think I can stand the pain of what has happened to me if we can have the truth. Please! Why do you hide from the real world?"

Althea stared at her dress, lying limp on the bed. She pursed her lips, thought for a long moment. "Well, I guess it was because I had to hide the truth so many times when I was a young girl." Delia said nothing, waiting for her mother to go on. "Mama—drank." There. Said, for the first time in forty years. "Well, not much of course, but just a little ladylike sherry and—" She stopped. "No, if we are to have the truth, she was a drunkard. She drank every few weeks for a whole day. She sat behind a door, there at Fairchance, and nobody could come in or go out." Her eyes grew distant, as if she were wandering in the halls of the past, looking at the huge, closed door looming, and she, small and frightened, sitting on the carpet runner outside. "When that door was closed, I closed myself down too. And told Addie to do the same. 'Don't worry, Little Addie,' I said. 'Mama is very tired and must take a nap. That is all. She is sleepy. If we do not think about it, do not worry, soon it will be all right.' "

"I tried to hide it from Papa, although of course he knew, though he did not ever mention it. If she was having a 'bad day,' I did not speak of it and was very, very cheerful and pleasant. Papa and I talked of hunting pheasants and haying the fields. We both played hide and seek from it, I guess."

"When Mama came out, pale and distant and half-ill, I came out of hiding again. Until the next time." Delia looked at her mother sympathetically. "But the next time came too fast. And really, it was waiting for it that was the worst. Finally, it seemed easier just to hide all the time from the truth about Mama. Just pretend it never happens, that everything is fine. Pretending that all is fine got to be a habit, I guess." Her face looked drawn, and Delia noticed the small wrinkles lining her cheeks. She was sitting there, shivering in her chemise. Delia got up and went to the old wardrobe and took out a dressing gown and put it around her mother's shoulders.

"What a cross for Grandma to bear. We saw her so seldom and never knew," Delia said.

"Of course not. She was a wonderful woman." Althea settled the peignoir around her squarely. "And that is the sad thing. The now-and-then besottedness is what the people who knew about her will remember, not the kind, church-going mother I loved. It clouded everything."

Delia rose and went to the window. Was that Zach, bounding up the steps and into the house? What did he have to act so buoyant about? Leaving her, going like some dark Don Quixote to save the South. Well, she had promised to say goodbye, tomorrow at sunup. Her heart sank at the unanswered questions in her own life, then she forced herself to turn back to what her mother was saying.

"Everybody always thought I was a brave, noble Southern woman, never teary, never blue," Althea said in a small voice. "What I really am is just a sad little girl outside a big, bad door, shut out from love, and afraid, hiding my eyes with my hands." Big, silent tears rolled down her cheeks.

"Darling," she said, opening her arms to Delia. "Please, please forgive me. What you must have been through in this love affair. I have looked at you but not really seen you." They clung to each other, crying in the soft, masking darkness.

Morning dawned bright and clear. Rain clouds that had caused the showers and mists of the last few days were brushed from the skies by the wind, and the plantation bustled with energy as bright as the washed sky outside its windows.

The valise sat in the small room off the kitchen which Bartie Fryerson used as an office. Zach, his usual cynical look replaced with one of concerned determination, shut the door and stood before Delia. "Listen to me, Delia. I don't have much time, and somehow I have got to make you believe me."

"About what?" Delia asked.

"I am going to get Jake out of prison."

Delia opened her mouth in amazement.

"I don't have time to give you details but I have been convinced that I— need to take a different tack with my life."

Delia blinked once. "And?" she said.

"I'm disgusted with the Northwest plot, actually have been for some time. The South has had its chance to win and it hasn't done so; this plot is rank insanity." The clock chimed; he waited until it ceased. "I am going to pull a switch on Mawkins and his cohorts, and use all my passes to go to Richmond to get Jake out of that prison before he dies there. I may be able to repair some of the damage I've done with Jake and in this rotten plot. Even if I don't succeed, I have to take the chance."

Delia listened but was having trouble believing what she heard. "Even if what you say is in your heart, that would be a very dangerous thing to do. Whatever makes you think you could succeed with such a wild idea?"

Briefly, he outlined what he had in mind, finishing by saying, "I want you to return to Indiana with me this morning. I ask again, one last time. Be my wife. I do not in any way deserve your trust, but I ask and need it, desperately. You will not be involved in the dangerous actions, but I need your help there in perfecting these details quickly, and I need your strength to change my life. I have only a little more than a week! Please, Delia."

What he did not say was that he might never be able to ask again. With the desperation now in the war on both sides, in the heated battle that must be beginning at this very minute to stop an advance on Richmond by the North, a man trying to pass through the lines would be in mortal danger.

She looked at him, but she did not answer immediately. "I'll tell you after breakfast," was all she said.

It was an odd breakfast. There was the one old gentleman, Althea's father, talking about historical curiosities to take his mind off the passing of his beloved but alcoholic wife. There was his daughter Althea refusing to even look at Zach Scott, who was eating large amounts of the none-too-plentiful food on the table to compensate for a couple of meals he'd missed lately. Then there was Uncle Bartie, just back from Natchez, who was full of the alarums and rumors of the faltering war effort.

"Well, if they would just let Nathan Bedford Forrest have his head, he'd ride hell out of the Yankees," he said to his brother. "He's the only general has a grain of sense in his skull."

"At least they had the courage to replace Bragg," Frank Fryerson said. "Did you know that Robert E. Lee was in the Mexican War with U.S. Grant?" He seemed to be addressing this question to Delia, and she shook her head that no, she did not know that these illustrious participants in the great drama engaging the nation were once comrades.

"But then how many of them were all on the same side in the days before the secession?" his brother retorted, unwilling to let the juicy piece of trivia rest, wanting to best it. "Why, Buell, Van Dorn, McClellan, D.H. Hill, Longstreet, Stonewall, all were in the Mexican War. At Churubusco, no less."

Althea's mind wrenched free of its turmoil for a moment, and she gave her uncle a dull look. As if anyone cared about Churubusco, whatever that was.

"Well, you just wait and see. We're goin' to pull this out of the fire yet," Uncle Bartie went on, helping himself to various dishes as Mavety served them.

"In Natchez they were sayin' that General Johnston is gettin' ready for a big assault. We're goin' to recapture Chattanooga and then Nashville and Memphis. Drat! The hominy's grainy, ain't it? But I was able to get fresh eggs. No mornin' meal's complete without an egg. That's what I always say, don't you, Althy?" Uncle Bartie beamed beneficently. "Hard to stomach that we don't have one chicken on the place, now. When the Yankees rode through in November, they emptied out the henhouse and rounded up the pigs. Tore through the smokehouse like the wrath of the Lord. Then the officers sat down and demanded that Mavety and the cook feed 'em."

"Did she do it, Uncle Bartie?" Althea wondered curiously.

"She feasted and feted 'em to beat all. We had brandied peaches and fruit cake and barbecue. They was fit to bust." His eyes were far off. "She invited 'em back anytime."

"How'd you like that?" Delia asked.

"I stayed back. Nursin' my pride. Then the Yankee captain told Mavety she and the other hands could go, that they were freed now." He looked up at the black woman, who was standing in the corner, awaiting the chance to serve. ''She said they were bein' paid and would stay. That somebody had to take care of the old folks in the Confederacy. She asked him if he had any old folks in his home, and tears came to his eyes. Then she invited them all back anytime. I think that was why they didn't burn our place like they did some. They hated opposition, wanted to feel accepted as human beings and not ogres. But they left us with not enough food to keep a pismire alive.'' He flashed his brother a challenging grin.

''And I suppose you think, Bartie, that I don't know that a pismire is an ant,'' Frank Fryerson said smugly.

''Still, we here in Mississippi have it easy compared to those in Virginia now. And in Georgia,'' Althea finally said. ''The Yankees are destroying as they go into a county. Burning half the fine old homes in the South.'' Visions of the shattered, dark hulk of Fairchance, wisps of smoke rising from its blackened, hand-hewn beams, passed through her mind.

Uncle Bartie patted her hand. ''Now, Althy, I don't want you worryin' about all that. The men are here to worry. Things are about to turn. Right at this moment, Calhoun and his friend are probably engaging the Yankees. In Natchez, folks were excited. Buzzin' that the telegraph says the two armies are lookin' for each other in a wildwoods called the Wilderness. They must be clashin' now.''

Somehow, of course, that did not reassure Althea but rather added to her apprehension. Her uncle was going on in his shaky, precise gentleman's voice. ''I trust General Lee implicitly. He will not settle for anything else but victory with honor! We will have our independence. And when we do, we're going to have to do something about this nigra question. We really should do a bit better with them after the war is over. Perhaps a gradual system to free them.''

Even Zach stopped eating to look at him with amazement at that comment.

''Now to what's important, Althy,'' Uncle Bartie went on. ''I was able to get some sugar in town and we'll have cook make some teacakes and have a little collation party for you next week. Invite all the quality people in. How about that?''

''We're in mourning, Bartie. Did you forget that?'' his brother said grumpily. ''Mourning in the best households goes on for at least three months, even in these war times. But we could have the refreshments ourselves today at tea.''

Althea looked at the both of them, about to register some sort of protest about the triviality of all they were saying, then shut her mouth. Talk about playing hide and seek. Her father and uncle were living in a dream world. The entire South was sitting outside a giant, closed door, as she had done, unable to face the awful things that were going on behind it. A bunch of children, playing a sad game of "pretend."

Zach put down his napkin. He would be leaving soon, thank God, and Althea would never see him again. The betrayal! Her spirit still ached to think of her daughter, so beautiful, so young and alone in her trouble. And she had not even known it. Delia had said last night she would not consider marrying the reprobate, and she, Althea, had to sit here and face him across the fried potatoes. Well, it had been a week, a month of surprise after surprise and not one of them good.

A chair scraped against the burnished hardwood floor. Delia rose to her feet. All turned to look at her. "Grandfather, Uncle Bartie, Mother, I have something to tell you all. This is a day of celebration. Zach and I"—she looked at him with veiled tenderness, watched the pleasure in his eyes— "are going to be married today." There was a startled communal gasp.

"He has been called back to handle some crucial family affairs"—surely she could say that without endangering the mission—"and he has asked me to go with him as his wife. We've loved each other for many months, and I have acceded to his wishes."

Zach stood and took her hand, speechless. A new kind of determination and satisfaction in his own worth had made him know that he would go north and act even if she did not come. Still, he had hoped against hope.

"Well," said Uncle Bartie, recovering after a long moment. "The rules of mourning may be broken for wartime marriages. We'll call the gentry in tomorrow and have a reception party for you—"

"No, although I thank you, Uncle," Delia said firmly. "Time is pressing at our backs. Will you have one of the hands drive us to Natchez within the hour?"

"Within the hour? Well, I s'pose so," Bartie said wonderingly.

Althea remained in her chair in the bustle that followed, as chairs scraped and servants flew about following orders, as Delia kissed her mother on the cheek and whispered, "I hope you understand. I'm not sure I do myself. I have to believe him and give it a chance," then flew up the stairs to pack a small valise.

"Well, I think we have had enough surprises to last this family for a year," Althea finally said to the empty room.

*   *   *   *

The Twenty First Georgia rose from their beds on the ground in Ewell's command.

"Clear as a churchbell," Calhoun Dugger said, looking around.

"May I offer you some coffee, suh?" Sergeant Boone Epworth said, bowing low and emptying his canteen into Calhoun's cup. "We are fresh out of prime Java beans today, but I can supply sweet potato brew."

"Much obliged, suh. And may I offer you some of our finest parched corn?" Willie said, showing his haversack supply. "Our Virginny ham did not come in on the train last night and the waffles and syrup are plum gone."

They laughed a little, slung on their rifles and checked their ammunition rounds, which in Epworth's case were tied around his waist with a rope.

"I was close to the Old Man at his morning campfire," Epworth told them. "Ewell was talkin' to a artilleryman."

"And what are General Ewell's instructions from headquarters," Calhoun wanted to know.

"Just barge on down the pike over there." Epworth pointed. "And if you encounter Yankees, kill 'em."

"Good instructions. Just the kind I like," Willie offered.

"That's what General Ewell said," Epworth laughed. Then, one final sally into the game of pretending to be gentlemen warriors. Boone Epworth bowed low and pointed at his feet. "Perchance, kind sirs, you might scare me up some footwear. My bootery lacks *dis*-tinction." They laughed and looked at his feet, which like about a third of the regiment's were unshod. Calluses a half an inch thick protected the soles, and his feet were stained dark brown.

All of them hurried to join the column; Doles' Brigade fell in and they began to march down the pike. A mile or two later, with the sun rising in the bright May sky, Willie and Calhoun could see General Ewell in the distance ahead raising his hand to stop the forward motion.

At a crossroads were a group of friendly Butternut cavalrymen, and the general conferred with them. Word finally filtered back from those who had overheard. "Yankees ahead, two miles, heading south. In the path of Lee's other troops. We are to go forward."

"Sounds like somebody else may be bargin' down this pike, or 'tother one over there," Willie said, as officers barked orders and the column started up again.

The Fourteenth Indiana had slept near the site where they were stationed a year ago, at the Battle of Chancellorsville. Now, in the bright glare of morning, John McClure, Isaac Crim and Tommy Thompson stared at a skeleton lying face down amidst Virginia creeper and last fall's leaves. It wore the fragments of a blue infantry uniform with sergeant's stripes on the sleeve.

"Tom Kidd of Company I," Crim had said. He called to a few men from I Company. "They can bury—what's left," he said, returning. They wandered about, looking at the shreds and forlorn pieces of disaster, mule skeletons, broken caissons, rotting haversacks, canteens.

"Look," Thompson said. "The lilacs are in bloom by the ruins of that old farmhouse. They were blooming when we left southern Indiana. What do you s'pose another lilac season will bring?"

"Waal, I hope to God it brings us all home," John McClure said. "I want to see m'self with Mary Jane in our new home. Mebbe a maybasket on the doorknob, stew in the pot, biscuits in the oven. And homemade cherry preserves. I got to get to know Annie again. I'm a little worried about her from what they write. But most of all I want to see Mary Jane. She has writ me so faithful-like, and been the mother of our fambly—what's left of it. I want to live through this for her."

"I saw somebody interesting today—in the reserve units," Crim said. "Van Dyke's contraband Negro."

"He's in the army?" McClure asked.

"Twenty First Colored Regiment," Crim told him. "They are showing signs of being good soldiers, so some folks say. Up to now they have been digging fortifications, but now they will stand reserve when we go in. Prob'bly fight."

"If they don't up and run," McClure said with some displeasure in his voice. It was one thing having Clemson Smith cooking and cleaning up like a servant, or even barbering, but when he took a good rifle and fought in the Army of the Potomac just like everybody else, that was another thing.

"They're formin' new colored regiments every day, don'tcha know," Thompson added.

"Waal, we'll test 'em," John McClure said. "Grant has got enough bloody jobs and dirty trench digging to keep a whole lot of nigras busy."

"Far as I'm concerned, they can stand in my place if there's shootin' and getting shot up to be done," Crim said.

"That, too," McClure agreed.

Now, with the rest of Hancock's force, they moved out, pressing relentlessly forward until they should encounter Lee. First Hancock, gentlemanly and smiling, then the divisions, one at a time, with the Fourteenth's, (Gibbons' Division) first, as usual, Colonel Carroll leading. They marched south out of Chancellorsville, then west, then south down Brock Road to Todd's Tavern. There they halted. The battle was underway in at least two spots nearby and Hancock, their commander, awaited orders from Ulysses S. Grant. Soon they received them, met the southerners advancing from their side of the field, and the Battle of the Wilderness was underway.

*   *   *   *

Jewell Simpson, fanning the fire over which a huge lard-rendering pot was hung, hallooed over to the shed where her husband Archie and nephew Bob McClure were completing the slaughtering of a two-hundred-twenty pound hog.

"You men 'bout ready with that fat?" No answer. They must not have been able to hear her.

"Go up, Mary Jane," she said to her niece, who was setting up crocks on boards between saw horses. "Tell 'em the fire's 'bout hot enough."

Mary Jane walked determinedly up the slight rise to the smoke shed. She was a little tired; they had all been up since dawn on this fine May day.

Before breakfast she and Annie had made the fire, heating stones hot as embers and shovelling them into water in a huge barrel to make it boil. As the sun rose, a shot a few yards off announced that Uncle Archie had killed the hog; soon he and Bob were lifting it with sawhorses and a pulley and hanging it up to cut its artery so the blood could drain out.

Annie stayed outside to feed the barrel with hot stones and keep the water boiling while Aunt Jewel served the rest breakfast, which Mary Jane could not eat a bite of. Then they were ready to scald the carcass.

Uncle Archie and Bob hauled the hog up and dunked it into the barrel feet first to scald its coarse hair off. Sweating by now, as the sun rose higher, Bob pulled the carcass out, and they all took up scrapers to get the rest of the hair the water had missed.

Then, hog in the air again, so Bob could make a cut down the middle to take out the entrails, pulling them in blue, bloody ropes—Mary Jane could not watch, and even Annie turned away.

"Dad-blatted trouble to get pork chops," Annie mumbled.

Then the pig was up and over the pulley rope again for three hours to cure a bit, while the family did the farm chores. As Mary Jane made the beds, she hummed a little tune. Soon, she told herself, she would take this very quilt, with its Rose of Sharon patterns, to the new bed she and Annie had picked out in Vincennes at the store. And take the Hogue dresser her grandmother had just given her, made by her father for her own dear mother—she smoothed the circular roses on the quilt. "Tiny, tiny stitches," she murmured in admiration. She used similar stitches in this dress she had made herself, which was still fresh and neat even though they'd butchered this morning, because she had stood a few feet back from the slaughtering. She was a great stickler for neatness and modesty too. She wondered if Martha Baird McClure, her great-grandmother who made the quilt, had liked to sew as much as she, Mary Jane, did. Was she modest and picky, too? Sometimes you wondered about the olden days people.

Martha Baird McClure had quilted the piece when she first came to Indiana. Pattern was supposed to commemorate the Lord, the Rose of Sharon, the Bright and Mornin' Star, as it calls him in the Bible. Mary Jane remembered her mother, who was a Quaker, wrapping it around her one night when she, Mary Jane, was a little girl and had a fever, and singing a hymn about the Rose of Sharon. It had comforted her immeasurably.

Was it the memory of her mother or of Jesus, the Rose of Sharon, that made Mary Jane feel so loved when she touched the quilt? She did not know or care. It was one of the only McClure things Aunt Jewell had allowed in the house. "So, so purty," Mary Jane said, and for a moment lay down and pulled its soft, white surface to her cheek.

"I'll put you on John's bed," she said, speaking to the quilt in a playful mood. "You be good to him. He's a-gonna need a lot of sleep after lyin' on the ground so long."

She would give him the new bed she was ordering; she and Annie would take the smaller rope ones. This little old bed would do for her, it was a small single bed they called the 'dyin' bed,' of all things. It was the one her grandmother Lizzie McClure had died in, and before her others in her Elliot family. All their names were scratched on the bottom of the bed all the way back to 1790, as well as the babies born in it—well, she had learned to sleep there without all the memories crowdin' round.

Livin', that was what she was thinking of on this breeze-washed, bird-filled day. The curtains flapped in the mild air.

She had raised herself reluctantly off the bed and gone to see about the larding. Aunt Jewell would be wondering where she was, and they would both have all the work they needed, stirring the pork fat the men would bring to the huge pot above the hot, hardwood fire.

Now, outside again, she tied an apron around her waist, noticing with chagrin that it did not protect the pretty ruffled bottom of her dress. Uncle Archie and Bob were coming with a huge trough of fat.

"They cut the hams and shoulders and the side meat a'ready," Annie announced. She was carrying her own, smaller bowl of fat. "The pork chops do look good." Mary Jane smiled at her sister. Seemed like lately Annie was growing almost human. She could speak without spitting out wild words, praise as well as scorn things in her day. They would be so happy before that hearth fire. When she went to see the carpenter, he'd drawn up a plan. She had a letter half written to John, telling him about the way the wood smelled in the carpenter's shop, where the shavings curled around your finger. The shavings for their new home would be like that soon, too.

Uncle Archie and Bob slid the fat into the kettle. "Last time I'll do this here," Bob said, cheerfully. He did this a lot lately, reminding the family that he was, yes, really was going to Oregon this summer when Reverend Paden, now a widower, went west with his family. Aunt Jewell frowned; she did not like to be reminded.

The men left to continue cutting the meat. Annie stirred the pot while Mary Jane let her thoughts ramble to the fall, when the three of them would gather for autumn dinners. Surely some of these very hams would be left. Aunt Jewell would give them some, if she was asked. "Applesauce would be good with the hams," she said out loud. "And cornbread and cherry preserves. John always liked cherry best. I could use the ham bone with black-eyed peas."

"And what if John don't come home?" Annie said in a somber tone.

"Girl, what do you mean?" Mary Jane said, picking up wood to feed the fire. "We have to pray and hope every minute. Don't let another thought come to you but that we will be around the fire this fall."

The girl refused to be squelched. Ever since the awe-filled day in the orphanage, she found she felt better when she voiced her deep fears. "They say there's a big battle in a place called the Wilderness. Both armies fightin' to the death—"

In some way the family dyin' bed flashed into Mary Jane's mind. What if he should be shot, like Tommy Brooks. They would send him home to—she brushed it aside, purposefully. "Look to the future. It's a-comin' soon. Think of the Hogue teacups, and us sippin'."

"You could sip here," her aunt said morosely. "We got cups, too." The fire burned high around the pot. "Watch no pieces of chitterlin' with water in 'em get in," Aunt Jewell warned Annie, who was stirring the rind and fat into the pot.

"Now, how am I a-goin' to know whether they's water or not in the pieces," Annie wanted to know.

"Jest watch the water. If it spits, it is right mean."

The strong, heavy smell of frying pork fat enveloped them, sending clouds of greasy steam about their faces.

"Waal, I jest hope John don't get hit, now so near the end," Annie said again. "We'd have to wait two days to git the news."

"Think about the tea party," Mary Jane said. Then grease spurted out in a small stream, spattering her apron and the bottom of her pretty dress. She looked down in dismay for an instant at her spoiled frock, then stooped to put more sticks into the fire.

"Or of a summer's night," she went on, the three of us will be on the porch. I'm havin' him build a little porch where we can sit and watch the lettuce grow in the evening, and then at night see lightnin' bugs flicker all across the fields." A small, tentative smile lit her tired face. "An' Aunt Jewell and Grandma Catherine there with us, in the dark, eatin' peanut brittle and drinking tea from the cups that belonged to both of their people." Her eyes got dreamy. "I can see it now. They're not mad atall."

"That's cause it's dark and they can't see each other," Annie grumped.

Jewell was a little tired and irritated herself. "Now, I'm sick and tired of hearin' all that. I tole you I am not, never, no never, goin' to sit down to a party with that crochety, snoot-in-air abolitionist bag o' bones."

Mary Jane could stand the old line no longer. She raised her hands in admonition and disgust, the logs dropped onto the edge of the fire and one fell against the edge of the pot. The pot swayed and spilled grease into the fire, which flamed up frightfully, and Mary Jane's skirt, spotted with lard already, became a grease-laden wick and caught flame.

She ran, shrieking agonizingly, up the rise towards her Uncle Arch, her aunt and sister pursuing in horror. Her uncle ran towards her. As long as she ran, the wind against her face blew out the flames. Then, when she could run not one pace more she stopped, and in that instant became a living torch. Not one part of her body was not aflame.

Archie McClure reached her, finally. She was screaming short, toneless, out of breath shrieks with an agony that reminded him of a woman in hard labor, and he pushed her onto the ground where he rolled her until the flames stopped. Dully, she saw the sky and scorched white violets under her head, smelled her own still smoldering hair and through the hideous veil of pain that was her whole existence mumbled something.

"What is it, Sister?" Bob McClure, leaning low, asked. Tenderly he picked her up, as Annie and his mother stood by sobbing. His uncle Arch's hands were so burned he could not lift anything; he was staring in disbelief at their pocked, smoking surface where blisters were already rising.

"Ashamed," she muttered. Annie, tears coursing down her face, came forward and saw that her blackened body now had only a few shreds of cotton on it. The fearsome fire had burnt both apron and skirt off. Annie lifted her own skirt and ripped off the petticoat to cover her sister's form.

"What else?" Bob asked. The blackened, twisting lips answered something.

"Say it again, pet," Archie Simpson said, coming up to her there, in her brother's arms.

"Rose of Sharon, Bright and Morning Star," she managed to get out, and pointed towards the house.

"Must be out of her head," Bob said sadly, then carried the precious bundle like a baby in his arms into the house.

*   *   *   *

Night settled over the Wilderness battlefield, but Calhoun and Willie and the rest of the Twenty First Georgia had no rest in the gloomy, humid aftermath of battle.

About one o'clock in the afternoon the Yankee line hit Ewell's units full force west of the Brock Road, and Doles' Brigade were rushed to a forward position. Two other brigades near Doles' were driven strongly back and began a wild retreat; Doles had to fall back. But not for long; the Rebels rallied and pushed the Yankees back beyond the original defense line.

An exhausting, continuing musketry skirmish, one of the worst of the war, followed. Calhoun and Willie and the rest of the men were pushed to the point of complete exhaustion advancing, changing front, shooting and pulling out scores of Confederate wounded who were caught in a wildfire which swept the overcharged battlefield.

And now across the field, the men of the Fourteenth, equally exhausted from firing at the Rebels all along the other side of Brock Road in the same skirmish, lay on their arms among the units of Hancock's Division.

John McClure looked up at Major Will Houghton, who was walking about, giving encouraging words for the action which would come, inevitably, awfully on the morrow.

"Too wrought up to sleep, major," McClure said.

"I know," Houghton told him. "Did you know they captured a bundle of our Northern men?"

"Yes, the newswalkers came from the other regiments and told about it." He sat up, putting his arms about his knees and Houghton sat down in the same position.

"Those men moanin' out there between the lines are pitiful as babes," McClure said.

"Yes. It's the ones with stomach or thigh wounds. They can't move back to the ambulances. Terrible to be shot after three years, when it's almost time to go home."

"I know," McClure said, shifting his weight to try to get comfortable. "And that I aim to avoid. I am playin' it as safe as possible—" he caught Houghton's eye—"waal, within the limits of honor, acourse. Little more'n a month—my sisters and I got plans for livin' normal."

"And so you will, John," Houghton said with a kind smile.

The afternoon's fighting had been a welter of confusion, with the fronts changing so rapidly that the wounded of both sides now lay in darkness, uncared for in a sort of no man's land between the lines.

Carrying his canteen, with two blankets on his back, Walter McClure crawled on his hands and knees beyond the Northern lines. Although Surgeon Burkhart had long since gone to serve in the hospital in Philadelphia, and Walter's help as an assistant medical aide was not needed, he was driven to action by the awful cries of the wounded.

If the snipers saw him, Walter told himself grimly, or the guards came this way, he could end up in Salisbury or Andersonville. Or worse.

He pressed on until he came to a Confederate lieutenant, who, with his eyes shut, was trying not to cry out from the pain of what seemed to be a shattered leg.

"What can I do for you?" Walter asked him.

"Water. I am very thirsty and cannot move," the lieutenant murmured through cracked-dry lips. Walter knelt beside him and held his head up, pouring water from the canteen into his mouth. Then, gently, he set him down, putting one of the blankets under his head. Getting to his hands and knees again, Walter circulated in an area between the lines, giving whatever aid and comfort he could. He was gratified to see that others, with uniforms of both gray and blue, were doing the same thing for their fellow human beings.

At 4:30 a.m. Calhoun and Willie, hearing the roar of Rebel artillery bombarding the Union lines, roused themselves, and pulling parched corn and dried beef out of their haversacks, quickly began to eat.

"That's a signal to Early to begin an attack," Boone Epworth said, as he came by checking the rifles and ammunition.

"Well, I don't suppose we'll have to wait long to join him," Willie said resignedly.

"No, there'll be action enough for all o' us," Boone said.

The firing was continuous all along a front five miles wide on that second day of the Battle of the Wilderness; Southerners like Calhoun and Willie loaded and shot amidst saplings in the woods, across ravines and behind hastily thrown-up breastworks. The Northern army, including the Fourteenth Indiana answered them shot for shot and loaded and blazed away hour after hour in the hellhole of the second-growth forest, with their comrades falling and dying about them, often with multiple wounds.

John McClure found himself all alone, shooting from behind a tree, early in the afternoon. "Jest like ol Dan'l McClure and the rest of the ancestors," he said. "Injeean style. Lord help us." He saw a gray hat, aimed and shot at it. A soldier dressed in gray fell out from behind a tree, just sort of leaned over and collapsed.

"God in heaven," McClure said. "I shot a man." He could see the soldier's chest heaving. Was he dying? In a state of almost hypnotic fascination, McClure wandered out from behind his own tree, uncaring that he was jeopardizing his safety should someone else be watching him from behind another tree.

"Always said it would be impossible to go to war if you could see the man you was a-shootin'," he mumbled. He drew nearer and bent down. The man was young, like the boy John himself had been when he came to this war. The Rebel had the stubble of a first beard on his chin and wore the crazy half-Zouave, half Butternut uniform of the Louisiana Tigers, a long-defunct unit whose men were scattered throughout other regiments. John knelt, bent low; the boy groaned once and bubbled blood. Then he was silent. The bullet must have entered a lung.

"Should get his wallet, take out his papers and send somethin' home so they'll know," John said aloud, numbly. But he couldn't. He stood up, suddenly. Horror struck him as he suddenly imagined a home and loved ones in Louisiana. He began to run for the Northern lines. "Has a home, his own Mary Jane waitin' for him," he said.

Within the hour he was wounded in the side. "Law of averages caught up," he told himself, as he lay on his back looking at the glare of the sun behind clouds of battlefield smoke. "Son-of-a-bitch bullet that's been chasin' me since Rich Mountain finally located the target."

He lay for over an hour, drifting in and out of consciousness. Aside from the terrible pain which radiated all the way to his fingertips and in the other direction through his groin, he felt a strange sense of comfort. Out of it, out of the battle, out of the war. Grass above his head, poplar saplings around him. He thought of himself as a child, lying on his back staring at the clouds and feeling the earth throbbing beneath him. It was disorienting to look at the sky; this one was full of amber smoke—smoke. He smelled it and then thought "God, the brush has caught fire again." He tried to prop himself up on one shoulder, lay down choked with the enormity of his pain, fainted, awoke, and saw fingers of flame heading towards him. He began to scream, over and over.

In the chorus of screams from the terrified men about him, he heard the pop-pop of ammunition; those were the bullets on their bodies. The poor devils were being burned alive. Heat incinerated everything—he had better say his prayer to meet his God. He couldn't seem to move; he went blank every time he did. This was the end. Damn it, he wished he hadn't a done that with that girl in Alexandria. The world, alive with terrible, choking smoke and searing heat and the smell of burned flesh seemed to turn and tumble about him, and then—he felt strong arms pulling him rapidly from the back, felt awful, wrenching stabs of pain, and he knew someone had come to save him.

Bullets whined about them. Whoever it was had to be in danger from wrathful Rebels—"Who's there?" he called back through pain and bouts of unconsciousness as he bumped along. No way to look— "Who is it?"

"Me, Whiteskin. For once the Indians are rescuing the settlers." It was Walter McClure's voice.

John McClure was too overcome by fright, pain and relief to be surprised. "Redskin?"

Finally they reached the lines and Walter McClure set his cousin up under a tree. He began to treat the wound, which was deep but not bleeding profusely any more.

"Why did you save me? Risk yourself?" John McClure asked, dully.

Walter was cutting away the shredded remains of John McClure's trousers. "Because you were going to die," he said matter-of-factly.

John McClure could not answer. He could only control the pain in his voice, which wanted to keep screaming, by clenching his fists and grinding his teeth. "You're probing, aren't yooooo?" he finally yelled.

"No—I'm—done," Walter grunted, "and here it is." The forceps he raised for John to see held a Minie ball. "If it shattered part of your thigh bone, best we get it out as soon as possible. It was not as deep as it might have been."

He came around and looked his cousin in the eye.

"Redskin, I—" John began, then tears came to his eyes, tears of relief, gratitude, mortification.

"Whiteskin," Walter said matter-of-factly, "I really saved you so I could have the satisfaction of knowing you would jounce thirty or forty miles to the hospital over bad roads in the ambulance wagons I saw back there. They don't have any springs."

John looked up into Walter McClure's eyes and saw the kindness in them. He marvelled. An Indian had saved his life. Just as Christian as anybody else. What could you make of that?

This Indian would not even take thanks for saving his life, after all John had done to hurt him. He had the forgiving grace to make a joke out of pulling him from hell, risking his own life in the process. What could you make of that?

Yes, and now that he looked, there was something familiar about the eyes. They were sharp and black, like his own. And the hair, damn it. No doubt about it. You could see through to the scalp. Poor son-of-a-bitch had the McClure thin reddish-brown hair, too.

"Waal, Redskin," John McClure said, as Walter helped him to the rear and the wagons, "When this is all over, you will have to come down and see me in my new house. Mebbe my sister Mary Jane can make you some chocolate cake and lemonade. Consider this an invite." Which was about as clear a way as any in southern Indiana to say, "I'm sorry and I was wrong."

William Houghton, back of the Northern front lines as the Battle of the Wilderness raged on, watched the men of the Fourteenth Indiana cook their first meal in two days. As the artillery boomed and shells shrieked in front of him on the Union Center, as John McClure and other of the scores of wounded of the regiment were being borne to the rear and away to the hospitals, Houghton thought of the irony of it all. On the very eve of mustering out, some were being carried to coffins while their tent-mates fried pork and boiled coffee. Landon, G's devil-may-care lieutenant, back in action after months in the hospital, had been seriously wounded in the foot and was out of the war now. The names of the wounded were circulated; there were nods, but no grief. "We are inured," he thought. "Our sympathies have deadened, like the roots of teeth which have borne pain too long. War does that."

He thought of home, of having made some sort of beginning of peace with his mother, of the friendship by mail that had developed between him and Lizzie Kelso, of returning to court her. Finally of Gus, far away at Chattanooga, a major on Harrow's staff, advancing still as the war blazed away there. Someone handed him a cup of coffee, made from a huge coffee urn that a corporal in Company E had dragged back from behind Rebel lines, under a shower of bullets during one of the lulls in fighting.

"Brave, foolish boys," Houghton thought. "No one will ever know what you have done, decimated the way you are. Spit in Treason's eye, kicked her shins, trod her toes. No one will ever know what you did. Others will get the credit."

David Beem, listening to the frenzy as Longstreet's troops hit and hit again to try to breach the Northern line, through the incessant artillery and musketry that had not ceased since it began the day before at noon—thought of Mahala and the peaceful hills around Spencer, where deer roamed through greening grass at that very moment. And he thought of Harrold, near him here, grim and grimy, squatting on his haunches drinking coffee, lacing it with whisky he had somehow found on a dead Rebel—which he, Davey Boy, was not supposed to see—and the others who helped him form the company the day Sumter was fired on. And the law office to which he would return if. . .

He saw it all, the shingle, the creaky chair, the leather books with gold-edged pages. "The other side of the moon," he thought. "We will be returning to the other side of the moon and we'll be strangers there, abandoned by the tide of all this, cast ashore. Part of us will always walk these hills of Virginia, where we left our blood, our friends, our youth."

Houghton, Beem, Crim, Thompson, Harrold, Colonel Coons—all of them waited for the time to come, as it always had in these battles, when headquarters would call for one reliable, intelligent striking unit, one brigade in all the Army of the Potomac they could count on not to fail, to send on the crucial mission which would determine the battle.

All of them in the Fourteenth Indiana Regiment, keystone of the Gibraltar Brigade, now diminished in size to a couple of hundred men, but still a unit in the real sense of the word, waited. Then the call came, as they knew it must.

The fire sweeping through woods and fields since mid-morning had reached the embankments of the Northern army and burnt the very logs which entrenched it. Soldiers stayed and fought until their arms and faces blistered, until blinded by smoke they retreated; Southerners swarmed over the Yankee entrenchments. The Rebel tide swept on, threatening to breach Grant's entire line.

"Gibraltar Brigade, advance!" General Sprig Carroll had received his orders and given them to his colonels. Colonel Coons, gallant and gentlemanly as ever, raised his sword. With a yell, the men of the Fourteenth, Fourth and Eighth Ohio and Seventh West Virginia regiments swarmed into the gap, fighting hand to hand, pushing Longstreet's men back, seizing the colors that had been placed on the breast-works, capturing Rebel officers.

"How in God's name have these men behaved with passable decency and even nobility in every situation, for three years?" Coons asked in wonder as he stood with Carroll watching his Fourteenth retire along with the rest of the Brigade, and the dejected Rebels pull back in certain knowledge that they had lost the opportunity to win the day.

And Sprig Carroll, whom the men called "Brick" because of his shock of red hair, born and bred in New Jersey, said, "You grow men in Indiana like you grow corn, head and shoulders above everybody else's. The Iron Brigade has Indiana men at its heart, too."

"Our Northern soldiers are the bravest army the world has known," Coons said and Carroll nodded, his head held high.

Later that evening Willie and Calhoun sadly carried the broken body of their friend Boone Epworth to the embalmers' tent to arrange for shipment home. Under heavy fire, he had been almost shot to pieces by canister as he bravely bore a message from General Ewell to one of his subordinates about the afternoon attack.

"The Yanks have Parrott guns," Willie said sadly, after they had completed their arrangements and were standing under the sign marked "Undertaking," next to the vertical display of open coffins which stood side by side to mark the trade. "They have the new rifles now, some of 'em even breechloaders. They've got the shoes and the beefsteak. But the Confederate Army has the best men an army can field."

Calhoun nodded proudly. Turning their backs on the coffins which stood by the tent, stacked ten feet high, they returned to the exhausted Confederate camp.

*   *   *   *

Mary Jane McClure lay in the narrow, wooden bed. The Rose of Sharon quilt was pulled back and neatly folded at the bottom; she had gestured that she did not want her charred, oozing flesh spoiling the blanket so they had put her on the sheet. Now she lay there, moaning, half conscious, covered by a sheet propped up with bricks.

Bob had ridden to Wheatland and returned with Dr. Campbell. Now Campbell was shaking his head. "You must try to wash her off, and— unguent is here somewhere." He knelt to his bag. "She must have this unguent put all over her flesh. It may help." Still kneeling, he pulled out a metal cylinder from his physician's bag.

"What is that?" Jewell Simpson asked, apprehensively watching him wiping off what appeared to be a long metal needle on the end of the cylinder.

"We can ease her pain. This is something new we use to get morphine into patients. A needle syringe. Turn your back while I use it." He searched the blackened flesh for an area that was not charred, and finding it, inserted the needle in soft flesh.

Gradually the girl relaxed. The rest of the family gathered around her.

"What is the hope, doctor?" Jewell Simpson asked. Her own dress was still dirty, soot-blackened. She had to put out the lard fire, which had spread around the pot towards the dry grass before she could dash water on it.

"Shh," Campbell said, his hands to his lips. "She can still hear us."

"Aaahn," Mary Jane said. They bent low.

"Annie." She managed to articulate it with her pained, twisted lips. Annie bent low.

"What's she saying?" Jewell wanted to know.

Annie stood up straight. "Grandma Catherine. She wants Grandma Catherine." Jewell licked her lips. Then she nodded. Short, affirmative nods, that the girl did not even wait to see before she went to saddle the horse.

Mary Jane lay in a dream world in which demons, angels, her own parents and people like Abraham Lincoln came and went, with the only constant being brutal, unremitting pain. Infection set in deep in the sores on the poor remnant of her skin, black as untanned leather, and she raged in fever. Next to her bed, but on opposite sides, were her Aunt Jewell and Grandmother Catherine. They took turns reading from the Bible, and their tears wet and crinkled its parchment paper.

She drifted in a haze for a day and half, and then her head cleared. She opened her eyelids and her eyes were bright. She tried to speak.

Grandmother Catherine bent low. "What, love, say it again." She worked at deciphering the labored, distorted words.

"What is it?" Jewell Simpson asked.

Catherine's eyes met hers. "She says 'too short.' "

"Life?"

"I think so," Catherine said, her eyes going to the darkened window.

Jewell emitted her breath, slowly. "Mebbe she's right after all." The girl tried to raise her right hand, struggled mightily, and grasped her grandmother's wrist. Then she raised her left hand and took her aunt's hand. With a mighty effort that included some little anger, she plumped them together, Grandma Catherine's on top of Aunt Jewell's. There they stayed for several minutes, until she went to sleep, fitful with pain.

A little after dawn two days after she was burnt, Doctor Campbell came back. He prepared another dose of morphine. "She has sunk so low. So many burns, so many her whole body is one large burn, and shock," he muttered. "It won't be long. Can't ever be sure of these doses." His eyes met Catherine Hogue's.

Then he gave the girl the morphine injection. Peacefully, within minutes, Mary Jane McClure died with those she loved, finally, all at her side.

John McClure lay patiently while Surgeon Burkhart examined his wound in the hospital in Philadelphia.

"Ah, Private McClure, you have been well cared for," he said. He had been on the spot to receive with particular care the scores of wounded from the Fourteenth Indiana Regiment. All about him nurses bustled in with fresh linen; cots were being set up to receive the hundreds of casualties from the fighting at the Wilderness.

"Redskin—that is, Walter, bound me up," John McClure said, and then went on to tell the surgeon how Walter saved his life. Emotionally and physically spent, he could not finish the story, but turned his face away, fighting with tightened lips for control of his sobs.

"I was so wrong about him. I knowed it for a long while," he said in a broken voice.

"I know, son," Surgeon Burkhart said. "I think the war has taught many lessons. A man we fight with, we cannot finally hate. Mr. Lincoln says we all are equal." Then, proudly, he said, "They have finally made me supervising surgeon. German or not, I am an officer and surgeon in the United States Army."

Burkhart finished his wraparound bandaging and lay John McClure back gently on his pillow. John looked up soberly at the physician. "Did you know that Van Dyke's contraband Negro is with the Army of the Potomac? Twenty Second Colored Regiment."

"Ah, is that so?" the surgeon asked, pleased.

"A lot is changed, ain't it?"

"Yes, I think it has," the surgeon replied, pulling the sheet up under John McClure's chin.

May, 1864

Delia Scott stood in Lettie Hogue's small flat in Vincennes. When Delia had appeared at the door a short time before, Lettie thought she seemed weary-looking and pale. Now in the evening light of the lamps and with closer inspection, Lettie could see Delia's mouth was firmly set and her eyes vibrant. Weary she might be, but still, she appeared happier than Lettie had seen her in many months.

As soon as she came in, Delia explained to her surprised friend that she and Zach had been married a few days ago in the Church of the Trinity in Natchez. Lettie accepted the story joyfully. She understood it completely. Eventually one must trust love, and all love involves risk. "The boldest risks are for the greatest loves," she said, smiling into her friend's eyes. Then Lettie told of the desperate adventure she and Zach were involved in to free Jacob Joe.

Lettie buttoned the top buttons on the dressing gown she had hurriedly slipped on when the knock had come at the door. "This love will have the test of risk indeed," she now told her friend.

"Lettie, we have only a few hours to make these arrangements. Zach is meeting with Willis Mawkins to receive the final plans for the conspiracy. He must not know that we are married, that Zach has any notion of turn-coating to save Jake."

"Of course not. But don't fret; Willis will be dense about this. He is only shrewd about politics and money. About people or their feelings—he is as dull as a scarecrow." She was sitting on the couch, looking in her friend's eyes with a sense of wonder.

"Lettie, we need your help," Delia said. There was urgency in her friend's voice, and Lettie nodded quick affirmation of her desire to help.

"As I've said," Delia went on, "Zach will be bearing a message about the prison uprising in the Northwest to the President of the Confederacy. That letter is Zach's ticket into the south," she continued, "but it could also be his doom. He must pass through Yankee territory. If he were to be caught with the letter on his person, whatever he tries to explain, he could be seized as a spy.''

Lettie nodded, deeply aware of the danger.

"But there is more," Delia went on. "I think you must know Zach will never take that letter all the way south. He will give it to Northern authorities and pretend to carry the message verbally. The message is sealed and in cipher. It contains the dates and numbers of troops involved in the freeing of the prisoners at Camp Douglas when the Knights of the Golden Circle and Sons of Liberty start the uprising. At least it is supposed to—we will not know its contents. And the officials may not be able to break the cipher, even after Zach gives it to them."

"No, I suppose not," Lettie murmured. She scanned her friend's pale face, wondering exactly how she could help.

"Is there any way you can get Mawkins to tell you this information? The Northern authorities must know it soon to be able to act upon the treason."

"Treason? You are calling it that, Delia?" Lettie wondered. "Your family, your mother and Calhoun—"

"I was always the black sheep, the one who held back while they were praising Dixie," Delia said, color returning to her cheeks. "This—Northwest Conspiracy—is preposterous and will do untold damage as well as prolong the war. You know that."

Lettie held up her hand and smiled. "My dear, you don't need to convince me. I just wanted to know where you stood in the ranks."

"Lettie, help us. Mawkins is going east on the train with Zach. He's changed this part of the plan—I don't think he trusts Zach completely. Or maybe it's all just too important, anyway, they will part in New York so Mawkins can buy guns and Zach can deliver the plans. Mawkins will only give the letter to Zach when they reach the city. If you were there, perhaps with Mawkins, Zach could give the letter to you and—"

"Me?" Lettie said, dismayed. "Are you saying I would be with Willis again?"

"I think you still have some hold on him."

"Well, of course," Lettie conceded, sitting down suddenly on the settee. "He is around here every week like a sniffing dog, talking at me in his oily voice, wanting me to learn his love lessons all over again." She put her hand on her forehead and laughed ruefully.

"Yes," Delia said, continuing to look at her with knowing eyes, as if she wanted Lettie to sense what she intended.

"Oh. You want me to use my—power over Willis? Is that it?"

Delia nodded, a small smile playing about her lips.

Lettie thought a moment. She reached for a pecan and caramel cluster from a dish on the table. "Well, it would be a suitable revenge, wouldn't it?

Use his own weakness against him. Seduce him. Play the part to the hilt, teasing him, hanging on his arm—'' She was obviously tempted by the idea. "Holding him off through the long train ride, toying—'' She waved the pecan cluster in the air and then bit into it sharply. "What would I do once I got the letter?''

"You may be able to worm the complete plan out of Mawkins. If you can't, take only the letter Zach gives you to the Provost Marshall of New York City as soon as you can slip away from him. There is a good chance they will be able to crack the cipher code.'' Delia sat down beside her on the settee. "Oh, Lettie, say you'll do it. We'll pave the way with the authorities in New York City. They will be expecting you.''

"How will that happen?'' Lettie asked.

"We will see Thomas Jefferson Brooks tonight to ask him to help us with his contacts in Washington. He can go all the way to the top, and I feel sure he would do it. We have telegraphed him that we are taking the night train to Loogootee. We'll not be observed there.''

"I should think not,'' Lettie retorted sarcastically. "Willis in his new incarnation as a potentate never goes there. Chicago, Indianapolis, Canada, but not Loogootee. He's an important person now.''

"Then you'll—do it?''

"Why not?'' she said, shrugging. "I'll go to his flat tonight. I'll beg him to take me back, say I yearn for his—instructions again. Promise all I have—but I'll get him to tell me about New York. Say I must go with him. Be put up in a suite. Get a new bonnet.''

"I hope and pray he will let you go.''

"Trust me. I know his weak points. He believes he has to exchange goods for services.'' She looked up, merriment in her eyes. "Have a caramel?''

"Don't mind if I do.'' Delia took two. "I haven't felt like eating for several weeks but now—I can't get filled up.''

"Oh?'' Lettie said, giving her a bright, inquiring smile. Delia shrugged, grinned and nodded. No need concealing it.

"You are a risk taker,'' Lettie said. "And the stakes are higher than I knew.'' She hugged her friend.

"Mr. Brooks, I have lied to you,'' Zach Scott said. He and Delia sat in the parlor at Loogootee. It was midnight; May frog and insect sounds and the smell of new-plowed earth drifted in through the open window.

"Yes, I telegraphed you that I urgently needed to meet with you on a matter of highest importance to our business orders in the South,'' Zach went on, as Brooks looked at him earnestly, wondering what this confession was about.

"I do have orders for you, but there are other matters far more significant. First of all, I want you to know that Delia and I are married."

Thomas Jefferson Brooks got up to give surprised congratulations, which were graciously accepted by both the bride and groom.

"What I tell you is in the utmost confidence for all of us," Zach went on. Brooks nodded gravely.

"I have been an ardent Copperhead." He did not lower his eyes, but neither did Thomas Jefferson Brooks.

"I think I knew that," Brooks said. "I believe you helped organize the Hindostan Castle. Tommy spied you out." He smiled, sadly, wistfully.

"Mr. Brooks, we're sorry," Delia said. "It has been a year since you lost your son, hasn't it? He was a friend of Jacob Joe's."

"Yes. Tommy was with your brother-in-law, I believe, in the Eightieth Indiana, when both were new recruits." His gaze returned to Zach. "But you said you were a Copperhead. Past tense? Overnight conversion to religion?" He did not mean to be sarcastic, but mention of Tommy and Copperheads made him irritable. The pain of his son's death, and anger at the Copperheads who caused it, were still strong as a toothache. Perhaps time would dull it, but he doubted it would ever be far from his mind.

"I have taken a new lease on life, and I see things in a different way now." Zach took Delia's hand, as if for security. He leaned close to Brooks, whose bright, perceptive eyes glowed with scrutinizing energy in the dim, lamp-lit room.

"Mr. Brooks, there is a well-developed plot to bring Confederate troops from Canada to free thousands of prisoners held in Union prisons in the Northwest. I was privy to information on it. It will be executed soon."

Brooks was taken aback. There were always fears about prisoners running wild, but an organized scheme?

"I can assure you it's true. In my position as castle organizer, I have been asked to carry information about it and purchase arms for its execution in the East, but instead I am turning the information over to the United States government."

"Good, good for you, lad. Tommy would have been proud of his friend's brother."

Zach went on, his brows knit intensely. "I know I can trust you not to breathe even the slightest hint of what I've just said. My life is at stake, along with that of others. But beyond that, I am going to use the trust that has been placed in me by the Confederates for my own purposes."

Brooks looked at him questioningly. Delia disengaged her arm and rose to go to a dark corner of the room. Her eyelids were so heavy she was drifting off, in spite of the importance of it all.

"I am going to free my brother from Castle Thunder in Richmond. He is in mortal danger because of the squalor and illness there."

"How in the name of goodness will you do that?" Brooks asked, thunderstruck. The Richmond prisons were invulnerable—well, almost. Recently several men had tunnelled under one of them and escaped in the street crowds to go north. Perhaps it could be done but—

"The plan that my cohorts have dreamed up allows me to pass through the lines dressed as a sutler. I will have surgical equipment for field hospitals, morphine, chloroform, which the Rebels need desperately, hidden under pies."

"Ah, a good scheme," Brooks chuckled. "I have reason to know about sutlers' pies. They are usually as awful as wet canvas. If yours are any good, you may not get past the first soldiers you meet."

"I will do a little business for form's sake and use my documents to get to Richmond. Then in the confusion I feel sure is everywhere there now, I will find my brother."

"You will have help—"

"Yes. Delia's cousin is a nurse in a Confederate hospital and has been attending Jake. She's been in touch with us, and I know she will help. I intend to spirit my brother away to the Northern lines. It is here I need, implore you for, aid."

Thomas Jefferson Brooks looked toward the corner, where, out of the corner of his eye, he saw Delia lying on the settee. His mother-in-law, Hannah Poore, entered the room in a dressing gown. The lamp in her hand cast a halo of light on her strong, lined face and shadowed hair that was still predominately brown, even though she was in her eighties.

"I heard talking and couldn't sleep," she said. She looked at the new Mrs. Scott asleep in the corner, then came to offer her hand to the visitor.

"Do you know Mr. Zach Scott, Mother Poore?" Thomas Jefferson Brooks asked, rising.

"I have not had that pleasure, though his father, John Robert Scott, was my dear friend and companion of many years," she said, and her eyes misted at the sudden remembrance.

"I hope to reflect honor on my father's memory someday," Zach said. "As for now, I am here giving a list of customers for food lots for summer delivery," he went on and, as if to make his story honest for the newcomer in the room, took out the sheaf of orders he had secured for Brooks interests in Natchez during the last few weeks.

Thomas Jefferson Brooks looked through them and nodded. "Good work, son. I think you have done the Duggers and all the rest of us proud."

"What do you hear from your grandsons in the service, Mrs. Poore?" Zach asked.

"The telegraph says the Battle of the Wilderness is sure to be a Union victory. But others are saying we have lost thousands of men and hardly escaped. I have not heard from Will Houghton in the Fourteenth. Eustace, in the Eightieth, where your brother served, is at Dalton, Georgia, with Sherman. The Eightieth is in the midst of bitter fighting."

"And Colonel Lewis?"

Thomas Jefferson Brooks answered this. "His health is still not good, but he is active in my business interests, here in Loogootee. He hopes to visit the Eightieth Indiana soon. And he helps to look after Tommy's widow Libby and his little son. We have had another sadness. Tom's baby girl caught the fever and died last week."

"So many children seem to have had it. In Vincennes several died," Zach said. Delia murmured in her sleep; they all looked over towards her.

"We have had three long days of journeying," Zach said. "I will be taking her to Rivertides tomorrow and then—I go east."

Hannah Poore continued nodding her head, as if affirming her pleasure in seeing the son John Robert Scott had written so anxiously of. He had been—what was it? Difficult. Never mind, he seemed a good and useful man now. "Your father and I lived so many trying, glorious times on the underground railroad in the old days," Hannah said finally. "I cannot help but wish he had lived to see the slaves free, finally. How glad he would have been."

Zach and Brooks nodded.

"How much we risked," Hannah said, her eyes far away. "He, his very life at times, going to Tennessee to free kidnapped slaves. He yearned for what the war has brought."

Delia stirred and rose from her catnap and came to offer her hand to Mrs. Poore. "We all must learn to risk, if we love, a friend of mine tells me," she said. Soon they were strolling to the kitchen, arm in arm, to build the stove fire up a bit and heat cocoa.

"Now what can I do to help you free your brother and expose this plot?" Thomas Jefferson Brooks said, opening a box and offering Zach a cigar.

"You have met President Lincoln."

"Indeed I have," Brooks answered, nodding gravely. "He was gracious enough to accept my report on sutlers for the government."

"I need—could you—would you—refer this matter of the conspiracy directly to him?"

Brooks looked steadily at the young man without answering, and Zach went on. "The provost in New York City will relay it to a higher power and that should be the President of the United States. He must be prepared in advance for what is to come. No one at the lesser levels of government should know, I think. It is all too important. Later on Governor Morton can be informed."

"You are right. Morton is as blabber-mouthed as a village gossip anyway," Brooks said, holding a match to the end of a cigar and puffing to ignite it.

"Then, to the matter of my brother," Zach went on. "President Lincoln is probably the only one who can guarantee my safe conduct. He must know we will bring the final plans to Federal officers in New York to be delivered to him as soon as we get them. Then I must have a pass and a sutler's license that will take me through the Northern lines. The Confederates I can deal with, but if I am caught by Northern officers, I could be detained as a spy. Some spies have been known to be summarily executed on the spot if they are caught. Anyway, precious time will pass, Jake will get sicker." For the first time the enormity of what he was thinking affected him, and he sank on the settee, his long arms hanging almost to the ground.

From the kitchen came noises: clattering pans, cups being drawn out of a cabinet, the soft purring and giggling of women's companionable voices.

"I don't think I can send your message to President Lincoln, son," Thomas Jefferson Brooks said, finally, looking earnestly at Zach.

"No, sir? No?" Zach said, disappointed.

Brooks rose and stood before him. "No, that would be too dangerous. I think I'd better bear this message myself and give it to the President personally." His smile was wide.

Zach rose to clasp the older man's hand gratefully.

"Now," Brooks said, looking for his spectacles. "Rough out your plan again with its details. Let me see any substantiation you have in writing. I will catch the morning train east tomorrow. I want to be as definite as I can about what may happen."

It was two hours and several cups of cocoa later that Hannah Chute Poore, who had been determined to hear nothing but had learned everything she needed to know, escorted the tired newlyweds to the guest bedroom in Brooks House. They would have a few hours of quiet sleep before they must return to Vincennes. And tomorrow morning Thomas would be going east, he said, on important business; John Robert's son Zachary was also journeying to the coast to do something good for his twin brother. All very secret. Risky.

Nothing ventured, nothing gained, she thought. It is always that way, she told herself. Especially when dreams must be bought, or won. The war has been about that—so very much ventured, so very much risked. Tommy and so many others dead, the land disfigured and rent until the very soil cried out for respite.

And the gain? The future would know that. The nation would surely be sewn back together like a quilt. But would the seams make the quilt stronger or weaker? Already colored people were pouring into camps, heading north to dubious welcome. How in the world would they all be assimilated? Only the future would prove whether the frightening risk had been worth it. She headed for her room, sighing over the memory of a Congestoga wagon full of children and supplies, risking it all as they jolted painfully over rough roads in Pennsylvania to a flatboat on the Ohio into wilderness country, long ago, when dreams were new.

Willis Mawkins' eyes were gloomy. He sat facing Zach Scott on a train bouncing along towards New York City.

"At this moment, Vallandigham may be meeting in Canada with the commissioners from the Confederacy," he said in a voice so low that Zach could scarcely hear it over the noise of the train. "Hines is setting it up."

Zach nodded. Mawkins had told him, in their brief conference in Vincennes, that the Canadian Confederate supporters had forwarded part of the promised $90,000 to him to distribute to various leaders of the Knights of the Golden Circle and the new Sons of Liberty lodges. Mawkins had a sizable chunk, he did not say how much, in his own valise for the gun purchases in New York.

In that morning conversation at Vincennes, Zach had pressed as hard as he could for details. Had the membership in the castles grown since he left? How many could be counted on? Mawkins had mentioned the 85,000 in Illinois, 50,000 in Indiana—a little less in Ohio, that he had talked of before, but were these how many were really ripe for rising, could they be counted on? Mawkins shook his head noncommittally and departed, and Zach left to take Delia out to Rivertides. He was nonplussed.

Was Mawkins evasive because he did not know himself what the conspiracy could count on? Had he lost his trust in Zach for some reason? Or was it just that his personal life was intruding on business and he was nervously wondering how to handle his affair with Lettie? Thank God Mawkins agreed to take her to New York City. She could be the key to all this. The cipher letter must get through to Northern authorities, and he could not be involved in handling it. It was going to be hard enough when all this was over to prove he had, ultimately, been not a traitor. The situation would be irretrievably complicated if it was proved he possessed that letter, even for a short while. It was probably the single most treasonable letter of the war.

Now, though, as they passed through Pennsylvania, looking out at the tree-clad mountains west of Harrisburg, on a trip that would see them in New York City tomorrow morning, Zach felt reassured. Mawkins was moody and skittish, but did not seem to be really untrusting of his first lieutenant. Mawkins expected the plot to go forward, and he had no reason to distrust Zach's part in it.

"Are you carrying the gun I gave you?" Mawkins asked He poked a silver toothpick skillfully about in his gums.

"Yes," Zach said, indicating a holster inside his coat, where the baby dragoon pistol was hidden.

"I have mine, and it is loaded," Mawkins said coolly. Zach tried not to look alarmed. The cool, calculating manner of the man as he cleaned his teeth and talked about the loaded gun reminded him that this was a dangerous escapade he was committed to. He was jeopardizing Lettie, too. What would Mawkins do if he felt his plot was betrayed? He was perfectly capable of silencing anyone who endangered the Confederacy and even more importantly, his own growing power, and the money that was somehow involved in all of this.

"Vallandigham will be a key," Mawkins continued. "He was banished by Burnside and has been gone from Ohio for over a year. He will surely return from Canada back home, and when he does, it will be the signal for a general revolt in Ohio. The rest of the states in the Northwest will fall like a house of cards."

Zach sighed a little. It was the same old plan he had heard for three years, but this time it had the potential to do real damage. Exactly when? It would have to be this summer, Zach told himself. But exactly when? He searched carefully for words. "I suppose they—we—won't wait long."

Mawkins wet his lips and put the toothpick in its little velvet case. "Can't. Grant is still fighting. He says he will fight every day until he gets to Richmond. If we are to stop disaster, it has to be soon. There are Southern units waiting to break through again around Knoxville. If they do, some of Hood's men are planning to ride straight north, join the prisoners and sweep the Northwest—but I have said too much."

Zach waited expectantly for more, but Mawkins turned his face to the window. The whoo-oo of the whistle, lonely and plaintive, sounded ahead of them. The train hurtled on in the echoing darkness, heading into a tunnel under a giant mountain.

Lettie Hogue slipped into the seat beside Mawkins. In the blackness which masked all things, she put her hand on his knee. Then, she pressed her lips to his and ran a finger up the inseam of his trousers, high enough to make him jump and reach for her breast. She teasingly continued her ministrations. Daylight appeared dimly in the small hole ahead; and as the train leapt towards it, she slowly withdrew her hand. When the train emerged into the bright sunlight again, Lettie was sitting primly with her hands folded in her lap.

Willis Mawkins leaned over her, whispered in her ear. "Tonight? In the hotel in Philadelphia?"

She tilted her chin to whisper in his ear, but first delivered a delicate, provocative kiss to his earlobe. "I want to trust you, Willis. I so want to. Help me to trust you," she whispered.

Across from them, Zach, pretending to look out the window, allowed himself just the smallest fraction of a smile.

The next morning, as they boarded the train into New York City, she brushed past Zach. Quickly she said, "Nothing last night. He would tell me nothing. I even cried to convince him to trust me with his inmost secrets so we could be one. But at least his stubbornness relieved me of what would have been a terrible duty. I'm still promising myself to him, trying to find out exact times and places. But he seems adamant. I'm afraid we may have to depend on the letter."

Zach nodded and helped her into one of the cars. Mawkins had gone ahead to stow the baggage. Lettie and Zach allowed a woman and two children and an old Irishman to board between them, so they would not seem to have been together. Up to this point, they were still supposed to be loyal parts of the Northwest Conspiracy, and Mawkins had said they must not arouse suspicion.

In a matter of hours, Zach thought, they would be in New York City. There was no way of knowing whether Thomas Jefferson Brooks had reached Washington, whether he had talked to Lincoln, whether Lincoln was even there. Probably he was, with all the war reports from the Wilderness fighting coming in hourly. Brooks and Zach had agreed that no matter what, they would meet in the Willard Hotel in Washington day after tomorrow. They would be willing to wait for each other one full day to complete their arrangements.

The train lurched forward; Zach, standing with one hand on an aisle seat, endured its start-up jolts with his hand to his head. He was not ready to sit down yet. He had not slept at all in the hotel last night. Bags were under his eyes. Sometimes he still wondered why in the Devil he was here. It was trying to have to always make moral decisions. Much easier when he could just be selfish and evil if he wanted to. He smiled a little, the old, scornful Zach smile. Probably he had been hypnotized in Mississippi. His smile grew broader as he mocked himself with that idea. That was it. Drugged in the mud. O-goo, or whoever that voodoo bastard was, had mesmerized him and was still riding around on his back, making him do this ridiculous, farcical, comic opera act. Then he thought of Delia and something reassuring seemed to spread through his whole body and mind. No, it was real.

What was happening was the most real thing that had ever happened in his life.

He had reached his seat. Mawkins was a seat forward; there he was looking up at him with his small, shrewd eyes. Zach took out a small pillow he had brought in his carpet bag. He coughed a couple of times. Drat! Was his perennial hacking cough returning? He had brought a bagful of handkerchiefs. It was embarrassing to be on a clandestine adventure, risking your life like a corsair, and have to be always hawking and spitting.

Well, it was just as well they weren't sitting together; he certainly didn't feel like talking to Mawkins. Perhaps he could get a nap. In a matter of hours they would be in New York City. They needed to be at their very best to carry off their complicated, dangerous plot. "O-goo," he thought sardonically, "if you're here, get the hell out. I've got enough trouble without a big, black voodoo spirit riding around on my back." He began to chuckle and then laughed so hard to himself, that Lettie, sitting across the aisle, sent him a quizzical look. Then he closed his eyes to snatch sleep before the real voodoo, back-country breakdown party began for all of them in the biggest city in America.

Dora Lavenham slumped wearily onto her bed. Outside in the streets of Richmond, young people were singing. A group of cadets from Virginia Military Institute had come into town on a short leave. It was well known they were trying to see action in the Rebel army, were training the old men of the city in military defense tactics. They wore bandbox-bright uniforms and fresh faces, and their winning ways were charming the young women of Richmond. Some of these boys and girls were strolling along, taking the spring air.

"Nursery rhyme children," she thought, "escaped from their nurses, playing toy soldier and ring-around-the-rosie in the balmy evening." How far away that all seemed. The casualties of the Wilderness campaign were beginning to find their way into the hospitals, and they were awful, maimed in ways that she had never seen. The canister explosions tore them to pieces and she was weary, weary, with taking care of them, poor, poor things. Tears came to her eyes. The wounded men said they had become fighting automatons. The papers said that even now Grant was fighting again at Spotsylvania near the Wilderness and that the Rebel forces were entrenching in a series of works they called the Mule Shoe. That they were fighting hand to hand, day after day, like two grim wrestlers stripped and sweating for their lives.

For their lives. Jacob Joe was weak, and, like most of the prisoners who had survived the winter starving and sick, spent a good deal of his day in bed. There was not enough to eat, not enough to feed the prisoners, and since they were no longer exchanging those held by the enemy, he seemed to be losing the will to live, like so many others she had seen on both sides of the war. When the will to live left, it was only a matter of weeks.

Recently she had been doing the most awful, deceitful thing. She was making up letters from Sophie, telling him his lost love had made an awful mistake, pouring out love. Dora's own love. "I adore you, everything about you." She was so eloquent he had rallied a bit, and now she went as often as she could, dragging herself after the endless day of caring for these new and horrible wounded, gone to see her love. Caution to the winds! It was his life she was fighting for.

A month ago she had written home and found a way to give her letter to one of the few prisoners who had been scheduled for exchange before the new rule went in. She had begged for help from anyone for Jacob Joe. Had it ever reached Louisville? She prayed that somehow it had. She held tight to fraying shreds of hope. What could they do anyway? There was no exchanging. But some of Delia's friends knew Governor Morton. Could he do something, anything? She did not know.

Perhaps Jacob Joe would not catch the varioloid that still claimed victims, perhaps there would be better food tomorrow to give him, perhaps she herself would not wear out and sicken looking at these weeping, agonized, blanched faces of indescribable pain.

Perhaps, oh God forgive her for praying it, perhaps Grant would hurry and end it all so they could all go home.

A teenaged, chiming female voice suddenly rang clear outside the window. "Now, suh, don't tease a body so. Just come on back to our humble house and we will see if we can find a little supper for you, maybe goin' to defend our noble cause and all for the first time. I think papa has loaned our piece of bacon out to the neighbors for their beans but maybe it is back by now! We can divide it eight ways, I do declare!"

Laughter rang out through the dusky Virginia night, then a hush and the sound of thunder rumbling in. The weather was changing.

Dora Lavenham sprawled on her bed, dazed with exhaustion, until her roommate and friend Betsy came in and gently put her feet on the bed. Drifting in and out of horrid dreams of canister exploding and tearing off men's arms and noses, Dora finally fell into a deep sleep at 4:30 a.m.

At that exact moment 4:30 a.m. May 12, 1864, a dim, gray dawn lit the sky which had drizzled rain almost all night on the battlefield camp of the Army of the Potomac. Carroll's Brigade, led by the Fourteenth Indiana, was approaching the fallen trees and jagged tree branch abatis which marked the muleshoe-shaped entrenchments of the Rebel Army near Spotsylvania. Major William Houghton, carrying a message on horseback behind the front lines, heard the cheers of the men and tried to watch them go forward, but fog obscured his view. "I've never seen anything like this," he thought. "They are operating in the darkness. I can see the musketry and exploding shells, flashing like heat lightning in a cloud. But what are they doing? Are they closing on the barricades? I hear Rebel shouts of warning." Then there were the sounds he had come to know well, of men clashing in explosive, terrible conflict.

It was not until he reached headquarters with his message that he learned. The Gibraltar Brigade and a few other units had surprised the Rebels, whose line of sight was obstructed by the depth of their trenches and embankments, especially in the fog. The hand-picked assault group had gone into the very midst of the entrenchments, fighting hand-to-hand, bayoneting as they had never done before, going up through Rebel chins, down through their breasts, smashing heads with their rifle butts. Lines behind them were firing as fast as they could.

The attack was a rousing success. The Second Corps had captured 4,000 prisoners of Ewell's corps and several pieces of artillery. One thing more he learned: losses in the Fourteenth had included both killed and wounded, again, and John Coons, Colonel of the Fourteenth Indiana, was mortally wounded leading the charge.

"We are a last man's club," Houghton thought, as he checked ammunition supplies for the corps, one of his new duties. "One by one we have dropped on the woods and fields of this infernal state. Over 400 men killed or wounded in the Fourteenth. Half of what started out to Virginia. There won't be a man of us left to return to southern Indiana in three weeks if Grant keeps on this way. He says he intends to fight it out on this line if it takes all summer." Still, the smile playing about his lips was filled with pride of accomplishment and wonder, not anger.

Two hours later the furious fighting for the muleshoe salient had not diminished. As Doles' Brigade of Southerners were flushed out of their bastion they turned to fight against the Yankees who had been fed by their generals in a steady stream into the center of the salient, claiming the very emplacements Doles' brigade had just left.

Now, Calhoun and Willie were fighting against the Yankees just yards away, separated only by the trenches. Minie balls flew faster than the raindrops which pelted down on and off, and shell and canister and musketry exploded so violently that a massive tree twenty-two inches in diameter was felled in the midst of it all.

Calhoun inched forward with the remnants of the Twenty First Georgia, slipping and sliding in the mud that boiled with blood and riveting water. Bodies were all around, mouths open to the rain, eyes open and staring.

Yankee artillerymen, sensing that the Rebels were sitting ducks in the middle of the muleshoe, aimed directly into the salient, and shells and cannister exploded everywhere. Calhoun fell into the mud, at Willie's feet, a piece of his skull shot off by a small, round case shot. Willie bent to turn him over.

Yet, incredibly, Calhoun was still conscious. "A real battle. Can't say it wasn't—," his friend murmured. Willie gazed in dull horror at his friend's broken skull. "Tell Delia—" Calhoun said, and died. Willie turned instantly back to the battle, advancing. To falter was to die, even when the companion of your childhood expired. He could not think of him, or notice that Calhoun's body was trampled on by other Confederate and finally Yankee soldiers, who used the bodies to gain footing, that finally a blue-clad young man from Massachusetts fell dead on top of him, and soon both the bodies were shoved so far down in the soft mud that they were out of sight in one common grave.

*   *   *   *

Frank Fryerson lay in the large bedroom in his brother's plantation in Mississippi. His heart, weakened by years of hard work, long hours in the saddle and tobacco smoking, was finally giving out. Althea Dugger sat by his side. They had been carrying on the most remarkable conversation over the last twenty-four hours, as it became apparent he could not rise and that his vital organs were slowing down.

He was calmer than Althea would have expected, more resigned. Her father was not overtly religious, although he had attended church irregularly when custom decreed, but he was not afraid to die. She had brought soup, cleaned his bed, instructed the colored servant to tend to his personal needs and bathing, and much of the time they had just talked, for the first time in her life. Perhaps it was the new freedom she had felt since she had told Delia the great, sad secret of her life—that her mother drank. Somehow, since she had told the truth, even to one person, she found she could be speak honestly in several areas of her life. It was as if honesty was an ink, which once spilled out of the bottle, seeped into all the areas of her life and colored them with the need for healthy truth.

Added to that was the grave sickness of the man she called Father. Illness, she thought, is the obliterator of all roles. When she herself went through the pangs of childbirth, she had clung to slaves for succor as if they were her own sisters, as now her strong father clung to her.

They had spoken of his coming to Tennessee from North Carolina, of the house he had helped build with his own hands, hewn the beams with pride, watched the clinch nails for the doors forged and worked the bellows for the nailsmith himself. How he rode to Kentucky to get the best horses for the stable, had brought them back, and with them the first slaves for Fairchance.

"You did not have slaves in North Carolina?"

"No. The Fryersons were townfolk. I and my brother grew up as lawyer's sons, you remember, and although we had over fifty acres around our house in the village, we hired what we wanted done. Townsfolk," he seemed to drift away, for a moment, then said, 'but the land called to us out here.' "

"Bartie went south before I did, then later I went west almost to the river. I do not regret a single thing we did. The clearing was worst. First the brush clearing, the mistletoe clinging to everything, fighting you when you went to pull it down. The grubbing of the trees, with oxen, the land resisting us every step. Your mother and you girls cooked over open fires. Do you remember that?"

"Open fires—" Althea said, musingly. "I remember the smoke always in the air, the huge piles of burning wood so hot it singed your face. And the people bringing hampers out to the men who drove the oxen. The rains kept coming and dousing the fires, and you cursed." She smiled.

"I was so eager to open the land to the plow. Then, that was a struggle, with the ground as hard as a slab of slate. I spent the last of the money I had on the best share I could get, and it was well worth it." He took the glass she offered him.

"First we stayed in the cabin, then, finally, the house stood," Althea said, her mind wandering in the past, "like a vision of a fairy palace." She sighed, unreconciled to what had happened to Fairchance. Fire was a brutal punisher. It destroyed twice: when the flames ate up what you loved and later, as it flashed uncalled for and revolting, over and over in your memory.

She went on. "You sent to New Orleans and got the piano and I polished it myself, every day. And all the other beautiful things, the music box, the candelabra, that we got when the cotton crops came in. I can see Mama with the Meissen china, the blue onion soup bowls, ladling out good soup." But she did not smile. "If it was a day Mama came to dinner," she added.

"Althy, do not blame your mama for the way she was. I know you do. But Stella was a good woman. Took care of all the people like they were her kin and loved you and Addie beyond anything."

"I know, Papa," Althea said. "I never said she didn't." She took a bottle of drops to the little table and stood looking at the live oaks outside the window.

"Seems to me that drinking is in the blood," her father said philosophically. "Her father before her was like that, too, and I 'spect one of your children could be. It goes like that, like sugar in the blood, through the family. Did I hear that Calhoun drinks too much?''

"I think so, Papa, but I really don't know. I do not know my children's hearts." She turned towards the wan face with the red hair speckled with gray above the bedquilt. "It bothers me. There he is, so far away, hardly ever writing, and I have not been able to say, I see things differently now you're gone. I'm sorry I tried to live your life for you. Sorry I did not listen to your fears and hopes, sorry. . .'' Her voice trailed off.

"It's all right, Althy," her father said, clutching at the quilt with his claw-like hands. "I have an odd idea 'bout that. Sometimes loved ones know more than we give them credit for. When we say 'I'm sorry,' it travels across the miles and even across time. Maybe he knows and forgives you." Her father smiled wanly.

They spoke about other things, and finally she asked him what she should do about Fairchance.

"Why, go live there, Althy. Go live there and rebuild the house. It is good land. You legally own it now, don't you? Your sister Addie had her share already, don't worry about her. Baled her out, we did, earlier." He raised his hand a little in admonition. "Go there, Althy."

"Go there myself? Papa, you know Rivertides is my home."

"Not any more. The war has changed it all. Your children will want to run it, don't you think?''

"Perhaps," she conceded, thinking of Delia's joy in managing the fields above the river. Things were changed now that this child of hers was married. But what would she, Althea, do? She was silent, considering. "I have a letter here," she told her father. "It is from the major in the Yankee army I spoke to you about several times, the one who watched the plantation, who helped me so?''

"Major Bachelder. Was that his name, Althy?''

"Yes." She took the letter out and smiled. "First he said that our old slave Jason has been captured once more and will go to trial for arson, probably be in prison for the rest of his life. Then he—Edward—says he wants to marry me, Papa. He says he has loved me since he first saw me and we worked to together to replant the plantation.''

"He is not married, Althy?" her father's voice seemed to be diminishing, as if it were coming to her from a distance.

"Yes," she sighed. "But he says he will separate from his wife anyway when he returns. They were estranged even before the war. He will seek a divorce.''

"Divorce!"

"You are as shocked as I," Althea said calmly. "Of course, it could never be."

"Why not?" her father asked. His voice was stronger; he was obviously calling on stored energies to voice strong sentiments.

"Well, divorce just isn't done, Papa," Althea told him, pulling a chair up so she could look earnestly at him. "You know what a stickler you are, and Uncle too, about all that. Why, you won't even allow me to take off my mourning black to work out among the daisies in the garden."

"That's different, girl," her father said as firmly as he could. He was silent for a while. "Times are turnin' flip-flops," he said.

"That's obvious," Althea said bitterly. "The old life is dying, dead. My daughter has run off to get married, there isn't even enough to feed the ten workers Uncle has left here, and Fairchance is ashes. None of this," and she swept her hands towards the Mississippi River, to the west, "will ever rise again. They have pushed our noses in our own—unpleasant institutions, and we will never get them off the ground."

Her father's voice rang through the room. "Nonsense. Of course it will rise."

"What do you mean?" she cried angrily, forgetting she was talking to a sick person. "They have utterly destroyed us, and when the reconstruction, as they are calling it, comes, they will keep us as servants so their Northern industries can flourish. They have taken all that made us prosperous, and nothing is left. You and Uncle live in a dream world."

"Listen to me, girl," Frank Fryerson said in a ringing voice which caused him pain. "None of this ever depended on slavery." She looked at him in disbelief. "Not for me, it didn't. There were slaves and so I had them, but if I had the body to equal my mind at this moment, I'd go right back and get the bank to back me and build Fairchance again with paid labor."

Althea looked confused. "I didn't think you cared, Papa. I thought you had put it all out of your life, and just wanted to be left alone to your few comforts, and Uncle Bartie and his antiquities."

"My body is worn out. But my mind—I'd buy new machinery, new land cultivators and grow cotton and hemp and try a hundred new things. Spit in their faces. Rise up like the Phoenix from the ashes! That's the way we'll win the war."

"Win the war!" Althea exclaimed.

"Oh, yes. Well, we will sign the articles of capitulation and we will be humbled and poor for a while. But your children, and their children's children will see a new South."

She looked at him, frowning wearily. It was hard to imagine anything past the devastated countryside, the exhausted, hungry people.

"Sherman may burn Atlanta and Chattanooga and New Orleans, and the cities of Texas may be in Northern hands, but they will rise. Ashes are a fertilizin' force, you know." He was laboring, pausing, grunting in pain as he spoke. "We can have—shoe factories and woollen mills and steel manu-factories just like Massachusetts does." His voice was beginning to fade. "It's just that we were—too lazy, girl, when we had other human bein's to tote and carry for us."

She rose, her finger to her lips, and tucked the quilt under his chin. His eyes were closing.

"We should have shook off the old way a long while back. Men can't live that way—it stunts the growth of a person to live dependent on others. Slavery was like—baccy smokin'. Gives you a bad habit and makes you lean on it ever after. Now we can build, build again, and this time on our own. It's all in the building. After that, the decaying sets in. Marry your Yankee—"

"No, Papa," she protested.

"Do you—love him?" He coughed, tried to breathe through failing lungs.

She was silent a moment. "I think so. I would need to be with him again, to talk. But Edward is the sweetest, most wonderful, gentle man—"

"Yes. You love him. Do as you want, Althy. You have always done your duty, been the one to keep us all together, sacrificed. I remember you helpin' the people set food on the table when your Ma was—poorly. Now follow your heart. See if he will stay with you at Fairchance. Build. Build again. It is all in the building, girl."

He was asleep. The next day he quietly slipped away from them, and as Althea helped her uncle and Mavety prepare for the second funeral within a few weeks in the house, she realized she alone was faced with the task of closing out her parents' life in these difficult times. Addie, little Addie, was never any help. The papers were in Memphis; it was there she must return to settle— everything in her existence.

John McClure woke from one of the many naps he took in the convales-cent ward in Philadelphia's three-story Soldiers' Hospital. He had not had the fever, and yet he thought he must be delirious; beside him stood his Grandmother Catherine and his Aunt Jewell. Together they were and smil-ing, gently, sadly down at him.

"Think I must've died and gone to heaven," he said, scratching his head with his good arm bewilderedly.

"No, John," Grandmother Catherine said. "We are here because— something has happened to bring us together, the whole family, after all these years."

Before he could say anything, Jewell Simpson told him, "Somethin' terrible, John, but we come to tell it to you right out, first hand and the both of us." And so, haltingly, with many tears, Jewell told the sad story of Mary Jane's accident and of the bravery of her dying, and they all sat together for hours in the failing light in the hospital and talked of the loveliness of spirit of the simple girl who had wanted nothing more than to have her family together, and loving, and through her death, so sadly, had achieved her dream.

And John, too, wept at his own loss, and at the awful realization that beauty and innocence can go so quickly out of the world, like a candle blown out by the wind.

Finally, as the women nurses lit the lamps, Walter McClure came about to check the beds of the men of the Gibraltar Brigade, more of whom were now coming in from Spotsylvania, and John McClure pulled him by the sleeve.

"Grandma, Aunt Jewell, I want you to meet my"—he thought about saying cousin and then decided on "my friend, Walter. Walter McClure. He's a McClure, too."

He looked up at Walter and Walter shook hands with relatives who would never know of his connection with him, because there really was no good reason for their knowing. As Walter stood nodding at these women with the tear-stained faces, he thought that he would in fact not need his relationship with the McClures at all any more. He must go on his own, to find his way in Miami society as it grew towards the future. He had written his mother he would be returning, not to teach, as he had always thought, but to study for medical school to go west to the reservations of tribal peoples. Thomas Jefferson Brooks had offered to pay for his education, and he had decided to accept the offer. But first, a summer getting reacquainted with Peru, Indiana. Nobody better taunt him when he bought his ice cream—

"Pleased to meet you. All of us McClures are good people," he said, winking at John so he would put the name question on ice.

"Durn tootin'," John McClure said, letting them all help prop him up in his cot. "Surgeon Burkhart says I will be released in two weeks. To go home to—what?" His heart was heavy, almost sick with dull grief over his sister.

"Yes, the regiment will be getting mustered out right about then," Walter said, "and we'll all be going home. I heard from Captain Beem today that his wife has a little house ready for him to come home to and his law partners are planning a welcome home celebration."

"Home," McClure said, as if the word were a gift to him, wrapped in white satin ribbon. And yet that ribbon was now fringed with black. The idea that soon the fulfillment of three years of yearning would finally be realized struggled with the grief that sat in his stomach like a lump of suet.

He had to go on, of course, one had to. That was the rock-bottom truth after every funeral. The living are after all, still alive. And he was young. It was all ahead—

"When we get back, I want Redskin—that is, Walter, to come down to God's country and we'll have a coon shoot back in the woods—"

"Thanks, John," Walter said smiling, "but I don't kill animals. Lots of my relatives do, though, and you can come up to Peru sometime. We'll take you out to my Miami ancestors' fishtraps in the Wabash. Best fishing in the world." And then he thought about that. He didn't really want John in Peru. It wouldn't fit. Anyway, now that he had been granted equality by his cousin, he wasn't even sure he liked him well enough to have him visit. "Maybe I could just come and you could show me your farm." He nodded his goodbyes and went on down the rows of beds.

"Yes. My farm." John said the words and wondered what they meant. What would it be like without Mary Jane's strength in his life? But then— He had beat the law of averages. Do the very best you can and things'll generally turn out—

"What are you lookin' to do, John?" Grandma Catherine wanted to know.

"Waal, I want you to give a letter to the carpenter that is making the house Mary Jane planned. Tell him to get started, jest as he had 'spected to this week. Uncle Arch can handle the money part of it; he's still trustee. I can oversee most of the housebuildin' when I get back, and we'll move in. Me and Annie, and Bob, if he don't leave or gets tired of Oregon. And mebbe someday I'll have someone to share it with."

His grandmother smiled as she watched his eyes come alive, and he saw her and shrugged, a little embarrassed. Having little else to do in the hospital, he had been writing letters to an old school friend, Frances Purcell, and she had answered back, long friendly letters. Only trouble was, she was related to the Duggers, whom he had never liked very well. Snakes in the bluegrass. Well, you couldn't have everything.

"Tell me the other news from home, Grandma Catherine," he said with a sigh. It would take his mind off the grief and shock of all this.

"Well, your cousin Zach Scott has married Delia Dugger from down at Duggerville." He looked at his grandmother. Could she read minds?

"Half the county is gabbing about it, but most think it's a good match for him. Don't know about her," Catherine sniffed. "Horace and Clarissa are as happy as two peas in a pod over by Corydon. Young Montmorency is gettin' sent to a boys' academy around Boston 'to complete his education in the liberal arts and sciences,' so says his mother." Catherine rolled her eyes.

"Annie says if he ever shows his pie-face around these parts again, she's a-going to paste it flat,'' Aunt Jewell said. ''An' I tole her she had my permission.''

''Well, I don't know about that,'' Catherine said, a little stiffly.

John looked at them, then laughed so hard his side wound hurt. ''You can harness two mares side by side, but you cain't make 'em pull together all the time,'' he thought. Then, he asked, ''How's my cousin, Jacob Joe Scott?''

''No one in the North has ever heard a word. We get information from the Dugger relatives in Louisville that he is still alive, but poorly in health. Scant information it is.''

''And Aunt Lettie?'' John wanted to know.

''She's fine, I guess,'' Catherine said. Haven't seen my own daughter in a right smart spell. ''I've been helping Esther with cooking for the extra hands at spring plowing—and then there was the trouble with Mary Jane.

''She waren't at the funeral,'' Jewell said dully. The doings of Lettie Hogue had really ceased to interest her very much.

''She had gone to Indianapolis to carry her millinery employer's books to the state house for audit,'' Catherine said.

She lied. Only Catherine, of course, of all the people in Knox County knew that Lettie had slipped out of town on the train and crossed the country on the cars ''on an errand of mercy you just have to trust me about, Mother.'' What she did not know was that at the very moment they spoke, Lettie was coming home from New York City. To understand that, we need to retrace our steps a bit.

*   *   *   *

Willis Mawkins, Zach Scott, and Lettie Hogue arrived in the big city on time and disembarked in the sulphur-smelling station. Picking cinders off their clothing, they walked up the stairs. ''I think I'll stop by the comfort parlor, Willis,'' Lettie had said in the fluttery little way she had adopted for this trip.

''I need to be excused, too. Mawkins, watch the luggage and I'll be back so you can make a visit yourself,'' Zach told the other man. Before Mawkins could protest, they were off to the public necessaries in the New York train terminal.

''We have just a moment,'' Zach told Lettie as they slipped behind a potted plant near a soda stall. ''Here,'' he said, reaching inside his coat, ''is the letter. He just gave it to me, as we came into the city. Sealed and within another envelope, which is also sealed. So there would be no chance for me to open it. We all trust each other so much,'' he snorted.

''Now it is up to me to find the provost office here, once I slip away,'' Lettie said, tucking the letter in her bosom. ''I have found out one thing: the time is the Democratic Convention in Chicago in July.''

"I suspected as much. Any indication as to numbers of Confederate troops involved?"

"No. They'll have to crack the code to get that." She looked at him a moment. "I'll say goodbye now. Give Willis this note from me. It should keep him from searching the city when I disappear." She put a piece of perfumed stationery in Zach's hands. "Go ahead, read it. It'll only take a moment," Lettie commanded with a smile.

Zach quickly drew the note out.

Willis—

I discover I do not have the heart for renewing our trysting times.

I needed to find out that our affair is over. I will make my way back alone, as I am determined not to further compromise myself or to be beholden to you for my lodging. I hope we can meet in Vincennes as friendly acquaintances.

Goodby,
Lettie

Zach put the note in his pocket as Lettie turned from him. She vanished into the crowd within a few seconds, leaving only the scent of her perfume in the air to remind him she had risked her safety and still might forfeit it, to help him in his desperate scheme.

Mawkins read the note, wadded it up, and cursed a string of oaths.

"What's the matter, Willis?" Zach asked innocently.

"The guinea hen has flown the coop," Mawkins said. "Never mind," he continued almost to himself. "If she don't have the sense to appreciate a gentleman's ability to do for her, why, I guess I know those who will. Right in this very city."

"Ungrateful, was she?" Zach asked.

"The little bitch didn't know she was journeyin' with a rich man."

"Oh?" Zach said, almost as if he didn't believe Mawkins.

"I have close to $100,000 in my valise here." He just could not resist bragging about it, could he, Zach told himself.

"For the guns? Will it take that much?" Zach asked him. He knew very well it wouldn't.

"Keep your voice down when you talk of the guns. Of course it won't. But I do have my expenses, don't you know?" His eyes became slits. "They leave it to me to hand out the cash to the Knights of the Golden

Circle. As I see fit. And expense money is due me for what I have done in this war. I see it as givin' me my due. Of course, there may be some of it for you, depending on how all this turns out.''

"Of course, Willis." Zach pulled out a pocket watch. "I must get my ticket to Washington and then, let me see, are my Confederate papers in order?''

"Shut up, I told you." No one was listening as they sat in this deserted corner of the station, but Mawkins was always afraid government spies were about.

Zach picked up a saddlebag he had reclaimed from the baggage car, the only baggage he would carry from here on in. He opened it. "Lets see— vials of chloroform, morphine, flasks of alcohol, very 'scace' item, ten full kits of the finest scalpels and surgical tools." They took up almost the entire case, with maps of the route he was to take on top, along with a steamship ticket to go to the Northern-held Harrison's Landing on the James, his striking out point for the South. He would add a few food rations in Washington; right now the bags were almost too heavy to carry on the train.

He went on checking off the plans as he understood them. "I am to get pies in Washington, plenty of them there, you said, to cover the surgical supplies and—here are my papers. A Yankee sutler's license for Hancock's corps, with forged signature. That's my safe conduct through the Northern lines. And a Rebel sutlers' license, and other, secret papers for passage through all the Southern lines. Signed by—Captain Thomas Hines, and— James Seddons, the Secretary of War of the Confederate States of America." He raised one of the flasks of alcohol. "Mr. Seddons, your health." He toasted the distinguished Confederate without ever taking the cork out of the flask. Then he turned in the other direction, towards the north. "Tom Hines, here's to you and old times. May your ventures prosper all of us.''

Mawkins looked at him oddly, and Zach reprimanded himself. Probably he was getting too devil-may-care and smart-pants. He'd better be a good boy. Solemnly, he shook Mawkins's hand and said, "I'll hope to see you back in southern Indiana, when you have completed your task, and I have delivered this message of deliverance to our Cause. All the best of luck, Mawkins.''

There! Zach thought, relieved, watching Mawkins head for the station door to get a hack. His worst fear was that for some reason Mawkins would want to see the message again, but no, he had just gone to get his guns and wait for his faithful retainer's return. What would Mawkins do if and when he found Zach had betrayed him, when he did not return to take the guns? Zach ran a finger around the inside of his collar, which was frayed and irritating his neck. When he got back to Vincennes, he would have to tell

Mawkins that he had delivered the letter and then decided to go to free his brother; with the South cut off the way it was, Mawkins would never know the difference until it was too late. Besides, he would not, could not challenge Zach too much without endangering the plot. And Zach would, of course, lay low, severing all connections with the Sons of Liberty-Knights of the Golden Circle.

Zach stepped along smartly to the ticket booth. "One ticket to Washington City," he said, and the buck-toothed ticket seller shoved the piece of paper over the marble counter.

Up the stairs and across the tracks to another line he bounded. His spirits began to lift. Ha! That much of the voodoo hoe-down was over. And not even one person had rolled in the mud and turned into a chicken. Well, if Lettie could just get to the provost's office, and get her message delivered, they'd be halfway home. Home. The word resonated in his mind, and he saw both the old Scott homestead across from Fort Knox, and Delia at Rivertides. She must be in the garden now, transplanting the delphinium she loved. Well, outdoors somewhere. Not horseback riding, surely. Not now. He grinned sheepishly. What in the world was a prospective father doing going through the lines to Richmond with a chance of getting shot? "Oh-goo," he told himself sarcastically. The spell of the big black spirit extended all the way to New York City. That must be it. Nothing else could explain such shenanigans. Smiling at the ridiculousness of what he was thinking and whistling as if he had not a care in the world, he boarded the train to Washington City.

Two days later, sitting in the tearoom of the Willard Hotel, Zach glanced at his watch a little nervously. It was almost noon, two hours past the hour he and Thomas Jefferson Brooks had agreed to meet. Time was drifting by; it would take him the best part of a week, at least, to make his way through the tortuous path mapped out for him to get to Richmond. He had his small food and camping supply, pies (apple and peach, the best) and now he needed to know he would not be shot if he went.

He ordered more coffee and was stirring it absently when he finally heard Brooks' voice. "Double double, toil and trouble," Brooks said, then slid into a chair beside him. "My back hurts," the older man commented. "I used to pole a flatboat hour after hour on the Mississippi. Did you know I was a boatman? Made enough money to come to Indiana that way."

Zach smiled that he hadn't, but he could easily believe that this tough old man was one of the legendary boatman Mike Fink's comrades.

"Now about my desire to buy your hosiery line for my daughter's store," Brooks said in a moderately loud, for-the-public, voice. Confederate spies were known to come in and out of Washington, almost at will. When the people who you were fighting looked and talked almost exactly like you, it made spying a lot easier.

Then, whispering, "Awful things kept happening on the trip out. The cars overturned in Ohio. Six women were injured and a child killed. It was worse than when the stagecoaches overturned. They brought out wagons and took us up the road to a stop further up and we caught another train." He let his thoughts wander for a moment, then continued.

"Then, when I got here, I couldn't get to see the President. I stayed here at the Willard. I went up the first afternoon I arrived here, then all day yesterday, and the secretary, or standing guard said that President Lincoln was receiving dispatches from Spotsylvania. That the situation was changing rapidly, though we were winning, it seemed. But I kept in my place. Had someone go get me a meat pie for dinner.

"Finally, I got desperate yesterday afternoon late. I asked a guard for the President's usual schedule, if he ever took recreation. He told me that most days Mr. Lincoln liked to go target shooting before breakfast in the yard of the army barracks. Actually, he had told me that himself, when I met him. I went out this morning at 6:30 o'clock and sure enough, there he was. I posted myself at the wrought-iron fence."

"How faithful a friend you have been," Zach said. "Surely you did not need to do any of this."

"Not let him know of a plot to our national war effort? Of course I would! Besides," his eyes grew solemn, sad. "your brother was Tommy's friend, and anytime I can do something along that line, it almost seems as if I'm doing it for Tommy. Well, Lincoln had a large rifle, handsomely set with silver on the stock. Fine shot too. Rang close to the bullseye. Not many were out; the morning was dreary and windy with a hint of rain. I called out, 'Mr. Lincoln.' He did not look up but called for the targets to be reset. I suppose he gets many gawkers at his private moments. But I would not be dissuaded. " 'Mr. Lincoln, it's I, Thomas Jefferson Brooks. The sutlers—remember?'

"He looked up across the barracks yard with the kindest smile I think I've ever seen. 'How is the corn in Southern Indiana, Mr. Brooks. Have the squirrels been at the seed this spring?' " Zach, listening intently, smiled broadly.

"I answered that they had not got at mine, but that was because the groundhogs got it all already. The President laughed and came to the fence, waving off his guards. I knew I had to speak carefully and quickly. 'Mr. President,' I whispered low, 'I have come all the way from Indiana on the train because I have specific news of a treasonous plot in the Northwest, given me by one who was trusted by the Knights of the Golden Circle, but is now bent on helping us.' He said nothing, only inspected his gun stock.

" 'I need an hour with you as soon as possible. They are buying guns to arm the prisoners in Camp Douglas at this very moment.' "

"He told the guard to bring me to the White House at once and I have been there with him ever since. He had gotten wind of the conspiracy; our intelligence is very good, but not all of the details you gave. It confirmed his suspicions. As I was talking to him news came from the provost marshall in New York City. Miss Hogue came yesterday and gave them the paper, and it was being transmitted to Washington by the Secret Service."

Zach had a small coughing fit, and when he had finished hacking and discreetly spitting, said, "So Lettie got her mission done. Did she—get out of town?"

"The provost had her escorted by guards in civilian clothes and put on the train for Indiana this morning. I am sure she is on her way there now."

"What will they do with Mawkins?"

"Nothing yet. They have decided to let the plot spin itself out with constant observation. Then they can act when it reaches a climax. Mawkins will be dealt with later. There is every reason, the President's aides said, to let him deal his treasonous hands for a while. They'll decide when to call the bets."

Zach breathed a sigh of relief and picked up a glass. He poured ice water into it and then drained it. "And my mission to save Jacob Joe? What of that?" he asked as he set the glass down.

"I told him in detail what you had in mind, and he said it was foolhardy, dangerous and not promising of success. And then he wished you well and said he would get a secret pass and a Northern sutler's license drafted at once. Zach, it will be from the President of the United States himself. He said, 'Too many brothers have been split by this conflict. If one set can be reunited, then I am well pleased.' "

"If," Zach repeated. "Many miles and a swamp full of trouble lie between here and Richmond."

"Yes, I am afraid for you. If I were a better pray-er I'd pray for you. But I expect Grandmother Poore is on her knees for all of us. She seemed to sense something big and troublesome was in the wind."

"I will need all the help I can get," Zach said, rising from the table.

Thomas Jefferson Brooks, frankly wearied by all of the confusion and exertion, excused himself to his room upstairs and Zach went immediately to prepare to depart the town, to get the steamboat for Harrison's Landing, and the land of danger.

He made an uneventful trip on the steamboat to the area of the James River in Virginia, near Richmond, captured early in the war and held ever since by the North. And, in that settlement of a thousand ship masts and smokestacks and a melee of military confusion, he bought the best horse he could find and carefully loaded on the saddle bags.

Then, out of Harrison's Landing, he made his way along a road crowded with army and private wagons, sleeping in a deserted barn off the road. The next day he reached the extent of the Northern army's lines within the hour, was stopped by the guards, then taken, finally to the Officer of the Day. Showing the sutler's wares in the saddlebag, the pies, the scalpels, and the morphine, he came to a moment when he had to decide which pass to show. He had Mawkins' forged Northern pass hidden on his person, but it was for Hancock's Second Corps. It might have worked. But the new one, made just yesterday at Lincoln's command, was up-to-the-minute. These people were serious; he had better pull out the big guns. The new pass was the one he used.

"This pass says you are with Sheridan's Cavalry. Why are you not with them?" the captain asked.

Zach had read the Washington papers, talked to folk at Willard's, thought about this a lot. "They are travelling light, as Grant has ordered, with only a few supply wagons. I was sent away earlier, asked to find emergency supplies for the surgeon and his field hospital, bring 'em through the lines."

"Sheridan is God knows where. He hit the Rebels at Yellow Tavern near Richmond, but he could not penetrate, and the Rebs are after him. He's wheeling about the countryside just west of here, trying to find safety. You can't locate him, I tell you."

"Sheridan trusts me to get through. I'm a daredevil. If I could swim, I would've gone down Niagara in a barrel." That sounded good. It made Zach feel expansive. "When I travelled with Sheridan earlier, I had my wagon destroyed by the Rebels. Mounted a horse and took a gun and fought with the troops in the Valley. What a fight that was!" He added a few details he had taken the time to bone up on.

The captain was not impressed. "This is an awful time to be travelling this way. The Rebels are nervous as ticks and ready to shoot anything wearing blue around Richmond. Why don't you just wait? He is likely headed for Harrison's Landing."

"That could be a week, maybe two. Can't wait. Sheridan needs these surgical supplies now. After all, his cavalrymen are out there, some wounded. They are my friends."

Carefully the officer scanned Zach's face, trying to decide just what type of man would try to infiltrate this bloody war zone. Or was this man a Rebel spy? The papers looked authentic. "Grant has some of his best generals trying to break through to Richmond, without much luck. He may be coming down soon himself. The fire on Jeff Davis is stoked hot. You will have to cut through Rebel lines that are pulled as taut as a clothesline. Don't you know that?''

"I am prepared to bear the risk.'' Zach coughed a little.

The captain sighed, and took out a handkerchief to mop his forehead. He did not want to take the responsibility. He was a small, corpulent man whose stomach bulged over his pants, and this May evening was stuffy, hot after recent rains.

"You will have to ask the colonel.'' And so he took Zach to a spiffily dressed colonel with long handlebar mustachios, the very picture of military smartness, who sat at a table outside a tent paring his fingernails.

Zach told his story again. When he was done, the colonel looked at the captain. "Government keeps certifying these damned pie sellers to trot around as if they are General Hancock himself. I thought they were supposed to stop doing that after the investigations.'' He clamped down with vehemence on his thumbnail.

The captain nodded nervously and took out his handkerchief again. The colonel read the papers. Without looking at Zach he asked, coolly,

"Why do you have pies on top of scalpels?''

"This mission for Sheridan is semi-secret. Important.'' He winked. "I don't want to have to answer every Tom, John and Billy's questions by showing them the real stuff. Pies'll do for most.'' His voice was husky from the coughing. Damn it! How irritating. He cleared his throat and spat.

The colonel squinted at his little finger, then carefully trimmed. "The sutler papers are in order,'' he said to the captain. "They say he's loyal. If this damned fool wants to go get his ass blown off to get through the lines to sell his wares, let him do it. Simple Simon, go forth! Sheridan's probably back at the coast by now!'' He dashed his fingernail scrapings off the table in a grand sweep and wrote out the pass for Zach to pass through his lines. Zach did not even have to call on Abraham Lincoln's personal letter to escape from the Army of the Potomac.

He looked at the map Mawkins had given him and headed the horse towards the road into the nearby Blackwater Swamp. It loomed ahead, a sea of tall swamp grass broken by thickets of gloomy trees with roots in the water and, on its highest ground, land farmed when the waters of Blackwater Creek were not overflowing.

It was the no man's land of the war, the bug-infested, impenetrable lowlands area where men of both armies hid out: deserters from the ranks, civilian desperados, blockade pirates and camp followers who had accumulated private hoards they did not want detected.

Following a trail west through the swamp, watching all the little intricate trails Mawkins had marked for him on the map, Zach passed through miles of swamp grass and tall reeds, flat marshes where water birds raised and lowered their feet and frog gurrumphing was a resounding, ceaseless clamor. Late in the afternoon he came to a rise which looked healthier and freer of gnats and mosquitoes than the bogs he'd been passing through.

Further up the hill was a strung-out frame house which looked either half built or half fallen down, he could not tell which. He would steer clear of that. No telling who was in it, and he would not know which role to play, North or South. He would tether his horse here near the stream, eat a cold supper, and sleep until first light tomorrow. His goal was Petersburg, near Richmond, and it was only a few miles further. The town was in a state of confusion trying to meet what was sure to be a final, massive northern invasion, and he could enter unobserved, pick up some information about the status of security in Richmond, and head on into the city.

He ate a little cold meat and bread. Then he stood and bent over with coughing as one of his hacking fits, the first all day in this beneficially humid croup-tent of a swamp, overtook him. When his breathing calmed, he went to check the saddlebags. He did this every few hours, as if to reassure himself that the passes, the tickets to his own security, were in order. He dug down.

Yes, the important, life-saving passes were safely hidden, authentic Northern Sheridan pass under the lining of a scalpel case, Southern War Office pass under the paper lining of morphine tablets. And the precious— and dangerous, here in the South— Lincoln personal pass, most important of all, in an invisible slit in the side of the saddlebag. Then, the everyday passes— the forged Mawkins passes, one for a Southern sutler, and the other for a Northern sutler to Hancock's Division. He lay those on the very top, strapped the bag shut and then—knew no more. Someone hit him on the head with a blunt instrument from behind.

When he awoke, it was to the jarring din of a banjo. He had been dragged unconscious into the lamp-lit interior of the cabin up the hill, and now was bound about his arms. His head throbbing, he looked around the dimness of the cabin at a circle of faces, none of which was particularly interested in him. All were dressed in blue, blue-army issue shirts, worn blue trousers, Yankee-issue foraging caps. Probably a hard-headed spy unit. Where were those Yankee passes? For a moment his mind clouded, then he recalled they were safe in the saddlebags. Or were they?

A man with sergeant's stripes on his sleeve came over and stood staring down at him. "So yer cranium's still in one piece, huh? You announce your arrival everwhere you go with that there coughin', Johnny?"

Zach decided to take the plunge. They said the Indians always respected you if you had indomitable courage even when they threatened you; this

Yankee spy unit, or whoever they were, needed to know he had gumption. "I'm not Johnny, Reb that is. I'm Billy Yank."

"Oh, you are, are you? Well one of your papers says you're passin' through as a Southern sutler. The other one says you're a sutler for Hancock's Corps. Now which are we to believe?"

Well, they had found the passes which were out on top of his saddlebag gear. "And we have et all your pie. Don't know what all that other stuff underneath it is." No interest in the surgical apparatus and medical supplies. That stuff was worth money; apparently they did not care about it. Spies, certainly, then, not contrabanders. If they were spies, they were stupid ones. Well, anyway, they had not discovered the authentic stashed passes. Good.

"Unloose me and I'll tell you who I am," Zach said. The private returned to the rest of the blue-clads in the cabin, who had put down the banjo and were now playing poker at the table. They held a whispered conference and the private came and cut the ropes Zach was bound with.

He was taken to stand by the table, where the men were slapping down aces and jacks and smoking cigars and cigarettes. One clean-shaven man wearing a cavalry sergeant stripes, was taking snuff and drinking whisky. A plate of sandwiches was at his elbow. This spy outfit was certainly not doing without the amenities of life, Zach noted.

"And you are?" the cavalryman asked.

"Zach Scott of Indiana, sirs. I am a sutler delivering emergency medical supplies to General Sh—Hancock." He had almost said Sheridan. They had found the Hancock pass. "Let's keep the story straight, Zach," he told himself sternly. "You've got to think on your feet. You've usually been pretty good at that."

"Zach Scott of Indiana," the man said in a measured voice that showed his suspicion, "Hancock is still back by the Rapidan." He put away his snuffbox and sneezed discreetly.

"Yes, but not for long." Several pairs of eyes looked at him for the first time.

"Well, yes," he went on rapidly, beginning to feel the part that he was beginning to play. "I was ordered to get some emergency medical supplies for the Second Corps in Washington. And they told me—ah—not to return to the camps near Spotsylvania but to—ah—meet them down the way." His voice had grown a little high pitched and strained. Damn!

"Oh, they did, did they?" said a dark, Italian-looking blue-clad across the table from the cavalryman. He stubbed out a cigarette and looking at Zach with coolly appraising eyes. "Scott of Indiana, you stumble like a drunken uncle, don't you?"

Zach told himself to think fast. There was a need for a diversion. "Well, yes," Zach said, continuing the high-pitched voice. He added effeminate, rather girl-like, fluttery little gestures with his hands, "They said that they had orders from General Grant that they would be moving all of the Northern troops south to Richmond on May 19."

There was a silence around the table. No one played a card. It was almost as if the men were testing the information, wondering what to do with the fact that in four more days the Army of the Potomac would be near Richmond. And they might, for all he knew. The rumor was as good as any he had heard at the Willard.

Zach burbled on. "But of course, sirs, I'm not breaking secrecy because obviously you are on the right side." He tittered nervously and hitched up his trousers.

The sergeant took out the snuffbox again and put it on the table. He tapped it with his index finger. "What are you, a goddamned pederast or what? Is he a little lady, men?" They guffawed.

"OK, Sallie Sue, or whoever you are, tell us what you know about Grant's movement south. Spill the navy beans, girlie pooh."

Zach looked intensely frightened. "Oh sirs, you know I am nervous even talking about all this secret information entrusted to me on this emergency mission even with you, loyal soldiers of Abraham Lincoln."

The men sat stock still for a moment, then the one with the sergeant's stripes began to chortle. The others took it up and soon all were laughing around the table, whooping and slapping their knees. All but the Italian-looking man, who casually lit another cigarette and sat watching the smoke rise without speaking.

"You goddamned bubble head," said the man who had unbound him. "We're Confederate spies, roustabouts, wearin' Yankee blue."

"Oh, no, sirs," Zach said, waving his hand about like a seal flipper. "Say not so, and I have just run off at the mouth—"

"And now you've just told us the one piece of information the government in Richmond has been pinin' to get aholt of." The "private" came over and slapped him on the back in exuberant jollity, harder than he needed to. The men were still laughing, bent over with the enormity of the joke.

Zach looked sufficiently crestfallen. Behind his fallen face he thought, coldly, "Bubble head, am I? As if I could possibly be fooled by you, you pack of clowns. What Northern soldier that I've ever heard of takes snuff? A decidedly Southern habit, disgusting as it is. The minute I saw that I knew you were Rebels. And what Yankee soldier even out in the swamp wears shoes two sizes too big, and a Zouave uniform from 1861? We'll show you who's girly-pooh or not." But he looked timorous and continued to fake his nervous little laugh and looked in his pocket for a comb to slick up his pretty, curly locks.

The next morning the "sergeant" told the Italian Rebel, "Benelli, go with this Scott of Indiana to Richmond. Find the colonel in charge of defendin' the city. Tell him what this faggot told us. They will find it very interestin'." The dark-eyed, taciturn Italian took off his blue coat and put on the nondescript homespun brown shirt of a farmer. He picked a felt farmer's hat from a group of different hats on pegs in the logs. Then he went to Zach with a pistol and marched him towards the horse. But before he allowed Zach to mount, he carefully inspected the saddlebags. Zach did not know how much the man had seen in the bags, and it was to worry him all morning.

They headed northwest, out of the swamp, following the railroad line to Petersburg, travelling until the sun was high. They stopped in a tangled woods outside of the town of Petersburg, which was not far from Richmond. "We will get the lay of the land before we travel further," the Italian said, leading them into a patch of woods. He let Zach dismount, go for a trip to the woods in range of the pistol; then he made Zach gather firewood and cook meat and beans.

He sat with his pistol held obviously in his hand, watching Zach put pieces of good beefsteak in a frying pan. "I do not think you are a pederast, Scott of Indiana," he said in a low voice. "The others were fools to think so. But then that is no suprise. Only one or two are spying for the government. The rest are deserters." He looked keenly at Zach, studying him from head to foot. "About your news concerning Grant's army, I do not know."

Zach did not look up.

"Nor do I think you are a Union licensed sutler. I have found papers in the saddlebag that say you are from Sheridan's army, not Hancock's. The man who carries two passes probably needs them because he is a spy."

He sprang up to put the pistol at Zach's head. "Who are you? Tell me or I shoot. Do not tell me a lie; I will know it. I was intelligence gatherer for the liberation army in Italy. I was with Garibaldi, and believe me, I know every sort of deception there is. Speak true."

It was the moment Zach had dreaded, meeting a shrewd, savvy spy who was every bit as much of a deceiver as he was. There was only one course. "Well, and would you like to see one more pass, this one the real one?"

The man looked dubious, but he lowered the pistol a little.

"Now, just let me inch my way back here to the horse, get into my saddlebags, sir—"

"Rico is my name. Rico Benelli, but I am Rico to all. Confederate States of America, Secret Service. And I am watching you with my pistol."

"Good. And sir, would you mind—turning the steak, please? I'm hungry and it will take a moment to tell my tale."

Never taking his eyes off the saddlebags for a moment, Rico did turn the steaks in the pans and stir the beans. Good spying did not mean going without dinner.

Zach returned with the pass from the Confederate Secretary of War and Tom Hines and showed it to the Italian. He told him he was delivering a verbal message from powerful elements in Canada to the government in Richmond. Gesturing for Zach to continue cooking, he digested the information.

"And yet," he said, "the other passes were forged. We spies must pass in and out of parts as the actor in the comic opera. Is that not true? It is the spy's job to deceive. The better he does it, the better he is at his job."

Zach nodded, smiling a little. He could not quarrel with that description. Rico went on.

"Your accents are from the North and yet you seem on some sort of message-carrying mission which you will not reveal except to highest authorities in the South. Why should I trust you to tell me you are a Confederate? Best I shoot you, right out and kill all the parts you play."

"No, no," Zach insisted. "I tell you I have been trusted all the war as a Northern supporter of the South. I rode with John Morgan in his invasion of the Northwest."

"Ah, now I have you there. My brother rode with Morgan. He was with the Eighth Kentucky Regiment. Is now in a Northern prison," the man said. Zach began spooning up the food, putting it onto the tin plates the man provided from his own gear.

"I knew the regiment well," Zach said. And as they ate, he went on to detail his experience, mentioning the few names he recalled in the unit.

"And yet you could have learned that from the tales told about Morgan. Many spies do. Tell me what the colonel was like."

"Handsome face to win any woman who sees him. The very picture of Southern gallantry and honor. Finest clothing. When I knew him he had just been given new Spanish riding boots and a crop of embossed morocco. But inside the fancy picture is a man with a strong need to be praised. He risked his men in the raid unnecessarily on a pipe dream."

"My brother said so, too," Rico murmured. "If I could just be sure."

"Have you seen his signature?" Zach wanted to know.

"Yes, I have a personal letter from him, sent when he was in prison, regretting my brother's capture."

Zach put down his plate and reached deep into the pockets of his brown trousers. There, creased almost to the point of tearing, was a piece of folded paper. It was the pass from John Hunt Morgan, given to him by Hines. He gave it to Benelli.

Rico read it, and then put down his plate, as if what he had to tell Zach could not be said with common food in the hand. "Ah, my friend. I finally see you are a comrade, not an adversary. In Italy we learn the word *fedele*. It is everything in our work to build the Italian nation. Do you know it?''

Zach said he did not, but wondered what it had to do with spying. Rico Benelli clapped him on the back in a comradely way and chuckled.

So, the Italian had come to trust him, Zach thought, with mild amusement. That was because he had it over the man; Rico Benelli was a good, committed man of honor and he, Zach Scott, had been evil for as long as he could remember, until, perhaps, lately.

Rico picked up his plate again and began to fork in steak and beans; Zach silently followed his example. Finally Rico spoke again. ''Loyalty is everything we do in my home. First is *fedele* to family, of course. Highest *fedele*. Then to state. We do not know country as you. That is why I come to the South in her struggle for freedom. For rights for the state!'' He rose and kicked the ashes of the fire about.

''Spying is not really for the clods you saw back at the cabin. It is for the shrewd and what you call it—stealthy.'' He covered the fire with sand, spread the embers out and buried them, and scrubbed the plates with more sand, saving the water in the canteens.

''Beyond that,'' he continued, looking seriously at Zach, ''among spies on the same side, is *fedele*. Loyalty. None of those bushwhackers at the hut—'' he gestured over his shoulder through the swamp—'understood that. Perhaps you, with your cleverness will.''

He picked Zach up from the fireside, grabbing him by the hand.

''We travel together to Richmond. I shall be your guide, through Petersburg and beyond, right to President Davis's office.'' As they walked towards the horses, talking and joking, Zach worried about how in the world he was going to handle this new turn of events. He had done his job too well! How was he going to get his new comrade out of the way before Rico took him right up to the door of the war office and introduced him to President Jefferson Davis himself. Then he would have to produce a momentous message letter which he no longer possessed, which was in the hands of the Northern authorities, being acted on in some secretive way, at this very moment. The last person in the world he needed to encounter was the President of the Confederate States of America.

The next day, they came into the streets of Richmond. It had been a tedious ride from Petersburg, through the fortifications surrounding that town. Various units of the Confederate Army clogged the road with ambulance and supply wagons from a calvary battle nearby. Detachments of Stuart's cavalry thundered by with grim, angry eyes and slouch hats pulled low. They were seeking units of the Northern general, Sheridan, who might still be in the area. Sheridan's men had just shot their leader, Jeb Stuart, one of the great generals of the Confederacy, and they sought bloody retribution.

Refugees who had not fled Petersburg before were leaving, heading away from the town which was increasingly in the way of what was shaping up as a great battle for Richmond.

Zach and Benelli had been stopped several times by suspicious scouting parties of the Confederate army and once by the captain of a regiment trying to trace Sheridan. Always Benelli handled it with whispered conversations and by showing his own papers.

Now they were approaching the capital of the Confederacy on the southeast, past old defense trenches from the Seven Days' Battles. These entrenchments looked like simple mounds of dirt, but they were being fortified with logs and abatis. "The big battle will come," Benelli said. "If not next month, then next year. We will fight it out on this line, as General Grant has said, before the very gates. These old trenches—" he gestured towards the mounds—"which a horse can jump over, are giving way to the new-style embattlements, with shredded metal beams, spears like—how you say it—porcupine quills from them and logs piled and intertwined to the skies. There are mines being set just below the surface of the ground. And water batteries on the river. If we must defend ourselves, at least we will do it with the latest in military science."

They rode into the city itself. Zach's curiosity overcame his anxiety to be rid of the scout who represented danger to him, no matter how charming he was. "Rico, you are in and out of Richmond all the time. Tell me what I am seeing," Zach said.

Rico began to rise a little in the saddle, to point at sights. "There, on that big hill, is the capital of the Confederacy. We will see it now, then I will show you the town a little before we complete our errand." They rode a short way up Capitol Square, saw the state house, a large building with Ionic pillars, a graceful church with a tall spire and an equestrian statue of Washington outside it and various stately mansions. They guided their horses down the steep road, proceeded up the narrow, sedate, main streets of Richmond, with two-and-three story, Federal-style buildings, lamplights, and trees in square boxes on the brick sidewalks.

Rico pointed out sights along the way. "And there, on your right, is New Military Hospital. They have, they say, some of the best surgeons in the Confederacy now, and women acting as nurses."

"Women, you say?" Zach's voice, in spite of itself, emerged with a fringe of frayed emotion. He was within yards of his mission, close to Jake. Was this the right hospital? There were several. He must try to sound casual. "Who is—kept in there?"

Rico raised his eyebrows a fraction of an inch at the question. "Why, the convalescents and desperate cases of the battles west of here. Some patients from other theatres, as the Yankees seize more territory south. And the prisoners, political ones, who are in the tobacco warehouses.'' Zach began to cough again, a long, chest-burning fit.

Rico leaned back in his saddle in a moment, continuing his travel discourse. ''And there on the corner, my friend, underneath that street lamp, is the Alps cafe. It is, even in the midst of all this confusion and despair, an oasis of quiet pleasure.''

''Could we get a cup of coffee there?''

''Well, if not coffee, then sassafras tea or some substitute. Would you like to rein and have a social moment?'' They hitched their horses. ''Take off your hat. There will be ladies there. We in the Mediterranean are very—how do you say—observant, of the fairer sex.'' Rico put his teamster's hat on his saddle; Zach took off his own. They walked towards the entrance of the cafe.

''Wait a moment, Rico. I need to check the saddlebags,'' Zach said, turning around. Rico stood watching. Did some part of him still not trust Zach? He certainly had been confiding, telling his life story in Italy, and Zach had come to like him immensely. Still—what must be done must be done. Using the horse as a screen, he pulled a packet of morphine from its long, flat box, palmed it into his shirt sleeve and picked up a flask of whisky.

Inside, young, finely-dressed recruits with soft, unbearded cheeks chatted with weary-looking officers whose Butternut uniforms were threadbare and soiled. Mud-spattered teamsters sat with their feet stretched out on chairs, and there was about it all an air of desperation, like a cafe in the path of an approaching tidal wave.

''Coffee, please,'' Rico said.

A faded woman in an old-fashioned forties' calico dress out of the attic stood rather defiantly before them. ''Hit's made of dried sweet taters today. Is that a' right?''

Rico raised his hands in a shrugging gesture and smiled that disarming smile. The waitress simpered a little in spite of herself and left to get the drinks. ''Too bad, my Italian friend,'' Zach thought. ''You are the best part of all this trip so far. Will you hate me when you find I have again fooled you?'' His expression grew sober. Spying was a desperately dangerous business. Rico could be capable of, might have to, track him down and kill him when he learned of the deception. The worst parts of this mission, by far, were yet ahead.

The cups of hot potato coffee came; Rico took a long gulping drink and made a face. ''Ugh. That is Devil's brew,'' he said.

Zach took out his flask of whisky. He knew it was a rarity in the Confederacy these days, along with everything else. "Let me doctor your drink a little. After all, I deal in surgical supplies. I'm surprised your bushwhacking cronies left this medicine in the bag." He poured a little whisky in his own brew and set the flask in his lap. He went on talking.

"I think I told you I was of Scotch Irish descent. They said one of the things my grandfather Scott always did at a wake was to make Irish coffee."

The Italian looked interested. "A little coffee, a little whisky, a little sugar. I even have some of that," Zach continued, taking out a cube he had filched from the Willard hotel. "May I?"

Rico nodded eagerly. "Why don't you call over Calico Katy," Zach suggested, "and we'll order another round. It would be a pity to leave the flask unemptied."

Rico gestured to the waitress and in a minute or two, after he had thoroughly stirred the sugar into the old and fresh drinks, Zach handed Rico his.

Zach carefully husbanded his first drink while Rico emptied both of his. It took about ten minutes for the morphine powder that Zach had put into the other man's whisky to take effect and send Rico into a slump over the cups.

Zach rose, putting a greenback on the table. "My friend is so satisfied with your substitute coffee that he has fallen asleep on it," Zach said to the faded waitress. "He has been in the saddle many hours. Let him sleep it off, will you?" He gave her a greenback and walked quickly out of the cafe. Then he swung onto his horse and reached over to Rico's mount and took the teamster's hat off the saddle horn.

"Now, to the hospital," Zach thought. "Down the street here, right, then left." It was about four P.M. when he came to it; mule wagons with Conestoga-like coverings were disgorging their wounded at the door, while white-shirted orderlies with stretchers bustled about. No one noticed when a man dressed like a supply teamster—at least he had a large teamster's hat on— entered the back door.

A matron with her hair pulled back in a bun bustled by. She had stacks of linen sheets in her arms. "Pardon me, ma'am—"

"Sir, I am very busy. New cases are coming in all the time." Her voice was irritated, strident. "We have them in the halls on straw couches. Then there is the desperate matter of feeding them. I do not have one instant to—"

"Please tell Miss Dora Lavenham I need to see her at once. It is about Mr. Scott." The woman looked at him without replying for an instant, then emitted an exasperated sigh.

He stood in a back hall. The kitchen was through a door to his left; from it came the odor of cooking cabbage. No other smells were mixed with the cabbage. "Last stock of somebody's potato hole," Zach thought. Through another door he could just catch sight of a row of beds, pallets really, with men lying on them covered with bloody bandages. God, he had been playing at lodge-building for three years while some of these men bled their lives out. He felt ashamed, and yet he wasn't sure which side he would have fought on, when one came down to it. He didn't feel strongly enough to take up a musket at any time, except to shoot a loud-mouth at a rally. He was suddenly struck with the incongruity of being in this odd place, the contrast to his old life. "Playing a part. You are acting," he told himself. But he only half believed that.

A short, very slight woman with brown hair escaping all around her face from a not-too-tidy hair clasp suddenly came around the door of the wounded corridor. "Now what is it?" she demanded nervously, hardly looking at him. "Is Mr. Scott worse?"

"This Mr. Scott is very well indeed, Miss Lavenham," Zach said in a very low voice coming up to within a few inches of her face. "Especially considering he has come all the way from Vincennes, Indiana, to answer your call to help his brother."

"What?" Dora Lavenham looked in amazement into the face of the tall man in front of her and saw calm strength, bravery, and--an angular version of Jacob Joe's face. "You are Zach," she said, after a moment. And then she went to an old broken-down chair which stood discarded in the kitchen hall and sat down on it. She put her head down in her hands. The heat of the kitchen, the smells all day of festering wounds, the men taken out of the ambulances dead, and now this. She was not going to faint when help was finally here.

Finally she looked up with wondering eyes sparkling in the gloom of the gathering twilight. "Who would have thought you—" She did not finish.

"Who indeed, Miss Lavenham?" Zach answered and stared steadily at her.

Late May, 1864

Chapter Twenty-Two

Althea Dugger stood with Major Edward Bachelder on a little rise near where the ruins of Fairchance lay shadowed with late afternoon light.

"Squirrels run around, wrens make nests above us in dogwood trees over there," Althea murmured. "The slave cabins are empty and the doors are coming off their hinges. In such a short time nature reclaims its own. It is as if nobody ever conceived and bore children on this space or laughed and lived or died here."

"There are so many places like this," Bachelder said. "I think of their occupants, and even though I know the South started all this, I feel the loss. I know that so much is swept away."

"Do you, Edward?" Althea looked up at him earnestly. She had arrived on the steamboat that afternoon from Natchez and gone at once to see if he would take her out to the property. He spoke to his superiors about it, and at four o'clock they let him take the owner of the land burned by the convicted felon out to her property.

"Swept away," she murmured. "Everything." The sky was particularly beautiful tonight, with long, pink fingers fading into mauve and gray on the horizon beyond the newly-plowed cornfields. Why was nature always so mockingly exquisite, she asked herself, when the heart was dull with pain?

Edward Bachelder stooped and picked up something from the ruins. He put it in his pocket and strolled over to what had been the well, now buried under a criss-cross of burnt beams. Then he came back, with a smile on his lips. "The water still wells up there, fresh and cold," he said.

What a friend he was. On the way out, she had told him about Delia's marriage and that Zach had left to carry on some sort of mysterious business, Althea knew not what. She told him of the loss of her own mother and father, explained the affairs of the estate she would investigate tomorrow. Now she sighed, pained almost beyond speaking.

"I did not tell you the worst. Could not make myself form the words. I received a telegram before I left Natchez. My son Calhoun was killed at the

Battle of Spotsylvania.'' Bachelder touched her shoulder gently feeling her anguish.

''Willie McClure wired that he had asked for Delia in his last breath. That he died a brave, heroic death defending the road to Richmond.''

''The road to Richmond has been a long, long way for all of us. I am sorry, Althea.'' He put his arm about her.

''I did not get to say goodbye when he left. I think he thought I never knew him.'' She leaned her head on Bachelder's chest. ''Perhaps I didn't,'' she went on. ''But I am proud, so proud of him. All of them, out there, fighting for the life of the Cause, day after day of grim struggle when the odds are so bad.''

''Proud. Well, I suppose so,'' he said softly. ''I would think you would be angry. You and all the mothers across this land. Secretly angry at your Cause, too.''

''I am,'' she answered, beginning to weep. ''We all, North and South talk brave, we all believe in whatever it is we're fighting for. But the basic part of it is—they'll never come home again. Never. And they hadn't even started to live.'' She wept silently against his shoulder until it was wet with her tears.

''I never used to be able to cry,'' she said. He stroked her hair, held her close.

''And now that I can there is so much to weep for that I think I will cry forever. All, all swept away. I have nothing left except a new honesty with myself. That is new. It is something.''

''There is something else,'' Bachelder said. ''You have Fairchance.'' He reached in his pocket and took out the object he had found amidst the wreckage of the plantation. It was a skeleton key. He handed it to her. Then he pulled her into his arms, kissed her deeply. She put her arms about his neck. ''You have my love. Does that mean anything to you?'' he wanted to know.

She pulled back and looked at him earnestly. ''Yes, Edward. Yes, it does.'' She turned her face up to his again to be kissed and he lightly kissed her lips and touched the tears on her cheek, as if each was precious to him.

''Papa said after the war we would build again. That it is in the South that the fair chances will be found. What do you think?'' she asked.

''I know that I do not yearn to go to Massachusetts,'' he said, looking away towards the sunset.

''Could you stay with me here, Edward?'' she asked, looking up into his calm eyes, so steady, so honest. ''After it all is all over?''

''How would you feel about a bridegroom who is a Yankee?'' he asked, smiling.

For the first time all day a slight smile lit Althea's face. "I think the questions is, how would you feel about a bride who is a grandmother?"

Arm in arm they strolled to the old slave quarters to see if any were still in habitable condition. They would have to hire some hands, good ones. There would be wages to pay and homes to build. There was important groundwork to lay if they were going to make a cotton farm work in the new age that was certainly coming.

*   *   *   *

That same day Dora Lavenham found Zach behind a wagon in the stable. He had slept the night before in a dark corner of the old building, amidst a collection of worn-out wagons collapsing from overuse and lack of repair. He had passed unnoticed in the shadows; outside the confusion of ambulance arrivals and departures, shouts of teamsters and the shoeing of emaciated mules and horses kept the two old men who worked in the hospital yard unceasingly busy.

Dora brought bread and a little cheese. "It's all there is today. We never know. Someone found a case of eggs and Betsy is out getting them for the worst cases. A judge sent in several bottles of wine and some biscuits yesterday. We go where we must to get whatever food is available."

"Have you talked to Jake?" Zach asked, eating hungrily.

"No, and I won't. I know he is alive, because Assistant Surgeon Wilson, who is a Northerner and lives at the prison, tells me so."

"Why don't you speak to him?" Zach demanded a little irritably. He felt grubby and dishevelled. His teamster's hat—Rico's hat—was on his head.

"We must be with him when he sees you for the first time. He is too ill to deceive, to keep a plot secret. What do you have in mind for getting him out of here?"

Zach dotted at bread crumbs in his palm with his finger, eager to get the last traces. "I really had not planned that far. I thought if I could get here— you'd know what to do." He looked at her.

She frowned and began to pace about, doing puttering little things in case anyone should chance to come in and see her talking there. "I will have to find a way to get a wagon. Did you say last night you had—opium in your saddlebags?"

Zach walked to the door and took the chance of peeking out. "No, morphine and chloroform. And surgical instrument kits, several new sets."

"Good. They will be our gold. I'll go immediately to make arrangements." Suddenly Zach started and slipped into the shadows of the horse barn. "What is the matter?" Dora wondered.

"I thought I saw someone." He peered around the corner again, holding himself in the shadows. "Yes. Damn it. It's Rico. He's asking for me. I know it."

He ripped the hat off his head and tossed it into the darkness in back of him. "Was I seen last evening? Does anyone know I'm here?"

"Well, Betsy, but she's completely trustworthy. No one else that I know of. But he will have trouble getting anyone to answer anything today. The casualties are straining us to the snapping point."

Zach looked up. "Is there a loft here?"

"I have never noticed, but yes, there seems to be a loft door. For hay, when we have it. It is almost empty now."

"I will wait until this place is empty and swing myself up there. In the meantime, arrange as fast as you can for a wagon. We can be an ambulance team. The details—" He was climbing on a stack of wooden crates, reaching for the loft door.

"Leave them to me," she said and hurried into the hospital.

Assistant Surgeon Wilson was tiredly changing dressings on men with stomach wounds. They moaned almost constantly; some were delirious. The bayonet wounds were the first he had ever seen. Men fighting toe to toe as they had at the Wilderness, with bright steel blades, could inflict real wounds, wounds that were infecting. Some of the shrapnel was in the stomach wounds; many of them were hopeless; others had been fired at at point blank range and had powder burns as well as horrible, shredded faces.

"Miss Lavenham. We have some textbook cases here," he said. She looked at him exasperatedly. Textbook cases. It was always like that with him.

"I believe I have the skill to operate on some of these men to stem the infection and remove the shrapnel. If only we had some anaesthesia. The blockade running is so ineffective now we cannot get our medicines in."

"Our," Dora thought. He was himself from Rhode Island, a captured enemy of all these patients. Yet he served them; they had become his whole life. He wrapped clean linen strips around a man's suppurating wound. The man refused to look at it, clamping his eyes tight and making a fist as the surgeon lifted him up, rolled him back.

"Sir, I need your help," Dora said. The surgeon paused in his wrapping and looked up.

"My patient Jacob Joe Scott has varioloid."

"Yes, so do scores of them over in Castle Thunder. The disease is reactivating." He resumed his wrapping.

"Mr. Scott is in mortal danger."

"I know, Miss Lavenham," the surgeon said with controlled patience. "You know the rules. No one there can come in here with varioloid."

"We may lose him if he stays there."

"But we have over a thousand wounded in these hospital buildings and more coming in every hour. We do not know how to feed them, we have no anaesthesia to operate with. The Confederacy says it can't think of prisoners any more, especially since the North refuses to trade."

Dora was silent a moment, watching his skill with the patient, then said, "What would you do with four large bottles of chloroform and several hundred papers of morphine?"

The surgeon tied the bandage off and turned to face the matron. "I would open the surgery immediately and begin to take care of these shrapnel wounds. I would clean them, as the doctors are doing in the North now to stop the pus formation, if I could find something like boric acid. They have discovered that the wounds heal better cleaned, without the pus."

"Would rubbing alcohol suit for that?"

"Miss Lavenham, can you get these things?" the surgeon asked eagerly.

"I can," Dora said firmly, "if you can get a signed permit for me to take an ambulance to get Jacob Joe Scott. And get me the ambulance to do it."

"You know I am a Yankee doctor. That I operate at the mercy of these people here."

"Our Confederate surgeons are overburdened to the point of dropping. They do not know rank or even nation any more."

He emitted a long breath. "You are right. Can you tell me where you got these medical supplies and instruments?"

"No," she said decisively. "There are also several new sets of surgical tools. We must act rapidly. I want the ambulance by ten o'clock, a team of the best mules you can find harnessed to it, standing right by the barn in the stableyard."

"Oh, you do, do you?" The patient who had been wrapped moaned deeply, then yipped, almost like a dog. Wounds in the gut were especially agonizing.

"Morphine, did you say?" Surgeon Wilson asked, looking at the patient.

"Several hundred papers. Enough for several days in this ward."

"Chloroform?"

"Four large bottles. Surgery for a week, I would say, for the shrapnel section."

"Ah. I will get your team. It should not be impossible with the teams coming in. And we will admit Mr. Jacob Joe Scott this afternoon in return for your service in this medicine matter. Find a way to isolate him."

Dora averted her eyes. "About that, Dr. Wilson. I may not return until the morrow."

"The morrow? I do not understand."

"I may wish to—take Mr. Scott to private quarters to give him special care." The surgeon stared at her. "That is a part of my arrangement with you. That you will raise no questions with anyone until I return. Simply treat my absence with Mr. Scott with complete silence."

"He is a prisoner of the Confederacy."

"He will be a dead prisoner of the Confederacy if we do not give him some specialized care." The surgeon smiled tiredly.

"You—care for him, don't you?"

"Yes, I do. But first of all, he is my patient. I shall do for him what I have to, and I think you understand. I shall go now, Doctor, and get the supplies I promised and meet you as soon as possible in the yard of the stable. Remember to have the written release." She leaned close to him. "Please, sir," she whispered, "breathe not a word of this. I implore you."

He nodded and went down the line to continue his bandaging.

The supply room was dark and cluttered, with dirty bandages lying about in sickening heaps and amputated limbs stacked in the corner. "I thought I had learned to stand the smells and sights," Dora told herself, making her way through the mess with a basket on her arm. "Four years of war, and we still haven't conquered the problems of waste and cleanup." The orderlies who usually removed the hospital offal were not about. Every man who could walk was either at the front or helping prepare for the defense of Petersburg and Richmond. Intelligence said Grant would be moving towards Richmond, and the defense of nearby Petersburg, and the capital itself, was beginning in earnest.

In the corner in an old bureau were the uniforms of hospital personnel: nurses' aprons and surgeons' shirts. At the bottom was a clean white orderly's shirt with the crest of New Hospital embroidered on it. "Ah, thank you Ladies Aid of the Baptist church. This will hold us in good stead," Dora thought. She put it in her basket and rushed out the supply room door. Just around the corner she almost bumped into the dark man with the Mediterranean look, whom Zach feared to see.

She backed away with more calmness than she felt and entered the kitchen to get her breath. Suddenly, just when she needed her, there was Betsy Pickering.

"Betsy," she whispered, "Are we bound friends? You have said so—"

"Of course," the tall woman said, looking at her friend with real concern. "You are the only reason I have been able to endure this Hades and still be alive to help these men."

"Trust me that I am involved in something decent and good to help Jake.

You are the only one I have taken into my confidence about him. Will you help me?'' Her friend nodded. ''Go to that man who is in the hall near the supply room. See if you can find out what he wants. Should he ask questions about seeing a stranger around, deny that we have done it. I fear he will ruin what I want to do for Jake. We must get that man away from the hospital.''

She followed behind and, stepping behind a screen, listened as Betsy confronted the swarthy visitor. ''Sir, can I help you?'' Her voice showed courage and aplomb, more than Dora was feeling at the moment. ''We are not showing visitors through the hospital just now.''

His eyes grew evasive, then he bowed. ''Miss, I am from the War Department's extended services. I am seeking information about a man named Scott.''

''Oh?'' Betsy asked, without blinking.

''Six feet or so, he is, blonde curly hair and a sharp nose. Would such a man have been about your hospital, perhaps asking questions?''

''Sir, I can assure you I have seen no such person, and I am about a good deal,'' Betsy said, with a conviction that surprised even Dora. ''Perhaps he has gone to one of the other hospitals.'' And, as an afterthought, to seem more realistic, ''May I contact you should we have the information you seek?''

''Yes. Rico Benelli is my name. You may reach me with a letter left at the War Department Secret Service.'' He bowed and went out the back door. After Dora was sure he was out of earshot, she crept from behind the door.

''Jake is very ill, Betsy,'' she said. ''I am going to try to help him. If you do not hear from me for a while, don't worry. I will be out of touch, but I'll contact you eventually. I promise you. If you do not say anything my absence, no one will. If they ask, say I've gone into a private home, ill with exhaustion. Meanwhile, I have to ask you to assume my head matron's job. I'm sorry, indeed, to leave you at this time with it.''

''All very mysterious, my dear,'' Betsy said. ''Are you sure you will be safe?''

Dora nodded briskly.

''There is happiness in your eyes,'' her friend said, smiling. ''I cannot understand it at all, but I know it has to do with your love for him. But since we are living in a madhouse, nothing seems very strange to me. If you say so, I will not notice if you vanish from the face of the earth. And, really, I doubt anyone else will. As a matter of fact, a townswoman, probably ashamed at her inactivity up to now, came in a few moments ago to volunteer. That will be a help.'' She kissed her friend. ''The earth is swallowing us all,'' she said, pensively. ''Have your moment of joy.''

''She thinks I am spiriting Jacob Joe off so we can be married,'' Dora thought wonderingly. ''That will suit as well as anything while I am gone.'' She went, as casually as she could, to tell Zach that much to her surprise the plans seemed to have been made to their satisfaction.

Forty-five minutes later an ambulance wagon bearing New Hospital's tower and cross crest pulled up at the door of the stable. The stable master, trying to keep some account of comings and goings, asked Assistant Surgeon Wilson, who held the reins, where he was bound to.

"To pick up a couple of sick prisoners at Castle Thunder," Surgeon Wilson said noncommittally.

"So we're admittin' them again. You've sartainly taken the best o' the mules," the old man said. "Them come in with the wounded from Stuart's battle." He strutted around, bowlegged, hitching at his worn out jean trousers. "Someun tole that this team come up from Tennessee, confiscated Yankee issue."

"Well, perhaps that accounts for their fatness," the surgeon said uneasily. "We'll have them back in a twinkling." The stablemaster nodded and loped his way down past the assortment of vehicles and wounded on crutches, many of them half-dazed, some still untreated, with stiff, bloody bandages and dirty clothing. They limped about the yard seeking relief from the fetid air of the hospital. A woman was boiling linen in a huge pot over an open fire.

The surgeon leapt down. He handed Dora the written release order which would be demanded at the prison. "I had to sign it myself. No one else was around."

Dora moistened her lips. "I hope that does not cause difficulty—well, we shall deal as best we can. Here," Dora went on, handing him her basket. "All I said is within. May it bring relief to some of the poor men inside."

"Who will drive?" the surgeon said without much interest.

"I have an orderly," Dora said evenly. "A new one from the countryside." Zach came out of the barn and nodded gravely. The surgeon's full interest was on the basket. After examining it and without a goodbye, he headed almost at a run towards the infirmary.

"Now, let us see if all is well within," Zach said, peering under the canvas cover. "Wooden bunks, dirty floor—nothing more." He turned his head aside and coughed, spat on the ground. Oddly, the cough was some better. Turmoil, starvation and mortal danger must be good for it. "Good enough for our purposes," he said. He looked around, determined that he was not observed, and began lifting all kinds of empty boxes into the back of the wagon. Crates, bushel baskets, even a couple of blankets went in.

"What are you doing?" Dora wanted to know.

"We must have something to hide Jake behind," Zach told her. "Now we are about ready—" he paused in mid sentence and sprang into the wagon. "Goddamn it," he said.

"Mr. Scott!" Dora said, confounded by his sudden oath. "What is it?"

"The Italian is watching the stableyard. I do not think he saw me. You will have to drive."

She turned her head and confirmed that the dark-skinned man had not been shunted off, as they had hoped. "Me, drive?" she asked. "I have never driven a mule! You cannot mean it!"

"Do you want to save Jacob Joe, Miss Lavenham?" He was drawing tight the entry hole of the wagon's canvas cover from the inside.

"Of course," Dora said in an agonized voice.

"Then get up there and take the reins and say 'gee up' to those mules." In a few moments anyone who cared to notice would have seen a team of mules proceeding unevenly out of the hospital stableyard with a determined matron, gritting her teeth, holding the reins.

"Ah, my friend of the sleeping drops," Rico Benelli said to himself softly. Contrary to what Zach thought, he had caught sight of Zach standing by the wagon.

"You are a true man of the Code of *fedele*, like Garibaldi and the Red-shirts," he murmured. "You follow the rules. If you deceive, you do it grandly. For that I admire you, even after what you did in the cafe. So, I cannot for the life of me imagine what you are doing raiding a hospital in a plot with a woman. You are going to—an unlikely spot, if what the surgeon said to the other nurse is right. What can it be about? When I do find out, and if you plan to hurt the poor, faltering Cause in some grand way, comrades we shall be no longer."

He touched the pistol strapped in a holster at a side. Then he hastened to his horse, moved quickly into the saddle and headed up the street at a rapid pace, taking a different route from the mule wagon but with a determination that showed that, with ears long attuned to overhearing, he knew in advance its destination was Castle Thunder prison.

Jacob Joe Scott drifted in and out of feverish dreams. In them he wandered in the home of his childhood, calling for aid. He went into the old parlor. Everything seemed tall and looming. His grandmother's old weaving loom, his mother's chair by the fire, cast long, eerie shadows. But the fire was out, and its ashes were cold.

"Pa," Jacob Joe's child-self said anxiously. No answer. He moved into the dining room, with its big, old-fashioned, hewn-oak table and deacons' benches.

Then, up the stairs, into his grandparents' bedroom, with the four-poster bed and handmade, almost black wardrobe brought from Kentucky. No one there? He felt the childish anxiety of being left alone in the pit of his stomach. Abandonment! It had no name for his child-self in the dream, but the child felt its bone-deep anxieties and reached for the only comforts he knew. Ma! Pa! Somebody! I am alone! Find me and take me in your arms! Silence, deep and still as dust. There was no one home to help. Then, suddenly he knew someone was in the house. Something evil. He felt, rather than heard, lurching steps slowly coming up the stairs behind him.

"Greetings," Rico said to the clerk of the prison. He pulled out his identification passes. "I am looking for a man named Scott. Scott of Indiana is what he calls himself. He has sharp nose, yellow curly hair. Have you seen such a man?"

"With all the dikes they have to plug, I wouldn't think the War Department would have time for snooping around this little pond," the young Confederate soldier said, looking over the passes. "We do have someone who fits your description almost exactly, but the hair is not really curly. Scott of Indiana. He is a prisoner here."

"Ah?" Rico Benelli said, surprised.

"Would you like to see him? I can take you to him."

"I suppose I would," Benelli said, wondering what it could mean. "If I do not have to be seen. I am on secret business."

Jacob Joe's dream-self stepped through a little closet door that connected the grandparents' room with his own small chamber. Panic seized him. Something black, he could not see its exact form in the shadows, was coming after him.

"Somebody help me," he called in that wordless way a person does in dreams, yearning for salvation from he knew not who. There, the thing had gone down the hall; his dream-self crept out of his room and went for the door to the attic. He pulled at the latch. No! It was jammed. He rattled and rattled. The thing had turned and was coming inexorably down the hall. It was the sureness of its pursuit that was the most frightening, Something horrible was determined to catch him.

"Somebody, help! Help!" he screamed and the door latch finally gave. Up, up the stairs. Oh, no, there it was behind him, and he heard it grunting, felt fear engulf him like floodwater, causing him to thrash about on his cot. He reached the top of the attic steps and backed into the corner, over old books and trunks and papers, waiting, unable even to scream as the thing advanced like the shadow of death to cover him.

He awoke, beaded all over with sweat and shaking with weakness, tried to sit straight up in bed but slumped down again. The clerk brought Rico Benelli to a chair against the wall, not far from the bunk. Few prisoners were in the sleeping room; it was exercise time in the yard. The few who remained were too sick to notice anything, and Benelli's gray kersey clothing suggested he was just another new prisoner.

It was dim in the room on this gray day; the prisoner the prison clerk pointed to was thirty feet away; Benelli did not wish to observe him too obviously. One must wait patiently until opportunity presented itself. Finally the man in the bunk opened his eyes.

"Clerk? Are you the new bed clerk?" the young man called in a faltering voice.

Benelli rose. "Can I get something for you, my friend?" He approached the bed with casual officiousness, came closer and looked into a face remarkably similar to "Scott of Indiana's." "Ah," he thought. "Two Scotts of Indiana, and they are alike enough to be brothers." But this one, ah, this one, was pinched and fevered. Very ill, this Scott was indeed. His heart wrenched as the truth hit him and the face of his own brother, strong in the saddle in a village street in Italy, came to him.

"Water," Jacob Joe said in a dull voice. "Can you get me some water?" A pitcher of tepid water stood nearby on a table, and Benelli poured some of it into a dirty glass. He propped Jacob Joe up and trickled water through his parched, cracked lips. "I dreamt awful things," Jake murmured, then suddenly looked into the face of the "bed clerk."

"I am delirious. Are you an angel?" he asked with an innocent smile on his face. "I have been praying to God to see me through, and perhaps He has sent you."

"Ah, my friend, I do not know. But you keep on praying." The prisoner's eyes closed and Rico Benelli gently put him down.

Rico turned on his heel. He walked to the prison clerk's office. "Should anyone come asking about me, do not mention that I have been here. I have found out what I wanted to know. I shall remain for a while in the barracks room, eh?"

The clerk looked at him without smiling. He had enough to do without the Secret Service pulling its intrigues down around his ears.

Rico Benelli sat on his chair, musing. The stench in this barracks room was execrable. With everyone heading off to be involved in the defense of Petersburg, with the constant turmoil in the streets of Richmond as the men went to and from battle, there were no attendants here at the prison to remove slops, to clean, even to provide basic food. There were only these few soldiers whose guns were at the ready in case of a prison revolt.

Now, if these two Scotts of Indiana were related, as it seemed, and if the one were very ill and in mortal danger in this terrible place (and who was not), had he complicated the matter with his inquiries? Just suppose that the tall Scott of Indiana was coming in the ambulance to—take his brother to the hospital for care. That could be it. To break the rules and take his brother to care with the woman nurse. Ah, that would be a noble thing to do, and he would not hinder it. But when another Scott came, looking like the first one, would not the clerk be suspicious? He had called attention to it all. Would the clerk hinder the removal?

As Rico thought about all this there was a clatter in the hallway. He turned about. Yes, there they were the woman nurse and tall Scott of Indiana, carrying a litter. And whatever it was would be botched because of him. The highest part of the Code of *Fedele* was family loyalty. And he was about to ruin it all.

He strode to the clerk's office. The young soldier was looking suspiciously at the release form signed by the Northern surgeon. Scott of Indiana stood, dressed as an orderly, his head down as the woman bravely fronted the clerk.

"I tell you we have orders to remove him, corporal," the woman nurse was saying, "and we must hurry. Those are our orders." The soldier was about to offer a rejoinder when Rico Benelli walked up.

"Ah, my party is here, I see. We have important business to perform, and this Scott man in the prison is to be taken to the hospital. He will be questioned there about a matter of interest to the War Department." He moved to stand in front of Scott of Indiana. Had the clerk noticed the similarity of face of this man to the prisoner? Pah, some spy this Northerner was! Why had this tall Scott not realized there would be a similarity? Perhaps illness had changed his relative. The clerk did not seem to notice; it was dark as ink in this dingy office, without the lamps, anyway.

But it wasn't only the clerk he had to worry about. At the same moment he had spoken, Dora Lavenham turned to him with astonishment. He could feel Zach moving towards him menacingly.

"It is imperative I help you get this man out of here," Rico said convincingly to them. "I have gone in and seen that he is very ill indeed, and I think we had better hurry," he said, taking Dora by the arm. As he walked her out the door, he said sternly to the clerk, "Your prison is a pigsty. President Davis has given orders that we are to provide basic necessities for these prisoners even in these troubled times. I hope I do not have to report you. Removing this man for questioning will certainly be in the name of humanity as well as practicality."

Good. Zach was not going to make an immediate scene; he was following with the stretcher. Rico could hear his measured breathing as they walked down the hall.

The corporal's voice was following them out the door, apologizing.

"Suh, the War Department has given s' many contradictory orders lately. And with all the confusion, they seem to have jus' bout forgotten us.''

"It is all right. I know you are trying to do your job,'' Rico said, closing the door. Dora had shut her mouth and was walking as if in a dream beside him. She did not know if she was being aided in some way by this enemy, or had been kidnapped in the midst of the plot by the Secret Service of the Confederacy, but she did know she was within a few yards of her ailing love and she was not going to stop.

Finally, Rico turned to see Zach's eyes burning at his back. He was accompanying him, but it was with outrage and suspicion. "Keep your back to the window of the clerk's office,'' Rico finally whispered. "Do not let your face be seen by the corporal.''

Zach moved close to Rico Benelli's ear as they advanced down the rows of pallets. "What in the name of God are you doing?'' Zach hissed. "If you think I am going to let you fox this now—''

"Not at all, Scott of Indiana,'' Rico said coolly. "I am not foxing anything. You have almost foxed yourself by not remembering how much you look like your brother. We have covered that now.'' He took the other end of the stretcher just as they reached Jacob Joe's bunk.

Jacob Joe opened his eyes but did not look up. He seemed only vaguely aware that people were by his bedside. "Help me, angel,'' he said to Benelli. "The black thing seems to have come out of my dream and is chasing me, even here,'' His fever-tortured voice came as if from a sepulchre. "I am alone, all alone.''

Rico answered him in deeply compassionate tones. "Not any more, my friend. We are here.'' Dora stood stock-still behind him. She finally perceived what Zach, too, was beginning to understand: Rico Benelli was there to help them. Zach moved forward and bent to his brother.

"Jake, we're going to take you out,'' he said. Jacob Joe's sight seemed to clear and he looked up into his brother's eyes.

"Why, it's Zach. I was in the attic! It was after me! I called and nobody came.'' Tears came to his eyes. "Brother, it was you! It was you 'I was looking for all along to come and save me!'' Carefully Zach picked up his brother's wasted form and placed it gently on the stretcher.

"Do not turn towards the hospital,'' Dora told the Italian who sat beside her holding the reins. Zach and Jacob Joe rode in the hospital wagon behind the boxes.

"Ah, and why not?'' Benelli asked.

"We are not taking him there. He is going home.''

"Home?'' Benelli asked, arching his eyebrows.

"Yes. Stop the team. You can get off here. We are taking him to the Northern lines."

The Italian raised the hand that was not on the reins in the air.

"Surely you will not hinder us, sir, after we have all come so far," Dora said, looking over at him with fear in her eyes.

"You are appealing to my gallantry, young woman. But what you are really asking is that I aid the escape of a prisoner of the Confederacy." He looked about at the streets of Richmond. Black men, shovels over their shoulders, were weaving their way around them and the other ambulance and provision wagons in all the streets.

Ahead of their mule wagon was a wagon piled high with furniture, driven by a woman. Portraits and children stuck out between upside-down chairs and trunks of clothing. A Scottie dog yapped incessantly on top of the heap and a small black boy danced about the scene waving his hands in jubilation. As Rico turned his eyes about, he could see the kaleidoscope of life in a decaying, dying Richmond: soldiers marching towards the front, well-dressed senators with somber looks on their faces making their way towards the strife-ridden meetings of the Confederate Congress, families by the side of the road with provisions tied up in sheets waiting for the move to safer ground. All this had happened to them before, more than once; when and if this emergency was over, it might happen again.

"Butler, General Butler, he a-comin' to Richmond soon," the small colored boy called up to the wagon, before he ran on down the street.

"Yes, and even if he does not, some other general will finally do it. Perhaps my effectiveness to the Cause is over," Rico murmured. "You need a driver," he said to Dora. "The tall Scott is my friend. I go with you now in the name of the Code of *Fedele*."

"I do not understand," Dora said.

"You do not need to," the Italian answered her, pulling the wagon around the household evacuation in front of them. "Just see you are ready to meet the Southern army officers. We will be heading for Northern lines with an ambulance marked 'CSA hospital.' The story you tell must be your own and it better be good. I can be of little help to you there."

Dora looked up to him steadily. "I will be ready," she said. "Pray God Jacob Joe lives long enough for us to get him through to safety."

*   *   *   *

"You were not at Mary Jane's funeral, though I would have thought to see you there." Reverend David Paden was saying at that same moment as he helped Lettie Hogue down from the wagon she had driven to Upper Indiana Church.

"No. I was not in town." That was enough to say to him, or anyone.

Thomas Jefferson Brooks had returned from Washington, saying that their work had been done well. President Lincoln thanked them both sincerely for their part in exposing the Confederacy plot. Northern agents said Clement Vallandigham was showing signs of returning to Ohio to begin an uprising for the South, but he would be watched closely now. Soldiers would be all about Chicago for the Democratic National Convention in a few weeks to act on whatever plot might develop. And as for Mawkins— he had returned with his guns, nursing anger at her and at his co-plotter, who had never shown up. He would be allowed to hang himself with his own rope.

Reverend Paden guided Lettie to the new plot in the McClure section by the walnut and oak trees at the edge of the cemetery and stood as she knelt to place a basket of large purple violets and red tulips on the raw, red-brown earth.

"I picked them in the woods over by the old Dan'l McClure house," Lettie said. "I don't know his descendants who live there now, though Mother does, but I don't think they'd mind. There are strings and sticks marking out rooms for a new house up the road a piece here where John and Annie will live, on their part of the Dan'l lands."

"So I hear." David Paden's tall, gangling frame seemed particularly awkward, as if its limbs did not quite know where to go, as he stood by, letting her minister to the memory of her loved niece.

Finally she picked up her basket and turned to him. "There will be a stone set soon?" she asked.

"Yes. It is to have two hands clasped in prayer on it. And the verse, 'Though she were dead, yet shall she live.' "

"It's 'he' in the Bible verse."

"Your mother wanted it the other way."

Lettie searched his face, set like a stone itself. "Your wife has been gone six weeks now, and I have not even written you a note."

"I did not expect you to. Considering." It seemed a long while since his stormy, outrageous pursuit of her, the festival where she had forgiven him, the weeks while the board deliberated in secret over the fate of its minister's disgrace, then the firm reprimand and removal. "I owed Alice something, but I gave her little, there at the end. I will not lie and say that there was love between us these last years. She was a cold, often condemning woman, but she was ill and deserved better. I have not paid my accounts yet, nor will I for a long while."

"And now you are going to Oregon. Along that long trail."

"Yes. There is a new church, a new start. Bob McClure will drive us. He is eager to go west, since he missed the war, he says. Two of my older children are staying here. They do not wish to go. So five of them and I will go on the trail in a month or so."

"You'll get to say goodbye to the boys in the Fourteenth Indiana," Lettie said thoughtfully. "They—and the others who went at the start of the war—will be mustered out in a week or two and will be home by then."

"Yes," Paden sighed. "Will we even know them? Will they know us?" Lettie shook her head, wondering too. It had been a long four years. The open sores still ran raw; the castles of the Knights of the Golden Circle and its new child, the Sons of Liberty, still met and chanted their hatred. What would it mean when the boys came back to a southern Indiana still rent with politics and argument over Negroes? Some even said there would be treason trials.

"We will need to stitch and sew," Paden said. "It is easy to tear and rend, but stitching and sewing the dream of America back together will take many years. We may not see it in our lifetime." He bent to sweep sticks off the new grave. "Still, it is a good dream, the best the world has seen. I rather think we will find it stronger, finally, than it ever was, because now it is for all people." They began to walk back through the cemetery, through the rows of stones marking four generations of pioneer people.

He did not look at her, but said as he walked, "Perhaps when things are torn and repaired staunchly, the new wholeness is stronger than the old. I have to believe so, or I could not live with my own shame."

Lettie thought about what he'd said. It had been so hard for her to confront her own burden of sin, to try to throw it out like old dishwater, which you fling, and fling, into the wind, and which yet flies back in your face. How much harder it must be for him, a minister of the Gospel! She could not rightly think of the pain it must have caused him.

They stopped to look at a robin's nest in a small thorn tree by the Emison plot. "See here, these babies, opening wide their mouths and squawking," Lettie said, "and the mother flying harried and worried away into the walnut grove to get worms for them."

"Yes," David Paden answered. "And below us the ants make their little tunnels and the beetles climb through grass." He looked at her thoughtfully. "I think they must be doing this on the new-grown grass at Gettysburg, where some of our Knox County boys rest. Do you?"

"Think the grass is growing now? They have made a Federal cemetery there. The grass grows best where it has been plowed under. And fertilized, but at what cost! Yes, I expect it is very green, and robins build their nests, too, on whatever little shreds of trees are growing back."

"And at Antietam, and Bull Run and Fredericksburg and the towns along the Mississippi," Paden went on, looking past the church, off towards where the Wabash River flowed. "The grass will grow back there, thick and lush, the bluegrass and the rye. And the redoubts will mound over with it and it will reach its roots and spreaders out into the burned woods and the gashed trenches, and it will heal them all, with its lushness and its promise of life which will not be quenched. And finally, it will cover the shallow graves, as it does here.'' They reached the edge of the cemetery again.

Lettie looked over the trees to the road and beyond it, to the Dan'l property. ''John McClure wrote that there were forget-me-nots growing at the Wilderness, beside the bodies of the Northern and Southern dead who had fallen a year before, on the very same spot, at the Battle of Chancellorsville,'' she said.

''Forget-me-nots,'' David Paden said, softly. ''Knox County will not forget, I think. Nor any other county or village in the land.''

They stood a long time at the edge of the peaceful churchyard, watching the birds swoop and soar and bees flit, finding the white cups of mayapples growing at the foot of a tree near the old, wooden church.

''Come with me, Lettie,'' David Paden said, finally, looking into her green eyes, drinking in the sight of the sunlight on her hair. ''I think you know that even when I was most horrid to you, scorching you with my lust—'' his voice broke—''it was because I loved and admired you.''

''Was it?'' Lettie said, turning her face from him. ''I did not think so then. You are fooling yourself. Do not bring it up—''

''Perhaps I am. I love you, Lettie. I love who you are, what you have done with a ridiculous, impossible mess.'' He did not touch her, but she felt the warmth of his yearning, the rise of responding longing in herself. It had always been so with her feeling for him. His mastery of the pulpit, his eloquent speech and his nearness to the heart of God, so she had thought, inspired her, pulled her to intense admiration and—desire.

''I loved your ministry,'' she said, looking into his pale blue, scholar's eyes behind the spectacles. ''I loved the power you brought to the Word. I worshipped you, I think, when I should have been worshipping God. Your own love, supposedly born of Christian fire, flamed and went out of control. How close the two are.''

''Everything you say is true. I think it every day of my life, over my children's beds, over my wife's grave—'' He abruptly wheeled about and leaned against a tree so she would not see his anguish.

''Don't''—she said. His shoulders were hunched, his hand still, despairing against the rough bark. ''David—''It was the first time she had used his Christian name. ''I have overcome one blighted love and found myself. I do not intend to lose so soon all I have gained, when I am not sure I could sort out love and lust in what we are. You may be looking for a mother for your children, you may only want—what you wanted that moonlit night. I don't think I could ever tell.''

He turned to look at her with pained eyes. Then he recovered himself and said with some dignity, ''I have done it again. I have poured out my heart like syrup on a plate, when I said I would not. I lied the other time, on the moonlit night, and now you think I lie again. I don't blame you, really. Goodbye Lettie.''

He helped her into the wagon and she clucked to the horses and drove off down the dusty road, never looking back, although he stood stock-still for many moments watching after her until the wagon was out of sight around the bend of the road.

* * * *

"I am Dora Lavenham, matron at New Hospital at Richmond. I am on a commissary mission." Her head held high, Dora stared into the cool, suspicious eyes of a captain of a Southern cavalry unit at the crossroads near Petersburg.

"You are near the Yankee lines, ma'am," the captain said with scant courtesy.

"We have had word of a supply of large hams and a wagonload of dried beans, flour and several other things, contributed from the cellar of a doctor out in the country here two miles or so."

"The lines are fluctuating every hour."

"I think we are safe in this Blackwater country."

"Almost all the Blackwater country is now in Yankee hands," the man said with irritation. He had small, sharp eyes and hardly any chin. He leaned forward on the horse confidingly with the confidence of a hill man born to the saddle. "You're in no man's land. S'posed to be Confederate territory, but Yankee scouts were here last night." He looked at the pass Dora showed him and told Dora his band was part of a raiding party of Stuart's cavalry. "We ain't 'bout to let you breach the lines, such as they are."

It was the third such encounter the hospital wagon had endured in the last four hours. At each stop they had to show passes to pickets in the bulging, irregular line. Tiredly Dora pulled a strand of hair back from her forehead and dabbed with a wrinkled handkerchief at perspiration on her forehead. Such heat! Thank God they had found a stream, so Jacob Joe could have plenty of fresh water. He was holding his own the last time she looked, though still out of his head. All this lurching and stopping couldn't help.

The cavalryman had his pistol out and was intent on forcing them to return. "I am going to turn you around, ma'am," the chinless man said. Up to this point in the encounter Rico Benelli had been a silent driver. He had given his teamster's pass for Dora to show at the two other encounters; it served to let them through. It seemed now, though, this tough Butternut was going to be hard to crack.

"I shall have to show him the Secret Service papers," Rico murmured in a cool voice. Dora sent him a frantic glance. She knew what the stakes were for him. Once it was known that a Secret Service man was in the area, his identity was compromised. An escape as important as this must eventually be found out; his name would be linked. He would not be able to return to the South; he could certainly not come with them to the North.

"Corporal, I have papers I wish you to see," Rico said. The corporal turned his snorting horse and, pistol at the ready, came to survey the papers.

"What is this all about?" he said.

"I am on President Davis's business," Rico said in a voice as smooth as coal oil. "We are getting supplies, but also something he wishes brought back to the capital. We are taking the swamp routes because they are less travelled. I am willing to assume the risk of encountering Yankees. At this stage in the war—" he shrugged.

The corporal studied the papers and nodded acquiescence as he handed them back. Rico clicked the reins at the mules to begin their forward motion.

Dora breathed a sigh of relief. "I think I shall spell Zach in the rear," she said. "He will be needing a breath of air."

"If you are to go back, you must do it within the hour. I shall not be able to accompany you as we near the Northern lines. It is too dangerous."

"What will you do, Rico?" Dora asked him, real apprehension in her voice.

"Vanish into the swamp forever." Evening was coming, and frogs began their vesper chorus about the wagon. He smiled a sad little smile. "At least until the war is over, I think. There are many places, many shacks up these lonely byways, many people willing to give me shelter. I am a man without a country now."

"You have done all this for us."

"I have done it for honor's sake," Rico said. "Above all in this war the South has had a sense of honor. I will take that home to my own people—if I can." He looked over his shoulder, past the waving swamp grass that stretched, an undulating ocean, behind him. Then he drew up the reins. "Now go, Miss Dora, to your patient in the rear and tell Scott of Indiana to come up here with me." Silently, she planted a kiss of gratitude on his cheek.

Behind the boxes in the covered ambulance wagon, a pallet had been made. On it Jacob Joe tossed and turned, out of his head. Dora lifted his head periodically and forced water between his cracked, bleeding lips. She spoke to him in soft tones.

"We will be out soon. Only a few more miles. Night is coming, and we will wait here. You can rest, rest, without the bumping. The night is warm, but it is cool here." She rose and, raising her skirt, took off her petticoat of lace, tore it at the seam, and put it on nails across the opening of the wagon. "There," she said to Jacob Joe, not sure just how well he heard her, "the awful mosquitoes will not get you." Her voice was dreamy, soothing. It was as if she were talking to a small child.

She looked at the flushed, thin face, once as round and rosy as a child's. She felt knit to him, soul to soul, because of these months of his awful trial in the prison. Nothing would ever change that, even though he loved another woman.

She took his hot hand in her own, leaning close to him. Through long months of nursing, she had learned what a leveler illness is. Fever, distress, know neither social classes, nor the impressiveness of a man's house or the size of his fortune. Lying helpless on a bed of pain, with eyes wide open and appealing for help, all are children. That is how it is, she thought, wetting a rag with water and wiping his forehead.

She leaned closer to his ear, began her encouraging whispers again. He must hold on! "Think of getting through, of going home. Home, Jacob Joe, home! The shady lane to the house you've told me about so often." His breathing was shallow, forced.

"Do you remember that night so long ago when we went to hear the silly speech about phrenology in the lecture hall? How you told me you left and went out and saw—the vision? Your grandmother, beckoning with her two fingers held together. Ah, Jacob Joe, it was all of us. One again. You and Zach, brother to brother." She would not have dared to say it could he really understand. Saying it comforted her now. "And one nation, North and South, when peace comes." Thank God! He seemed to be breathing a little more deeply. Perhaps he would sleep. They had pulled off the road, into a little rise with trees and she could hear the sounds of camp being made, the mules snuffling as they were unhitched.

She continued her whispers. "One, Jacob Joe, all of us. Perhaps, even you and Sophie. You, so good, so true, so wonderful of all men—" she sighed and looked longingly at his beloved face, hoping, willing him to live, for—another woman. "You can find the love you deserve." How could they marry? Perhaps there would be an annulment. Divorce was a possibility in cases of abandonment, as Sophie's was. "You could even"—each word was like a weight on her heart. But anything to encourage him to live— "marry Sophie after all."

Jacob Joe's eyes opened slowly. He stared straight ahead into the gloom of the wagon, focusing on the points of light where the men were building a fire. "Marry Sophie?" he said in a cracked whisper. "Why would I do that? Terrible mistake—I love Dora, after all. Is that bacon frying?" His eyelids fluttered and closed.

Dora's desperate composure crumbled. She put her head on Jacob Joe's chest and sobbed with joy and relief, listening to the beating of his heart, strong and even against the background noises of the camp at night and the gallumph of the frogs echoing through the stillness of the Blackwater swamp.

When morning came, Rico Benelli was gone, evaporated into the mist which surrounded the wagon. Jacob Joe seemed stronger, his fever down. Zach went to a remote farmhouse which somehow had escaped the ravages of food-raiding. He bought fresh eggs, ham, even new potatoes and they all enjoyed a feast which the invalid, too, seemed to appreciate.

Then on, on they rode, winding for hours over the remote roads, following the map which Rico had drawn. How odd that they could not go straight to the lines, but must describe a large arc east and south, then back north to the Northern lines of Burnside. But they had to travel remote roads to avoid interception. Dora rode in the wagon, holding her love's hand. Jacob Joe was awake for longer and longer periods, but they did not speak. The bond between them was too deep now for words. Sometimes she wept, silently, against her will, at the trouble they and all the poor, worn nation had known, her tears falling on his hands. Once he reached out to pat her hand with comfort.

By eleven o'clock they were seeing only stragglers along the road; after twelve they saw no one but swamp birds and occasional farmers. At two o'clock they reached higher ground, finally a crossroads. Dora went to sit beside Zach. They started up a road which traversed higher ground now, towards Bermuda Hundred, to the lines of General Ben Butler, who had recently threatened Richmond, but was now withdrawn to lines nearer the Federal gunboats.

Trees blocked the view around the bend in the road; suddenly they were among Northern soldiers who were astonished to see a Confederate ambulance, a nurse, and a teamster in the Northern lines.

Soon Zach was taken to one of General Butler's assistants, a flippant young adjutant. "I cannot imagine what kind of pass a passel of Rebels and mules can have," the adjutant demanded sourly. He looked at the pass, then read it aloud, and disrespect passed into wonder. " 'Please allow Zachary Scott of Indiana and his party to come into the lines of the United States government. More, see to the aid of his brother should he be with him. Like Joshua, Mr. Scott has crossed the River Jordan and stormed a hostile city in the land of the enemy. He is bringing out his brother, and we pray that they all have arrived safely in the Promised Land. Abraham Lincoln Washington City' "

"I shall see to your comfort, sir," the adjutant said, nodding respectfully.

hollow-eyed, stood in the dress uniform of a Union soldier of the Eightieth Indiana Regiment. He was determined to rejoin his beloved regiment, which was with Sherman in Georgia. Beside him stood his taller, more muscular brother dressed in a black frock coat, matching trousers and ivory silk vest.

By the piano and fireplace, throughout the parlor, were the flowers of summer the bride herself had cultivated on her return from Virginia: lilies, red-pink tea roses, hydrangeas. Their sweet odor filled the rooms, affirming love and sweet hope in the midst of all too short life, as they always do at weddings and funerals.

Delia Dugger Scott, just beginning to show as an obviously expectant mother, bent to pick a white lily and pinned it into the clip which held her luxuriant black-brown hair. She stood beside her aunt, Addie Lavenham, whose face was calm but inscrutable. After all, it had not been long since she watched her other daughter marry in this very parlor, unhappily as it turned out. Well, Sophie was trying again. She was in Texas trying to find her wayfaring boy as he travelled from town to town on the card-playing circuit. Addie was stoically keeping up appearances.

Other guests sat in the impoverished but fadedly elegant salon. John R. McClure of Knox County, Colonel Lewis Brooks, formerly of the Fourteenth and Eightieth Indiana Regiments, Major Edward Bachelder, dear and trusted friend of Althea Dugger, the aunt of the bride, and a few other family friends of the city at the falls of the Ohio stole glances at the stairs where the bride was to appear.

Now Althea Dugger began Lohengrin, its stately measured strains with all their personal implications for life and happiness resounding through the room, causing tears in the eyes of most of the women. The maid of honor, Miss Pickering, recently of the Confederate hospital service, descended the staircase. Then, on the arm of her uncle from Memphis, the radiant bride entered the room, wearing a simple dotted Swiss gown, her hair encircled with a ring of pink stock flowers and white roses which held a delicate white veil.

Jacob Joe Scott turned about and his heart leapt. "It is my dream, but all different. I had the face confused. This is the true one, the one which lit the prison hall, beamed above my sickbed." He took her hand, as they both turned to face the Episcopal minister. Jacob Joe was glad that Colonel Lewis Brooks was at his back; he did not wish him to see one of his lieutenants weep. Sentimental tears, always close to the surface, flowed freely as he professed his vows to the woman he deeply loved—who literally was his life.

John McClure was drinking a small glass of blackberry wine at the reception. Dora and Jacob Joe stood beside a tiered cake looking at miniature versions of themselves standing on its top layer. The little groom wore a bright blue uniform and carried a sword by his side, the bride had bright, doll eyes. Jacob Joe, laughing, plucked the toy groom off the cake and handed it to Corporal Eustace Brooks.

"Don't look like anybody I know," Eustace said. He had grown taller, more muscular in the last months. This was his first furlough; from here he would go to be with his family for a week. This time he would be able to go home with pride. At the recent battle of Rescaca in Georgia he had been part of a company personally commended for bravery by the commanding general. With a smile, he handed the toy soldier to John McClure, who pretended to scrutinize it carefully.

"Member of the infantry, I'd say. Not the Fourteenth though. He still has all his arms and legs and his uniform ain't full of holes and rotting."

Colonel Lewis Brooks came up bearing a small glass plate heaped high with bread-and-butter and cucumber sandwiches, fondant candy and salted nuts.

"I miss the old Fourteenth," he said to McClure. "I received a letter from Captain Beem. He is well settled in his law practice. Jess Harrold is still mending from being wounded so often."

"Yep," McClure said. "An' Joe Roseman had a letter from Redskin McClure. He is fixin' to go to doctor school."

"I think my father had something to do with that," Colonel Lewis Brooks smiled. "He was impressed with all you McClures. Henderson Simpson is still with the One Hundred Twentieth Indiana?"

"Yes," John answered. "Aunt Jewell had a letter from him from Arkansas. They made him a sergeant. When he comes home he'll be so sharp he'll cut the whole countryside up."

"Perhaps some day we'll have a reunion or two, talk about the old battles."

"I ain't goin' to be ready for that for a right smart spell," John McClure answered laconically. "Still gettin' the powder off my brain. And the fumes of hospital boric acid out of my nose."

"Lieutenant Scott," Eustace Brooks said, turning to the bridegroom, who was putting a sterling silver knife into the first tier of the cake, "where will you be going—after this is all over?"

"Well, they say the government may offer lands as veterans' bonuses. North and west. Perhaps in Michigan, up in the wild forests where Indians still live."

"Michigan, you say?" Eustace looked interested.

"Or one of the frontiers like it. Fortunes to be made. Eh, brother?" He looked at Zach, who was picking through nuts on the table.

"We're thinking about it," Zach said. "It would be hard to get Delia to leave Rivertides, I think. Since Calhoun is gone, it means the place will have to be sold. But Delia's mother had a letter from Willie McClure, and he wants to buy it when and if he returns and they should want to sell. For himself and his sister Ruby Jean. Says money has come to him from Archie's estate." He did not add that he and Delia had something to do with that, looking into the estate privately.

Lewis Brooks turned to John McClure. "Willie McClure? A relative?"

"Waal, yes. The first old lady McClure, Grandmother Jane, had four sons and a daughter. All o' em multiplied like mice, and there's a McClure in every third house in southern Indiana. But Miz Dugger tells me Willie is my cousin, descended from the old man Will. He's a Rebel. Mebbe even fought against me, so they say." He glanced long and hard at Althea Dugger. He still could not get over the easy way these people back home moved in and out of the war, as if it were a painting, how they consorted with the enemy. He himself was eating with Copperheads today. They did make good cake. "But I s'pose if, *when*, the Rebels lose and Willie McClure takes some kind o' loyalty oath, he can reform like any other sinner, even buy property from decent folks."

"All that remains to be seen," Lewis Brooks said, picking up the last of his sandwich. "There are battles yet to be fought. Robert E. Lee has a heart of iron."

"But we have the men and machines," the bridegroom said. John McClure looked intently at his cousin and friend, Jacob Joe Scott. "Jake, why have you re-joined?"

"I want to march into Richmond. Take it, see the buildings where I was imprisoned opened wide, see the city humbled, on its knees."

"I can understand that. But how do you know the Eightieth Indiana will be one of the units to go into Richmond if we win?"

"I just have that feeling," Jacob Joe said easily. "Sometimes I get feelings. They usually turn out to be true." He turned to feed his bride more cake, but she had crossed the room to see her Dugger relatives.

Jacob Joe went into the front parlor to where a man was standing apart, looking out the window at the streets of Louisville. Tilghman Vistal, finally released from Salisbury Prison through the relentless efforts of the Quakers, had honored Jacob Joe by coming to his wedding.

"Tilgh, it looks like you are conducting an inspection of the buildings of Louisville. Shall we condemn any?" Jacob Joe asked genially. His friend was almost as lean and spare as he had been in Castle Thunder.

"No, my friend, although like every other place in America, it is Vanity Fair. I can hardly think of all the building and getting and spending that is going to take place once the fighting ceases. But that was not what I was fixing on.'' Jacob Joe looked at him expectantly.

''I was looking at freedom. Men walking about as they please, women and children bustling about to shop or carry a book to a friend or take a course of learning.''

Jacob Joe sighed. ''Yes. Being able to walk out the door when you want to. That is the definition of freedom.'' A moment passed in comfortable silence. ''I went to the war to give the slaves that freedom. I was one of the few, I think,'' Jacob Joe said.

''And yet it has happened. Strange are the ways of Almighty God.''

Jacob Joe nodded.

''And are they free?''

''The slaves?''

''Yes. Are they free?'' Vistal wanted to know.

Jacob Joe thought about it. Thousands of black people were wandering about, starving, being beaten by itinerant ''Confederate vigilantes.'' Others were in Federal camps, some being taught to read, others just being held like animals in a compound. But some were filtering into Northern cities and into the West, with a determination to start a life. ''Well, they have some freedom.''

''There is no such thing as some freedom,'' Vistal said, taking off his glasses and wiping his eyes.

''I guess not,'' Jacob Joe said. As always, Vistal was sorting out meanings. ''Well, our children will have to worry about that,'' he said to Vistal. Jacob Joe offered his hand to his friend, but his eyes sought his bride, across the room with her relatives.

''Sometimes dreams do come true,'' Althea Dugger said, hugging Dora. ''I have always had trouble accepting pure joy fully, but that is what I feel today for you, dear one. You are so well suited.''

''Like hand and glove,'' Dora said, pulling back her veil. ''Major Bachelder, I hear you have been helping my aunt at Fairchance.''

''I know its fields now almost as if they were mine,'' Edward Bachelder said. His worn, blue staff officer's uniform of the western army, two years' old, with shiny elbows and knees contrasted with Jacob Joe's bright new Yankee blue. ''I have decided to resettle in the South when the war is over.''

''And, aunt, what are your plans?'' Dora wanted to know.

''We shall see when all is quiet again,'' Althea said softly, looking with love at Major Bachelder. ''Man proposes, God disposes,'' she murmured, turning her eyes to the bridal table.

Dora continued looking at Althea. It was obvious that something strong and lasting had developed between her aunt and this kind, quiet man. Her mother had told her there might be a marriage, once he was free of a bitterly unhappy marriage.

"Odd," Dora thought. "It seems strange to think that any marriage, begun beautifully, as this one was today, amidst prayers and blossoms and friends' good wishes, could end." Still, many did. But a marriage forged the way hers and Jacob Joe's had been, through suffering and salvation, was likely to be of true steel. How she loved him! She looked at him, joking with his friends, and fervently thanked God that, most of all, he could laugh again.

Delia came up and put her arm about Dora's waist. "Twenty inches, my dear," she said. "Perhaps one day mine will be like that again."

"Soon the time will come," Dora said with a smile, "when you will stay at home. So no prying eyes can see your condition, as Mama says. Confinement—"

Delia laughed. "I don't intend to have a confinement, cousin. I'm proud of myself. Motherhood should be shown off as the finest thing in the world."

"Well, perhaps so," Dora said, smiling broadly. It was a new idea, but it made sense. There was so much new these days!

"Zach and I start home in a little while," Delia told her cousin. They would be opening up Zach and Jacob Joe's house, which had been sitting dormant for months, feather dusted only occasionally by Ella, the emotional hired girl. Ella would be glad, Jacob Joe said, when they returned to the house. She would have someone to cook cherry pies for, then.

"You are so kind to have invited me to be with you. It will make the months fly," Dora said.

"Of course! It's your home now. We will sort the future out when Jacob Joe returns. In the meantime, Mother can manage Rivertides and I will help Zach learn what farming is. He doesn't know a hoe from a hoecake." She smiled broadly at her tall, dashing husband, who was looking as if he would like to escape all the folderol of the wedding reception about now.

Delia excused herself and went to speak to John McClure, who was having another little glass of blackberry wine and staring into a small container of rice he would soon be throwing at the bride and groom.

"I may be seeing you soon, Mr. McClure," Delia said.

"Will I have that pleasure, Mrs. Scott?" John said, with his best manners.

"I am to visit my dear friend Lettie Hogue at the old George McClure home a week from today. She said it was very important, that your family would be there, and that I could not know what I would find until I came."

"Then best I don't inform you, eh?" John said with a smile.

"Couldn't if I wanted to, anyways, 'cause I don't quite know what she means. But I got an inkling. See you, then, Mrs. Scott—cousin."

His smile was broad and confident, but it was a good thing Delia did not know what he was thinking. That a Dugger, Copperheads that they always were, would end up a cousin-in-law of his. Well, Zach seemed to have found religion or something. Mebbe he'd become a phrenologist or spiritualist. Whatever it was, Zach now supported the Union, or at least he didn't work against it. 'Bout time. As a returning veteran with a side that still ached like hell, John McClure would have probably found time to beat the crap out of Zach otherwise if he so much as mentioned states' rights, cousin or not.

*   *   *   *

A sleek new cross country wagon with a white, canvas top stopped in front of George McClure's old home on a drizzly day late in the next week. On its two seats rode five children, and from its cover hole a dog had put out his head and was yapping at everyone in sight.

Reverend David Paden walked beside it, guiding a team of sturdy horses that had been the gift of Upper Indiana Church on his leaving.

Zach had driven Delia out and, as requested, she stood outside the house under huge elm trees for Lettie to emerge and explain why Delia's presence was desired. John McClure and his sister Annie were helping Bob bring out his own trunk.

"Now mind you, Bob," Annie was saying, "Don't slip in the mud. And don't forget to take these hermits I made you." Bob McClure looked warily into a small, decorated box. Hermit cookies as hard as knots of wood stared up at him, Annie's parting gift to the brother who would be soon taking to the Oregon Trail.

"I tole you, Annie, to quit that bossin'," John McClure said. "You are worse'n a sergeant. One thing Bob ain't goin' to miss is your brassy voice."

Catherine Hogue banged the screen door behind her as she stepped quickly down the walk to the wagon. She was carrying a basket; soon others were traipsing down the walk behind her— brother Billy, Esther and Effie, now a beautiful young lady with aloof eyes. And behind them was Horace Hogue and his wife Clarissa. Clarissa was enormous with child, which the proud Horace could not resist patting now and then. Montmorency walked casually behind his mother. Annie eyed him with wary eyes. Under threats from all parties involved, they had declared a truce.

Jewell Simpson clucked about the wagon, looking inside at the gear which seemed to swell its insides to bulging—sacks and barrels of provisions, clothing trunks, bedding and even a cage of chickens. "Now, Bob, I have sent paregoric and citronella and spirits of ipecac and Smith Brothers cough drops for you, and mind you eat some of the transparent apples we sent so you don't get bound up on the trail,'' his aunt told him.

David Paden smiled. Seeing all these milling McClures reminded him of the warmth of the community he would be leaving. ''I'll miss you all,'' he said to Catherine Hogue.

''Yes,'' she answered, ''seems like the McClures move as easy as they breathe. We came in among the first into Knox County. I crossed the Buffalo Trace with Ma and Pa in a wagon not too different from that. They had come from Caintuck and before that, from Pennsylvania and Northern Ireland. West, ever west the road lies.'' She pursed her lips and looked towards Illinois and the road which led eventually to the Pacific.

Lettie Hogue came out of the house, a sunbonnet in hand. Without stopping to speak to Delia, she bounded up on the one seat left on the driving board of the covered wagon.

''Letitia Hogue,'' Delia said in an astonished voice, coming over to the wagon. ''You have invited me to come over here to see you leave Knox County to go west.''

David Paden was swinging her valise into the hole of the wagon. ''I'm to have a new bride as soon as we get to Illinois,'' he said.

Delia shook her head in disbelief, but Catherine Hogue walked over, smiling. ''He certainly did some convincing to win this bride, but I couldn't convince the both of them to stay and have a southern Indiana wedding.''

''I can recommend it, Sister,'' Horace Hogue said, his arm around Clarissa.

''Just as well we skip the festivities, I opine,'' Jewell Simpson said with a small toss of the head. And then, a little more cordially, ''Bob has a present in his carpetbag. Mind you ask him for it after you've seen the preacher.''

Lettie stepped down to kiss Jewell, who tut-tutted and then kissed her back on the cheek. ''And Annie,'' Lettie said, solemnly planting a kiss on each cheek as she went around the group, ''Uncle Billy, Aunt Esther, Clarissa, Horace.'' She held Horace at arms' length and sighed, realizing how far away Oregon was, how she might never, ever see his child.

Catherine Hogue stood apart a bit, under the tree where, as a young girl she had spread a picnic dinner on the first day in this new land of Indiana, over sixty years ago.

''Mother—'' here Lettie broke down. She clasped her mother in her arms and they wept together silently, with small wrenching sobs.

Then Catherine drew back, trying to think of something to say. ''Glad the rain has stopped. The roads could get bad,'' she offered vacantly. If she said what was really in her heart, she would weep again. She turned and looked down the road, to Vincennes and beyond. It was a long one, so many miles, chuckholes, ditches, puddles would be between her and this daughter she loved. "We have something for you—here," she finally said.

She waved for her grandson John McClure, who had been keeping in the shadows to come up. He brought a book and opened it for Lettie to the inscription.

"This book given to George McClure, January 15, 1710, by his father, Alexander McClure, Physician Dunleigh, Ireland," he read. "Not the George that's our ancestor, but another one. His great-uncle, somebody said." He handed the little, worn book, still open, to Lettie. "*Pilgrim's Progress*. I took it through the war."

Lettie looked at the inscription with interest. "What's this other thing? I can hardly make it out."

Catherine Hogue came forward and put a long, graceful finger on the writing. "Pluck up a good heart, O Christian, for Greater is He that is in thee, than he that is in the world," she read. Her eyes caught her daughter's, and in that gaze were all the ancestral memories of the Scotch women who had seen their daughters leave for Northern Ireland, the Jane McClure who had left her Irish home to cross the ocean to Pennsylvania, the Jean McClure who had left the grave of father and babies to come to Indiana.

"I will never see you again," Catherine said, turning away. "I feel it in my heart."

"Oh, Mother," Lettie said. "I will write." But her eyes went to David Paden. He was checking the horse's harness one last time.

"You will write," Catherine said softly. "So they all said. But they hardly ever do. Still, I'm not alone." Lettie looked at Horace, silently bequeathing their mother to his care.

"Yes, I have Horace," Catherine went on, "and Billy's family. They say I must stay here as long as I live. He has paid me back; the house is in the family again, where it belongs. I hope after all this trouble it stays there." She waved at the hills and woods that stretched on to the Wabash River. "And I have this county—my home. Land has an identity of its own. As long as I am here, near the church where my loved ones lie, near the fields where my husband plowed, and my children played, and especially as long as I am near this house,"—she gestured back towards the ancestral mansion of George McClure, "I have all the associations as deep as a river and as wide as the sky." She hugged Lettie one more time, then retreated to the consoling branches of the old tree.

The Paden children squirmed and laughed and fussed on the wagon seat. David Paden stood expectantly by the horses; John McClure shuffled his feet. His family responsibility about over, he was ready to go up the road to visit Fannie Purcell, the childhood companion to whom he had taken a great shine. And Annie and Montmorency were sending each other challenging looks. They had invited other young people in the neighborhood in for a horse race and chocolate cake later that afternoon as the first walls went up on John and Annie's new house around on the Upper Indiana Road. The faces of her relatives ringed about Lettie, loving, expectant.

One last goodbye. She went to Delia. "Write me when the young one has come. Do you wish for a girl?"

"If we have a girl, she shall be Letitia," Delia said. They turned to face David Paden and the wagon; Delia walked her friend towards it.

"Will this odd match ever work?" Delia whispered, almost to herself.

Lettie smiled. "I could have asked you the same thing once. In fact, I think I did." She looked at the tall, solemn minister. "We have grown to need each other. And to trust each other." They were almost at the wagon. "Besides," Lettie said with a wry little smile, "someone told me once that you must be daring if you wish to find love. Those who love the most are willing to risk the most."

Delia nodded and kissed her friend goodbye. Soon the little group stood in front of the beautiful old home from Revolutionary War times, watching the covered wagon lumber down the road and out of sight, going west.

Two weeks later, Hannah Poore, on the arm of her grandchildren Susie Niblack and Seymour Brooks, slowly made her way through long grass to the Brooks family plot in the little cemetery in Mt. Pleasant. No one had cut the grass this summer. They were all busy, she thought, and most of the younger ones were off at war. It was important to keep cemeteries up. Understanding, reverencing the lives of those who have come before throws the present into perspective, as a magic lantern show throws images on the wall. We must pay our due to the past before we can fully live in our own day and age.

Thomas Jefferson Brooks and his wife Susan followed. Turning to the left, they all came to the wrought iron fence. There, not far from the graves of his brother Daniel Brooks who had owned the circus, and his wife, was Tommy's grave.

"Virginia Creeper has grown on it now," Susie said, poignantly. "It doesn't take long, does it?"

Seymour, hands in pockets, wandered about, kicking at some of the old nameless sandstones which marked the graves of folks reburied from Hindostan Falls, throwing acorns at other stones. His mother Susan Brooks, her eyes impassive, knelt with scissors to trim the vines away from her babies' graves. Love shown in her eyes, little troubled with grief. She had done this service so often, and she felt a gentle comfort in it. It meant she had not forgotten them, and thus they lived, in a small way yet, here.

Hannah Poore had not been out for many months. She took a small trowel out of her dress pocket and knelt on Tommy's grave.

"What are you doing, Mother Poore?" Thomas Jefferson Brooks asked.

"Trimming away the weeds so the grape hyacinths can grow. They don't like too much crowding."

Thomas Jefferson Brooks cleared his throat. He looked down at the grave. "Well, Son," he said, "your regiment is doing itself up proud. Sherman is getting ready to take Atlanta, and Eustace and your friend Jacob Joe Scott are right with him. I wish you—"

"Pa, don't—" Susie said, pulling on the arm of the old man. He stood silent, composing himself.

Hannah Poore thought that she had never understood why people talked to the departed in graveyards. As if they could hear! Well, Thomas never had been straight on all that. Maybe it made him feel better.

Susan Brooks rose from her duties and cried out in surprise. "Look at this," she said.

"What is it?" Thomas wanted to know.

"Look. A new, double stone. Says 'Colonel Lewis Brooks and his beloved consort, Amanda'."

Thomas Jefferson Brooks walked over a few paces and stared at the stone. So premature! Lewis and Amanda were alive and well and building their own farm down the road near Hindostan. Susie had the answer. "A salesman was through Loogootee the other day offering a special price on stones if you ordered in advance. You could get your own inscription."

"That's creepy," young Seymour Brooks said, wiping his glasses on a handkerchief.

"Lewis, ever practical," Thomas Jefferson Brooks said. "He doesn't care if he rests in peace out here for forty years while he's still trotting around. Leave it to Lewis." He began to laugh; the others took up the laughter and soon the dells and woods were ringing with the laughter of the Brooks clan.

William Houghton had come to the graveyard in the wagon with them, but he had not gone to the Brooks plot. Instead, he bounded like a boy through the edges of Brooks cemetery, down the steep hill and across the ravine to what was called the New Cemetery on the next hill. Mt. Pleasant had never been able to contain its dead in one plot because of the hills which encircled the village; so the resting places spread across a series of rises.

Though he was no longer on active duty, he wore his major's uniform complete with sword. He walked now, hat in hand, among the gravestones. "So peaceful here," he thought. The day was oddly cool for August, the sky a leaden gray. Just a touch of fall wafted in the air. Queen Anne's lace, bending a little in the breeze, made the fields all the way to Hindostan Falls and the river snowy. Above him, in maple trees, catbirds called.

The Houghtons were buried here, and other of the key families of this piece of Martin County. He passed their stones without really noticing. He was seeking one stone in particular, the goal of his pilgrimage on this day.

He had not been out since his return. So many things to attend to, visiting Beem in Spencer and meeting his wife, reacquainting himself with his own parents, helping Beem and Cavins write the record of the Fourteenth for the Adjutant General, calling on Lizzie Kelso, writing to his two brothers Walter and Eugene, now in the army too. And keeping up with Gus, too, who was the Assistant Adjutant General now with Sherman's army in Georgia, readying for the final push to end the war. The last letter Houghton received from Van Dyke said his friend might be a career officer. Adjutant General! So he had ended where he wished to be.

Houghton stopped a moment to look at the sky, the horizon. It was still hard to believe he was home. The peace of this scene, smoke rising from the kitchen chimney of the old Brooks home across the ravine, the clop-clop of hoofs and the jangling of harness as someone cultivated in the field next to him—it was unreal. The Fourteenth had fought its last battle at Cold Harbor in Virginia and its men were scattered to the winds, but until the moment of his death they would be the ultimate reality in his life, above parents, wife, any children he might have. When you had lived in the throat of death the way he had, known the inmost hearts and ultimate bravery of the men he had called comrade, that experience was a fist around your heart that would never loosen its hold, binding you to echoes of the past, to half-heard musketry, to tones fading around campfires long extinguished. That was the way it was now; that was the way he knew it would be.

He found the grave he wanted. Well, two graves. There was the monument of his old friend, George Reilly, and next to it the stone he had come to see. Will Houghton stood back and surveyed the carving. Bascomb Reilly, Born 1846. Fell Battle of Antietam, September 17, 1862. Short years—he had helped to enroll this boy just a few miles from here at a table in the middle of Loogootee, he had buried him, he had disinterred him. Associations crowded in on him: Bo's frightened face at the Battle of Greenbrier, Bo's shock at seeing someone he loved die, Bo singing himself to sleep with a hymn, and then Bo grimacing, swearing, and shooting at Bloody Lane. Finally, Bo's decent, young, freckled face, composed in death after he had volunteered to face mortal danger behind the lines.

There was honor here that Houghton, for all his experience in the war, did not yet understand. He had sought honor on every battlefield, thought he had seen it many times, but now knew, at last, that the very quintessence of the word lived in the life of Bo Reilly and others like him. The great land had been split in two; boys not yet out of their teens had bound it up with their own deaths. Greater honor has no land or age.

William Houghton came to attention. There, alone in the long grass, he put his hat on his head and came to attention. Sharply, he saluted.

"Here's to you, Bo," he said, in a hoarse voice. Then, ceremonial sword jingling at his side, with a small, accepting smile on his lips, he walked slowly away over the hill to join the rest.